THE MAN
IN THE
IRON MASK

ALEXANDRE DUMAS

AIRMONT BOOKS
NEW YORK

An Airmont Classic
specially selected for the Airmont Library
from the immortal literature of the world

ISBN: 0-8049-0150-3

AIRMONT PUBLISHING CO., INC.,   New York, N.Y.

THE MAN
IN THE
IRON MASK

ALEXANDRE DUMAS

Introduction

Alexandre Dumas is best known as the creator of those devil-may-care heroes, the three musketeers. One might wonder how their author could see even these colorful soldiers-of-fortune through some forty-four volumes of free-wheeling romance, intrigue, and battle. On the other hand, a glance at Alexandre's parentage suggests that he could hardly have done otherwise. His father was the greatest swashbuckler of them all.[1]

This father, Alexandre Davy de la Pailleterie, was the mulatto son of a French marquis. He refused aid from his father and enlisted in the Queen's Dragoons as a private under the name of his mother, Dumas. During the French Revolution he was promoted, within twenty months, from private to commander-in-chief of the Army of the Western Pyrenees. The General's exploits more than rival those of Porthos: a giant of a man, he could toss a hesitant soldier bodily over a wall, crush a steel helmet between his hands or a horse between his legs.

Headstrong in battle, he frequently outstripped his men. In one engagement he single-handedly routed an entire Austrian division, earning the name *schwartzer Teufel* (Black Devil). This same impetuous nature which made his reputation in battle was his

---

[1] A fascinating account of Dumas *pere*, his father, and his son is presented in *The Titans* by Andre Maurois (New York: Harper, 1957).

3

undoing as a commander of armies. Combined with a simple frankness and strong humanitarian feelings, this impetuosity soon put the General in Napoleon's disfavor. He died a poor and broken man, at the age of forty-four, just four years after the birth of Alexandre.

Alexandre Dumas was born in 1802. He soon began to show many of the characteristics of his father: physical size, intelligence, a love of action, and, above all, a free and romantic spirit. By the age of six, young Dumas had read the Bible, *Robinson Crusoe, Arabian Nights*, and a number of volumes of mythology. Despite this early start, he could not be considered bookish; much of his later youth was spent in the outdoors he loved, hunting and roaming in the woods.

The meager income earned by Alexandre's mother barely enabled the two of them to subsist. As soon as he was old enough, Dumas added to the family income by working as a lawyer's messenger. It was during this early period that two important events occurred in his life: he attended a traveling-company presentation of *Hamlet* in his village of Villers-Cotterets, and he made the acquaintance of Adolphe de Leuven, an aspiring playwright and devotee of the theater. His desire whetted by this taste of theater, Alexandre resolved to seek his fortune in Paris.

Through one of the few friends of his father, Alexandre was granted a job as copy boy for the Duc d'Orleans. By the age of twenty he had written three plays and had received as many rejections. However, he added to his list of friends and tutors one Lassagne, chief clerk for the Duc d'Orleans and a talented critic of literature and the theater.

Lassagne and de Leuven were gifted mentors and rebels against the classic tradition. Dumas, although largely innocent of the classic tradition, recognized the need for emotion—the human element—in drama. The break-through came when the young Romantic was twenty-seven, with the success of his first accepted play *Henri III et sa cour. Christine*, his subsequent effort, was saved from almost certain failure by a post-first-night revision. With the aid of Victor Hugo and de Vigny, the play was salvaged into a moderate success.

Within the year, Dumas' reputation was made with the overwhelming success of *Anthony*. The tremendous response to this play brought money and fame—fame that placed Dumas as an equal with Hugo and almost destroyed their friendship. Thereafter, success followed success.

The theatrical conquests of Dumas were equaled only by the number of his feminine conquests. His natural son, the young Alexandre who was born during the early years in Paris, was well cared for, as was the child's mother and the mother of Dumas himself. However, despite the extent of his income, Dumas was never to become wealthy because of the many women he loved and supported during his life.

While Dumas had written some historical books and accounts of his travels, including impressions from a sojourn with Garibaldi, it was not until 1844 that he firmly demonstrated himself as a novelist. By this time, the historical novel as a genre was established; Hugo and de Vigny, among others, had seen to that. It remained for Dumas to inject his own flavor of romance and adventure—humanity—to the type. This he did, in eight volumes, with *The Three Musketeers*.

It is doubtful that any author equaled the productivity of Dumas in his next eight years. He had found his place, and it seemed that he was determined to include all of French history in his scope. Over one hundred volumes were published between 1844 and 1851. Obviously no man could do this alone; hence, Dumas gained the reputation as Dumas and Company, manufacturers of novels.

The criticism was, in part, due to jealousy. Many novels of the period were run first as serials in the newspapers. Because of his popular appeal, Dumas had a monopoly with his stories in the French newspapers. This control cut off the income of established as well as new writers of the day.

The criticism was in part true. Dumas did have collaborators, as did most major writers of his day; in fact, Dumas was not above hiring the better ones away from Hugo, de Vigny, or Balzac. From all we know, however, it is not true that Dumas merely bought and signed the manuscripts of his collaborators. The best evidence in support of this statement is the fact that most of these collaborators, at one time or another, attempted without success to produce novels on their own. They were the plot sketchers and the character inventors, but it took the master himself to breathe life into the raw material. A particularly bilious accusation, fought through the courts, brought forth the judgment of libel that Dumas sought against one accuser.

The novels of Dumas, especially those dealing with the musketeers, have universal appeal. They express artlessly the author's boundless *joie de vivre*, his love of action, strength, and generosity. On the other hand, the many one and two word paragraphs probably reflect the influence of the newspaper serialization, since authors were paid by the line, regardless of the number of words.

In no other way did Dumas show an awareness of money: he earned fortunes and he threw them away. He was often hounded by creditors, and he died a poor man. Likewise, while in his lifetime he was the superior in popularity and even the envy of the great Victor Hugo, Honoré de Balzac, and de Vigny, today he is not classed as their literary equal. He was the man of action and adventure, not the refiner of literary works. His fondest wish—to be admitted to the French Academy—was never achieved by himself; it was gained by his son, Alexandre Dumas *fils*.

While he was the author of some three hundred volumes, Alexandre Dumas *pere* is best known for his series on the musketeers. *The Three Musketeers* (1844) was originally published in eight volumes. This was followed by *Twenty Years After* (1845) in ten volumes, and *The Viscount Bragelonne* (1848-50) in twenty-six volumes. Interspersed among these volumes were the numerous Monte Cristo books.

The Man in the Iron Mask is a sequence lifted from the latter part of *The Viscount Bragelonne*. It begins in the mature years of the musketeers and follows them to the end. In this volume, we again admire the quiet Athos, the strong and simple Porthos, the devious Aramis, and the highly principled and impetuous captain of the king's musketeers, d'Artagnan.

The Man in the Iron Mask is an intrigue, initiated by the scheming Aramis, which places the friends in opposite camps and dearly tests their principles against their camaraderie. Each, however, lives a full life in the eyes of Dumas, and each achieves what is important to him. Not even a king's musketeer could ask for more.

Dumas himself seems to be telling us what he deems important in a man, as he speaks through d'Artagnan near the end of the book. This indomitable musketeer, audacious even in his humbled concession, says to his king:

"Do not imagine that I bear malice; no, you have tamed me, as you say; but it must be confessed that in taming me you have lessened me,—by bowing me, you have convicted me of weakness. If you knew how well it suits me to carry my head high, and what a pitiful mien I shall have while scenting the dust of your carpets! Oh Sire, I regret sincerely, and you will regret as I do, those times when the King of France saw in his vestibules all those insolent gentlemen, lean, always swearing—cross-grained mastiffs, who could bite mortally in days of battle. Those men were the best of courtiers for the hand which fed them—they would lick it; but for the hand that struck them, oh! the bite that followed." *

ROBERT L. HILLERICH, M.S., Ed.D.

* From Chapter 53, "King Louis XIV"

Chapter 1 — THE PRISONER

Since Aramis' singular transformation into a confessor of the order, Baisemeaux was no longer the same man. Up to that period, the place which Aramis had held in the worthy governor's estimation was that of a prelate whom he respected and a friend to whom he owed a debt of gratitude; but now he felt himself an inferior, and that Aramis was his master. He himself lighted a lantern, summoned a turnkey, and said, returning to Aramis:

"I am at your orders, monseigneur."

Aramis merely nodded his head, as much to say, "Very good," and signed to him with his hand to lead the way. Baisemeaux advanced, and Aramis followed him. It was a beautiful starry night; the steps of three men resounded on the flags of the terraces, and the clinking of the keys hanging from the jailer's girdle made itself heard up to the stories of the towers, as if to remind the prisoners that liberty was out of their reach. It might have been said that the alteration effected in Baisemeaux had extended itself even to the prisoners. The turnkey, the same who, on Aramis' first arrival, had shown himself so inquisitive and curious, had now become not only silent, but even impassible. He held his head down, and seemed afraid to keep his ears open. In this wise they reached the basement of the Bertaudiere, the two first stories of which were mounted silently and somewhat slowly; for Baisemeaux, though far from disobeying, was far from exhibiting any eagerness to obey. On arriving at the door Baisemeaux showed a disposition to enter the prisoner's chamber; but Aramis, stopping him on the threshold, said:

"The rules do not allow the governor to hear the prisoner's confession."

Baisemeaux bowed, and made way for Aramis, who took the lantern and entered; and then signed to them to close the door behind him. For an instant he remained standing, listening whether Baisemeaux and the turnkey had retired; but as soon as he was assured by the sound of their dying footsteps that they had left the tower, he put the lantern on the table and gazed around. On a bed of green serge, similar in all respects to the other beds in the Bastile, save that it was newer, and under curtains half-drawn, reposed a young man, to whom we have already once before introduced Aramis. According to custom, the prisoner was without a light. At the hour of curfew he was bound to extinguish his lamp, and we perceive how much he was favored in being allowed to keep it burning, even till then. Near the bed a large leather armchair, with twisted legs, sustained his clothes. A little table—without pens, books, paper, or ink—stood neglected in sadness near the window; while several plates, still unemptied, showed that the prisoner had scarcely touched his recent repast. Aramis saw that the young man was stretched upon his bed, his face half-concealed by his arms. The arrival of a visitor did not cause any change of position; either he was waiting in expectation or was asleep. Aramis lighted the candle from the lantern, pushed back the armchair, and approached the bed with an evident mixture of interest and respect. The young man raised his head.

"What is it?" said he.

"Have you not desired a confessor?" replied Aramis.

"Yes."

"Because you are ill?"

"Yes."

"Very ill?"

The young man gave Aramis a piercing glance, and answered: "I thank you." After a moment's silence, "I have seen you before," he continued.

Aramis bowed.

Doubtless, the scrutiny the prisoner had just made of the cold, crafty, and imperious character stamped upon the features of the bishop of Vannes was little reassuring to one in his situation, for he added:

"I am better."

"And then?" said Aramis.

"Why, then, being better, I have no longer the same need of a confessor, I think."

"Not even of the haircloth, which the note you found in your bread informed you of?"

The young man started; but before he had either assented or denied Aramis continued:

"Not even of the ecclesiastic from whom you were to hear an important revelation?"

"If it be so," said the young man, sinking again on his pillow, "it is different; I listen."

Aramis then looked at him more closely, and was struck with the easy majesty of his mien, one which can never be acquired unless Heaven has implanted it in the blood or heart.

"Sit down, monsieur," said the prisoner. Aramis bowed, and obeyed.

"How does the Bastile agree with you?" asked the bishop.

"Very well."

"You do not suffer?"

"No."

"You have nothing to regret?"

"Nothing."

"Not even your liberty?"

"What do you call liberty, monsieur?" asked the prisoner, with the tone of a man who is preparing for a struggle.

"I call liberty the flowers, the air, light, the stars, the happiness of going whithersoever the nervous limbs of twenty years of age may wish to carry you."

The young man smiled, whether in resignation or contempt it was difficult to tell.

"Look," said he, "I have in that Japanese vase two roses gathered yesterday evening in the bud from the governor's garden; this morning they have blown and spread their vermilion chalice beneath my gaze; with every opening petal they unfold the treasures of their perfume, filling my chamber with a fragrance that embalms it. Look, now, on these two roses; even among roses these are beautiful, and the rose is the most beautiful of flowers. Why, then, do you bid me desire other flowers when I possess the loveliest of all?"

Aramis gazed at the young man in surprise.

"If *flowers* constitute liberty," sadly resumed the captive, "I am free, for I possess them."

"But the air!" cried Aramis; "air so necessary to life!"

"Well, monsieur," returned the prisoner, "draw near to the window; it is open. Between heaven and earth the wind whirls on its storms of hail and lightning, wafts its warm mists, or breathes in gentle breezes. It caresses my face. When mounted on the back of this armchair, with my arm around the bars of the window to sustain myself, I fancy I am swimming in the wide expanse before me."

The countenance of Aramis darkened as the young man continued:

"Light I have; what is better than light? I have the sun, a friend who comes to visit me every day, without the permission of the governor or the jailer's company. He comes in at the window, and traces in my room a square the shape of the window, and which lights up the hangings of my bed down to the border. This luminous square increases from ten o'clock till midday, and decreases from one till three slowly, as if, having hastened to come, it sorrowed at leaving me. When its last ray disappears I have enjoyed its presence for four hours. Is not that sufficient?

I have been told that there are unhappy beings who dig in quarries, and laborers who toil in mines, and who never behold it at all."

Aramis wiped the drops from his brow.

"As to the stars, which are so delightful to view," continued the young man, "they all resemble one another, save in size and brilliancy. I am a favored mortal, for if you had not lighted that candle you would have been able to see the beautiful stars which I was gazing at from my couch before your arrival, and whose rays were playing over my eyes."

Aramis lowered his head; he felt himself overwhelmed with the bitter flow of that sinister philosophy which is the religion of the captive.

"So much, then, for the flowers, the air, the daylight, and the stars," tranquilly continued the man; "there remains but my exercise. Do I not walk all day in the governor's garden if it is fine—here if it rains? in the fresh air if it is warm; in the warm, thanks to my winter stove, if it be cold? Ah, monsieur, do you fancy," continued the prisoner, not without bitterness, "that men have not done everything for me that a man can hope for or desire?"

"Men!" said Aramis. "Be it so; but it seems to me you forget Heaven."

"Indeed I have forgotten Heaven," murmured the prisoner, with emotion; "but why do you mention it? Of what use is it to talk to a prisoner of Heaven?"

Aramis looked steadily at this singular youth, who possessed the resignation of a martyr with the smile of an atheist.

"Is not Heaven in everything?" he murmured, in a reproachful tone.

"Say, rather, at the end of everything," answered the prisoner firmly.

"Be it so," said Aramis; "but let us return to our starting-point."

"I desire nothing better," returned the young man.

"I am your confessor."

"Yes."

"Well, then, you ought, as a penitent, to tell me the truth."

"All that I wish is to tell it you."

"Every prisoner has committed some crime for which he has been imprisoned. What crime, then, have *you* committed?"

"You asked me the same question the first time you saw me," returned the prisoner.

"And then, as now, you evaded giving me an answer."

"And what reason have you for thinking that I shall now reply to you?"

"Because this time I am your confessor."

"Then, if you wish me to tell what crime I have committed, explain to me in what a crime consists. For as my conscience does not accuse me, I aver that I am not a criminal."

"We are often criminals in the sight of the great of the earth, not alone for having ourselves committed crimes, but because we know that crimes have been committed."

The prisoner manifested the deepest attention.

"Yes, I understand you," he said, after a pause; "yes, you are right, monsieur; it is very possible that in that light I am a criminal in the eyes of the great of the earth."

"Ah! then you know something," said Aramis, who thought he had pierced not merely through a defect in, but through the joints of the harness.

"No, I am not aware of anything," replied the young man; "but sometimes I think—and I say to myself——"

"What do you say to yourself?"

"That if I were to think any further I should either go mad or I should divine a great deal."

"And then—and then?" said Aramis impatiently.

"Then I leave off."

"You leave off?"

"Yes; my head becomes confused, and my ideas melancholy; I feel *ennui* overtaking me; I wish——"

"What?"

"I don't know; but I do not like to give myself up to longing for things which I do not possess, when I am so happy with what I have."

"You are afraid of death?" said Aramis, with a slight uneasiness.

"Yes," said the young man, smiling.

Aramis felt the chill of that smile, and shuddered.

"Oh, as you fear death, you know more about matters than you say," he cried.

"And you," returned the prisoner, "who bid me to ask to see you; you, who, when I did ask to see you, came here promising a world of confidence; how is it that, nevertheless, it is you who are silent, and 'tis I who speak? Since, then, we both wear masks, either let us both retain them or put them aside together."

Aramis felt the force and justice of the remark, saying to himself:

"This is no ordinary man; I must be cautious. Are you ambitious?" said he suddenly to the prisoner, aloud, without preparing him for the alteration.

"What do you mean by ambition?" replied the youth.

"It is," replied Aramis, "a feeling which prompts a man to desire more than he has."

"I said that I was contented, monsieur; but, perhaps, I deceive myself. I am ignorant of the nature of amibition; but it is not impossible I may have some. Tell me your mind; 'tis all I wish."

"An ambitious man," said Aramis, "is one who covets what is beyond his station."

"I covet nothing beyond my station," said the young man, with an assurance of manner which for the second time made the bishop of Vannes tremble.

He was silent. But, to look at the kindling eye, the knitted brow, and the reflective attitude of the captive, it was evident that he expected something more than silence—a silence which Aramis now broke.

"You lied the first time I saw you," said he.

"Lied!" cried the young man, starting up on his couch, with such a tone in his voice, and such a lightning in his eyes, that Aramis recoiled in spite of himself.

"I *should* say," returned Aramis, bowing, "you concealed from me what you knew of your infancy."

"A man's secrets are his own, monsieur," retorted the prisoner, "and not at the mercy of the first chance comer."

"True," said Aramis, bowing still lower than before, " 'tis true. Pardon me, but to-day, do I still occupy the place of a chance comer? I beseech you to reply, monseigneur."

This title slightly disturbed the prisoner; but nevertheless he did not appear astonished that it was given him.

"I do not know you, monsieur," said he.

"Oh, if I but dared, I would take your hand and would kiss it!"

The young man seemed as if he were going to give Aramis his hand; but the light which beamed in his eyes faded away and he coldly and distrustfully withdrew his hand again.

"Kiss the hand of a prisoner," he said, shaking his head; "to what purpose?"

"Why did you tell me," said Aramis, "that you were happy here? Why, that you aspired to nothing? Why, in a word, by thus speaking, do you prevent me from being frank in my turn?"

The same light shone a third time in the young man's eyes, but died ineffectually away as before.

"You distrust me," said Aramis.

"And why say you so, monsieur?"

"Oh, for a very simple reason; if you know what you ought to know, you ought to mistrust everybody."

"Then be not astonished that I am mistrustful, since you suspect me of knowing what I know not."

Aramis was struck with admiration at this energetic resistance.

"Oh, monseigneur, you drive me to despair!" said he, striking the armchair with his fist.

"And, on my part, I do not comprehend you, monsieur."

"Well, then, try to understand me."

The prisoner looked fixedly at Aramis.

"Sometimes it seems to me," said the latter, "that I have before me the man whom I seek, and then——"

"And then your man disappears—is it not so?" said the prisoner, smiling. "So much the better."

Aramis rose.

"Certainly," said he; "I have nothing further to say to a man who mistrusts me as you do."

"And I, monsieur," said the prisoner, in the same tone, "have nothing to say to a man who will not understand that a prisoner ought to be mistrustful of everybody."

"Even of his old friends," said Aramis. "Oh, monseigneur, you are *too* prudent!"

"Of my old friends?—you one of my old friends—you?"

"Do you no longer remember," said Aramis, "that you once saw, in the village where your early years were spent——"

"Do you know the name of the village?" asked the prisoner.

"Noisy-le-Sec, monseigneur," answered Aramis firmly.

"Go on," said the young man, with an immovable aspect.

"Stay, monseigneur," said Aramis; "if you are positively resolved to carry on this game, let us break off. I am here to tell you many things, 'tis true; but you must allow me to see that, on your side, you have a desire to know them. Before revealing the important matters I conceal, be assured I am in need of some encouragement, if not candor; a little sympathy, if not confidence. But you keep yourself intrenched in a pretended ignorance which paralyzes me. Oh, not for the reason you think; for, ignorant as you may be, or indifferent as you feign to be, you are none the less what you are, monseigneur, and there is nothing—nothing, mark me—which can cause you not to be so."

"I promise you," replied the prisoner, "to hear you without impatience. Only it appears to me that I have a right to repeat the question I have already asked—'Who *are* you?'"

"Do you remember, fifteen or eighteen years ago, seeing at

Noisy-le-Sec a cavalier, accompanied by a lady in black silk, with flame-colored ribbons in her hair?"

"Yes," said the young man; "I once asked the name of this cavalier, and they told me he called himself the Abbé d'Herblay. I was astonished that the abbé had so warlike an air, and they replied that there was nothing singular in that, seeing that he was one of Louis XIII.'s musketeers."

"Well," said Aramis, "that musketeer and abbé, afterward bishop of Vannes, is your confessor now."

"I know it; I recognized you."

"Then, monseigneur, if you know that, I must further add a fact of which you are ignorant—that if the king were to know this evening of the presence of this musketeer, this abbé, this bishop, this confessor, *here*—he, who has risked everything to visit you, would to-morrow see glitter the executioner's ax at the bottom of a dungeon more gloomy and more obscure than yours."

While hearing these words, delivered with emphasis, the young man had raised himself on his couch, and gazed more and more eagerly at Aramis.

The result of his scrutiny was that he appeared to derive some confidence from it.

"Yes," he murmured, "I remember perfectly. The woman of whom you speak came once with you, and twice afterward with another."

He hesitated.

"With another woman, who came to see you every month—is it not so, monseigneur?"

"Yes."

"Do you know who this lady was?"

The light seemed ready to flash from the prisoner's eyes.

"I am aware that she was one of the ladies of the court," he said.

"You remember that lady well, do you not?"

"Oh, my recollection can hardly be very confused on this head," said the young prisoner. "I saw that lady once with a gentleman about forty-five years old. I saw her once with you, and with the lady dressed in black. I have seen her twice since with the same person. These four people, with my master, and old Perronnette, my jailer, and the governor of the prison, are the only persons with whom I have ever spoken, and, indeed, almost the only persons I have ever seen."

"Then, you were in prison?"

"If I am a prisoner here, there I was comparatively free, although in a very narrow sense—a house which I never quitted, a garden surrounded with walls I could not clear, these constituted my residence; but you know it, as you have been there. In a word, being accustomed to live within these bounds, I never cared to leave them. And so you will understand, monsieur, that, not having seen anything of the world, I have nothing left to care for; and, therefore, if you relate anything, you will be obliged to explain everything to me."

"And I will do so," said Aramis, bowing, "for it is my duty, monseigneur."

"Well, then, begin by telling me who was my tutor."

"A worthy and, above all, an honorable gentleman, monseigneur; fit guide both for body and soul. Had you ever any reason to complain of him?"

"Oh, no; quite the contrary. But this gentleman of yours often used to tell me that my father and mother were dead. Did he deceive me, or did he speak the truth?"

"He was compelled to comply with the orders given him."

"Then he lied?"

"In one respect. Your father is dead."

"And my mother?"

"She is dead for you."

"But, then, she lives for others, does she not?"

"Yes."

"And I—I, then" (the young man looked sharply at Aramis), "am compelled to live in the obscurity of a prison?"

"Alas! I fear so."

"And that, because my presence in the world would lead to the revelation of a great secret?"

"Certainly, a very great secret."

"My enemy must indeed be powerful, to be able to shut up in the Bastile a child such as I then was."

"He is."

"More powerful than my mother, then?"

"And why do you ask that?"

"Because my mother would have taken my part."

Aramis hesitated.

"Yes, monseigneur; more powerful than your mother."

"Seeing, then, that my nurse and preceptor were carried off, and that I, also, was separated from them—either they were, or I am, very dangerous to my enemy?"

"Yes; a peril from which he freed himself, by causing the nurse and preceptor to disappear," answered Aramis quietly.

"Disappear!" cried the prisoner—"but how did they disappear?"

"In the surest possible way," answered Aramis—"they are dead."

The young man turned visibly pale, and passed his hand tremblingly over his face.

"From poison?" he asked.

"From poison."

The prisoner reflected a moment.

"My enemy must, indeed, have been very cruel, or hard beset by necessity, to assassinate those two innocent people, my sole support; for the worthy gentleman and the poor nurse had never harmed a living being."

"In your family, monseigneur, necessity is stern. And so it is necessity which compels me, to my great regret, to tell you that this gentleman and the unhappy lady have been assassinated."

"Oh, you tell me nothing I am not aware of," said the prisoner, knitting his brows.

"How?"

"I suspected it."

"Why?"

"I will tell you."

At this moment the young man, supporting himself on his two elbows, drew close to Aramis' face, with such an expression of dignity, of self-command, and of defiance even, that the bishop felt the electricity of enthusiasm strike in devouring flashes from that sacred heart of his into his brain of adamant.

"Speak, monseigneur. I have already told you that by conversing with you I endanger my life. Little value as it has, I implore you to accept it as the ransom of your own."

"Well," resumed the young man, "this is why I suspected that they killed my nurse and my preceptor."

"Whom you used to call your father?"

"Yes; whom I called my father, but whose son I well knew I was not."

"Who caused you to suppose so?"

"For the same reason that you, monsieur, are too respectful for a friend, he was also too respectful for a father."

"I, however," said Aramis, "have no intention to disguise myself."

The young man nodded assent, and continued:

"Undoubtedly, I was not destined to perpetual seclusion," said the prisoner; "and that which makes me believe so, above all, now, is the care that was taken to render me as accomplished a cavalier as possible. The gentleman attached to my person taught me everything he knew himself—mathematics, a little geometry, astronomy, fencing, and riding. Every morning I went through military exercises, and practiced on horseback. Well, one morning, during summer, it being very hot, I went to sleep in the hall. Nothing up to that period, except the respect paid me, had enlightened me, or even roused my suspicions. I lived as children, as birds, as plants, as the air and the sun do. I had just turned my fifteenth year——"

"This, then, is eight years ago?"

"Yes, nearly; but I have ceased to reckon time."

"Excuse me; but what did your tutor tell you to encourage you to work?"

"He used to say that a man was bound to make for himself, in the world, that fortune which Heaven had refused him at his birth. He added, that, being a poor, obscure orphan, I had no one but myself to look to; and that nobody either did, or ever would, take any interest in me. I was then in the hall I have spoken of, asleep from fatigue in fencing. My preceptor was in his room on the first floor, just over me. Suddenly I heard him exclaim, and then he called: 'Perronnette! Perronnette!' It was my nurse whom he called."

"Yes, I know it," said Aramis. "Continue, monseigneur."

"Very likely she was in the garden, for my preceptor came hastily downstairs. I rose, anxious at seeing him anxious. He opened the garden-door, still crying out, 'Perronnette! Perronnette!' The windows of the hall looked into the court; the shutters were closed; but through a chink in them I saw my tutor draw near a large well, which was almost directly under the windows of his study. He stooped over the brim, looked into the well, again cried out, and made wild and affrighted gestures. Where I was, I could not only see, but hear—and see and hear I did."

"Go on, I pray you," said Aramis.

"Dame Perronnette came running up, hearing the governor's cries. He went to meet her, took her by the arm, and drew her quickly toward the edge; after which, as they both bent over it together, 'Look, look,' cried he, 'what a misfortune!' "

" 'Calm yourself, calm yourself,' said Perronnette; 'what is the matter?'

" 'The letter!' he exclaimed; 'do you see that letter?' pointing to the bottom of the well.

" 'What letter?' she cried.

" 'The letter you see down there; the last letter from the queen.'

"At this word I trembled. My tutor—he who passed for my

father, he who was continually recommending me modesty and humility—in correspondence with the queen.

" 'The queen's last letter!' cried Perronnette, without showing more astonishment than at seeing this letter at the bottom of the well; 'but how came it there?'

" 'A chance, Dame Perronnette—a singular chance. I was entering my room, and on opening the door, the window, too, being open, a puff of air came suddenly and carried off this paper —this letter of her majesty's; I darted after it, and gained the window just in time to see it flutter a moment in the breeze and disappear down the well.'

" 'Well,' said Dame Perronnette; 'and if the letter has fallen into the well 'tis all the same as if it was burned; as the queen burns all her letters every time she comes——'

"And so, you see, this lady who came every month was the queen," said the prisoner.

" 'Doubtless, doubtless,' continued the old gentleman; 'but this letter contained instructions—how can I follow them?'

" 'Write immediately to her; give her a plain account of the accident, and the queen will no doubt write you another letter in place of this.'

" 'Oh! the queen would never believe the story,' said the good gentleman, shaking his head; 'she will imagine that I want to keep this letter instead of giving it up like the rest, so as to have a hold over her. She is so distrustful, and Monsieur de Mazarin so— This devil of an Italian is capable of having us poisoned at the first breath of suspicion.' "

Aramis almost imperceptibly smiled.

" 'You know, Dame Perronnette, they are both so suspicious in all that concerns Philippe.'

" 'Philippe' was the name they gave me," said the prisoner.

" 'Well, 'tis no use hesitating,' said Dame Perronnette, 'somebody must go down the well.'

" 'Of course; so that the person who goes down may read the paper as he is coming up.'

" 'But let us choose some villager who cannot read, and then you will be at ease.'

" 'Granted; but will not any one who descends guess that a paper must be important for which we risk a man's life? However, you have given me an idea, Dame Perronnette; somebody shall go down the well, but that somebody shall be myself.'

"But at this notion Dame Perronnette lamented and cried in such a manner, and so implored the old nobleman, with tears in her eyes, that he promised her to obtain a ladder long enough to reach down, while she went in search of some stout-hearted youth, whom she was to persuade that a jewel had fallen into the well, and that this jewel was wrapped in a paper. 'And as paper,' remarked my preceptor, 'naturally unfolds in water, the young man would not be surprised at finding nothing, after all, but the letter wide open.'

" 'But perhaps the writing will be already effaced by that time,' said Dame Perronnette.

" 'No consequence, provided we secure the letter. On returning it to the queen she will see at once that we have not betrayed her; and, consequently, as we shall not rouse the distrust of Mazarin, we shall have nothing to fear from him.'

"Having come to this resolution, they parted. I pushed back the shutter, and, seeing that my tutor was about to re-enter, I threw myself on my couch, in a confusion of brain caused by all I had just heard. My governor opened the door a few moments after, and thinking I was asleep, gently closed it again. As soon as ever it was shut I rose, and listening, heard the sound of re-tiring footsteps. Then I returned to the shutter, and saw my tutor and Dame Perronnette go out together. I was alone in the house. They had hardly closed the gate before I sprang from the window and ran to the well. Then, just as my governor had leaned over, so leaned I. Something white and luminous glistened in the green and quivering ripples of the water. The brilliant disk fascinated and allured me; my eyes became fixed, and I could hardly breathe. The well seemed to draw me in with its large mouth and icy breath; and I thought I read, at the bottom of the water, characters of fire traced upon the letter the queen had touched. Then, scarcely knowing what I was about, and urged on by one of those instinctive impulses which drive men upon their destruction, I lowered the cord from the windlass of the well to within about three feet of the water, leaving the bucket dangling, and at the same time taking infinite pains not to disturb that coveted letter, which was beginning to change its white tint for a greenish hue—proof enough that it was sinking—and then, with the rope weltering in my hands, slid down into the abyss. When I saw myself hanging over the dark pool, when I saw the sky lessening above my head, a cold shudder came over me, a chill fear got the better of me, I was seized with giddiness, and the hair rose on my head; but my strong will still reigned supreme over all the terror and disquietude. I gained the water, and at once plunged into it, holding on by one hand, while I immersed the other and seized the dear letter, which, alas! came in two in my grasp. I concealed the two fragments in my body-coat, and, helping myself with my feet against the sides of the pit, and clinging on with my hands, agile and vigorous as I was, and, above all, pressed for time, I regained the brink, drenching it as I touched it with the water that streamed off me. I was no sooner out of the well with my prize than I rushed into the sunlight, and took refuge in a kind of shrubbery at the bottom of the garden. As I entered my hiding-place, the bell which resounded when the great gate was opened, rang. It was my preceptor come back again. I had but just time. I calculated that it would take ten minutes before he would gain my place of concealment, even if, guessing where I was, he came straight to it; and twenty if he were obliged to look for me. But this was time enough to allow me to read the cherished letter, whose fragments I hastened to unite again. The writing was already fading, but I managed to decipher it all."

"And what read you there, monseigneur?" asked Aramis, deeply interested.

"Quite enough, monsieur, to see that my tutor was a man of noble rank, and that Perronnette, without being a lady of quality, was far better than a servant; and also to perceive that I must myself be high-born, since the queen, Anne of Austria, and Mazarin, the prime minister, commended me so earnestly to their care."

Here the young man paused, quite overcome.

"And what happened?" asked Aramis.

"It happened, monsieur," answered he, "that the workmen they had summoned found nothing in the well, after the closest search; that my governor perceived that the brink was all watery; that I was not so dried by the sun as to escape Dame Perronnette's observing that my garments were moist; and, lastly, that I was seized with a violent fever, owing to the chill and the excitement of my discovery, an attack of delirium supervening, during which I related the whole adventure; so that, guided by my avowal, my governor found under the bolster the two pieces of the queen's letter."

"Ah!" said Aramis, "now I understand."

"Beyond this, all is conjecture. Doubtless the unfortunate lady and gentleman, not daring to keep the occurrence secret, wrote all to the queen, and sent back to her the torn letter."

"After which," said Aramis, "you were arrested and removed to the Bastile."

"As you see."

"Then your two attendants disappeared?"

"Alas!"

"Let us not take up our time with the dead, but see what can be done with the living. You told me you were resigned."

"I repeat it."

"Without any desire for freedom?"

"As I told you."

"Without ambition, sorrow, or thought?"

The young man made no answer.

"Well," asked Aramis, "why are you silent?"

"I think I have spoken enough," answered the prisoner, "and that now it is your turn. I am weary."

Aramis gathered himself up, and a shade of deep solemnity spread itself over his countenance. It was evident that he had reached the crisis in the part he had come to the prison to play.

"One question," said Aramis.

"What is it? Speak."

"In the house you inhabited there were neither looking-glasses nor mirrors?"

"What are those two words, and what is their meaning?" asked the young man. "I have no sort of knowledge of them."

"They designate two pieces of furniture which reflect objects; so that, for instance, you may see in them your own lineaments, as you see mine now, with the naked eye."

"No; then there was neither a glass nor a mirror in the house," answered the young man.

Aramis looked round him.

"Nor is there here either," he said; "they have again taken the same precaution."

"To what end?"

"You will know directly. Now, you have told me that you were instructed in mathematics, astronomy, fencing, and riding; but you have not said a word about history."

"My tutor sometimes related to me the principal deeds of the King St. Louis, King Francis I., and King Henry IV."

"Is that all?"

"Very nearly."

"This also was done by design, then; just as they deprived you of mirrors, which reflect the present, so they left you in ignorance of history, which reflects the past. Since your imprisonment, books have been forbidden you; so that you are unacquainted with a number of facts, by means of which you would be able to reconstruct the shattered edifice of your recollections and your hopes."

"It is true," said the young man.

"Listen, then; I will in a few words tell you what has passed

in France during the last twenty-three or twenty-four years;
that is, from the probable date of your birth; in a word, from
the time that interests you."

"Say on."

And the young man resumed his serious and attentive attitude.

"Do you know who was the son of Henry IV.?"

"At least, I know who his successor was."

"How?"

"By means of a coin dated 1610, which bears the effigy of
Henry IV.; and another of 1612, bearing that of Louis XIII. So
I presumed that, there being only two years between the two
dates, Louis was Henry's successor."

"Then," said Aramis, "you know that the last reigning monarch was Louis XIII.?"

"I do," answered the youth, slightly reddening.

"Well, he was a prince full of noble ideas and great projects,
always, alas! deferred by trouble of the times and the struggle
that his minister, Richelieu, had to maintain against the great
nobles of France. The king himself was of a feeble character, and
died young and unhappy."

"I know it."

"He had been long anxious about having an heir; a care which
weighs heavily on princes, who desire to leave behind them
more than one pledge that their thoughts and their works will
be continued."

"Did the king, then, die childless?" asked the prisoner, smiling.

"No, but he was long without one, and for a long while thought
he should be the last of his race. This idea had reduced him to
the depths of despair, when suddenly, his wife, Anne of Austria——"

The prisoner trembled.

"Did you know," said Aramis, "that Louis XIII.'s wife was
called Anne of Austria?"

"Continue," said the young man, without replying to the
question.

"When suddenly," resumed Aramis, "the queen announced an
interesting event. There was great joy at the intelligence, and
all prayed for her happy delivery. On the 5th of September,
1638, she gave birth to a son."

Here Aramis looked at his companion, and thought he observed him turning pale.

"You are about to hear," said Aramis, "an account which few

could now give; for it refers to a secret which they think buried with the dead, or entombed in the abyss of the confessional."

"And you will tell me this secret," broke in the youth.

"Oh!" said Aramis, with unmistakable emphasis, "I do not know that I ought to risk this secret by intrusting it to one who has no desire to quit the Bastile."

"I hear you, monsieur."

"The queen, then, gave birth to a son. But while the court was rejoicing over the event, when the king had shown the new-born child to the nobility and people, and was sitting gayly down to table, to celebrate the event, the queen, who was alone in her room, was again taken ill and gave birth to a second son."

"Oh!" said the prisoner, betraying a better acquaintance with affairs than he had owned to, "I thought that Monsieur was only born a——"

Aramis raised his finger.

"Let me continue," said he.

The prisoner sighed impatiently, and paused.

"Yes," said Aramis, "the queen had a second son, whom Dame Perronnette, the midwife, received in her arms."

"Dame Perronnette!" murmured the young man.

"They ran at once to the banqueting-room, and whispered to the king what had happened; he rose and quitted the table. But this time it was no longer happiness that his face expressed, but something akin to terror. The birth of twins changed into bitterness the joy to which that of an only son had given rise, seeing that in France (a fact you are assuredly ignorant of), it is the oldest of the kings' sons who succeeds his father."

"I know it."

"And that the doctors and jurists assert that there is ground for doubting whether he who first makes his appearance is the elder by the law of Heaven and of nature."

The prisoner uttered a smothered cry, and became whiter than the coverlet under which he hid himself.

"Now you understand," pursued Aramis, "that the king, who, with so much pleasure, saw himself repeated in one, was in despair about two; fearing that the second might dispute the first's claim to seniority, which had been recognized only two hours before; and so this second son, relying on party interests and caprices, might one day sow discord and engender civil war in the kingdom; by these means destroying the very dynasty he should have strengthened."

"Oh, I understand! I understand!" murmured the young man.

"Well," continued Aramis, "this is what they relate, what they declare; this is why one of the queen's two sons, shamefully parted from his brother, shamefully sequestered, is buried in the profoundest obscurity; this is why that second son has disappeared, and so completely that not a soul in France, save his mother, is aware of his existence."

"Yes, his mother, who has cast him off," cried the prisoner, in a tone of despair.

"Except, also," Aramis went on, "the lady in the black dress; and, finally, excepting——"

"Excepting yourself. Is it not? You who come and relate all this; you, who rouse in my soul curiosity, hatred, ambition, and, perhaps, even the thirst of vengeance; except you, monsieur, who, if you are the man whom I expect, whom the note I have received applies to; whom, in short, Heaven ought to send me, must possess about you——"

"What?" asked Aramis.

"A portrait of the king, Louis XIV., who at this moment reigns upon the throne of France."

"Here is the portrait," replied the bishop, handing the prisoner a miniature in enamel, on which Louis was depicted lifelike, with a handsome, lofty mien. The prisoner eagerly seized the portrait, and gazed at it with devouring eyes.

"And now, monseigneur," said Aramis, "here is a mirror."

Aramis left the prisoner time to recover his ideas.

"So high! so high!" murmured the young man, eagerly comparing the likeness of Louis with his own countenance reflected in the glass.

"What do you think of it?" at length said Aramis.

"I think that I am lost," replied the captive; "the king will never set me free."

"And I—I demand," added the bishop, fixing his piercing eyes significantly upon the prisoner, "I demand which of the two is the king; the one whom this miniature portrays, or whom the glass reflects?"

"The king, monsieur," sadly replied the young man, "is he who is on the throne, who is not in prison; and who, on the other hand, can cause others to be entombed there. Royalty is power; and you see well how powerless I am."

"Monseigneur," answered Aramis, with a respect he had not yet manifested, "the king, mark me, will, if you desire it, be he who, quitting his dungeon, shall maintain himself upon the throne, on which his friends will place him."

"Tempt me not, monsieur," broke in the prisoner bitterly.

"Be not weak, monseigneur," persisted Aramis; "I have brought all the proofs of your birth; consult them; satisfy yourself that you are a king's son; and then let us act."

"No, no; it is impossible."

"Unless, indeed," resumed the bishop ironically, "it be the destiny of your race that the brothers excluded from the throne should be always princes void of courage and honesty, as was your uncle, Monsieur Gaston d'Orleans, who ten times conspired against his brother, Louis XIII."

"What!" cried the prince, astonished, "my uncle Gaston 'conspired against his brother;' conspired to dethrone him?"

"Exactly, monseigneur; for no other reason. I tell you the truth."

"And he had friends—devoted ones?"

"As much so as I am to you."

"And, after all, what did he do? Failed!"

"He failed, I admit; but always through his own fault; and for the sake of purchasing—not his life—for the life of the king's brother is sacred and inviolable—but his liberty, he sacrificed the lives of all his friends, one after another. And so, at this day, he is the very shame of history, and the detestation of a hundred noble families in this kingdom."

"I understand, monsieur; either by weakness or treachery, my uncle slew his friends."

"By weakness; which, in princes, is always treachery."

"And cannot a man fail, then, from incapacity and ignorance? Do you really believe it possible that a poor captive such as I, brought up, not only at a distance from the court, but even from the world—do you believe it possible that such a one could assist those of his friends who should attempt to serve him?"

And, as Aramis was about to reply, the young man suddenly cried out, with a violence which betrayed the temper of his blood:

"We are speaking of friends; but how can *I* have any friends —I, whom no one knows, and have neither liberty, money, nor influence, to gain any?"

"I fancy I had the honor to offer myself to your royal highness."

"Oh, do not style me so, monsieur; 'tis either treachery or cruelty. Bid me not think of aught else than these prison walls, which confine me; let me again love, or, at least, submit to my slavery and my obscurity."

"Monseigneur, monseigneur, if you again utter these desperate words—if, after having received proof of your high birth,

you still remain poor-sighted in body and soul, I will comply
with your desire, I will depart, and renounce forever the service of a master to whom so eagerly I came to devote my assistance and my life!"

"Monsieur," cried the prince, "would it not have been better
for you to have reflected, before telling me all that you have
done, that you have broken my heart forever!"

"And so I desired to do, monseigneur."

"To talk to me about power, grandeur, and even royalty. Is
a prison the fitting place? You wish to make me believe in
splendor, and we are lying hidden in night; you boast of glory,
and we are smothering our words in the curtains of this miserable bed; you give me glimpses of absolute power, and I hear
the step of the jailer in the corridor—that step which, after
all, makes you tremble more than it does me. To render me
somewhat less incredulous, free me from the Bastile; let me
breathe the fresh air; give me my spurs and trusty sword, then
we shall begin to understand each other."

"It is precisely my intention to give you all this, monseigneur,
and more; only, do you desire it?"

"A word more," said the prince. "I know there are guards in
every gallery, bolts to every door, cannon and soldiery at every
barrier. How will you overcome the sentries—spike the guns?
How will you break through the bolts and bars?"

"Monseigneur—how did you get the note which announced
my arrival to you?"

"You can bribe a jailer for such a thing as a note."

"If we can corrupt one turnkey, we can corrupt ten."

"Well, I admit that it may be possible to release a poor captive from the Bastile; possible so to conceal him that the king's
people shall not again insnare him; possible, in some unknown
retreat, to sustain the unhappy wretch in some suitable manner."

"Monseigneur!" said Aramis, smiling.

"I admit that, whoever would do thus much for me, would
seem more than mortal in my eyes; but as you tell me I am a
prince, brother of a king, how can you restore me the rank and
power which my mother and my brother have deprived me of?
And as, to effect this, I must pass a life of war and hatred, how
will you make me prevail in those combats—render me invulnerable by my enemies? Ah! monsieur, reflect upon this; place
me, to-morrow, in some dark cavern in a mountain's base; yield
me the delight of hearing in freedom the sounds of river and
plain, of beholding in freedom the sun of the blue heavens, or

the stormy sky, and it is enough. Promise me no more than this, for, indeed, more you cannot give, and it would be a crime to deceive me, since you call yourself my friend."

Aramis waited in silence.

"Monseigneur," he resumed, after a moment's reflection, "I admire the firm, sound sense which dictates your words; I am happy to have discovered my monarch's mind."

"Again, again! oh! for mercy's sake," cried the prince, pressing his icy hands upon his clammy brow, "do not play with me! I have no need to be a king to be the happiest of men."

"But I, monseigneur, wish you to be a king for the good of humanity."

"Ah!" said the prince, with fresh distrust inspired by the word, "ah! with what, then, has humanity to reproach my brother?"

"I forgot to say, monseigneur, that if you would allow me to guide you, and if you consent to become the most powerful monarch on earth, you will have promoted the interests of all the friends whom I devote to the success of your cause, and these friends are numerous."

"Numerous?"

"Less numerous than powerful, monseigneur."

"Explain yourself."

"It is impossible; I will explain, I swear before Heaven, on that day that I see you sitting on the throne of France."

"But my brother?"

"You shall decree his fate. Do you pity him?"

"Him, who leaves me to perish in a dungeon? No, I pity him not."

"So much the better."

"He might have himself come to this prison, have taken me by the hand and have said, 'My brother, Heaven created us to love, not to contend with one another. I come to you. A barbarous prejudice has condemned you to pass your days in obscurity, far from all men, and deprived of every joy. I will make you sit down beside me; I will buckle round your waist our father's sword. Will you take advantage of this reconciliation to put down or to restrain me? Will you employ that sword to spill my blood?' 'Oh! never,' I would have replied to him. 'I look on you as my preserver, and will respect you as my master. You give me far more than Heaven bestowed; for through you I possess liberty and the privilege of loving and being loved in this world.' "

"And you would have kept your word, monseigneur?"

"On my life! While now—now that I have guilty ones to punish."

"In what manner, monseigneur?"

"What do you say as to the resemblance that Heaven has given me to my brother?"

"I say that there was in that likeness a providential instruction which the king ought to have heeded; I say that your mother committed a crime in rendering those different in happiness and fortune whom nature created so similar in her womb; and I conclude that the object of punishment should be only to restore the equilibrium."

"By which you mean——"

"That if I restore you to your place on your brother's throne, he shall take yours in prison."

"Alas! there is so much suffering in prison, especially to a man who has drunk so deeply of the cup of enjoyment."

"Your royal highness will always be free to act as you may desire; and if it seems good to you, after punishment, may pardon."

"Good. And now, are you aware of one thing, monsieur?"

"Tell me, my prince."

"It is that I will hear nothing further from you till I am clear of the Bastile."

"I was going to say to your highness that I should only have the pleasure of seeing you once again."

"And then?"

"The day when my prince leaves these gloomy walls."

"Heavens! how will you give me notice of it?"

"By myself coming to fetch you." .

"Yourself?"

"My prince, do not leave this chamber save with me, or if in my absence you are compelled to do so, remember that I am not concerned in it."

"And so I am not to speak a word of this to any one whatever, save to you?"

"Save only to me."

Aramis bowed very low; the prince offered his hand.

"Monsieur," he said, in a tone that issued from his heart, "one word more, my last. If you have sought me for my destruction, if you are only a tool in the hands of my enemies, if from our conference, in which you have sounded the depths of my mind, anything worse than captivity result, that is to say, if death befall me, still receive my blessing, for you will have ended my roubles and given me repose from the tormenting fever that as preyed upon me these eight years."

"Monseigneur, wait the result ere you judge me," said Armis.

"I say that, in such a case, I bless and forgive you. If, on the other hand, you are come to restore me to that position in the unshine of fortune and glory to which I was destined by Heaven; if by your means I am enabled to live in the memory of man, and confer luster on my race by deeds of valor, or by solid benefits bestowed upon my people; if, from my present depths of sorrow, aided by your generous hand, I raise myself to the very height of honor, then to you, whom I thank with blessings, to you will I offer half my power and my glory; though you would still be but partly recompensed, and your share must always remain incomplete, since I could not divide with you the happiness received at your hands."

"Monseigneur," replied Aramis, moved by the pallor and excitement of the young man, "the nobleness of your heart fills me with joy and admiration. It is not you who will have to thank me, but rather the nation whom you will render happy, the posterity whose name you will make glorious. Yes; I shall indeed have bestowed upon you more than life, as I shall have given you immortality."

The prince offered his hand to Aramis, who sank upon his knee and kissed it.

"It is the first act of homage paid to our future king," said he. "When I see you again, I shall say, 'Good-day, sire.'"

"Till then," said the young man, pressing his wan and wasted fingers over his heart—"till then, no more dreams, no more strain upon my life—it would break! Oh, monsieur, how small is my prison—how low the window—how narrow are the doors! To think that so much pride, splendor, and happiness should be able to enter in and remain here!"

"Your royal highness makes me proud," said Aramis, "since you infer it is I who brought all this."

And he rapped immediately on the door. The jailer came to open it with Baisemeaux, who, devoured by fear and uneasiness, was beginning, in spite of himself, to listen at the door. Happily, neither of the speakers had forgotten to smother his voice, even in the most passionate outbreaks.

"What a confessor!" said the governor, forcing a laugh. "Who would believe that a mere recluse, a man almost dead, could have committed crimes so numerous, and so long to tell of?"

Aramis made no reply. He was eager to leave the Bastile, where the secret which overwhelmed him seemed to double the weight of the walls. As soon as they reached Baisemeaux's quarters:

"Let us proceed to business, my dear governor," said Aramis.

"Alas!" replied Baisemeaux.

"You have to ask me for my receipt for one hundred and fifty thousand livres," said the bishop.

"And to pay over the first third of the sum," added the poor governor, with a sigh, taking three steps toward his iron strongbox.

"Here is the receipt," said Aramis.

"And here is the money," returned Baisemeaux, with a threefold sigh.

"The order instructed me only to give a receipt; it said nothing about receiving the money," rejoined Aramis. "Adieu, Monsieur le Gouverneur."

And he departed, leaving Baisemeaux almost more than stifled with joy and surprise at this regal present so liberally bestowed by the confessor-extraordinary to the Bastile.

Chapter 2 — HOW MOUSTON HAD BECOME FATTER WITHOUT GIVING PORTHOS NOTICE THEREOF, AND OF THE TROUBLES WHICH CONSEQUENTLY BEFELL THAT WORTHY GENTLEMAN

Since the departure of Athos for Blois, Porthos and D'Artagnan were seldom together. One was occupied with harassing duties for the king, the other had been making many purchases of furniture which he intended to forward to his estate, and by aid of which he hoped to establish in his various residences something of that court luxury which he had witnessed in all its dazzling brightness in his majesty's society. D'Artagnan, ever faithful, one morning, during an interval of service, thought about Porthos, and being uneasy at not having heard anything of him for a fortnight, directed his steps toward his hotel, and pounced upon him just as he was getting up. The worthy baron had a pensive—nay, more than pensive—a melancholy air. He was sitting on his bed, only half-dressed, and with legs dangling over the edge, contemplating a host of garments, which, with their fringes, lace, embroidery, and slashes of ill-assorted hues, were strewed all over the floor. Porthos, sad and reflective as La Fontaine's hare, did not observe D'Artagnan's entrance, which was, moreover, screened at this moment by M. Mouston, whose personal corpulency, quite enough at any time to hide one man from another, was effectually doubled by a scarlet coat which the intendant was holding up for his master's inspection, by the sleeves, that he might the better see it all over. D'Artagnan stopped at the threshold and looked at the pensive Porthos, and then, as the sight of the innumerable garments strewing the floor caused mighty sighs to heave from the bosom of that excellent gentleman, D'Artagnan thought it time to put an end to these dismal reflections, and coughed by way of announcing himself.

"Ah!" exclaimed Porthos, whose countenance brightened with joy, "ah! ah! Here is D'Artagnan. I shall then get hold of an idea!"

At these words, Mouston, doubting what was going on behind him, got out of the way, smiling kindly at the friend of his master, who thus found himself freed from the material obstacle which had prevented his reaching D'Artagnan. Porthos made his sturdy knees crack again in rising, and crossing the room in two strides, found himself face to face with his friend, whom he folded to his breast with a force of affection that seemed to increase with every day.

"Ah!" he repeated, "you are always welcome, dear friend; but just now you are more welcome than ever."

"But you seem in the dumps here?" exclaimed D'Artagnan.

Porthos replied by a look expressive of dejection.

"Well, then, tell me all about it, Porthos, my friend, unless it is a secret."

"In the first place," returned Porthos, "you know I have no secrets from you. This, then, is what saddens me."

"Wait a minute, Porthos; let me first get rid of all this litter of satin and velvet."

"Oh, never mind," said Porthos contemptuously; "it is all trash."

"Trash, Porthos! Cloth at twenty livres an ell! Gorgeous satin! regal velvet!"

"Then you think these clothes are——"

"Splendid, Porthos, splendid! I'll wager that you alone in France have so many; and suppose you never had any more made, and were to live a hundred years, which wouldn't astonish

me, you could still wear a new dress the day of your death,
without being obliged to see the nose of a single tailor from
now till then."

Porthos shook his head.

"Come, my friend," said D'Artagnan, "this unnatural melancholy in you frightens me. My dear Porthos, pray get out of it
then. And the sooner the better."

"Yes, my friend, so I will; if, indeed, it is possible."

"Perhaps you have received bad news from Bracieux?"

"No; they have felled the wood, and it has yielded a third
more than the estimate."

"Then has there been a falling off in the pools of Pierrefonds?"

"No, my friend; they have been fished, and there is enough
left to stock all the pools in the neighborhood."

"Perhaps your estate at Vallon has been destroyed by an
earthquake?"

"No, my friend; on the contrary, the ground was struck with
lightning a hundred paces from the château, and a fountain
sprung up in a place entirely destitute of water."

"What in the world *is* the matter, then?"

"The fact is, I have received an invitation for the *fête* at
Vaux," said Porthos, with a lugubrious expression.

"Well, do you complain of that? The king has caused a hundred mortal heart-burnings among the courtiers by refusing invitations. And so, my dear friend, you are really going to Vaux?"

"Indeed I am!"

"You will see a magnificent sight."

"Alas! I doubt it, though."

"Everything that is grand in France will be brought together
there."

"Ah!" cried Porthos, tearing out a lock of his hair in despair.

"Eh! good heavens, are you ill?" cried D'Artagnan.

"I am as well as the Pont-Neuf. It isn't that."

"But what is it, then?"

" 'Tis that I have no clothes."

D'Artagnan stood petrified.

"No clothes! Porthos, no clothes!" he cried, "when I see at
least fifty suits on the floor."

"Fifty, truly; but not one which fits me."

"What, not one that fits you? But are you not measured, then,
when you give an order?"

"To be sure he is," answered Mouston; "but, unfortunately,
I have grown stouter!"

"What, *you* stouter?"

"So much so that I am now bigger than the baron. Would you believe it, monsieur?"

"Parbleu! it seems to me that is quite evident."

"Do you see, stupid?" said Porthos, "that is quite evident."

"Be still, my dear Porthos," resumed D'Artagnan, becoming slightly impatient. "I don't understand why your clothes should not fit you, because Mouston has grown stouter."

"I am going to explain it," said Porthos. "You remember having related to me the story of the Roman general, Antony, who had always seven wild boars kept roasting, each cooked up to a different point; so that he might be able to have his dinner at any time of the day he chose to ask for it. Well, then, I resolved, as at any time I might be invited to court to spend a week, I resolved to have always seven suits ready for the occasion."

"Capitally reasoned, Porthos—only a man must have a fortune like yours to gratify such whims. Without counting the time lost in being measured, the fashions are always changing."

"That is exactly the point," said Porthos, "in regard to which I flatter myself I had hit on a very ingenious device."

"Tell me what it is; for I don't doubt your genius."

"You remember what Mouston once was, then?"

"Yes; when he used to call himself Mousqueton."

"And you remember, too, the period when he began to grow fatter?"

"No, not exactly. I beg your pardon, my good Mouston."

"Oh! you are not in fault, monsieur," said Mouston graciously. "You were in Paris, and as for us, we were at Pierrefonds."

"Well, well, my dear Porthos, there was a time when Mouston began to grow fat. Is that what you wished to say?"

"Yes, my friend; and I greatly rejoice over the period."

"Indeed, I believe you do!" exclaimed D'Artagnan.

"You understand," continued Porthos, "what a world of trouble it spared me."

"No, I do not, though."

"Look here, my friend. In the first place, as you have said, to be measured is a loss of time, even though it occur only once a fortnight. And then, one may be traveling; and then you wish to have seven suits always with you. In short, I have a horror of letting any one take my measure. Confound it! either one is a nobleman or not. To be scrutinized and scanned by a fellow who completely analyzes you, by inch and line—'tis degrading!

Here, they find you too hollow; there, too prominent. They recognize your strong and weak points. See, now, when we leave the measurer's hands, we are like those strongholds whose angles and different thicknesses have been ascertained by a spy."

"In truth, my dear Porthos, you possess ideas entirely your own."

"Ah! you see when a man is an engineer——"

"And has fortified Belle-Isle—'tis natural, my friend."

"Well, I had an idea, which would doubtless have proved a good one, but for Mouston's carelessness."

D'Artagnan glanced at Mouston, who replied by a slight movement of his body, as if to say, "You will see whether I am at all to blame in all this."

"I congratulated myself, then," resumed Porthos, "at seeing Mouston get fat; and I did all I could, by means of substantial feeding, to make him stout—always in the hope that he would come to equal myself in girth, and could then be measured in my stead."

"Ah!" cried D'Artagnan. "I see—that spared you both time and humiliation."

"Consider my joy when, after a year and a half's judicious feeding—for I used to feed him up myself—the fellow——"

"Oh! I lent a good hand myself, monsieur," said Mouston humbly.

"That's true. Consider my joy when, one morning, I perceived Mouston was obliged to squeeze in, as I once did myself, to get through the little secret door that those fools of architects had made in the chamber of the late Madame du Vallon, in the Château of Pierrefonds. And, by the way, about that door, my friend, I should like to ask you, who know everything, why these wretches of architects, who ought by rights to have the compasses in their eye came to make doorways through which nobody but thin people could pass?"

"Oh, those doors," answered D'Artagnan, "were meant for gallants, and they have generally slight and slender figures."

"Madame du Vallon had no gallant!" answered Porthos majestically.

"Perfectly true, my friend," resumed D'Artagnan; "but the architects were imagining the possibility of your marrying again."

"Ah! that is possible," said Porthos. "And now I have received an explanation how it is that doorways are made too narrow, let us return to the subject of Mouston's fatness. But see how the two things apply to each other. I have always no-

ed that ideas run parallel. And so, observe this phenomenon,
'Artagnan. I was talking to you of Mouston, who is fat, and it
d us on to Madame du Vallon——"

"Who was thin?"

"Hum! Is it not marvelous?"

"My dear friend, a savant of my acquaintance, Monsieur
ostar, has made the same observation as you have, and he
lls the process by some Greek name which I forget."

"What! my remark is not then original?" cried Porthos,
tounded. "I thought I was the discoverer."

"My friend, the fact was known before Aristotle's days—that
to say, nearly two thousand years ago."

"Well, well, 'tis no less true," said Porthos, delighted at the
ea of having concurred with the sages of antiquity.

"Wonderfully—but suppose we return to Mouston. It seems
me, we have left him fattening under our very eyes."

"Yes, monsieur," said Mouston.

"Well," said Porthos, "Mouston fattened so well that he grati-
d all my hopes by reaching my standard; a fact of which I
as well able to convince myself by seeing the rascal, one day,
a waistcoat of mine, which he had turned into a coat—a
aistcoat, the mere embroidery of which was worth a hundred
stoles."

" 'Twas only to try it on, monsieur," said Mouston.

"From that moment I determined to put Mouston in com-
unication with my tailors, and to have him measured instead
myself."

"A capital idea, Porthos; but Mouston is a foot and a half
orter than you."

"Exactly! They measured him down to the ground, and the
d of the skirt came just below my knee."

"What a wonder you are, Porthos! Such a thing could happen
ly to you."

"Ah! yes; pay your compliments; there is something to do it
on. It was exactly at that time—that is to say, nearly two
ars and a half ago—that I set out for Belle-Isle, instructing
ouston (so as always to have, in every event, a pattern of
ery fashion) to have a coat made for himself every month."

"And did Mouston neglect complying with your instructions?
a! that would not be right, Mouston."

"No, monsieur; quite the contrary, quite the contrary!"

"No, he never forgot to have his coats made; but he for-
t to inform me that he had got stouter!"

"But it was not my fault, monsieur! your tailor never to me."

"And this to such an extent, monsieur," continued Portho "that the fellow in two years has gained eighteen inches girth, and so my last dozen coats are all too large, from a fo to a foot and a half!"

"But the rest; those which were made when you were of t same size?"

"They are no longer the fashion, my dear friend. Were I put them on, I should look like a fresh arrival from Siam, a as though I had been two years away from court."

"I understand your difficulty. You have how many new su —nine? thirty-six? and yet not one to wear. Well, you mu have a thirty-seventh made, and give the thirty-six to Mousto

"Ah! monsieur!" said Mouston, with a gratified air. "T truth is, that monsieur has always been very generous to me

"Do you mean to think that I hadn't that idea, or that I w deterred by the expense? But it wants only two days to t *fête;* I received the invitation yesterday, made Mouston p hither with my wardrobe, and only this morning discovered n misfortune; and from now till the day after to-morrow, the isn't a single fashionable tailor who will undertake to make me suit."

"That is to say, one covered all over with gold, isn't it?"

"I wish it so! all over."

"Oh, we shall manage it. You won't leave for three days. T invitations are for Wednesday, and this is only Sunday mor ing."

" 'Tis true; but Aramis has strongly advised me to be at Va twenty-four hours beforehand."

"How, Aramis?"

"Yes, it was Aramis who brought me the invitation."

"Ah! to be sure, I see. You are invited on the part Monsieur Fouquet?"

"By no means; by the king, dear friend. The letter bears t following, as large as life: 'Monsieur le Baron du Vallon is i formed that the king has condescended to place him on the in tation list——' "

"Very good; but you leave with Monsieur Fouquet?"

"And when I think," cried Porthos, stamping on the flo "when I think I shall have no clothes, I am ready to burst wi rage. I should like to strangle somebody or destroy something

"Neither strangle anybody nor destroy anything, Porthos;

will manage it all; put on one of your thirty-six suits, and come with me to a tailor."

"Pooh! my agent has seen them all this morning."

"Even Monsieur Percerin?"

"Who is Monsieur Percerin?"

"Only the king's tailor."

"Oh! ah! yes," said Porthos, who wished to appear to know the king's tailor, but now heard his name mentioned for the first time; "to Monsieur Percerin's, by Jove! I thought he would be too much engaged."

"Doubtless he will be, but be at ease, Porthos; he will do for me what he won't do for another. Only you must allow yourself to be measured."

"Ah!" said Porthos, with a sigh, " 'tis vexatious, but what would you have me do?"

"Do? as others do; as the king does."

"What! do they measure the king, too? Does *he* put up with it?"

"The king is a beau, my good friend, and so are you, too, whatever you may say about it."

Porthos smiled triumphantly.

"Let us go to the king's tailor," he said; "and, since he measures the king, I think, by my faith! I may well allow him to measure me."

Chapter 3 — WHO M. JEAN PERCERIN WAS

The king's tailor, M. Jean Percerin, occupied a rather large house in the Rue St. Honoré, near the Rue de l'Arbre Sec. He was a man of great taste in elegant stuffs, embroideries, and velvet, being hereditary tailor to the king. The preferment of his house reached as far back as the time of Charles IX.; from whose reign dated, as we know, fancies in *bravery* difficult enough to gratify. The Percerin of that period was a Huguenot, like Ambroise Paré, and had been spared by the Queen of Navarre, the beautiful Margot, as they used to write and say, too, in those days; because, in sooth, he was the only one who could make for her those wonderful riding-habits which she loved to wear, seeing that they were marvelously well suited to hide certain anatomi-

cal defects which the Queen of Navarre used very studiously to
conceal. Percerin being saved, made, out of gratitude, some beautiful black bodices, very inexpensive indeed for Queen Catherine, who ended by being pleased at the preservation of a Huguenot, on whom she had long looked with aversion. But Percerin was a very prudent man; and having heard it said that
there was no more dangerous sign for a Protestant than to be
smiled upon by Catherine; and having observed that her smiles
were more frequent than usual, he speedily turned Catholic with
all his family; and having thus become irreproachable, attained the lofty position of master tailor to the crown of
France. Under Henry III., gay king as he was, this position was
as good as the height of one of the loftiest peaks of the Cordil-
leras. Now Percerin had been a clever man all his life, and by
way of keeping up his reputation beyond the grave, took very
good care not to make a bad death of it, and so contrived to die
very skillfully; and that at the very moment he felt his powers
of invention declining. He left a son and daughter, both worthy of
the name they were called upon to bear; the son, a cutter as un-
erring and exact as the square rule; the daughter, apt at embroidery and at designing ornaments. The marriage of Henry IV.
and Marie de Medici, and the exquisite court-mourning for the
aforementioned queen, together with a few words let fall by M.
de Bassompierre, king of the beaus of the period, made the
fortune of the second generation of Percerins. M. Concino Concini, and his wife, Galligai, who subsequently shone at the French
court, sought to Italianize the fashion, and introduced some
Florentine tailors; but Percerin, touched to the quick in his
patriotism and his self-esteem, entirely defeated these for-
eigners, and that so well that Concino was the first to give up his
compatriots, and held the French tailor in such esteem that he
would never employ any other, and thus wore a doublet of his
on the very day that Vitry blew out his brains with his pistol at
the Pont du Louvre.

And this is the doublet, issuing from M. Percerin's work-
shop, which the Parisians rejoiced in hacking into so many
pieces with the human flesh it covered. Notwithstanding the
favor Concino Concini had shown Percerin, King Louis XIII. had
the generosity to bear no malice to his tailor, and to retain him
in his service. At the time that Louis the Just afforded this great
example of equity, Percerin had brought up two sons, one of
whom made his *début* at the marriage of Anne of Austria, invented that admirable Spanish costume, in which Richelieu
danced a saraband, made the costumes for the tragedy of "Mi-

rame," and stitched on to Buckingham's mantle those famous pearls which were destined to be scattered about the pavement of the Louvre. A man becomes easily notable who has made the dresses of M. de Buckingham, M. de Cinq-Mars, Mlle. Ninon, M. de Beaufort, and Marion de Lorme. And thus Percerin III. had attained the summit of his glory when his father died. This same Percerin III., old, famous, and wealthy, yet further dressed Louis XIV.; and having no son, which was a great cause of sorrow to him, seeing that with himself his dynasty would end, he had brought up several hopeful pupils. He possessed a carriage, a countryhouse, men-servants the tallest in Paris, and, by special authority from Louis XIV., a pack of hounds. He worked for Mm. de Lyonne and Letellier, under a sort of patronage; but politic man as he was, and versed in state secrets, he never succeeded in fitting M. Colbert. This is beyond explanation; it is matter for intuition.

Great geniuses of every kind live upon unseen, intangible ideas; they act without themselves knowing why. The great Percerin (for, contrary to the rule of dynasties, it was, above all, the last of the Percerins who deserved the name of Great), the great Percerin was inspired when he cut a robe for the queen, or a coat for the king; he could mount a mantle for Monsieur, the clock of a stocking for madame; but, in spite of his supreme talent, he could never hit the measure of M. Colbert.

"That man," he used often to say, "is beyond my art; my needle never can hit him off."

We need scarcely say that Percerin was M. Fouquet's tailor, and that the surintendant highly esteemed him. M. Percerin was nearly eighty years old, nevertheless still fresh, and at the same time so dry, the courtiers used to say that he was positively brittle. His renown and his fortune were great enough for M. le Prince, that king of fops, to take his arm when talking over the fashions; and for those least eager to pay never to dare to leave their accounts in arrears with him; for Master Percerin would for the first time make clothes upon credit, but the second never, unless paid for the former order.

It is easy to see at once that a tailor of such standing, instead of running after customers, made difficulties about obliging any fresh ones. And so Percerin declined to fit *bourgeois*, or those who had but recently obtained patents of nobility. A story used to circulate that even M. de Mazarin, in exchange for Percerin supplying him with a full suit of ceremonial vestments as cardinal, one fine day slipped letters of nobility into his pocket.

It was to the house of this great lord of tailors that D'Artagnan took the despairing Porthos; who, as they were going along, said to his friend:

"Take care, my good D'Artagnan, not to compromise the dignity of a man such as I am with the arrogance of this Percerin, who will, I expect, be very impertinent; for I give you notice, my friend, that if he is wanting in respect to me I will chastise him."

"Presented by me," replied D'Artagnan, "you have nothing to fear, even though you were what you are not."

"Ah! 'tis because——"

"What? Have you anything against Percerin, Porthos?"

"I think that I once sent Mouston to a fellow of that name."

"And then?"

"The fellow refused to supply me."

"Oh, a misunderstanding, no doubt, which 'tis pressing to set right. Mouston must have made a mistake."

"Perhaps."

"He has confused the names."

"Possibly. That rascal Mouston never can remember names."

"I will take it all upon myself."

"Very good."

"Stop the carriage, Porthos; here we are."

"Here! how here? We are at the Halles; and you told me the house was at the corner of the Rue de l'Arbre Sec."

" 'Tis true; but look."

"Well, I do look, and I see——"

"What?"

"*Pardieu!* that we are at the Halles."

"You do not, I suppose, want our horses to clamber up on the top of the carriage in front of us."

"No."

"Nor the carriage in front of us to mount on the one in front of it. Nor that the second should be driven over the roofs of the thirty or forty others which have arrived before us?"

"No, you are right, indeed. What a number of people. And what are they all about?"

" 'Tis very simple. They are waiting their turn."

"Bah! Have the comedians of the Hotel de Bourgogne shifted their quarters?"

"No; their turn to obtain an entrance to Monsieur Percerin's house."

"And we are going to wait, too?"

"Oh, we shall show ourselves more ready and less proud than they."

"What are we to do, then?"

"Get down, pass through the footmen and lackeys, and enter the tailor's house, which I will answer for our doing, if you go first."

"Come, then," said Porthos.

They both alighted and made their way on foot toward the establishment. The cause of the confusion was, that M. Percerin's doors were closed, while a servant standing before them was explaining to the illustrious customers of the illustrious tailor that just then M. Percerin could not receive anybody. It was bruited about outside still, on the authority of what the great lackey had told some great noble whom he favored, in confidence, that M. Percerin was engaged upon five dresses for the king, and that, owing to the urgency of the case, he was meditating in his office on the ornaments, colors, and cut of these five suits. Some, contented with this reason, went away again, happy to repeat it to others; but others, more tenacious, insisted on having the doors opened, and among these last three Blue Ribbons, intended to take parts in a ballet, which should inevitably fail unless the said three had their costumes shaped by the hand of the great Percerin himself. D'Artagnan pushing on Porthos, who scattered the groups of people right and left, succeeded in gaining the counter, behind which the journeymen tailors were doing their best to answer queries. (We forgot to mention that at the door they wanted to put off Porthos like the rest, but D'Artagnan, showing himself, pronounced merely these words, "The king's order," and was let in with his friend.) The poor fellows had enough to do, and did their best to reply to the demands of the customers in the absence of their master, leaving off drawing a stitch to turn a sentence; and when wounded pride, or disappointed expectation, brought down upon them too cutting rebukes, he who was attacked made a dive and disappeared under the counter. The line of discontented lords formed a very remarkable picture. Our captain of musketeers, a man of sure and rapid observation, took it all in at a glance; but having run over the groups, his eye rested on a man in front of him. This man, seated upon a stool, scarcely showed his head above the counter which sheltered him. He was about forty years of age, with a melancholy aspect, pale face, and soft, luminous eyes. He was looking at D'Artagnan and the rest, with his chin resting upon his hand, like a calm and inquiring amateur. Only on perceiving, and doubtless recognizing, our captain, he pulled his hat down over his eyes. It was this action, perhaps, that attracted D'Artagnan's attention. If so, the gentleman who had

pulled down his hat produced an effect entirely different from
what he had desired. In other respects his costume was plain,
and his hair evenly cut enough for customers, who were not
close observers, to take him for a mere tailor's apprentice,
perched behind the board, and carefully stitching cloth or velvet.
Nevertheless, this man held up his head too often to be very
productively employed with his fingers. D'Artagnan was not deceived—not he; and he saw at once that if this man was working at anything, it certainly was not at velvet.

"Eh!" said he, addressing this man, "and so you have become
a tailor's boy, Monsieur Molière?"

"Hush, Monsieur d'Artagnan!" replied the man softly, "you
will make them recognize me."

"Well, and what harm?"

"The fact is, there is no harm, but——"

"You were going to say there is no good in doing it either,
is it not so?"

"Alas! no; for I was occupied in looking at some excellent
figures."

"Go on—go on, Monsieur Molière. I quite understand the interest you take in it—I will not disturb your study."

"Thank you."

"But on one condition: that you tell me where Monsieur
Percerin really is."

"Oh! willingly; in his own room. Only——"

"Only that one can't enter it?"

"Unapproachable."

"For everybody?"

"For everybody. He brought me here so that I might be at
my ease to make my observations, and then he went away."

"Well, my dear Monsieur Molière, but you will go and tell
him I am here."

"I!" exclaimed Molière, in the tone of a courageous dog from
which you snatched the bone it has legitimately gained; "I disturb myself. Ah! Monsieur d'Artagnan, how hard you are upon
me!"

"If you don't go directly and tell Monsieur Percerin that I am
here, my dear Molière," said D'Artagnan, in a low tone, "I
warn you of one thing; that I won't exhibit to you the friend I
have brought with me."

Molière indicated Porthos by an imperceptible gesture:

"This gentleman, is it not?"

"Yes."

Molière fixed upon Porthos one of those looks which penetrate the minds and hearts of men. The subject doubtless appeared very promising to him, for he immediately rose and led the way into the adjoining chamber.

Chapter 4 — THE PATTERNS

During all this time the crowd was slowly rolling away, leaving at every angle of the counter either a murmur or a menace, as the waves leave foam or scatter seaweed on the sands when they retire with the ebbing tide. In about ten minutes Molière reappeared, making another sign to D'Artagnan from under the hangings. The latter hurried after him, with Porthos in the rear, and after threading a labyrinth of corridors, introduced him to M. Percerin's room. The old man, with his sleeves turned up, was gathering up in folds a piece of gold-flowered brocade, so as the better to exhibit its luster. Perceiving D'Artagnan, he put the silk aside, and came to meet him, by no means radiant with joy, and by no means courteous, but, take it altogether, in a tolerably civil manner.

"The captain of the musketeers will excuse me, I am sure, for I am engaged."

"Eh! yes, on the king's costumes; I know that, my dear Monsieur Percerin. You are making three, they tell me."

"Five, my dear monsieur, five."

"Three or five, 'tis all the same to me, my dear monsieur; and I know that you will make them most exquisitely."

"Yes, I know. Once made, they will be the most beautiful in the world, I do not deny it; but that they may be the most beautiful in the world, they must first be made; and to do this, captain, I am pressed for time."

"Oh, bah! there are two days yet; 'tis much more than you require, Monsieur Percerin," said D'Artagnan, in the coolest possible manner.

Percerin raised his head with the air of a man little accustomed to be contradicted, even in his whim; but D'Artagnan did not pay the least attention to the airs which the illustrious tailor began to assume.

"My dear Monsieur Percerin," he continued, "I bring you a customer."

"Ah! ah!" exclaimed Percerin crossly.

"Monsieur le Baron du Vallon de Braceiux de Pierrefonds," continued D'Artagnan.

Percerin attempted to bow, which found no favor in the eyes of the terrible Porthos, who, from his first entry into the room, had been regarding the tailor askance.

"A very good friend of mine," concluded D'Artagnan.

"I will attend to monsieur," said Percerin, "but later."

"Later? But when?"

"When I have time."

"You have already told my valet as much," broke in Porthos discontentedly.

"Very likely," said Percerin; "I am nearly always pushed for time."

"My friend," returned Porthos sententiously, "there is always time when one chooses to find it."

Percerin turned crimson; a very ominous sign indeed in old men blanched by age.

"Monsieur is very free to confer his custom elsewhere."

"Come, come, Percerin," interposed D'Artagnan, "you are not in a good temper to-day. Well, I will say one more word to you, which will bring you on your knees; monsieur is not only a friend of mine, but more, a friend of Monsieur Fouquet."

"Ah! ah!" exclaimed the tailor, "that is another thing."

Then, turning to Porthos, "Monsieur le Baron is attached to the surintendant?" he inquired.

"I am attached to myself," shouted Porthos, at the very moment that the tapestry was raised to introduce a new speaker in the dialogue. Molière was all observation, D'Artagnan laughed, Porthos swore.

"My dear Percerin," said D'Artagnan, "you will make a dress for the baron. 'Tis I who ask you."

"To you I will not say nay, captain."

"But that is not all; you will make it for him at once."

" 'Tis impossible before eight days."

"That, then, is as much as to refuse, because the dress is wanted for the *fête* at Vaux."

"I repeat that it is impossible," returned the obstinate old man.

"By no means, dear Monsieur Percerin; above all, if *I* ask you," said a mild voice at the door, a silvery voice which made D'Artagnan prick up his ears. It was the voice of Aramis.

"Monsieur d'Herblay!" cried the tailor.

"Aramis!" murmured D'Artagnan.

"Ah, poor bishop!" said Porthos.

"Good-morning, D'Artagnan; good-morning, Porthos; good-morning, my dear friends," said Aramis. "Come, come, Monsieur Percerin, make the baron's dress; and I will answer for it you will gratify Monsieur Fouquet." And he accompanied the words with a sign, which seemed to say, "Agree, and dismiss them."

It appeared that Aramis had over Master Percerin an influence superior even to D'Artagnan's, for the tailor bowed in assent, and turning round upon Porthos:

"Go and get measured on the other side," said he rudely.

Porthos colored in a formidable manner. D'Artagnan saw the storm coming, and, addressing Molière, said to him, in an undertone:

"You see before you, my dear monsieur, a man who considers himself disgraced if you measure the flesh and bones that Heaven has given him; study his type for me, Master Aristophanes, and profit by it."

Molière had no need of encouragement, and his gaze dwelt upon the Baron Porthos.

"Monsieur," he said, "if you will come with me, I will make them take your measure without the measure touching you."

"Oh!" said Porthos, "how do you make that out, my friend?"

"I say that they shall apply neither line nor rule to the seams of your dress. It is a new method we have invented for measuring people of quality, who are too sensitive to allow low-born fellows to touch them. We know some susceptible persons who will not put up with being measured, a process which, as I think, wounds the natural dignity of man; and if perchance monsieur should be one of these——"

"*Corbœuf!* I believe I am, too."

"Well, that is a capital coincidence, and you will have the benefit of our invention."

"But how in the world can it be done?" asked Porthos, delighted.

"Monsieur," said Molière, bowing, "if you will deign to follow me, you will see."

Aramis observed this scene with all his eyes. Perhaps he fancied, from D'Artagnan's liveliness, that he would leave with Porthos, so as not to lose the conclusion of a scene so well begun. But, clear-sighted as he was, Aramis deceived himself. Porthos and Molière left together alone. D'Artagnan remained with Percerin. Why? From curiosity, doubtless; probably to enjoy a little longer the society of his good friend, Aramis. As Molière and Porthos disappeared, D'Artagnan drew near the bishop of Vannes, a proceeding which appeared particularly to disconcert him.

"A dress for you, also, is it not, my friend?"

Aramis smiled.

"No," said he.

"You will go to Vaux, however?"

"I shall go, but without a new dress. You forget, dear D'Artagnan, that a poor bishop of Vannes is not rich enough to have new dresses for every *fête*."

"Bah!" said the musketeer, laughing, "and do we write no more poems now, either?"

"Oh, D'Artagnan!" exclaimed Aramis, "I have long given over all these follies."

"True," repeated D'Artagnan, only half-convinced.

As for Percerin, he had relapsed into his contemplation of the brocades.

"Don't you perceive," said Aramis, smiling, "that we are greatly boring this good gentleman, my dear D'Artagnan?"

"Ah! ah!" murmured the musketeer, aside; "that is, I am boring you, my friend." Then, aloud, "Well, then, let us leave; I have no further business here, and if you are as disengaged as I, Aramis——"

"No, not I—I wished——"

"Ah! you had something particular to say to Monsieur Percerin? Why did you not tell me so at once?"

"Something particular, certainly," repeated Aramis; "but not for you, D'Artagnan. But, at the same time, I hope you will believe that I can never have anything so particular to say that a friend like you may not hear it."

"Oh, no, no! I am going," said D'Artagnan, imparting to his voice an evident tone of curiosity; for Aramis' annoyance, well dissembled as it was, had not a wit escaped him; and he knew that, in that impenetrable mind, every thing, even the most apparently trivial, was designed to some end; an unknown one, but one which, from the knowledge he had of his friend's character, the musketeer felt must be important.

On his part, Aramis saw that D'Artagnan was not without suspicion, and pressed him.

"Stay, by all means," he said; "this is what it is." Then, turning toward the tailor: "My dear Percerin," said he, "I am even very happy that you are here, D'Artagnan."

"Oh, indeed!" exclaimed the Gascon, for the third time, even less deceived this time than before.

Percerin never moved. Aramis roused him violently by

snatching from his hands the stuff upon which he was engaged:
"My dear Percerin," said he, "I have, near at hand, Monsieur
Lebrun, one of Monsieur Fouquet's painters."

"Ah, very good," thought D'Artagnan; "but why 'Lebrun'?"

Aramis looked at D'Artagnan, who seemed to be occupied
with an engraving of Mark Antony.

"And you wish to have made for him a dress similar to those
of the Epicureans?" answered Percerin.

And while saying this, in an absent manner, the worthy tailor
endeavored to recapture his piece of brocade.

"An Epicurean's dress?" asked D'Artagnan, in a tone of in-
quiry.

"I see," said Aramis, with a most engaging smile; "it is written that our dear D'Artagnan shall know all our secrets this evening. Yes, friend, you have surely heard speak of Monsieur Fouquet's Epicureans, have you not?"

"Undoubtedly. Is it not a kind of poetical society, of which
La Fontaine, Loret, Pellisson, and Molière are members, and
which holds its sittings at St. Mandé?"

"Exactly so. Well, we are going to put our poets in uniform,
and enroll them in a regiment for the king."

"Oh, very well; I understand. A surprise Monsieur Fouquet
is getting up for the king. Be at ease; if that is the secret about
Monsieur Lebrun, I will not mention it."

"Always agreeable, my friend. No, Monsieur Lebrun has nothing to do with this part of it; the secret which concerns him is
far more important than the other."

"Then, if it is so important as all that, I prefer not to know
it," said D'Artagnan, making a show of departure.

"Come in, Monsieur Lebrun, come in," said Aramis, opening a
side-door with his right hand, and holding back D'Artagnan
with his left.

"I' faith, I, too, am quite in the dark," quoth Percerin.

Aramis took an "opportunity," as is said in theatrical matters.

"My dear Monsieur de Percerin," Aramis continued, "you are
making fine dresses for the king, are you not? One in brocade,
one in hunting-cloth, one in velvet, one in satin, and one in Florentine stuffs?"

"Yes; but how do you know all that, monseigneur?" said Percerin, astounded.

"It is all very simple, my dear monsieur. There will be a hunt,
a banquet, concert, promenade, and reception; these five kinds
of dress are required by etiquette."

"You know everything, monseigneur."

"And a great many more things, too," murmured D'Artagnan.

"But," cried the tailor, in triumph, "what you do not know, monseigneur—prince of the church though you are—what nobody will know—what only the king, Mademoiselle de la Valliere, and myself do know, is the color of the materials and nature of the ornaments, and the cut, the *ensemble*, the finish of it all."

"Well," said Aramis, "that is precisely what I have come to ask you, dear Percerin."

"Ah, bah!" exclaimed the tailor, terrified, though Aramis had pronounced these words in his sweetest and most honeyed voice. The request appeared, on reflection, so exaggerated, so ridiculous, so monstrous to M. Percerin that first he laughed to himself, then aloud, and finished with a shout. D'Artagnan followed his example, not because he found the matter so "very funny," but in order not to allow Aramis to cool.

"At the outset I appear to be hazarding an absurd question, do I not?" said Aramis. "But D'Artagnan, who is incarnate wisdom itself, will tell you that I could not do otherwise than ask you this."

"Let us see," said the attentive musketeer, perceiving, with his wonderful instinct, that they had only been skirmishing till now, and that the hour of battle was approaching.

"Let us see," said Percerin incredulously.

"Why, now," continued Aramis, "does Monsieur Fouquet give the king a *fête*? Is it not to please him?" "Assuredly," said Percerin. D'Artagnan nodded assent. "By delicate attentions? by some happy device? by a succession of surprises, like that of which we were talking, the enrollment of our Epicureans?"

"Admirable."

"Well, then, this is the surprise we intend. Monsieur Lebrun here is a man who draws most exactly."

"Yes," said Percerin; "I have seen his pictures, and observed that the dresses were highly elaborated. That is why I at once agreed to make him a costume—whether to agree with those of the Epicureans, or an original one."

"My dear monsieur, we accept your offer, and shall presently avail ourselves of it; but just now, Monsieur Lebrun is not in want of the dresses you will make for him, but of those you are making for the king."

Percerin made a bound backward, which D'Artagnan—calmest and most appreciative of men—did not consider overdone so many strange and startling aspects wore the proposal which Aramis had just hazarded.

"The king's dresses! Give the king's dresses to any mortal whatever! Oh! for once, monseigneur, your grace is mad!" cried the poor tailor, in extremity.

"Help me now, D'Artagnan," said Aramis, more and more calm and smiling. "Help me now to persuade monsieur, for *you* understand, do you not?"

"Eh, eh! not exactly, I declare."

"What! you do not understand that Monsieur Fouquet wishes to afford the king the surprise of finding his portrait on his arrival at Vaux; and that the portrait, which will be a striking resemblance, ought to be dressed exactly as the king will be on the day it is shown?"

"Oh! yes, yes," said the musketeer, nearly convinced, so plausible was this reasoning. "Yes, my dear Aramis, you are right; it is a happy idea. I will wager it is one of your own, Aramis."

"Well, I don't know," replied the bishop; "either mine or Monsieur Fouquet's." Then, scanning Percerin, after noticing D'Artagnan's hesitation, "Well, Monsieur Percerin," he asked, "what do you say to this?"

"I say that——"

"That you are, doubtless, free to refuse. I know well—and I by no means count upon compelling you, my dear monsieur. I will say more, I even understand all the delicacy you feel in taking up with Monsieur Fouquet's idea; you dread appearing to flatter the king. A noble spirit, Monsieur Percerin, a noble spirit!"

The tailor stammered.

"It would, indeed, be a very pretty compliment to pay the young prince," continued Aramis; "but as the surintendant told me, 'If Percerin refuse, tell him that it will not at all lower him in my opinion, and I shall always esteem him, only——' "

" 'Only?' " repeated Percerin, rather troubled.

" 'Only,' " continued Aramis, 'I shall be compelled to say to the king'—you understand, my dear Monsieur Percerin, that these are Monsieur Fouquet's words—'I shall be constrained to say to the king, Sire, I had intended to present your majesty with your portrait, but owing to a feeling of delicacy, slightly exaggerated perhaps, although creditable, Monsieur Percerin opposed the project.' "

"Opposed!" cried the tailor, terrified at the responsibility which would weigh upon him; "I to oppose the desire, the will of Monsieur Fouquet when he is seeking to please the king! Oh, what a hateful word you have uttered, monseigneur. Oppose!

Oh, 'tis not I who said it, Heaven have mercy on me! I call the captain of the musketeers to witness it! Is it not true, Monsieur d'Artagnan, that I have opposed nothing?"

D'Artagnan made a sign, indicating that he wished to remain neutral. He felt that there was an intrigue at the bottom of it, whether comedy or tragedy; he was at his wits' end at not being able to fathom it, but in the meanwhile wished to keep clear.

But already Percerin, goaded by the idea that the king should be told he stood in the way of a pleasant surprise, had offered Lebrun a chair, and proceeded to bring from a wardrobe four magnificent dresses, the fifth being still in the workmen's hands; and these masterpieces he successively fitted upon four lay figures, which, imported into France in the time of Concini, had been given to Percerin II. by Marshal d'Onoro, after the discomfiture of the Italian tailors, ruined in their competition. The painter set to work to draw and then to paint the dress. But Aramis, who was closely watching all the phases of his toil, suddenly stopped him.

"I think you have not quite got it, my dear Lebrun," he said; "your colors will deceive you, and on canvas we shall lack that exact resemblance which is absolutely requisite. Time is necessary for attentively observing the finer shades."

"Quite true," said Percerin, "but time is wanting, and on that head, you will agree with me, monseigneur, I can do nothing."

"Then the affair will fail," said Aramis quietly, "and that because of a want of precision in the colors."

Nevertheless, Lebrun went on copying the materials and ornaments with the closest fidelity—a process which Aramis watched with ill-concealed impatience.

"What in the world, now, is the meaning of this imbroglio?" the musketeer kept saying to himself.

"That will certainly never do," said Aramis. "Monsieur Lebrun, close your box, and roll up your canvas."

"But, monsieur," cried the vexed painter, "the light is abominable here."

"An idea, Monsieur Lebrun, an idea! If we had a pattern of the materials for example, and with time, and a better light——"

"Oh, then," cried Lebrun, "I would answer for the effect."

"Good!" said D'Artagnan, "this ought to be the knotty point of the whole thing; they want a pattern of each of the materials. *Mordioux!* will this Percerin give it now?"

Percerin, beaten in his last retreat, and duped, moreover, by the feigned good-nature of Aramis, cut out five patterns and handed them to the bishop of Vannes.

"I like this better. That is your opinion, is it not?" said Aramis to D'Artagnan.

"My dear Aramis," said D'Artagnan, "my opinion is that you are always the same."

"And, consequently, always your friend," said the bishop, in a charming tone.

"Yes, yes," said D'Artagnan aloud; then, in a low voice, "If I am your dupe, double Jesuit that you are, I will not be your accomplice; and to prevent it, 'tis time I left this place."

"Adieu, Aramis," he added aloud, "adieu; I am going to rejoin Porthos."

"Then wait for me," said Aramis, pocketing the patterns, "for I have done, and shall not be sorry to say a parting word to our friend."

Lebrun packed up, Percerin put back the dresses into the closet, Aramis put his hand on his pocket to assure himself the patterns were secure—and they all left the study.

Chapter 5 — WHERE, PROBABLY, MOLIÈRE FORMED HIS FIRST IDEA OF THE BOURGEOIS GENTILHOMME

D'Artagnan found Porthos in the adjoining chamber; but no longer an irritated Porthos, or a disappointed Porthos, but Porthos radiant, blooming, fascinating, and chatting with Molière, who was looking upon him with a species of idolatry and as a man would who had not only never seen anything better, but not even ever anything so good. Aramis went straight up to Porthos and offered him his delicate white hand, which lost itself in the gigantic hand of his old friend—an operation which Aramis never hazarded without a certain uneasiness. But the friendly pressure having been performed not too painfully for him, the bishop of Vannes passed over to Molière.

"Well, monsieur," said he, "will you come with me to St. Mandé?"

"I will go anywhere you like, monseigneur," answered Molière.

"To St. Mandé!" cried Porthos, surprised at seeing the proud

bishop of Vannes fraternizing with a journeyman tailor. "Wha
Aramis, are you going to take this gentleman to St. Mandé?"

"Yes," said Aramis, smiling, "our work is pressing."

"And, besides, my dear Porthos," continued D'Artagnan, "Mor
sieur Molière is not altogether what he seems."

"In what way?" asked Porthos.

"Why, this gentleman is one of Monsieur Percerin's chi
clerks, and is expected at St. Mandé to try on the dresses whi
Monsieur Fouquet has ordered for the Epicureans."

" 'Tis precisely so," said Molière.

"Yes, monsieur."

"Come, then, my dear Monsieur Molière," said Aramis, "th
is, if you have done with Monsieur du Vallon?"

"We have finished," replied Porthos.

"And you are satisfied?" asked D'Artagnan.

"Completely so," replied Porthos.

Molière took his leave of Porthos with much ceremony, ar
grasped the hand which the captain of the musketeers furtive
offered him.

"Pray, monsieur," concluded Porthos mincingly, "above a
be exact."

"You will have your dress after to-morrow, Monsieur
Baron," answered Molière.

And he left with Aramis.

Then D'Artagnan, taking Porthos' arm:

"What has this tailor done for you, my dear Porthos," l
asked, "that you are so pleased with him?"

"What has he done for me, my friend—done for me?" cri
Porthos enthusiastically.

"Yes, I ask you, what has he done for you?"

"My friend, he has done that which no tailor ever yet a
complished; he has taken my measure without touching me."

"Ah, bah! tell me how he did it."

"First, then, they went, I don't know where, for a number
lay figures, of all heights and sizes, hoping there would be one
suit mine, but the largest—that of the drum-major of the Swi
Guard—was two inches too short, and half a foot too slender

"Indeed!"

"It is exactly as I tell you, D'Artagnan; but he is a great ma
or, at the very least, a great tailor, is this Monsieur Molièr
He was not at all put at fault by the circumstance."

"What did he do, then?"

"Oh! it is a very simple matter. I' faith, 'tis an unheard

thing that people should have been so stupid as not to have discovered this method from the first. What annoyance and humiliation they would have spared me!"

"Not to speak of the dresses, my dear Porthos."

"Yes, thirty dresses."

"Well, my dear Porthos, come tell me Monsieur Molière's plan."

"Molière? You call him so, do you? I shall make a point of recollecting his name."

"Yes; or Poquelin, if you prefer that."

"No; I like Molière best. When I wish to recollect his name I shall think of Volière (an aviary); and as I have one at Pierrefonds——"

"Capital!" returned D'Artagnan. "And Monsieur Molière's plan?"

" 'Tis this: Instead of pulling me to pieces, as all these rascals do—of making me bend in my back, and double my joints—all of them low and dishonorable practices——"

D'Artagnan made a sign of approbation with his head.

" 'Monsieur,' he said to me," continued Porthos, " 'a gentleman ought to measure himself. Do me the pleasure to draw near this glass,' and I drew near the glass. I must own I did not exactly understand what this good Monsieur Volière wanted with me."

"Molière."

"Ah, yes, Molière—Molière. And as the fear of being measured still possessed me, 'Take care,' said I to him, 'what you are going to do with me; I am very ticklish, I warn you.' But he, with his soft voice (for he is a courteous fellow, we must admit, my friend), he, with his soft voice, 'Monsieur,' said he, 'that your dress may fit you well, it must be made according to your figure. Your figure is exactly reflected in his mirror. We shall take the measure of this reflection.' "

"In fact," said D'Artagnan, "you saw yourself in the glass. But where did they find one in which you could see your whole figure?"

"My good friend, it is the very glass in which the king sees himself."

"Yes; but the king is a foot and a half shorter than you are."

"Ah! well, I know not how that may be; it would no doubt be a way of flattering the king; but the looking-glass was too large for me. 'Tis true that its height was made up of three Venetian plates of glass, placed one above another, and its breadth of three similar pieces in juxtaposition."

"Oh, Porthos! what excellent words you have command of. Where in the world did you make the collection?"

"At Belle-Isle. Aramis explained them to the architect."

"Ah! very good. Let us return to the glass, my friend."

"Then, this good Monsieur Volière——"

"Molière."

"Yes, Molière—you are right. You will see, now, my dear friend, that I shall recollect his name too well. This excellent Monsieur Molière set to work tracing out lines on the mirror, with a piece of Spanish chalk, following in all the make of my arms and my shoulders, all the while expounding this maxim, which I thought admirable: 'It is necessary that a dress do not incommode its wearer.'"

"In reality," said D'Artagnan, "that is an excellent maxim, which is, unfortunately, seldom carried out in practice."

"That is why I found it all the more astonishing, when he expatiated upon it."

"Ah! he expatiated?"

"Parbleu!"

"Let me hear his theory."

"'Seeing that,' he continued, 'one may, in awkward circumstances, or in a troublesome position, have one's doublet on one's shoulder, and not desire to take one's doublet off——'"

"True," said D'Artagnan.

"'And so,' continued Monsieur Volière——"

"Molière."

"Molière, yes. 'And so,' went on Monsieur Molière, 'you want to draw your sword, monsieur, and you have your doublet on your back. What do you do?'"

"'I take it off,' I answered.

"'Well, no,' he replied.

"'How, no?'

"'I say that the dress should be so well made that it can in no way incumber you, even in drawing your sword.'

"'Ah! ah!'

"'Throw yourself on guard,' pursued he.

"I did it with such wondrous firmness that two panes of glass burst out of the window.

"''Tis nothing, nothing,' said he. 'Keep your position.'

"I raised my left arm in the air, the forearm gracefully bent, the ruffle drooping, and my wrist curved, while my right arm, half-extended, securely covered my waist with the elbow and my breast with the wrist."

"Yes," said D'Artagnan; " 'tis the true guard—the academic guard."

"You have said the very word, dear friend. In the meanwhile, Volière——"

"Molière."

"Hold! I should certainly, after all, prefer to call him—what did you say his other name was?"

"Poquelin."

"I prefer to call him Poquelin."

"And how will you remember this name better than the other?"

"You understand, he calls himself Poquelin, does he not?"

"Yes."

"I shall recall to mind Madame Coquenard."

"Good."

"I shall change *Coc* into *Poc, nard* into *lin;* and instead of Coquenard I shall have Poquelin."

" 'Tis wonderful!" cried D'Artagnan, astounded. "Go on, my friend; I am listening to you with admiration."

"This Coquelin sketched my arm on the glass."

"I beg your pardon—Poquelin."

"What did I say, then?"

"You said Coquelin."

"Ah! true. This Poquelin, then, sketched my arm on the glass; but he took his time over it; he kept looking at me a good deal. The fact is, that I was very handsome.

" 'Does it weary you?' he asked.

" 'A little,' I replied, bending a little in my hands, 'but I could yet hold out an hour.'

" 'No, no, I will not allow it; the willing fellows will make it a duty to support your arms, as of old, men supported those of the prophet.'

" 'Very good,' I answered.

" 'That will not be humiliating to you?'

" 'My friend,' said I, 'there is, I think, a great difference between being supported and being measured.' "

"The distinction is full of sense," interrupted D'Artagnan.

"Then," continued Porthos, "he made a sign; two lads approached; one supported my left arm, while the other, with infinite address, supported my right."

" 'Another, my man,' cried he. A third approached. 'Support monsieur by the waist,' said he. The *garçon* complied."

"So that you were at rest?" asked D'Artagnan.

"Perfectly; and Pocquenard drew me on the glass."

"Poquelin, my friend."

"Poquelin—you are right. Stay; decidedly I prefer calling him Volière."

"Yes; and then it was over, wasn't it?"

"During that time Volière drew me on the mirror."

" 'Twas delicate in him."

"I much like the plan; it is respectful, and keeps every one in his place."

"And there it ended?"

"Without a soul having touched me, my friend."

"Except the three *garçons* who supported you."

"Doubtless; but I have, I think, already explained to you the difference there is between supporting and measuring."

" 'Tis true," answered D'Artagnan, who said afterward, to himself, "I' faith, I greatly deceive myself, or I have been the means of a good windfall to that rascal Molière, and we shall assuredly see the scene hit off to the life in some comedy or other."

Porthos smiled.

"What are you laughing at?" asked D'Artagnan.

"Must I confess? Well, I was laughing over my good fortune."

"Oh, that is true; I don't know a happier man than you. But what is this last piece of luck that has befallen you?"

"Well, my dear fellow, congratulate me."

"I desire nothing better."

"It seems that I am the first who has had his measure taken in that manner."

"Are you sure of it?"

"Nearly so. Certain signs of intelligence which passed between Volière and the other *garçons* showed me the fact."

"Well, my friend, that does not surprise me from Molière," said D'Artagnan.

"Volière, my friend."

"Oh, no no, indeed! I am very willing to leave you to say Volière; but myself, I shall continue to say Molière. Well, this, I was saying, does not surprise me, coming from Molière, who is a very ingenious fellow, and inspired you with this grand idea."

"It will be of great use to him by and by, I am sure."

"Won't it be of use to him, indeed! I believe you, it will, and not a little so; for, you see, my friend Molière is of all known tailors the man who best clothes our barons, comtes, and marquises—according to their measure."

On this observation, neither the application nor depth of which shall we discuss, D'Artagnan and Porthos quitted M. de Percerin's house and rejoined their carriage, wherein we will leave them, in order to look after Molière and Aramis at St Mandé.

Chapter 6 — THE BEEHIVE, THE BEES, AND THE HONEY

The bishop of Vannes, much annoyed at having met D'Artagnan at M. Percerin's, returned to St. Mandé in no very good humor. Molière, on the other hand, quite delighted at having made such a capital rough sketch, and at knowing where to find its original again, whenever he should desire to convert his sketch into a picture, Molière arrived in the merriest of moods. All the first story of the left wing was occupied by the most celebrated Epicureans in Paris, and those on the freest footing in the house— every one in his compartment, like the bees in their cells, employed in producing the honey intended for that royal cake which M. Fouquet proposed to offer His Majesty Louis XIV. during the *fête* at Vaux. Pellisson, his head leaning on his hand, was engaged in drawing out the plan of the prologue to the "Fâcheux," a comedy in three acts, which was to be put on the stage by Poquelin de Molière, as D'Artagnan called him, or Coquelin de Volière, as Porthos styled him. Loret, with all the charming innocence of a gazetteer—the gazetteers of all ages have always been so artless!—Loret was composing an account of the *fêtes* of Vaux, before those *fêtes* had taken place. La Fontaine, sauntering about from one to the other, a wandering, absent, boring, unbearable shade, who kept buzzing and humming at everybody's shoulder a thousand poetic abstractions. He so often disturbed Pellisson that the latter, raising his head crossly said:

"At least, La Fontaine, supply me with a rhyme, since you have the run of the gardens at Parnassus."

"What rhyme do you want?" asked the *Fabler*, as Mme. de Sévigne used to call him.

"I want a rhyme to *lumière*."

"*Ornière*," answered La Fontaine.

"Ah! but, my good friend, one cannot talk of *wheel-ruts* when celebrating the delights of Vaux," said Loret.

"Besides, it doesn't rhyme," answered Pellisson.

"How! doesn't rhyme?" cried La Fontaine, in surprise.

"Yes; you have an abominable habit, my friend—a habit which will ever prevent your becoming a poet of the first order. You rhyme in a slovenly manner."

"Oh, oh! you think so, do you, Pellisson?"

"Yes, I do, indeed. Remember that a rhyme is never good so long as one can find a better."

"Then I will never write anything again but in prose," said La Fontaine, who had taken up Pellisson's reproach in earnest. "Ah! I often suspected I was nothing but a rascally poet. Yes, 'tis the very truth."

"Do not say so; your remark is too sweeping, and there is much that is good in your 'Fables.' "

"And to begin," continued La Fontaine, following up his idea, "I will go and burn a hundred verses I have just made."

"Where are your verses?"

"In my head."

"Well, if they are in your head you cannot burn them."

"True," said La Fontaine; "but if I do not burn them——"

"Well, what will happen if you do not burn them?"

"They will remain in my mind, and I shall never forget them."

"The deuce!" cried Loret; "what a dangerous thing! One would go mad with it!"

"The deuce! the deuce!" repeated La Fontaine; "what can I do?"

"I have discovered the way," said Molière, who had entered just at this point of the conversation.

"What way?"

"Write them first, and burn them afterward."

"How simple it is! Well, I should never have discovered that. What a mind that devil Molière has!" said La Fontaine. Then, striking his forehead, "Oh, thou wilt never be aught but an ass, Jean La Fontaine!" he added.

"*What* are you saying there, my friend?" broke in Molière, approaching the poet, whose aside he had heard.

"I say I shall never be aught but an ass," answered La Fontaine, with a heavy sigh and swimming eyes. "Yes, my friend," he added, with increasing grief, "it seems that I rhyme in a slovenly manner."

"Oh, 'tis wrong to say so."

"Nay, I am a poor creature!"

"Who said so?"

"*Parbleu!* 'twas Pellisson; did you not, Pellisson?"

Pellisson, again lost in his work, took good care not to answer.

"But if Pellisson said you were so," cried Molière, "Pellisson has seriously offended you."

"Do you think so?"

"Ah! I advise you, as you are a gentleman, not to leave an insult like that unpunished."

"How?" exclaimed La Fontaine.

"Did you ever fight?"

"Once only, with a lieutenant in the light horse."

"What wrong had he done you?"

"It seems he had run away with my wife."

"Ah! ah!" said Molière, becoming slightly pale; but, as at La Fontaine's declaration, the others had turned round, Molière kept upon his lips the rallying smile which had so nearly died away, and continuing to make La Fontaine speak, "and what was the result of the duel?"

"The result was, that on the ground my opponent disarmed me, and then made an apology, promising never again to set foot in my house."

"And you considered yourself satisfied?" said Molière.

"Not at all; on the contrary, I picked up my sword. 'I beg your pardon, monsieur,' I said. 'I have not fought you because you were my wife's friend, but because I was told I ought to fight. So, as I have never known any peace save since you made her acquaintance, do me the pleasure to continue your visits as heretofore, or, *morbleu!* let us set to again.' And so," continued La Fontaine, "he was compelled to resume his friendship with madame, and I continue to be the happiest of husbands."

All burst out laughing. Molière alone passed his hand across his eyes. Why? Perhaps to wipe away a tear, perhaps to smother a sigh. Alas! we know that Molière was a moralist, but he was not a philosopher.

" 'Tis all the same," he said, returning to the topic of the conversation, "Pellisson has insulted you."

"Ah, truly; I had already forgotten it."

"And I am going to challenge him on your behalf."

"Well, you can do so, if you think it indispensable."

"I do think it indispensable, and I am going to——"

"Stay!" exclaimed La Fontaine. "I want your advice."

"Upon what? this insult?"

"No; tell me really, now, whether *lumière* does not rhyme
with *ornière*."

"I should make them rhyme—ah! I knew you would—and I
have made a hundred thousand such rhymes in my time."

"A hundred thousand!" cried La Fontaine, "four times as
many as La Pucelle, which Monsieur Chaplain is meditating.
Is it also on this subject too that you have composed a hundred
thousand verses?"

"Listen to me, you eternally absent creature," said Molière.

"It is certain," continued La Fontaine, "that *legume*, for instance, rhymes with *posthume*."

"In the plural, above all."

"Yes, above all, in the plural, seeing that then it rhymes not
with three letters, but with four; as *ornière* does with *lumière*."

"Put *ornières* and *lumières* in the plural, my dear Pellisson,"
said La Fontaine, clapping his hand on the shoulder of his
friend, whose insult he had quite forgotten, "and they will
rhyme."

"Hem!" cried Pellisson.

"Molière says so, and Molière is a judge of it; he declares he
has himself made a hundred thousand verses."

"Come," said Molière, laughing, "he is off now."

"It is like *rivage*, which rhymes admirably with *herbage*, I
would take my oath of it."

"But—" said Molière.

"I tell you all this," continued La Fontaine, "because you are
preparing a *divertissement* for Vaux, are you not?"

"Yes, the 'Fâcheux.'"

"Ah, yes, the 'Fâcheux;' yes, I recollect. Well, I was thinking
a prologue would admirably suit your *divertissement*."

"Doubtless it would suit capitally."

"Ah! you are of my opinion?"

"So much so that I have asked you to write this prologue."

"You asked *me* to write it?"

"Yes, you, and on your refusal begged you to ask Pellisson,
who is engaged upon it at this moment."

"Ah! that is what Pellisson is doing, then?"

"I' faith, my dear Molière, you might indeed often be right."

"When?"

"When you call me absent. It is a wretched defect; I will cure
myself of it, and do your prologue for you."

"But seeing that Pellisson is about it——"

"Ah! true, double rascal that I am! Loret was indeed right in
saying I was a poor creature."

"It was not Loret who said so, my friend."

"Well, then, whoever said so, 'tis the same to me. And so your *divertissement* is called the 'Fâcheux?' Well can you not make *heureux* rhyme with *fâcheux?*"

"If obliged, yes."

"And even with *capricieux.*"

"Oh, no, no!"

"It would be hazardous, and yet why so?"

"There is too great a difference in the cadences."

"I was fancying," said La Fontaine, leaving Molière for Loret—"I was fancying——"

"What were you fancying?" said Loret, in the middle of a sentence. "Make haste."

"You are writing the prologue to the 'Fâcheux,' are you not?"

"No! *mordieu!* it is Pellisson."

"Ah, Pellisson!" cried La Fountaine, going over to him. "I was fancying," he continued, "that the nymph of Vaux——"

"Ah! beautiful!" cried Loret. "The nymph of Vaux! thank you, La Fontaine; you have just given me the two concluding verses of my paper."

"Well, if you can rhyme so well, La Fontaine," said Pellisson, "tell me now in what way you would begin my prologue?"

"I should say, for instance, 'Oh! nymph, who—' After 'who' I should place a verb in the second person singular of the present indicative; and should go on thus: 'this grot profound.'"

"But the verb, the verb," asked Pellisson.

"To admire the greatest king of all kings round," continued La Fontaine.

"But the verb, the verb," obstinately insisted Pellisson. "This second person singular of the present indicative?"

"Well, then; quittest:

> " 'O, nymph, who quittest now this grot profound,
>   To admire the greatest king of all kings round.' "

"You would put 'who quittest,' would you?"

"Why not?"

" 'Gentlest,' after 'you who?' "

"Ah! my dear fellow," exclaimed La Fontaine, "you are a shocking pedant!"

"Without counting," said Molière, "that the second verse, 'king of all kings round,' is very weak, my dear La Fontaine."

"Then you see clearly I am nothing but a poor creature—a shuffler, as you said."

"I never said so."

"Then, as Loret said."

"And it was not Loret, neither; it was Pellisson."

"Well, Pellisson was right a hundred times over. But what annoys me more than anything, my dear Molière, is, that I fear we shall not have our Epicurean dresses."

"You expected yours, then, for the *fête*?"

"Yes, for the *fête*, and then for after the *fête*. My housekeeper told me that my own is rather faded."

"*Diable!* your housekeeper is right; rather more than faded."

"Ah, you see," resumed La Fontaine, "the fact is, I left it on the floor in my room, and my cat——"

"Well, your cat——"

"She kittened upon it, which has rather altered its color."

Molière burst out laughing; Pellisson and Loret followed his example. At this juncture the bishop of Vannes appeared, with a roll of plans and parchments under his arm. As if the angel of death had chilled all gay and sprightly fancies—as if that wan form had scared away the Graces to whom Xenocrates sacrificed—silence immediately reigned through the study, and every one resumed his self-possession and his pen. Aramis distributed the notes of invitation, and thanked them in the name of M. Fouquet.

"The surintendant," he said, "being kept to his room by business, could not come and see them, but begged them to send him some of the fruits of their day's work, to enable him to forget the fatigue of his labor in the night."

At these words all settled to work. La Fontaine placed himself at a table, and set his rapid pen running over the vellum; Pellisson made a fair copy of his prologue; Molière gave fifty fresh verses, with which his visit to Percerin had inspired him; Loret, his article on the marvellous *fêtes* he predicted; and Aramis, laden with his booty like the king of the bees, that great black drone, decked with purple and gold, re-entered his apartment, silent and busy. But before departing: "Remember, gentlemen," said he, "we all leave to-morrow evening."

"In that case I must give notice at home," said Molière.

"Yes; poor Molière!" said Loret, smiling, "he loves his home."

"'*He* loves,' yes," replied Molière, with his sad, sweet smile. "'He loves,' that does not mean they love *him*."

"As for me," said La Fontaine, "they love me at Château Thierry, I am very sure."

Aramis here re-entered, after a brief disappearance.

"Will any one go with me?" he asked. "I am going by Paris, after having passed a quarter of an hour with Monsieur Fouquet. I offer my carriage."

"Good," said Molière, "I accept it. I am in a hurry."

"I shall dine here," said Loret. "Monsieur de Gourville has promised me some crawfish."

"He has promised me some whitings. Find a rhyme for that, La Fontaine."

Aramis went out laughing, as only he could laugh, and Molière followed him. They were at the bottom of the stairs when La Fontaine opened the door and shouted out:

> "He has promised us some whitings,
> In return for all our writings."

The shouts of laughter reached the ears of Fouquet at the moment Aramis opened the door of the study. As to Molière, he had undertaken to order the horses, while Aramis went to exchange a parting word with the surintendant.

"Oh, how they are laughing there!" said Fouquet, with a sigh.

"Do you not laugh, monseigneur?"

"I laugh no longer now, Monsieur d'Herblay."

"The *fête* is approaching; money is departing."

"Have I not told you that was my business?"

"Yes; you promised me millions."

"You shall have them the day after the king's *entrée* into Vaux."

Fouquet looked closely at Aramis, and passed his icy hand across his moistened brow. Aramis perceived that the surintendant either doubted him or felt he was powerless to obtain the money. How could Fouquet suppose that a poor bishop, ex-abbé, ex-musketeer, could find any?

"Why doubt me?" said Aramis.

Fouquet smiled, and shook his head.

"Man of little faith!" added the bishop.

"My dear Monsieur d'Herblay," answered Fouquet, "if I fall——"

"Well, if you 'fall'?"

"I shall, at least, fall from such a height that I shall shatter myself in falling." Then, giving himself a shake, as though to escape from himself, "Whence come you," said he, "my friend?"

"From Paris—from Percerin."

"And what have you been doing at Percerin's, for I suppose you attach no such great importance to our poets' dresses?"

"No; I went to prepare a surprise."

"Surprise?"

"Yes; which you are to give to the king."

"And will it cost much?"

"Oh! a hundred pistoles you will give Lebrun."

"A painting? Ah! all the better! And what is this painting to represent?"

"I will tell you; then, at the same time, whatever you may say of it, I went to see the dresses for our poets."

"Bah! and they will be rich and elegant?"

"Splendid! There will be few great monseigneurs with so good. People will see the difference there is between the courtiers of wealth and those of friendship."

"Ever generous and graceful, dear prelate."

"In your school."

Fouquet grasped his hand.

"And where are you going?" he said.

"I am off to Paris, when you shall have given a certain letter."

"For whom?"

"Monsieur de Lyonne."

"And what do you want with Lyonne?"

"I wish to make him sign a *lettre de cachet*."

"'*Lettre de cachet!*' Do you desire to put somebody in the Bastile?"

"On the contrary—to let somebody out."

"And who?"

"A poor devil—a youth, a lad who has been Bastiled these ten years for two Latin verses he made against the Jesuits."

"'Two Latin verses!' And for 'two Latin verses' the miserable being has been in prison for ten years?"

"Yes."

"And has committed no other crime?"

"Beyond this, he is as innocent as you or I."

"On your word?"

"On my honor!"

"And his name is?"

"Seldon."

"Yes, but it is too bad. You knew this, and you never told me."

"'Twas only yesterday his mother applied to me, monseigneur."

"And the woman is poor?"

"In the deepest misery."

"Oh, Heaven!" said Fouquet, "you sometimes bear with such injustice on earth that I understand why there are wretches who doubt in your existence. Stay, Monsieur d'Herblay."

And Fouquet, taking a pen, wrote a few rapid lines to his colleague, Lyonne. Aramis took the letter and made ready to go.

"Wait," said Fouquet. He opened his drawer, and took out ten government notes which were there, each for a thousand francs. "Stay," he said; "set the son at liberty, and give this to the mother; but, above all, tell her not——"

"What, monseigneur?"

"That she is ten thousand livres richer than I. She would say I am but a poor surintendant. Go, and I hope that God will bless those who are mindful of His poor!"

"So also do I hope," replied Aramis, kissing Fouquet's hand. And he went out quickly, carrying off the letter for Lyonne and the notes for Seldon's mother, and taking up Molière, who was beginning to lose patience.

Chapter 7 — ANOTHER SUPPER AT THE BASTILE

Seven o'clock sounded from the great clock of the Bastile, that famous clock, which, like all the accessories of the state prison, the very use of which is a torture, recalled to the prisoners' minds the destination of every hour of their punishment. The timepiece of the Bastile, adorned with figures, like most of the clocks of the period, represented St. Peter in bonds. It was the supper hour of the unfortunate captives. The doors, grating on their enormous hinges, opened for the passage of the baskets and trays of provisions, the delicacy of which, as M. de Baisemeaux has himself taught us, was regulated by the condition in life of the prisoner. We understand, on this head, the theories of M. de Baisemeaux, sovereign dispenser of gastronomic delicacies, head-cook of the royal fortress, whose trays, full laden, were ascending the steep staircases, carrying some consolation to the prisoners in the bottom of honestly filled bottles. This same hour was that of M. de Gouverneur's supper also. He had a guest to-day, and the spit turned more heavily than usual. Roast partridges flanked with quails and flanking a larded leveret; boiled fowls, ham, fried and sprinkled with white wine,

cardons of Guipuzcoa and *la bisque ècrivisses*—these, together
with the soups and *hors d'œuvre*, constituted the governor's
bill of fare. Baisemeaux, seated at table, was rubbing his hands
and looking at the bishop of Vannes, who, booted like a cavalier,
dressed in gray and sword at side, kept talking of his hunger
and testifying the liveliest impatience. M. de Baisemeaux de
Montlezun was not accustomed to the unbending movements of
his greatness, my lord of Vannes, and this evening Aramis, becoming quite sprightly, volunteered confidence on confidence.
The prelate had again a little touch of the musketeer about
him. The bishop just trenched on the borders only of license in
his style of conversation. As for M. de Baisemeaux, with the
facility of vulgar people, he gave himself up entirely upon this
point of his guest's freedom.

"Monsieur," said he, "for indeed to-night I dare not call you
monseigneur."

"By no means," said Aramis; "call me monsieur; I am
booted."

"Do you know, monsieur, of whom you remind me this evening?"

"No, faith!" said Aramis, taking up his glass; "but I hope I
remind you of a capital guest."

"You remind me of two, monsieur. François, shut the window; the wind may annoy his greatness."

"And let him go," added Aramis. "The supper is completely
served, and we shall eat it very well without waiters. I like extremely to be *tête-à-tête* when I am with a friend."

Baisemeaux bowed respectfully.

"I like extremely," continued Aramis, "to help myself."

"Retire, François," cried Baisemeaux. "I was saying that your
greatness puts me in mind of two persons: one very illustrious,
the late cardinal, the great Cardinal de la Rochelle, who wore
boots like you."

"Indeed!" said Aramis; "and the other?"

"The other was a certain musketeer, very handsome, very
brave, very adventurous, very fortunate, who, from being abbé,
turned musketeer, and from musketeer turned abbé." Aramis
condescended to smile. "From abbé," continued Baisemeaux,
encouraged by Aramis' smile—"from abbé, bishop—and from
bishop——"

"Ah! stay there, I beg!" exclaimed Aramis.

"I say, monsieur, that you gave me the idea of a cardinal."

"Enough, dear Monsieur Baisemeaux. As you said, I have

n the boots of a cavalier, but I do not intend, for all that, to
mbroil myself with the church this evening."

"But you have wicked intentions, however, monseigneur."

"Oh, yes, wicked, I own, as everything mundane is."

"You traverse the town and the streets in disguise?"

"In disguise, as you say."

"And do you still make use of your sword?"

"Yes, I should think so; but only when I am compelled. Do
ne the pleasure to summon François."

"Have you no wine there?"

" 'Tis not for wine, but because it is hot here, and the win-
ow is shut."

"I _shut the windows at supper-time, so as not to hear the
ounds or the arrival of couriers."

"Ah, yes. You hear them when the window is open?"

"But too well, and that disturbs me. You understand."

"Nevertheless, I am suffocated. François!" François entered.
Open the windows, I pray you, Master François," said Aramis.
You will allow him, dear Monsieur Baisemeaux."

"You are at home here," answered the governor. The window
/as opened. "Do you not think," said M. de Baisemeaux, "that
ou will find yourself very lonely, now Monsieur de la Fere has
eturned to his household gods at Blois? He is a very old friend,
; he not?"

"You know it as I do, Baisemeaux, seeing that you were in the
nusketeers with us."

"Bah! with my friends I reckon neither bottles of wine nor
ears."

"And you are right. But I do more than love Monsieur de la
ere, dear Baisemeaux; I venerate him."

"Well, for my part, though 'tis singular," said the governor,
I prefer Monsieur d'Artagnan to him. There is a man for you
/ho drinks long and well! That kind of people allow you, at
east, to penetrate their thoughts."

"Baisemeaux, make me tipsy to-night; let us have a debauch
s of old, and if I have a trouble at the bottom of my heart, I
romise you, you shall see it as you would a diamond at the bot-
om of your glass."

"Bravo!" said Baisemeaux, and he poured out a glass of wine
nd drank it off at a draught, trembling with joy at the idea of
eing, by hook or by crook, in the secret of some high archie-
iscopal misdemeanor. While he was drinking he did not see
vith what attention Aramis was noting the sounds in the great

court. A courier came in about eight o'clock, as François brough
in the fifth bottle, and, although the courier made a great noise
Baisemeaux heard nothing.

"The devil take him!" said Aramis.

"What! who?" asked Baisemeaux. "I hope 'tis neither th
wine you drink nor he who is the cause of your drinking it."

"No; it is a horse, who is making noise enough in the cour
for a whole squadron."

"Pooh! some courier or other," replied the governor, redou
bling his numerous bumpers. "Yes; and may the devil take him
and so quickly that we shall never hear him speak more! Hur
rah! hurrah!"

"You forget me, Baisemeaux; my glass is empty," said
Aramis, showing his dazzling goblet.

"Upon honor, you delight me. François, wine!"

François entered.

"Wine, fellow! and better."

"Yes, monsieur, yes; but a courier has just arrived."

"Let him go to the devil, I say!"

"Yes, monsieur, but——"

"Let him leave his news at the office; we will see it to-morrow
To-morrow, there will be time to-morrow; there will be day
light," said Baisemeaux, chanting the words.

"Ah, monsieur!" grumbled the soldier, François, in spite o
himself, "Monsieur!"

"Take care," said Aramis, "take care!"

"Of what, dear Monsieur d'Herblay?" said Baisemeaux
half-intoxicated.

"The letter which the courier brings to the governor of a for
tress is sometimes an order."

"Nearly always."

"Do not orders issue from the ministers?"

"Yes, undoubtedly; but——"

"And what do these ministers do but countersign the signa
ture of the king?"

"Perhaps you are right. Nevertheless, 'tis very tiresome when
you are sitting before a good table, *tête-à-tête* with a friend—
Ah! I beg your pardon, monsieur; I forgot it is I who engag
you at supper, and that I speak to a future cardinal."

"Let us pass over that, dear Baisemeaux, and return to ou
soldier, to François."

"Well, what has François done?"

"He has demurred."

"He was wrong, then."

"However, he *has* demurred, you see; 'tis because there is something extraordinary in this matter. It is very possible that it was not François who was wrong in demurring, but you, who will be wrong in not listening to him."

"Wrong? I to be wrong before François? that seems rather hard."

"Pardon me, merely an irregularity. But I thought it my duty to make an observation which I deem important."

"Oh! perhaps you are right," stammered Baisemeaux. "The king's order is sacred; but as to orders that arrive when one is at supper, I repeat that the devil——"

"If you had said as much to the great cardinal—hem! my dear Baisemeaux, and if his order had any importance."

"I do it that I may not disturb a bishop. *Mordioux!* am I not, then, excusable?"

"Do not forget, Baisemeaux, that I have worn the soldier's coat, and I am accustomed to see everywhere obedience."

"You wish, then——"

"I wish that you should do your duty, my friend; yes, at least, before this soldier."

" 'Tis mathematically true," exclaimed Baisemeaux. François still waited. "Let them send this order of the king's up to me," he repeated, recovering himself. And he added, in a low tone, "Do you know what it is? I will tell you something about as interesting as this. 'Beware of fire near the powder-magazine;' or, 'Look close after such a one, who is clever at escaping.' Ah! if you only knew, monseigneur, how many times I have been suddenly awakened from the very sweetest and deepest slumber by messengers arriving at full gallop to tell me, or, rather, bring me a slip of paper containing these words: 'Monsieur de Baisemeaux, what news?' 'Tis clear enough that those who waste their time writing such orders have never slept in the Bastile. They would know better; the thickness of my walls, the vigilance of my officers, the number of rounds we go. But, indeed, what can you expect, monseigneur? It is their business to write and torment me when I am at rest, and to trouble me when I am happy," added Baisemeaux, bowing to Aramis. "Then let them do their business."

"And do you do yours," added the bishop, smiling.

François re-entered; Baisemeaux took from his hands the minister's order. He slowly undid it, and as slowly read it. Aramis pretended to be drinking, so as to be able to watch his host through the glass. Then, Baisemeaux having read it:

"What was I just saying?" he exclaimed.

"What is it?" asked the bishop.

"An order of release! There, now; excellent news, indeed, to disturb us!"

"Excellent news for him whom it concerns, you will, at least agree, my dear governor."

"And at eight o'clock in the evening!"

"It is charitable."

"Oh! charity is all very well, but it is for that fellow who says he is so weary and tired, but not for me who am amusing myself," said Baisemeaux, exasperated.

"Will you lose by him, then? And is the prisoner who is to be set at liberty a high payer?"

"Oh, yes, indeed; a miserable, five-franc rat!"

"Let me see it," asked M. d'Herblay. "It is no indiscretion?"

"By no means; read it."

"There is 'Urgent' on the paper; you have seen that, I suppose?"

"Oh, admirable! 'Urgent!'—a man who has been here ten years! It is *urgent* to set him free to-day, this very evening, at eight o'clock!—*urgent!*" And Baisemeaux, shrugging his shoulders with an air of supreme disdain, flung the order on the table, and began eating again. "They are fond of these dodges!" he said, with his mouth full; "they seize a man some fine day, maintain him for ten years, and write to you, 'Watch this fellow well,' or, 'Keep him very strictly.' And then, as soon as you are accustomed to look upon the prisoner as a dangerous man, all of a sudden, without cause or precedent, they write, 'Set him at liberty;' and actually add to their missive, 'urgent.' You will own, my lord, 'tis enough to make any one shrug his shoulders!"

"What do you expect? It is they who write," said Aramis, "and it is for you to execute the order."

"Good! good! execute it! Oh, patience! You must not imagine that I am a slave."

"Gracious Heaven! my very good Monsieur Baisemeaux, who ever said so? Your independence is known."

"Thank Heaven!"

"But your good heart also is known."

"Ah! don't speak of it."

"And your obedience to your superiors. Once a soldier, you see, Baisemeaux, always a soldier."

"And so I shall strictly obey; and to-morrow morning, at daybreak, the prisoner referred to shall be set free."

"To-morrow?"

"At dawn."

"Why not this evening, seeing that the *lettre de cachet* bears, both on the direction and inside, *'urgent'?*"

"Because this evening we are at supper, and our affairs are urgent, too."

"Dear Baisemeaux, booted though I be, I feel myself a priest, and charity has higher claims upon me than hunger and thirst. This unfortunate man has suffered long enough, since you have just told me that he has been your prisoner these ten years. Abridge his suffering. His good time has come; give him the benefit quickly. God will repay you in paradise with years of felicity."

"You wish it?"

"I entreat you."

"What! in the very middle of our repast?"

"I implore you; such an action is worth ten Benedicites."

"It shall be as you desire, only our supper will get cold."

"Oh! never heed that."

Baisemeaux leaned back to ring for François, and, by a very natural motion, turned round toward the door. The order had remained on the table; Aramis seized the opportunity, when Baisemeaux was not looking, to change the paper for another, folded in the same manner, and which he took from his pocket.

"François," said the governor, "let the major come up here with the turnkeys of the Bertaudiere."

François bowed and quitted the room, leaving the two companions alone.

Chapter 8 — THE GENERAL OF THE ORDER

There was now a brief silence, during which Aramis never removed his eyes from Baisemeaux for a moment. The latter seemed only half-decided to disturb himself thus in the middle of supper, and it was clear he was seeking some pretext, whether good or bad, for delay, at any rate, till after dessert. And it appeared also that he had hit upon a pretext at last.

"Eh! but it is impossible!" he cried.

"How, impossible?" said Aramis. "Give me a glimpse of this impossibility."

" 'Tis impossible to set a prisoner at liberty at such an hour. Where can he go to, he, who is unacquainted with Paris?"

"He will go wherever he can."

"You see, now, one might as well set a blind man free."

"I have a carriage, and will take him wherever he wishes."

"You have an answer for everything. François, tell Monsieur le Major to go and open the cell of Monsieur Seldon, No. 3, Bertaudiere."

"Seldon!" exclaimed Aramis very naturally. "You said Seldon, I think?"

"I said Seldon, of course. 'Tis the name of the man they set free."

"Oh! you mean to say Marchiali?" said Aramis.

"Marchiali? Oh! yes, indeed. No, no; Seldon."

"I think you are making a mistake, Monsieur Baisemeaux."

"I have read the order."

"And I, also."

"And I saw 'Seldon' in letters as large as that," and Baisemeaux held up his finger.

"And I read 'Marchiali,' in characters as large as this," said Aramis, also holding up two fingers.

"To the proof; let us throw a light on the matter," said Baisemeaux, confident he was right. "There is the paper, you have only to read it."

" 'I read 'Marchiali,' " returned Aramis, spreading out the paper. "Look."

Baisemeaux looked, and his arms dropped suddenly.

"Yes, yes," he said, quite overwhelmed; "yes, Marchiali. 'Tis plainly written Marchiali! Quite true!"

"Ah!"

"How! the man of whom we have talked so much? The man whom they are every day telling me to take such care of?"

"There is 'Marchiali,' " repeated the inflexible Aramis.

"I must own it, monseigneur. But I understand nothing about it."

"You believe your eyes, at any rate."

"To tell me very plainly there is 'Marchiali.' "

"And in a good handwriting, too."

" 'Tis a wonder! I still see this order and the name of Seldon, Irishman. I see it. Ah! I even recollect that under this name there was a blot of ink."

"No, there is no ink; no, there is no blot."

"Oh! but there was, though; I know it, because I rubbed the powder that was over the blot."

"In a word, be it how it may, dear Monsieur Baisemeaux," said Aramis, "and whatever you may have seen, the order is signed to release Marchiali, blot or no blot."

"The order is signed to release Marchiali," replied Baisemeaux mechanically, endeavoring to regain his courage.

"And you are going to release this prisoner. If your heart dictates to you to deliver Seldon also, I declare to you I will not oppose it the least in the world."

Aramis accompanied this remark with a smile, the irony of which effectually dispelled Baisemeaux's confusion of mind, and restored his courage.

"Monseigneur," he said, "this Marchiali is the very same prisoner whom the other day a priest, confessor of *our order*, came to visit in so imperious and so secret a manner."

"I don't know that, monsieur," replied the bishop.

" 'Tis no such long time ago, dear Monsieur d'Herblay."

"It is true. But *with us*, monsieur, it is good that the man of to-day should no longer know what the man of yesterday did."

"In any case," said Baisemeaux, "the visit of the Jesuit confessor must have given happiness to this man."

Aramis made no reply, but recommenced eating and drinking. As for Baisemeaux, no longer touching anything that was on the table, he again took up the order and examined it in every way. This investigation, under ordinary circumstances, would have made the ears of the impatient Aramis burn with anger; but the bishop of Vannes did not become incensed for so little, above all, when he had murmured to himself that to do so was dangerous.

"Are you going to release Marchiali?" he said. "What mellow and fragrant sherry this is, my dear governor."

"Monseigneur," replied Baisemeaux, "I shall release the prisoner Marchiali when I have summoned the courier who brought the order, and above all, when, by interrogating him, I have satisfied myself."

"The order is sealed, and the courier is ignorant of the contents. What do you want to satisfy yourself about?"

"Be it so, monseigneur; but I shall send to the ministry, and Monsieur de Lyonne will either confirm or withdraw the order."

"What is the good of all that?" asked Aramis coldly.

"What good?"

"Yes; what is your object, I ask?"

"The object of never deceiving one's self, monseigneur; nor being wanting in the respect which a subaltern owes to his superior officers, nor infringing the duties of that service which one has voluntarily accepted."

"Very good; you have just spoken so eloquently that I cannot but admire you. It is true that a subaltern owes respect to his superiors; he is guilty when he deceives himself, and he should be punished if he infringe either the duties or laws of his office."

Baisemeaux looked at the bishop with astonishment.

"It follows," pursued Aramis, "that you are going to ask advice, to put your conscience at ease in the matter?"

"Yes, monseigneur."

"And if a superior officer gives you orders, you will obey?"

"Never doubt it, monseigneur."

"You know the king's signature well, Monsieur de Baisemeaux?"

"Yes, monseigneur."

"Is it not on this order of release?"

"It is true, but it may——"

"Be forged, you mean?"

"That is evident, monseigneur."

"You are right. And that of Monsieur de Lyonne?"

"I see it plain enough on the order; but for the same reason that the king's signature may have been forged, so also, even more likely, may Monsieur de Lyonne's."

"Your logic has the stride of a giant, Monsieur de Baisemeaux," said Aramis; "and your reasoning is irresistible. But on what special grounds do you base your idea that these signatures are false?"

"On this: the absence of counter-signatures. Nothing checks his majesty's signature; and Monsieur de Lyonne is not there to tell me he has signed."

"Well, Monsieur de Baisemeaux," said Aramis, bending an eagle glance on the governor, "I adopt so frankly your doubts, and your mode of clearing them up, that I will take a pen if you will give me one."

Baisemeaux gave him a pen.

"And a sheet of white paper," added Aramis.

Baisemeaux handed some paper.

"Now, I—I, also—I, here present—incontestably, I—am going to write an order to which I am certain you will give credence, incredulous as you are."

Baisemeaux turned pale at this icy assurance of manner. It seemed to him that that voice of the bishop's, but just now so playful and so gay, had become funereal and sad; that the wax-lights changed into the tapers of a mortuary chapel, and the glasses of wine into chalices of blood.

Aramis took a pen, and wrote. Baisemeaux, in terror, read over his shoulder.

"A. M. D. G.," wrote the bishop; and he drew a cross under these four letters, which signify *ad majorem Dei gloriam,* "to the greater glory of God;" and thus he continued, "It is our pleasure that the order brought to Monsieur de Baisemeaux de Montlezun, governor, for the king, of the castle of the Bastile, be held by him good and effectual, and be immediately carried into operation.

"(Signed)   D'HERBLAY,

"General of the Order, by the grace of God."

Baisemeaux was so profoundly astonished that his features remained contracted, his lips parted, and his eyes fixed. He did not move an inch, nor articulate a sound. Nothing could be heard in that large chamber but the buzzing of a little moth, which was fluttering about the candles. Aramis, without even deigning to look at the man whom he had reduced to so miserable a condition, drew from his pocket a small case of black wax; he sealed the letter, and stamped it with a seal suspended at his breast, beneath his doublet, and when the operation was concluded, presented—still in silence—the missive to M. de Baisemeaux. The latter, whose hands trembled in a manner to excite pity, turned a dull and meaningless gaze upon the letter. A last gleam of feeling played over his features, and he fell, as if thunderstruck, on a chair.

"Come, come," said Aramis, after a long silence, during which the governor of the Bastile had slowly recovered his senses, "do not lead me to believe, dear Baisemeaux, that the presence of the general of the order is as terrible as His, and that men die merely from having seen Him. Take courage, rouse yourself; give me your hand, and obey."

Baisemeaux, reassured if not satisfied, obeyed, kissed Aramis' hand, and rose.

"Immediately?" he murmured.

"Oh, there is no pressing haste, my host; take your place again, and do the honors over this beautiful dessert."

"Monseigneur, I shall never recover such a shock as this; I who have laughed, who have jested with you! I, who have dared to treat you on a footing of equality!"

"Say nothing about it, old comrade," replied the bishop, who perceived how strained the cord was, and how dangerous it would have been to break it, "say nothing about it. Let us each live in our own way; to you, my protection and my friendship; to me, your obedience. Having exactly fulfilled these two requirements, let us live happily."

Baisemeaux reflected; he perceived, at a glance, the consequence of this withdrawal of a prisoner by means of a forged order; and, putting in the scale the guarantee offered him by the official order of the general, did not consider it of any value.

Aramis divined this.

"My dear Baisemeaux," said he, "you are a simpleton. Lose this habit of reflection when I give myself the trouble to think for you."

And at another gesture he made, Baisemeaux bowed again.

"How shall I set about it?" he said.

"What is the process for releasing a prisoner?"

"I have the regulations."

"Well, then, follow the regulations, my friend."

"I go with my major to the prisoner's room, and conduct him, if he is a personage of importance."

"But this Marchiali is not an important personage," said Aramis carelessly.

"I don't know," answered the governor; as if he would have said, "It is for you to instruct me."

"Then, if you don't know it, I am right; so act toward Marchiali as you act toward one of obscure station."

"Good; the regulations so provide. They are to the effect that the turnkey, or one of the lower officials, shall bring the prisoner before the governor, in the office."

"Well, 'tis very wise, that; and then?"

"Then we return to the prisoner the valuables he wore at the time of his imprisonment, his clothes and papers, if the minister's orders have not otherwise directed."

"What was the minister's order as to this Marchiali?"

"Nothing; for the unhappy man arrived here without jewels, without papers, and almost without clothes."

"See how simple it all is. Indeed, Baisemeaux, you make a mountain of everything. Remain here, and make them bring the prisoner to the governor's house."

Baisemeaux obeyed. He summoned his lieutenant, and gave him an order, which the latter passed on, without disturbing himself about it, to the next whom it concerned.

Half an hour afterward they heard a gate shut in the court; it was the door to the dungeon, which had just rendered up its prey to the free air. Aramis blew out all the candles which lighted the room but one, which he left burning behind the door. This flickering glare prevented the sight from resting steadily on any object. It multiplied tenfold the changing forms and shadows of the place, by its wavering uncertainty. Steps drew near.

"Go and meet your men," said Aramis to Baisemeaux.

The governor obeyed. The sergeant and turnkeys disappeared. Baisemeaux re-entered, followed by a prisoner. Aramis had placed himself in the shade; he saw without being seen. Baisemeaux, in an agitated tone of voice, made the young man acquainted with the order which set him at liberty. The prisoner listened, without making a single gesture or saying a word.

"You will swear ('tis the regulation that requires it)," added the governor, "never to reveal anything that you have seen or heard in the Bastile?"

The prisoner perceived a crucifix; he stretched out his hands, and swore with his lips.

"And now, monsieur, you are free, whither do you intend going?"

The prisoner turned his head, as if looking behind him for some protection, on which he ought to rely. Then was it that Aramis came out of the shade.

"I am here," he said, "to render the gentleman whatever service he may please to ask."

The prisoner slightly reddened, and, without hesitation, passed his arm through that of Aramis.

"God have you in His holy keeping," he said, in a voice the firmness of which made the governor tremble as much as the form of the blessing astonished him.

Aramis, on shaking hands with Baisemeaux, said to him:

"Does my order trouble you? Do you fear their finding it here, should they come to search?"

"I desire to keep it, monseigneur," said Baisemeaux. "If they found it here, it would be a certain indication I should be lost, and, in that case, you would be a powerful and a last auxiliary to me."

"Being your accomplice, you mean?" answered Aramis, shrugging his shoulders. "Adieu, Baisemeaux," said he.

The horses were in waiting, making the carriage shake again with their impatience. Baisemeaux accompanied the bishop to the bottom of the steps. Aramis caused his companion to mount before him, then followed, and without giving the driver any further order, "Go on," said he. The carriage rattled over the pavement of the courtyard. An officer with a torch went before the horses, and gave orders at every post to let them pass. During the time taken in opening all the barriers, Aramis barely breathed, and you might have heard his "sealed heart knock against his ribs." The prisoner, buried in a corner of the carriage, made no more sign of life than his companion. At length, a jolt more severe than the others announced to them that they had cleared the last watercourse. Behind the carriage closed the last gate, that in the Rue St. Antoine. No more walls either on the right or left; heaven everywhere, liberty everywhere, and life everywhere. The horses, kept in check by a vigorous hand, went quietly as far as the middle of the faubourg. There they began to trot. Little by little, whether they warmed over it, or whether they were urged, they gained in swiftness, and, once past Bercy, the carriage seemed to fly, so great was the ardor of the coursers. These horses ran thus as far as Villeneuve St. George's, where relays were waiting. Then, four instead of two whirled the carriage away in the direction of Melun, and pulled up for a moment in the middle of the forest of Senart. No doubt the order had been given the postilion beforehand, for Aramis had no occasion even to make a sign.

"What is the matter?" asked the prisoner, as if waking from a long dream.

"The matter is, monseigneur," said Aramis, "that before going further it is necessary your royal highness and I should converse."

"I will wait an opportunity, monsieur," answered the young prince.

"We could not have a better, monseigneur; we are in the middle of a forest, and no one can hear us."

"The postilion?"

"The postilion of this relay is deaf and dumb, monseigneur."

"I am at your service, Monsieur d'Herblay."

"Is it your pleasure to remain in the carriage?"

"Yes; we are comfortably seated, and I like this carriage, for it has restored me to liberty."

"Wait, monseigneur; there is yet a precaution to be taken."

"What?"

"We are here on the highway; cavaliers or carriages traveling like ourselves might pass, and, seeing us stopping, deem us in some difficulty. Let us avoid offers of assistance, which would embarrass us."

"Give the postilion orders to conceal the carriage in one of the side avenues."

" 'Tis exactly what I wished to do, monseigneur."

Aramis made a sign to the deaf and dumb driver of the carriage, whom he touched on the arm. The latter dismounted, took the leaders by the bridle, and led them over the velvet sward and the mossy grass of a winding alley, at the bottom of which, on this moonless night, the deep shades formed a curtain blacker than ink. This done, the man lay down on a slope near his horses, who, on either side, kept nibbling the young oak shoots.

"I am listening," said the young prince to Aramis; "but what are you doing there?"

"I am disarming myself of my pistols, of which we have no further need, monseigneur."

Chapter 9 — THE TEMPTER

"My prince," said Aramis, turning in the carriage toward his companion, "weak creature as I am, so unpretending in genius, so low in the scale of intelligent beings, it has never yet happened to me to converse with a man without penetrating his thoughts through that living mask which has been thrown over our mind, in order to retain its expression. But to-night, in this darkness, in the reserve which you maintain, I can read nothing on your features, and something tells me that I shall have great difficulty in wresting from you a sincere declaration. I beseech you, then, not for love of me, for subjects should never weigh as anything in the balance which princes hold, but for love of yourself, to retain every syllable, every inflection which, under our present grave circumstances will all have a sense and value as important as any ever uttered in the world."

"I listen," repeated the young prince, "decidedly, without either eagerly seeking or fearing anything you are about to say to me."

And he buried himself still deeper in the thick cushions of the carriage, trying to deprive his companion not only of the sight of him, but even of the very idea of his presence.

Black was the darkness which fell wide and dense from the

summits of the intertwining trees. The carriage, covered in by this vast roof, would not have received a particle of light, not even if a ray could have struggled through the wreaths of mist which were rising in the avenue of the wood.

"Monseigneur," resumed Aramis, "you know the history of the government which to-day controls France. The king issued from an infancy imprisoned like yours, obscure as yours, and confined as yours; only, instead of ending, like yourself, this slavery in a prison—this obscurity in solitude—these straitened circumstances in concealment, he was fain to bear all these miseries, humiliations, and distresses in full daylight, under the pitiless sun of royalty, or an elevation so flooded with light, where every stain appears a miserable blemish, and every glory a stain. The king has suffered; it rankles in his mind; and he will avenge himself. He will be a bad king. I say not that he will pour out blood, like Louis XI., or Charles IX.; for he has no mortal injuries to avenge; but he will devour the means and substance of his people; for he has himself undergone wrongs in his own interest and money. In the first place, then, I quite acquit my conscience, when I consider openly the merits and faults of this prince; and if I condemn him, my conscience absolves me."

Aramis paused. It was not to listen if the silence of the forest remained undisturbed, but it was to gather up his thoughts from the very bottom of his soul—to leave the thoughts he had uttered sufficient time to eat deeply into the mind of his companion.

"All that Heaven does, Heaven does well," continued the bishop of Vannes; "and I am so persuaded of it that I have long been thankful to have been chosen depositary of the secret which I have aided you to discover. To a just Providence was necessary an instrument, at once penetrating, persevering, and convincing, to accomplish a great work. I am this instrument. I possess penetration, perseverance, conviction; I govern a mysterious people, who has taken for its motto the motto of God, '*Patiens quia ætermus.*'" The prince moved. "I divine, monseigneur, why you are raising your head, and are surprised at the people I have under my command. You did not know you were dealing with a king—oh! monseigneur, king of a people very humble, much disinherited; humble, because they have no force save when creeping; disinherited, because never, almost never in this world, do my people reap the harvest they sow, nor eat the fruit they cultivate. They labor for an abstract idea; they heap together all the atoms of their power, to form one man; and round this man, with the sweat of their labor, they create a misty halo, which his genius shall, in turn, render a glory gilded with the rays of all the crowns in Christendom. Such is the man you have beside you, monseigneur. It is to tell you that he has drawn you from the abyss for a great purpose, and that he desires, for this sublime purpose, to raise you above the powers of the earth—above himself."

The prince lightly touched Aramis' arm.

"You speak to me," he said, "of that religious order whose chief you are. For me, the result of your words is, that the day you desire to hurl down the man you shall have raised, the event will be accomplished; and that you will keep under your hand your creation of yesterday."

"Undeceive yourself, monseigneur," replied the bishop. "I should not take the trouble to play this terrible game with your royal highness if I had not a double interest in gaining it. The day you are elevated, you are elevated forever; you will overturn the footstool, as you rise, and will send it rolling so far that not even the sight of it will ever again recall to you its right to gratitude."

"Oh, monsieur!"

"Your movement, monseigneur, arises from an excellent disposition. I thank you. Be well assured, I aspire to more than gratitude. I am convinced that, when arrived at the summit, you will judge me still more worthy to be your friend; and then, monseigneur, we two will do such great deeds that ages hereafter shall long speak of them."

"Tell me plainly, monsieur—tell me without disguise—what am to-day, and what you aim at my being to-morrow."

"You are the son of King Louis XIII., brother of Louis XIV., natural and legitimate heir to the throne of France. In keeping you near him, as Monsieur has been kept—Monsieur, your younger brother—the king reserved to himself the right of being legitimate sovereign. The doctors only could dispute his legitimacy. But the doctors always prefer the king who is to the king who is not. Providence has willed that you should be persecuted; and this persecution to-day consecrates you King of France. You had, then, a right to reign, seeing that it is disputed; you had a right to be proclaimed, seeing that you have been concealed; and you possess royal blood, since no one has dared to shed yours, as your servants' has been shed. Now, see, then, what this Providence, which you have so often accused of having in every way thwarted you, has done for you. It has given you the features, figure, age, and voice of your brother; and

the very causes of your persecution are about to become those
of your triumphant restoration. To-morrow, after to-morrow
—from the very first, regal phantom, living shade of Louis XIV.
you will sit upon his throne, whence the will of Heaven, con
fided in execution to the arm of man, will have hurled him
without hope of return."

"I understand," said the prince; "my brother's blood wil
not be shed, then?"

"You will be sole arbiter of his fate."

"The secret of which they made an evil use against me?"

"You will employ it against him. What did he do to concea
it? He concealed you. Living image of himself, you will defeat
the conspiracy of Mazarin and Anne of Austria. You, my prince
will have the same interest in concealing him, who will, as a prisoner, resemble you, as you will resemble him as king."

"I fall back on what I was saying to you. Who will guard
him?"

"Who guarded you?"

"You know this secret—you have made use of it with regard
to myself. Who else knows it?"

"The queen-mother and Madame de Chevreuse."

"What will they do?"

"Nothing, if you choose."

"How is that?"

"How can they recognize you, if you act in a manner that
no one can recognize you?"

" 'Tis true; but there are grave difficulties."

"State them, prince."

"My brother is married; I cannot take my brother's wife."

"I will cause Spain to consent to a divorce; it is in the inter
est of your new policy; it is human morality. All that is really
noble and really useful in this world will find its account
therein."

"The imprisoned king will speak."

"To whom do you think he will speak—to the walls?"

"You mean, by walls, the men in whom you put confidence."

"If need be, yes. And, besides, your royal highness——"

"Besides?"

"I was going to say that the designs of Providence do not stop
on such a fair road. Every scheme of this caliber is completed
by its results, like a geometrical calculation. The king, in prison
will not be for you the cause of embarrassment that you have
been for the king enthroned. His soul is naturally proud and
impatient; it is, moreover, disarmed and enfeebled, by being

ccustomed to honors, and by the license of supreme power. The
ame Providence which has willed that the concluding step in
he geometrical calculation I have had the honor of describing
o your royal highness should be your accession to the throne,
nd the destruction of him who is hurtful to you has also de-
ermined that the conquered one shall soon end both his
wn and your sufferings. Therefore, his soul and body have been
dapted for but a brief agony. Put into prison as a private in-
ividual, left alone with your doubts, deprived of everything,
ou have exhibited a solid, enduring principle of life in with-
tanding all this. But your brother, a captive, forgotten, and in
onds, will not long endure the calamity; and Heaven will re-
ume his soul at the appointed time—that is to say, *soon*."

At this point in Aramis' gloomy analysis, a bird of night ut-
ered from the depths of the forest that prolonged and plaintive
ry which makes every creature tremble.

"I will exile the deposed king," said Philippe, shuddering; "it
ill be more human."

"The king's good pleasure will decide the point," said Aramis.
But has the problem been well put? Have I brought out the
olution according to the wishes or the foresight of your royal
ighness?"

"Yes, monsieur, yes; you have forgotten nothing—except,
ndeed, two things."

"The first?"

"Let us speak of it at once, with the same frankness we have
lready conversed in. Let us speak of the causes which may
ring about the ruin of all the hopes we have conceived. Let us
peak of the risks we are running."

"They would be immense, infinite, terrific, insurmountable,
f, as I have said, all things did not concur in rendering them
f absolutely no account. There is no danger either for you or
or me, if the constancy and intrepidity of your royal highness
re equal to that perfection of resemblance to your brother
hich nature has bestowed upon you. I repeat it, there are no
angers, only obstacles; a word, indeed, which I find in all
anguages, but have always ill-understood, and, were I king,
ould have obliterated as useless and absurd."

"Yes, indeed, monsieur; there is a very serious obstacle, an
nsurmountable danger, which you are forgetting."

"Ah!" said Aramis.

"There is conscience, which cries aloud; remorse, which never
ies."

"True, true," said the bishop; "there is a weakness of heart

of which you remind me. You are right, too, for that indeed is an
immense obstacle. The horse afraid of the ditch leaps into the
middle of it, and is killed. The man who tremblingly crosses his
sword with that of another leaves loopholes whereby his enemy
has him in his power."

"Have you a brother?" said the young man to Aramis.

"I am alone in the world," said the latter, with a hard, dry
voice.

"But, surely, there is some one in the world whom you love?"
added Philippe.

"No one—yes, I love you."

The young man sank into so profound a silence that the mere
sound of his respiration seemed like a roaring tumult for
Aramis.

"Monseigneur," he resumed, "I have not said all I had to say
to your royal highness; I have not offered you all the salutary
counsels and useful resources which I have at my disposal.
It is useless to flash bright visions before the eyes of one who
seeks and loves darkness; useless, too, is it to let the magnif-
ience of the cannon's roar be heard in the ears of one who
loves repose and the quiet of the country. Monseigneur, I have
your happiness spread out before me in my thoughts; listen
to my words: precious they indeed are, in their import and
their sense, for you who look with such tender regard upon the
bright heavens, the verdant meadows, the pure air. I know a
country instinct with delights of every kind, an unknown paradise, a secluded corner of the world—where alone, unfettered
and unknown, in the thick covert of the woods, amid flowers
and streams of rippling water, you will forget all the misery that
human folly has so recently allotted you. Oh! listen to me, my
prince. I do not jest. I have a heart, and mind, and soul, and
can read to the depths of your own. I will not take you, incomplete for your task, in order to cast you into the crucible of my
own desires, or my caprice, or my ambition. Everything or nothing. You are chilled and galled, sick at heart, almost overcome
by the excess of emotion which but one hour's liberty was produced in you. For me, that is a certain and unmistakable sign
that you do not wish to continue at liberty. Would you prefer a more humble life, a life more suited to your strength?
Heaven is my witness that I wish your happiness to be the result
of the trial to which I have exposed you."

"Speak, speak!" said the prince, with a vivacity which did
not escape Aramis.

"I know," resumed the prelate, "in the Bas-Poiton, a canton, of which no one in France suspects the existence. Twenty leagues of country is immense, is it not? Twenty leagues, monseigneur, all covered with water and herbage, and reeds of the most luxuriant nature; the whole studded with islands covered with woods of the densest foliage. These large marshes, covered with reeds as with a thick mantle, sleep silently and calmly beneath the sun's soft and genial rays. A few fishermen with their families indolently pass their lives away there, with their large rafts of poplars and alders, the flooring formed of reeds, and the roof woven out of thick rushes. These barks, these floating-houses, are wafted to and fro by the changing winds. Whenever they touch a bank, it is but by chance; and so gently, too, that the sleeping fisherman is not awakened by the shock. Should he wish to land, it is merely because he has seen a large flight of land-rails or plovers, of wild ducks, teal, widgeon, or woodcocks, which fall an easy prey to his nets or his gun. Silver shad, eels, greedy pike, red and gray mullet, fall in masses into his nets; he has but to choose the finest and largest, and return the others to the waters. Never yet has the foot of man, be he soldier or simple citizen, never has any one, indeed, penetrated into that district. The sun's rays there are soft and tempered, in plots of solid earth, whose soil is rich and fertile, grows the vine, which nourishes with its generous juice its black and white grapes. Once a week a boat is sent to fetch the bread which has been baked at an oven—the common property of all. There—like the seigneurs of early days—powerful because of your dogs, your fishing-lines, your guns, and your beautiful reed-built house, would you live, rich in the produce of the chase, in the plenitude of perfect security. There would years of your life roll away, at the end of which, no longer recognizable, for you would have been perfectly transformed, you would have succeeded in acquiring a destiny accorded to you by Heaven. There are a thousand pistoles in this bag, monseigneur—more, far more, than sufficient to purchase the whole marsh of which I have spoken; more than enough to live there as many years as you have days to live; more than enough to constitute you the richest, the freest and the happiest man in the country. Accept it, as I offer it to you—sincerely, cheerfully. Forthwith, without a moment's pause, I will unharness two of my horses, which are attached to the carriage yonder, and they, accompanied by my servant—my deaf and dumb attendant—shall conduct you—traveling throughout the night, sleeping during the day—to the locality I have mentioned; and I shall, at least, have the satisfaction of knowing that I have rendered to my prince the service that he himself most preferred. I shall have made one man happy; and Heaven for that will hold me in better account than if I had made one man powerful; for that is far more difficult And now, monseigneur, your answer to this proposition? Here is the money. Nay, do not hesitate. At Poiton you can risk nothing, except the chance of catching the fevers prevalent there; and even of them the so-called wizards of the country may cure you, for the sake of your pistoles. If you play the other game you run the chance of being assassinated on a throne, or of being strangled in a prison. Upon my soul, I assure you, now I begin to compare them together, I should hesitate which of the two I should accept."

"Monsieur," replied the young prince, "before I determine let me alight from this carriage, walk on the ground, and consult that still voice within me which Heaven bids address us all. Ten minutes is all I ask, and then you shall have your answer."

"As you please, monseigneur," said Aramis, bending before him with respect, so solemn and august in its tone and address had been the voice which had just spoken.

Chapter 10 — CROWN AND TIARA

Aramis was the first to descend from the carriage; he held the door open for the young man. He saw him place his foot on the mossy ground with a trembling of the whole body, and walk round the carriage with an unsteady and almost tottering step It seemed as if the poor prisoner was unaccustomed to walk on God's earth. It was the 15th of August, about eleven o'clock night; thick clouds, portending a tempest, overspread the heavens, and shrouded all light and prospect beneath their heavy folds. The extremities of the avenues were imperceptibly detached from the copse by a lighter shadow of opaque gray which, upon closer examination became visible in the midst of the obscurity. But the fragrance which ascended from the grass fresher and more penetrating than that which exhaled from the trees around him; the warm and balmy air which enveloped him for the first time for many years past; the ineffable enjoyment liberty in an open country, spoke to the prince in so seducing a language, that, notwithstanding the great caution, we would almost say the dissimulation of his character, of which we have tried to give an idea, he could not restrain his emotion, and breathed a sigh of joy. Then, by degrees, he raised his aching head and inhaled the perfumed air, as it was wafted in gentle gusts across his uplifted face. Crossing his arms on his chest, as if to control this new sensation of delight, he drank in·delicious draughts of that mysterious air which penetrates at night-time through lofty forests. The sky he was contemplating, the murmuring waters, the moving creatures; was not this reality? Was not Aramis a madman to suppose that he had aught else to dream of in this world? Those exciting pictures of country life, so free from cares, from fears, and troubles, that ocean of happy days which glitters incessantly before all youthful imaginations, are real allurements wherewith to fascinate a poor, unhappy prisoner, worn out by prison life, and emaciated by the close air of the Bastile. It was the picture, it will be remembered, drawn by Aramis, when he offered the thousand pistoles which he had with him in the carriage to the prince, and the enchanted Eden which the deserts of Bas-Poiton hid from the eyes of the world. Such were the reflections of Aramis as he watched, with an anxiety impossible to describe, the silent progress of the emotions of Philippe, whom he perceived gradually becoming more and more absorbed in his meditations. The young prince was offering up an inward prayer to Heaven, to be divinely guided in this trying moment, upon which his life or death depended. It was an anxious time for the bishop of Vannes, who had never before been so perplexed. His iron will, accustomed to overcome all obstacles, never finding itself inferior or vanquished on any occasion, to be foiled in so vast a project from not having foreseen the influence which a view of Nature in all its luxuriance would have on the human mind! Aramis, overwhelmed by anxiety, contemplated with emotion the painful struggle which was taking place in Philippe's mind. This suspense lasted the whole ten minutes which the young man had requested. During this space of time, which appeared an eternity, Philippe continued gazing with an imploring and sorrowful look toward the heavens; Aramis did not remove the piercing glance he had fixed on Philippe. Suddenly the young man bowed his head. His thoughts returned to the earth, his looks perceptibly hardened, his brow contracted, his mouth assuming an expression of fierce courage; and then again his look became fixed, but this time it wore a worldly expression, hardened by covetousness, pride, and strong desire. Aramis' look then became as soft as it had before been gloomy. Philippe, seizing his hand in a quick, agitated manner, exclaimed:

"Let us go where the crown of France is to be found."

"Is this your decision, monseigneur?" asked Aramis.

"It is."

"Irrevocably so?"

Philippe did not even deign to reply. He gazed earnestly at the bishop, as if to ask him if it were possible for a man to waver after having once made up his mind.

"Those looks are flashes of fire which portray character," said Aramis, bowing over Philippe's hand; "you will be great, monseigneur, I will answer for that."

"Let us resume our conversation. I wish to discuss two points with you; in the first place, the dangers or the obstacles we may meet with. That point is decided. The other is the conditions you intend imposing on me. It is your turn to speak, Monsieur d'Herblay."

"The conditions, monseigneur?"

"Doubtless. You will not allow so mere a trifle to stop me, and you will not do me the injustice to suppose that I think you have no interest in this affair. Therefore, without subterfuge or hesitation, tell me the truth."

"I will do so, monseigneur. Once a king——"

"When will that be?"

"To-morrow evening—I mean in the night."

"Explain yourself."

"When I shall have asked your highness a question."

"Do so."

"I sent to your highness a man in my confidence, with instructions to deliver some closely written notes, carefully drawn up, which will thoroughly acquaint your highness with the different persons who compose and will compose your court."

"I perused all the notes."

"Attentively?"

"I know them by heart."

"And understand them? Pardon me, but I may venture to ask that question of a poor, abandoned captive of the Bastile. It will not be requisite in a week's time to further question a mind like yours, when you will then be in full possession of liberty and power."

"Interrogate me, then, and I will be a scholar repeating his lesson to his master."

"We will begin with your family, monseigneur."

"My mother, Anne of Austria, all her sorrows, her painful malady. Oh! I know her—I know her!"

"Your second brother?" asked Aramis, bowing.

"To these notes," replied the prince, "you have added portraits so faithfully painted that I am able to recognize the persons whose characters, manners, and history you have so carefully portrayed. Monsieur, my brother, is a fine, dark young man, with a pale face; he does not love his wife, Henriette, whom I, Louis XIV., loved a little, and still flirt with, even although she made me weep on the day she wished to dismiss Mademoiselle de la Valliere from her service in disgrace."

"You will have to be careful with regard to watchfulness of the latter," said Aramis; "she is sincerely attached to the actual king. The eyes of a woman who loves are not easily deceived."

"She is fair, has blue eyes, whose affectionate gaze will reveal her identity. She halts slightly in her gait; she writes a letter every day, to which I have to send an answer by Monsieur de St. Aignan."

"Do you know the latter?"

"As if I saw him, and I know the last verses he composed for me, as well as those I composed in answer to his."

"Very good. Do you know your ministers?"

"Colbert, an ugly, dark-browed man, but intelligent enough; his hair covering his forehead, a large, heavy, full head; the mortal enemy of Monsieur Fouquet."

"As for the latter, we need not disturb ourselves about him."

"No; because, necessarily, you will require me to exile him, I suppose?"

Aramis, struck with admiration at the remark, said:

"You will become very great, monseigneur."

"You see," added the prince, "that I know my lesson by heart, and with Heaven's assistance, and yours afterward, I shall seldom go wrong."

"You have still an awkward pair of eyes to deal with, monseigneur."

"Yes, the captain of the musketeers, Monsieur d'Artagnan, your friend."

"Yes; I can well say 'my friend.'"

"He who escorted La Valliere to Le Chaillot; he who delivered up Monk, fastened in an iron box, to Charles II.; he who so faithfully served my mother; he to whom the crown of France owes so much that it owes everything. Do you intend to ask me to exile him also?"

"Never, sire. D'Artagnan is a man to whom, at a certain given time, I will undertake to reveal everything; but be on your guard with him; for if he discovers our plot before it is revealed to him, you or I will certainly be killed or taken. He is a bold, enterprising man."

"I will think over it. Now tell me about Monsieur Fouquet; what do you wish to be done with regard to him?"

"One moment more, I entreat you, monseigneur; and forgive me if I seem to fail in respect in questioning you further."

"It is your duty to do so, and, more than that, your right also."

"Before we pass to Monsieur Fouquet, I should very much regret forgetting another friend of mine."

"Monsieur du Vallon, the Hercules of France, you mean; oh! as far as he is concerned, his fortune is safe."

"No; it is not he whom I intended to refer to."

"The Comte de la Fere, then?"

"And his son, the son of all four of us."

"That poor boy who is dying of love for La Valliere, whom my brother so disloyally deprived him of? Be easy on that score, I shall know how to restore him. Tell me only one thing, Monsieur d'Herblay; do men, when they love, forget the treachery that has been shown them? Can a man ever forgive the woman who has betrayed him? Is that a French custom, or is it one of the laws of the human heart?"

"A man who loves deeply, as deeply as Raoul loves Mademoiselle de la Valliere, finishes by forgetting the fault or crime of the woman he loves; but I do not know if Raoul will be able to forget."

"I will see after that. Have you anything further to say about your friend?"

"No; that is all."

"Well, then, now for Monsieur Fouquet. What do you wish me to do for him?"

"To continue him as surintendant, as he has hitherto acted, I entreat you."

"Be it so; but he is the first minister at present."

"Not quite so."

"A king, ignorant and embarrassed as I shall be, will, as a matter of course, require a first minister of state."

"Your majesty will require a friend."

"I have only one, and that is yourself."

"You will have many others by and by, but none so devoted, none so zealous for your glory."

"You will be my first minister of state."

"Not immediately, monseigneur, for that would give rise to too much suspicion and astonishment."

"Monsieur de Richelieu, the first minister of my grandmother, Marie de Medici, was simply bishop of Luçon, as you are bishop of Vannes."

"I perceive that your royal highness has studied my notes to great advantage; your amazing perspicacity overpowers me with delight."

"I am perfectly aware that Monsieur de Richelieu, by means of the queen's protection, soon became cardinal."

"It would be better," said Aramis, bowing, "that I should not be appointed first minister until your royal highness has procured my nomination as cardinal."

"You shall be nominated before two months are past, Monsieur d'Herblay. But that is a matter of very trifling moment; you would not offend me if you were to ask more than that, and you would cause me serious regret if you were to limit yourself to that."

"In that case, I have something still further to hope for, monseigneur."

"Speak, speak!"

"Monsieur Fouquet will not keep long at the head of affairs, he will soon get old. He is fond of pleasure, consistently so with his labors, thanks to that amount of youthfulness which he still retains; but this youthfulness will disappear at the approach of the first serious annoyance, or at the first illness he may experience. We will spare him the annoyance, because he is an agreeable and noble-hearted man; but we cannot save him from ill-health. So it is determined. When you shall have paid all Monsieur Fouquet's debts, and restored the finances to a sound condition, Monsieur Fouquet will be able to remain the sovereign ruler in his little court of poets and painters, but we shall have made him rich. When that has been done, and I shall have become your royal highness' prime minister, I shall be able to think of my own interests and yours."

The young man looked at his interrogator.

"Monsieur de Richelieu, of whom we were speaking just now, was very blamable in the fixed idea he had of governing France alone, unaided. He allowed two kings, King Louis XIII. and himself, to be seated upon the same throne, while he might have installed them more conveniently upon two separate and distinct thrones."

"Upon two thrones?" said the young man thoughtfully.

"In fact," pursued Aramis quietly, "a cardinal, prime minister of France, assisted by the favor and by the countenance of His Most Christian Majesty the King of France, a cardinal to whom the king, his master, lends the treasures of the state, his army, his counsel, such a man would be acting with twofold injustice in applying these mighty resources to France alone. Besides," added Aramis, "you will not be a king such as your father was; delicate in health, slow in judgment, whom all things wearied; you will be a king governing by your brain and by your sword; you will have in the government of the state no more than you could manage unaided; I should only interfere with you. Besides, our friendship ought never to be, I do not say impaired, but in any way affected, by a secret thought. I shall have given you the throne of France, you will confer on me the throne of St. Peter. Whenever your loyal, firm, and mailed hand shall have joined in ties of intimate association the hand of a pope such as I shall be, neither Charles V., who owned two-thirds of the habitable globe, nor Charlemagne, who possessed it entirely, will be able to reach to half your stature. I have no alliances, I have no predictions; I will not throw you into persecutions of heretics, nor will I cast you into the troubled waters of family dissension; I will simply say to you: The whole universe is our own; for me the minds of men, for you their bodies. And as I shall be the first to die, you will have my inheritance. What do you say of my plan, monseigneur?"

"I say that you render me happy and proud, for no other reason than that of having comprehended you thoroughly. Monsieur d'Herblay, you shall be cardinal, and when cardinal, my prime minister; and then you will point out to me the necessary steps to be taken to secure your election as pope, and I will take them. You can ask what guarantees from me you please."

"It is useless. I shall never act except in such a manner that you are the gainer; I shall never ascend the ladder of fortune, fame, or position, until I shall have first seen you placed upon the round of the ladder immediately above me; I shall always hold myself sufficiently aloof from you to escape incurring your jealousy, sufficiently near to sustain your personal advantage and to watch over your friendship. All the contracts in the world are easily violated, because the interest included in them inclines more to one side than to another. With us, however, i will never be the case; I have no need of any guarantees."

"And so—my dear brother—will disappear?"

"Simply. We will remove him from his bed by means of a
lank which yields to the pressure of the finger. Having retired
 rest as a crowned sovereign, he will awaken in captivity.
lone you will rule from that moment, and you will have no in-
rest dearer and better than that of keeping me near you."

"I believe it. There is my hand on it, Monsieur d'Herblay."

"Allow me to kneel before you, sire, most respectfully. We
ill embrace each other on the day we shall both have on our
mples, you the crown, and I the tiara."

"Still, embrace me this very day also, and be, for and toward
e, more than great, more than skillful, more than sublime in
enius; be kind and indulgent—be my father!"

Aramis was almost overcome as he listened to his voice; he
ncied he detected in his own heart an emotion hitherto un-
nown to him; but this impression was speedily removed.

"His father!" he thought; "yes, his holy father."

And they resumed their places in the carriage, which sped
pidly along the road leading to Vaux-le-Vicomte.

Chapter 11 — THE CHATEAU
DE VAUX-LE-VICOMTE

The Château of Vaux-le-Vicomte, situated about a league from
Melun, had been built by Fouquet in 1655, at a time when
ere was a scarcity of money in France; Mazarin had taken all
at there was, and Fouquet expended the remainder. However,
 certain men have fertile, false, and useful vices, Fouquet, in
attering broadcast millions of money in the construction of
is palace, had found means of gathering, as the result of his
nerous profusion, three illustrious men together: Levan, the
chitect of the building; Lenôtre, the designer of the gardens;
d Lebrun, the decorator of the apartments. If the Château
Vaux possessed a single fault with which it could be re-
oached, it was its grand, pretentious character. It is even at
e present day proverbial to calculate the number of acres of
ofing, the reparation of which would, in our age, be the ruin
 fortunes cramped and narrowed as the epoch itself. Vaux-le-
comte, when its magnificent gates, supported by Caryatides,
ve been passed through, has the principal front of the main

building, opening upon a vast so-called court of honor, inclosed
by deep ditches, bordered by a magnificent stone balustrade.
Nothing could be more noble in appearance than the fore-court
of the middle, raised upon the flight of steps, like a king upon
his throne, having around it four pavilions forming the angles,
the immense Ionic columns of which rose majestically to the
whole height of the building. The friezes ornamented with ara-
besques, and the pediments which crowned the pilasters, con-
ferred richness and grace upon every part of the building, while
the domes which surmounted the whole added proportion and
majesty. This mansion, built by a subject, bore a far greater
resemblance to those royal residences which Wolsey fancied he
was called upon to construct, in order to present them to his
master from the fear of rendering him jealous. But if magnificence and splendor were displayed in any one particular part
of this palace more than in another—if anything could be preferred to the wonderful arrangement of the interior, to the profusion of the paintings and statues—it would be the park and
gardens of Vaux. The *jets d'eau,* which were regarded as wonderful in 1653, are still so, even at the present time; the cascades awakened the admiration of kings and princes; and as
for the famous grotto, the theme of so many poetical effusions,
the residence of that illustrious nymph of Vaux whom Pellisson
made converse with La Fontaine, we must be spared the description of all its beauties. We will do as Despreaux did—we
will enter the park, the trees of which are of eight years' growth
only, and whose summits even yet, as they proudly tower aloft,
blushingly unfold their leaves to the earliest rays of the rising
sun. Lenôtre had accelerated the pleasure of the Mecænas of
his period; all the nurserygrounds had furnished trees whose
growth had been accelerated by careful culture and rich manure.
Every tree in the neighborhood which presented a fair appearance of beauty or stature had been taken up by its roots
and transplanted to the park. Fouquet could well afford to pur
chase trees to ornament his park, since he had bought up three
villages and their appurtenances (to use a legal word) to in
crease its extent. M. de Scudéry said of this palace that, for the
purpose of keeping the grounds and gardens well watered, M
Fouquet had divided a river into a thousand fountains, and
gathered the waters of a thousand fountains into torrents. The
same M. de Scudéry said a great many other things, in his "Clé
lie," about this palace of Valterre, the charms of which he de
scribes most minutely. We should be far wiser to send our cu

ous readers to Vaux to judge for themselves than to refer them to "Clélie;" and yet there are as many leagues from Paris to Vaux as there are volumes of the "Clélie."

This magnificent palace had been got ready for the reception of the greatest reigning sovereign of the time. M. Fouquet's friends had transported thither, some their actors and their dresses, others their troops of sculptors and artists; not forgetting others with their ready-mended pens—floods of impromptus were contemplated. The cascades, somewhat rebellious nymphs though they were, poured forth their waters brighter and clearer than crystal; they scattered over the bronze tritons and nereids their waves of foam, which glistened like fire in the rays of the sun. An army of servants were hurrying to and fro in squadrons in the courtyard and corridors; while Fouquet, who had only that morning arrived, walked all through the palace with a calm, observant glance, in order to give his last orders, after his intendants had inspected everything.

It was, as we have said, the 15th of August. The sun poured down its burning rays upon the heathen deities of marble and bronze; it raised the temperature of the water in the conch shells, and ripened, on the walls, those magnificent peaches, of which the king fifty years later spoke so regretfully, when, at Marly, on an occasion of a scarcity of the finer sort of peaches being complained of, in the beautiful gardens there—gardens which had cost France double the amount that had been expended on Vaux—the *great king* observed to some one:

"You are far too young to have eaten any of Monsieur Fouquet's peaches."

"Oh, fame! Oh, the blazonry of renown! Oh, the glory of this earth! That very man whose judgment was so sound and accurate where merit was concerned—he who had swept into his coffers the inheritance of Nicolas Fouquet, who had robbed him of Lenôtre and Lebrun, and had sent him to rot for the remainder of his life in one of the state prisons—merely remembered the peaches of that vanquished, crushed, forgotten enemy! It was to little purpose that Fouquet had squandered thirty millions of francs in the fountains of his gardens, in the crucibles of his sculptors, in the writing-desks of his literary friends, in the portfolios of his painters; vainly had he fancied that thereby he might be remembered. A peach—a blushing, rich-flavored fruit, nestling in the trellis-work on the garden-wall, hidden beneath its long, green leaves—this small vegetable production, that a dormouse would nibble up without a thought, was sufficient to recall to the memory of this great monarch the mournful shade of the last surintendant of France.

With a perfect reliance that Aramis had made arrangements fairly to distribute the vast number of guests throughout the palace, and that he had not omitted to attend to any of the internal regulations for their comfort, Fouquet devoted his entire attention to the *ensemble* alone. In one direction De Gourville showed him the preparations which had been made for the fireworks; in another, Molière led him over the theater; at last, after he had visited the chapel, the salons, and the galleries, and was again going downstairs, exhausted with fatigue, Fouquet saw Aramis on the staircase. The prelate beckoned to him. The surintendant joined his friend, and, with him, paused before a large picture scarcely finished. Applying himself, heart and soul, to his work, the painter, Lebrun, covered with perspiration, stained with paint, pale from fatigue and inspiration of genius, was putting the last finishing touches with his rapid brush. It was the portrait of the king, whom they were expecting, dressed in the court suit which Percerin had condescended to show beforehand to the bishop of Vannes. Fouquet placed himself before this portrait, which seemed to live, as one might say, in the cool freshness of its flesh and in its warmth of color. He gazed upon it long and fixedly, estimated the prodigious labor that had been bestowed upon it, and, not being able to find any recompense sufficiently great for this Herculean effort, he passed his arm round the painter's neck, and embraced him. The surintendant, by this action, had utterly ruined a suit of clothes worth a thousand pistoles, but he had satisfied, more than satisfied, Lebrun. It was a happy moment for the artist; it was an unhappy one for M. Percerin, who was walking behind Fouquet, and was engaged in admiring in Lebrun's painting the suit that he had had made for his majesty, a perfect *objet d'art*, as he called it, which was not to be matched except in the wardrobe of the surintendant. His distress and his exclamations were interrupted by a signal which had been given from the summit of the mansion. In the direction of Melun, in the still empty open plain, the sentinels of Vaux had perceived the advancing procession of the king and the queens. His majesty was entering into Melun with his long train of carriages and cavaliers.

"In an hour—" said Aramis to Fouquet.

"In an hour!" replied the latter, sighing.

"And the people ask one another what is the good of these royal *fêtes!*" continued the bishop of Vannes, laughing, with his false smile.

"Alas! I, too, who am not the people, ask the same thing."

"I will answer you in twenty-four hours, monseigneur. Assume a cheerful countenance, for it should be a day of true rejoicing."

"Well, believe me or not, as you like, D'Herblay," said the surintendant, with a swelling heart, pointing at the *cortège* of Louis, visible in the horizon, "he certainly loves me but very little, nor do I care much for him; but I cannot tell you how it is, that since he is approaching toward my house——"

"Well, what?"

"Well, then, since I know he is on his way here, as my guest, he is more sacred than ever for me; he is my acknowledged sovereign, and as such is very dear to me."

"Dear? yes," said Aramis, playing upon the word, as the Abbé Tenay did, at a later period, with Louis XV.

"Do not laugh, D'Herblay; I feel that if he were really to wish it, I could love that young man."

"You should not say that to me," returned Aramis, "but rather to Monsieur Colbert."

"To Monsieur Colbert!" exclaimed Fouquet. "Why so?"

"Because he would allow you a pension out of the king's privy purse, as soon as he becomes surintendant," said Aramis, preparing to leave as soon as he had dealt this last blow.

"Where are you going?" returned Fouquet, with a gloomy look.

"To my own apartment, in order to change my costume, monseigneur."

"Whereabouts are you lodging, D'Herblay?"

"In the blue room, on the second story."

"The room immediately over the king's room?"

"Precisely."

"You will be subject to very great restraint there. What an idea to condemn yourself to a room where you cannot stir or move about."

"During the night, monseigneur, I sleep or read in my bed."

"And your servants?"

"I have only one person with me. I find my reader quite sufficient. Adieu, monseigneur; do not overfatigue yourself; keep yourself fresh for the arrival of the king."

"We shall see you by and by, I suppose, and shall see your friend Du Vallon also?"

"He is lodging next to me, and is at this moment dressing."

And Fouquet, bowing, with a smile, passed on like a com-

mander-in-chief who pays the different outposts a visit after the
enemy has been signaled in sight.

Chapter 12 — THE WINE OF MELUN

The king had, in point of fact, entered Melun with the intention of merely passing through the city. The youthful monarch
was most eagerly anxious for amusements; only twice during
the journey had he been able to catch a glimpse of La Valliere,
and, suspecting that his only opportunity of speaking to her
would be after nightfall, in the gardens, and after the ceremonial of reception had been gone through, he had been very
desirous to arrive at Vaux as early as possible. But he reckoned
without his captain of the musketeers, and without M. Colbert.
Like Calypso, who could not be consoled at the departure of
Ulysses, our Gascon could not console himself for not having
guessed why Aramis had asked Percerin to show him the king's
new costumes. "There is not a doubt," he said to himself, "that
my friend, the bishop of Vannes, had some motive in that"; and
then he began to rack his brains most uselessly. D'Artagnan, so
intimately acquainted with all the court intrigues, who knew the
position of Fouquet better even than Fouquet himself did,
had conceived the strangest fancies and suspicions at the an-
nouncement of the *fête,* which would have ruined a wealthy
man, and which became if possible, utter madness even, for a
man so destitute as he was. And then, the presence of Aramis,
who had returned from Belle-Isle, and been nominated by M.
Fouquet inspector-general of all the arrangements; his perseverance in mixing himself up with all the surintendant's affairs;
his visits to Baisemeaux—all this suspicious singularity of conduct had excessively troubled and tormented D'Artagnan during the last several weeks.

"With men of Aramis' stamp," he said, "one is never the
stronger except sword in hand. So long as Aramis continued a
soldier, there was hope of getting the better of him; but since
he has covered his cuirass with a stole, we are lost. But what can
Aramis' object possibly be?" And D'Artagnan plunged again
into deep thought. "What does it matter to me, after all," he
continued, "if his only object is to overthrow Monsieur Colbert? And what else can he be after?" And D'Artagnan rubbed

forehead—that fertile land whence the plowshare of his
ils had turned up so many and such admirable ideas in his
he. He at first thought of talking the matter over with Col-
rt, but his friendship for Aramis, the oath of earlier days,
und him too strictly. He revolted at the bare idea of such a
ing, and, besides, he hated the financier too cordially. Then,
ain, he wished to unburden his mind to the king; but yet the
ig would not be able to understand the suspicions which had
t even a shadow of reality at their base. He resolved to ad-
ess himself to Aramis, direct, the first time he met him. "I
ll take him," said the musketeer, "between a couple of can-
es, suddenly, and when he least expects it, I will place my
nd upon his heart, and he will tell me— What will he tell me?
es, he will tell me something, for, *mordioux!* there is some-
ng in it, I know."

Somewhat calmer, D'Artagnan made every preparation for
e journey, and took the greatest care that the military house-
ld of the king, as yet very inconsiderable in numbers, should
well officered and well disciplined in its meager and limited
oportions. The result was that, through the captain's arrange-
ents, the king, on arriving at Melun, saw himself at the head
the musketeers, his Swiss guards, as well as a picket of the
ench guards. It might almost have been called a small army.

Colbert looked at the troops with great delight; he even
shed there had been a third more in number.

"But why?" said the king.

"In order to show greater honor to Monsieur Fouquet," re-
ed Colbert.

"In order to ruin him the sooner," thought D'Artagnan.

When this little army appeared before Melun, the chief mag-
rates came out to meet the king, and to present him with the
ys of the city, and invited him to enter the Hôtel de Ville, in
der to partake of the wine of honor. The king, who expected
pass through the city and to proceed to Vaux without delay,
came quite red in the face from vexation.

"Who was fool enough to occasion this delay?" muttered the
ig, between his teeth, as the chief magistrate was in the mid-
e of a long address.

"Not I, certainly," replied D'Artagnan, "but I believe it was
onsieur Colbert."

Colbert, having heard his name pronounced, said:

"What was Monsieur d'Artagnan good enough to say?"

"I was good enough to remark that it was you who stopped

the king's progress, so that he might taste the vin de Brie. W
I right?"

"Quite so, monsieur."

"In that case, then, it was you whom the king called so
name or other."

"What name?"

"I hardly know; but wait a moment—idiot, I think it was
no, no; it was fool or stupid. Yes; his majesty said that t
man who had thought of the vin de Melun was something
the sort."

D'Artagnan, after this broadside, quietly caressed his mu
tache; M. Colbert's large head seemed to become larger a
larger than ever. D'Artagnan, seeing how ugly anger made hi
did not stop halfway. The orator still went on with his spee
while the king's color was visibly increasing.

"*Mordioux!*" said the musketeer coolly, "the king is goi
to have an attack of determination of blood to the head. Whe
the deuce did you get hold of that idea, Monsieur Colbe
You have no luck."

"Monsieur," said the financier, drawing himself up, "my z
for the king's service inspired me with the idea."

"Bah!"

"Monsieur, Melun is a city, an excellent city, which pa
well, and which it would be imprudent to displease."

"There, now! I, who do not pretend to be a financier, s
only one idea in your idea."

"What was that, monsieur?"

"That of causing a little annoyance to Monsieur Fouqu
who is making himself quite giddy on his donjons yonder,
waiting for us."

This was a home-stroke, hard enough, in all conscience. C
bert was completely thrown out of his saddle by it, and retir
thoroughly discomfited. Fortunately, the speech was now at
end; the king drank the wine which was presented to him, a
then every one resumed the progress through the city. The ki
bit his lips in anger, for the evening was closing in, and
hope of a walk with La Valliere was at an end.

In order that the whole of the king's household should en
Vaux, four hours, at least, were necessary, owing to the differ
arrangements. The king, therefore, who was boiling with imp
tience, hurried forward as much as possible, in order to rea
it before nightfall. But, at the moment he was setting off aga
other and fresh difficulties arose.

"Is not the king going to sleep at Melun?" said Colbert, in a low tone of voice, to D'Artagnan.

M. Colbert must have been badly inspired that day, to address himself in that manner to the chief of the musketeers; for the latter guessed that the king's intention was very far from that of remaining where he was. D'Artagnan would not allow him to enter Vaux except he were well and strongly accompanied, and desired that his majesty would not enter except with all the escort. On the other hand, he felt that these delays would irritate that impatient character beyond measure. In what way could he possibly reconcile these two difficulties? D'Artagnan took up Colbert's remark, and determined to repeat it to the king.

"Sire," he said, "Monsieur Colbert has been asking me if your majesty does not intend to sleep at Melun."

"Sleep at Melun! What for?" exclaimed Louis XIV. "Sleep at Melun! Who, in Heaven's name, can have thought of such a thing, when Monsieur Fouquet is expecting us this evening?"

"It was simply," replied Colbert quickly, "the fear of causing your majesty any delay; for according to established etiquette, you can not enter any place, with the exception of your own royal residences, until the soldiers' quarters have been marked out by the quartermaster, and the garrison properly distributed."

D'Artagnan listened with the greatest attention, biting his mustache to conceal his vexation; and the queens listened attentively also. They were fatigued, and would have liked to have gone to rest without proceeding any further; and especially, in order to prevent the king walking about in the evening with M. de St. Aignan and the ladies of the court, for, if etiquette required the princesses to remain within their own rooms, the ladies of honor, as soon as they had performed the services required of them, had no restrictions placed upon them, but were at liberty to walk about as they pleased. It will easily be conjectured that all these rival interests, gathering together in vapors, must necessarily produce clouds, and that the clouds would be followed by a tempest. The king had no mustache to gnaw, and therefore kept biting the handle of his whip instead, with ill-concealed impatience. How could he get out of it? D'Artagnan looked as agreeable as possible, and Colbert as sulky as he could. Whom was there he could get in a passion with?

"We will consult the queen," said Louis XIV., bowing to the royal ladies. And this kindness of consideration, which softened

Maria Theresa's heart, who was of a kind and generous disposition, when left to her own free will replied:

"I shall be delighted to do whatever your majesty wishes."

"How long will it take us to get to Vaux?" inquired Anne of Austria, in slow and measured accents, and placing her hand upon her bosom, where the seat of her pain lay.

"An hour for your majesties' carriages," said D'Artagnan, "the roads are tolerably good."

The king looked at him.

"And a quarter of an hour for the king," he hastened to add.

"We should arrive by daylight?" said Louis XIV.

"But the billeting of the king's military escort," objected Colbert softly, "will make his majesty lose all the advantage of his speed, however quick he may be."

"Double ass that you are!" thought D'Artagnan; "if I had any interest or motive in demolishing your credit, I could do it in ten minutes. If I were in the king's place," he added, aloud, "I should, in going to Monsieur Fouquet, leave my escort behind me; I should go to him as a friend; I should enter accompanied only by my captain of the guards; I should consider that I was acting more nobly, and should be invested with a still more sacred character by doing so."

Delight sparkled in the king's eyes.

"That is indeed a very good suggestion. We will go to see a friend as friends; those gentlemen who are with the carriages can go slowly; but we who are mounted will ride on."

And he rode off, accompanied by all those who were mounted. Colbert hid his ugly head behind his horse's neck.

"I shall be quits," said D'Artagnan, as he galloped along, "by getting a little talk with Aramis this evening. And then, Monsieur Fouquet is a man of honor. *Mordioux!* I have said so, and it must be so."

And this was the way how, toward seven o'clock in the evening, without announcing his arrival by the din of trumpets, and without even his advanced guard, without outriders or musketeers, the king presented himself before the gate of Vaux, where Fouquet, who had been informed of his royal guest's approach, had been waiting for the last half-hour, with his head uncovered, surrounded by his household and his friends.

Chapter 13 — NECTAR AND AMBROSIA

M. Fouquet held the stirrup of the king, who, having dismounted, bowed most graciously, and more graciously still held out his hand to him, which Fouquet, in spite of a slight resistance on the king's part, carried respectfully to his lips. The king wished to wait in the first courtyard for the arrival of the carriages, nor had he long to wait, for the roads had been put into excellent order by the surintendant, and a stone would hardly have been found of the size of an egg the whole way from Melun to Vaux; so that the carriages, rolling along as though on a carpet, brought the ladies to Vaux, without jolting or fatigue, by eight o'clock. They were received by Mme. Fouquet, and at the moment they made their appearance a light as bright as day burst forth from all the trees and vases and marble statues. This species of enchantment lasted until their majesties had retired into the palace. All these wonders and magical effects which the chronicler has heaped up, or, rather, preserved, in his recital, at the risk of rivaling the creations of a romancist; these splendors whereby night seemed conquered and nature corrected, together with every delight and luxury combined for the satisfaction of all the senses, as well as of the mind, Fouquet did, in real truth, offer to his sovereign in that enchanting retreat of which no monarch could, at that time, boast of possessing an equal. We do not intend to describe the grand banquet, at which all the royal guests were present, nor the concerts, nor the fairy-like and magical transformations and metamorphoses; it will be more than enough for our purpose to depict the countenance which the king assumed, and which, from being gay, soon wore a gloomy, constrained, and irritated expression. He remembered his own residence, royal though it was, and the mean and indifferent style of luxury which prevailed there, and which comprised only that which was merely useful for the royal wants, without being his own personal property. The large vases of the Louvre, the old furniture and plate of Henry II., of Francis I., of Louis XI., were merely historical monuments of earlier days; they were nothing but specimens of art, the relics of his predecessors; while with Fouquet the value of the article was as much in the workmanship as in the article itself. Fouquet eat from a gold service, which artists in his own employ had modeled and cast for himself alone. Fouquet drank wines of which the King of France did not even know the name, and drank them out of goblets each more precious than the whole royal cellar.

What, too, can be said of the apartments, the hangings, the pictures, the servants and officers, of every description, of his household? What can be said of the mode of service in which etiquette was replaced by order; stiff formality by personal unrestrained comfort; the happiness and contentment of the guest became the supreme law of all who obeyed the host. The perfect swarm of busily engaged persons moving about noiselessly; the multitude of guests—who were, however, even less numerous than the servants who waited on them—the myriad of exquisitely prepared dishes, of gold and silver vases; the floods of dazzling light, the masses of unknown flowers of which the hothouses had been despoiled, and which were redundant with all the luxuriance of unequaled beauty; the perfect harmony of everything which surrounded them, and which, indeed, was no more than the prelude of the promised *fête*, more than charmed all who were there, and who testified their admiration over and over again, not by voice or gesture, but by deep silence and rapt attention, those two languages of the courtier which acknowledge the hand of no master powerful enough to restrain them.

As for the king, his eyes filled with tears; he dared not look at the queen. Anne of Austria, whose pride, as it ever had been, was superior to that of any creature breathing, overwhelmed her host by the contempt with which she treated everything handed to her. The young queen, kindhearted by nature and curious by disposition, praised Fouquet, eat with an exceedingly good appetite, and asked the names of the different fruits which were placed upon the table. Fouquet replied that he was not aware of their names. The fruits came from his own stores; he had often cultivated them himself, having an intimate acquaintance with the cultivation of exotic fruits and plants. The king felt and appreciated the delicacy of the reply, but was only the more humiliated at it; he thought that the queen was a little too familiar in her manners, and that Anne of Austria resembled Juno a little too much, in being too proud and haughty; his chief anxiety, however, was himself, that he might remain cold and distant in his behavior, bordering slightly on the limits of extreme disdain or of simple admiration.

But Fouquet had foreseen all that; he was, in fact, one of those men who foresee everything. The king had expressly declared that so long as he remained under M. Fouquet's roof he did not wish his own different repast to be served in accordance with the usual etiquette, and that he would, consequently, dine with the rest of the society; but by the thoughtful attention of the surintendant, the king's dinner was served up separately, if one may so express it, in the middle of the general table; the dinner, wonderful in every respect, from the dishes of which it was composed, comprised everything the king liked, and which he generally preferred to anything else. Louis had no excuse— he, indeed, who had the keenest appetite in his kingdom—for saying that he was not hungry. Nay, M. Fouquet even did better still; he certainly, in obedience to the king's expressed desire, seated himself at the table, but as soon as the soups were served, he rose and personally waited on the king, while Mme. Fouquet stood behind the queen-mother's armchair. The disdain of Juno and the sulky fits of temper of Jupiter could not resist this excess of kindly feeling and polite attention. The queen eat a biscuit dipped in a glass of San Lucar wine; and the king eat of everything, saying to M. Fouquet:

"It is impossible, Monsieur le Surintendant, to dine better anywhere."

Whereupon, the whole court began, on all sides, to devour the dishes spread before them, with such enthusiasm that it looked like a cloud of Egyptian locusts settling down upon the uncut crop.

As soon, however, as his hunger was appeased, the king became dull and gloomy again; the more so in proportion to the satisfaction he fancied he had manifested, and particularly on account of the deferential manner which his courtiers had shown toward Fouquet. D'Artagnan, who eat a good deal and drank but little, without allowing it to be noticed, did not lose a single opportunity, but made a great number of observations which he turned to good profit.

When the supper was finished the king expressed a wish not to lose the promenade. The park was illuminated; the moon, too, as if she had placed herself at the orders of the lord of Vaux, silvered the trees and lake with her bright, phosphoric light. The air was soft and balmy; the graveled walks through the thickly set avenues yielded luxuriously to the feet. The *fête* was complete in every respect, for the king, having met La Valliere in one of the winding paths of the wood, was able to press her by the hand and say, "I love you," without any one overhearing him except M. d'Artagnan, who followed, and M. Fouquet, who preceded him.

The night of magical enchantments stole on. The king, having requested to be shown his room, there was immediately a movement in every direction. The queens passed to their own apartments, accompanied by the music of theorbos and lutes; the king found his musketeers awaiting him on the grand flight of steps, for M. Fouquet had brought them on from Melun, and had invited them to supper. D'Artagnan's suspicions at once disappeared. He was weary, he had supped well, and wished, for once in his life, thoroughly to enjoy a *fête* given by a man who was in every sense of the word a king.

"Monsieur Fouquet," he said, "is the man for me."

The king was conducted with the greatest ceremony to the chamber of Morpheus, of which we owe some slight description to our readers. It was the handsomest and the largest in the palace. Lebrun had painted on the vaulted ceiling the happy, as well as disagreeable, dreams with which Morpheus affects kings as well as other men. Everything that sleep gives birth to that is lovely, its perfumes, its flowers and nectar, the wild voluptuousness or deep repose of the senses, had the painter enriched with his frescoes. It was a composition as soft and pleasing in one part as dark and gloomy and terrible in another. The poisoned chalice, the glittering dagger suspended over the head of the sleeper; wizards and pantoms with hideous masks, those half-dim shadows more terrific than the brightness of flame or the blackness of night; these, and such as these, he had made the companions of his more pleasing pictures. No sooner had the king entered the room than a cold shiver seemed to pass through him, and on Fouquet asking him the cause of it, the king replied, as pale as death:

"I am sleepy, that is all."

"Does your majesty wish for your attendants at once?"

"No; I have to talk with a few persons first," said the king. "Will you have the goodness to tell Monsieur Colbert I wish to see him?"

Fouquet bowed, and left the room.

Chapter 14 — A GASCON AND A GASCON AND A HALF

D'Artagnan had determined to lose no time, and, in fact, he never was in the habit of doing so. After having inquired for

Aramis, he had looked for him in every direction, until he had succeeded in finding him. Besides, no sooner had the king entered into Vaux than Aramis had retired to his own room, meditating, doubtlessly, some new piece of gallant attention for his majesty's amusement. D'Artagnan desired the servants to announce him, and found on the second story (in a beautiful room called the blue room, on account of the color of its hangings) the bishop of Vannes in company with Porthos and several of the modern Epicureans. Aramis came forward to embrace his friend, and offered him the best seat. As it was after awhile generally remarked among those present that the musketeer was reserved, and wished for an opportunity for conversing secretly with Aramis, the Epicureans took their leave. Porthos, however, did not stir; for true it is, that, having dined exceedingly well, he was fast asleep in his armchair; and the freedom of conversation therefore was not interrupted by a third person. Porthos had a deep, harmonious snore, and people might talk in the midst of its loud bass without fear of disturbing him. D'Artagnan felt that he was called upon to open the conversation.

"Well, and so we have come to Vaux," he said.

"Why, yes, D'Artagnan. And how do you like the place?"

"Very much, and I like Monsieur Fouquet also."

"Is he not a charming host?"

"No one could be more so."

"I am told that the king began by showing a great distance in his manner toward Monsieur Fouquet, but that his majesty became much more cordial afterward."

"You did not notice it, then, since you say you have been told so?"

"No; I was engaged with those gentlemen who have just left the room about the theatrical performances and the tournaments which are to take place to-morrow."

"Ah, indeed! you are the comptroller-general of the *fêtes* here, then?"

"You know I am a friend of all kinds of amusement where the exercise of the imagination is required; I have always been a poet in one way or another."

"Yes, I remember the verses you used to write; they were charming."

"I have forgotten them, but I am delighted to read the verses of others, when those others are known by the names of Molière, Pellisson, La Fontaine, etc."

"Do you know what idea occurred to me this evening, Aramis?"

"No; tell me what it was, for I should never be able to guess it, you have so many."

"Well, the idea occurred to me that the true King of France is not Louis XIV."

"What!" said Aramis involuntarily, looking the musketeer full in the eyes.

"No; it is Monsieur Fouquet."

Aramis breathed again, and smiled.

"Ah! you are like all the rest, jealous!" he said. "I would wager that it was Monsieur Colbert who turned that pretty phrase."

D'Artagnan, in order to throw Aramis off his guard, related Colbert's misadventure with regard to the vin de Melun.

"He comes of a mean race, does Colbert," said Aramis.

"Quite true."

"When I think, too," added the bishop, "that that fellow will be your minister within four months, and that you will serve him as blindly as you did Richelieu or Mazarin——"

"And as you serve Monsieur Fouquet," said D'Artagnan.

"With the difference, though, that Monsieur Fouquet is not Monsieur Colbert."

"True, true," said D'Artagnan, as he pretended to become sad and full of reflection; and then, a moment after, he added, "Why do you tell me that Monsieur Colbert will be minister in four months?"

"Because Monsieur Fouquet will have ceased to be so," replied Aramis.

"He will be ruined, you mean?" said D'Artagnan.

"Completely so."

"Why does he give these *fêtes*, then?" said the musketeer, in a tone so full of thoughtful consideration, and so well assumed, that the bishop was for the moment deceived by it. "Why did you not dissuade him from it?"

The latter part of the phrase was just a little too much, and Aramis' former suspicions were again aroused.

"It is done with the object of humoring the king."

"By ruining himself?"

"Yes, by ruining himself for the king."

"A singular calculation, that."

"Necessity."

"I don't see that, dear Aramis."

"Do you not? Have you not remarked Monsieur Colbert's

daily increasing antagonism, and that he is doing his utmost to drive the king to get rid of the surintendant?"

"One must be blind not to see it."

"And that a cabal is formed against Monsieur Fouquet?"

"That is well known."

"What likelihood is there that the king would join a party formed against a man who will have spent everything he had to please him?"

"True, true," said D'Artagnan slowly, hardly convinced, yet curious to broach another phase of the conversation. "There are follies and follies," he resumed, "and I do not like those you are committing."

"What do you allude to?"

"As for the banquet, the ball, the concert, the theatricals, the tournaments, the cascades, the fireworks, the illuminations, and the presents—these are well and good, I grant; but why were not these expenses sufficient? Was it necessary to have new liveries and costumes for your whole household?"

"You are quite right. I told Monsieur Fouquet that myself; he replied that if he were rich enough, he would offer the king a newly erected chateau, from the vanes at the top of the house to the very cellar; completely new inside and out; and that, as soon as the king had left, he would burn the whole building and its contents, in order that it might not be made use of by any one else."

"How completely Spanish!"

"I told him so, and he then added this: 'Whoever advises me to spare expense I shall look upon as my enemy.'"

"It is positive madness; and that portrait, too!"

"What portrait?" said Aramis.

"That of the king; and the surprise as well."

"What surprise?"

"The surprise you seem to have in view, and on account of which you took some specimens away, when I met you at Percerin's."

D'Artagnan paused. The shaft was discharged, and all he had to do was to wait and watch its effect.

"That is merely an act of graceful attention," replied Aramis.

D'Artagnan went up to his friend, took hold of both his hands, and looking him full in the eyes, said:

"Aramis, do you still care for me a very little?"

"What a question to ask!"

"Very good. One favor, then. Why did you take some patterns of the king's costumes at Percerin's?"

"Come with me and ask poor Lebrun, who has been working upon them for the last two days and two nights."

"Aramis, that may be the truth for everybody else, but for me——"

"Upon my word, D'Artagnan, you astonish me!"

"Be a little considerate for me. Tell me the exact truth; you would not like anything disagreeable to happen to me, would you?"

"My dear friend, you are becoming quite incomprehensible! What suspicion can you possibly have got hold of?"

"Do you believe in my instinctive feelings? Formerly you used to have faith in them. Well, then, an instinct tells me that you have some concealed project on foot."

"I—a project?"

"I am convinced of it."

"What nonsense!"

"I am not only sure of it, but I would even swear it."

"Indeed, D'Artagnan, you cause me the greatest pain. Is it likely, if I have any project in hand, that I ought to keep secret from you, I should tell you about it? If I had one that I could and ought to have revealed, should I not have already told it to you?"

"No, Aramis, no. There are certain projects which are never revealed until the favorable opportunity arrives."

"In that case, my dear fellow," returned the bishop, laughing, "the only thing now is, that the 'opportunity' has not yet arrived."

D'Artagnan shook his head with a sorrowful expression.

"Oh, friendship, friendship!" he said, "what an idle word you are! Here is a man, who, if I were but to ask it, would suffer himself to be cut in pieces for my sake."

"You are right," said Aramis nobly.

"And this man, who would shed every drop of blood in his veins for me, will not open the smallest corner in his heart. Friendship, I repeat, is nothing but a mere unsubstantial shadow and a lure, like everything else in this world which is bright and dazzling."

"It is not thus you should speak of *our* friendship," replied the bishop, in a firm, assured voice; "for ours is not of the same nature as those you have been speaking of."

"Look at us, Aramis; three out of the old 'four.' You are deceiving me; I suspect you; and Porthos is fast asleep. An admirable trio of friends, don't you think so? A beautiful relic of former times."

"I can only tell you one thing, D'Artagnan, and I swear it on the Bible; I love you just as I used to do. If I ever suspect you, it is on account of others, and not on account of either of us. In everything I may do, and should happen to succeed in, you will find your fourth. Will you promise me the same favor?"

"If I am not mistaken, Aramis, your words—at the moment you pronounce them—are full of generous feeling."

"That is possible."

"You are conspiring against Monsieur Colbert. If that be all, *mordioux!* tell me so at once. I have the instrument in my own hand, and will pull out the tooth easily enough."

Aramis could not restrain a smile of disdain which passed across his noble features.

"And supposing that I were conspiring against Colbert, what harm would there be in that?"

"No, no; that would be too trifling a matter for you to take in hand, and it was not on that account you asked Percerin for those patterns of the king's costumes. Oh! Aramis we are not enemies, remember, but brothers. Tell me what you wish to undertake, and, upon the word of a D'Artagnan, if I cannot help you, I will swear to remain neutral."

"I am undertaking nothing," said Aramis.

"Aramis, a voice speaks within me, and seems to enlighten my darkness; it is a voice which has never yet deceived me. It is the king you are conspiring against."

"The king?" exclaimed the bishop, pretending to be annoyed.

"Your face will not convince me; the king, I repeat."

"Will you help me?" said Aramis, smiling ironically.

"Aramis, I will do more than help you—I will do more than remain neutral—I will save you."

"You are mad, D'Artagnan."

"I am the wiser of the two, in this matter."

"You to suspect me of wishing to assassinate the king!"

"Who spoke of that at all?" said the musketeer.

"Well, let us understand each other. I do not see what any one can do to a legitimate king, as ours is, if he does not assassinate him."

D'Artagnan did not say a word.

"Besides, you have your guards and your musketeers here," said the bishop.

"True."

"You are not in Monsieur Fouquet's house, but in your own."

"True; but in spite of that, Aramis, grant me, for pity's sake, but one single word of a true friend."

"A friend's word is the truth itself. If I think of touching, even with my finger, the son of Anne of Austria, the true king of this realm of France—if I have not the firm intention of prostrating myself before his throne—if in every idea I may entertain to-morrow, here at Vaux, will not be the most glorious day my king ever enjoyed—may Heaven's lightning blast me where I stand!"

Aramis had pronounced these words, with his face turned toward the alcove of his own bedroom, where D'Artagnan, seated with his back toward the alcove, could not suspect that any one was lying concealed. The earnestness of his words, the studied slowness with which he pronounced them, the solemnity of his oath, gave the musketeer the most complete satisfaction. He took hold of both Aramis' hands, and shook them cordially. Aramis had endured reproaches without turning pale, and had blushed as he listened to words of praise. D'Artagnan, deceived, did him honor; but D'Artagnan, trustful and reliant, made him feel ashamed.

"Are you going away?" he said, as he embraced him, in order to conceal the flush on his face.

"Yes; my duty summons me. I have to get the watchword. It seems I am to be lodged in the king's anteroom. Where does Porthos sleep?"

"Take him away with you, if you like, for he snores like a park of artillery."

"Ah! he does not stay with you, then?" said D'Artagnan.

"Not the least in the world. He has his room to himself, but I don't know where."

"Very good!" said the musketeer, from whom this separation of the two associates removed his last suspicion; and he touched Porthos lightly on the shoulder. The latter replied by a terrible yawn.

"Come," said D'Artagnan.

"What, D'Artagnan, my dear fellow, is that you? What a lucky chance! Oh, yes—true, I had forgotten; I am at the *fête* at Vaux."

"Yes; and your beautiful dress, too."

"Yes, it was very attentive on the part of Monsieur Coquelin de Volière, was it not?"

"Hush!" said Aramis. "You are walking so heavily you will make the flooring give way."

"True," said the musketeer; "this room is above the dome, I think."

"And I did not choose it for a fencing-room, I assure you," added the bishop. "The ceiling of the king's room has all the sweetness and calm delights of sleep. Do not forget, therefore, that my flooring is merely the covering of his ceiling. Good-night, my friends, and in ten minutes I shall be fast asleep."

And Aramis accompanied them to the door, laughing quietly all the while. As soon as they were outside he bolted the door hurriedly, closed up the chinks of the windows, and then called out:

"Monseigneur! monseigneur!"

Philippe made his appearance from the alcove, as he pushed aside a sliding panel placed behind the bed.

"Monsieur d'Artagnan entertains a great many suspicions, it seems," he said.

"Ah! you recognized Monsieur d'Artagnan, then?"

"Before you called him by his name, even."

"He is your captain of musketeers."

"He is very devoted to *me*," replied Philippe, laying a stress upon the personal pronoun.

"As faithful as a dog; but he bites sometimes. If D'Artagnan does not recognize you before *the other* has disappeared, rely upon D'Artagnan to the end of the world; for, in that case, if he has seen nothing, he will keep his fidelity. If he sees, when it is too late, he is a Gascon, and will never admit that he has been deceived."

"I thought so. What are we to do now?"

"You will go and take up your post at our place of observation, and watch the moment of the king's retiring to rest, so as to learn how that ceremony is performed."

"Very good. Where shall I place myself?"

"Sit down on this folding-chair. I am going to push aside a portion of the flooring; you will look through the opening, which answers to one of the false windows made in the dome of the king's apartment. Can you see?"

"Yes," said Philippe, starting as at the sight of an enemy; "I see the king."

"What is he doing?"

"He seems to wish some man to sit down close to him."

"Monsieur Fouquet?"

"No, no; wait a moment——"

"Look at the notes and portraits, my prince."

"The man whom the king wishes to sit down in his presence is Monsieur Colbert."

"Colbert sit down in the king's presence!" exclaimed Aramis; "it is impossible."

"Look!"

Aramis looked through the opening in the flooring.

"Yes," he said. "Colbert himself. Oh, monseigneur! what can we be going to hear—and what can result from this intimacy?"

"Nothing good for Monsieur Fouquet, at all events."

The prince did not deceive himself.

We have seen that Louis XIV. had sent for Colbert, and that Colbert had arrived. The conversation began between them by the king, according to him one of the highest favors that he had ever done; it was true, the king was alone with his subject.

"Colbert," said he, "sit down."

The intendant, overcome with delight—for he feared he should be dismissed—refused this unprecedented honor.

"Does he accept?" said Aramis.

"No; he remains standing."

"Let us listen, then."

And the future king and the future pope listened eagerly to the simple mortals whom they held under their feet, ready to crush them if they had liked.

"Colbert," said the king, "you have annoyed me exceedingly to-day."

"I know it, sire."

"Very good; I like that answer. Yes, you knew it, and there was courage in having done it."

"I ran the risk of displeasing your majesty, but I risked also concealing what were your true interests from you."

"What! you were afraid of something on my account?"

"I was, sire, even if it were nothing more than an indigestion," said Colbert; "for people do not give their sovereign such banquets as the one of to-day, except it be to stifle them under the weight of good living."

Colbert waited the effect which this coarse jest would produce upon the king, and Louis XIV., who was the vainest and the most fastidiously delicate man in his kingdom, forgave Colbert the joke.

"The truth is," he said, "that Monsieur Fouquet has given me too good a meal. Tell me, Colbert, where does he get all the money required for this enormous expenditure—can you tell?"

"Yes, I do know, sire."

"Will you be able to prove it with tolerable certainty?"

"Easily; to the very farthing."

"I know you are very exact."

"It is the principal qualification required in an intendant of finances."

"But all are not so."

"I thank your majesty for so flattering a compliment from your own lips."

"Monsieur Fouquet, therefore, is rich—very rich—and I suppose every man knows he is so."

"Every one, sire; the living as well as the dead."

"What does that mean, Monsieur Colbert?"

"The living are witnesses of Monsieur Fouquet's wealth—they admire and applaud the result produced; but the dead, wiser and better informed than we are, know how that wealth was obtained, and they rise up in accusation."

"So that Monsieur Fouquet owes his wealth to some cause or other."

"The occupation of an intendant very often favors those who practice it."

"You have something to say to me more confidentially, I perceive; do not be afraid, we are quite alone."

"I am never afraid of anything under the shelter of my own conscience, and under the protection of your majesty," said Colbert, bowing.

"If the dead, therefore, were to speak——"

"They do speak sometimes, sire; read."

"Ah!" murmured Aramis, in the prince's ear, who, close beside him, listened without losing a syllable, "since you are placed here, monseigneur, in order to learn your vocation of a king, listen to a piece of infamy—of a nature truly royal. You are about to be a witness of one of those scenes which the foul fiend alone can conceive and execute. Listen attentively—you will find your advantage in it."

The prince redoubled his attention, and saw Louis XIV. take from Colbert's hands a letter which the latter held out to him.

"The late cardinal's handwriting," said the king.

"Your majesty has an excellent memory," replied Colbert, bowing; "it is an immense advantage for a king who is destined for hard work to recognize handwritings at the first glance."

The king read Mazarin's letter, and, as its contents are already known to the reader, in consequence of the misunder-

standing between Mme. de Chevreuse and Aramis, nothing
ther would be learned if we stated them here again.

"I do not quite understand," said the king, greatly intere

"Your majesty has not yet acquired the habit of
through the public accounts."

"I see that it refers to money which had been given to
sieur Fouquet."

"Thirteen millions. A tolerably good sum."

"Yes. Well, and these thirteen millions are wanting to
ance the total of the accounts. That is what I do not very
understand. How was this deficit possible?"

"Possible, I do not say; but there is no doubt about the
that it really is so."

"You say that these thirteen millions are found to be
ing in the accounts?"

"I do not say so, but the registry does."

"And this letter of Monsieur Mazarin indicates the em
ment of that sum, and the name of the person with whom i
deposited?"

"As your majesty can judge for yourself."

"Yes; and the result is, then, that Monsieur Fouquet ha
yet restored the thirteen millions."

"That results from the accounts, certainly, sire."

"Well, and, consequently——"

"Well, sire, in that case, inasmuch as Monsieur Fouque
not yet given back the thirteen millions, he must have a
priated them to his own purposes; and with those thi
millions one could incur four times and a little more as
expense, and make four times as great a display as your
jesty was able to do at Fontainebleau, where we only
three millions altogether, if you remember."

For a blunderer, the souvenir he had evoked was a
skillfully contrived piece of baseness; for, by the re
brance of his own *fête*, he, for the first time, perceived i
feriority compared with that of Fouquet. Colbert received
again at Vaux what Fouquet had given him at Fontaine
and, as a good financier, he returned it with the best po
interest. Having once disposed the king's mind in that
Colbert had nothing of much importance to detain him
felt that such was the case, for the king, too, had again
into a dull and gloomy state. Colbert awaited the first
from the king's lips with as much impatience as Philipp
Aramis did from their place of observation.

"Are you aware what is the usual natural consequence

this, Monsieur Colbert?" said the king, after a few moments' reflection.

"No, sire, I do not know."

"Well, then, the fact of the appropriation of the thirteen millions, if it can be proved——"

"But it is so already."

"I mean if it were to be declared and certified, Monsieur Colbert."

"I think it will be to-morrow, if your majesty——"

"Were we not under Monsieur Fouquet's roof, you were going to say, perhaps?" replied the king, with something of nobleness in his manner.

"The king is in his own palace, wherever he may be, and especially in houses which his own money has paid for."

"I think," said Philippe, in a low tone, to Aramis, "that the architect who constructed this dome ought, anticipating what use could be made of it, so to have contrived that it might easily be made to fall on the heads of scoundrels such as that Monsieur Colbert."

"I thought so, too," replied Aramis; "But Monsieur Colbert is so very near the king at this moment."

"That is true, and that would open the succession."

"Of which your younger brother would reap all the advantage, monseigneur. But stay, let us keep quiet, and go on listening."

"We shall not have long to listen," said the young prince.

"Why not, monseigneur?"

"Because, if I were the king, I should not reply anything further."

"And what would you do?"

"I should wait until to-morrow morning to give myself time for reflection."

Louis XIV. at last raised his eyes, and finding Colbert attentively waiting for his next remarks, said, hastily changing the conversation:

"Monsieur Colbert, I perceive it is getting very late, and I shall now retire to bed. By to-morrow morning I shall have made up my mind."

"Very good, sire," returned Colbert, greatly incensed, though he restrained himself in the presence of the king.

The king made a gesture of adieu, and Colbert withdrew with respectful bow.

"My attendants," cried the king; and, as they entered the apartment, Philippe was about to quit his post of observation.

"A moment longer," said Aramis to him, with his accustom▪
gentleness of manner. "What has just now taken place is on▪
a detail, and to-morrow we shall have no occasion to think an▪
thing more about it; but the ceremony of the king's retiring ▪
rest, the etiquette observed in addressing the king, that inde▪
is of the greatest importance. Learn, sire, and study well ho▪
you ought to go to bed of a night. Look! look!"

Chapter 15 — COLBERT

History will tell us, or, rather, history has told us, of the va▪
ous events of the following day, of the splendid *fêtes* given ▪
the surintendant to his sovereign. There was nothing b▪
amusement and delight allowed to prevail throughout the who▪
of the following day; there was a promenade, a banquet, a cor▪
edy to be acted, and a comedy, too, in which, to his gre▪
amazement, Porthos recognized M. Coquelin de Volière as o▪
of the actors, in the piece called "Les Fâcheux." Full of pr▪
occupation, however, from the scene of the previous evenin▪
and hardly recovered from the effects of the poison which Co▪
bert had then administered to him, the king, during the who▪
of the day, so brilliant in its effects, so full of unexpected a▪
startling novelties, in which all the wonders of the "Arabi▪
Nights' Entertainments" seemed to be reproduced for his esp▪
cial amusement—the king, we say, showed himself cold, r▪
served, and taciturn. Nothing could smooth the frowns up▪
his face; every one who observed him noticed that a deep fee▪
ing of resentment of remote origin, increased by slow degree▪
as the source becomes a river, thanks to the thousand threa▪
of water which increase its body, was keenly alive in the dept▪
of the king's heart. Toward the middle of the day only did ▪
begin to resume a little serenity of manner, and by that tir▪
he had, in all probability, made up his mind. Aramis, who f▪
lowed him, step by step, in his thoughts, as in his walk, co▪
cluded that the event that he was expecting would not be lo▪
before it was announced. This time Colbert seemed to walk ▪
concert with the bishop of Vannes, and had he received f▪
every annoyance which he inflicted on the king a word of dire▪
tion from Aramis, he could not have done better. During t▪
whole of the day the king, who, in all probability, wished to fr▪

himself from some of the thoughts which disturbed his mind, seemed to seek La Valliere's society as actively as he seemed to show his anxiety to flee that of M. Colbert or M. Fouquet. The evening came. The king had expressed a wish not to walk in the park until after cards in the evening. In the interval between supper and the promenade, cards and dice were introduced. The king won a thousand pistoles, and, having won them, put them in his pocket, and then rose, saying:

"And now, gentlemen, to the park."

He found the ladies of the court already there. The king, we have before observed, had won a thousand pistoles, and had put them in his pocket; but M. Fouquet had somehow contrived to lose ten thousand, so that among the courtiers there was still left a hundred and ninety thousand francs profit to divide, a circumstance which made the countenances of the courtiers and the officers of the king's household the most joyous countenances in the world. It was not the same, however, with the king's face; for, notwithstanding his success at play, to which he was by no means insensible, there still remained a slight shade of dissatisfaction. Colbert was waiting for or upon him at the corner of one of the avenues; he was most probably waiting there in consequence of a rendezvous which had been given him by the king, as Louis XIV., who had avoided him, or who had seemed to avoid him, suddenly made him a sign, and they then struck into the depths of the park together. But La Valliere, too, had observed the king's gloomy aspect and kindling glances; she had remarked this—and as nothing which lay hidden or smoldering in his heart was impenetrable to her affection—she understood that this repressed wrath menaced some one; she prepared to withstand the current of his vengeance, and intercede like an angel of mercy. Overcome by sadness, nervously agitated, deeply distressed at having been so long separated from her lover, disturbed at the sight of that emotion which she had divined, she accordingly presented herself to the king with an embarrassed aspect, which in his then disposition of mind the king interpreted unfavorably. Then, as they were alone—nearly alone, inasmuch as Colbert, as soon as he perceived the young girl approaching, had stopped and drawn back a dozen paces—the king advanced toward La Valliere and took her by the hand.

"Mademoiselle," he said to her, "should I be guilty of an indiscretion if I were to inquire if you were indisposed? for you seem to breathe as if you were oppressed by some secret cause of uneasiness, and your eyes are filled with tears."

"Oh! sire, if I be indeed so, and if my eyes are indeed full of tears, I am sorrowful only at the sadness which seems to oppress your majesty."

"My sadness? You are mistaken, mademoiselle; no, it is not sadness I experience."

"What is it, then, sire?"

"Humiliation."

"Humiliation? Oh, sire, what a word for you to use!"

"I mean, mademoiselle, that wherever I may happen to be, no one else ought to be the master. Well, then, look round you on every side, and judge whether I am not eclipsed—I, the King of France—before the king of these wide domains. Oh!" he continued, clinching his hands and teeth, "when I think that this king——"

"Well, sire?" said Louise, terrified.

"That this king is a faithless, unworthy servant, who becomes proud and self-sufficient with property which belongs to me, and which he has stolen! And, therefore, am I about to change this impudent minister's *fête* into a sorrow and mourning, of which the nymph of Vaux, as the poets say, shall not soon lose the remembrance."

"Oh! your majesty——"

"Well, mademoiselle, are you about to take Monsieur Fouquet's part?" said Louis impatiently.

"No, sire; I will only ask whether you are well informed. Your majesty has more than once learned the value of accusations made at court."

Louis XIV. made a sign for Colbert to approach.

"Speak, Monsieur Colbert," said the young prince, "for I almost believe that Mademoiselle de la Valliere has need of your assurance before she can put any faith in the king's word. Tell mademoiselle what Monsieur Fouquet has done; and you, mademoiselle, will perhaps have the kindness to listen. It will not be long."

Why did Louis XIV. insist upon it in such a manner? A very simple reason—his heart was not at rest; his mind was not thoroughly convinced; he imagined there was some dark, hidden, tortuous intrigue concealed beneath these thirteen millions of francs; and he wished that the pure heart of La Valliere, which had revolted at the idea of a theft or robbery, should approve—even were it only by a single word—the resolution he had taken, and which, nevertheless, he hesitated about carrying into execution.

"Speak, monsieur," said La Valliere to Colbert, who had advanced; "speak, since the king wishes me to listen to you. Tell me, what is the crime with which Monsieur Fouquet is charged?"

"Oh! not very heinous, mademoiselle," he returned; "a simple abuse of confidence."

"Speak, speak, Colbert; and when you shall have related it, leave us, and go and inform Monsieur d'Artagnan that I have certain orders to give him."

"Monsieur d'Artagnan, sire!" exclaimed La Valliere; "but why send for Monsieur d'Artagnan? I entreat you to tell me."

"*Pardieu!* in order to arrest this haughty, arrogant Titan, who, true to his menace, threatens to scale my heaven."

"Arrest Monsieur Fouquet, do you say?"

"Ah! does that surprise you?"

"In his own house?"

"Why not? If he be guilty, he is guilty in his own house as anywhere else."

"Monsieur Fouquet, who at this moment is ruining himself for his sovereign?"

"In plain truth, mademoiselle, it seems as if you were defending this traitor."

Colbert began to chuckle silently. The king turned round at the sound of this suppressed mirth.

"Sire," said La Valliere, "it is not Monsieur Fouquet I am defending; it is yourself."

"Me! you defend me?"

"Sire, you would be dishonoring yourself if you were to give such an order."

"Dishonor myself!" murmured the king, turning pale with anger. "In plain truth, mademoiselle, you show a strange persistence in what you say."

"If I do so, sire, my only motive is that of serving your majesty," replied the noble-hearted girl; "for that I would risk, I would sacrifice my very life, without the slightest reserve."

Colbert seemed inclined to grumble and complain. La Valliere, that timid, gentle lamb, turned round upon him, and with a glance like lightning imposed silence upon him.

"Monsieur," she said, "when the king acts well, whether, in doing so, he does either myself or those who belong to me an injury, I have nothing to say; but were the king to confer a benefit either upon me or mine, and if he acted badly, I should tell him so."

"But it appears to me, mademoiselle," Colbert ventured to say, "that I, too, love the king."

"Yes, monseigneur, we both love him, but each in a different manner," replied La Valliere, with such an accent that the heart of the young king was powerfully affected by it. "I love him so deeply that the whole world is aware of it; so purely that the king himself does not doubt my affection. He is my king and my master; I am the humblest of his servants. But he who touches his honor touches my life. Therefore, I repeat, that they dishonor the king who advise him to arrest Monsieur Fouquet under his own roof."

Colbert hung down his head, for he felt that the king had abandoned him. However, as he bent his head he murmured:

"Mademoiselle, I have only one word to say."

"Do not say it, then, monsieur; for I would not listen to it. Besides, what could you have to tell me? That Monsieur Fouquet has been guilty of certain crimes? I know he has, because the king has said so; and from the moment the king said, 'I think so,' I have no occasion for other lips to say, 'I affirm it.' But, were Monsieur Fouquet the vilest of men, I should say aloud, 'Monsieur Fouquet's person is sacred to the king, because he is the king's host.' Were his house a den of thieves, were Vaux a cave of coiners or robbers, his home is sacred, his palace is inviolable, since his wife is living in it, and that is an asylum whch even executioners would not dare to violate."

La Valliere paused, and was silent. In spite of himself, the king could not but admire her; he was overpowered by the passionate energy of her voice, by the nobleness of the cause she advocated. Colbert yielded, overcome by the inequality of the struggle. At last the king breathed again more freely, shook his head, and held out his hand to La Valliere.

"Mademoiselle," he said gently, "why do you decide against me? Do you know what this wretched fellow will do, if I give him time to breathe again?"

"Is he not a prey which will always be within your grasp?"

"And if he escapes, and takes to flight?" exclaimed Colbert.

"Well, monsieur, it will always remain on record, to the king's eternal honor, that he allowed Monsieur Fouquet to flee; and the more guilty he may have been, the greater will the king's honor and glory appear, when once compared with such misery and such shame."

Louis kissed La Valliere's hand as he knelt before her.

"I am lost," thought Colbert; then suddenly his face brightened up again. "Oh! no, no, not yet," he said to himself.

And while the king, protected from observation by the thick covert of an enormous lime, pressed La Valliere to his breast, with all the ardor of ineffable affection, Colbert tranquilly looked among the papers in his pocketbook, and drew out of it a paper folded in the form of a letter, slightly yellow, perhaps, but which must have been very precious, since the intendant smiled as he looked at it; he then bent a look, full of hatred, upon the charming group which the young girl and the king formed together—a group which was revealed for a moment, as the light of the approaching torches shone upon it. Louis noticed the light reflected upon La Valliere's white dress.

"Leave me, Louise," he said, "for some one is coming."

"Mademoiselle, mademoiselle, some one is coming!" cried Colbert, to expedite the young girl's departure.

Louise disappeared rapidly among the trees; and then, as the king, who had been on his knees before the young girl, was rising from his humble posture, Colbert exclaimed:

"Ah! Mademoiselle de la Valliere has let something fall."

"What is it?" inquired the king.

"A paper—a letter—something white; look there, sire."

The king stooped down immediately and picked up the letter, crumpling it in his hand as he did so; and at the same moment the torches arrived, inundating the darkness of the scene with a flood of light as bright as day.

Chapter 16 — JEALOUSY

The torches we have just referred to, the eager attention which every one displayed, and the new ovation paid to the king by Fouquet, arrived in time to suspend the effect of a resolution which La Valliere had already considerably shaken in Louis XIV.'s heart. He looked at Fouquet with a feeling almost of gratitude for having given La Valliere an opportunity of showing herself so generously disposed, so powerful in the influence he exercised over his heart. The moment of the last and greatest display had arrived. Hardly had Fouquet conducted the king toward the château than a mass of fire burst from the dome of Vaux, with a prodigious uproar, pouring a flood of dazzling light on every side, and illumining the remotest corners of the gardens. The fireworks began. Colbert, at twenty paces from the king, who was surrounded and fêted by the owner of Vaux, seemed, by the obstinate persistence of his gloomy thoughts, to do his utmost to recall Louis' attention, which the magnificence of the spectacle was already, in his opinion, too easily diverting. Suddenly, just as Louis was on the point of holding it out to Fouquet, he perceived in his hand the paper which, as he believed, La Valliere had dropped at his feet as she hurried away. The still stronger magnet of love drew the young prince's attention toward the souvenir of his idol; and, by the brilliant light, which increased momentarily in beauty, and drew forth from the neighboring villages loud exclamations of admiration, the king read the letter, which he supposed was a loving and tender epistle which La Valliere had destined for him. But as he read it a deathlike pallor stole over his face, and an expression of deep-seated wrath, illumined by the many-colored fires which rose brightly and soaringly around the scene, produced a terrible spectacle, which every one would have shuddered at, could they only have read into his heart, which was torn by the most stormy and most bitter passions. There was no truce for him now, influenced as he was by jealousy and mad passion. From the very moment when the dark truth was revealed to him, every gentler feeling seemed to disappear; pity, kindness of consideration, the religion of hospitality, all were forgotten. In the bitter pang which wrung his heart, still too weak to hide his sufferings, he was almost on the point of uttering a cry of alarm, and calling his guards to gather round him. This letter which Colbert had thrown down at the king's feet, the reader has doubtless guessed, was the same that had disappeared with the porter, Toby, at Fontainebleau, after the attempt which Fouquet had made upon La Valliere's heart. Fouquet saw the king's pallor, and was far from guessing the evil; Colbert saw the king's anger, and rejoiced inwardly at the approach of the storm. Fouquet's voice drew the young prince from his wrathful reverie.

"What is the matter, sire?" inquired the surintendant, with an expression of graceful interest.

Louis made a violent effort over himself, as he replied:

"Nothing."

"I am afraid your majesty is suffering."

"I am suffering, and have already told you so, monsieur; but it is nothing."

And the king, without waiting for the termination of the fireworks, turned toward the château. Fouquet accompanied him and the whole court followed after them, leaving the remain of the fireworks burning for their own amusement. The surintendant endeavored again to question Louis XIV., but could no succeed in obtaining a reply. He imagined there had been some misunderstanding between Louis and La Vallière in the park, which had resulted in a slight quarrel; and that the king, who was not ordinarily sulky by disposition, but completely absorbed by his passion for La Vallière, had taken a dislike to every one because his mistress had shown herself offended with him. This idea was sufficient to console him; he had even a friendly and kindly smile for the young king when the latter wished him good-night. This, however, was not all the king had to submit to; he was obliged to undergo the usual ceremony, which on that evening was marked by the closest adherence to the strictest etiquette. The next day was the one fixed for the departure; it was but proper that the guests should thank their host, and should show him a little attention in return for the expenditure of his twelve millions. The only remarks approaching to amiability which the king could find to say to M. Fouquet, as he took leave of him, were in these words:

"Monsieur Fouquet, you shall hear from me. Be good enough to desire Monsieur d'Artagnan to come here."

And the blood of Louis XIII., who had so profoundly dissimulated his feelings, boiled in his veins; and he was perfectly ready to get M. Fouquet's throat cut, with the same readiness, indeed, as his predecessor had caused the assassination of le Maréchal d'Ancre; and so he disguised the terrible resolution he had formed beneath one of those royal smiles which are the lightning flashes indicating *coups d'état*. Fouquet took the king's hand and kissed it; Louis shuddered throughout his whole frame, but allowed M. Fouquet to touch his hand with his lips. Five minutes afterward D'Artagnan, to whom the royal order had been communicated, entered Louis XIV.'s apartment. Aramis and Philippe were in theirs, still eagerly attentive, and still listening with all their ears. The king did not even give the captain of the musketeers time to approach his armchair, but ran forward to meet him.

"Take care," he exclaimed, "that no one enters here."

"Very good, sire," replied the captain, whose glance had for a long time past analyzed the ravages on the king's countenance. He gave the necessary order at the door; but, returning to the king, he said:

"Is there something fresh the matter, your majesty?"

"How many men have you here?" inquired the king, without making any other reply to the question addressed to him.

"What for, sire?"

"How many men have you, I say?" repeated the king, stamping upon the ground with his foot.

"I have the musketeers."

"Well, and what others?"

"Twenty guards and thirteen Swiss."

"How many men will be required to——"

"To do what, sire?" replied the musketeer, opening his large, calm eyes.

"To arrest Monsieur Fouquet."

D'Artagnan fell back a step.

"To arrest Monsieur Fouquet!" he burst forth.

"Are you going to tell me that it is impossible?" exclaimed the king, with cold and vindictive passion.

"I never say that anything is impossible," replied D'Artagnan, wounded to the quick.

"Very well; do it, then."

D'Artagnan turned on his heel, and made his way toward the door; it was but a short distance, and he cleared it in half a dozen paces; when he reached it he suddenly paused, and said:

"Your majesty will forgive me, but, in order to effect this arrest, I should like written directions."

"For what purpose—and since when has the king's word been insufficient for you?"

"Because the word of a king, when it springs from a feeling of anger, may possibly change when the feeling changes."

"A truce to set phrases, monsieur; you have another thought besides that."

"Oh! I, at least, have certain thoughts and ideas, which, unfortunately, others have not," D'Artagnan replied impertinently.

The king, in the tempest of his wrath, hesitated, and drew back in the face of D'Artagnan's frank courage, just as a horse crouches on his haunches under the strong hand of a bold and experienced rider.

"What is your thought?" he exclaimed.

"This, sire," replied D'Artagnan: "You cause a man to be arrested when you are still under his roof, and passion is alone the cause of that. When your anger shall have passed away you will regret what you have done; and then I wish to be in a position to show you your signature. If that, however, should fail to be a reparation, it will, at least, show us that the king is wrong to lose his temper."

"Wrong to lose his temper!" cried the king, in a loud, passionate voice. "Did not my father, my grandfather, too, before me, lose their temper at times, in Heaven's name?"

"The king, your father, and the king, your grandfather, never lost their temper when under the protection of their own palace."

"The king is master, wherever he may be."

"That is a flattering, complimentary phrase, which cannot proceed from any one but Monsieur Colbert; but it happens not to be the truth. The king is at home in every man's house when he has driven its owner out of it."

The king bit his lips, but said nothing.

"Can it be possible?" said D'Artagnan; "here is a man who is positively ruining himself in order to please you, and you wish to have him arrested! *Mordioux!* Sire, if my name was Fouquet, and people treated me in that manner, I would swallow, at a single gulp, all the fireworks and other things, and I would set fire to them, and blow myself and everybody else up to the sky. But it is all the same; it is your wish, and it shall be done."

"Go," said the king; "but have you men enough?"

"Do you suppose I am going to take a whole host to help me? Arrest Monsieur Fouquet! why, that is so easy that a very child might do it. It is like drinking a glass of bitters; one makes an ugly face, and that is all."

"If he defends himself?"

"He? not at all likely. Defend himself when such extreme harshness as you are going to practice makes the man a very martyr! Nay, I am sure that if he has a million of francs left, which I very much doubt, he would be willing enough to give it in order to have such a termination as this. But what does that matter? It shall be done at once."

"Stay," said the king; "do not make his arrest a public affair."

"That will be more difficult."

"Why so?"

"Because nothing is easier than to go up to Monsieur Fouquet in the midst of a thousand enthusiastic guests who surround him, and say, 'In the king's name, I arrest you.' But to go up to him, to turn him first one way and then another, to drive him up into one of the corners of the chessboard, in such a way that he cannot escape; to take him away from his guests, and keep him a prisoner for you, without one of them, alas! having heard anything about it—that indeed is a real difficulty, the greatest of all, in truth; and I hardly see how it is to be done."

"You had better say it is impossible, and you will have

finished much sooner. Heaven help me, but I seem to be surrounded by people who prevent me doing what I wish."

"I do not prevent your doing anything. Are you decided?"

"Take care of Monsieur Fouquet, until I shall have made up my mind by to-morrow morning."

"That shall be done, sire."

"And return, when I rise in the morning, for further orders and now leave me to myself."

"You do not even want Monsieur Colbert, then?" said the musketeer, firing this last shot as he was leaving the room. The king started. With his whole mind fixed on the thought of revenge, he had forgotten the cause and substance of the offense

"No, no one," he said; "no one here! Leave me."

D'Artagnan quitted the room. The king closed the door with his own hands, and began to walk up and down his apartment a a furious pace, like a wounded bull in an arena, dragging after him the colored streamers and iron darts. At last he began to take comfort in the expression of his violent feelings.

"Miserable wretch that he is! not only does he squander my finances, but with his ill-gotten plunder he corrupts secretaries friends, generals, artists, and all, and tries to rob me of the one to whom I am most attached. And that is the reason why that perfidious girl so boldly took his part! Gratitude! and who can tell whether it was not a stronger feeling—love itself?"

He gave himself up for a moment to his bitter reflections.

"A satyr!" he thought, with that abhorrent hate with which young men regard those more advanced in life who still think of love. "A man who has never found opposition or resistance in any one, who lavishes his gold and jewels in every direction, and who retains his staff of painters in order to take the portraits of his mistresses in the costume of goddesses."

The king trembled with passion, as he continued:

"He pollutes and profanes everything that belongs to me He destroys everything that is mine. He will be my death at last, I know. That man is too much for me; he is my mortal enemy, and he shall fall! I hate him—I hate him—I hate him!" and as he pronounced these words he struck the arm of the chair in which he was sitting violently, over and over again, and then rose like one in an epileptic fit. "To-morrow! to-morrow! oh, happy day!" he murmured, "when the sun rises, no other rival will that bright orb have but me. That man shall fall so low that when people look at the utter ruin which my anger shall have wrought they will be forced to confess at least, that am indeed greater than he."

The king, who was incapable of mastering his emotions any longer, knocked over with a blow of his fist a small table placed close to his bedside, and in the bitterness of feeling from which he was suffering, almost weeping, and half-suffocated by his passion, he threw himself on his bed, dressed as he was, and bit the sheets in the extremity of his passion, trying to find repose of body, at least, there. The bed creaked beneath his weight, and, with the exception of a few broken sounds which escaped from his overburdened chest, absolute silence soon reigned in the chamber of Morpheus.

Chapter 17 — HIGH TREASON

The ungovernable fury which took possession of the king at the sight and at the perusal of Fouquet's letter to La Valliere by degrees subsided into a feeling of pain and extreme weariness. Youth, invigorated by health and lightness of spirits, and requiring that what it loses should be immediately restored—youth knows not those endless, sleepless nights which enable us to realize the fable of the vulture unceasingly feeding on Prometheus. In instances where the man of middle life, in his acquired strength of will and purpose, and the old man, in his state of exhaustion, find an incessant augmentation of their bitter sorrow, a young man, surprised by the sudden appearance of a misfortune, weakens himself in sighs, and groans, and tears, in direct struggles with it, and is thereby far sooner overthrown by the inflexible enemy with whom he is engaged. Once overthrown, his struggles cease. Louis could not hold out more than a few minutes, at the end of which he had ceased to clinch his hands, and to burn up with his looks the invisible objects of his hatred; he soon ceased to attack with his violent imprecations not M. Fouquet alone, but even La Valliere herself; from fury he subsided into despair, and from despair to prostration. After he had thrown himself for a few minutes to and fro convulsively on his bed, his nerveless arms fell quietly down; his head lay languidly on his pillow; his limbs, exhausted from his excessive emotions, still trembled occasionally, agitated by slight muscular contractions; and from his breast only faint and unfrequent sighs still issued. Morpheus, the tutelary deity of the apartment, toward whom Louis raised his eyes, wearied by his anger and reddened by his tears, showered down upon him the sleep-inducing poppies with which his hands were filled; so that the king gently closed his eyes and fell asleep. Then it seemed to him, as it often happens in that first sleep, so light and gentle, which raises the body above the couch, the soul above the earth—it seemed to him, we say, as if the god Morpheus, painted on the ceiling, looked at him with eyes resembling human eyes; that something shone brightly, and moved to and fro in the dome above the sleeper; that the crowd of terrible dreams which thronged together in his brain, and which were interrupted for a moment, half-revealed a human face, with a hand resting against the mouth, and in an attitude of deep and absorbed meditation. And, strange enough, too, this man bore so wonderful a resemblance to the king himself that Louis fancied he was looking at his own face reflected in a mirror; with the exception, however, that the face was saddened by a feeling of the profoundest pity. Then it seemed to him as if the dome gradually retired, escaping from his gaze, and that the figures and attributes painted by Lebrun became darker and darker as the distance became more and more remote. A gentle, easy movement, as regular as that by which a vessel plunges beneath the waves, had succeeded to the immovableness of the bed. Doubtless the king was dreaming, and in this dream the crown of gold, which fastened the curtains together, seemed to recede from his vision, just as the dome, to which it remained suspended, had done, so that the winged genius which, with both its hands, supported the crown, seemed, though vainly so, to call upon the king, who was fast disappearing from it. The bed still sunk. Louis, with his eyes open, could not resist the deception of this cruel hallucination. At last, as the light of the royal chamber faded away into darkness and gloom, something cold, gloomy, and inexplicable in its nature seemed to infect the air. No paintings, nor gold, nor velvet hangings were visible any longer; nothing but walls of a dull-gray color, which the increasing gloom made darker every moment. And yet the bed still continued to descend, and after a minute, which seemed in its duration almost an age to the king, it reached a stratum of air black and still as death, and then it stopped. The king could no longer see the light in his room, except as from the bottom of a well we can see the light of day.

"I am under the influence of a terrible dream," he thought. "It is time to awaken from it. Come! let me wake up."

Every one has experienced what the above remark conveys; there is hardly a person who, in the midst of a nightmare hose influence is suffocating, has not said to himself, by the lp of that light which still burns in the brain when every human light is extinguished, "It is nothing but a dream, after all." his was precisely what Louis XIV. said to himself; but when he said, "Come, come! wake up!" he perceived that not only as he already awake, but still more, that he had his eyes open so; he then looked all round him. On his right hand and on his ft two armed men stood silently, each wrapped in a huge oak, and the face covered with a mask; one of them held small lamp in his hand, whose glimmering light revealed the sadest picture a king could look upon. Louis could not help saying to himself that his dream still lasted and that all he had to to cause it to disappear was to move his arms or to say something aloud. He darted from his bed, and found himself upon e damp, moist ground. Then, addressing himself to the man ho held the lamp in his hand, he said:

"What is this, monsieur, and what is the meaning of this st?"

"It is no jest," replied, in a deep voice, the masked figure at held the lantern.

"Do you belong to Monsieur Fouquet?" inquired the king, eatly astonished at his situation.

"It matters very little to whom we belong," said the antom; "we are your masters now; that is sufficient."

The king, more impatient than intimidated, turned to the her masked figure.

"If this is a comedy," he said, "you will tell Monsieur Fouet that I find it unseemly and improper, and that I desire it ould cease."

The second masked person to whom the king had addressed mself was a man of huge stature and vast circumference. He ld himself erect and motionless as a block of marble.

"Well," added the king, stamping his foot, "you do not anwer!"

"We do not answer you, my good monsieur," said the giant, a stentorian voice, "because there is nothing to answer."

"At least, tell me what you want?" exclaimed Louis, folding s arms with a passionate gesture.

"You will know by and by," replied the man who held the mp.

"In the meantime, tell me where I am."

"Look."

Louis looked all around him; but by the light of the lamp hich the masked figure raised for the purpose, he could perceive nothing but the damp walls, which glistened here and there with the slimy traces of the snail.

"Oh, oh! a dungeon!" said the king.

"No, a subterranean passage."

"Which leads——"

"Will you be good enough to follow us?"

"I shall not stir from hence!" cried the king.

"If you are obstinate, my dear young friend," replied the taller and stouter of the two, "I will lift you in my arms, will roll you up in a cloak, and if you are stifled there, why, so much the worse for you."

And as he said this he disengaged from beneath his cloak a hand of which Milo of Cortona would have envied him the possession, on the day when he had that unhappy idea of rending his last oak. The king dreaded violence, for he could well believe that the two men into whose power he had fallen had not gone so far with any idea of drawing back, and that they would consequently be ready to proceed to extremities, if necessary. He shook his head, and said:

"It seems I have fallen into the hands of a couple of assassins. Move on, then."

Neither of the men answered a word to this remark. The one who carried the lantern walked the first, the king followed him, while the second masked figure closed the procession. In this manner they passed along a winding gallery of some length, with as many staircases leading out of it as are to be found in the mysterious and gloomy palaces of Ann Radcliff's creation. All these windings and turnings, during which the king heard the sound of falling water on his head, ended at last in a long corridor closed by an iron door. The figure with the lamp opened the door with one of the keys he wore suspended at his girdle, where, during the whole of the time, the king had heard them rattle. As soon as the door was opened and admitted the air, Louis recognized the balmy odors which are exhaled by the trees after a hot summer's day. He paused hesitatingly for a moment or two; but his huge companion who followed him thrust him out of the subterranean passage.

"Another blow," said the king, turning toward the one who had just had the audacity to touch his sovereign. "What do you intend to do with the King of France?"

"Try and forget that word," replied the man with the lamp, in a tone which as little admitted of a reply as one of the famous decrees of Minos.

"You deserve to be broken on the wheel for the word you

have just made use of," said the giant, as he extinguished the lamp his companion handed to him; "but the king is too kind-hearted."

Louis, at that threat, made so sudden a movement that it seemed as if he meditated flight; but the giant's hand was in a moment placed on his shoulder, and fixed him motionless where he stood.

"But tell me, at least, where we are going," said the king.

"Come," replied the former of the two men, with a kind of respect in his manner, and leading his prisoner toward a carriage which seemed to be in waiting.

The carriage was completely concealed amid the trees. Two horses, with their feet fettered, were fastened by a halter to the lower branches of a large oak.

"Get in," said the same man, opening the carriage-door and letting down the step. The king obeyed, seated himself at the back of the carriage, the padded door of which was shut and locked immediately upon him and his guide. As for the giant, he cut the fastenings by which the horses were bound, harnessed them himself, and mounted on the box of the carriage, which was unoccupied. The carriage set off immediately at a quick trot, turned into the road to Paris, and in the forest of Senart found a relay of horses fastened to the trees in the same manner the first horses had been, and without a postilion. The man on the box changed the horses, and continued to follow the road toward Paris with the same rapidity, and entered the city about three o'clock in the morning. The carriage proceeded along the Faubourg St. Antoine, and after having called out to the sentinel, "By the king's order," the driver conducted the horses into the circular inclosure of the Bastile, looking out upon the court-yard, called La Cour du Gouvernement. There the horses drew up, reeking with sweat, at the flight of steps, and a sergeant of the guard ran forward.

"Go and wake the governor," said the coachman, in a voice of thunder.

With the exception of this voice, which might have been heard at the entrance of the Faubourg St. Antoine, everything remained as calm in the carriage as in the prison. Ten minutes afterward M. de Baisemeaux appeared in his dressing-gown on the threshold of the door.

"What is the matter now?" he asked, "and whom have you brought me there?"

The man with the lantern opened the carriage-door, and said two or three words to the one who acted as driver, who imme-

diately got down from his seat, took up a short musket which
he kept under his feet, and placed its muzzle on the prisoner's
chest.

"And fire at once if he speaks!" added aloud the man who
alighted from the carriage.

"Very good," replied his companion, without any other remark.

With this recommendation, the person who had accompanied
the king in the carriage ascended the flight of steps, at the top
of which the governor was awaiting him.

"Monsieur d'Herblay!" said the latter.

"Hush!" said Aramis. "Let us go into your room."

"Good heavens! what brings you here at this hour?"

"A mistake, my dear Monsieur de Baisemeaux," Aramis replied quietly. "It appears that you were quite right the other
day."

"What about?" inquired the governor.

"About the order of release, my dear friend."

"Tell me what you mean, monsieur—no, monseigneur," said
the governor, almost suffocated by surprise and terror.

"It is a very simple affair. You remember, dear Monsieur Baisemeaux, that an order of release was sent to you."

"Yes, for Marchiali."

"Very good; we both thought that it was for Marchiali."

"Certainly; you will recollect, however, that I would not believe it, but that you compelled me."

"Oh! Baisemeaux, my good fellow, what a word to make use
of!—strongly recommended, that was all."

"Strongly recommended, yes; strongly recommended to give
him up to you; and that you carried him off with you in your
carriage."

"Well, my dear Monsieur de Baisemeaux, it was a mistake; it
was discovered at the ministry, so that I now bring you an order from the king to set at liberty—Seldon, that poor Scotch fellow, you know."

"Seldon! Are you sure this time?"

"Well, read it yourself," added Aramis, handing him the order.

"Why," said Baisemeaux, "this order is the very same that
has already passed through my hands."

"Indeed?"

"It is the very one I assured you I saw the other evening.
Parbleau! I recognize it by the blot of ink."

"I do not know whether it is that; but all I know is, that I bring it for you."

"But, then, about the other?"

"What other?"

"Marchiali."

"I have got him here with me."

"But that is not enough for me. I require a new order to take him back again."

"Don't talk such nonsense, my dear Baisemeaux; you talk like a child! Where is the order you received respecting Marchiali?"

Baisemeaux ran to his iron chest and took it out. Aramis seized hold of it, coolly tore it in four pieces, held them to the lamp, and burned them.

"Good heavens! what are you doing?" exclaimed Baisemeaux, in an extremity of terror.

"Look at your position a little quietly, my dear governor," said Aramis, with his imperturbable self-possession, "and you will see how very simple the whole affair is. You no longer possess any order justifying Marchiali's release."

"I am a lost man!"

"Far from it, my good fellow, since I have brought Marchiali back to you, and it is just the same as if he had never left."

"Ah!" said the governor, completely overcome by terror.

"Plain enough, you see; and you will go and shut him up immediately."

"I should think so, indeed."

"And you will hand over this Seldon to me, whose liberation is authorized by this order. Do you understand?"

"I—I——"

"You do understand, I see," said Aramis. "Very good."

Baisemeaux clasped his hands together.

"But why, at all events, after having taken Marchiali away from me, do you bring him back again?" cried the unhappy governor, in a paroxysm of terror, and completely dumfounded.

"For a friend such as you are," said Aramis—"for so devoted a servant, I have no secrets;" and he put his mouth close to Baisemeaux's ear, as he said, in a low tone of voice, "You know the resemblance between that unfortunate fellow and——"

"And the king?—yes."

"Very good; the very first use that Marchiali made of his liberty was to persist— Can you guess what?"

"How is it likely I should guess?"

"To persist in saying that he was the King of France; to

dress himself up in clothes like those of the king; and then pretend to assume that he was the king himself."

"Gracious heavens!"

"That is the reason why I have brought him back again, my dear friend. He is mad, and lets every one see how mad he is."

"What is to be done, then?"

"That is very simple; let no one hold any communication with him. You understand that when his peculiar style of madness came to the king's ears, the king, who had pitied his terrible affliction, and saw how his kindness of heart had been repaid by such black ingratitude, became perfectly furious; so that, now—and remember this very distinctly, dear Monsieur de Baisemeaux, for it concerns you most closely—so that there is now, I repeat, sentence of death pronounced against all those who may allow him to communicate with any one else but me or the king himself. You understand, Baisemeaux, sentence of death!"

"You need not ask me whether I understand."

"And now, let us go down, and conduct this poor devil back to his dungeon again, unless you prefer he should come up here."

"What would be the good of that?"

"It would be better, perhaps, to enter his name in the prison-book at once."

"Of course, certainly; not a doubt of it."

"In that case, have him up."

Baisemeaux ordered the drums to be beaten, and the bell to be rung, as a warning cry to every one to retire, in order to avoid meeting a prisoner, about whom it was desired to observe a certain mystery. Then, when the passages were free, he went to take the prisoner from the carriage, at whose breast Porthos, faithful to the directions which had been given him, still kept his musket leveled.

"Ah! is that you, miserable wretch?" cried the governor, as soon as he perceived the king. "Very good, very good!"

And immediately, making the king get out of the carriage, he led him, still accompanied by Porthos, who had not taken off his mask, and Aramis, who again resumed his, up the stairs, to the second Bertaudiere, and opened the door of the room in which Philippe for six long years had bemoaned his existence. The king entered into the cell without pronouncing a single word; he was pale and haggard. Baisemeaux shut the door upon him, turned the key twice in the lock, and then returned to Aramis.

"It is quite true," he said, in a low tone, "that he has a rather strong resemblance to the king; but still less so than you said."

"So that," said Aramis, "you would not have been deceived by the substitution of the one for the other?"

"What a question!"

"You are a most valuable fellow, Baisemeaux," said Aramis; "and now set Seldon free."

"Oh, yes! I was going to forget that. I will go and give orders at once."

"Bah! to-morrow will be time enough."

"'To-morrow!' oh, no! This very minute."

"Well, go off to your affairs, I shall go away to mine. But it is quite understood, is it not?"

"What 'is quite understood?'"

"That no one is to enter the prisoner's cell, except with an order from the king—an order which I will myself bring."

"Quite so. Adieu, monseigneur."

Aramis returned to his companion.

"Now, Porthos, my good fellow, back again to Vaux, and as fast as possible."

"A man is light and easy enough when he has faithfully served his king, and, in serving him, saved his country," said Porthos. "The horses will be as light as if they had nothing at all behind them. So let us be off."

And the carriage, lightened of a prisoner, who might well be—as he in fact was—very heavy for Aramis, passed across the drawbridge of the Bastile, which was raised again immediately behind it.

Chapter 18 — A NIGHT AT THE BASTILE

Pain, anguish, and suffering in human life are always in proportion to the strength with which a man is endowed. We will not pretend to say that Heaven always apportions to a man's capability of endurance the anguish with which He afflicts him; such, indeed, would not be exact, since Heaven permits the existence of death, which is sometimes the only refuge open to those who are too closely pressed—too bitterly afflicted, as far as the body is concerned. Suffering is in proportion to the strength which has been accorded to a person; in other words, the weak suffer more where the trial is the same, than the strong. And what are the elementary principles, we may ask, which compose human strength? Is it not—more than anything else—exercise, habit, experience? We shall not even take the trouble to demonstrate that, for it is an axiom in morals, as in physics. When the young king, stupefied and crushed in every sense and feeling, found himself led to a cell in the Bastile, he fancied that death itself is but a sleep; that it, too, has its dreams as well; that the bed had broken through the flooring of his room at Vaux; that death had resulted from the occurrence; and that, still carrying out his dream, as the king, Louis XVI., now no longer living, was dreaming one of those horrors, impossible to realize in life, which is termed dethronement, imprisonment, and insult toward a sovereign who formerly wielded unlimited power. To be present at—an actual witness, too—of this bitterness of death; to float, undecisively, in an incomprehensible mystery, between resemblance and reality; to hear everything, to see everything, without interfering with a single detail of agonizing suffering, was—so the king thought within himself—a torture far more terrible, since it might last forever.

"Is this what is termed eternity—hell?" he murmured, at the moment the door closed upon him, which Baisemeaux had himself shut.

He did not even look round him; and in the room, leaning with his back against the wall, he allowed himself to be carried away by the terrible supposition that he was already dead, as he closed his eyes, in order to avoid looking upon something even worse still.

"How can I have died?" he said to himself, sick with terror. "The bed might have been let down by some artificial means. But no! I do not remember to have received any contusion, nor any shock either. Would they not rather have poisoned me at one of my meals, or with the fumes of wax, as they did my ancestress, Jeanne d'Albret?"

Suddenly, the chill of the dungeon seemed to fall like a cloak upon Louis' shoulders.

"I have seen," he said, "my father lying dead upon his funeral couch, in his regal robes. That pale face, so calm and worn; those hands, once so skillful, lying nerveless by his side; those limbs stiffened by the icy grasp of death; nothing there betokened a sleep peopled with dreams. And yet how numerous were the dreams which Heaven might have sent that royal corpse—him, whom so many others had preceded, hurried away by him into eternal death! No, that king was still the king; he was enthroned still upon that funeral couch, as upon a velvet armchair; he had not abdicated aught of his majesty. God, who had not punished him, cannot, will not punish me who have done nothing."

A strange sound attracted the young man's attention. He looked round him, and saw on the mantel-shelf, just below an enormous crucifix, coarsely painted in fresco on the wall, a rat of enormous size engaged in nibbling a piece of dry bread, but fixing, all the time, an intelligent and inquiring look upon the new occupant of the cell. The king could not resist a sudden impulse of fear and disgust; he moved back toward the door, uttering a loud cry; and, as if he but needed this cry, which escaped from his breast almost unconsciously, to recognize himself, Louis knew that he was alive and in full possession of his natural senses.

"A prisoner!" he cried. "I—I, a prisoner!"

He looked round him for a bell to summon some one to him.

"There are no bells at the Bastile," he said, "and it is in the Bastile I am imprisoned. In what way can I have been made a prisoner? It must have been owing to a conspiracy of Monsieur Fouquet. I have been drawn to Vaux, as into a snare. Monsieur Fouquet cannot be acting alone in this affair. His agent— That voice that I but just now heard was Monsieur d'Herblay's; I recognized it. Colbert was right then. But what is Fouquet's object? To reign in my place and stead? Impossible! Yet, who knows?" thought the king, relapsing into gloom again. "Perhaps my brother, the Duc d'Orleans, is doing that which my uncle wished to do during the whole of his life against my father. But the queen? My mother, too? And La Valliere? Oh! La Valliere, she will have been abandoned to madame. Dear, dear girl! Yes, it is—it must be so. They must have shut her up as they have me. We are separated forever!"

And at this idea of separation the poor lover burst into a flood of tears, and sobs, and groans.

"There is a governor in this place," the king continued, in a fury of passion. "I will speak to him, I will summon him to me."

He called, but no voice replied to his. He seized hold of his chair, and hurled it against the massive oaken door. The wood resounded against the door, and awakened many a mournful echo in the profound depths of the staircase; but from a human creature, not one.

This was a fresh proof for the king of the slight regard in

which he was held at the Bastile. Therefore, when his first fit of
anger had passed away, having remarked a barred window
through which there passed a stream of light, lozenge-shaped,
which must be, he knew, the bright orb of approaching day,
Louis began to call out, at first gently enough, then louder
and louder still; but no one replied to him. Twenty other attempts which he made, one after another, obtained no other or
better success. His blood began to boil within him, and mount
to his head. His nature was such that, accustomed to command,
he trembled at the idea of disobedience. By degrees his anger
increased more and more. The prisoner broke the chair, which
was too heavy for him to lift, and made use of it as a battering-
ram to strike against the door. He struck so loudly, and so re-
peatedly, that the perspiration soon began to pour down his
face. The sound became tremendous and continuous; some
stifled, smothered cries replied in different directions. This
sound produced a strange effect upon the king. He paused to listen to it; it was the voices of the prisoners, formerly his victims, now his companions. The voices ascended like vapors
through the thick ceilings and the massive walls, and rose in accusation against the author of this noise, as doubtless their sighs
and tears accused, in whispered tones, the author of their captivity. After having deprived so many people of their liberty, the
king came among them to rob them of their rest. This idea almost drove him mad; it redoubled his strength, or, rather, his
will, bent upon obtaining some information, or a conclusion to
the affair. With a portion of the broken chair he recommenced
the noise. At the end of an hour Louis heard something in
the corridor, behind the door of his cell, and a violent blow,
which was returned upon the door itself, made him cease his
own.

"Are you mad?" said a rude, brutal voice. "What is the matter with you this morning?"

"This morning!" thought the king; but he said aloud politely, "Monsieur, are you the governor of the Bastile?"

"My good fellow, your head is out of sorts," replied the voice;
"but that is no reason why you should make such a terrible disturbance. Be quiet, *mordioux!*"

"Are you the governor?" the king inquired again.

He heard a door on the corridor close; the jailer had just left,
not even condescending to reply a single word. When the king
had assured himself of his departure, his fury knew no longer
any bounds. As agile as a tiger, he leaped from the table to the
window, and struck the iron bars with all his might. He broke

a pane of glass, the pieces of which fell clanking into the court-yard below. He shouted with increasing hoarseness, "The governor! the governor!" This excess lasted fully an hour, during which time he was in a burning fever. With his hair in disorder and matted on his forehead, his dress torn and whitened, his linen in shreds, the king never rested until his strength was utterly exhausted, and it was not until then that he clearly understood the pitiless thickness of the walls, the impenetrable nature of the cement, invincible to all other influence but that of time, and possessed of no other weapon but despair. He leaned his forehead against the door, and let the feverish throbbings of his heart calm by degrees; it had seemed as if one single additional pulsation would have made it burst.

"A moment will come when the food which is given to the prisoners will be brought to me. I shall then see some one; I shall speak to him, and get an answer."

And the king tried to remember at what hour the first repast of the prisoners was served at the Bastile; he was ignorant even of this detail. The feeling of remorse at this remembrance smote him like the keen thrust of a dagger, that he should have lived for twenty-five years a king, and in the enjoyment of every happiness, without having bestowed a moment's thought on the misery of those who had been unjustly deprived of their liberty. The king blushed from very shame. He felt that Heaven, in permitting this fearful humiliation, did no more than render to the man the same torture as was inflicted by that man upon so many others. Nothing could be more efficacious for re-awakening his mind to religious influences than the prostration of his heart, and mind, and soul beneath the feeling of such acute wretchedness. But Louis dared not even kneel in prayer to God to entreat Him to terminate his bitter trial.

"Heaven is right," he said; "Heaven acts wisely. It would be cowardly to pray to Heaven for that which I have so often refused to my own fellow-creatures."

He had reached this stage of his reflections, that is, of his agony of mind, when a similar noise was again heard behind his door, followed this time by the sound of the key in the lock, and of the bolts being withdrawn from their staples. The king bounded forward to be nearer to the person who was about to enter, but, suddenly reflecting that it was a movement unworthy of a sovereign, he paused, assumed a noble and calm expression, which for him was easy enough, and waited with his back turned toward the window, in order, to some extent, to conceal his agitation from the eyes of the person who was about enter-

ing. It was only a jailer with a basket of provisions. The king
looked at the man with restless anxiety, and waited until he
spoke.

"Ah!" said the latter, "you have broken your chair. I said
you had done so! Why, you must have become quite mad."

"Monsieur," said the king, "be careful what you say; it will
be a very serious affair for you."

The jailer placed the basket on the table, and looked at his
prisoner steadily.

"What do you say?" he said.

"Desire the governor to come to me," added the king, in accents full of calm dignity.

"Come, my boy," said the turnkey, "you have always been
very quiet and reasonable, but you are getting vicious, it seems,
and I wish you to know it in time. You have broken your chair,
and made a great disturbance; that is an offense punishable by
imprisonment in one of the lower dungeons. Promise me not to
begin over again, and I will not say a word about it to the governor."

"I wish to see the governor," replied the king, still control-
ling his passion.

"He will send you off to one of the dungeons, I tell you; so
take care."

"I insist upon it, do you hear?"

"Ah, ah! your eyes are becoming wild again. Very good! I
shall take away your knife."

And the jailer did what he said, quitted the prisoner, and
closed the door, leaving the king more astounded, more
wretched, and more isolated than ever. It was useless, though
he tried it, to make the same noise again on his door, and
equally useless that he threw the plates and dishes out of the
window; not a single sound was heard in answer. Two hours
afterward he could not be recognized as a king, a gentleman, a
man, a human being; he might rather be called a madman,
tearing the door with his nails, trying to tear up the flooring of
his cell, and uttering such wild and fearful cries that the old
Bastile seemed to tremble to its very foundations for having
revolted against its master. As for the governor, the jailer did
not even think of disturbing him; the turnkeys and the sentinels had reported the occurrence to him, but what was the good
of it? were not these madmen common enough in the fortress?
and were not the walls still stronger than they? M. de Baisemeaux, thoroughly impressed with what Aramis had told him,
and in perfect conformity with the king's order, hoped only

that one thing might happen; namely, that the madman Marchiali might be mad enough to hang himself to the canopy of his bed, or to one of the bars of the window. In fact, the prisoner was anything but a profitable investment for M. Baisemeaux, and became more annoying than agreeable to him. These complications of Seldon and Marchiali—the complications, first of setting at liberty and then imprisoning again, the complications arising from the strong likeness in question—had at last found a very proper *dénouement*. Baisemeaux even thought he had remarked that D'Herblay himself was not altogether dissatisfied at it.

"And then, really," said Baisemeaux to his next in command, "an ordinary prisoner is already unhappy enough in being a prisoner; he suffers quite enough indeed to induce one to hope charitably enough that his death may not be far distant. With still greater reason, then, when the prisoner has gone mad, and might bite and make a terrible disturbance in the Bastile; why, in that case, it is not simply an act of mere charity to wish him dead; it would be almost a good, and even commendable action, to quietly put him out of his misery."

And the good-natured governor thereupon sat down to his late breakfast.

Chapter 19 — THE SHADOW OF M. FOUQUET

D'Artagnan, still confused and oppressed by the conversation he had just had with the king, could not resist asking himself if he were really in possession of his senses, if he were really and truly at Vaux, if he, D'Artagnan, were really the captain of the musketeers and M. Fouquet the owner of the château in which Louis XIV. was at that moment partaking of his hospitality. These reflections were not those of a drunken man, although everything was in prodigal profusion at Vaux, and the surintendant's wines had met with a distinguished reception at the *fête*. The Gascon, however, was a man of calm self-possession; and no sooner did he touch his bright steel blade than he knew how to adopt morally the cold, keen weapon as his guide of action.

"Well," he said, as he quitted the royal apartment, "I seem now to be mixed up historically with the destinies of the king and the minister; it will be written that Monsieur d'Artagnan, a younger son of a Gascon family, placed his hand on the shoulder of Monsieur Nicolas Fouquet, the surintendant of finances of France. My descendants, if I have any, will flatter themselves with the distinction which this arrest will confer, just as the members of the De Luynes family have done with regard to the estates of the poor Maréchal d'Ancre. But the question is, to execute the king's direction in a proper manner. Any man would know how to say to Monsieur Fouquet, 'Your sword, monsieur.' But it is not every one who would be able to take care of Monsieur Fouquet without others knowing anything about it. How am I to manage, then, so that Monsieur le Surintendant pass from the height of favor to the direst disgrace; that Vaux be turned into a dungeon for him; that after having been steeped to his lips, as it were, in all the perfumes and incense of Assuerus, he is transferred to the gallows of Haman—in other words, of Enguerraud de Marigny?"

And at this reflection D'Artagnan's brow became clouded with perplexity. The musketeer had certain scruples on the matter, it must be admitted. To deliver up to death (for not a doubt existed that Louis hated Fouquet mortally) the man who had just shown himself so delightful and charming a host in every way, was a real case of conscience.

"It almost seems," said D'Artagnan to himself, "that if I am not a poor, mean, miserable fellow, I should let Monsieur Fouquet know the opinion the king has about him. Yet, if I betray my master's secret, I shall be a false-hearted, treacherous knave, a traitor, too—a crime provided for and punishable by military laws—so much so, indeed, that twenty times, in former days when wars were rife, I have seen many a miserable fellow strung up to a tree for doing, in a small degree, what my scruples counsel me to do to a greater extent now. No, I think that a man of true readiness of wit ought to get out of this difficulty with more skill than that. And now, let us admit that I do possess a little readiness of invention—it is not at all certain, though—for, after having for forty years absorbed so large a quantity, I shall be lucky if there were to be a pistole's worth left."

D'Artagnan buried his head in his hands, tore his mustache in sheer vexation, and added:

"What can be the reason of Monsieur Fouquet's disgrace? There seem to be three good ones: the first, because Monsieur Colbert doesn't like him; the second, because he wished to fall in love with Mademoiselle de la Valliere, and, lastly, because the king likes Monsieur Colbert and loves Mademoiselle de la Valliere. Oh, he is a lost man! But shall I put my foot on his neck, I of all men, when he is falling a prey to the intrigues of a set of women and clerks? For shame! If he be dangerous, I will lay him low enough; if, however, he be only persecuted, I will look on. I have come to such a decisive determination that neither king nor living man shall change my opinion. If Athos were here, he would do as I have done. Therefore, instead of going cold-bloodedly up to Monsieur Fouquet, and arresting him off-hand and shutting him up altogether, I will try and conduct myself like a man who understands what good manners are. People will talk about it, of course; but they shall talk well of it, I am determined."

And D'Artagnan, drawing by a gesture peculiar to himself his shoulder-belt over his shoulder, went straight off to M. Fouquet, who, after he had taken leave of his guests, was preparing to retire for the night and to sleep tranquilly after the triumphs of the day. The air was still perfumed, or infected, whichever way it may be considered, with the odor of the fireworks. The wax-lights were dying away in their sockets, the flowers fell unfastened from the garlands, the groups of dancers and courtiers were separating in the saloons. Surrounded by his friends, who complimented him and received his flattering remarks in return, the surintendant half-closed his wearied eyes. He longed for rest and quiet; he sank upon the bed of laurels, which had been heaped up for him for so many days past; it might almost have been said that he seemed bowed beneath the weight of the new debts which he had incurred for the purpose of giving the greatest possible honor to this *fête*. Fouquet had just retired to his room, still smiling, but more than half-dead. He could listen to nothing more, he could hardly keep his eyes open; his bed seemed to possess a fascinating and irresistible attraction for him. The god Morpheus, the presiding deity of the dome painted by Lebrun, had extended his influence over the adjoining rooms, and showered down his most sleep-inducing poppies upon the master of the house. Fouquet, almost entirely alone, was being assisted by his *valet de chambre* to undress, when M. D'Artagnan appeared at the entrance of the room. D'Artagnan had never been able to succeed in making himself common at court; and notwithstanding he was seen everywhere and on all occasions, he never failed to produce an effect wherever and whenever he made his appearance. Such is the happy privilege of certain natures, which in that respect resemble either thunder or lightning; every one recognizes them; but their appearance never fails to arouse surprise and astonishment, and whenever they occur, the impression is always left that the last was the loudest or brightest and most violent.

"What! Monsieur d'Artagnan?" said Fouquet, who had already taken his right arm out of the sleeve of his doublet.

"At your service," replied the musketeer.

"Come in, my dear Monsieur d'Artagnan."

"Thank you."

"Have you come to criticise the *fête?* You are ingenious enough in your criticisms, I know."

"By no means."

"Are not your men looked after properly?"

"In every way."

"You are not comfortably lodged, perhaps?"

"Nothing could be better."

"In that case, I have to thank you for being so amiably disposed, and I must not fail to express my obligations to you for all your flattering kindness."

These words were as much as to say, "My dear D'Artagnan, pray go to bed, since you have a bed to lie down on, and let me do the same."

D'Artagnan did not seem to understand it.

"Are you going to bed already?" he said to the surintendant.

"Yes; have you anything to say to me?"

"Nothing, monsieur, nothing at all. You sleep in this room, then?"

"Yes, as you see."

"You have given a most charming *fête* to the king."

"Do you think so?"

"Oh, beautiful!"

"Is the king pleased?"

"Enchanted."

"Did he desire you to say as much to me?"

"He would not choose so unworthy a messenger, monsieur."

"You do not do yourself justice, Monsieur d'Artagnan."

"Is that your bed there?"

"Yes; but why do you ask? Are you not satisfied with you own?"

"May I speak frankly to you?"

"Most assuredly."

"Well, then, I am not."

Fouquet started, and then replied:

"Will you take my room, Monsieur d'Artagnan?"

"What! deprive you of it, monseigneur? Never!"

"What am I to do, then?"

"Allow me to share yours with you."

Fouquet looked at the musketeer fixedly.

"Ah! ah!" he said, "you have just left the king."

"I have, monseigneur."

"And the king wishes you to pass the night in my room?"

"Monseigneur——"

"Very well, Monsieur d'Artagnan, very well. You are master here."

"I assure you, Monseigneur, that I do not wish to abuse——"

Fouquet turned to his valet, and said:

"Leave us."

When the man had left he said to D'Artagnan.

"You have something to say to me?"

"I?"

"A man of your superior intelligence cannot have come to talk with a man like myself, at such an hour as the present without grave motives."

"Do not interrogate me."

"On the contrary. What do you want with me?"

"Nothing more than the pleasure of your society."

"Come into the garden, then," said the surintendant suddenly, "or into the park."

"No," replied the musketeer hastily, "no!"

"Why?"

"The fresh air——"

"Come, admit at once that you arrest me," said the surintendant to the captain.

"Never!" said the latter.

"You intend to look after me, then?"

"Yes, monseigneur; I do, upon my honor."

"Upon your honor? Ah! that is quite another thing. So I am to be arrested in my own house!"

"Do not say such a thing."

"On the contrary, I will proclaim it aloud."

"If you do so, I shall be compelled to request you to be silent."

"Very good! Violence toward me, and in my own house, too!"

"We do not seem to understand each other at all. Stay a moment; there is a chessboard there; we will have a game, if you have no objection."

"Monsieur d'Artagnan, I am in disgrace, then?"

"Not at all; but——"

"I am prohibited, I suppose, from withdrawing from you sight?"

"I do not understand a word you are saying, monseigneur and if you wish me to withdraw, tell me so."

"My dear Monsieur d'Artagnan, your mode of action i enough to drive me mad; I was almost sinking for want o sleep, but you have completely awakened me."

"I shall never forgive myself, I am sure; and if you wish t reconcile me with myself, why, go to sleep in your bed in m presence; I shall be delighted at it."

"I am under surveillance, I see."

"I will leave the room if you say such a thing as that."

"You are beyond my comprehension."

"Good-night, monseigneur," said D'Artagnan, as he pre tended to withdraw.

Fouquet ran after him.

"I will not lie down," he said. "Seriously, and since you re fuse to treat me as a man, and since you finesse with me, I wi try and set you at bay, as a hunter does a wild boar."

"Bah!" cried D'Artagnan, pretending to smile.

"I shall order my horses, and set off for Paris," said Fouque sounding the heart of the captain of the musketeers.

"If that be the case, monseigneur, it is very different."

"You will arrest me, then?"

"No; but I shall go with you."

"That is quite sufficient, Monsieur d'Artagnan," returne Fouquet, in a cold tone of voice. "It is not idly that you hav acquired your reputation as a man of intelligence and full o resources; but with me that is quite superfluous. Let us tw come to the point. Grant me a service. Why do you arres me? What have I done?"

"Oh! I know nothing about what you have done; but I d not arrest you—this evening, at least."

"This evening!" said Fouquet, turning pale, "but tomorrow?

"It is not to-morrow just yet, monseigneur. Who can eve answer for the morrow?"

"Quick, quick, captain! let me speak to Monsieur d'Herblay.

"Alas! that is quite impossible, monseigneur. I have stri orders to see that you hold no communication with any one.

"With Monsieur d'Herblay, captain—with your friend."

"Monseigneur, is Monsieur d'Herblay the only person wit whom you ought to be prevented holding any communication?

Fouquet colored, and then, assuming an air of resignatio he said:

"You are right, monsieur; you have taught me a lesson that I ought not to have provoked. A fallen man cannot assert his right to anything, even from those whose fortunes he may have made; for a still greater reason, he cannot claim anything from those to whom he may never have had the happiness of doing a service."

"Monseigneur!"

"It is perfectly true, Monsieur d'Artagnan; you have always acted in the most admirable manner toward me—in such a manner, indeed, as most becomes the man who is destined to arrest me. You, at least, have never asked me anything."

"Monseigneur," replied the Gascon, touched by his eloquent and noble tone of grief, "will you—I ask it as a favor—pledge me your word as a man of honor that you will not leave this room?"

"What is the use of it, dear Monsieur d'Artagnan, since you keep watch and ward over me? Do you suppose that I should struggle against the most valiant sword in the kingdom?"

"It is not that at all, monseigneur; but that I am going to look for Monsieur d'Herblay, and, consequently, to leave you alone."

Fouquet uttered a cry of delight and surprise.

"To look for Monsieur d'Herblay! to leave me alone!" he exclaimed, clasping his hands together.

"Which is Monsieur d'Herblay's room? The blue room, is it not?"

"Yes, my friend, yes."

"Your friend! thank you for that word, monseigneur; you confer it upon me to-day, at least, if you have never done so before."

"Ah! you have saved me."

"It will take me a good ten minutes to go from hence to the blue room, and to return?" said D'Artagnan.

"Nearly so."

"And then to wake Aramis, who sleeps very soundly when he is asleep, I put that down at another five minutes; making a total of fifteen minutes' absence. And now, monseigneur, give me your word that you will not in any way attempt to make your escape, and that when I return I shall find you here again."

"I give it you, monsieur," replied Fouquet, with an expression of the warmest and deepest gratitude.

D'Artagnan disappeared. Fouquet looked at him as he quitted the room, waited with a feverish impatience until the door was

closed behind him, and, as soon as it was shut, flew to his key,
opened two or three secret doors concealed in various articles o
furniture in the room, looked vainly for certain papers, whic
doubtless he had left at St. Mandé, and which he seemed t
regret not having found in them; then, hurriedly seizing hol
of letters, contracts, paper writings, he heaped them up into
pile, which he burned in the extremest haste upon the marbl
hearth of the fireplace, not even taking time to draw from th
interior of it the vases and pots of flowers with which it wa
filled. As soon as he had finished, like a man who has just es
caped an imminent danger, and whose strength abandons him a
soon as the danger is past, he sunk down, completely overcom
on a couch. When D'Artagnan returned he found Fouquet in th
same position; the worthy musketeer had not the slightes
doubt that Fouquet, having given his word, would not even
think of failing to keep it, but he had thought it most likely tha
Fouquet would turn his (D'Artagnan's) absence to the best ad
vantage in getting rid of all the papers, memorandums, an
contracts, which might possibly render his position, which wa
even now serious enough, still more dangerous than ever. An
so, lifting up his head like a dog who gains the scent, he per
ceived a certain odor resembling smoke which he fully relie
upon finding in the atmosphere, and having found it, he mad
a movement of his head in token of satisfaction. When D'A
tagnan had entered Fouquet had, on his side, raised his hea
and not one of D'Artagnan's movements had escaped him. An
then the looks of the two men met, and they both saw that the
had understood each other without exchanging a syllable.

"Well!" asked Fouquet, the first to speak, "and Monsieu
d'Herblay?"

"Upon my word, monseigneur," replied D'Artagnan, "Mon
sieur d'Herblay must be desperately fond of walks by nigh
and composing verses by moonlight in the park of Vaux, wit
some of your poets, in all probability, for he is not in his ow
room."

"What! not in his own room?" cried Fouquet, whose la
hope had thus escaped him; for, unless he could ascertain
what way the bishop of Vannes could assist him, he perfectl
well knew that in reality he could not expect assistance fro
any one but him.

"Or, indeed," continued D'Artagnan, "if he is in his ow
room, he has very good reasons for not answering."

"But surely you did not call him in such a manner that I
could have heard you?"

"You can hardly suppose, monseigneur, that, having already exceeded my orders, which forbid me leaving you a single moment—you can hardly suppose, I say, that I should have been mad enough to rouse the whole house and allow myself to be seen in the corridor of the bishop of Vannes, in order that Monsieur Colbert might state with positive certainty that I gave you time to burn your papers."

"My papers?"

"Of course; at least, that is what I should have done in your place; when any one opens a door for me, I always avail myself of it."

"Yes, yes, and I thank you, for I have availed myself of it."

"And you have done perfectly right. Every man has his own peculiar secrets with which others have nothing to do. But let us return to Aramis, monseigneur."

"Well, then, I tell you, you could not have called loud enough, or Aramis would have heard you."

"However softly any one may call Aramis, monseigneur, Aramis always hears when he has an interest in hearing. I repeat what I said before—Aramis was not in his own room, or Aramis had certain reasons for not recognizing my voice, of which I am ignorant, and of which you even may be ignorant yourself, notwithstanding your liege-man is his greatness the Lord Bishop of Vannes."

Fouquet drew a deep sigh, rose from his seat, made three or four turns in his room, and finished by seating himself, with an expression of extreme dejection, upon his magnificent bed with velvet hangings, and trimmed with the costliest lace. D'Artagnan looked at Fouquet with feelings of the deepest and sincerest pity.

"I have seen a good many men arrested in my life," said the musketeer sadly; "I have seen both Monsieur de Cinq-Mars and Monsieur de Chalais arrested, though I was very young then. I have seen Monsieur de Condé arrested with the princes; I have seen Monsieur de Retz arrested; I have seen Monsieur Broussel arrested. Stay a moment, monseigneur, it is disagreeable to have to say, but the very one of all those whom you most resemble at this moment was that poor fellow, Broussel. You were very near doing as he did, putting your dinner-napkin in your portfolio, and wiping your mouth with your papers. *Mordioux!* Monseigneur Fouquet, a man like you ought not to be dejected in this manner. Suppose your friends saw you?"

"Monsieur d'Artagnan," returned the surintendant, with a

smile full of gentleness, "you do not understand me; it is precisely because my friends do not see me that I am such as you see me now. I do not live, exist even, isolated from others; I am nothing when left to myself. Understand that throughout my whole life I have passed every moment of my time in making friends, whom I hoped to render my stay and support. In times of prosperity, all these cheerful, happy voices—and rendered so through and by my means—formed in my honor a concert of praises and kindly actions. In the least disfavor, these humbler voices accompanied in harmonious accents the murmur of my own heart. Isolation I have never yet known. Poverty (a phantom I have sometimes beheld, clad in rags, awaiting me at the end of my journey through life)—this poverty has been the specter with which many of my own friends have trifled for years past, which they poetize and caress, and which has attracted me toward them. Poverty! I accept it, acknowledge it, receive it, as a disinherited sister; for poverty is not solitude, nor exile, nor imprisonment. Is it likely I shall ever be poor, with such friends as Pellisson, as La Fontaine, as Molière? with such a mistress as— Oh! if you knew how utterly lonely and desolate I feel at this moment, and how you who separate me from all I love, seem to resemble the image of solitude, of annihilation, and of death itself!"

"But I have already told you, Monsieur Fouquet," replied D'Artagnan, moved to the depths of his soul, "that you exaggerate matters a great deal too much. The king likes you."

"No, no!" said Fouquet, shaking his head.

"Monsieur de Colbert hates you."

"Monsieur de Colbert! What does that matter to me?"

"He will ruin you."

"Oh! I defy him to do that, for I am ruined already."

At this singular confession of the surintendant, D'Artagnan cast his glance all round the room; and although he did not open his lips, Fouquet understood him so thoroughly that he added:

"What can be done with such wealth of substance as surrounds us, when a man can no longer cultivate his taste for the magnificent? Do you know what good the greater part of the wealth and the possessions which we rich enjoy confer upon us? merely to disgust us, by their very splendor even, with everything which does not equal this splendor. Vaux! you will say, and the wonders of Vaux! What then? What boot these wonders? If I am ruined, how shall I fill with water the urns which my Naiads bear in their arms, or force the air into the lungs of my Tritons? To be rich enough, Monsieur d'Artagnan, a man must be too rich."

D'Artagnan shook his head.

"Oh! I know very well what you think," replied Fouquet quickly. "If Vaux were yours, you would sell it, and would purchase an estate in the country; an estate which should have woods, orchards, and land attached, and that this estate should be made to support its master. With forty millions you might——"

"Ten millions," interrupted D'Artagnan.

"Not a million, my dear captain. No one in France is rich enough to give two millions for Vaux, and to continue to maintain it as I have done; no one could do it, no one would know how."

"Well," said D'Artagnan, "in any case, a million is not abject misery."

"It is not far from it, my dear monsieur. But you do not understand me. No; I will not sell my residence at Vaux; I will give it to you, if you like;" and Fouquet accompanied these words with a movement of the shoulders to which it would be impossible to do justice.

"Give it to the king; you will make a better bargain."

"The king does not require me to give it to him," said Fouquet; "he will take it away from me with the most perfect ease and grace, if it please him to do so; and that is the reason why I should prefer to see it perish. Do you know, Monsieur d'Artagnan, that if the king did not happen to be under my roof, I would take this candle, go straight to the dome, and set fire to a couple of huge chests of fuses and fireworks which are in reserve there, and would reduce my palace to ashes?"

"Bah!" said the musketeer negligently. "At all events, you would not be able to burn the gardens, and that is the best part about the place."

"And yet," resumed Fouquet thoughtfully, "what was I saying? Great heavens! burn Vaux! destroy my palace! But Vaux is not mine; these wonderful creations are, it is true, the property, as far as sense of enjoyment goes, of the man who has paid for them; but as far as duration is concerned, they belong to those who created them. Vaux belongs to Lebrun, to Lenôtre, to Pellisson, to Levan, to La Fontaine, to Molière; Vaux belongs to posterity, in fact. You see, Monsieur d'Artagnan, that my very house ceases to be my own."

"That is all well and good," said D'Artagnan; "the idea is agreeable enough, and I recognize Monsieur Fouquet himself in it. That idea, indeed, makes me forget that poor fellow, Broussel, altogether; and I now fail to recognize in you the whining complaints of that old frondeur. If you are ruined, monsieur, look at the affair manfully, for you, too, *mordioux!* belong to posterity, and have no right to lessen yourself in any way. Stay a moment; look at me, I who seem to exercise in a degree a kind of superiority over you, because I arrest you; fate, which distributes their different parts to the comedians of this world, accorded to me a less agreeable and less advantageous part to fill than yours has been; I am one of those who think that the parts which kings and powerful nobles are called upon to act are infinitely of more worth than the parts of beggars or lackeys. It is far better on the stage—on the stage, I mean, of another theater than the theater of this world—it is far better to wear a fine coat and to talk fine language than to walk the boards shod with a pair of old shoes, or to get one's backbone gently caressed by a sound thrashing with a stick. In one word, you have been a prodigal with money, you have ordered and been obeyed—have been steeped to the lips in enjoyment; while I have dragged my tether after me, have been commanded and have obeyed, and have drudged my life away. Well, although I may seem of such trifling importance beside you, monseigneur, I do declare to you that the recollection of what I have done serves me as a spur, and prevents me from bowing my old head too soon. I shall remain unto the very end a good trooper; and when my turn comes I shall fall perfectly straight, all in a heap, still alive, after having selected my place beforehand. Do as I do, Monsieur Fouquet; you will not find yourself the worse for it; that happens only once in a lifetime to men like yourself, and the chief thing is to do it well when the chance presents itself. There is a Latin proverb—the words have escaped me, but I remember the sense of it very well, for I have thought over it more than once, which says, 'The end crowns the work!' "

Fouquet rose from his seat, passed his arm round D'Artagnan's neck, and clasped him in a close embrace, while with the other hand he pressed his hand.

"An excellent homily," he said, after a moment's pause.

"A soldier's, monseigneur."

"You have a regard for me in telling me all that."

"Perhaps."

Fouquet resumed his pensive attitude once more, and then, a moment after, he said:

"Where can Monsieur d'Herblay be? I dare not ask you to send for him."

"You would not ask me, because I would not do it, Monsieur Fouquet. People would learn it, and Aramis, who is not mixed up with the affair, might possibly be compromised and included in your disgrace."

"I will wait here till daylight," said Fouquet.

"Yes; that is best."

"What shall we do when daylight comes?"

"I know nothing at all about it, monseigneur."

"Monsieur d'Artagnan, will you do me a favor?"

"Most willingly."

"You guard me, I remain, you are acting in the full discharge of your duty, I suppose?"

"Certainly."

"Very good, then; remain as close to me as my shadow, if you like; and I infinitely prefer such a shadow to any one else."

D'Artagnan bowed to this compliment.

"But, forget that you are Monsieur d'Artagnan, captain of the musketeers; forget that I am Monsieur Fouquet, surintendant of the finances, and let us talk about my affairs."

"That is rather a delicate subject."

"Indeed?"

"Yes; but, for your sake, Monsieur Fouquet, I will do what may almost be regarded as an impossibility."

"Thank you. What did the king say to you?"

"Nothing."

"Ah! is that the way you talk?"

"The deuce!"

"What do you think of my situation?"

"Nothing."

"However, unless you have some ill feeling against me——"

"Your position is a difficult one."

"In what respect?"

"Because you are under your own roof."

"However difficult it may be, yet I understand it very well."

"Do you suppose that with any one else but yourself I should have shown so much frankness?"

"What! so much frankness, do you say? you, who refuse to tell me the slightest thing?"

"At all events, then, so much ceremony and consideration."

"Ah! I have nothing to say in that respect."

"One moment, monseigneur; let me tell you how I should

have behaved toward any one else but yourself. It might b
that I happened to arrive at your door just as your guests c
your friends had left you—or, if they had not yet gone, I shoul
wait until they were leaving, and should then catch them on
after the other, like rabbits; I should lock them up quietl
enough; I should steal softly along the carpet of your corrido
and with one hand upon you, before you suspected the slightes
thing about it, I should keep you safely until my master'
breakfast in the morning. In this way, I should just the sam
have avoided all publicity, all disturbance, all opposition; bu
there would also have been no warning for Monsieur Fouquet
no consideration for his feelings, none of those delicate con
cessions which are shown by persons who are essentially cour
teous in their natures, whenever the decisive moment ma
arrive. Are you satisfied with that plan?"

"It makes me shudder."

"I thought you would not like it. It would have been ver
disagreeable to have made your appearance to-morrow, with
out any preparation, and to have asked you to deliver up you
sword."

"Oh, monsieur, I should have died from sheer shame an
anger!"

"Your gratitude is too eloquently expressed. I have not don
enough to deserve it, I assure you."

"Most certainly, monsieur, you will never get me to believ
that."

"Well, then, monseigneur, if you are satisfied with what
have done, and have somewhat recovered from the shock whic
I prepared you for as much as I possibly could, let us allo
the few hours that remain to pass away undisturbed. You ar
harassed, and require to arrange your thoughts; I beg yo
therefore, to go to sleep, or pretend to go to sleep, either o
your bed or in your bed; I shall sleep in this armchair; an
when I fall asleep, my rest is so sound that a cannon would n
wake me."

Fouquet smiled.

"I except, however," continued the musketeer, "the case
a door being opened, whether a secret door or any other, or th
case of any one going out of or coming into the room. For any
thing like that my ear is as quick and sensitive as possible. An
creaking noise makes me start. It arises, I suppose, from a na
ural antipathy to anything of the kind. Move about as muc
as you like; walk up and down in any part of the room; writ
efface, destroy, burn—nothing like that will prevent me fro

going to sleep, or even prevent me from snoring; but do not touch either the key or the handle of the door! for I should start up in a moment, and that would shake my nerves terribly."

"Monsieur d'Artagnan," said Fouquet, "you are certainly the most witty and the most courteous man I ever met with; and you will leave me only one regret, that of having made your acquaintance so late."

D'Artagnan drew a deep sigh, which seemed to say, "Alas! you have, perhaps, made it too soon." He then settled himself in his armchair, while Fouquet, half-lying on his bed and leaning on his arm, was meditating upon his adventure. In this way, both of them, leaving the candles burning, awaited the first dawn of day; and when Fouquet happened to sigh too loudly, D'Artagnan only snored the louder. Not a single visit, not even from Aramis, disturbed their quietude; not a sound even was heard throughout the vast palace. Outside, however, the guards of honor on duty, and the patrols of the musketeers, paced up and down; and the sound of their feet could be heard on the gravel-walks. It seemed to act as an additional soporific for the sleepers; while the murmuring of the wind through the trees, and the unceasing music of the fountains, whose waters fell tumbling into the basins, still went on uninterruptedly, without being disturbed at the slight noises and matters of trifling moment which constitute the life and death of human nature.

Chapter 20 — THE MORNING

In opposition to the sad and terrible destiny of the king imprisoned in the Bastile, and tearing, in sheer despair, the bolts and bars of his dungeon, the rhetoric of the chroniclers of old would not fail to present, as a complete antithesis, the picture of Philippe lying asleep beneath the royal canopy. We do not pretend to say that such rhetoric is always bad, and always scatters, in places it should not, the flowers with which it embellishes and enlivens history. But we shall, on the present occasion, carefully avoid polishing the antithesis in question, but shall proceed to draw another picture as carefully as possible, to serve as a companion to the one we have drawn in the last chapter. The young prince descended from Aramis' room, in the same way the king had descended from the apartment dedi-

cated to Morpheus. The dome gradually and slowly sunk down
under Aramis' pressure, and Philippe stood beside the royal bed,
which had ascended again after having deposited its prisoner
in the secret depths of the subterranean passage. Alone, in the
presence of all the luxury which surrounded him; alone, in the
presence of his power; alone, with the part he was about to be
forced to act, Philippe for the first time felt his heart, and
mind, and soul expand beneath the influence of a thousand
varied emotions, which are the vital throbs of a king's heart.
But he could not help changing color when he looked upon the
empty bed, still tumbled by his brother's body. This mute accomplice had returned, after having completed the work it had
been destined to perform; it returned with the traces of the
crime; it spoke to the guilty author of that crime, with the
frank and unreserved language which an accomplice never fears
using toward his companion in guilt; for it spoke the truth.
Philippe bent over the bed, and perceived a pocket-handker-
chief lying on it, which was still damp from the cold sweat
which had poured from Louis XIV.'s face. This sweat-bestained
handkerchief terrified Philippe, as the blood of Abel had terrified Cain.

"I am now face to face with my destiny," said Philippe, with
his eyes on fire and his face lividly white. "Is it likely to be
more terrifying than my captivity has been sad and gloomy?
When I am compelled to follow out, at every moment, the
sovereign power and authority I have usurped, shall I never
cease to listen to the scruples of my heart? Yes; the king has
lain on his bed; it is indeed his head that has left its impression
on this pillow; his bitter tears which have stained this handkerchief; and yet I hesitate to throw myself on the bed, or to press
in my hand the handkerchief which is embroidered with my
brother's arms. Away with this weakness! let me imitate Monsieur d'Herblay, whose thoughts are of and for himself alone,
who regards himself as a man of honor, so long as he injures or
betrays his enemies only. I—I alone should have occupied this
bed, if Louis XIV. had not, owing to my mother's criminal
abandonment of me, stood in my way; and this handkerchief
embroidered with the arms of France, would, in right and justice, belong to me alone, if, as Monsieur d'Herblay observes, I
had been left in my place in the royal cradle. Philippe, son of
France, take your place on that bed! Philippe, sole King of
France, resume the blazonry which is yours! Philippe, sole heir
presumptive to Louis XIII., your father, show yourself without

pity or mercy for the usurper who, at this moment, has not even to suffer the agony of the remorse of all that you have had to submit to!"

With these words, Philippe, notwithstanding an instinctive repugnance of feeling, and in spite of the shudder of terror which mastered his will, threw himself on the royal bed, and forced his muscles to press the still warm place where Louis XIV. had lain, while he buried his burning face in the handkerchief still moistened by his brother's tears. With his head thrown back and buried in the soft down of his pillow, Philippe perceived above him the crown of France, suspended, as we have stated, by angels with outspread golden wings.

A man may be ambitious of lying in a lion's den, but can hardly hope to sleep there quietly. Philippe listened attentively to every sound; his heart panted and throbbed at the very suspicion of approaching terror and misfortune; but confident in his own strength, which was confirmed by the force of an overpowering, resolute determination, he waited until some decisive circumstance should permit him to judge for himself. He hoped that some imminent danger would be revealed for him, like those phosphoric lights of the tempest which show the sailors the altitude of the waves against which they have to struggle. But nothing approached. Silence, the mortal enemy of restless hearts, the mortal enemy of ambitious minds, shrouded in the thickness of its gloom during the remainder of the night the future King of France, who lay there sheltered beneath his stolen crown. Toward the morning a shadow, rather than a body, glided into the royal chamber; Philippe expected his approach, and neither expressed nor exhibited any surprise.

"Well, Monsieur d'Herblay?" he said.

"Well, sire, all is done."

"How?"

"Exactly as we expected."

"Did he resist?"

"Terribly; tears and entreaties."

"And then?"

"A perfect stupor."

"But at last?"

"Oh, at last, a complete victory, and absolute silence."

"Did the governor of the Bastile suspect anything?"

"Nothing."

"The resemblance, however——"

"That was the cause of the success."

"But the prisoner cannot fail to explain himself. Think well of that. I have, myself, been able to do that, on a former occasion."

"I have already provided for everything. In a few days, sooner, if necessary, we will take the captive out of his prison, and will send him out of the country, to a place of exile so remote——"

"People can return from their exile, Monsieur d'Herblay."

"To a place of exile so distant, I was going to say, that human strength and the duration of human life would not be enough for his return."

And once more a cold look of intelligence passed between Aramis and the young king.

"And Monsieur du Vallon?" asked Philippe, in order to change the conversation.

"He will be presented to you to-day, and confidentially will congratulate you on the danger which that conspirator has made you run."

"What is to be done with him?"

"With Monsieur du Vallon?"

"Yes; confer a dukedom on him, I suppose?"

"A dukedom," replied Aramis, smiling in a significant manner.

"Why do you laugh, Monsieur d'Herblay?"

"I laugh at the extreme caution of your idea."

"Cautious—why so?"

"Your majesty is doubtless afraid that poor Porthos may probably become a troublesome witness, and you wish to get rid of him."

"What! in making him a duke?"

"Certainly; you would assuredly kill him, for he would die from joy, and the secret would die with him."

"Good heavens!"

"Yes," said Aramis phlegmatically; "I should lose a very good friend."

At this moment, and in the middle of this idle conversation, under the light tone of which the two conspirators concealed their joy and pride at their mutual success, Aramis heard something which made him prick up his ears.

"What is that?" said Philippe.

"The dawn, sire."

"Well?"

"Well, before you retired to bed last night, you probably decided to do something this morning at the break of day?"

"Yes, I told my captain of the musketeers," replied the young man hurriedly, "that I should expect him."

"If you told him that he will certainly be here, for he is a most punctual man."

"I hear a step in the vestibule."

"It must be he."

"Come, let us begin the attack," said the young king resolutely.

"Be cautious, for Heaven's sake; to begin the attack, and with D'Artagnan, would be madness. D'Artagnan knows nothing, he has seen nothing; he is a hundred miles from suspecting our mystery in the slightest degree, but if he comes into this room the first this morning, he will be sure to detect something which has taken place, and which he would think his business to occupy himself about. Before we allow D'Artagnan to penetrate into this room, we must air the room thoroughly, or introduce so many people into it that the keenest scent in the whole kingdom may be deceived by the traces of twenty different persons."

"But how can I send him away, since I have given him a rendezvous?" observed the prince, impatient to measure swords with so redoubtable an antagonist.

"I will take care of that," replied the bishop; "and in order to begin, I am going to strike a blow which will completely stupefy our man."

"He, too, is striking a blow, for I hear him at the door," added the prince hurriedly.

And, in fact, a knock at the door was heard at that moment. Aramis was not mistaken; for it was indeed D'Artagnan who adopted that mode of announcing himself.

We have seen how he passed the night in philosophizing with M. Fouquet; but the musketeer was very wearied even of feigning to fall asleep, and as soon as the dawn illumined with its pale-blue light the sumptuous cornices of the surintendant's room D'Artagnan rose from his armchair, arranged his sword, brushed his coat and hat with his sleeve, like a private soldier getting ready for inspection.

"Are you going out?" said Fouquet.

"Yes, monseigneur. And you?"

"No; I shall remain."

"You give me your word?"

"Certainly."

"Very good. Besides, my only reason for going out is to try and get that reply—you know what I mean?"

"That sentence, you mean——"

"Stay, I have something of the old Roman in me. This morning, when I got up, I remarked that my sword had not caught in one of the *aiguilettes,* and that my shoulder-belt had slipped quite off. That is an infallible sign."

"Of prosperity?"

"Yes, be sure of it; for every time that that confounded belt of mine stuck fast to my back, it always signified a punishment from Monsieur de Tréville, or a refusal of money by Monsieur de Mazarin. Every time my sword hung fast to my shoulder-belt, it always predicted some disagreeable commission or another for me to execute, and I have had showers of them all my life through. Every time, too, my sword danced about in its sheath, a duel, fortunate in its result, was sure to follow; whenever it dangled about the calves of my legs, it was a slight wound; every time it fell completely out of the scabbard, I was booked, and made up my mind that I should have to remain on the field of battle, with two or three months under the surgeon's care into the bargain."

"I never knew your sword kept you so well informed," said Fouquet, with a faint smile, which showed how he was struggling against his own weaknesses. "Is your sword bewitched, or under the influence of some charm?"

"Why, you must know that my sword may almost be regarded as part of my own body. I have heard that certain men seem to have warnings given them by feeling something the matter with their legs, or by a throbbing of their temples. With me it is my sword that warns me. Well, it told me of nothing this morning. But, stay a moment—look here, it has just fallen of its own accord into the last hole of the belt. Do you know what that is a warning of?"

"No."

"Well, that tells me of an arrest that will have to be made this very day."

"Well," said the surintendant, more astonished than annoyed by this frankness, "if there is nothing disagreeable predicted to you by your sword, I am to conclude that it is not disagreeable for you to arrest me."

"You—arrest you?"

"Of course. The warning——"

"Does not concern you, since you have been arrested ever since yesterday. It is not you I shall have to arrest, be assured of that. That is the reason why I am delighted, and also the reason why I said that my day will be a happy one."

And with these words, pronounced with the most affectionate graciousness of manner, the captain took leave of Fouquet in order to wait upon the king. He was on the point of leaving the room, when Fouquet said to him:

"One last mark of your kindness."

"What is it, monseigneur?"

"Monsieur d'Herblay; let me see Monsieur d'Herblay."

"I am going to try and get him to come to you."

D'Artagnan did not think himself so good a prophet. It was written that the day would pass away and realize all the predictions that had been made in the morning. He had accordingly knocked, as we have seen, at the king's door. The door opened. The captain thought that it was the king who had just opened it himself, and this supposition was not altogether inadmissible, considering the state of agitation in which he had left Louis XIV. the previous evening; but instead of his royal master, whom he was on the point of saluting with the greatest respect, he perceived the long, calm features of Aramis. So extreme was his surprise that he could hardly refrain from uttering a loud exclamation.

"Aramis!" he said.

"Good-morning, dear D'Artagnan," replied the prelate coldly.

"You here!" stammered out the musketeer.

"His majesty desires you to report that he is still sleeping after having been greatly fatigued during the whole night."

"Ah!" said D'Artagnan, who could not understand how the bishop of Vannes, who had been so indifferent a favorite the previous evening, had become, in half a dozen hours, the largest mushroom of fortune which had ever sprung up in a sovereign's bedroom. In fact, to transmit the orders of the king even to the mere threshold of that monarch's room, to serve as an intermediary of Louis XIV., so as to be able to give a single order in his name at a couple of paces from him, he must be greater than Richelieu had ever been to Louis XIII. D'Artagnan's expressive eye, half-opened lips, his curling mustache, said as much indeed in the plainest language to the chief favorite, who remained calm and perfectly unmoved.

"Moreover," continued the bishop, "you will be good enough, Monsieur le Capitaine des Mousquetaires, to allow those only to pass into the king's room this morning who have special permission. His majesty does not wish to be disturbed just yet."

"But," objected D'Artagnan, almost on the point of refusing to obey this order, and particularly of giving unrestrained passage to the suspicions which the king's silence had aroused—

"but, Monsieur l'Evêque, his majesty gave me a rendezvo
for this morning."

"Later, later," said the king's voice, from the bottom of t
alcove—a voice which made a cold shudder pass through t
musketeer's veins. He bowed, amazed, confused, and stupefi
by the smile with which Aramis seemed to overwhelm him,
soon as those words had been pronounced.

"And then," continued the bishop, "as an answer to what y
were coming to ask the king, my dear D'Artagnan, here is
order of his majesty, which you will be good enough to atten
to forthwith, for it concerns Monsieur Fouquet."

D'Artagnan took the order which was held out to him.

"To be set at liberty!" he murmured. "Ah!" and he utter
a second "Ah!" still more full of intelligence than the forme
for this order explained Aramis' presence with the king, ar
that Aramis, in order to have obtained Fouquet's pardon, mu
have made considerable progress in the royal favor, and th
this favor explained, in its tenor, the hardly conceivable assu
ance with which M. d'Herblay issued the orders in the king
name. For D'Artagnan it was quite sufficient to have unde
stood something in order to understand everything. He bow
and withdrew a couple of steps, as if he were about to leave.

"I am going with you," said the bishop.

"Where to?"

"To Monsieur Fouquet; I wish to be a witness of his d
light."

"Ah! Aramis, how you puzzled me just now!" said D'A
tagnan again.

"But you understand now, I suppose?"

"Of course I understand," he said aloud; but then adde
in a low tone, to himself, almost hissing the words between h
teeth, "No, no, I do not understand yet. But it is all the sam
for here is the order for it." And then he added "I will lead t
way, monseigneur;" and he conducted Aramis to Fouquet
apartments.

Chapter 21 — THE KING'S FRIEND

Fouquet was waiting with anxiety; he had already sent aw
many of his servants and his friends, who, anticipating the usu

hour of his ordinary receptions, had called at his door to inquire after him. Preserving the utmost silence respecting the danger which hung suspended over his head, he only asked them, as he did every one indeed who came to the door, where Aramis was. When he saw D'Artagnan return, and when he perceived the bishop of Vannes behind him, he could hardly restrain his delight; it was fully equal to his previous uneasiness. The mere sight of Aramis was a complete compensation to the surintendant for the unhappiness he had undergone in being arrested. The prelate was silent and grave; D'Artagnan completely bewildered by such an accumulation of events.

"Well, captain, so you have brought Monsieur d'Herblay to me?"

"And something better still, monseigneur."

"What is that?"

"Liberty."

"I am free?"

"Yes, by the king's order."

Fouquet resumed his usual serenity, that he might interrogate Aramis with his look.

"Oh, yes, you can thank Monsieur l'Evêque de Vannes," pursued D'Artagnan, "for it is indeed to him that you owe the change that has taken place in the king."

"Oh!" said Fouquet, more humiliated at the service than grateful at its success.

"But you," continued D'Artagnan, addressing Aramis—"you, who have become Monsieur Fouquet's protector and patron, can you not do something for me?"

"Anything you like, my friend," replied the bishop, in a calm voice.

"One thing only, then, and I shall be perfectly satisfied. How have you managed to become the favorite of the king, you, who have never spoken to him more than twice in your life?"

"From a friend such as you are," said Aramis, "I cannot conceal anything."

"Ah! very good; tell me, then."

"Very well. You think that I have seen the king only twice, while the fact is I have seen him more than a hundred times; only we have kept it very secret, that is all."

And without trying to remove the color which at this revelation made D'Artagnan's face flush scarlet, Aramis turned toward M. Fouquet, who was as much surprised as the musketeer.

"Monseigneur," he resumed, "the king desires me to inform

you that he is more than ever your friend, and that your beau
tiful *fête,* so generously offered by you on his behalf, h
touched him to the very heart."

And thereupon he saluted M. Fouquet with so much reve
ence of manner that the latter, incapable of understanding
man whose diplomacy was of so prodigious a character, r
mained incapable of uttering a single syllable, and equally in
capable of thought or movement. D'Artagnan fancied he pe
ceived that these two men had something to say to each othe
and he was about to yield to that feeling of instinctive polit
ness which in such a case hurries a man toward the door, whe
he feels his presence is an inconvenience for others; but b
eager curiosity, spurred on by so many mysteries, counsele
him to remain.

Aramis thereupon turned toward him and said, in a qui
tone:

"You will not forget, my friend, the king's order respectir
those whom he intends to receive this morning on rising."

These words were clear enough, and the musketeer unde
stood them; he therefore bowed to Fouquet, and then to Ar
mis—to the latter with a slight admixture of ironical respect—
and disappeared.

No sooner had he left than Fouquet, whose impatience ha
hardly been able to wait for that moment, darted toward th
door to close it, and then, returning to the bishop, he said:

"My dear D'Herblay, I think it now high time you shoul
explain to me what has passed, for in plain and honest trut
I do not understand anything."

"We will explain all that to you," said Aramis, sitting dow
and making Fouquet sit down also. "Where shall I begin?"

"With this, first of all. Why does the king set me at liberty?

"You ought rather to ask me what was his reason for havir
you arrested."

"Since my arrest I have had time to think over it, and m
idea is that it arises out of some slight feeling of jealousy. M
fête put Monsieur Colbert out of temper, and Monsieur Co
bert discovered some cause of complaint against me; Bell
Isle, for instance."

"No; there is no question at all just now of Belle-Isle."

"What is it, then?"

"Do you remember those receipts for thirteen millio
which Monsieur de Mazarin contrived to get stolen from you

"Yes, of course."

"Well, you are already pronounced to be a public robber."

"Good heavens!"

"Oh, that is not all. Do you also remember that letter you wrote to La Valliere?"

"Alas! yes."

"And that proclaims you a traitor and suborner."

"Why should he have pardoned me, then?"

"We have not yet arrived at that part of our argument. I wish you to be quite convinced of the fact itself. Observe this well: the king knows you to be guilty of an appropriation of public funds. Oh, of course *I* know that you have done nothing of the kind; but, at all events, the king has not seen the receipts, and he cannot do otherwise than believe you criminal."

"I beg your pardon, I do not see——"

"You will see presently, though. The king, moreover, having read your love letter to La Valliere, and the offers you there made her, cannot retain any doubt of your intentions with regard to that young lady; you will admit that, I suppose?"

"Certainly. But conclude."

"In a few words. The king is, therefore, a powerful, implacable, and eternal enemy for you."

"Agreed. But am I, then, so powerful that he has not dared to sacrifice me, notwithstanding his hatred, with all the means which my weakness, or my misfortunes, may have given him as a hold upon me?"

"It is clear, beyond all doubt," pursued Aramis coldly, "that the king has quarreled irreconcilably with you."

"But, since he absolves me——"

"Do you believe it likely?" asked the bishop, with a searching look.

"Without believing in his sincerity of heart, I believe in the truth of the fact."

Aramis slightly shrugged his shoulders.

"But why, then, should Louis XIV. have commissioned you to tell me what you have just stated?"

"The king charged me with nothing for you."

"With nothing!" said the surintendant, stupefied. "But that order, then——"

"Oh, yes! You are quite right. There is an order, certainly;" and these words were pronounced by Aramis in so strange a tone that Fouquet could not resist starting.

"You are concealing something from me, I see. What is it?"

Aramis softly rubbed his white fingers over his chin, but said nothing.

"Does the king exile me?"

"Do not act as if you were playing at the game children play at when they have to try and guess where a thing has been hidden, and are informed by a bell being rung when they are approaching near to it, or going away from it."

"Speak, then."

"Guess."

"You alarm me!"

"Bah! that is because you have not guessed, then."

"What did the king say to you? In the name of our friendship, do not deceive me."

"The king has not said a word to me."

"You are killing me with impatience, D'Herblay. Am I still surintendant?"

"As long as you like."

"But what extraordinary empire have you so suddenly acquired over his majesty's mind?"

"Ah! that is it."

"You make him do as you like."

"I believe so."

"It is hardly credible."

"So any one would say."

"D'Herblay, by our alliance, by our friendship, by everything you hold dearest in the world, speak openly, I implore you. By what means have you succeeded in overcoming Louis XIV.'s prejudices, for he did not like you, I know?"

"The king will like me *now*," said Aramis, laying stress upon the last word.

"You have something particular, then, between you?"

"Yes."

"A secret, perhaps?"

"Yes, a secret."

"A secret of such a nature as to change his majesty's interests?"

"You are indeed a man of superior intelligence, monseigneur, and have made a very accurate guess. I have, in fact, discovered a secret, of a nature to change the interests of the King of France."

"Ah!" said Fouquet, with the reserve of a man who does not wish to ask any questions.

"And you shall judge of it yourself," pursued Aramis; "and you shall tell me if I am mistaken with regard to the importance of this secret."

"I am listening, since you are good enough to unbosom yourself to me; only do not forget that I have asked you nothing which may be indiscreet in you to communicate."

Aramis seemed, for a moment, as if he were collecting himself.

"Do not speak," said Fouquet; "there is still time enough."

"Do you remember," said the bishop, casting down his eyes, "the birth of Louis XIV.?"

"As if it were yesterday."

"Have you ever heard anything particular respecting his birth?"

"Nothing, except that the king was not really the son of Louis XIII."

"That does not matter to us, or the kingdom either; he is the son of his father, says the French law, whose father is recognized by the law."

"True; but it is a grave matter, when the quality of races is called into question."

"A mere secondary question, after all. So that, in fact, you have never learned or heard anything in that particular?"

"Nothing."

"That is where my secret begins. The queen, you must know, instead of being delivered of one son, was delivered of two children."

Fouquet looked up suddenly, as he replied:

"And the second is dead?"

"You will see. These twins seemed likely to be regarded as the pride of their mother and the hope of France; but the weak nature of the king, his superstitious feelings, made him apprehend a series of conflicts between two children whose rights were equal; so he put out of the way—he suppressed—one of the twins."

"Suppressed, do you say?"

"Be patient. Both the children grew up; the one on the throne, whose minister you are—the other, who is my friend, in gloom and isolation."

"Good heavens! What are you saying, Monsieur d'Herblay? And what is this poor prince doing?"

"Ask me, rather, what he has done."

"Yes, yes."

"He was brought up in the country, and then thrown into a fortress which goes by the name of the Bastile."

"Is it possible?" cried the surintendant, clasping his hands.

"The one was the most fortunate of men; the other the most unhappy and most miserable of all living beings."

"Does his mother not know this?"

"Anne of Austria knows it all."

"And the king?"

"Knows absolutely nothing."

"So much the better," said Fouquet.

This remark seemed to make a great impression on Aramis; he looked at Fouquet with the most anxious expression of countenance.

"I beg your pardon; I interrupted you," said Fouquet.

"I was saying," resumed Aramis, "that this poor prince was the unhappiest of human beings, when Heaven, whose thoughts are over all His creatures, undertook to come to his assistance."

"Oh! in what way—tell me."

"You will see. The reigning king—I say the reigning king—you can guess very well why?"

"No. Why?"

"Because both of them, being legitimately entitled from their birth, ought both to have been kings. Is not that your opinion?"

"It is, certainly."

"Unreservedly so?"

"Most unreservedly; twins are one person in two bodies."

"I am pleased that a legist of your learning and authority should have pronounced such an opinion. It is agreed, then, that both of them possessed the same rights, is it not?"

"Incontestably so; but, gracious heavens! what an extraordinary circumstance."

"We are not at the end of it yet. Patience."

"Oh! I shall find 'patience' enough."

"Heaven wished to raise up for that oppressed child an avenger, or a supporter, or vindicator, if you prefer it. It happened that the reigning king, the usurper—you are quite of my opinion, I believe, that it is an act of usurpation quietly to enjoy, and selfish to assume the right over an inheritance to which a man has only the right of one half?"

"Yes, usurpation is the word."

"In that case, I continue. It was Heaven's will that the usurper should possess, in the person of his first minister, a man of great talent, of large and generous nature."

"Well, well," said Fouquet, "I understand you; you have relied upon me to repair the wrong which has been done to this unhappy brother of Louis XIV. You have thought well; I will help you. I thank you, D'Herblay, I thank you."

"Oh, no, it is not that at all; you have not allowed me to finish," said Aramis, perfectly unmoved.

"I will not say another word, then."

"Monsieur Fouquet, I was observing, the minister of the reigning sovereign was suddenly taken into the greatest aversion, and menaced with the ruin of his fortune, with loss of liberty, with loss of life even, by intrigue and personal hatred, to which the king gave too readily an attentive ear. But Heaven permits (still, however, out of consideration for the unhappy prince who had been sacrificed) that Monsieur Fouquet should in his turn have a devoted friend who knew this state secret, and felt that he possessed strength and courage enough to divulge this secret, after having had the strength to carry it locked up in his own heart for twenty years."

"Do not go on any further," said Fouquet, full of generous feelings. "I understand you, and can guess everything now. You went to see the king when the intelligence of my arrest reached you; you implored him; he refused to listen to you; then you threatened him with that secret, threatened to reveal it, and Louis XIV., alarmed at the risk of its betrayal, granted to the terror of your indiscretion what he refused to your generous intercession. I understand, I understand; you have the king in your power; I understand."

"You understand nothing as yet," replied Aramis, "and again you have interrupted me. And then, too, allow me to observe that you pay no attention to logical reasoning, and seem to forget what you ought most to remember."

"What do you mean?"

"You know upon what I laid the greatest stress at the beginning of our conversation?"

"Yes; his majesty's hate, invincible hate for me; yes, but what feeling of hate could resist the threat of such a revelation?"

"Such a revelation, do you say? that is the very point where your logic fails you. What! do you suppose that if I had made such a revelation to the king, I should have been alive now?"

"It is not ten minutes ago since you were with the king?"

"That may be. He might not have had the time to get me killed outright, but he would have had the time to get me gagged and thrown into a dungeon. Come, come, show a little consistency in your reasoning, *mordieu!*"

And by the mere use of this word, which was so thoroughly his old musketeer's expression, forgotten by one who never

seemed to forget anything, Fouquet could not but understand
to what a pitch of exaltation the calm, impenetrable bishop of
Vannes had wrought himself. He shuddered at it.

"And then," replied the latter, after having mastered his
feelings, "should I be the man I really am, should I be the
true friend you regard me as, if I were to expose you, you
whom the king hates already bitterly enough, to a feeling still
more than ever to be dreaded in that young man? To have
robbed him is nothing; to have addressed the woman he loves
is not much; but to hold in your keeping both his crown and
his honor, why, he would rather pluck out your heart with his
own hands."

"You have not allowed him to penetrate your secret, then?"

"I would sooner, far sooner, have swallowed at one draught
all the poisons that Mithridates drank in twenty years, in order
to try and avoid death, than have betrayed my secret to the
king."

"What have you done, then?"

"Ah! now we are coming to the point, monseigneur. I think
I shall not fail to excite a little interest in you. You are listening, I hope."

"How can you ask me if I am listening? Go on."

Aramis walked softly all round the room, satisfied himself
that they were alone, and that all was silent, and then returned and placed himself close to the armchair in which Fouquet was seated, awaiting with the deepest anxiety the revelations he had to make.

"I forgot to tell you," resumed Aramis, addressing himself
to Fouquet, who listened to him with the most absorbed attention—"I forgot to mention a most remarkable circumstance respecting these twins, namely, that God had formed them so
startlingly, so miraculously, like each other that it would be
utterly impossible to distinguish the one from the other. Their
own mother would not be able to distinguish them."

"Is it possible?" exclaimed Fouquet.

"The same noble character in their features, the same carriage, the same stature, the same voice."

"But their thoughts, degree of intelligence, their knowledge of human life?"

"There is inequality there, I admit, monseigneur. Yes; for
the prisoner of the Bastile is, most incontestably, superior in
every way to his brother; and if, from his prison, this unhappy
victim were to pass to the throne, France would not, from the

earliest period of its history, perhaps, have had a master more powerful by his genius and true nobleness of character."

Fouquet buried his face in his hands, as if he were overwhelmed by the weight of this immense secret. Aramis approached him.

"There is a further inequality," he said, continuing his work of temptation, "an inequality which concerns yourself, monseigneur, between the twins, both sons of Louis XIII., namely, the last comer does not know Monsieur Colbert."

Fouquet raised his head immediately—his features were pale and distorted. The bolt had hit its mark—not his heart, but his mind and comprehension.

"I understand you," he said to Aramis; "you are proposing a conspiracy to me?"

"Something like it."

"One of those attempts which, as you said at the beginning of this conversation, alters the fate of empires?"

"And of the surintendant, too; yes, monseigneur."

"In a word, you propose that I should agree to the substitution of the son of Louis XIII. who is now a prisoner in the Bastile, for the son of Louis XIII. who is now at this moment asleep in the chamber of Morpheus?"

Aramis smiled with the sinister expression of the sinister thought which was passing through his brain.

"Exactly," he said.

"Have you thought," continued Fouquet, becoming animated with that strength of talent which in a few seconds originates and matures the conception of a plan, and with that largeness of view which foresees all its consequences, and embraces all its results at a glance—"have you thought that we must assemble the nobility, the clergy, and the third estate of the realm; that we shall have to depose the reigning sovereign, to disturb by so frightful a scandal the tomb of their dead father, to sacrifice the life, the honor of a woman, Anne of Austria, the life and peace of mind and heart of another woman, Maria Theresa; and suppose that all were done, if we were to succeed in doing it——"

"I do not understand you," continued Aramis coldly. "There is not a single word of the slightest use in what you have just said."

"What!" said the surintendant, surprised, "a man like you refuse to view the practical bearings of the case! Do you confine yourself to the childish delight of a political illusion, and neglect the chances of its being carried into execution; in other words, the reality itself, is it possible?"

"My friend," said Aramis, emphasizing the word with a kind of disdainful familiarity, "what does Heaven do in order to substitute one king for another?"

"Heaven!" exclaimed Fouquet—"Heaven gives directions to its agent, who seizes upon the doomed victim, hurries him away, and seats the triumphant rival on the empty throne. But you forget that this agent is called death. Oh! Monsieur d'Herblay, in Heaven's name, tell me if you have had the idea——"

"There is no question of that, monseigneur; you are going beyond the object in view. Who spoke of Louis XIV.'s death? who spoke of adopting the example which Heaven sets in following out the strict execution of its decrees? No, I wish you to understand that Heaven effects its purposes without confusion or disturbance, without exciting comment or remark, without difficulty or exertion; and that men inspired by Heaven succeed like Heaven itself in all their undertakings, in all they attempt, in all they do."

"What do you mean?"

"I mean, my *friend*," returned Aramis, with the same intonation on the word friend that he had applied to it the first time— "I mean that if there has been any confusion, scandal, and even effort in the substitution of the prisoner for the king, I defy you to prove it."

"What!" cried Fouquet, whiter than the handkerchief with which he wiped his temples, "what do you say?"

"Go to the king's apartment," continued Aramis tranquilly, "and you who know the mystery, I defy even you to perceive that the prisoner of the Bastile is lying in his brother's bed."

"But the king?" stammered Fouquet, seized with horror at the intelligence.

"What king?" said Aramis, in his gentlest tone, "the one who hates you, or the one who likes you?"

"The king—of yesterday."

"The king of yesterday! Be quite easy on that score; he has gone to take the place in the Bastile which his victim has occupied for such a long time past."

"Great God! And who took him there?"

"I."

"You?"

"Yes; and in the simplest way. I carried him away last night; and while he was descending into gloom, the other was ascending into light. I do not think there has been any disturbance created in any way. A flash of lightning without thunder never awakens any one."

Fouquet uttered a thick, smothered cry, as if he had been struck by some invisible blow, and clasping his head between his clinched hands, he murmured:

"You did that?"

"Cleverly enough, too. What do you think of it?"

"You dethroned the king? imprisoned him, too?"

"Yes, that has been done."

"And such an action has been committed here, at Vaux?"

"Yes, here, at Vaux, in the chamber of Morpheus. It would almost seem that it had been built in anticipation of such an act."

"And at what time did it occur?"

"Last night, between twelve and one o'clock."

Fouquet made a movement as if he were on the point of springing upon Aramis; he restrained himself.

"At Vaux, under my roof!" he said, in a half-strangled voice.

"I believe so; for it is still your house, and is likely to continue so, since Monsieur Colbert cannot rob you of it now."

"It was under my roof, then, monsieur, that you committed this crime?"

"This crime?" said Aramis, stupefied.

"This abominable crime!" pursued Fouquet, becoming more and more excited, "this crime more execrable than an assassination! this crime which dishonors my name forever, and entails upon me the horror of posterity!"

"You are not in your senses, monsieur," replied Aramis, in an irresolute tone of voice; "you are speaking too loudly; take care!"

"I will call out so loudly that the whole world shall hear me."

"Monsieur Fouquet, take care!"

Fouquet turned round toward the prelate, whom he looked at full in the face.

"You have dishonored me," he said, "in committing so foul an act of treason, so heinous a crime upon my guest, upon one who was peacefully reposing beneath my roof. Oh! woe, woe is me!"

"Woe to the man, rather, who, beneath your roof, meditated the ruin of your fortune, your life! Do you forget that?"

"He was my guest, my sovereign."

Aramis rose, his eyes literally bloodshot, his mouth trembling convulsively.

"Have I a man out of his senses to deal with?" he said.

"You have an honorable man to deal with."

"You are mad."

"A man who will prevent you consummating your crime."

"You are mad, I say."

"A man who would sooner, oh! far sooner, die; who would kill you even, rather than allow you to complete his dishonor."

And Fouquet snatched up his sword, which D'Artagnan had placed at the head of his bed, and clinched it resolutely in his hand. Aramis frowned, and thrust his hand into his breast as if in search of a weapon. This movement did not escape Fouquet, who, full of nobleness and pride in his magnanimity, threw his sword to a distance from him, and approached Aramis so close as to touch his shoulder with his disarmed hand.

"Monsieur," he said, "I would sooner die here on the spot than survive this terrible disgrace; and if you have any pity left for me, I entreat you to take my life."

Aramis remained silent and motionless.

"You do not reply?" said Fouquet.

Aramis raised his head gently, and a glimmer of hope might be seen once more to animate his eyes.

"Reflect, monseigneur," he said, "upon everything we have to expect. As the matter now stands, the king is still alive, and his imprisonment saves your life."

"Yes," replied Fouquet; "you may have been acting on my behalf, but I will not, do not accept your services. But, first of all, I do not wish your ruin. You will leave this house."

Aramis stifled the exclamation which almost escaped his broken heart.

"I am hospitable toward all who are dwellers beneath my roof," continued Fouquet, with an air of inexpressible majesty; "you will not be more fatally lost than he whose ruin you have consummated."

"You will be so," said Aramis, in a hoarse, prophetic voice, "you will be so, believe me."

"I accept the augury, Monsieur d'Herblay; but nothing shall prevent me, nothing shall stop me. You will leave Vaux—you must leave France; I give you four hours to place yourself out of the king's reach."

"Four hours?" said Aramis scornfully and incredulously.

"Upon the word of Fouquet, no one shall follow you before the expiration of that time. You will, therefore, have four hours' advance of those whom the king may wish to dispatch after you."

"Four hours!" repeated Aramis, in a thick, smothered voice.

"It is more than you will need to get on board a vessel and flee to Belle-Isle, which I give you as a place of refuge."

"Ah!" murmured Aramis.

"Belle-Isle is as much mine for you as Vaux is mine for the king. Go, D'Herblay, go! as long as I live, not a hair of your head shall be injured."

"Thank you," said Aramis, with a cold irony of manner.

"Go at once, then, and give me your hand, before we both hasten away; you to save your life, I to save my honor."

Aramis withdrew from his breast the hand he had concealed there; it was stained with his blood. He had dug his nails into his flesh, as if in punishment for having nursed so many projects, more vain, insensate, and fleeting than the life of man himself. Fouquet was horror-stricken, and then his heart smote him with pity. He threw open his arms as if to embrace him.

"I had no arms," murmured Aramis, as wild and terrible in his wrath as the shade of Dido.

And then, without touching Fouquet's hand, he turned his head aside, and stepped back a pace or two. His last word was an imprecation, his last gesture a curse, which his blood-stained hand seemed to invoke, as it sprinkled on Fouquet's face a few drops of blood which flowed from his breast. And both of them darted out of the room by the secret staircase which led down to the inner courtyard. Fouquet ordered his best horses, while Aramis paused at the foot of the staircase which led to Porthos' apartment. He reflected profoundly and for some time, while Fouquet's carriage left the stone-paved courtyard at full gallop.

"Shall I go alone?" said Aramis to himself, "or warn the prince? Oh, fury! Warn the prince, and then—do what? Take him with me? To carry this accusing witness about with me everywhere? War, too, would follow—civil war, implacable in its nature! And without any resource save myself—it is impossible! What could he do without me? Oh! without me he would be utterly destroyed. Yet who knows—let destiny be fulfilled—condemned he was, let him remain so, then. Good or evil Spirit—gloomy and scornful Power, whom men call the Genius of man, thou art a power more restlessly uncertain, more baselessly useless, than the wild wind in the mountains; Chance thou term'st thyself, but thou art nothing; thou inflamest everything with thy breath, crumblest mountains at thy approach, and suddenly art thyself destroyed at the presence of the cross of dead wood, behind which stands another power invisible like thyself—whom thou deniest, perhaps, but whose avenging hand is on thee, and hurls thee in the dust, dishonored

and unnamed! Lost!—I am lost! What can be done? Flee to
Belle-Isle? Yes, and leave Porthos behind me, to talk and
relate the whole affair to every one! Porthos, too, who will
have to suffer for what he has done. I will not let poor Porthos
suffer. He seems like one of the members of my own frame,
and his grief or misfortune would be mine as well. Porthos shall
leave with me, and shall follow my destiny. It must be so."

And Aramis, apprehensive of meeting any one to whom his
hurried movements might appear suspicious, ascended the
staircase without being perceived. Porthos, so recently returned
from Paris, was already in a profound sleep; his huge body
forgot its fatigue, as his mind forgot its thoughts. Aramis entered, light as a shadow, and placed his nervous grasp on the
giant's shoulder.

"Come, Porthos," he cried, "come!"

Porthos obeyed, rose from his bed, opened his eyes, even
before his intelligence seemed to be aroused.

"We are going off," said Aramis.

"Ah!" returned Porthos.

"We shall go mounted, and faster than we have ever gone
in our lives!"

"Ah!" repeated Porthos.

"Dress yourself, my friend."

And he helped the giant to dress himself, and thrust his gold
and diamonds into his pocket. While he was thus engaged, a
slight noise attracted his attention, and on looking up, he saw
D'Artagnan watching them through the half-opened door.
Aramis started.

"What the devil are you doing there in such an agitated
manner?" said the musketeer.

"Hush!" said Porthos.

"We are going off on a mission of great importance," added
the bishop.

"You are very fortunate," said the musketeer.

"Oh, dear me!" said Porthos, "I feel so wearied; I would far
sooner have been fast asleep. But the service of the king——"

"Have you seen Monsieur Fouquet?" said Aramis to D'Artagnan.

"Yes, this very minute, in a carriage."

"What did he say to you?"

" 'Adieu,' nothing more."

"Was that all?"

"What else do you think he could say? Am I worth anything
now, since you have all got into such high favor?"

"Listen," said Aramis, embracing the musketeer. "Your good times are returning again. You will have no occasion to be jealous of any one."

"Ah, bah!"

"I predict that something will happen to you to-day which will increase your importance more than ever."

"Really?"

"You know that I know all the news?"

"Oh, yes!"

"Come, Porthos, are you ready? Let us go."

"I am quite ready, Aramis."

"Let us embrace D'Artagnan first."

"Most certainly."

"But the horses?"

"Oh! there is no want of them here. Will you have mine?"

"No; Porthos has his own stud. So, adieu, adieu!"

The two fugitives mounted their horses beneath the captain of the musketeer's eyes, who held Porthos' stirrup for him, and gazed after them until they were out of sight.

"On any other occasion," thought the Gascon, "I should say that those gentlemen were making their escape; but in these days politics seem so changed that that is what is termed going on a mission. I have no objection; let me attend to my own affairs, that is quite enough;" and he philosophically entered his apartments.

Chapter 22 — SHOWING HOW THE COUNTERSIGN WAS RESPECTED AT THE BASTILE

Fouquet tore along as fast as his horses could drag him. On his way he trembled with horror at the idea of what had just been revealed to him.

"What must have been," he thought, "the youth of those extraordinary men, who, even as age is stealing fast upon them, still are able to conceive such plans, and can carry them out without flinching?"

At one moment he could not resist the idea that all that Aramis had just been recounting to him was nothing more than a dream, and whether the fable itself was not the snare; so that when Fouquet arrived at the Bastile, he might possibly find an order of arrest, which would send him to join the de-

throned king. Strongly impressed with this idea, he gave certain
sealed orders on his route, while fresh horses were being har
nessed to his carriage. These orders were addressed to M. d'Ar
tagnan and to certain others whose fidelity to the king was far
above suspicion.

"In this way," said Fouquet to himself, "prisoner or not, I
shall have performed the duty which I owe to my honor. The
orders will not reach them until after my return, if I should
return free, and, consequently they will not have been un
sealed. I shall take them back again. If I am delayed, it will
be because some misfortune will have befallen me; and in that
case assistance will be sent for me as well as for the king."

Prepared in this manner, the surintendant arrived at the
Bastile; he had traveled at the rate of five leagues and a half
the hour. Every circumstance of delay which Aramis had es
caped in his visit to the Bastile befell Fouquet. It was useless
his giving his name, equally useless his being recognized; he
could not succeed in obtaining an entrance. By dint of entreat
ies, threats, commands, he succeeded in inducing a sentine
to speak to one of the subalterns, who went and told the major
As for the governor, they did not even dare to disturb him
Fouquet sat in his carriage, at the outer gate of the fortress
chafing with rage and impatience, awaiting the return of the
officers, who at last reappeared with a sufficiently sulky air.

"Well," said Fouquet impatiently, "what did the major say?"

"Well, monsieur," replied the soldier, "the major laughed
in my face. He told me that Monsieur Fouquet was at Vaux
and that even were he at Paris, Monsieur Fouquet would no
get up at so early an hour as the present."

"*Mordieu!* you are a perfect set of fools," cried the minis
ter, darting out of the carriage; and before the subaltern had
had time to shut the gate, Fouquet sprang through it and ran
forward in spite of the soldier, who cried out for assistance
Fouquet gained ground, regardless of the cries of the man, who
however, having at last come up with Fouquet, called out to the
sentinel of the second gate:

"Look out! look out, sentinel!"

The man crossed his pike before the minister; but the lat
ter, robust and active, and hurried away, too, by his passion
wrested the pike from the soldier and struck him a violent
blow on the shoulder with it. The subaltern, who approached
too closely, received his part of the blows as well. Both of them
uttered loud and furious cries, at the sound of which the whole
of the first body of the advanced guard poured out of the guard

house. Among them there was one, however, who recognized the surintendant, and who called out: "Monseigneur! ah, monseigneur! Stop, stop, you fellows-"

And he effectually checked the soldiers, who were on the point of revenging their companions. Fouquet desired them to open the gate, but they refused to do so without the countersign; he desired them to inform the governor of his presence, but the latter had already heard the disturbance at the gate. He ran forward, followed by his major, and accompanied by a picket of twenty men, persuaded that an attack was being made on the Bastile. Baisemeaux also recognized Fouquet immediately, and dropped his sword, which he had held brandishing about in his hand.

"Ah, monseigneur!" he stammered, "how can I excuse——"

"Monsieur," said the surintendant, flushed with anger, and heated by his exertions, "I congratulate you. Your watch and ward are admirably kept."

Baisemeaux turned pale, thinking that this remark was said ironically, and portended a furious burst of anger. But Fouquet had recovered his breath, and, beckoning the sentinel and the subaltern, who were rubbing their shoulders, toward him, he said: "There are twenty pistoles for the sentinel, and fifty for the officer. Pray receive my compliments, gentlemen. I will not fail to speak to his majesty about you. And now, Monsieur Baisemeaux, a word with you."

And he followed the governor to his official residence, accompanied by a murmur of general satisfaction. Baisemeaux was already trembling with shame and uneasiness. Aramis' early visit, from that moment, seemed to possess consequences which a functionary such as he (Baisemeaux) was, was perfectly justified in apprehending. It was quite another thing, however, when Fouquet, in a sharp tone of voice, and with an imperious look, said:

"You have seen Monsieur d'Herblay this morning?"

"Yes, monseigneur."

"And are you not horrified at the crime of which you have made yourself an accomplice?"

"Well," thought Baisemeaux, "good so far," and then he added, aloud: "But what crime, monseigneur, do you allude to?"

"That for which you can be quartered alive, monsieur—do not forget that! But this is not a time to show anger. Conduct me immediately to the prisoner."

"To what prisoner?" said Baisemeaux tremblingly.

"You pretend to be ignorant? Very good—it is the best thin
for you, perhaps, to do; for if, in fact, you were to admit you
participation in it, it would be all over with you. I wish, there
fore, to seem to believe in your assumption of ignorance."

"I entreat you, monseigneur——"

"That will do. Lead me to the prisoner."

"To Marchiali?"

"Who is Marchiali?"

"The prisoner who was brought back this morning by Mon
sieur d'Herblay."

"He is called Marchiali?" said the surintendant, his convic
tion somewhat shaken by Baisemeaux's cool manner.

"Yes, monseigneur; that is the name under which he wa
inscribed here."

Fouquet looked steadily at Baisemeaux, as if he would rea
his very heart, and perceived, with that clear-sightedness whic
men possess who are accustomed to the exercise of power, tha
the man was speaking with the most perfect sincerity. Besides, i
observing his face for a few moments, he could not believe tha
Aramis would have chosen such a confidant.

"It is the prisoner," said the surintendant to him, "whom
Monsieur d'Herblay carried away the day before yesterday?

"Yes, monseigneur."

"And whom he brought back this morning?" added Fouque
quickly; for he understood immediately the mechanism of Ara
mis' plan.

"Precisely, monseigneur."

"And his name is Marchiali, you say?"

"Yes, Marchiali."

"If monseigneur has come here to remove him, so much th
better, for I was going to write about him."

"What has he done, then?"

"Ever since this morning he has annoyed me extremely. H
has had such terrible fits of passion as almost to make me b
lieve that he would bring the Bastile itself down about our ears

"I will soon relieve you of his presence," said Fouquet.

"Ah, so much the better."

"Conduct me to his prison."

"Will monseigneur give me the order?"

"What order?"

"An order from the king."

"Wait until I sign you one."

"That will not be sufficient, monseigneur. I must have an o
der from the king."

Fouquet assumed an irritated expression.

"As you are so scrupulous," he said, "with regard to allowing prisoners to leave, show me the order by which this one was set at liberty."

Baisemeaux showed him the order to release Seldon.

"Very good," said Fouquet; "but Seldon is not Marchiali."

"But Marchiali is not at liberty, monseigneur; he is here."

"But you said that Monsieur d'Herblay carried him away and brought him back again."

"I did not say so."

"So surely did you say it that I almost seem to hear it now."

"It was a slip of my tongue, then, monseigneur."

"Take care, Monsieur de Baisemeaux, take care!"

"I have nothing to fear, monseigneur; I am acting according to strict regulation."

"Do you dare to say so?"

"I would say so in the presence of an apostle himself. Monsieur d'Herblay brought me an order to set Seldon at liberty; and Seldon is free."

"I tell you that Marchiali has left the Bastile."

"You must prove that, monseigneur."

"Let me see him."

"You, monseigneur, who govern this kingdom, know very well that no one can see any of the prisoners without an express order from the king."

"Monsieur d'Herblay has entered, however."

"That is to be proved, monseigneur."

"Monsieur de Baisemeaux, once more I warn you to pay particular attention to what you are saying."

"All the documents are there, monseigneur."

"Monsieur d'Herblay is overthrown."

"Overthrown?—Monsieur d'Herblay! Impossible!"

"You see that he has undoubtedly influenced you."

"No, monseigneur; what does, in fact, influence me is the king's service. I am doing my duty. Give me an order from him, and you shall enter."

"Stay, Monsieur le Gouverneur, I give you my word that if you allow me to see the prisoner, I will give you an order from the king at once."

"Give me it now, monseigneur."

"And that, if you refuse me, I will have you and all your officers arrested on the spot."

"Before you commit such an act of violence, monseigneur, you will reflect," said Baisemeaux, who had turned very pale, "that we will only obey an order signed by the king, and that it will be just as easy for you to obtain one to see Marchiali as to obtain one to do me so much injury; me, too, who am perfectly innocent."

"True, true!" cried Fouquet furiously; "perfectly true. Monsieur de Baisemeaux," he added, in a sonorous voice, drawing the unhappy governor toward him, "do you know why I am so anxious to speak to the prisoner?"

"No, monseigneur; and allow me to observe that you are terrifying me out of my senses; I am trembling all over, and feel as if I were going to faint."

"You will stand a better chance of fainting outright, Monsieur Baisemeaux, when I return here at the head of ten thousand men and thirty pieces of cannon."

"Good heavens, monseigneur, you are losing your senses!"

"When I have roused the whole population of Paris against you and your cruel towers, and have battered open the gates of this place, and hanged you up to the bars of that tower in the corner there."

"Monseigneur, monseigneur! for pity's sake!"

"I give you ten minutes to make up your mind," added Fouquet, in a calm voice. "I will sit down here, in this armchair, and wait for you; if in ten minutes' time you still persist, I leave this place, and you may think me as mad as you like; but you will see."

Baisemeaux stamped his foot on the ground, like a man in a state of despair, but he did not reply a single syllable; whereupon Fouquet seized a pen and ink, and wrote:

"Order for Monsieur le Prévot des Marchands to assemble the municipal guard and to march upon the Bastile for the king's service."

Baisemeaux shrugged his shoulders. Fouquet wrote:

"Order for the Duc de Bouillon and Monsieur le Prince de Condé to assume the command of the Swiss guards, of the King's guards, and to march upon the Bastile for the king's service.'

Baisemeaux reflected. Fouquet still wrote:

"Order for every soldier, citizen, or gentleman to seize and apprehend, wherever he may be found, Le Chevalier d'Herblay Evêque de Vannes, and his accomplices, who are: 1st, Mon sieur de Baisemeaux, governor of the Bastile, suspected of the crimes of high treason and rebellion—"

"Stop, monseigneur!" cried Baisemeaux; "I do not understand a single thing of the whole matter; but so many misfortunes, even were it madness itself that had set them at work, might happen here in a couple of hours that the king, by whom I shall be judged, will see whether I have been wrong in withdrawing the countersign before so many imminent catastrophes. Come with me to the keep, monseigneur, you shall see Marchiali.'

Fouquet darted out of the room, followed by Baisemeaux, as he wiped the perspiration from his face.

"What a terrible morning!" he said, "what a disgrace!"

"Walk faster," replied Fouquet.

Baisemeaux made a sign to the jailer to precede them. He was afraid of his companion, which the latter could not fail to perceive.

"A truce to this child's play," he said roughly. "Let the man remain here, take the keys yourself, and show me the way. Not a single person, do you understand, must hear what is going to take place here."

"Ah!" said Baisemeaux, undecided.

"Again!" cried Fouquet. "Ah! say 'no' at once, and I will leave the Bastile and will myself carry my own dispatches."

Baisemeaux bowed his head, took the keys, and, unaccompanied, except by the minister, ascended the staircase. The higher they advanced up the spiral staircase, certain smothered murmurs became distinct cries and fearful imprecations.

"What is that?" asked Fouquet.

"That is your Marchiali," said the governor, "that is the way these madmen call out."

And he accompanied that reply with a glance more indicative of injurious allusions, as far as Fouquet was concerned, than of politeness. The latter trembled; he had just recognized in one cry more terrible than any that had preceded it, the king's voice. He paused on the staircase, snatching the bunch of keys from Baisemeaux, who thought this new madman was going to dash out his brains with one of them.

"Ah!" he cried, "Monsieur d'Herblay did not say a word about that."

"Give me the keys at once!" cried Fouquet, tearing them from his hand. "Which is the key of the door I am to open?"

"That one."

"A fearful cry, followed by a violent blow against the door, made the whole staircase resound with the echo.

"Leave this place," said Fouquet to Baisemeaux, in a threatening tone.

"I ask nothing better," murmured the latter. "There will be a couple of madmen face to face, and the one will kill the other, I am sure."

"Go!" repeated Fouquet. "If you place your foot on this staircase before I call you, remember that you shall take the place of the meanest prisoner in the Bastile."

"This job will kill me, I am sure it will," muttered Baisemeaux, as he withdrew with tottering steps.

The prisoner's cries became more and more terrible. When Fouquet had satisfied himself that Baisemeaux had reached the bottom of the staircase, he inserted the key in the first lock. It was then that he heard the hoarse, choking voice of the king, crying out, in a frenzy of rage, "Help! help! I am the king." The key of the second door was not the same as the first, and Fouquet was obliged to look for it on the bunch. The king, however, furious and almost mad with rage and passion, shouted at the top of his voice:

"It was Monsieur Fouquet who brought me here. Help me against Monsieur Fouquet! I am the king! Help the king against Monsieur Fouquet!"

These cries tore the minister's heart with mingled emotions. They were followed by a shower of terrible blows leveled against the door with a part of the broken chair with which the king had armed himself. Fouquet at last succeeded in finding the key. The king was almost exhausted; he could hardly articulate distinctly, as he shouted:

"Death to Fouquet! death to the traitor Fouquet!"

The door flew open.

Chapter 23 — THE KING'S GRATITUDE

The two men were on the point of darting toward each other when they suddenly and abruptly stopped, as a mutual recognition took place, and each uttered a cry of horror.

"Have you come to assassinate me, monsieur?" said the king when he recognized Fouquet.

"The king in this state!" murmured the minister.

Nothing could be more terrible, indeed, than the appearance of the young prince at the moment Fouquet had surprised him; his clothes were in tatters; his shirt, open and torn to rags, was stained with sweat and with the blood which streamed from his lacerated breast and arms. Haggard, ghastly pale, his hair in disheveled masses, Louis XIV. presented the most perfect picture of despair, hunger, and fear combined that could possibly be united in one figure. Fouquet was so touched, so acted and disturbed by it, that he ran toward him with his arms stretched out and his eyes filled with tears. Louis held up the massive piece of wood of which he had made such a furious use.

"Sire," said Fouquet, in a voice trembling with emotion, "do you not recognize the most faithful of your friends?"

"A friend—you!" repeated Louis, gnashing his teeth in a manner which betrayed his hate and desire for speedy vengeance.

"The most respectful of your servants," added Fouquet, throwing himself on his knees.

The king let his rude weapon fall from his grasp. Fouquet approached him, kissed his knees and took him in his arms with inconceivable tenderness.

"My king, my child," he said, "how you must have suffered!"

Louis, recalled to himself by the change of situation, looked at himself, and ashamed of the disordered state of his apparel, ashamed of his conduct, and ashamed of the air of pity and protection that was shown toward him, drew back. Fouquet did not understand this movement; he did not perceive that the king's feelings of pride would never forgive him for having been a witness of such an exhibition of weakness.

"Come, sire," he said, "you are free."

"Free?" repeated the king. "Oh! you set me at liberty, then, after having dared to lift up your hand against me!"

"You do not believe that!" exclaimed Fouquet indignantly; "you cannot believe me to be guilty of such an act."

And rapidly, warmly even, he related the whole particulars of the intrigue, the details of which are already known to the reader. While the recital continued Louis suffered the most horrible anguish of mind; and when it was finished the magnitude of the danger he had run struck him far more than the importance of the secret relative to his twin brother.

"Monsieur," he said suddenly, to Fouquet, "this double birth is a falsehood; it is impossible—you cannot have been the dupe of it."

"Sire!"

"It is impossible, I tell you, that the honor, the virtue of m
mother can be suspected. And my first minister has not yet don
justice on the criminals?"

"Reflect, sire, before you are hurried away by your anger,
replied Fouquet. "The birth of your brother—"

"I have only one brother—and this is *Monsieur.* You kno
it as well as myself. There is a plot, I tell you, beginning wit
the governor of the Bastile."

"Be careful, sire, for this man has been deceived as ever
one else has by the prince's likeness to yourself."

"Likeness? Absurd!"

"This Marchiali must be singularly like your majesty to b
able to deceive every one's eye," Fouquet persisted.

"Ridiculous!"

"Do not say so, sire; those who had prepared everything i
order to face and deceive your ministers, your mother, you
officers of state, the members of your family, must be quit
confident of the resemblance between you."

"But where are these persons, then?" murmured the kin

"At Vaux."

"At Vaux! and you suffer them to remain there?"

"My most pressing duty seemed to be your majesty's releas
I have accomplished that duty; and now, whatever your majest
may command shall be done. I await your orders."

Louis reflected for a few moments.

"Muster all the troops in Paris," he said.

"All the necessary orders are given for that purpose," replie
Fouquet.

"You have given orders?" exclaimed the king.

"For that purpose, yes, sire; your majesty will be at the hea
of ten thousand men in less than an hour."

The only reply the king made was to take hold of Fouquet
hand with such an expression of feeling that it was very eas
to perceive how strongly he had, until that remark, maintaine
his suspicions of the minister, notwithstanding the latter's i
tervention.

"And with these troops," he said, "we shall go at once a
besiege in your house the rebels who by this time will have e
tablished and intrenched themselves there."

"I should be surprised if that were the case," replied Fouque

"Why?"

"Because their chief—the very soul of the enterprise, havin
been unmasked by me, the whole plan seems to me to have mi
carried."

"You have unmasked this false prince also?"

"No; I have not seen him."

"Whom have you seen, then?"

"The leader of the enterprise, not that unhappy young man; the latter is merely an instrument, destined through his whole life to wretchedness, I plainly perceive."

"Most certainly."

"It is Monsieur l'Abbé d'Herblay, Evêque de Vannes."

"Your friend."

"He was my friend, sire," replied Fouquet nobly.

"An unfortunate circumstance for you," said the king, in a less generous tone of voice.

"Such friendships, sire, had nothing dishonorable in them so long as I was ignorant of the crime."

"You should have foreseen it."

"If I am guilty, I place myself in your majesty's hands."

"Ah! Monsieur Fouquet, it was not that I meant," returned the king, sorry to have shown the bitterness of his thought in such a manner. "Well, I assure you that, notwithstanding the mask with which the villain covered his face, I had something like a vague suspicion that it might be he. But with this chief of the enterprise there was a man of prodigious strength, the one who menaced me with a force almost herculean—what is he?"

"It must be his friend, the Baron du Vallon, formerly one of the musketeers."

"The friend of D'Artagnan? the friend of the Comte de la Fere? Ah!" exclaimed the king, as he paused at the name of the latter, "we must not forget the connection that existed between the conspirators and Monsieur de Bragelonne."

"Sire, sire, do not go too far. Monsieur de la Fere is the most honorable man in France. Be satisfied with those whom I deliver up to you."

"With those whom you deliver up to me, you say? Very good, or you will deliver up those who are guilty to me."

"What does your majesty understand by that?" inquired Fouquet.

"I understand," replied the king, "that we shall soon arrive at Vaux with a large body of troops, that we will lay violent hands upon that nest of vipers, and that not a soul shall escape."

"Your majesty will put these men to death!" cried Fouquet.

"To the very meanest of them."

"Oh, sire!"

"Let us understand each other, Monsieur Fouquet," said the

king haughtily. "We no longer live in times when assassination was the only and the last resource which kings had in their power. No, Heaven be praised! I have parliaments who sit and judge in my name, and I have scaffolds on which my supreme authority is carried out."

Fouquet turned pale.

"I will take the liberty of observing to your majesty that any proceedings instituted respecting these matters would bring down the greatest scandal upon the dignity of the throne. The august name of Anne of Austria must never be allowed to pass the lips of the people accompanied by a smile."

"Justice must be done, however, monsieur."

"Good, sire; but the royal blood cannot be shed on a scaffold."

"The royal blood! You believe that?" cried the king, with fury in his voice, stamping his foot on the ground. "This double birth is an invention; and in that invention particularly do I see Monsieur d'Herblay's crime. It is the crime I wish to punish, rather than their violence or their insult."

"And punish it with death, sire?"

"With death, yes, monsieur."

"Sire," said the surintendant, with firmness, as he raised his head proudly, "your majesty will take the life, if you please, of your brother, Philippe of France; that concerns you alone, and you will doubtless consult the queen-mother upon the subject. Whatever she may command will be perfectly correct. I do not wish to mix myself up in it, not even for the honor of your crown, but I have a favor to ask of you, and I beg to submit it to you."

"Speak," said the king, in no little degree agitated by his minister's last words. "What do you require?"

"The pardon of Monsieur d'Herblay and of Monsieur du Vallon."

"My assassins?"

"Two rebels, sire, that is all."

"Oh! I understand, then, you ask me to forgive your friends."

"My friends!" said Fouquet, deeply wounded.

"Your friends, certainly; but the safety of the state require that an exemplary punishment should be inflicted on the guilty.

"I will not permit myself to remind your majesty that I have just restored you to liberty, and have saved your life."

"Monsieur!"

"I will not allow myself to remind your majesty that ha

Monsieur d'Herblay wished to carry out his character of an assassin, he could very easily have assassinated your majesty this morning in the forest of Senart, and all would have been over."

The king started.

"A pistol bullet through the head," pursued Fouquet, "and the disfigured features of Louis XIV., which no one could have recognized, would be Monsieur d'Herblay's complete and entire justification."

The king turned pale and giddy at the idea of the danger he had escaped.

"If Monsieur d'Herblay," continued Fouquet, "had been an assassin, he had no occasion to inform me of his plan in order to succeed. Freed from the real king, it would have been impossible to guess the false king. And if the usurper had been recognized by Anne of Austria, he would still have been a son for her. The usurper, as far as Monsieur d'Herblay's conscience was concerned, was still a king of the blood of Louis XIII. Moreover, the conspirator, in that course, would have had security, secrecy, and impunity. A pistol-bullet would have procured him all that. For the sake of Heaven, sire, grant me his forgiveness!"

The king, instead of being touched by the picture he had drawn, so faithful in all its details, of Aramis' generosity, felt himself most painfully and cruelly humiliated by it. His unconquerable pride revolted at the idea that a man had held suspended at the end of his finger the thread of his royal life. Every word that fell from Fouquet's lips, and which he thought most efficacious in procuring his friend's pardon, seemed to pour another drop of poison into the already ulcerated heart of Louis XIV. Nothing could bend or soften him. Addressing himself to Fouquet, he said:

"I really don't know, monsieur, why you should solicit the pardon of these men. What good is there is asking that which can be obtained without solicitation?"

"I do not understand you, sire."

"It is not difficult, either. Where am I now?"

"In the Bastile, sire."

"Yes; in a dungeon. I am looked upon as a madman, am I not?"

"Yes, sire."

"And no one is known here but Marchiali?"

"Certainly."

"Well, change nothing in the position of affairs. Let the madman rot in the dungeon of the Bastile and Monsieur d'Herblay and Monsieur du Vallon will stand in no need of my forgiveness. Their new king will absolve them."

"Your majesty does me a great injustice, sire, and you are wrong," replied Fouquet dryly; "I am not child enough, nor is Monsieur d'Herblay silly enough to have omitted to make all these reflections; and if I had wished to make a new king, as you say, I had no occasion to have come here to force open all the gates and doors of the Bastile, to free you from this place. That would show a want of common sense even. Your majesty's mind is disturbed by anger; otherwise you would be far from offending, groundlessly, the very one of your servants who has rendered you the most important service of all."

Louis perceived that he had gone too far, that the gates of the Bastile were still closed upon him; while, by degrees, the floodgates were gradually being opened behind which the generous-hearted Fouquet had restrained his anger.

"I did not say that to humiliate you, Heaven knows, monsieur!" he replied. "Only you are addressing yourself to me, in order to obtain a pardon, and I answer you according as my conscience dictates. And so, judging by my conscience, the criminals we speak of are not worthy of consideration or forgiveness."

Fouquet was silent.

"What I do is as generous," added the king, "as what you have done, for I am in your power. I will even say it is more generous, inasmuch as you place before me certain conditions upon which my liberty, my life, may depend; and to reject which is to make a sacrifice of them both."

"I was wrong, certainly," replied Fouquet. "Yes—I had the appearance of extorting a favor; I regret it, and entreat your majesty's forgiveness."

"And you are forgiven, my dear Monsieur Fouquet," said the king, with a smile, which restored the serene expression of his features, which so many circumstances had altered since the preceding evening.

"I have my own forgiveness," replied the minister, with some degree of persistence; "but Monsieur d'Herblay and Monsieur du Vallon?"

"They will never obtain theirs, as long as I live," replied the inflexible king. "Do me the kindness not to speak of it again."

"Your majesty shall be obeyed."

"And you will bear me no ill-will for it?"

"Oh, no, sire; for I anticipated it as being most likely."

"You had 'anticipated' that I should refuse to forgive those gentlemen?"

"Certainly; and all my measures were taken in consequence."

"What do you mean to say?" cried the king, surprised.

"Monsieur d'Herblay came, as may be said, to deliver himself into my hands. Monsieur d'Herblay left to me the happiness of saving my king and my country. I could not condemn Monsieur d'Herblay to death, nor could I, on the other hand, expose him to your majesty's most justifiable wrath; it would have been just the same as if I had killed him myself."

"Well, and what have you done?"

"Sire, I gave Monsieur d'Herblay the best horses in my stables, and four hours' start over all those your majesty might, probably, dispatch after him."

"Be it so!" murmured the king. "But still, the world is wide enough and large enough for those whom I may send to overtake your horses, notwithstanding the 'four hours' start' which you have given to Monsieur d'Herblay."

"In giving him those four hours, sire, I knew I was giving him his life, and he will save his life."

"In what way?"

"After having galloped as hard as possible, with the four hours' start, before your musketeers, he will reach my château of Belle-Isle, where I have given him a safe asylum."

"That may be; but you forget that you have made me a present of Belle-Isle."

"But not for you to arrest my friends."

"You take it back again, then?"

"As far as that goes—yes, sire."

"My musketeers will capture it, and the affair will be at an end."

"Neither your musketeers nor your whole army could take Belle-Isle," said Fouquet coldly. "Belle-Isle is impregnable."

The king became perfectly livid; a lightning flash seemed to dart from his eyes. Fouquet felt that he was lost, but he was not one to shrink when the voice of honor spoke loudly within him. He bore the king's wrathful gaze; the latter swallowed his rage, and after a few moments' silence said:

"Are we going to return to Vaux?"

"I am at your majesty's orders," replied Fouquet, with a low bow; "but I think that your majesty can hardly dispense with changing clothes previous to appearing before your court."

"We shall pass by the Louvre," said the king. "Come."

And they left the prison, passing before Baisemeaux, who looked completely bewildered as he saw Marchiali once more leave; and, in his helplessness, tore out the few remaining hairs he had left. It was perfectly true, however, that Fouquet wrote and gave him an authority for the prisoner's release, and that the king wrote beneath it, "Seen and approved, Louis;" a piece of madness that Baisemeaux, incapable of putting two ideas together, acknowledged by giving himself a terrible blow with his fist on his jaws.

Chapter 24 — THE FALSE KING

In the meantime, usurped royalty was playing out its part bravely at Vaux. Philippe gave orders that for his *petit lever*, the *grandes entrées*, already prepared to appear before the king, should be introduced. He determined to give this order, notwithstanding the absence of M. d'Herblay, who did not return, and our readers know for what reason. But the prince, not believing that absence could be prolonged, wished, as all rash spirits do, to try his valor and his fortune when far from all protection and all counsel. Another reason urged him to this—Anne of Austria was about to appear; the guilty mother was about to stand in the presence of her sacrificed son. Philippe was not willing, if he had a weakness, to render the man a witness of it before whom he was bound thenceforth to display so much strength. Philippe opened his folding-doors, and several persons entered silently. Philippe did not stir while his *valets de chambre* dressed him. He had watched, the evening before, all the habits of his brother, and played the king in such a manner as to awaken no suspicion. He was then completely dressed in his hunting costume when he received his visitors. His own memory and the notes of Aramis announced everybody to him, first of all Anne of Austria, to whom Monsieur gave his hand, and then madame with M. de St. Aignan. He smiled at seeing these countenances, but trembled on recognizing his mother. That figure, so noble, so imposing, ravaged by pain, pleaded in his heart the cause of that famous queen who had immolated a child to reasons of state. He found his mother still handsome. He knew that Louis XIV. loved her, and he promised himself to love her likewise,

d not to prove a cruel chastisement for her old age. He con-
mplated his brother with a tenderness easily to be understood.
he latter had usurped nothing over him, had cast no shade
er his life. A separate branch, he allowed the stem to rise
ithout heeding its elevation or the majesty of its life. Philippe
omised himself to be a kind brother to this prince, who re-
ired nothing but gold to minister to his pleasures. He bowed
ith a friendly air to St. Aignan, who was all reverences and
niles, and tremblingly held out his hand to Henriette, is sis-
r-in-law, whose beauty struck him; but he saw in the eyes of
at princess an expression of coldness which would facilitate,
he thought, her future relations.

"How much more easy," thought he, "it will be to be the
other of that woman than her gallant, if she evinces toward
e a coldness that my brother could not have for her, and which
imposed upon me as a duty."

The only visit he dreaded at this moment was that of the
een; his heart—his mind—had just been shaken by so violent
trial that, in spite of their firm temperament, they would not,
rhaps, support another shock. Happily the queen did not come.
hen commenced, on the part of Anne of Austria, a political
ssertation upon the welcome M. Fouquet had given to the
use of France. She mixed up hostilities with compliments
ldressed to the king, and questions as to his health, with little
aternal flatteries and diplomatic artifices.

"Well, my son," said she, "are you convinced with regard to
onsieur Fouquet?"

"St. Aignan," said Philippe, "have the goodness to go and
quire after the queen."

At these words, the first Philippe had pronounced aloud, the
ght difference that there was between his voice and that of
e king was sensible to maternal ears, and Anne of Austria
oked earnestly at her son. St. Aignan left the room, and Phi-
ppe continued:

"Madame, I do not like to hear Monsieur Fouquet ill-spoken
, you know I do not—and you have even spoken well of him
urself."

"That is true; therefore, I only question you on the state of
ur sentiments with respect to him."

"Sire," said Henriette, "I, on my part, have always liked Mon-
ur Fouquet. He is a man of good taste—he is a superior man."

"A surintendant who is never sordid or niggardly," added
onsieur; "and who pays in gold all the orders I have on him."

"Every one in this thinks too much of himself, and nobo
for the state," said the old queen. "Monsieur Fouquet, it is
fact, Monsieur Fouquet is ruining the state."

"Well, mother," replied Philippe, in rather a lower key, "
you likewise constitute yourself the buckler of Monsieur C
bert?"

"How is that?" replied the old queen, rather surprised.

"Why, in truth," replied Philippe, "you speak that just
your old friend, Madame de Chevreuse, would speak."

"Why do you mention Madame de Chevreuse to me?" sa
she, "and what sort of humor are you in to-day toward me?"

Philippe continued:

"Is not Madame de Chevreuse always in league against som
body? Has not Madame de Chevreuse been to pay you a visi
mother?"

"Monsieur, you speak to me now in such a manner that I c
almost fancy I am listening to your father."

"My father did not like Madame de Chevreuse, and had go
reason for not liking her," said the prince. "For my part, I li
her no better than he did; and if she thinks proper to com
here as she formerly did, to sow divisions and hatreds und
the pretext of begging money, why——"

"Well, what?" said Anne of Austria proudly, herself provo
ing the storm.

"Well," replied the young man firmly, "I will drive Madan
de Chevreuse out of my kingdom—and with her all who medd
with secrets and mysteries."

He had not calculated the effect of this terrible speech,
perhaps, he wished to judge of the effect of it, like those wh
suffering from a chronic pain, and seeking to break the mono
ony of that suffering, touch their wound to procure a sharp
pang. Anne of Austria was near fainting; her eyes, open b
meaningless, ceased to see for several seconds; she stretch
out her arms toward her other son, who supported and embrace
her without fear of irritating the king.

"Sire," murmured she, "you treat your mother cruelly."

"In what, madame?" replied he. "I am only speaking of M
dame de Chevreuse; does my mother prefer Madame de Ch
vreuse to the security of the state and to the security of n
person? Well, then, madame, I tell you Madame de Chevreu
is returned to France to borrow money, and that she address
herself to Monsieur Fouquet to sell him a certain secret."

"A certain secret!" cried Anne of Austria.

"Concerning pretended robberies that Monsieur le Surintendant had committed, which is false," added Philippe.

"Monsieur Fouquet rejected her offers with indignation, preferring the esteem of the king to all complicity with intriguers.
Then Madame de Chevreuse sold the secret to Monsieur Colbert, and as she is insatiable, and was not satisfied with having
extorted a hundred thousand crowns from that clerk, she has
flown still higher, and has endeavored to find still deeper springs.
Is that true, madame?"

"You know all, sire," said the queen, more uneasy than irritated.

"Now," continued Philippe, "I have good reason to dislike
his fury, who comes to my court to plan the dishonor of some
and the ruin of others. If God has suffered certain crimes to
be committed, and has concealed them in the shade of His clem-
ency, I will not permit Madame de Chevreuse to have the power
to counteract the designs of God."

The latter part of the speech had so agitated the queen-
mother that her son had pity on her. He took her hand and
kissed it tenderly; she did not feel that in that kiss, given in
spite of repulsions and bitterness of the heart, there was a pardon for eight years of horrible suffering. Philippe allowed the
silence of a moment to swallow the emotions that had just de-
veloped themselves. Then, with a cheerful smile:

"We will not go to-day," said he; "I have a plan."

And turning toward the door, he hoped to see Aramis, whose
absence began to alarm him. The queen-mother wished to leave
the room.

"Remain where you are, mother," said he; "I wish you to
make your peace with Monsieur Fouquet."

"I bear no ill-will toward Monsieur Fouquet; I only dreaded
his prodigalities."

"We will put that to rights, and will take nothing of the surintendant but his good qualities."

"What is your majesty looking for?" said Henriette, seeing
the king's eyes constantly turned toward the door, and wishing
to let fly a little poisoned arrow at his heart, supposing he was
so anxiously expecting either La Valliere or a letter from her.

"My sister," said the young man, who had divined her thought,
thanks to that marvelous perspicuity of which fortune was from
that time about to allow him the exercise, "my sister, I am expecting a most distinguished man, a most able counselor, whom
I wish to present to you all, recommending him to your good
graces. Ah! come in, then, D'Artagnan."

"What does your majesty wish?" said D'Artagnan, appear ing.

"Where is Monsieur the Bishop of Vannes, your friend?"

"Why, sire——"

"I am waiting for him, and he does not come. Let him be sought for."

D'Artagnan remained for an instant stupefied; but soon reflecting that Aramis had left Vaux secretly, with a mission from the king, he concluded that the king wished to preserve the secret of it.

"Sire," replied he, "does your majesty absolutely require Monsieur d'Herblay to be brought to you?"

"Absolutely is not the word," said Philippe; "I do not want him so particularly as that; but if he can be found——"

"I thought so," said D'Artagnan, to himself.

"Is this Monsieur d'Herblay, bishop of Vannes?"

"Yes, madame."

"A friend of Monsieur Fouquet?"

"Yes, madame; an old musketeer."

Anne of Austria blushed.

"One of the four braves who formerly performed such won ders."

The old queen repented of having wished to bite; she broke off the conversation, in order to preserve the rest of her teeth.

"Whatever may be your choice, sire," said she, "I have no doubt it will be excellent."

All bowed in support of that sentiment.

"You will find in him," continued Philippe, "the depth and penetration of Monsieur de Richelieu, without the avarice of Monsieur de Mazarin."

"A prime minister, sire?" said Monsieur in a fright.

"I will tell you all about that, brother; but it is strange that Monsieur d'Herblay is not here!"

He called out:

"Let Monsieur Fouquet be informed that I wish to speak to him—oh! before you, before you; do not retire."

M. de St. Aignan returned, bringing satisfactory news of the queen, who only kept her bed from precaution, and to have strength to carry out all the king's wishes. While everybody was seeking M. Fouquet and Aramis, the new king quietly continued his experiments, and everybody, family, officers, servants, had not the least suspicion, his air, voice, and manners were so like the king's. On his side, Philippe, applying to all countenances the faithful notice and design furnished by his accomplice, Ara mis, conducted himself so as not to give birth to a doubt in the minds of those who surrounded him. Nothing from that time could disturb the usurper. With what strange facility had Providence just reversed the most elevated fortune of the world to substitute the most humble in its stead! Philippe admired the goodness of God with regard to himself, and seconded it with all the resources of his admirable nature. But he felt, at times, something like a shadow gliding between him and the rays of his new glory. Aramis did not appear. The conversation had languished in the royal family; Philippe, preoccupied, forgot to dismiss his brother and Mme. Henriette. The latter were astonished, and began, by degrees, to lose all patience. Anne of Austria stooped toward her son's ear, and addressed some words to him in Spanish. Philippe was completely ignorant of that language, and grew pale at this unexpected obstacle. But, as if the spirit of the imperturbable Aramis had covered him with his infallibility, instead of appearing disconcerted, Philippe rose.

"Well, what?" said Anne of Austria.

"What is all that noise?" said Philippe, turning round toward the door of the second staircase.

And a voice was heard, saying:

"This way, this way! A few steps more, sire!"

"The voice of Monsieur Fouquet!" said D'Artagnan, who was standing close to the queen-mother.

"Then Monsieur d'Herblay cannot be far off," added Philippe.

But he then saw what he little thought to see so near to him. All eyes were turned toward the door at which M. Fouquet was expected to enter; but it was not M. Fouquet who entered. A terrible cry resounded from all corners of the chamber, a painful cry uttered by the king and all present. It is not given to men, even to those whose destiny contains the strangest elements, and accidents the most wonderful, to contemplate a spectacle similar to that which presented itself in the royal chamber at that moment. The half-closed shutters only admitted the entrance of an uncertain light passing through large velvet curtains lined with silk. In this soft shade the eyes were by degrees dilated, and every one present saw others rather with trust than with positive sight. There could not, however, escape in these circumstances one of the surrounding details; and the new object which presented itself appeared as luminous as if it had been enlightened by the sun. So it happened with Louis XIV., when he showed himself pale and frowning in the doorway of the secret stairs. The face of Fouquet appeared behind him, impressed with sorrow and sternness. The queen-mother, who perceived Louis XIV., and who held the hand of Philippe, uttered the cry of which we have spoken, as if she had beheld a phantom. Monsieur was bewildered, and kept turning his head in astonishment, from one to the other. Madame made a step forward, thinking she saw the form of her brother-in-law reflected in a glass. And, in fact, the illusion was possible. The two princes, both pale as death—for we renounce the hope of being able to describe the fearful state of Philippe—both trembling, and clinching their hands convulsively, measured each other with their looks, and darted their eyes, like poniards, into each other. The unheard-of resemblance of countenance, gesture, shape, height, even to the resemblance of costume, produced by chance—for Louis XIV. had been to the Louvre and put on a violet-colored dress—the perfect analogy of the two princes, completed the consternation of Anne of Austria. And yet she did not at once guess the truth. There are misfortunes in life that no one will accept; people would rather believe in the supernatural and the impossible. Louis had not reckoned upon these obstacles. He expected he had only to appear and be acknowledged. A living sun, he could not endure the suspicion of parity with any one. He did not admit that every torch should not become darkness at the instant he shone out with his conquering ray. At the aspect of Philippe, then, he was perhaps more terrified than any one round him, and his silence, his immobility, were, this time, a concentration and a calm which precede violent explosions of passion.

But Fouquet—who could paint his emotion and stupor in presence of this living portrait of his master? Fouquet thought Aramis was right, that this newly arrived was a king as pure in his race as the other, and that, for having repudiated all participation in this *coup d'état*, so skillfully got up by the general of the Jesuits, he must be a mad enthusiast, unworthy of ever again dipping his hands in a political work. And then it was the blood of Louis XIII. which Fouquet was sacrificing to the blood of Louis XIII.; it was to a selfish ambition he was sacrificing a noble ambition; it was to the right of keeping he sacrificed the right of having. The whole extent of his fault was revealed to him by the simple sight of the pretender. All which passed in the mind of Fouquet was lost upon the persons present. He had five minutes to concentrate his meditations upon this point of the case of conscience; five minutes, that is to say, five ages, during which the two kings and their family scarcely found time to breathe after so terrible a shock. D'Artagnan, leaning against the wall, in front of Fouquet, with his hand to his brow, asked himself the cause of such a wonderful prodigy. He could not have said at once why he doubted, but he knew assuredly that he had reason to doubt, and that in this meeting of the two Louis XIV.'s lay all the difficulty which, during late days, had rendered the conduct of Aramis so suspicious to the musketeer. These ideas were, however, enveloped in thick veils. The actors in this assembly seemed to swim in the vapors of a confused waking. Suddenly Louis XIV., more impatient and more accustomed to command, ran to one of the shutters, which he opened, tearing the curtains in his eagerness. A flood of living light entered the chamber, and made Philippe draw back to the alcove. Louis seized upon this movement with eagerness, and addressing himself to the queen:

"My mother," said he, "do you not acknowledge your son, since every one here has forgotten his king!"

Anne of Austria started, and raised her arms toward heaven, without being able to articulate a single word.

"My mother," said Philippe, with a calm voice, "do you not acknowledge your son?"

And this time, in his turn, Louis drew back.

As to Anne of Austria, struck in both head and heart with remorse, she lost her equilibrium. No one aiding her, for all were petrified, she sank back in her *fauteuil*, breathing a weak, trembling sigh. Louis could not endure this spectacle and this affront. He bounded toward D'Artagnan, upon whom the vertigo was beginning to gain, and who staggered as he caught at the door for support.

"*A moi, mousquetaire!*" said he. "Look us in the face, and say which is the paler, he or I!"

This cry roused D'Artagnan, and stirred in his heart the fiber of obedience. He shook his head, and, without more hesitation, he walked straight up to Philippe, upon whose shoulder he laid his hand, saying:

"Monsieur, you are my prisoner!"

Philippe did not raise his eyes toward heaven, nor stir from the spot, where he seemed nailed to the floor, his eye intensely fixed upon the king, his brother. He reproached him by a sublime silence with all his misfortunes past, with all his tortures to come. Against this language of the soul the king felt he had no power; he cast down his eyes, dragging away precipitately his brother and sister, forgetting his mother, sitting motionless within three paces of the son whom she left a second time to be condemned to death. Philippe approached Anne of Austria, and said to her, in a soft and nobly agitated voice:

"If I were not your son, I should curse you, my mother, for having rendered me so unhappy!"

D'Artagnan felt a shudder pass through the marrow of his bones. He bowed respectfully to the young prince, and said, as he bent:

"Excuse me, monseigneur, I am but a soldier, and my oaths are his who has just left the chamber."

"Thank you, Monsieur d'Artagnan. But what is become of Monsieur d'Herblay?"

"Monseiur d'Herblay is in safety, monseigneur," said a voice behind them; "and no one, while I live and am free, shall cause a hair to fall from his head."

"Monsieur Fouquet!" said the prince, smiling sadly.

"Pardon me, monseigneur," said Fouquet, kneeling, "but he who is just gone out from hence was my guest."

"Here are," murmured Philippe, with a sigh, "brave friends and good hearts. They make me regret the world. On, Monsieur d'Artagnan; I follow you."

At the moment the captain of the musketeers was about to leave the room with his prisoner, Colbert appeared, and, after remitting an order from the king to D'Artagnan, retired. D'Artagnan read the paper, and then crushed it in his hand with rage.

"What is it?" asked the prince.

"Read, monseigneur," replied the musketeer.

Philippe read the following words, hastily traced by the hand of the king:

Monsieur d'Artagnan will conduct the prisoner to the Iles Ste. Marguerite. He will cover his face with an iron visor, which the prisoner cannot raise without peril of his life."

"That is just," said Philippe, with resignation; "I am ready."

"Aramis was right," said Fouquet, in a low voice, to the musketeer, "this one is quite as much of a king as the other."

"More!" replied D'Artagnan. "He only wants you and me."

Chapter 25 — IN WHICH PORTHOS THINKS HE IS PURSUING A DUCHY

Aramis and Porthos, having profited by the time granted them by Fouquet, did honor to the French cavalry by their speed. Porthos did not clearly understand for what kind of mission he was forced to display so much velocity; but as he saw Aramis spurring on furiously, he, Porthos, spurred on in the same manner. They had soon, in this manner, placed twelve leagues between them and Vaux; they were then obliged to change horses, and organize a sort of post arrangement. It was during a relay that Porthos ventured to interrogate Aramis discreetly.

"Hush!" replied the latter; "know only that our fortune depends upon our speed."

As if Porthos had still been the musketeer, without a sou or a *maille* of 1626, he pushed forward. That magic word, "fortune," always means something in the human ear. It means *enough* for those who have nothing; it means *too much* for those who have enough.

"I shall be made a duke!" said Porthos aloud. He was speaking to himself.

"That is possible," replied Aramis, smiling after his own fashion, as the horse of Porthos passed him. The head of Aramis was, notwithstanding, on fire; the activity of the body had not yet succeeded in subduing that of the mind. All that there is in raging passions, in severe toothaches, or mortal threats twisted, gnawed, and grumbled in the thoughts of the vanquished prelate. His countenance exhibited very visible traces of this rude combat. Free upon the highway to abandon himself to every impression of the moment, Aramis did not fail to swear at every start of his horse, at every inequality in the road. Pale, at times inundated with boiling sweats, then again dry and icy, he beat his horses and made the blood stream from their sides. Porthos, whose dominant fault was not sensibility, groaned at this. Thus traveled they on for eight long hours, and then arrived at Orleans. It was four o'clock in the afternoon. Aramis, on observing this, judged that nothing demonstrated pursuit to be possible. It would be without example that a troop capable of taking him and Porthos should be furnished with relays sufficient to perform forty leagues in eight hours. Thus, admitting pursuit, which

was not at all manifest, the fugitives were five hours in advance
of their pursuers.

Aramis thought that there might be no imprudence in taking
a little rest, but that to continue would make the matter more
certain. Twenty leagues more, performed with the same rapidity, twenty more leagues devoured, and no one, not even D'Artagnan, could overtake the enemies of the king. Aramis felt
obliged, therefore, to inflict upon Porthos the pain of mounting
on horseback again. They rode on till seven o'clock in the evening, and had only one post more between them and Blois. But
here a diabolical accident alarmed Aramis greatly. There were
no horses at the post. The prelate asked himself by what
infernal machination his enemies had succeeded in depriving
him of the means of going further—he who never recognized
chance as a deity, he who found a cause for every result, he
preferred believing that the refusal of the postmaster, at such
an hour, in such a country, was the consequence of an order
emanating from above; an order given with a view of stopping
short the king-maker in the midst of his flight. But at the moment he was about to fly into a passion, so as to procure either
a horse or an explanation, he was struck with the recollection
that the Comte de la Fere lived in the neighborhood.

"I am not traveling," said he; "I do not want horses of a whole
stage. Find me two horses to go and pay a visit to a nobleman
of my acquaintance who resides near this place."

"What nobleman?" asked the postmaster.

"Monsieur le Comte de la Fere."

"Oh!" replied the postmaster, uncovering with respect, "a
very worthy nobleman. But, whatever may be my desire to
make myself agreeable to him, I cannot furnish you with horses
for all mine are engaged by Monsieur le Duc de Beaufort."

"Indeed!" said Aramis, much disappointed.

"Only," continued the postmaster, "if you will put up with a
little carriage I have, I will harness an old blind horse, who has
still his legs left, and will draw you to the house of Monsieur le
Comte de la Fere."

"That is worth a louis," said Aramis.

"No, monsieur, that is never worth more than a crown; that
is what Monsieur Grimaud, the comte's intendant, always pays
me when he makes use of that carriage, and I should not wish the
Comte de la Fere to have to reproach me with having imposed on one of his friends."

"As you please," said Aramis, "particularly as regards disobliging the Comte de la Fere; only I think I have a right to give you a louis for your idea."

"Oh! doubtless," replied the postmaster, with delight.

And he himself harnessed the old horse to the creaking carriage. In the meantime, Porthos was curious to behold. He imagined he had discovered the secret, and he felt pleased because a visit to Athos, in the first place, promised him much satisfaction, and, in the next, gave him the hope of finding at the same time a good bed and a good supper. The master, having got the carriage ready, ordered one of his men to drive the strangers to La Fere. Porthos took his seat by the side of Aramis, whispering in his ear:

"I understand."

"Ah, ah!" said Aramis, "and what do you understand, my friend?"

"We are going, on the part of the king, to make some great proposal to Athos."

"Pooh!" said Aramis.

"You need tell me nothing about it," added the worthy Porthos, endeavoring to place himself so as to avoid the jolting; "you need tell me nothing, I shall guess."

"Well, do, my friend; guess away."

They arrived at Athos' dwelling about nine o'clock in the evening, favored by a splendid moon. This cheerful light rejoiced Porthos beyond expression; but Aramis appeared annoyed by it in an equal degree. He could not help showing something of this to Porthos, who replied:

"Ay, ay! I guess how it is; the mission is a secret one."

These were his last words in the carriage. The driver interrupted him, by saying:

"Gentlemen, you are arrived."

Porthos and his companion alighted before the gate of the little château, where we are about to meet again with Athos and De Bragelonne, the latter of whom had disappeared since the discovery of the infidelity of La Valliere. If there be one saying more true than another, it is this: great griefs contain within themselves the germ of their consolation. This painful wound, inflicted upon Raoul, had drawn him nearer to his father again; and God knows how sweet were the consolations which flowed from the eloquent mouth and generous heart of Athos. The wound was not cicatrized, but Athos, by dint of conversing with his son and mixing a little more of his life with that of the young man, had brought him to understand that this pang of a first in-

fidelity is necessary to every human existence, and that no one
has loved without meeting with it. Raoul listened often, but
never understood. Nothing replaces in the deeply afflicted heart
the remembrance and thought of the beloved object. Raoul then
replied to the reasonings of his father:

"Monsieur, all that you tell me is true; I believe that no one
has suffered in the affections of the heart so much as you have;
but you are a man too great from intelligence, and too severely
tried by misfortunes, not to allow for the weakness of the soldier who suffers for the first time. I am paying a tribute which
I shall not pay a second time; permit me to plunge myself so
deeply in my grief that I may forget myself in it, that I may
drown even my reason in it."

"Raoul! Raoul!"

"Listen, monsieur. Never shall I accustom myself to the idea
that Louise, the most chaste and the most innocent of women,
has been able so basely to deceive a man so honest and so true
a lover as I am. Never can I persuade myself that I see that
sweet and good mask change into a hypocritical and lascivious
face. Louise lost! Louise infamous! Ah! monseigneur, that idea
is much more cruel to me than Raoul abandoned—Raoul unhappy!"

Athos then employed the heroic remedy. He defended Louise
against Raoul, and justified her perfidy by her love.

"A woman who would have yielded to a king because he is a
king," said he, "would deserve to be styled infamous; but Louise
loved Louis. Both young, they have forgotten, he his rank, she
her vows. Love absolves everything, Raoul. The two young people loved each other with sincerity."

And when he had dealt this severe poniard-thrust, Athos, with
a sigh, saw Raoul bound away under the cruel wound, and fly
to the thickest recesses of the wood, or the solitude of his
chamber, whence, an hour after, he would return, pale, trembling, but subdued. Then, coming up to Athos with a smile, he
would kiss his hand, like the dog who, having been beaten, caresses a good master, to redeem his fault. Raoul redeemed nothing but his weakness, and only confessed his grief. Thus passed
away the days that followed that scene in which Athos had so
violently shaken the indomitable pride of the king. Never, when
conversing with his son, did he make any allusion to that scene;
never did he give him the details of that vigorous lecture, which
might, perhaps, have consoled the young man, by showing him
his rival humbled. Athos did not wish that the offended lover
should forget the respect due to the king. And when De Brage

lonne, ardent, furious, and melancholy, spoke with contempt of royal words, of the equivocal faith which certain madmen draw from promises falling from thrones, when, passing over two centuries, with the rapidity of a bird which traverses a narrow strait, to go from one world to the other, Raoul ventured to predict the time in which kings would become less than other men, Athos said to him, in his serene, persuasive voice:

"You are right, Raoul; all that you say will happen; kings will lose their privileges, as stars which have completed their time lose their splendor. But when that moment shall come, Raoul, we shall be dead. And remember well what I say to you. In this world, all—men, women, and kings—must live for the present. We can only live for the future, for God."

This was the manner in which Athos and Raoul were, as usual, conversing, and walking backward and forward in the long alley of limes in the park, when the bell which served to announce to the comte either the hour of dinner or the arrival of a visitor, was rung; and, without attaching any importance to it, he turned toward the house with his son, and at the end of the alley they found themselves in the presence of Aramis and Porthos.

Chapter 26 — THE LAST ADIEUS

Raoul uttered a cry, and affectionately embraced Porthos. Aramis and Athos embraced like old men; and this embrace itself being a question for Aramis, he immediately said:

"My friend, we have not long to remain with you."

"Ah!" said the comte.

"Only time to tell you of my good fottune," interrupted Porthos.

"Ah!" said Raoul.

"Athos looked silently at Aramis, whose somber air had already appeared to him very little in harmony with the good news Porthos spoke of.

"What is the good fortune that has happened to you? Let us hear it," said Raoul, with a smile.

"The king has made me a duke," said the worthy Porthos, with an air of mystery, in the ear of the young man, "a duke by brevet."

But the asides of Porthos were always loud enough to be heard by everybody. His murmurs were in the diapason of ordinary roaring. Athos heard him, and uttered an exclamation which made Aramis start. The latter took Athos by the arm, and, after having asked Porthos' permission to say a word to his friend in private:

"My dear Athos," he began, "you see me overwhelmed with grief."

"With grief, my dear friend?" cried the comte. "Oh, what?"

"In two words. I have raised a conspiracy against the king; that conspiracy has failed, and at this moment I am, doubtless, pursued."

"You are pursued!—a conspiracy? Eh, my friend, what do you tell me?"

"A sad truth. I am entirely ruined!"

"Well, but Porthos—this title of duke—what does all that mean?"

"That is the subject of my severest pain; that is the deepest of my wounds. I have, believing in an infallible success, drawn Porthos into my conspiracy. He has thrown himself into it, as you know he would do, with all his strength, without knowing what he was about; and now, he is as much compromised as myself—as completely ruined as I am."

"Good God!"

And Athos turned toward Porthos, who was smiling complacently.

"I must make you acquainted with the whole. Listen to me," continued Aramis; and he related the history as we know it.

Athos, during the recital, several times felt the sweat break from his forehead.

"It was a great idea," said he, "but a great error."

"For which I am punished, Athos."

"Therefore, I will not tell you my entire thought."

"Tell it, nevertheless."

"It is a crime."

"Capital, I know it is. *Lèse majesté*."

"Porthos! poor Porthos!"

"What would you advise me to do? Success, as I have told you, was certain."

"Monsieur Fouquet is an honest man."

"And I am a fool for having so ill judged of him," said Aramis. "Oh, the wisdom of man! Oh, the vast millstone which grinds a world! and which is one day stopped by a grain of sand which has fallen, no one knows how, in its wheels."

"Say, by a diamond, Aramis. But the thing is done. How do you think of acting?"

"I am taking away Porthos. The king will never believe that that worthy man has acted innocently. He never can believe that Porthos has thought he was serving the king while acting as he has done. His head would pay for my fault. It shall not be so."

"You are taking him away, whither?"

"To Belle-Isle, at first. That is an impregnable place of refuge. Then I have the sea, and a vessel to pass over into England, where I have many relations."

"You? In England?"

"Yes, or else in Spain, where I have still more."

"But our excellent Porthos? You ruin him, for the king will confiscate all his property."

"All is provided for. I know how, when once in Spain, to reconcile myself with Louis XIV., and restore Porthos to favor."

"You have credit, seemingly, Aramis," said Athos, with a discreet air.

"Much; and at the service of my friends."

These words were accompanied by a warm pressure of the hand.

"Thank you," replied the comte.

"And while we are on that head," said Aramis, "you also are a malcontent; you also, Raoul, have griefs to lay to the king. Follow our example; pass over into Belle-Isle. Then we shall see, I guarantee upon my honor, that in a month there will be war between France and Spain on the subject of this son of Louis XIII., who is an Infante likewise, and whom France detains inhumanly. Now, as Louis XIV. would have no inclination for a war on that subject, I will answer for a transaction, the result of which must bring greatness to Porthos and to me, and a duchy in France to you, who are already a grandee of Spain. Will you join us?"

"No; for my part, I prefer having something to reproach the king with; it is a pride natural to my race to pretend to a superiority over royal races. Doing what you propose, I should become the obliged of the king; I should certainly be the gainer on that ground, but I should be a loser in my conscience. No, thank you!"

"Then give me two things, Athos—your absolution."

"Oh! I give it you if you have really wished to avenge the weak and the oppressed against the oppressor."

"That is sufficient for me," said Aramis, with a blush which was lost in the obscurity of the night. "And now, give me your two best horses to gain the second post, as I have been refused any under the pretext of the Duc de Beaufort being traveling in this country."

"You shall have the two best horses, Aramis; and I again recommend Porthos strongly to you."

"Oh! I have no fear on that head. One word more: do you think I am maneuvering for him as I ought?"

"The evil being committed, yes; for the king would not pardon him, and you have, whatever may be said, always a supporter in Monsieur Fouquet, who will not abandon you, he being himself compromised, notwithstanding his heroic action."

"You are right. And that is why, instead of gaining the sea at once, which would proclaim my fear and guilt, that is why I remain upon French ground. But Belle-Isle will be for me whatever ground I wish it to be—English, Spanish, or Roman; all will consist, with me, in the standard I shall think proper to unfurl."

"How so?"

"It was I who fortified Belle-Isle; and, while I defend it, nobody can take Belle-Isle from me. And then, as you have said just now, Monsieur Fouquet is there. Belle-Isle will not be attacked without the signature of Monsieur Fouquet."

"That is true. Nevertheless, be prudent. The king is both cunning and strong."

Aramis smiled.

"I again recommend Porthos to you," repeated the comte, with a cold persistence.

"Whatever becomes of me, comte," replied Aramis, in the same tone, "our brother, Porthos, will fare as I do."

Athos bowed while pressing the hand of Aramis, and turned to embrace Porthos with much emotion.

"I was born lucky, was I not?" murmured the latter, transported with happiness, as he folded his cloak round him.

"Come, my dear friend," said Aramis.

Raoul was gone out to give orders for the saddling of the horses. The group was already divided. Athos saw his two friends on the point of departure, and something like a mist passed before his eyes and weighed upon his heart.

"It is strange," thought he, "whence comes the inclination I feel to embrace Porthos once more?"

At that moment Porthos turned round, and he came toward his old friend with open arms. This last endearment was tender as in youth, as in times when the heart was warm, and life happy.

And then Porthos mounted his horse. Aramis came back once more to throw his arms round the neck of Athos. The latter watched them along the highroad, elongated by the shade, in their white cloaks. Like two phantoms, they seemed to be enlarged on departing from the earth, and it was not in the mist, but in the declivity of the ground that they disappeared. At the end of the perspective both seemed to have given a spring with their feet, which made them vanish, as if evaporated into the clouds.

"Then Athos, with an oppressed heart, returned toward the house, saying to De Bragelonne:

"Raoul, I don't know what it is that has just told me that I have seen these two men for the last time."

"It does not astonish me, monsieur, that you should have such a thought," replied the young man, "for I have at this moment the same, and think also that I shall never see Messieurs du Vallon and D'Herblay again." ·

"Oh! you," replied the comte, "you speak like a man rendered sad by another cause; you see everything in black; you are young, and if you chance never to see those old friends again, it will be because they no longer exist in the world in which you have many years to pass. But I——"

Raoul shook his head sadly, and leaned upon the shoulder of the comte, without either of them finding another word in their hearts, which were ready to overflow.

All at once a noise of horses and voices, from the extremity of the road to Blois, attracted their attention that way. Flambeau-bearers shook their torches merrily among the trees of their route, and turned round, from time to time, to avoid distancing the horsemen who followed them. These flames, this noise, this dust of a dozen richly-caparisoned horses formed a strange contrast in the middle of the night with the melancholy, unreal disappearance of the two shadows of Aramis and Porthos. Athos went toward the house; but he had hardly reached the parterre when the entrance-gate appeared in a blaze; all the flambeaus stopped and appeared to inflame the road. A cry was heard of "Monsieur le Duc de Beaufort!" and Athos sprang toward the door of his house. But the duke had already alighted from his horse, and was looking around him.

"I am here, monseigneur," said Athos.

"Ah! good evening, dear comte," said the prince, with that frank cordiality which won him so many hearts. "Is it too late for a friend?"

"Ah, my dear prince, come in!" said the comte.

And M. de Beaufort, leaning on the arm of Athos, they entered the house, followed by Raoul, who walked respectfully and modestly among the officers of the prince, with several of whom he was acquainted.

Chapter 27 — M. DE BEAUFORT

The prince turned round at the moment when Raoul, in order to leave him alone with Athos, was shutting the door, and preparing to go with the other officers into an adjoining apartment.

"Is that the young man I have heard Monsieur le Prince speak so highly of?" asked M. de Beaufort.

"It is, monseigneur."

"He is quite the soldier; let him stay, comte, we cannot spare him."

"Remain, Raoul, since monseigneur permits it," said Athos.

"*Ma foi!* he is tall and handsome!" continued the duke. "Will you give him to me, monseigneur, if I ask him of you?"

"How am I to understand you, monseigneur?" said Athos.

"Why, I call upon you to bid you farewell."

"Farewell?"

"Yes, in good truth. Have you no idea of what I am about to become?"

"Why, I suppose, what you have always been, monseigneur —a valiant prince, and an excellent gentleman."

"I am going to become an African prince—a Bedouin gentleman. The king is sending me to make conquests among the Arabs."

"What do you tell me, monseigneur?"

"Strange, is it not? I, the Parisian *par excellence*, I, who have reigned in the faubourgs, and have been called King of the Halles —I am going to pass from the Place Maubert to the minarets of Gigelli; I become from a *frondeur* an adventurer!"

"Oh, monseigneur, if you did not yourself tell me that——"

"It would not be credible, would it? Believe me, nevertheless, and we have but to bid each other farewell. This is what comes of getting into favor again."

"Into favor?"

"Yes. You smile. Ah, my dear comte, do you know why have accepted this enterprise, can you guess?"

"Because your highness loves glory above everything."

"Oh! no; there is no glory in firing muskets at savages. I see no glory in that, for my part, and it is more probable that I shall there meet with something else. But I have wished, and still wish earnestly, my dear comte, that my life should have that last *facet*, after all the whimsical exhibitions I have seen myself make during fifty years. For, in short, you must admit that it is sufficiently strange to be born the grandson of a king, to have made war against kings, to have been reckoned among the powers of the age, to have maintained my rank, to feel Henry IV. within me, to be great admiral of France—and then to go and get killed at Gigelli, among all those Turks, Saracens, and Moors."

"Monseigneur, you dwell strangely upon that subject," said Athos, in an agitated voice. "How can you suppose that so brilliant a destiny will be extinguished in that remote and miserable scene?"

"And can you believe, just and simple man as you are, that if I go into Africa for this ridiculous motive I will not endeavor to come out of it without ridicule? Will I not give the world cause to speak of me? And to be spoken of nowadays, when there are Monsieur le Prince, Monsieur de Turenne, and many others, my contemporaries, I, admiral of France, grandson of Henry IV., king of Paris, have I anything left but to get myself killed? *Mordieu!* I will be talked of, I tell you; I shall be killed whether or not; if not there, somewhere else."

"Why, monseigneur, this is only exaggeration; and hitherto you have demonstrated nothing of that kind but in bravery."

"*Peste!* my dear friend, there is bravery in facing scurvy, dysentery, locusts, and poisoned arrows, as my ancestor, St. Louis, did. Do you know those fellows still use poisoned arrows? And then, you know me of old, I fancy, and you know that when I once make up my mind to a thing, I do it in earnest."

"Yes, you made up your mind to escape from Vincennes."

"Ay, but you aided me in that, my master; and, apropos, I turn this way and turn that, without seeing my old friend, Monsieur Vaugrimaud. How is he?"

"Monsieur Vaugrimaud is still your highness' most respectful servant," said Athos, smiling.

"I have a hundred pistoles here for him, which I bring as a legacy. My will is made, comte."

"Ah! monseigneur, monseigneur!"

"And you may understand that if Grimaud's name were to

appear in my will——" The duke began to laugh; then, addressing Raoul, who, from the commencement of this conversation, had sunk into a profound reverie, "Young man," said he, "I know there is to be found here a certain De Vouvray wine, and I believe——"

Raoul left the room precipitately to order the wine. In the meantime, M. de Beaufort took the hand of Athos.

"What do you mean to do with him?" asked he.

"Nothing at present, monseigneur."

"Ah, yes, I know; since the passion of the king for La Valliere."

"Yes, monseigneur."

"That is all true, then, is it? I think I know her, that little La Valliere. She is not particularly handsome, if I remember right."

"No, monseigneur," said Athos.

"Do you know whom she reminds me of?"

"Does she remind your highness of any one?"

"She reminds me of a very agreeable girl, whose mother lived in the Halles."

"Ah! ah!" said Athos, smiling.

"Oh! the good old times," added M. de Beaufort. "Yes, La Valliere reminds me of that girl."

"Who had a son, had she not?"

"I believe she had," replied the duke, with careless naïveté, and a complaisant forgetfulness of which no words could translate the tone and the vocal expression. "Now, here is poor Raoul, who is your son, I believe?"

"Yes, he is my son, monseigneur."

"And the poor lad has been cut out by the king, and he frets?"

"Better than that, monseigneur, he abstains."

"You are going to let the boy rust in idleness? You are wrong. Come, give him to me."

"My wish is to keep him at home, monseigneur. I have no longer anything in the world but him, and as long as he likes to remain——"

"Well, well," replied the duke, "I could, nevertheless, have soon put matters to rights again. I assure you, I think he has in him the stuff of which maréchals of France are made; I have seen more than one produced from such."

"That is very possible, monseigneur; but it is the king who makes maréchals of France, and Raoul will never accept anything of the king."

Raoul interrupted this conversation by his return. He preceded Grimaud, whose still steady hands carried the plateau with one glass and a bottle of the duc's favorite wine. On seeing his old *protégé*, the duke uttered an exclamation of pleasure.

"Grimaud! Good-evening, Grimaud!" said he. "How goes it?"

The servant bowed profoundly, as much gratified as his noble interlocutor was.

"Two old friends!" said the duke, shaking honest Grimaud's shoulder after a vigorous fashion, which was followed by another still more profound and delighted bow from Grimaud.

"But what is this, comte, only one glass?"

"I should not think of drinking with your highness, unless your highness permitted me," replied Athos, with noble humility.

"*Mordieu!* you were right to bring only one glass; we will both drink out of it, like two brothers in arms. Begin, comte."

"Do me the honor," said Athos, gently putting back the glass.

"You are a charming friend," replied the Duc de Beaufort, who drank, and passed the goblet to his companion. "But that is not all," continued he, "I am still thirsty, and I wish to do honor to this handsome young man who stands here. I carry good luck with me, vicomte," said he to Raoul; "wish for something while drinking out of my glass, and the plague stifle me if what you wish does not come to pass!"

He held the goblet to Raoul, who hastily moistened his lips, and replied, with the same promptitude:

"I have wished for something, monseigneur."

His eyes sparkled with a gloomy fire, and the blood mounted to his cheeks; he terrified Athos, if only with his smile.

"And what have you wished for?" replied the duc, sinking back into his *fauteuil*, while with one hand he returned the bottle to Grimaud, and with the other gave him a purse.

"Will you promise me, monseigneur, to grant me what I wish for?"

"*Pardieu!* that is agreed upon."

"I wished, Monsieur le Duc, to go with you to Gigelli."

Athos became pale, and was unable to conceal his agitation. The duke looked at his friend, as if desirous to assist him to carry this unexpected blow.

"That is difficult my dear vicomte, very difficult," added he, in a lower tone of voice.

"Pardon me, monseigneur, I have been indiscreet," replied Raoul, in a firm voice; "but as you yourself invited me to wish——"

"To wish to leave me?" said Athos.

"Oh, monsieur—can you imagine——"

"Well, *mordieu!*" cried the duke, "the young vicomte is right. What can he do here? He will rot with grief."

Raoul blushed, and the excitable prince continued:

"War is a distraction; we gain everything by it; we can only lose one thing by it, life; then so much the worse."

"That is to say memory," said Raoul eagerly, "and that is to say, so much the better!"

He repented of having spoken so warmly when he saw Athos rise and open the window, which was, doubtless, to conceal an emotion. Raoul sprang toward the comte, but the latter had already overcome his emotion, and turned to the lights with a serene and impressive countenance.

"Well, come," said the duke, "let us see! Shall he go, or shall he not? If he goes, comte, he shall be my aid-de-camp my son."

"Monseigneur!" cried Raoul, bending his knee.

"Monseigneur!" cried Athos, taking the hand of the duke, "Raoul shall do just as he likes."

"Oh, no, monsieur; just as you like!" interrupted the young man.

"By *la Corbleu!*" said the prince, in his turn, "it is neither the comte nor the vicomte that shall have his way, it is I. I will take him away. The marine offers a superb future, my friend."

Raoul smiled again so sadly that this time Athos felt his heart penetrated by it, and replied to him by a severe look. Raoul comprehended it all; he recovered his calmness, and was so guarded that not another word escaped him. The duke at length rose, on observing the advanced hour, and said, with much animation:

"I am in great haste, but if I am told I have lost time in talking with a friend, I will reply I have gained a good recruit."

"Pardon me, Monsieur le Duc," interrupted Raoul, "do not tell the king so, for it is not the king I will serve."

"Eh! my friend, whom, then, will you serve? The times are past when you might have said, 'I belong to Monsieur de Beaufort.' No, nowadays we all belong to the king, great or small. Therefore, if you serve on board my vessel, there can be nothing equivocal in it, my dear vicomte; it will be the king you will serve."

Athos waited with a kind of impatient joy for the reply about to be made to this embarrassing question by Raoul, the intractable enemy of the king, his rival. The father hoped that the obstacle would overcome the desire. He was thankful to M. de Beaufort, whose lightness or generous reflection had thrown an impediment in the way of the departure of a son now his only joy. But Raoul, still firm and tranquil:

"Monsieur le Duc," replied he, "the objection you make I have already considered in my mind. I will serve on board your vessels, because you do me the honor to take me with you; but I shall there serve a more powerful master than the king, I shall serve God!"

"God! how so?" said the duke and Athos together.

"My intention is to make profession, and become a Knight of Malta," added De Bragelonne, letting fall, one by one, words more icy than the drops which fall from the bare trees after the tempests of winter.

Under this blow Athos staggered, and the prince himself was moved. Grimaud uttered a heavy groan, and let fall the bottle, which was broken without anybody paying attention to it. M. de Beaufort looked the young man in the face, and read plainly, though his eyes were cast down, the fire of resolution before which everything must give way. As to Athos, he was too well acquainted with that tender but inflexible soul; he could not hope to make it deviate from the fatal road it had just chosen. He could only press the hand the duke held out to him.

"Comte, I shall set off in two days for Toulon," said M. de Beaufort. "Will you meet me at Paris, in order that I may know your determination?"

"I will have the honor of thanking you there, *mon prince*, for all your kindnesses," replied the comte.

"And be sure to bring the vicomte with you, whether he follows me or does not follow me," added the duke; "he has my word, and I only ask yours."

Having thrown a little balm upon the wound of the paternal heart, he pulled the ear of Grimaud, whose eyes sparkled more than usual, and regained his escort in the parterre. The horses, rested and refreshed, set off with spirit through this beautiful night, and soon placed a considerable distance between their master and the château.

Athos and De Bragelonne were again face to face. Eleven o'clock was striking. The father and son preserved a profound silence toward each other, where an intelligent observer would

have expected cries and tears. But these two men were of such
a nature that all emotion plunged itself where it was lost for
ever when they had resolved to confine it to their own hearts
They passed, then, silently and almost breathlessly, the hour
which preceded midnight. The clock, by striking, alone pointed
out to them how many minutes had lasted the painful journey
made by their souls in the immensity of the remembrance
of the past and of the fears of the future. Athos rose first, say
ing:

"It is late—till to-morrow."

Raoul rose, and in his turn embraced his father. The latter
held him clasped to his breast, and said, in a tremulous
voice:

"In two days you will have left me, then—left me forever
Raoul!"

"Monsieur," replied the young man, "I had formed a deter
mination, that of piercing my heart with my sword; but you
would have thought that cowardly. I have renounced that de
termination, and therefore we must part."

"You leave me by going, Raoul."

"Listen to me again, monsieur, I implore you. If I do not go
I shall die here of grief and love. I know how long a time I have
to live thus. Send me away quickly, monsieur, or you will see
me basely die before your eyes—in your house—this is stronger
than my will—stronger than my strength—you may plainly
see that within one month I have lived thirty years, and that
I approach the end of my life."

"Then," said Athos coldly, "you go with the intention of get
ting killed in Africa? Oh, tell me, do not lie!"

Raoul grew deathly pale, and remained silent for two sec
onds, which were to his father two hours of agony. Then all at
once:

"Monsieur," said he, "I·have promised to devote myself to
God. In exchange for this sacrifice which I make of my youth
and my liberty, I will only ask of Him one thing, and that is to
preserve me for you, because you are the only tie which at
taches me to this world. God alone can give me the strength
not to forget that I owe you everything, and that nothing
ought to be with me before you."

Athos embraced his son tenderly and said:

"You have just replied to me on the word of honor of an
honest man; in two days we shall be with Monsieur de Beau
fort at Paris, and you will then do what will be proper for you
to do. You are free, Raoul: adieu."

And he slowly gained his bedroom. Raoul went down into the garden, and passed the night in the alley of limes.

Chapter 28 — PREPARATIONS FOR DEPARTURE

Athos lost no time in combating this immutable resolution. He gave all his attention to preparing, during the two days the duke had granted him, the proper appointments for Raoul. This labor chiefly concerned Grimaud, who immediately applied himself to it with the good-will and intelligence we know he possessed. Athos gave this worthy servant orders to take the route to Paris when the equipments should be ready, and not to expose himself to keeping the duke waiting, or to delay Raoul; so that the duke should not perceive his absence, he himself, the day after the visit of M. de Beaufort, set off for Paris with his son.

For the poor young man it was an emotion easily to be understood, thus to return to Paris among all the people who had known and loved him. Every face recalled a suffering to him who had suffered so much, to him who had loved so much, some circumstance of his love. Raoul, on approaching Paris, felt as if he were dying. Once in Paris, he really existed no longer. When he reached De Guiche's residence he was informed that De Guiche was with Monsieur. Raoul took the road to the Luxembourg, and when arrived, without suspecting that he was going to the place where La Valliere had lived, he heard so much music and respired so many perfumes, he heard so much joyous laughter, and saw so many dancing shadows, that, if it had not been for a charitable woman, who perceived him so dejected and pale beneath a doorway, he would have remained there a few minutes, and then would have gone away, never to return. But, as we have said, in the first antechambers he had stopped, solely for the sake of not mixing himself with all those happy existences which he felt were moving around him in the adjacent saloons. And as one of Monsieur's servants, recognizing him, had asked him if he wished to see Monsieur or Madame, Raoul had scarcely answered him, but had sunk down on a bench near the velvet doorway, looking at a clock, which had stood for nearly an hour. The servant had passed on, and another, better acquainted with him, had come up, and inter-

rogated Raoul whether he should inform M. de Guiche of his
being there. This name even did not rouse the recollections of
poor Raoul. The persistent servant went on to relate that De
Guiche had just invented a new game of lottery, and was teach-
ing it to the ladies. Raoul, opening his large eyes, like the absent man in Theophrastus, had made no answer, but his sadness
had increased by it two shades. With his head hanging down,
his limbs relaxed, his mouth half open for the escape of his
sighs, Raoul remained, thus forgotten, in the antechamber,
when all at once a lady's robe passed, rubbing against the doors
of a lateral saloon which opened upon the gallery. A lady, young,
pretty, and gay, scolding an officer of the household, entered
by that way, and expressed herself with much vivacity. The
officer replied in calm but firm sentences; it was rather a little
love pet than a quarrel of courtiers, and was terminated by a
kiss on the fingers of the lady. Suddenly, on perceiving Raoul,
the lady became silent, and pushing away the officer:

"Make your escape, Malicorne," said she; "I did not think
there was any one here. I shall curse you, if they have either
heard or seen us!"

Malicorne hastened away. The young lady advanced behind
Raoul, and stretching her joyous face over him as he lay:

"Monsieur is a gallant man," said she, "and no doubt——'
She here interrupted herself by uttering a cry:

"Raoul!" said she, blushing.

"Mademoiselle de Montalais!" said Raoul, more pale than
death.

He rose unsteadily, and tried to make his way across the
slippery mosaic of the floor; but she had comprehended the
savage and cruel grief; she felt that in the flight of Raoul there
was an accusation, or, at least, a suspicion against herself. A
woman, ever vigilant, she did not think she ought to let the opportunity slip of making a justification; but Raoul, though
stopped by her in the middle of the gallery, did not seem disposed to surrender without a combat. He took it up in a ton
so cold and embarrassed that if they had been thus surprised
the whole court would have had no doubt about the proceedings of Mlle. de Montalais.

"Ah! monsieur," said she, with disdain, "what you are doing
is very unworthy of a gentleman. My heart inclines me to
speak to you; you compromise me by a reception almost uncivil; you are wrong, monsieur; and you confound your friends
with your enemies. Farewell!"

Raoul had sworn never to speak of Louise, never even to look at those who might have seen Louise; he was going into another world, that he might never meet with anything Louise had seen, or anything she had touched. But after the first shock of his pride, after having had a glimpse of Montalais, the companion of Louise—Montalais, who reminded him of the turret of Blois and the joys of youth, all his reason faded away.

"Pardon me, mademoiselle; it enters not, it cannot enter into my thoughts to be uncivil."

"Do you wish to speak to me?" said she, with the smile of former days. "Well, come somewhere else; for we may be surprised."

"Oh!" said he.

She looked at the clock doubtingly, then, having reflected: "In my apartment," said she, "we shall have an hour to ourselves."

And taking her course, lighter than a fairy, she ran up to her chamber, followed by Raoul. Shutting the door, and placing in the hands of her *camériste* the mantle she had held upon her arm:

"You were seeking Monsieur de Guiche, were you not?" said she to Raoul.

"Yes, mademoiselle."

"I will go and ask him to come up here presently, after I have spoken to you."

"Do so, mademoiselle."

"Are you angry with me?"

Raoul looked at her for a moment, then, casting down his eyes:

"Yes," said he.

"You think I was concerned in the plot which brought about our rupture, do you not?"

"Rupture!" said he, with bitterness. "Oh, mademoiselle, there can be no rupture where there has been no love."

"An error," replied Montalaise: "Louise did love you."

Raoul started.

"Not with love, I know; but she liked you, and you ought have married her before you set out for London."

Raoul broke into a sinister laugh, which made Montalais shudder.

"You tell me that very much at your ease, mademoiselle. Do people marry whom they like? You forget that the king then sot for himself, as his mistress, her of whom we are speaking."

"Listen," said the young woman, pressing the cold hands of Raoul in her own, "you were wrong in every way; a man of your age ought never to leave a woman of hers alone."

"There is no longer any faith in the world, then," said Raoul.

"No, vicomte," said Montalais quietly. "Nevertheless, let me tell you that if instead of loving Louise coldly and philosophically, you had endeavored to awaken her to love——"

"Enough, I pray you, mademoiselle," said Raoul. "I feel that you are all, of both sexes, of a different age from me. You can laugh, and you can banter agreeably. I, mademoiselle, I loved Mademoiselle de—" Raoul could not pronounce her name— "I loved her; well, I put faith in her—now I am quits by loving her no longer."

"Oh, vicomte!" said Montalais, pointing to his reflection in a mirror.

"I know what you mean, mademoiselle; I am much altered, am I not? Well, do you know why? Because my face is the mirror of my heart; the inside has changed as you see the outside has."

"You are consoled, then," said Montalais sharply.

"No, I shall never be consoled."

"I don't understand you, Monsieur de Bragelonne."

"I care but little for that. I do not quite understand myself."

"You have not even tried to speak to Louise?"

"Who, I?" exclaimed the young man, with eyes flashing fire; "I? Why do you not advise me to marry her? Perhaps the king would consent now."

And he rose from his chair, full of anger.

"I see," said Montalais, "that you are not cured, and that Louise has one enemy the more."

"One enemy the more!"

"Yes; favorites are but little beloved at the Court of France."

"Oh! while she has her lover to protect her, is not that enough? She has chosen him of such a quality that her enemies cannot prevail against her." But, stopping all at once, "And then she has you for a friend, mademoiselle," added he with a shade of irony which did not glide off the cuirass.

"Who, I? Oh, no; I am no longer one of those whom Mademoiselle de la Valliere deigns to look upon; but——"

This *but*, so big with menace and storms; this *but*, which made the heart of Raoul beat, such griefs did it presage for her whom lately he loved so dearly; this terrible *but*, so s

ificant in a woman like Montalais, was interrupted by a
moderately loud noise heard by the speakers, proceeding from
the alcove behind the wainscoting. Montalais turned to listen,
and Raoul was already rising, when a lady entered the room
quietly by the secret door, which she closed after her.

"Madame!" exclaimed Raoul, on recognizing the sister-in-
law of the king.

"Stupid wretch!" murmured Montalais, throwing herself,
but too late, before the princess, "I have been mistaken in
an hour!"

She had, however, time to warn the princess, who was walking toward Raoul.

"Monsieur de Bragelonne, madame;" and at these words the
princess drew back, uttering a cry in her turn.

"Your royal highness," said Montalais, with volubility, "is
kind enough to think of this lottery, and——"

The princess began to lose countenance. Raoul hastened his
departure, without yet divining all; but he felt that he was in
the way. Madame was preparing a word of transition to recover
herself, when a closet opened in front of the alcove, and M. de
Guiche issued, all radiant, also from that closet. The most pale
of the four, we must admit, was still Raoul. The princess, however, was near fainting, and was obliged to lean upon the foot
of the bed for support. No one ventured to support her. This
scene occupied several minutes of terrible silence. But Raoul
broke it. He went up to the comte, whose inexpressible emotion made his knees tremble, and taking his hand:

"Dear comte," said he, "tell madame I am too unhappy not
to merit my pardon; tell her also that I have loved in the course
of my life, and that the horror of the treachery that has been
practiced on me renders me inexorable for all other treachery
that may be committed around me. This is why, mademoiselle,"
said he, smiling, to Montalais, "I never would divulge the secret of the visits of my friend to your apartment. Obtain from
madame—from madame, who is so clement and so generous—
obtain her pardon for you whom she has just surprised also.
You are both free, love each other, be happy!"

The princess felt for a moment the despair which cannot be
described; it was repugnant to her, nowithstanding the exquisite delicacy which Raoul had exhibited, to feel herself at
the mercy of an indiscretion. It was equally repugnant to her
to accept the evasion offered by this delicate deception. Agitated, nervous, she struggled against the double stings of the

two troubles. Raoul comprehended her position, and came on
more to her aid. Bending his knee before her:

"Madame," said he, in a low voice, "in two days I shall
far from Paris; in a fortnight I shall be far from France, whe
I shall never be seen again."

"Are you going away, then?" said she, with great delight.

"With Monsieur de Beaufort."

"Into Africa?" cried De Guiche, in his turn. "You, Raou
Oh, my friend—into Africa, where everybody dies!"

And, forgetting everything, forgetting that that forgetfulne
itself compromised the princess more eloquently than 1
presence:

"Ingrate," said he, "and you have not even consulted me

And he embraced him, during which time Montalais had 1
away madame, and disappeared herself.

Raoul passed his hand over his brow, and said, with a smil

"I have been dreaming!" Then, warmly, to De Guiche, wl
by degrees, absorbed him, "My friend," said he, "I conce
nothing from you, who are the elected of my heart. I am goi
to seek death in yonder country; your secret will not remain
my breast more than a year."

"Oh, Raoul, a man!"

"Do you know what is my thought, De Guiche? This is
'I shall live more, being buried beneath the earth, than I ha
lived for this month past. We are Christians, my friend, a
if such sufferings were to continue, I would not be answeral
for the safety of my soul.'"

De Guiche was anxious to raise objections.

"Not one word more on my account," said Raoul; "1
advice to you, dear friend; what I am going to say to you
of much greater importance."

"What is that?"

"Without doubt, you risk much more than I do, because y
love."

"Oh!"

"It is a joy so sweet to me to be able to speak to you th
Well, then, De Guiche, beware of Montalais."

"What, of that kind friend?"

"She was the friend of—her you know of. She ruined her
pride."

"You are mistaken."

"And now, when she has ruined her, she would ravish fr
her the only thing that renders that woman excusable in
eyes."

"What is that?"

"Her love."

"What do you mean by that?"

"I mean that there is a plot formed against her who is the mistress of the king—a plot formed in the very house of madame."

"Can you think so?"

"I am certain of it."

"By Montalais?"

"Take her as the least dangerous of the enemies I dread for —the other."

"Explain yourself clearly, my friend; and if I can understand you——"

"In two words. Madame has been jealous of the king."

"I know she has——"

"Oh, fear nothing—you are beloved—you are beloved, De Guiche; do you feel the value of these three words? They signify that you can raise your head, that you can sleep tranquilly, that you can thank God every minute of your life. You are beloved; that signifies that you may hear everything, even the counsel of a friend who wishes to preserve your happiness. You are beloved, De Guiche, you are beloved! You do not endure those atrocious nights, those nights without end, which, with arid eye and devoured heart, others pass through who are destined to die. You will live long, if you act like the miser who, bit by bit, crumb by crumb, collects and heaps up diamonds and gold. You are beloved! allow me to tell you what you must do that you may be beloved forever."

De Guiche contemplated for some time this unfortunate young man, half-mad with despair; there passed through his heart something still like remorse at his own happiness. Raoul suppressed his feverish excitement, to assume the voice and countenance of an impassible man.

"They will make her, whose name I should wish still to be able to pronounce—they will make her suffer. Swear to me that you will not second them in anything—but that you will defend her, when possible, as I would have done myself."

"I swear I will!" replied De Guiche.

"And," continued Raoul, "some day, when you shall have rendered her a great service—some day, when she shall thank you, promise me to say these words to her: 'I have done you this kindness, madame, by the warm desire of Monsieur de Bragelonne, whom you so deeply injured.' "

"I swear I will!" murmured De Guiche.

"That is all. Adieu! I set out to-morrow, or the day after, for Toulon. If you have a few hours to spare, give them to me."

"All, all!" cried the young man.

"Thank you."

"And what are you going to do now?"

"I am going to meet Monsieur le Comte at the house of Planchet, where we hope to find Monsieur d'Artagnan."

"Monsieur d'Artagnan?"

"Yes; I wish to embrace him before my departure. He is a brave man, who loves me dearly. Farewell, my friend; you are expected, no doubt; you will find me, when you wish, at the lodgings of the comte. Farewell!"

The two young men embraced. They who might have seen them both thus would not have hesitated to say, pointing to Raoul:

"That is the happy man!"

Chapter 29 — PLANCHET'S INVENTORY

Athos, during the visit made to the Luxembourg by Raoul, had gone to Planchet's residence to inquire after D'Artagnan. The gentleman, on arriving at the Rue des Lombards, found the shop of the grocer in great confusion; but it was not the encumberment of a lucky sale, or that of an arrival of goods. Planchet was not throned, as usual, upon sacks and barrels. No. A young man with a pen behind his ear, and another with an account-book in his hand, were setting down a number of figures, while a third counted and weighed. An inventory was being taken. Athos, who had no knowledge of commercial matters, felt himself a little embarrassed by the material obstacles and the majesty of those who were thus employed. He saw several customers sent away, and asked himself whether he who came to buy nothing, would not be more properly deemed importunate. He therefore asked very politely if he could see M. Planchet. The reply, pretty carelessly given, was that M. Planchet was packing his trunks. These words surprised Athos.

"How! his trunks?" said he; "is Monsieur Planchet going away?"

"Yes, monsieur, directly."

"Then, if you please, inform him that Monsieur le Comte de la Fere desires to speak to him for a moment."

At the mention of the comte's name one of the young men, no doubt accustomed to hear it pronounced with respect, immediately went to inform Planchet. It was at this moment that Raoul, after his painful scene with Montalais and De Guiche, arrived at the grocer's house. Planchet left his job directly he received the comte's message.

"Ah, Monsieur le Comte!" exclaimed he, "how glad I am to see you! What good star brings you here?"

"My dear Planchet," said Athos, pressing the hand of his son, whose sad look he silently observed, "we are come to learn of you— But in what confusion do I find you! You are as white as a miller. Where have you been rummaging?"

"Ah, *diable!* take care, monsieur; don't come near me till I have well shaken myself."

"What for? Flour or dust only whiten."

"No, no; what you see on my arms is arsenic."

"Arsenic?"

"Yes; I am making my provision for the rats."

"Ay, I suppose in an establishment like this the rats play a conspicuous part."

"It is not with this establishment I concern myself, Monsieur le Comte. The rats have robbed me of more here than they will ever rob me of again."

"What do you mean?"

"Why, you may have observed, monsieur, my inventory is being taken."

"Are you leaving trade, then?"

"Eh! *mon Dieu!* yes. I have disposed of my business to one of my young men."

"Bah! you are rich, then, I suppose?"

"Monsieur, I have taken a dislike to the city; I don't know whether it is because I am growing old, and as Monsieur d'Artagnan one day said, when we grow old we more often think of the things of our youth, but for some time past I have felt myself attracted toward the country and gardening; I was a countryman formerly."

And Planchet marked this confession with a little rather pretentious laugh for a man making profession of humility.

Athos made a gesture of approval, and then added:

"You are going to buy an estate, then?"

"I have bought one, monsieur."

"Ah! that is still better."

"A little house at Fontainebleau, with something like twent acres of land round it."

"Very well, Planchet. Accept my compliments on your ac quisition."

"But, monsieur, we are not comfortable here; the curse dust makes you cough. *Corbleu!* I should not wish to poiso the most worthy gentleman in the kingdom."

Athos did not smile at this little pleasantry which Planche had aimed at him, in order to try his strength in mundane face tiousness.

"Yes," said he, "let us have a little talk by ourselves—i your own room, for example. You have a room, have yo not?"

"Certainly, Monsieur le Comte."

"Upstairs, perhaps?"

And Athos, seeing Planchet a little embarrassed, wished t relieve him by going first.

"It is—but—" said Planchet, hesitating. Athos was mistake in the cause of this hesitation, and, attributing it to a fear th grocer might have of offering humble hospitality:

"Never mind, never mind," said he, still going up, "the dwell ing of a tradesman in this quarter is not expected to be a pa ace. Come on."

Raoul nimbly preceded him, and entered first. Two crie were heard simultaneously—we may say three. One of thes cries dominated over the others; it was uttered by a woma The other proceeded from the mouth of Raoul; it was an e clamation of surprise. He had no sooner made it than he shu the door sharply. The third was from fright; Planchet ha proffered it.

"I ask your pardon," added he; "madame is dressing."

Raoul had, no doubt, seen that what Planchet said was true for he turned round to go downstairs again.

"Madame—" said Athos. "Oh, pardon me, Planchet, I di not know that you had upstairs——"

"It is Trüchen," added Planchet, blushing a little.

"It is whom you please, my good Planchet; but pardon m rudeness."

"No, no; go up now, gentlemen."

"We will do no such thing," said Athos.

"Oh! madame, having notice, has had time——"

"No, Planchet; farewell."

"Eh! gentlemen, you would not disoblige me by thus stand

ing on the staircase, or by going away without having sat down?"

"If we had known you had a lady upstairs," replied Athos, with his customary coolness, "we would have asked permission to pay our respects to her."

Planchet was so disconcerted by this little extravagance that he forced the passage, and himself opened the door to admit the comte and his son. Trüchen was quite dressed: costume of the shop-keeper's wife, rich and coquettish; German eyes attacking French eyes. She ceded the apartment after two courtesies, and went down into the shop—but not without having listened at the door, to know what Planchet's gentlemen visitors would say of her. Athos suspected that, and, therefore, turned the conversation accordingly. Planchet, on his part, was burning to give explanations, which Athos avoided. But, as certain tenacities are stronger than all others, Athos was forced to hear Planchet recite his idyls of felicity, translated into a language more chaste than that of Longus. So Planchet related how Trüchen had charmed his ripe age, and brought good luck to his business, as Ruth did to Boaz.

"You want nothing now, then, but heirs to your property."

"If I had one, he would have three hundred thousand livres," said Planchet.

"Humph! you must have one, then," said Athos phlegmatically; "if only to prevent your little fortune being lost."

These words, *little fortune*, placed Planchet in his rank, like the voice of the sergeant when Planchet was but a *piqueur* in the regiment of Piedmont, in which Rochefort had placed him. Athos perceived that the grocer would marry Trüchen, and, in spite of fate, establish a family. This appeared the more evident to him when he learned that the young man to whom Planchet was selling his business was her cousin. Having heard all that was necessary of the happy prospects of the retiring grocer:

"What is Monsieur d'Artagnan about?" said he. "He is not at the Louvre."

"Ah! Monsieur le Comte. Monsieur d'Artagnan has disappeared."

"Disappeared?" said Athos, with surprise.

"Oh! monsieur, we know what that means."

"But I do not know."

"Whenever Monsieur d'Artagnan disappears it is always for some mission or some great affair."

"Has he said anything to you about it?"

"Never."

"You were acquainted with his departure for England formerly, were you not?"

"On account of the speculation," said Planchet heedlessly.

"The speculation!"

"I mean—" interrupted Planchet, quite confused.

"Well, well, neither your affairs nor those of your master are in question; the interest we take in him alone has induced me to apply to you. Since the captain of the musketeers is not here, and as we cannot learn from you where we are likely to find Monsieur d'Artagnan, we will take our leave of you. *Au revoir*, Planchet, *au revoir*. Let us be gone, Raoul."

"Monsieur le Comte, I wish I were able to tell you——"

"Oh, not at all; I am not the man to reproach a servant with discretion."

This word "servant" struck rudely on the ears of the *demi-millionnaire*, Planchet; but natural respect and *bon-homie* prevailed over pride.

"There is nothing indiscreet in telling you, Monsieur le Comte; Monsieur d'Artagnan came here the other day."

"Ah! ah!"

"And remained several hours consulting a geographica chart."

"You are right, then my friend; say no more about it."

"And the chart is there as a proof," added Planchet, who went to fetch from the neighboring wall, where it was suspended by a twist, forming a triangle with the bar of the window to which it was fastened—the plan consulted by the captain on his last visit to Planchet. This plan, which he brought to the comte, was a map of France, upon which the practiced eye of that gentleman discovered an itinerary, marked out with small pins; wherever a pin was missing, a hole denoted its having been there. Athos, by following with his eye the pins and holes, saw that D'Artagnan had taken the direction of the south, and gone as far as the Mediterranean, toward Toulon It was near Cannes that the marks and the punctured place ceased. The Comte de la Fere puzzled his brains for some time to divine what the musketeer could be going to do at Cannes, and what motive could have led him to examine the banks of the Var. The reflections of Athos suggested nothing His accustomed perspicacity was at fault. Raoul's research were not more successful than his father's.

"Never mind," said the young man to the comte, who lently, and with his finger, had made him understand the rou of D'Artagnan; "we must confess that there is a Providence always occupied in connecting our destiny with that of Monsieur d'Artagnan. There he is on the coast of Cannes, and you, monsieur, will, at least, conduct me as far as Toulon. Be assured that we shall meet with him more easily upon our route than upon this map."

Then, taking leave of Planchet, who was scolding his shopmen, even the cousin of Trüchen, his successor, the gentlemen set out to pay a visit to M. de Beaufort. On leaving the grocer's shop they saw a coach, the future depository of the charms of Mlle. Trüchen and the bags of crowns of Planchet.

"Every one journeys toward happiness by the route he chooses," said Raoul, in a melancholy tone.

"Road to Fontainebleau!" cried Planchet, to his coachman.

Chapter 30 — THE INVENTORY OF M. DE BEAUFORT

To have talked of D'Artagnan with Planchet, to have seen Planchet quit Paris to bury himself in his country retreat, had been for Athos and his son like a last farewell to the noise of the capital—to their life of former days. What, in fact, did these men leave behind them—one of whom had exhausted the past age in glory, and the other the present age in misfortune? egotistical aristocracy which Richelieu had constrained to contemporaries. They had only to pay a visit to M. de Beaufort, and arrange with him the particulars of the departure. The duke was lodged magnificently in Paris. He had one of those superb establishments pertaining to great fortunes, which certain old men remembered to have seen flourish in times of wasteful liberality in Henry III.'s reign. Then, really, several great nobles were richer than the king. They knew it, used it, and never deprived themselves of the pleasure of humiliating his royal majesty when they had an opportunity. It was this egotistical aristocracy which Richelieu had constrained to contribute, with its blood, its purse, and its duties, to what was from his time styled the king's service. From Louis XI.—that terrible mower down of the great—to Richelieu, how many families had raised their heads! How many from Richelieu to Louis XIV. had bowed their heads, never to raise them again! But M. de Beaufort was born a prince, and of a blood which is not shed upon scaffolds, unless by the decree of peoples. This prince had kept up a grand style of living. How did he maintain his horses, his people, and his table? Nobody knew; himself less than others. Only there were then privileges for the sons of kings, to whom nobody refused to become a creditor, whether from respect, devotedness, or persuasion that they would some day be paid.

Athos and Raoul found the mansion of the duke in as much confusion as that of Planchet. The duke, likewise, was making his inventory; that is to say, he was distributing to his friends everything of value he had in his house. Owing nearly two millions—an enormous amount in those days—M. de Beaufort had calculated that he could not set out for Africa without a good round sum; and, in order to find that sum, he was distributing to his old creditors plate, arms, jewels, and furniture, which was more magnificent than selling it, and brought him back double. In fact, how could a man to whom ten thousand livres were owing, refuse to carry away a present of six thousand, enhanced in merit from having belonged to a descendant of Henry IV.? And how, after having carried away that present, could he refuse ten thousand livres more to this generous noble? This, then, was what had happened. The duke had no longer a dwelling-house—that had become useless to an admiral whose place of residence is his ship; he had no longer need of superfluous arms, when he was placed amid his cannons; no more jewels, which the sea might rob him of; but he had three or four hundred thousand crowns fresh in his coffers. And throughout the house there was a joyous movement of people who believed they were plundering monseigneur. The prince had, in a supreme degree, the art of making happy the creditors the most to be pitied. Every distressed man, every empty purse, found with him patience and intelligence of his position. To some he said, "I wish I had what you have, I would give it you." And to others, "I have but this silver ewer, it is worth at least five hundred livres—take it." The effect of which was—so truly is courtesy a current payment—that the prince constantly found means to renew his creditors. This time he used no ceremony; it might be called a general pillage. He gave up everything. The Oriental fable of the poor Arab who carried away from the pillage of a palace a kettle at the bottom of which was concealed a bag of gold, and whom everybody allowed to pass without jealousy—this fable had become a truth in the prince's mansion. Many contractors paid themselves upon the offices of the duke. Thus, the provision de partment, who plundered the clothes-presses and the harness-rooms, attached very little value to things which tailors and saddlers set great store by. Anxious to carry home to their wives preserves given them by monseigneur, many were seen bounding joyously along, under the weight of earthen jars and bottles gloriously stamped with the arms of the prince. M. de Beaufort finished by giving away his horses and the hay from his lofts. He made more than thirty happy with kitchen utensils; and thirty more with the contents of his cellar. Still further: all these people went away with the conviction that M. de Beaufort only acted in this manner to prepare for a new fortune concealed beneath the Arab tents. They repeated to each other, while devastating his hotel that he was sent to Gigelli by the king to reconstruct his lost fortunes; that the treasures of Africa would be equally divided between the admiral and the King of France; that these treasures consisted in mines of diamonds, or other fabulous stones; the gold and silver mines of Mount Atlas did not even obtain the honor of being named. In addition to the mines to be worked—which could not be begun till after the campaign—there would be the booty made by the army. M. de Beaufort would lay his hands upon all the riches pirates had robbed Christendom of since the battle of Lepanto. The number of millions from these sources defied calculation. Why, then, should he who was going in quest of such treasures set any store by the poor utensils of his past life? And, reciprocally, why should they spare the property of him who spared it so little himself?

Such was the position of affairs. Athos, with his investigating glance, saw what was going on at once. He found the admiral of France a little exalted, for he was rising from a table of fifty covers, at which the guests had drunk long and deeply to the prosperity of the expedition; at which, with the dessert, the remains of the meal had been given to the servants, and the empty dishes and plates to the curious. The prince was intoxicated with his ruin and his popularity at the same time. He had drunk his old wine to the health of his future wine. When he saw Athos and Raoul:

"There is my aid-de-camp being brought to me!" he cried. "Come hither, comte; come hither, vicomte."

Athos tried to find a passage through the heaps of linen and plate.

"Ah! step over, step over!" said the duke, offering a full glass to Athos.

The latter took it; Raoul scarcely moistened his lips.

"Here is your commission," said the prince to Raoul. "I ha
prepared it, reckoning upon you. You will go on before me a
far as Antibes."

"Yes, monseigneur."

"Here is the order." And De Beaufort gave Raoul the orde
"Do you know anything of the sea?"

"Yes, monseigneur; I have traveled with Monsieur le Prince.

"That is well. All these barges and lighters must be in at
tendance to form an escort and carry my provisions. The arm
must be prepared to embark in a fortnight at latest."

"That shall be done, monseigneur."

"The present order gives you the right to visit and search a
the isles along the coast; you will there make the enrollment
and levies you may want for me."

"Yes, Monsieur le Duc."

"And as you are an active man, and will work freely, you wi
spend much money."

"I hope not, monseigneur."

"But I reckon you will. My intendant has prepared orde
of a thousand livres, drawn upon the cities of the south; he wi
give you a hundred of them. Now, dear vicomte, be gone."

Athos interrupted the prince.

"Keep your money, monseigneur; war is to be made amon
the Arabs with gold as well as lead."

"I wish to try the contrary," replied the duke; "and then yo
are acquainted with my ideas upon the expedition—plenty o
noise, plenty of fire, and, if so it must be, I shall disappear i
the smoke."

Having spoken thus, M. de Beaufort began to laugh; but h
mirth was not reciprocated by Athos and Raoul. He perceive
this at once.

"Ah!" said he, with the courteous egotism of his rank an
his age, "you are such people as a man should not see afte
dinner; you are cold, stiff and dry, when I am all fire, all sup
pleness, and all wine. No, devil take me! I should always se
you fasting, vicomte; and you, comte, if you wear such a fac
as that, you will see me no more."

He said this, pressing the hand of Athos, who replied:

"Monseigneur, do not talk so grandly because you happen t
have plenty of money. I predict that within a month you wi
be dry, stiff, and cold, in presence of your strong-box, and tha
then, having Raoul at your elbow, quite fasting, you will b
surprised to see him gay, animated, and generous, because h
will have new crowns to offer you."

"God grant it may be so!" cried the delighted duke. "Comte, stay with me!"

"No, I shall go with Raoul; the mission with which you charge him is a troublesome and a difficult one. Alone, it would be too much for him to execute. You do not observe, monseigneur, you have given him a command of the first order."

"Bah!"

"And in the marine."

"That may be true. But when people resemble him, do they not do all that is required of them?"

"Monseigneur, I believe you will find nowhere so much zeal and intelligence, so much real bravery, as in Raoul; but if he failed in your embarkation, you would only meet with what you deserve."

"Humph! you are scolding me, then."

"Monseigneur, to provision a fleet, to assemble a flotilla, to enroll your maritime force, would take an admiral a year. Raoul is a cavalry officer, and you allow him a fortnight!"

"I tell you he will get through."

"He may; but I will help him."

"To be sure you will; I reckoned upon you, and still further believe that when we are once at Toulon you will not let him depart alone."

"Oh!" said Athos, shaking his head.

"Patience! patience!"

"Monseigneur, permit us to take our leave."

"Be gone, then, and may good fortune attend you."

"Adieu, monseigneur; and may your good fortune attend you likewise."

"Here is an expedition admirably commenced!" said Athos to his son. "No provisions—no store flotilla! What can be done, thus?"

"Humph!" murmured Raoul; "if all are going to do as I am, provisions will not be wanted."

"Monsieur," replied Athos sternly, "do not be unjust and senseless in your egotism, or your grief, whichever you please to call it. If you set out for this war solely with the intention of getting killed in it, you stand in need of nobody, and it was scarcely worth while to recommend you to Monsieur de Beaufort. But when you have been introduced to the prince commandant—when you have accepted the responsibility of a post in his army, the question is no longer about you, but about all those poor soldiers, who, as well as you, have hearts and bodies, who will weep for their country and endure all the necessities

of their human condition. Remember, Raoul, that an officer is
a minister as useful as a priest, and that he ought to have more
charity than a priest."

"Monsieur, I know it, and have practiced it; I would have
continued to do so still, but——"

"You forget also that you are of a country which is proud of
its military glory; go and die if you like, but do not die without honor and without advantage to France. Cheer up, Raoul!
do not let my words grieve you; I love you, and wish to see you
perfect."

"I love your reproaches, monsieur," said the young man
mildly; "they alone may cure me, because they prove to me
that some one loves me still."

"And now, Raoul, let us be off; the weather is so fine, the
heavens are so pure, those heavens which we shall always find
above our heads, which you will see more pure still at Gigelli,
and which will speak to you of me there, as they speak to me
here of God."

The two gentlemen, after having agreed on this point,
talked over the wild freaks of the duke, convinced that France
would be served in a very incomplete manner, as regarded both
spirit and practice, in the ensuing expedition; and having
summed up his policy under the word vanity, they set forward,
in obedience to their will, rather than to their destiny. The sacrifice was accomplished.

Chapter 31 — THE SILVER DISH

The journey passed off pretty well. Athos and his son traversed
France at the rate of fifteen leagues per day; sometimes more,
sometimes less, according to the intensity of Raoul's grief. It
took them a fortnight to reach Toulon, and they lost all traces
of D'Artagnan at Antibes. They were forced to believe that the
captain of the musketeers was desirous of preserving an in-
cognito on his route, for Athos derived from his inquiries an
assurance that such a cavalier as he described had exchanged
his horse for a well-closed carriage on quitting Avignon. Raoul
was much affected at not meeting with D'Artagnan. His affectionate heart longed to take a farewell and receive consolation
from that heart of steel. Athos knew from experience that

D'Artagnan became impenetrable when engaged in any serious affair, whether on his own account or in the service of the king. He even feared to offend his friend, or thwart him by too pressing inquiries. And yet, when Raoul commenced his labor of classing the flotilla, and got together the *chalands* and lighters to send them to Toulon, one of the fishermen told the comte that his boat had been laid up to refit since a trip he had made on account of a gentleman who was in great haste to embark. Athos, believing that this man was telling a falsehood in order to be left at liberty to fish, and so gain more money when all his companions were gone, insisted upon having the details. The fisherman informed him that six days previously a man had come in the night to hire his boat, for the purpose of visiting the island of St. Honorat. The price was agreed upon, but the gentleman had arrived with an immense carriage case, which he insisted upon embarking, in spite of all the difficulties which opposed themselves to that operation. The fisherman had wished to retract. He had even threatened, but his threats had procured him nothing but a shower of blows from the gentleman's cane, which fell upon his shoulders sharp and long. Swearing and grumbling, he had recourse to the syndic of his brotherhood at Antibes, who administer justice among themselves and protect one another; but the gentleman had exhibited a certain paper, at the sight of which the syndic, bowing to the very ground, had enjoined obedience from the fisherman, and abused him for having been refractory. They then departed with the freight.

"But all this does not tell us," said Athos, "how you have injured your boat."

"This is the way. I was steering toward St. Honorat as the gentleman had desired me; but he changed his mind, and pretended that I could not pass to the south of the abbey."

"And why not?"

"Because, monsieur, there is in front of the square tower of the Benedictines, toward the southern point, the bank of the Moines."

"A rock?" asked Athos.

"Level with the water, and below the water; a dangerous passage, but one I have cleared a thousand times; the gentleman required me to land him at Ste. Marguerite's."

"Well?"

"Well, monsieur," cried the fisherman, with his Provençal accent, "a man is a sailor, or he is not; he knows his course, or he is nothing but a fresh-water lubber. I was obstinate, and wished to try the channel. The gentleman took me by the collar, and told me quietly he would strangle me. My mate armed himself with a hatchet, and so did I. We had the affront of the night before to pay him out for. But the gentleman drew his sword, and used it in such an astonishingly rapid manner that we neither of us could get near him. I was about to hurl my hatchet at his head, and I had a right to do so, hadn't I, monsieur? for a sailor aboard is master, as a citizen is in his chamber; I was going, then, in self-defense, to cut the gentleman in two, when, all at once—believe me or not, monsieur—the great carriage case opened of itself, I don't know, and there came out of it a sort of a phantom, his head covered with a black helmet and a black mask, something terrible to look upon, which came toward me threatening with its fist."

"And that was?" said Athos.

"That was the devil, monsieur; for the gentleman, with great glee, cried out, on seeing him, 'Ah! thank you, monseigneur!'"

"A strange story!" murmured the comte, looking at Raoul.

"And what did you do?" asked the latter of the fisherman.

"You must know, monsieur, that two poor men, such as we are, could be no match for two gentlemen; but when one of them is the devil, we had no chance. My companion and I did not stop to consult each other; we made but one jump into the sea, for we were within seven or eight hundred feet of the shore."

"Well, and then?"

"Why, and then, monseigneur, as there was a little wind from the southwest, the boat drifted into the sands of Ste. Marguerite's."

"Oh! but the two travelers?"

"Bah! you need not be uneasy about them! It was pretty plain that one was the devil, and protected the other; for when we recovered the boat, after she got afloat again, instead of finding these two creatures injured by the shock, we found nothing, not even the carriage or the case."

"Very strange! very strange!" repeated the comte. "But since that, what have you done, my friend?"

"I made my complaint to the governor of Ste. Marguerite's, who brought my finger under my nose, by telling me if I plagued him with such silly stories he would have me flogged."

"What! did the governor say so?"

"Yes, monsieur; and yet my boat was injured, seriously injured, for the prow is left upon the point of Ste. Marguerite's, and the carpenter asks a hundred and twenty livres to repair it."

"Very well," replied Raoul; "you will be exempted from the service. Go."

"We will go to Ste. Marguerite's, shall we?" said the comte to De Bragelonne, as the man walked away.

"Yes, monsieur, for there is something to be cleared up; that man does not seem to me to have told the truth."

"Nor to me either," said Raoul. "The story of the masked man and the carriage having disappeared may be told to conceal some violence these fellows have committed upon their passenger in the open sea, to punish him for his persistence in embarking."

"I formed the same suspicion; the carriage was more likely to contain property than a man."

"We shall see to that, Raoul. This gentleman very much resembles D'Artagnan; I recognize his mode of proceeding. Alas! we are no longer the young invincibles of former days. Who knows whether the hatchet or the iron bar of this miserable coaster has not succeeded in doing that which the best blades of Europe, balls, and bullets have not been able to do in forty years?"

That same day they set out for Ste. Marguerite's, on board a *chasse-marée* come from Toulon under orders. The impression they felt on landing was a singularly pleasing one. The isle was full of flowers and fruits. In its cultivated part it served as a garden for the governor. Orange, pomegranate, and fig-trees bent beneath the weight of their golden or purple fruits. All around this garden, in the uncultivated parts, the red partridges ran about in coveys among the brambles and tufts of junipers, and at every step of the comte and Raoul a terrified rabbit quitted his thyme and heath to scuttle away to his burrow. In fact, this fortunate isle was uninhabited. Flat, offering nothing but a tiny bay for the convenience of embarkation, and under the protection of the governor, who went shares with them, smugglers made use of it as a provisional *entrepôt*, at the expense of not killing the game or devastating the garden. With this compromise, the governor was in a situation to be satisfied with a garrison of eight men to guard his fortress, in which twelve cannons accumulated their coats of moldy green. The governor was a sort of happy farmer, harvesting wines, figs, oil, and oranges, preserving his citrons and *cédrates* in the sun of his casemates. The fortress, encircled by a deep ditch, its only guardian, arose like three heads upon turrets connected with one another by terraces covered with moss.

Athos and Raoul wandered for some time round the fence of the garden without finding any one to introduce them to the governor. They ended by making their own way into the garden. It was at the hottest time of the day. Everything sought shelter beneath grass or stone. The heavens spread their fiery veils as if to stifle all noises, to envelope all existences; the rabbit under the broom, the fly under the leaf, slept as the wave did beneath the heavens. Athos saw nothing living but a soldier, upon the terrace beneath the second and third court, who was carrying a basket of provisions on his head. This man returned almost immediately without his basket, and disappeared in the shade of his sentry-box. Athos supposed this man must have been carrying dinner to some one, and, after having done so, returned to dine himself. All at once they heard some one call out, and raising their heads, perceived in the frame of the bars of the window something of a white color, like a hand that was waved backward and forward—something shining, like a polished weapon struck by the rays of the sun. And before they were able to ascertain what it was, they saw a luminous train accompanied by a hissing sound in the air, which called their attention from the donjon to the ground. A second dull noise was heard from the ditch, and Raoul ran to pick up a silver plate which was rolling along the dry sand. The hand which had thrown this plate made a sign to the two gentlemen, and then disappeared. Athos and Raoul, approaching each other, commenced an attentive examination of the dusty plate, and they discovered, in characters traced upon the bottom of it with the point of a knife, this inscription:

"I am the brother of the King of France—a prisoner today —a madman to-morrow. French gentlemen and Christians, pray to God for the soul and the reason of the son of your masters."

The plate fell from the hands of Athos, while Raoul was endeavoring to make out the meaning of these dismal words. At the same instant they heard a cry from the top of the donjon. As quick as lightning, Raoul bent down his head, and forced down that of his father likewise. A musket-barrel glittered from the crest of the wall. A white smoke floated like a plume from the mouth of the musket, and a ball was flattened against a stone within six inches of the two gentlemen.

"*Cordieu!*" cried Athos. "What, are people assassinated here? Come down, cowards as you are!"

"Yes, come down!" cried Raoul furiously, shaking his fist at the castle.

One of the assailants—he who was about to fire—replied to these cries by an exclamation of surprise; and as his companion who wished to continue the attack, had re-seized his loaded musket, he who had cried out threw up the weapon, and the ball flew into the air. Athos and Raoul, seeing them disappear from the platform, expected they would come to them, and waited with a firm demeanor. Five minutes had not elapsed, when a stroke upon a drum called the eight soldiers of the garrison to arms, and they showed themselves on the other side of the ditch with their muskets in hand. At the head of these men was an officer, whom Athos and Raoul recognized as the one who had fired the first musket. The man ordered the soldiers to "make ready."

"We are going to be shot!" cried Raoul; "but, sword in hand, at least, let us leap the ditch. We shall kill at least two of these scoundrels, when their muskets are empty."

And, suiting the action to the word, Raoul was springing forward, followed by Athos, when a well-known voice resounded behind them:

"Athos! Raoul!"

"D'Artagnan!" replied the two gentlemen.

"Recover arms! *Mordioux!* cried the captain, to the soldiers. I was sure I could not be mistaken!"

"What is the meaning of this?" asked Athos. "What, were we to be shot without warning?"

"It was I who was going to shoot you, and if the governor missed you, I should not have missed you, my dear friends. How fortunate it is that I am accustomed to take a long aim, instead of firing at the instant I raise my weapon! I thought I recognized you. Ah! my dear friends, how fortunate!"

And D'Artagnan wiped his brow, for he had run fast, and emotion with him was not feigned.

"How!" said Athos. "And is the gentleman who fired at us the governor of the fortress?"

"In person."

"And why did he fire at us? What have we done to him?"

"*Pardieu!* You received what the prisoner threw to you?"

"That is true."

"That plate—the prisoner has written something on the bottom of it, has he not?"

"Yes."

"Good heavens! I was afraid he had."

And D'Artagnan, with all the marks of mortal disquietude
seized the plate, to read the inscription. When he had read it
fearful pallor spread over his countenance.

"Oh! good heavens!" repeated he. "Silence! Here is the gov
ernor."

"And what will he do to us? Is it our fault?"

"It is true, then?" said Athos, in a subdued voice. "Is i
true?"

"Silence! I tell you—silence! If he only believes you ca
read, if he only suspects you have understood! I love you, m
dear friends; I will be killed for you. But——"

" 'But—' " said Athos and Raoul.

"But I could not save you from perpetual imprisonment, i
I saved you from death. Silence, then! Silence again!"

The governor came up, having crossed the ditch upon a plan
bridge.

"Well!" said he, to D'Artagnan, "what stops us?"

"You are Spaniards—you do not understand a word o
French," said the captain eagerly, to his friends, in a low voic

"Well!" replied he, addressing the governor. "I was right
these gentlemen are two Spanish captains with whom
was acquainted at Ypres, last year; they don't know a wor
of French."

"Ah!" said the governor sharply, "and yet they were tryin
to read the inscription on the plate."

D'Artagnan took it out of his hands, effacing the character
with the point of his sword.

"How!" cried the governor—"what are you doing? I canne
read them now!"

"It is a state secret," replied D'Artagnan bluntly; "and a
you know that, according to the king's orders, it is under th
penalty of death any one should penetrate it, I will, if you lik
allow you to read it, and have you shot immediately afte
ward."

During this apostrophe—half-serious, half-ironical—Ath
and Raoul preserved the coolest, most unconcerned silence.

"But is it possible," said the governor, "that these gentl
men do not comprehend at least some words?"

"Suppose they do! If they do understand a few spoke
words, it does not follow that they should understand what
written. They cannot even read Spanish. A noble Spaniard, r
member, ought never to know how to read."

The governor was obliged to be satisfied with these explanations, but he was still tenacious.

"Invite these gentlemen to come to the fortress," said he.

"That I will willingly do. I was about to propose it to you."

The fact is, the captain had quite another idea, and would have wished his friends a hundred leagues off, and was obliged to make the best of it. He addressed the two gentlemen in Spanish, giving them a polite invitation, which they accepted. They all turned toward the entrance of the fort, and the incident being exhausted, the eight soldiers returned to their delightful leisure, for a moment disturbed by this unexpected adventure.

Chapter 32 — CAPTIVE AND JAILERS

When they had entered the fort, and while the governor was making some preparations for the reception of his guests:

"Come," said Athos, "let us have a word of explanation while we are alone."

"It is simply this," replied the musketeer. "I have conducted hither a prisoner, who the king commands shall not be seen. You came here, he has thrown something to you through the lattice of his window; I was at dinner with the governor, I saw the object thrown, and I saw Raoul pick it up. It does not take long to understand this. I understood it, and I thought you in intelligence with my prisoner. And then——"

"And then—you commanded us to be shot."

"*Ma foi!* I admit it; but if I was the first to seize a musket, fortunately I was the last to take aim at you."

"If you had killed me, D'Artagnan, I should have had the good fortune to die for the royal house of France, and it would be an honor to die by your hand—you, its noblest and most loyal defender."

"What the devil, Athos, do you mean by the royal house?" stammered D'Artagnan. "You don't mean that you, a well-informed and sensible man, can place any faith in the nonsense written by an idiot?"

"I do believe in it."

"With so much the more reason, my dear chevalier, from

your having orders to kill all those who do believe in it," said
Raoul.

"That is because," replied the captain of the musketeers—
"because every calumny, however absurd it may be, has the
almost certain chance of becoming popular."

"No, D'Artagnan," replied Athos promptly; "but because the
king is not willing that the secret of his family should tran
spire among the people, and cover with shame the execution
ers of the son of Louis XIII."

"Do not talk in such a childish manner, Athos, or I shall
begin to think you have lost your senses. Besides, explain to
me how it is possible Louis XIII. should have a son in the Isle
of Ste. Marguerite."

"A son whom you have brought hither masked, in a fishing
boat," said Athos. "Why not?"

D'Artagnan was brought to a pause.

"Ah! ah!" said he, "whence do you know that a fishing
boat——"

"Brought you to Ste. Marguerite's with the carriage contain
ing the prisoner—with a prisoner whom you styled mon
seigneur. Oh! I am acquainted with all that," resumed the
comte. D'Artagnan bit his mustache.

"If it were true," said he, "that I had brought hither in a
boat and with a carriage a masked prisoner, nothing proves
that this prisoner must be a prince—a prince of the house of
France."

"Oh! ask that of Aramis," replied Athos coolly.

"Of Aramis," cried the musketeer, quite at a stand. "Have
you seen Aramis?"

"After his discomfiture at Vaux, yes; I have seen Aramis, a
fugitive, pursued, ruined; and Aramis has told me enough to
make me believe in the complaints that this unfortunate young
man cut upon the bottom of the plate."

D'Artagnan's head sunk upon his breast with confusion.

"This is the way," said he, "in which God turns to nothing
that which men call their wisdom! A fine secret must that be
of which twelve or fifteen persons hold the tattered fragments
Athos, cursed be the chance which has brought you face to face
with me in this affair! for now——"

"Well," said Athos, with his customary mild severity
"is your secret lost because I know it? Consult your memory
my friend. Have I not borne secrets as heavy as this?"

"You have never borne one so dangerous," replied D'Ar
tagnan, in a tone of sadness. "I have something like a sinister

idea that all who are concerned with this secret will die, and die unfortunately."

"The will of God be done!" said Athos; "but here is your governor."

D'Artagnan and his friends immediately resumed their parts. The governor, suspicious and hard, behaved toward D'Artagnan with a politeness almost amounting to obsequiousness. With respect to the travelers, he contented himself with offering them good cheer, and never taking his eye from them. Athos and Raoul observed that he often tried to embarrass them by sudden attacks, or to catch them off their guard; but neither the one nor the other gave him the least advantage. What D'Artagnan had said was probable, if the governor did not believe it to be quite true. They rose from the table to repose awhile.

"What is this man's name? I don't like the looks of him," said Athos to D'Artagnan, in Spanish.

"De St. Mars," replied the captain.

"He is, then, I suppose the prince's jailer?"

"Eh! how can I tell? I may be kept at Ste. Marguerite's forever."

"Oh, no, not you!"

"My friend, I am in the situation of a man who finds a treasure in the midst of a desert. He would like to carry it away, but he cannot; he would like to leave it, but he dares not. The king will not dare to recall me, for no one else should serve him as faithfully as I should; he regrets not having me near him, from being aware that no one will be of so much service near his person as myself. But it will happen as it may please God."

"But," observed Raoul, "your not being certain proves that your situation here is provisional, and you will return to Paris."

"Ask these gentlemen," interrupted the governor, "what was their purpose in coming to Ste. Marguerite?"

"They came from learning there was a convent of Benedictines at Ste. Honorat which is considered curious; and from being told there was excellent shooting in the island."

"That is quite at their service, as well as yours," replied St. Mars.

D'Artagnan politely thanked him.

"When will they depart?" added the governor.

"To-morrow," replied D'Artagnan.

M. de St. Mars went to make his rounds, and left D'Artagnan alone with the pretended Spaniards.

"Oh!" exclaimed the musketeer, "here is a life with a society that suits me but little. I command this man, and he bores

me, *mordioux!* Come, let us have a shot or two at the rabbits
the walk will be beautiful, and not fatiguing. The isle is bu
a league and a half in length, upon a breadth of a league; a rea
park. Let us try to amuse ourselves."

"As you please, D'Artagnan; not for the sake of amusin
ourselves, but to gain an opportunity for talking freely."

D'Artagnan made a sign to a soldier, who brought the gen
tlemen some guns, and then returned to the fort.

"And now," said the musketeer, "answer me the questio
put to you by that black-looking St. Mars: What did you com
to do at the Lerin Isles?"

"To bid you farewell."

"Bid me farewell! What do you mean by that? Is Raoul go
ing anywhere?"

"Yes."

"Then I will lay a wager it is with Monsieur de Beaufort.

"With Monsieur de Beaufort it is, my dear friend; you a
ways guess right."

"From habit."

While the two friends were commencing their conversatio
Raoul, with his head hanging down and his heart oppresse
seated himself on a mossy rock, his gun across his knees, look
ing at the sea—looking at the heavens, and listening to th
voice of his soul—he allowed the sportsmen to attain a consi
erable distance from him. D'Artagnan remarked his absence.

"He has not recovered the blow," said he to Athos.

"He is struck to death."

"Oh! your fears exaggerate, I hope. Raoul is of a fine natur
Around all hearts as noble as his there is a second envelop
which forms a cuirass. The first bleeds, the second resists."

"No," replied Athos; "Raoul will die of it."

"*Mordioux!*" said D'Artagnan, in a melancholy tone.

And he did not add a word to this exclamation. Then, a mi
ute after:

"Why do you let him go?"

"Because he insists upon going."

"And why do you not go with him?"

"Because I could not bear to see him die."

D'Artagnan looked his friend earnestly in the face.

"You know one thing," continued the comte, leaning upo
the arm of the captain; "you know that in the course of m
life I have been afraid of but few things. Well, I have an ince
sant, gnawing, insurmountable fear that a day will arrive
which I shall hold the dead body of that boy in my arms."

"Oh!" murmured D'Artagnan, "oh!"

"He will die, I know, I have a perfect conviction of that; but I would not see him die."

"How is this, Athos? You come and place yourself in the presence of the bravest man you say you have ever seen, of your own D'Artagnan, of that man without an equal, as you formerly called him, and you come and tell him, with your arms folded, that you are afraid of witnessing the death of your son, you who have seen all that can be seen in this world! Why have you this fear, Athos? Man, upon this earth, must expect everything, and ought to face everything."

"Listen to me, my friend. After having worn myself out upon this earth of which you speak, I have preserved but two religions; that of life, my friendships, my duty as a father —that of eternity, love and respect for God. Now, I have within me the revelation that if God should decree that my friend or my son should render up his last sigh in my presence —oh! no; I cannot even tell you, D'Artagnan!"

"Speak, speak; tell me!"

"I am strong against everything, except against the death of those I love. For that only there is no remedy. He who does gains; he who sees others die loses. No; this it is—to know that I should no more meet upon earth him whom I now behold with joy; to know that there would nowhere be a D'Artagnan any more, nowhere again be a Raoul—oh! I am old, you see, I have no longer courage. I pray God to spare me in my weakness; but if He struck me so plainly and in that fashion, I should curse Him. A Christian gentleman ought not to curse his God, D'Artagnan; it is quite enough to have cursed a king!"

"Humph!" said D'Artagnan, a little confused by this violent tempest of grief.

"Let me speak to him, Athos. Who knows?"

"Try, if you please; but I am convinced you will not succeed."

"I will not attempt to console him, I will serve him."

"You will?"

"Doubtless, I will. Do you think this would be the first time a woman had repented of an infidelity? I will go to him, I tell you."

Athos shook his head, and continued his walk alone. D'Artagnan, cutting across the bramble, rejoined Raoul, and held out his hand to him.

"Well, Raoul! You have something to say to me?"

"I have a kindness to ask of you," replied De Bragelonne.

"Ask it, then."

"You will some day return to France?"

"I hope so."

"Ought I to write to Mademoiselle de la Valliere?"

"No, you must not."

"But I have so many things to say to her."

"Come and say them to her, then."

"Never!"

"Pray, what virtue do you attribute to a letter, which your speech might not possess?"

"Perhaps you are right."

"She loves the king," said D'Artagnan bluntly, "and she is an honest girl."

Raoul started.

"And you—you, whom she abandons, she, perhaps, loves better than she does the king, but after another fashion."

"D'Artagnan, do you believe she loves the king?"

"To idolatry. Her heart is inaccessible to any other feeling. You might continue to live near her, and would be her best friend."

"Ah!" exclaimed Raoul, with a passionate burst of repugnance for such a painful hope.

"Will you do so?"

"It would be base."

"That is a very absurd word, which would lead me to think slightly of your understanding. Please to understand, Raoul, that it is never base to do that which is imposed by a superior force. If your heart says to you, 'Go there, or die,' why, go there, Raoul. Was she base or brave, she whom you loved, in preferring the king to you, the king whom her heart commanded her imperiously to prefer to you? No, she was the bravest of women. Do, then, as she has done. Oblige yourself. Do you know one thing of which I am sure, Raoul?"

"What is that?"

"Why, that by seeing her closely with the eyes of a jealous man——"

"Well?"

"Well, you would cease to love her."

"Then I am decided, my dear D'Artagnan."

"To set off to see her again?"

"No; to set off that I may never see her again. I wish to love her forever."

"Humph! I must confess," replied the musketeer, "that is a conclusion which I was far from expecting."

"This is what I wish, my friend. You will see her again, and you will give her a letter which, if you think proper, will explain to her as to yourelf, what is passing in my heart. Read it; I prepared it last night. Something told me I should see you to-day."

He held the letter out, and D'Artagnan read it:

"MADEMOISELLE: You are not wrong in my eyes in not loving me. You have only been guilty of one fault toward me, that of having left me to believe you loved me. This error will cost me my life. I pardon you, but I cannot pardon myself. It is said that happy lovers are deaf to the complaints of rejected lovers. It will not be so with you, who did not love me, except with anxiety. I am sure that if I had persisted in endeavoring to change that friendship into love, you would have yielded out of a fear of bringing about my death, or of lessening the esteem I had for you. It is much more delightful to me to die, knowing you are free and satisfied. How much, then, will you love me, when you will no longer fear either my presence or my reproaches! You will love me, because, however charming a new love may appear to you, God has not made me in anything inferior to him you have chosen, and because my devotedness, my sacrifice, and my painful end will assure me, in your eyes, a certain superiority over him. I have allowed to escape, in the candid credulity of my heart, the treasure I possessed. Many people tell me that you loved me enough to lead me to hope you would have loved me much. That idea takes from my mind all bitterness, and leads me only to blame myself. You will accept this last farewell, and you will bless me for having taken refuge in the inviolable asylum where all hatred is extinguished, and where all love endures forever. Adieu, mademoiselle. If your happiness could be purchased by the last drop of my blood, I would shed that drop. I willingly make the sacrifice of it to my misery!

"RAOUL, VICOMTE DE BRAGELONNE."

"The letter is very well," said the captain. "I have only one fault to find with it."

"Tell me what that is?" said Raoul.

"Why, it is, that it tells everything, except the thing which exhales, like a mortal poison, from your eyes and from your heart; except the senseless love which still consumes you."

Raoul grew paler, but remained silent.

"Why did you not write simply these words:

" 'MADEMOISELLE: Instead of cursing you, I love you, a I die.' "

"That is true!" exclaimed Raoul, with a sinister kind of jo
And tearing the letter he had just taken back, he wrote t following words upon a leaf of his tablets:

"To procure the happiness of once more telling you I lov you, I commit the baseness of writing to you, and to puni myself for that baseness, I die."

And he signed it.
"You will give her these tablets, captain, will you not?"
"When?" asked the latter.
"On the day," said De Bragelonne, pointing to the last se tence, "on the day when you can place a date under the words."

And he sprung away quickly to join Athos, who was retur ing with slow steps.

As they re-entered the fort the sea rose with that rapid gus vehemence which characterizes the Mediterranean, the humor of the element became a tempest. Something shapele and tossed about violently by the waves, appeared just off t coast.

"What is that?" said Athos—"a wrecked boat?"
"No, it is not a boat," said D'Artagnan.
"Pardon me," said Raoul, "there is a bark gaining the p rapidly."
"Yes, there is a bark in the creek, which is prudently seeki shelter here; but that which Athos points to in the sand is a boat at all—it has run aground."
"Yes, yes, I see it."
"It is the carriage which I threw into the sea, after landi the prisoner."
"Well!" said Athos, "if you take my advice, D'Artagnan, y will burn that carriage, in order that no vestige of it may main, without which the fishermen of Antibes, who have lieved they had to do with the devil, will endeavor to pro that your prisoner was but a man."
"Your advice is good, Athos, and I will this night have carried out, or, rather, I will carry it out myself; but let us in, for the rain falls heavily, and the lightning is terrific."

As they were passing over the ramparts to a gallery of whi D'Artagnan had the key, they saw M. de St. Mars directing steps toward the chamber inhabited by the prisoner. Upon a sign from D'Artagnan, they concealed themselves in an angle of the staircase.

"What is it?" said Athos.

"You will see. Look. The prisoner is returning from chapel."

And they saw, by the red flashes of the lightning against the violet fog which the wind stamped upon the bankward sky, they saw pass gravely, at six paces behind the governor, a man clothed in black and masked by a visor of polished steel, soldered to a helmet of the same nature, which altogether enveloped the whole of his head. The fire of the heavens cast red reflections upon the polished surface, and these reflections, flying off capriciously, seemed to be angry looks launched by this unfortunate, instead of imprecations. In the middle of the gallery, the prisoner stopped for a moment, to contemplate the infinite horizon, to respire the sulphurous perfumes of the tempest, to drink in thirstily the hot rain, and to breathe a sigh resembling a smothered roar.

"Come on, monsieur," said St. Mars sharply, to the prisoner, for he already became uneasy at seeing him look so long beyond the walls. "Monsieur, come on!"

"Say monseigneur!" cried Athos, from his corner, with a voice so solemn and terrible that the governor trembled from head to foot.

Athos insisted upon respect being paid to fallen majesty. The prisoner turned round.

"Who spoke?" asked St. Mars.

"It was I," replied D'Artagnan, showing himself promptly. "You know that is the order."

"Call me neither monsieur nor monseigneur," said the prisoner, in his turn, in a voice that penetrated to the very soul of Raoul; "call me *Accursed!*"

He passed on, and the iron door creaked after him.

"That is truly an unfortunate man!" murmured the musketeer, in a hollow whisper, pointing out to Raoul the chamber inhabited by the prince.

Chapter 33 — PROMISES

Scarcely had D'Artagnan re-entered his apartment with his two friends than one of the soldiers of the fort came to inform him that the governor was seeking for him. The bark which Raoul had perceived at sea, and which appeared so eager to gain the port, came to Ste. Marguerite with an important dispatch for the captain of the musketeers. On opening it D'Artagnan recognized the writing of the king.

"I should think," said Louis XIV., "you will have completed the execution of my orders, Monsieur d'Artagnan; return, then, immediately to Paris, and join me at the Louvre."

"There is the end of my exile!" cried the musketeer, with joy. "God be praised! I am no longer a jailer."

And he showed the letter to Athos.

"So then, you must leave us?" replied the latter, in a melancholy tone.

"Yes, but to meet again, dear friend, seeing that Raoul is old enough now to go alone with Monsieur de Beaufort, and who will prefer his father going back in company with Monsieur d'Artagnan to forcing him to travel two hundred leagues solitarily to reach home at La Fere; would you not, Raoul?"

"Certainly," stammered the latter, with an expression of tender regret.

"No, no, my friend," interrupted Athos; "I will never quit Raoul till the day his vessel shall have disappeared on the horizon. As long as he remains in France he shall not be separated from me."

"As you please, dear friend; but we will, at least, leave Ste. Marguerite together; take advantage of the bark which will convey me back to Antibes."

"With all my heart; we cannot too soon be at a distance from this fort, and from the spectacle which saddened us so just now."

The three friends quitted the little isle, after paying their respects to the governor, and by the last flashes of the departing tempest they took their farewell of the white walls of the fort. D'Artagnan parted from his friends that same night, after having seen fire set to the carriage upon the shore by the orders of St. Mars, according to the advice the captain had given him. Before getting on horseback, and after leaving the arms of Athos:

"My friends," said he, "you bear too much resemblance to two soldiers who are abandoning their post. Something warns me that Raoul will require being supported by you in his rank. Will you allow me to ask permission to go over into Africa with a hundred good muskets? The king will not refuse me, and I will take you with me."

"Monsieur d'Artagnan," replied Raoul, pressing his hand with emotion, "thanks for that offer, which would give us more than we wish, either Monsieur le Comte or I. I, who am young, stand in need of labor of mind and fatigue of body; Monsieur le Comte wants the profoundest repose. You are his best friend. I recommend him to your care. In watching over him, you will hold both our souls in your hands."

"I must go; my horse is all in a fret," said D'Artagnan, with whom the most manifest sign of a lively emotion was the change of ideas into a conversation. "Come, comte, how many days longer has Raoul to stay here?"

"Three days, at most."

"And how long will it take you to reach home?"

"Oh! a considerable time," replied Athos. "I shall not like the idea of being separated too quickly from Raoul. Time will travel too fast of itself to require me to aid it by distance. I shall only make half stages."

"And why so, my friend? Nothing is more dull than traveling slowly; and hostelry life does not become a man like you."

"My friend, I came hither on post-horses, but I wish to purchase two animals of a superior kind. Now, to take them home fresh, it would not be prudent to make them travel more than seven or eight leagues a day."

"Where is Grimaud?"

"He arrived yesterday morning, with Raoul's appointments; and I have left him to sleep."

"That is, never to come back again," D'Artagnan suffered to escape him. "Till we meet again, then, dear Athos—and if you are diligent, well, I shall embrace you the sooner."

So saying, he put his foot in the stirrup, which Raoul held.

"Farewell!" said the young man, embracing him.

"Farewell!" said D'Artagnan, as he got into his saddle.

His horse made a movement which divided the cavalier from his friends. This scene had taken place in front of the house chosen by Athos, near the gates of Antibes, whither D'Artagnan, after his supper, had ordered the horses to be brought. The road began to extend there, white and undulating in the vapors of the night. The horse eagerly respired the strong, sharp perfume of the marshes. D'Artagnan put him into a trot; and Athos and Raoul turned toward the house. All at once they heard the rapid approach of a horse's steps, and at first believed it to be one of those singular repercussions which

deceive the ear at every turn in a road. But it was really the
return of the horseman. They uttered a cry of joyous surprise,
and the captain, springing to the ground like a young man,
seized within his arms the two beloved heads of Athos and
Raoul. He held them long embraced thus, without speaking a
word, or suffering the sigh which was bursting his breast to escape him. Then, as rapidly as he had come back, he set off
again, with a sharp application of his spurs to the sides of his
fiery horse.

"Alas!" said the comte, in a low voice, "alas! alas!"

"Evil presage!" on his side, said D'Artagnan to himself, making up for lost time. "I could not smile upon them. An
evil presage!"

The next day Grimaud was on foot again. The service commanded by M. de Beaufort was happily accomplished. The flotilla, sent to Toulon by the exertions of Raoul, had set out,
dragging after it in little nutshells, almost invisible, the wives
and friends of the fishermen and smugglers put in requisition
for the service of the fleet. The time, so short, which remained
for the father and son to live together, appeared to have doubled in rapidity, as the swiftness of everything increases which
inclines toward mixing with the gulf of eternity. Athos and
Raoul returned to Toulon, which began to be filled with the
noise of carriages, with the noise of arms, with the noise
of neighing horses. The trumpeters sounded their spirited
marches; the drummers signalized their strength; the streets
were overflowing with soldiers, servants, and trades-people.
The Duc de Beaufort was everywhere, superintending the embarkation with the zeal and interest of a good captain. He encouraged even the most humble of his companions; he scolded
his lieutenants, even those of the highest rank. Artillery, provisions, baggage, he insisted upon seeing all himself. He examined the equipment of every soldier; he assured himself of
the health and soundness of every horse. It was plain that,
light, boastful, egotistical, in his hotel, the gentleman became
the soldier again—the high noble, a captain—in face of the responsibility he had accepted. And yet, it must be admitted that,
whatever was the care with which he presided over the preparations for departure, it was easy to perceive careless precipi-
tation, and the absence of all the precaution which make the
French soldier the first soldier in the world, because, in that
world, he is the one most abandoned to his own physical and
moral resources. All things having satisfied, or appearing to

ave satisfied, the admiral, he paid his compliments to Raoul,
nd gave the last orders for sailing, which was ordered the next
morning at daybreak. He invited the comte and his son to dine
with him; but they, under a pretext of the service, kept them-
elves apart. Gaining their hostelry, situated under the trees of
he great place, they took their repast in haste, and Athos
ed Raoul to the rocks which dominated the city, vast gray
mountains, whence the view is infinite, and embraces a liquid
orizon, which appears, so remote is it, on a level with the
rocks themselves. The night was fine, as it always is in these
appy climates. The moon, rising behind the rocks, unrolled,
ike a silver sheet, upon the blue carpet of the sea. In the
oad, maneuvered silently the vessels which had just taken
heir rank to facilitate the embarkation. The sea, loaded with
phosphoric light, opened beneath the hulls of the barks which
ransported the baggage and munitions; every dip of the prow
lowed up this gulf of white flames; and from every oar
ropped liquid diamonds. The sailors, rejoicing in the largesses
f the admiral, were heard murmuring their slow and artless
ongs. Sometimes the grinding of the chains was mixed with
he dull noise of shot falling into the holds. These harmonies,
nd this spectacle, oppress the heart like fear, and dilate it
ke hope. All this life speaks of death. Athos had seated him-
elf with his son, upon the moss, among the brambles of the
romontory. Around their heads passed and repassed large bats,
arried along in the fearful whirl of their blind chase. The feet
f Raoul were across the edge of the cliff, and bathed in that
oid which is peopled by vertigo, and provokes to annihilation.
Vhen the moon had risen to its full height, creasing with its
ght the neighboring peaks, when the watery mirror was illu-
ained in its full extent, and the little red fires had made their
penings in the black masses of every ship, Athos collected all
is ideas and all his courage, and said:

"God has made all that we see, Raoul. He has made us also
—poor atoms mixed up with this great universe. We shine like
ose fires and those stars; we sigh like those waves; we suf-
er like those great ships, which are worn out in plowing the
aves, in obeying the wind which urges them toward an end,
s the breath of God blows us toward a port. Everything likes
 live, Raoul; and everything is beautiful in living things."

"Monsieur," said Raoul, "we have before us a beautiful spec-
acle."

"How good D'Artagnan is!" interrupted Athos suddenly,

"and what a rare good fortune it is to be supported during a whole life by such a friend as he is! That is what you have wanted, Raoul."

"A friend!" cried Raoul, "I have wanted a friend!"

"Monsieur de Guiche is an agreeable companion," resumed the comte coldly, "but I believe, in the times in which you live, men are more engaged in their own interests and their own pleasures than they were in our times. You have sought a secluded life; that is a great happiness, but you have lost your strength in it. We four, more weaned from these delicate abstractions which constitute our joy, we furnished much more resistance when misfortune presented itself."

"I have not interrupted you, monsieur, to tell you that I had a friend, and that that friend is Monsieur de Guiche. *Certes*, he is good and generous, and moreover he loves me. But I have lived under the guardianship of another friendship, monsieur, as precious and as strong as that of which you speak, since that is yours."

"I have not been a friend for you, Raoul," said Athos.

"Eh! monsieur, and in what respect not?"

"Because I have given you reason to think that life has but one face, because, sad and severe, alas! I have always cut off for you, without, God knows, wishing to do so, the joyous buds which incessantly spring from the tree of youth; so that at this moment I repent of not having made of you a more expansive, dissipated, animated man."

"I know why you say that, monsieur. No, it is not you who have made me what I am; it was love which took me at the time when children have only inclinations; it is the constancy natural to my character, which, with other creatures, is but a habit. I believe that I should always be as I was; I thought God had cast me in a path quite cleared, quite straight, bordered with fruits and flowers. I had watching over me your vigilance and your strength. I believed myself to be vigilant and strong. Nothing prepared me; I fell once, and that once deprived me of courage for the whole of my life. It is quite true that I wrecked myself. Oh, no, monsieur; you are nothing in my past but a happiness—you are nothing in my future but a hope. No, I have no reproach to make against life, such as you made it for me; I bless you, and I love you ardently."

"My dear Raoul, your words do me good. They prove to me that you will act a little for me in the time to come."

"I shall only act for you, monsieur."

"Raoul, what I have never hitherto done with respect to you

will henceforward do. I will be your friend, not your father. We will live in expanding ourselves, instead of living and holding ourselves prisoners, when you come back. And that will be soon, will it not?"

"Certainly, monsieur, for such an expedition cannot be long."

"Soon, then, Raoul, soon, instead of living moderately upon my income, I will give you the capital of my estates. It will suffice for launching you into the world till my death; and you will give me, I hope, before that time, the consolation of not seeing my race extinct."

"I will do all you shall command," said Raoul, much agitated.

"It is not necessary, Raoul, that your duty as aid-de-camp should lead you into too hazardous enterprises. You have gone through your ordeal; you are known to be good under fire. Remember that war with the Arabs is a war of snares, ambuscades, and assassinations."

"So it is said, monsieur."

"There is never much glory in falling in an ambuscade. It is a death which always implies a little rashness or want of foresight. Often, indeed, he who falls in it meets with but little pity. They who are not pitied, Raoul, have died uselessly. Still further, the conqueror laughs, and we Frenchmen ought not to allow stupid infidels to triumph over our faults. Do you clearly understand what I am saying to you, Raoul? God forbid I should encourage you to avoid encounters!"

"I am naturally prudent, monsieur, and I have very good fortune," said Raoul, with a smile which chilled the heart of his poor father; "for," the young man hastened to add, "in twenty combats in which I have been, I have only received one scratch."

"There is, in addition," said Athos, "the climate to be dreaded; that is an ugly end, that fever. King St. Louis prayed God to send him an arrow or the plague, rather than the fever."

"Oh, monsieur! with sobriety, with reasonable exercise——"

"I have already obtained from Monsieur de Beaufort a promise that his dispatches shall be sent off every fortnight to France. You, as his aid-de-camp, will be charged with expediting them, and will be sure not to forget me."

"No, monsieur," said Raoul, almost choked with emotion.

"Besides, Raoul, as you are a good Christian, and I am one also, we ought to reckon upon a more special protection of God

and His guardian angels. Promise me that if anything evil
should happen to you, on any occasion, you will think of me
at once."

"First, and at once! Oh, yes, monsieur."

"And will call upon me?"

"Instantly."

"You dream of me sometimes, do you not, Raoul?"

"Every night, monsieur. During my early youth I saw you
in my dreams, calm and mild, with one hand stretched out over
my head, and that it was that made me sleep so soundly—*formerly*."

"We love each other too dearly," said the comte, "that from
this moment, in which we separate, a portion of both our souls
should not travel with one and the other of us, and should now
dwell wherever we may dwell. Whenever you may be sad,
Raoul, I feel that my heart will be drowned in sadness; and
when you smile on thinking of me, be assured you will send me,
from however remote a distance, a ray of your joy."

"I will not promise you to be joyous," replied the young
man; "but you may be certain that I will never pass an hour
without thinking of you, not one hour, I swear, unless I be
dead."

Athos could contain himself no longer; he threw his arm
round the neck of his son, and held him embraced with all
the powers of his heart. The moon began to be now eclipsed by
twilight; a golden band surrounded the horizon, announcing the
approach of day. Athos threw his cloak over the shoulders of
Raoul, and led him back to the city, where burdens and porters
were already in motion, like a vast ant-hill. At the extremity of
the plateau, which Athos and De Bragelonne were quitting,
they saw a dark shadow moving uneasily backward and forward,
as if in indecision or ashamed to be seen. It was Grimaud, who,
in his anxiety, had tracked his master, and was waiting for him.

"Oh! my good Grimaud," cried Raoul, "what do you want?
You are come to tell us it is time to be gone, have you not?"

"Alone?" said Grimaud, addressing Athos and pointing to
Raoul in a tone of reproach, which showed to what an extent
the old man was troubled.

"Oh, you are right!" cried the comte. "No, Raoul, do not go
alone; no, he shall not be left alone in a strange land, without
some friendly hand to support him, some friendly heart to recall to him all he loved!"

"I?" said Grimaud.

"You—yes, you!" cried Raoul, touched to his inmost heart.

"Alas!" said Athos, "you are very old, my good Grimaud."

"So much the better," replied the latter, with an inexpressible depth of feeling and intelligence.

"But the embarkation is begun," said Raoul, "and you are not prepared."

"Yes," said Grimaud, showing the keys of his trunks, mixed with those of his young master.

"But," again objected Raoul, "you cannot leave Monsieur le Comte thus alone—Monsieur le Comte, whom you have never quitted."

Grimaud turned his dimmed eyes upon Athos and Raoul, as if to measure the strength of both. The comte uttered not a word.

"Monsieur le Comte will prefer my going," said Grimaud.

"I should," said Athos, by an inclination of the head.

At that moment the drums suddenly rolled, and the clarions filled the air with their inspiring notes. The regiments destined for the expedition began to debouch from the city. They advanced to the number of five, each composed of forty companies. Royal's marched first, distinguished by their white uniform, faced with blue. The ordonnance colors, quartered crosswise, violet and dead leaf, with a sprinkling of golden fleurs-de-lis, left the white-colored flag, with its fluer-de-lised cross, to dominate over the whole. Musketeers at the wings, with their forked sticks and their muskets on their shoulders; pikemen in the center, with their lances, fourteen feet in length, marched gayly toward the transports, which carried them in detail to the ships. The regiments of Picardy, Navarre, Normandy, and Royal Vaisseau followed after. M. de Beaufort had known well how to select his troops. He himself was seen closing the march with his staff—it would take a full hour before he could reach the sea. Raoul, with Athos, turned his steps slowly toward the beach, in order to take his place when the prince embarked. Grimaud, boiling with the ardor of a young man, superintended the embarkation of Raoul's baggage in the admiral's vessel. Athos, with his arm passed through that of the son he was about to lose, absorbed in melancholy meditation, was deaf to the noise around him. An officer came quickly toward them to inform Raoul that M. de Beaufort was anxious to have him by his side.

"Have the kindness to tell the prince," said Raoul, "that I request he will allow me this hour to enjoy the company of my father."

"No, no," said Athos, "an aid-de-camp ought not thus to quit his general. Please to tell the prince, monsieur, that the vicomte will join him immediately."

The officer set off at a gallop.

"Whether we part here or part there," added the comte, "it is no less a separation."

He carefully brushed the dust from his son's coat, and passed his hand over his hair as they walked along.

"But, Raoul," said he, "you want money. Monsieur de Beaufort's train will be splendid, and I am certain it will be agreeable to you to purchase horses and arms, which are very dear things in Africa. Now, as you are not actually in the service of the king or Monsieur de Beaufort, and are simply a volunteer, you must not reckon upon either pay or largesses. But I should not like you to want for anything at Gigelli. Here are two hundred pistoles; if you would please me, Raoul, spend them."

Raoul pressed the hand of his father, and at the turning of a street they saw M. de Beaufort, mounted upon a magnificent white *genet,* which replied by graceful curvets to the applause of the women of the city. The duc called Raoul, and held out his hand to the comte. He spoke to him for some time, with such a kindly expression that the heart of the poor father even felt a little comforted. It was, however, evident to both father and son that their walk was directed to nothing less than a punishment. There was a terrible moment—that at which, on quitting the sands of the shore, the soldiers and sailors exchanged the last kisses with their families and friends; a supreme moment, in which, notwithstanding the clearness of the heavens, the warmth of the sun, of the perfumes of the air, and the rich life that was circulating in their veins, everything appeared black, everything appeared bitter, everything created doubts of a God, while speaking by the mouth, even, of God. It was customary for the admiral and his suit to embark the last; the cannon waited to announce with its formidable voice, that the leader had placed his foot on board his vessel. Athos, forgetful of both the admiral and the fleet, and of his own dignity as a strong man, opened his arms to his son, and pressed him convulsively to his heart.

"Accompany us on board," said the duc, very much affected; "you will gain a good half hour."

"No," said Athos; "my farewell is spoken. I do not wish to speak a second."

"Then, vicomte, embark—embark quickly!" added the prince, wishing to spare the tears of these two men, whose hearts were bursting. And paternally, tenderly, very much as

Porthos might have done, he took Raoul in his arms and placed him in the boat; the oars of which, at a signal, immediately were dipped in the waves. Himself, forgetful of ceremony, he jumped into his boat, and pushed it off with a vigorous foot.

"Adieu!" cried Raoul.

Athos replied only by a sign, but he felt something burning on his hand; it was the respectful kiss of Grimaud—the last farewell of the faithful dog. This kiss given, Grimaud jumped from the step of the mole upon the stem of a two-oared yawl, which had just been taken in tow by a *chaland* served by twelve galley-oars. Athos seated himself on the mole, stunned, deaf, abandoned. Every instant took from him one of the features, one of the shades of the pale face of his son. With his arms hanging down, his eyes fixed, his mouth open, he remained confounded with Raoul—in one same look, in one same thought, in one same stupor. The sea, by degrees, carried away boats and faces, until at the distance at which men become nothing but points—loves, nothing but remembrances, Athos saw his son ascend the ladder of the admiral's ship, he saw him lean upon the rail of the deck, and place himself in such a manner as to be always an object in the eye of his father. In vain the cannon thundered, in vain from the ship sounded a long and loud tumult, responded to by immense acclamations from the shore, in vain did the noise deafen the ear of the father, and the smoke obscure the cherished object of all his aspirations. Raoul appeared to him up to the last moment; and the imperceptible atom, passing from black to pale, from pale to white, from white to nothing, disappeared for Athos—disappeared very long after for all the eyes of the spectators, had disappeared both gallant ships and swelling sails. Toward midday, when the sun devoured space, and scarcely the tops of the masts dominated the incandescent line of the sea, Athos perceived a soft aërial shadow rise, and vanish as soon as seen. This was the smoke of a cannon, which M. de Beaufort ordered to be fired as a last salute to the coast of France. The point was buried, in its turn, beneath the sky, and Athos returned painfully and slowly to his hostelry.

Chapter 34 — AMONG WOMEN

D'Artagnan had not been able to hide his feelings from his friends so much as he would have wished. The stoical soldier, the impassible man-at-arms, overcome by fear and presentiments, had yielded, for a few minutes, to human weakness. When, therefore, he had silenced his heart and calmed the agitation of his nerves, turning toward his lackey, a silent servant, always listening, in order to obey the more promptly:

"Rabaud," said he, "mind, we must travel thirty leagues a day."

"At your pleasure, captain," replied Rabaud.

And from that moment, D'Artagnan, accommodating his action to the pace of his horse, like a true centaur, employed his thoughts about nothing—that is to say, about everything. He asked himself why the king had sent for him back? why the Iron Mask had thrown the silver plate at the feet of Raoul? As to the first subject, the reply was negative; he knew right well that the king's calling him was from necessity. He still further knew that Louis XIV. must experience an imperious want of a private conversation with one whom the possession of such a secret placed on a level with the highest powers of the kingdom. But as to saying exactly what the king's wish was, D'Artagnan found himself completely at a loss. The musketeer had no other doubts, either, upon the reason which had urged the unfortunate Philippe to reveal his character and his birth. Philippe, hidden forever beneath a mask of iron, exiled to a country where the men seemed little more than slaves of the elements; Philippe, deprived even of the society of D'Artagnan, who had loaded him with honors and delicate attentions, had nothing more to see than specters and griefs in this world, and despair beginning to devour him, he poured himself forth in complaints, in the belief that his revelations would raise an avenger for him. The manner in which the musketeer had been near killing his two best friends, the destiny which had so strangely brought Athos to participate in the great state secret, the farewell of Raoul, the obscurity of that future which threatened to end in a melancholy death; all this threw D'Artagnan incessantly back to lamentable predictions and fore-

dings, which the rapidity of his pace did not dissipate, as it
ed formerly to do. D'Artagnan passed from these considera-
ns to the remembrance of the proscribed Porthos and
amis. He saw them both, fugitives, tracked, ruined—labori-
s architects of a fortune they must lose; and, as the king
lled for his man of execution in hours of vengeance and mal-
, D'Artagnan trembled at the idea of receiving some com-
ssion that would make his very heart bleed. Sometimes, when
cending hills, when the winded horse breathed hard from
s nostrils, and heaved his flanks, the captain, left to more
edom of thought, reflected upon the prodigious genius of
amis, a genius of astucity and intrigue, such as the Fronde
d the civil war had produced but two. Soldier, priest, and
lomatist; gallant, avaricious, and cunning; Aramis had
ver taken the good things of this life but as stepping-stones
rise to bad ones. Generous in spirit, if not high in heart, he
ver did ill but for the sake of shining a little more brilliantly.
ward the end of his career, at the moment of reaching the
al, like the patrician, Fuscus, he had made a false step upon
plank, and had fallen into the sea. But Porthos, the good,
rmless Porthos! To see Porthos hungry, to see Mousqueton
thout gold lace, imprisoned, perhaps; to see Pierrefonds,
acieux, razed to the very stones, dishonored even to the tim-
r—these were so many poignant griefs for D'Artagnan, and
ery time that one of these griefs struck him, he bounded
e a horse at the sting of the gadfly beneath the vaults of foli-
e where he has sought shade and shelter from the burning
n. Never was the man of spirit subjected to *ennui*, if his body
s exposed to fatigue; never did the man healthy of body fail
find life light, if he had something to engage his mind. D'Ar-
nan, riding fast, thinking as constantly, alighted from his
rse in Paris, fresh and tender in his muscles as the athlete
eparing for the gymnasium. The king did not expect him so
n, and had just departed for the chase toward Meudon.
Artagnan, instead of riding after the king, as he would for-
rly have done, took off his boots, had a bath, and waited till
majesty should return, dusty and tired. He occupied the
erval of five hours in taking, as people say, the air of the
use, and in arming himself against all ill chances. He learned
t the king, during the last fortnight, had been gloomy; that
queen-mother was ill and much depressed; that Monsieur,
king's brother, was exhibiting a devotional turn; that
dame had the vapors; and that M. de Guiche was gone to
of his estates. He learned that M. Colbert was radiant;

that M. Fouquet consulted a fresh physician every day, wh
still did not cure him, and that his principal complaint was o
which physicians do not usually cure, unless they are politic
physicians. The king, D'Artagnan was told, behaved in th
kindest manner to M. Fouquet, and did not allow him to l
ever out of his sight; but the surintendant, touched to th
heart, like one of those fine trees which a worm has puncture
was declining daily, in spite of the royal smile, that sun
court trees. D'Artagnan learned that Mlle. de la Valliere ha
become indispensable to the king, that the king, during h
sporting excursions, if he did not take her with him, wrote
her frequently, no longer verses, but, what was still mu
worse, prose, and that whole pages at a time. Thus, as the poet
cal Pleiad of the day said, "the first king in the world was se
descending from his horse with an ardor beyond compare
and on the crown of his hat scrawling bombastic phrase
which M. de St. Aignan, aid-de-camp in perpetuity, carried
La Valliere at the risk of foundering his horses. During th
time, deer and pheasants were left to the free enjoyment
their nature, hunted so lazily that, it was said, the art of vener
ran great risk of degenerating at the Court of France. D'A
tagnan then thought of the wishes of poor Raoul, of that d
sponding letter destined for a woman who passed her life
hoping, and as D'Artagnan loved to philosophize a little occ
sionally he resolved to profit by the absence of the king
have a minute's talk with Mlle. de la Valliere. This was a ve
easy affair; while the king was hunting, Louise was walking wi
some other ladies in one of the galleries of the Palais Roy
exactly where the captain of the musketeers had some guar
to inspect. D'Artagnan did not doubt that if he could but op
the conversation upon Raoul, Louise might give him groun
for writing a consolatory letter to the poor exile; and hope,
at least consolation for Raoul, in the state of heart in whi
he had left him, was the sun, was life to two men who we
very dear to our captain. He directed his course, therefore,
the spot where he knew he should find Mlle. de la Vallier
D'Artagnan found La Valliere the center of a circle. In h
apparent solitude, the king's favorite received, like a quee
more perhaps than the queen, a homage of which madame ha
been so proud, when all the king's looks were directed to h
and commanded the looks of the courtiers. D'Artagna
although no squire of dames, received, nevertheless, civiliti
and attentions from the ladies; he was polite, as a brave ma
always is, and his terrible reputation had conciliated as mu

iendship among the men as admiration among the women.
n seeing him enter, therefore, they immediately accosted
m; and, as is not unfrequently the case with fair ladies,
ened the attack by questions.

"Where *had* he been? What *had* become of him so long?
hy had they not seen him as usual make his fine horse curvet
such beautiful style, to the delight and astonishment of the
rious from the king's balcony?"

He replied that he had just come from the land of oranges.
is set all the ladies laughing. Those were times in which
erybody traveled, but in which, notwithstanding, a journey
a hundred leagues was a problem often solved by death.

"From the land of oranges?" cried Mlle. de Tonnay-
arente. From Spain?"

"Eh! eh!" said the musketeer.

"From Malta?" said Montalais.

"*Ma foi!* You are coming very near, ladies."

"Is it an island?" asked La Valliere.

"Mademoiselle," said D'Artagnan, "I will not give you the
uble of seeking any further; I come from the country
ere Monsieur de Beaufort is, at this moment, embarking
r Algiers."

"Have you seen the army?" asked several war-like fair ones.

"As plainly as I see you," replied D'Artagnan.

"And the fleet?"

"Yes; I saw everything."

"Have we, any of us, any friends there?" said Mlle. de
nnay-Charente coldly, but in a manner to attract attention
a question that was not without a calculated aim.

"Why," replied D'Artagnan, "yes; there were Monsieur
la Guillotiere, Monsieur de Manchy, Monsieur de Brage-
ne——"

La Valliere became pale.

"Monsieur de Bragelonne!" cried the perfidious Athenaïs.
h, what! is he gone to the wars—he?"

Montalais trod upon her toe, but in vain.

"Do you know what my opinion is?" continued she, address-
 D'Artagnan.

"No, mademoiselle; but I should like very much to know

"My opinion is, then, that all the men who go to this war
 desperate, desponding men whom love has treated ill; and
 o go to try if they cannot find black women more kind than
 r ones have been."

Some of the ladies laughed. La Valliere was evidently co
fused. Montalais coughed loud enough to waken the dead.

"Mademoiselle," interrupted D'Artagnan, "you are in err
when you speak of black women at Gigelli; the women the
are not black; it is true, they are not white—they are yellow

"Yellow!" exclaimed the bevy of fair beauties.

"Eh! do not disparage it. I have never seen a finer col
to match with black eyes and a coral mouth."

"So much the better for Monsieur de Bragelonne," sa
Mlle. de Tonnay-Charente,' with persistent malice. "He w
make amends for his loss. Poor fellow!"

A profound silence followed these words; and D'Artagn
had time to observe and reflect that women—those mi
doves—treat each other much more cruelly than tigers a
bears. But making La Valliere pale did not satisfy Athenaï
she determined to make her blush likewise. Resuming the co
versation without pause:

"Do you know, Louise," said she, "that that is a great sin
your conscience?"

"What sin, mademoiselle?" stammered the unfortunate gi
looking round her for support, without finding it.

"Eh! why?" continued Athenaïs, "the poor young man w
affianced to you; he loved you; you cast him off."

"Well, and that is a right every honest woman has," sa
Montalais, in an affected tone. "When we know we can n
constitute the happiness of a man, it is much better to cast hi
off."

"Cast him off! or refuse him!—that's all very well," sa
Athenaïs; "but that is not the sin Mademoiselle de la V
liere has to reproach herself with. The actual sin is sendi
poor De Bragelonne to the wars; and to wars in which death
to be met with." Louise pressed her hand over her icy bro
"And if he dies," continued her pitiless tormentor, "you w
have killed him. That is the sin."

Louise, half-dead, caught at the arm of the captain of t
musketeers, whose face betrayed unusual emotion.

"You wished to speak with me, Monsieur d'Artagnan," s
she, in a voice broken by anger and pain. "What had you
say to me?"

D'Artagnan made several steps along the gallery, holdi
Louise on his arm; then, when they were far enough remov
from the others:

"What I had to say to you, mademoiselle," replied he, "

...moiselle de Tonnay-Charente has just expressed; roughly ...d unkindly, it is true, but still in its entirety."

She uttered a faint cry, and, struck to the heart by this new ...und, she went on her way, like one of those poor birds which, ...ruck to death, seek the shade of the thicket to die in. She ...sappeared at one door, at the moment the king was entering ... another. The first glance of the king was directed toward ...e empty seat of his mistress. Not perceiving La Valliere, a ...own came over his brow; but as soon as he saw D'Artagnan, ...o bowed to him:

"Ah! monsieur," cried he, "you *have* been diligent. I am ...uch pleased with you."

This was the superlative expression of royal satisfaction. ...any men would have been ready to lay down their lives for ...ch a speech from the king. The maids of honor and the cour-...rs, who had formed a respectful circle round the king on his ...trance, drew back, on observing he wished to speak privately ...th his captain of the musketeers. The king led the way out of ...e gallery, after having again, with his eyes, sought everywhere ... La Valliere, whose absence he could not account for. The ...oment they were out of the reach of curious ears:

"Well, Monsieur d'Artagnan," said he, "the prisoner?"

"Is in his prison, sire."

"What did he say on the road?"

"Nothing, sire."

"What did he do?"

"There was a moment at which the fisherman—who took me ... his boat to Ste. Marguerite—revolted, and did his best to ... me. The the—prisoner defended me instead of attempting ... fly."

The king became pale.

"Enough!" said he; and D'Artagnan bowed.

Louis walked about his cabinet with hasty steps.

"Were you at Antibes," said he, "when Monsieur de Beau-...rt came there?"

"No, sire; I was setting off when Monsieur le Duc arrived."

"Ah!" which was followed by a fresh silence. "Whom did ...u see there?"

"A great many persons," said D'Artagnan coolly.

The king perceived that he was unwilling to speak.

"I have sent for you, Monsieur le Capitaine, to desire you ... go and prepare my lodgings at Nantes."

"At Nantes!" cried D'Artagnan.

"In Bretagne."

"Yes, sire; it is in Bretagne. Will your majesty make so long a journey as to Nantes?"

"The States are assembled there," replied the king. "I have two demands to make of them; I wish to be there."

"When shall I set out?" said the captain.

"This evening—to-morrow—to-morrow evening; for you must stand in need of rest."

"I have rested, sire."

"That is well. Then, between this and to-morrow evening, when you please."

D'Artagnan bowed as if to take his leave; but, perceiving the king very much embarrassed:

"Will your majesty," said he, stepping two paces forward, "take the court with you?"

"Certainly I shall."

"Then your majesty will, doubtless, want the musketeers?" And the eye of the king sunk beneath the penetrating glance of the captain.

"Take a brigade of them," replied Louis.

"Is that all? Has your majesty no other orders to give me?"

"No—ah! yes."

"I am all attention, sire."

"At the Castle of Nantes, which I hear is very ill arranged, you will adopt the practice of placing musketeers at the door of each of the principal dignitaries I shall take with me."

"Of the principal?"

"Yes."

"For instance, at the door of Monsieur de Lyonne?"

"Yes."

"At that of Monsieur Letellier?"

"Yes."

"Of Monsieur de Brienne?"

"Yes."

"And of Monsieur le Surintendant?"

"Without doubt."

"Very well, sire. By to-morrow I shall have set out."

"Oh, yes; but one more word, Monsieur d'Artagnan. At Nantes you will meet with Monsieur le Duc de Gesvres, captain of the guards. Be sure that your musketeers are placed before his guards arrive. Precedence always belongs to the first comer."

"Yes, sire."

"And if Monsieur de Gesvres should question you?"

"Question me, sire! Is it likely that Monsieur de Gesvres should question me?"

And the musketeer, turning cavalierly on his heel, disappeared.

"To Nantes!" said he to himself, as he descended the stairs. "Why did he not dare to say from thence to Belle-Isle?"

As he reached the great gates one of M. de Brienne's clerks came running after him, exclaiming:

"Monsieur d'Artagnan! I beg your pardon——"

"What is the matter, Monsieur Ariste?"

"The king has desired me to give you this order."

"Upon your cash-box?" asked the musketeer.

"No, monsieur; upon that of Monsieur Fouquet."

D'Artagnan was surprised, but he took the order, which was in the king's own writing, and was for two hundred pistoles.

"What!" thought he, after having politely thanked M. de Brienne's clerk, "Monsieur Fouquet is to pay for the journey, then? *Mordioux!* that is a bit of pure Louis XI.! Why was not his order upon the chest of Monsieur Colbert? He would have paid it with such joy."

And D'Artagnan, faithful to his principle of never letting an order at sight get cold, went straight to the house of M. Fouquet, to reecive his two hundred pistoles.

Chapter 35 — THE LAST SUPPER

The surintendant had no doubt received advice of the approaching departure, for he was giving a farewell dinner to his friends. From the bottom to the top of the house, the hurry of the servants bearing dishes, and the diligence of the *registres*, denoted an approaching change in both offices and kitchen. D'Artagnan, with his order in his hand, presented himself at he bureau, when, he was told, it was too late to pay cash, the hest was closed. He only replied:

"On the king's service."

The clerk, a little put out by the serious air of the captain, eplied that "that was a very respectable reason, but that the ustoms of the house were respectable likewise, and that in onsequence he begged the bearer to call again next day."

D'Artagnan asked if he could not see M. Fouquet. The clerk

replied that M. le Surintendant did not interfere with such
details, and rudely closed the outer door in D'Artagnan's face.
But the latter had foreseen this stroke, and placed his boot
between the door and the door-case, so that the lock did not
catch, and the clerk was still nose to nose with his interlocutor.
This made him change his tone, and say, with terrified politeness:

"If monsieur wishes to speak to Monsieur le Surintendant,
he must go to the antechamber; these are the offices, where
monseigneur never comes."

"Oh! very well. Where are they?" replied D'Artagnan.

"On the other side of the court," said the clerk, delighted at
being free.

D'Artagnan crossed the court, and fell in with a crowd of
servants.

"Monseigneur sees nobody at this hour," he was answered
by a fellow carrying a vermeil dish, in which were three pheasants and twelve quails.

"Tell him," said the captain, laying hold of the servant by
the end of his dish, "that I am Monsieur d'Artagnan, captain
of his majesty's musketeers."

The fellow uttered a cry of surprise, and disappeared,
D'Artagnan following him slowly. He arrived just in time to
meet M. Pellisson in the antechamber; the latter, a little pale,
came hastily out of the dining-room to learn what was the matter. D'Artagnan smiled.

"There is nothing unpleasant, Monsieur Pellisson, only a
little order to receive the money for."

"Ah!" said Fouquet's friend, breathing more freely; and
he took the captain by the hand, and, dragging him behind
him, led him into the dining-room, where a number of friends
surrounded the surintendant, placed in the center, and buried
in the cushions of a *fauteuil*. There were assembled all the
Epicureans who so lately, at Vaux, did the honors of the mansion of wit and money of M. Fouquet. Joyous friends, for
the most part faithful, they had not fled their protector at the
approach of the storm, and, in spite of the threatening heavens,
in spite of the trembling earth, they remained there, smiling,
cheerful, as devoted to misfortune as they had been to prosperity. On the left of the surintendant was Mme. de Belliere,
on his right was Mme. Fouquet; as if braving the laws of the
world, and putting all vulgar reasons of propriety to silence,
the two protecting angels of this man united to offer him, at
the moment of the crisis, the support of their intertwined arms.

Mme. de Belliere was pale, trembling, and full of respectful attentions for Mme. la Surintendante, who, with one hand on the hand of her husband, was looking anxiously toward the door by which Pellisson had gone out to bring in D'Artagnan. The captain entered at first full of courtesy, and afterward of admiration, when, with his infallible glance, he had divined as well as taken in the expression of every face. Fouquet raised himself up in his chair.

"Pardon me, Monsieur d'Artagnan," said he, "if I did not come to receive you when coming in the king's name."

And he pronounced the last words with a sort of melancholy firmness, which filled the hearts of his friends with terror.

"Monseigneur," replied D'Artagnan, "I only come to you, in the king's name, to demand payment of an order for two hundred pistoles."

The clouds passed from every brow but that of Fouquet, which still remained overcast.

"Ah, then," said he, "perhaps you are also setting out for Nantes?"

"I do not know whither I am setting out for, monseigneur."

"But," said Mme. Fouquet, recovered from her fright, "you are not going so soon, Monsieur le Capitaine, as not to do us the honor to take a seat with us?"

"Madame, I should esteem that a great honor done to me, but I am so pressed for time that, you see, I have been obliged to permit myself to interrupt your repast to procure payment of my note."

"The reply to which shall be gold," said Fouquet, making a sign to his intendant, who went out with the order which D'Artagnan handed to him.

"Oh!" said the latter, "I was not uneasy about the payment; the house is good."

A painful smile passed over the pale features of Fouquet.

"Are you in pain?" asked Mme. de Belliere.

"Do you feel your attack coming on?" asked Mme. Fouquet.

"Neither, thank you both," said Fouquet.

"Your attack?" said D'Artagnan, in his turn; "are you unwell, monseigneur?"

"I have a certain fever, which seized me after the *fête* at Vaux."

"Caught cold in the grottoes, at night, perhaps?"

"No, no; nothing but agitation, that was all."

"The too much heart you displayed in your reception of

the king," said La Fontaine quietly, without suspicion that he was uttering a sacrilege.

"We cannot devote too much heart to the reception of our king," said Fouquet mildly, to his poet.

"Monsieur meant to say the too great ardor," interrupted D'Artagnan, with perfect frankness and much amenity. "The fact is, monseigneur, that hospitality was never practiced as at Vaux."

Mme. Fouquet permitted her countenance to show clearly that if Fouquet had conducted himself well toward the king, the king had not rendered the like to the minister. But D'Artagnan knew the terrible secret. He alone, with Fouquet, knew it; those two men had not, the one the courage to complain, the other the right to accuse. The captain, to whom the two hundred pistoles were brought, was about to take leave, when Fouquet, rising, took a glass of wine, and ordered one to be given to D'Artagnan.

"Monsieur," said he, "to the health of the king, 'whatever may happen.'"

"And to your health, monseigneur, 'whatever may happen,'" said D'Artagnan.

He bowed, with these words of evil omen, to all the company, who rose as soon as they heard the sound of his spurs and boots at the bottom of the stairs.

"I, for a moment, thought it was me, and not my money, he wanted," said Fouquet, endeavoring to laugh.

"You!" cried his friends; "and what for, in the name of Heaven?"

"Oh! do not deceive yourselves, my dear brothers in Epicurus," said the surintendant; "I will not make a comparison between the most humble sinner on the earth and the God we adore, but remember, He gave one day to His friends a repast which is called the Last Supper, and which was nothing but a farewell dinner, like that which we are making at this moment."

A painful cry of denial arose from all parts of the table.

"Shut the doors," said Fouquet, and the servants disappeared. "My friends," continued Fouquet, lowering his voice, "what was I formerly? What am I now? Consult among yourselves, and reply. A man like me sinks when he does not continue to rise. What shall we say, then, when he really sinks? I have no more money, no more credit; I have no longer anything but powerful enemies, and powerless friends."

"Quick!" cried Pellisson. "Since you explain yourself with that frankness, it is our duty to be frank, likewise. Yes, you are ruined—yes, you are hastening to your ruin—stop. And, in the first place, what money have we left?"

"Seven hundred thousand livres," said the intendant.

"Bread," murmured Mme. Fouquet.

"Relays," said Pellisson, "relays, and fly!"

"Whither?"

"To Switzerland—to Savoy—but fly!"

"If monseigneur flies," said Mme. Belliere, "it will be said that he was guilty, and was afraid."

"More than that, it will be said that I have carried away twenty millions with me."

"We will draw up memoirs to justify you," said La Fontaine. "Fly!"

"I will remain," said Fouquet. "And, besides, does not everything serve me?"

"You have Belle-Isle," cried the Abbé Fouquet.

"And I am naturally going there, when going to Nantes," replied the surintendant. "Patience, then, patience!"

"Before arriving at Nantes, what a distance!" said Mme. Fouquet.

"Yes, I know that well," replied Fouquet. "But what is to be done there? The king summons me to the States. I know well it is for the purpose of ruining me; but to refuse to go would be to evince uneasiness."

"Well, I have discovered the means of reconciling everything," cried Pellisson. "You are going to set out for Nantes."

Fouquet looked at him with an air of surprise.

"But with friends; but in your own carriage as far as Orleans; in your barge as far as Nantes; always ready to defend yourself, if you are attacked; to escape, if you are threatened. In fact, you will carry your money against all chances; and while flying you will only have obeyed the king; then, reaching the sea when you like, you will embark for Belle-Isle, and from Belle-Isle you will shoot out wherever it may please you, like the eagle which rushes into space when it has been driven from its eyrie."

A general assent followed Pellisson's words.

"Yes, do so," said Mme. Fouquet, to her husband.

"Do so," said Mme. Belliere.

"Do it! do it!" cried all his friends.

"I will do so," replied Fouquet.

"This very evening?"

"In an hour?"

"Immediately."

"With seven hundred thousand livres you can lay the foundation of another fortune," said the Abbé Fouquet. "What is there to prevent our arming corsairs at Belle-Isle?"

"And, if necessary, we will go and discover a new world," added La Fontaine, intoxicated with projects and enthusiasm.

A knock at the door interrupted this concert of joy and hope. "A courier from the king," said the master of the ceremonies.

A profound silence immediately ensued, as if the message brought by this courier was nothing but a reply to all the projects given birth to an instant before. Every one waited to see what the master would do. His brow was streaming with perspiration, and he was really suffering from his fever at that instant. He passed into his cabinet, to receive the king's message. There prevailed, as we have said, such a silence in the chambers, and throughout the attendance, that from the dining-room could be heard the voice of Fouquet, saying, "That is well, monsieur." This voice was, however, broken by fatigue, trembling with emotion. An instant after Fouquet called Gourville, who crossed the gallery amid the universal expectation. At length he himself reappeared among his guests; but it was no longer the same pale, spiritless countenance they had beheld when he left them; from pale he had become livid, and from spiritless, annihilated. A living specter, he advanced with his arms stretched out, his mouth parched, like a shade that comes to salute friends of former days. On seeing him thus every one cried out, and every one rushed toward Fouquet. The latter, looking at Pellisson, leaned upon Mme. la Surintendante, and pressed the icy hand of the Marquise de Belliere.

"Well!" said he, in a voice which had nothing human in it.

"What has happened, my God?" said some one to him.

Fouquet opened his right hand, which was clinched, humid, and displayed a paper, upon which Pellisson cast a terrified glance. He read the following lines, written by the king's hand:

"'DEAR AND WELL-BELOVED MONSIEUR FOUQUET: Give us, upon that which you have left of ours, the sum of seven hundred thousand livres, of which we stand in need to prepare for our departure.

"'And, as we know your health is not good, we pray God to restore you to health, and to have you in His holy keeping.

LOUIS.

"'The present letter is to serve as a receipt.'"

A murmur of terror circulated through the apartment.

"Well!" cried Pellisson, in his turn, "you have received that letter?"

"Received it—yes."

"What will you do, then?"

"Nothing, since I have received it."

"But——"

"If I have received it, Pellisson, I have paid it," said the surintendant, with a simplicity that went to the heart of all present.

"You have paid it!" cried Mme. Fouquet. "Then we are ruined!"

"Come, no useless words," interrupted Pellisson. "After money, life. Monseigneur, to horse! to horse!"

"What, leave us!" at once cried both the women, with wild grief.

"Eh! monseigneur, in saving yourself you save us all. To horse!"

"But he cannot hold himself on. Look at him!"

"Oh! if he takes time to reflect——" said the intrepid Pellisson.

"He is right," murmured Fouquet.

"Monseigneur! monseigneur!" cried Gourville, rushing up the stairs four steps at once. "Monseigneur!"

"Well, what?"

"I escorted, as you desired, the king's courier with the money."

"Yes."

"Well, when I arrived at the Palais Royal, I saw——"

"Take breath, my poor friend, take breath; you are suffocating."

"What did you see?" cried the impatient friends.

"I saw the musketeers mounting on horseback," said Gourville.

"There, then!" cried all the voices at once; "there, then! is there an instant to be lost?" Mme. Fouquet rushed downstairs, calling for her horses; Mme. de Belliere flew after her, catching her in her arms, and saying:

"Madame, in the name of his safety, do not show anything, do not manifest any alarm."

Pellisson ran to have the horses put to the carriages. And, in the meantime, Gourville gathered in his hat all that the weeping friends were able to throw into it of gold and silver—the last offering, the pious alms made to misfortune by poverty.

The surintendant, dragged along by some, carried by others, was shut up in his carriage. Gourville took the reins and mounted the box. Pellisson supported Mme. Fouquet, who had fainted. Mme. de Belliere had more strength, and was well paid for it; she received Fouquet's last kiss. Pellisson easily explained this precipitate departure, by saying that an order from the king had summoned the minister to Nantes.

Chapter 36 — IN THE CARRIAGE OF M. COLBERT

As Gourville had seen, the king's musketeers were mounting and following their captain. The latter, who did not like to be confined in his proceedings, left his brigade under the orders of a lieutenant, and set off, on his part, upon post horses, recommending his men to use all diligence. However rapidly they might travel, they could not arrive before him. He had time, in passing along the Rue des Petits Champs, to see a thing which afforded him plenty of food for thought and conjecture. He saw M. Colbert coming out from his house to get into his carriage, which was stationed before the door. In this carriage D'Artagnan perceived the hoods of two women, and being rather curious, he wished to know the names of the women concealed beneath these hoods. To get a glimpse at them, for they kept themselves closely covered up, he urged his horse so near to the carriage that he drove him against the step with such force as to shake everything containing and contained. The terrified women uttered, the one a faint cry, by which D'Artagnan recognized a young woman, the other an imprecation, by which he recognized the vigor and *aplomb* which half a century bestows. The hoods were thrown back; one of the women was Mme. Vanel, the other was the Duchesse de Chevreuse. D'Artagnan's eyes were quicker than those of the ladies; he had seen and known them, while they did not recognize him; and as they laughed at their fright, pressing each others' hands:

"Humph!" said D'Artagnan, "the old duchess is not more difficult in her friendships than she was formerly. She paying her court to the mistress of Monsieur Colbert! Poor Monsieur Fouquet! that presages you nothing good!"

He rode on. M. Colbert got into his carriage, and this noble trio commenced a sufficiently slow pilgrimage toward the wood of Vincennes. Mme. de Chevreuse set down Mme. Vanel at her husband's house, and, left alone with M. Colbert, she chatted upon affairs while continuing her ride. She had an inexhaustible fund of conversation, had that dear duchess, and as she always talked for the ill of others, always with a view to her own good, her conversation amused her interlocutor, and did not fail to leave a favorable impression behind.

She taught Colbert, who, poor man! was ignorant of it, how great a minister he was, and how Fouquet would soon become nothing. She promised to rally around him, when he should become surintendant, all the old nobility of the kingdom, and questioned him as to the preponderance it would be proper to allow La Valliere to take. She praised him, she blamed him, she bewildered him. She showed him the secret of so many secrets that, for a moment Colbert feared he must have to do with the devil. She proved to him that she held in her hand the Colbert of to-day as she held the Fouquet of yesterday; and as he asked her very simply the reason of her hatred for the surintendant:

"Why do you yourself hate him?" said she.

"Madame, in politics," replied he, "the differences of system may bring about divisions between men. Monsieur Fouquet always appeared to me to practice a system opposed to the true interests of the king."

She interrupted him.

"I will say no more to you about Monsieur Fouquet. The journey the king is about to take to Nantes will give a good account of him. Monsieur Fouquet, for me, is a man quite gone by—and for you also."

Colbert made no reply.

"On his return from Nantes," continued the duchess, "the king, who is only anxious for a pretext, will find that the States have not behaved well—that they have made too few sacrifices. The States will say that the imposts are too heavy, and that the surintendant has ruined them. The king will lay all the blame on M. Fouquet, and then——"

"And then?" said Colbert.

"Oh! he will be disgraced. Is not that your opinion?"

Colbert darted a glance at the duchess, which plainly said, "If Monsieur Fouquet be only disgraced you will not be the cause of it."

"Your place, Monsieur Colbert," the duchess hastened to say, "must be quite a marked place. Do you perceive any one between the king and yourself, after the fall of Monsieur Fouquet?"

"I do not understand," said he.

"You will understand. To what does your ambition aspire?"

"I have none."

"It was useless, then, to overthrow the surintendant, Monsieur Colbert. That is idle."

"I had the honor to tell you, madame——"

"Oh, yes, I know, all about the interest of the king; but, if you please, we will speak of your own."

"Mine! that is to say, the affairs of his majesty."

"In short, are you, or are you not, ruining Monsieur Fouquet? Answer without evasion."

"Madame, I ruin nobody."

"I cannot, then, comprehend why you should purchase of me the letters of Monsieur Mazarin concerning Monsieur Fouquet. Neither can I conceive why you have laid those letters before the king."

Colbert, half-stupefied, looked at the duchess with an air of constraint.

"Madame," said he, "I can less easily conceive how you, who received the money, can reproach me on that head."

"That is," said the old duchess, "because we must will that which we wish for, unless we are not able to obtain what we wish."

"*Will!*" said Colbert, quite confounded by such coarse logic.

"You are not able, *hein!* Speak."

"I am not able, I allow, to destroy certain influences near the king."

"Which combat for Monsieur Fouquet? What are they? Stop; let me help you."

"Do, madame."

"La Valliere?"

"Oh, very little influence; no knowledge of business, and small means. Monsieur Fouquet has paid his court to her."

"To defend him would be to accuse herself, would it not?"

"I think it would."

"There is still another influence, what do you say to that?"

"Is it considerable?"

"The queen-mother, perhaps?"

"Her majesty, the queen-mother, has for Monsieur Fouquet a weakness very prejudicial to her son."

"Never believe that," said the old duchess, smiling.

"Oh!" said Colbert, with incredulity, "I have often experienced it."

"Formerly?"

"Very recently, madame, at Vaux. It was she who prevented the king from having Monsieur Fouquet arrested."

"People do not always entertain the same opinions, my dear monsieur. That which the queen may have wished recently, she would not, perhaps, to-day."

"And why not?" said Colbert, astonished.

"Oh! the reason is of very little consequence."

"On the contrary, I think it is of great consequence; for, if I were certain of not displeasing her majesty, the queen-mother, all my scruples would be removed."

"Well, have you never heard talk of a certain secret?"

"A secret?"

"Call it what you like. In short, the queen-mother has conceived a horror for all those who have participated, in one fashion or another, in the discovery of this secret, and Monsieur Fouquet I believe to be one of these."

"Then," said Colbert, "we may be sure of the assent of the queen-mother?"

"I have just left her majesty, and she assures me so."

"So be it, then, madame."

"But there is something further; do you happen to know a man who was the intimate friend of Monsieur Fouquet, a Monsieur d'Herblay, a bishop, I believe?"

"Bishop of Vannes."

"Well, this Monsieur d'Herblay, who also knew the secret, the queen-mother is having him pursued with the utmost rancor."

"Indeed!"

"So hotly pursued that if he were dead, she would not be satisfied with anything less than his head, to satisfy her he could never speak again."

"And is that the desire of the queen-mother?"

"An order is given for it."

"This Monsieur d'Herblay shall be sought for, madame."

"Oh! it is well known where he is."

Colbert looked at the duchess.

"Say where, madame."

"He is at Belle-Isle-en-Mer."

"At the residence of Monsieur Fouquet?"

"At the residence of Monsieur Fouquet."

"He shall be taken."

It was now the duchess' turn to smile.

"Do not fancy that so easy," said she, "and do not promis
it so lightly."

"Why not, madame?"

"Because Monsieur d'Herblay is not one of those peopl
who can be taken just when you please."

"He is a rebel, then."

"Oh, Monsieur Colbert, we folks have passed all our lives i
making rebels, and yet you see plainly that so far from bein
taken, we take others."

Colbert fixed upon the old duchess one of those fierce look
of which no words can convey the expression, accompanie
by a firmness which was not wanting in grandeur.

"The times are gone," said he, "in which subjects gaine
duchies by making war against the King of France. If Monsie
d'Herblay conspires, he will perish on the scaffold. That wi
give, or will not give, pleasure to his enemies—that is of ver
little importance to *us*."

And this *us*, a strange word in the mouth of Colbert, ma
the duchess thoughtful for a moment. She caught herself rec
oning inwardly with this man—Colbert had regained his s
periority in the conversation, and he was desirous of keeping i

"You ask me, madame," he said, "to have this Monsie
d'Herblay arrested?"

"I?—I ask you nothing of the kind!"

"I thought you did, madame. But as I have been mi
taken, we will leave him alone; the king has said nothing abo
him."

The duchess bit her nails.

"Besides," continued Colbert, "what a poor capture woul
this bishop be! A bishop game for a king! Oh, no, no; I will n
even take the least notice of him."

The hatred of the duchess now discovered itself.

"Game for a woman!" said she, "and the queen is a woma
If she wishes to have Monsieur d'Herblay arrested, she has h
reasons for it. Besides, is not Monsieur d'Herblay the friend
him who is destined to fall?"

"Oh, never mind that!" said Colbert. "This man shall
spared, if he is not the enemy of the king. Is that displeasing
you?"

"I say nothing."

"Yes; you wish to see him in prison, in the Bastile, for i
stance."

believe a secret better concealed behind the walls of the
le than behind those of Belle-Isle."

will speak to the king about it; he will clear up the
."

nd while waiting for that enlightenment, Monsieur l'E-
e de Cannes will have escaped. I would do so."

scaped? he—and whither would he escape? Europe is ours,
ll, if not in fact."

e will always find an asylum, monsieur. It is evident you
 nothing of the man you have to do with. You do not
 D'Herblay; you did not know Aramis. He was one of those
 musketeers who, under the late king, made Cardinal de
elieu tremble, and who, during the regency, gave so
 trouble to Monseigneur Mazarin."

ut, madame, what can he do, unless he has a kingdom to
 him?"

e has one, monsieur."

 kingdom? he? What, Monsieur d'Herblay?"

 repeat to you, monsieur, that if he wants a kingdom he
 has it or will have it."

ell, as you are so earnest that this rebel should not
 e, madame, I promise you he shall not escape."

elle-Isle is fortified, Monsieur Colbert, and fortfied by

 Belle-Isle were also defended by him, Belle-Isle is not
egnable; and if Monsieur l'Evêque de Cannes is shut up
 lle-Isle, well, madame, the place will be besieged, and he
 e taken."

ou may be very certain, monsieur, that the zeal which you
 y for the interests of the queen-mother will affect her
sty warmly, and that you will be magnificently rewarded
.; but what shall I tell her of your projects respecting this
"

hat when once taken, he shall be shut up in a fortress
 which her secret shall never escape."

ery well, Monsieur Colbert, and we may say that, dating
 this instant, we have formed a solid alliance, that is, you
, and that I am perfectly at your service."

 is I, madame, who place myself at yours. This Chevalier
 blay is a kind of Spanish spy, is he not?"

ore than that."

 secret ambassador?"

igher still."

"Stop—King Philip III. of Spain is a bigot. He is, perha
the confessor of Philip III."

"You must go much higher than that."

"*Mordieu!*" cried Colbert, who forgot himself so far as
swear in the presence of this great lady, of this old friend
the queen-mother—of the Duchesse de Chevreuse, in sh
"He must, then, be the general of the Jesuits?"

"I believe you have guessed at last," replied the duche

"Ah, then, madame, this man will ruin us all if we do
ruin him; and we must make haste to do it, too."

"That was my opinion, monsieur, but I did not dare to g
it you."

"And it is fortunate for us that he has attacked the thro
and not us."

"But, mark this well, Monsieur Colbert. Monsieur d'Herb
is never discouraged; and if he has missed one blow, he
be sure to make another; he will begin again. If he has
lowed an opportunity to escape of making a king for hims
sooner or later, he will make another, of whom, to a certai
you will not be prime minister."

Colbert knitted his brow with a menacing expression.

"I feel assured that a prison will settle this affair for us, m
ame, in a manner satisfactory for both."

The duchess smiled again.

"Oh! if you knew," said she, "how many times Aramis
got out of prison!"

"Oh!" replied Colbert, "we will take care he shall not get
this time."

"But you have not attended to what I said to you just n
Do you remember that Aramis was one of the four invinci
whom Richelieu dreaded? And at that period the four mus
eers were not in possession of that which they have no
money and experience."

Colbert bit his lips.

"We will renounce the idea of the prison," said he, in a lo
tone; "we will find a retreat from which the invincible will
possibly escape."

"That is well spoken, our ally!" replied the duchess. "Bu
is getting late; had we not better return?"

"The more willingly, madame, from my having my prepa
tions to make for setting out with the king."

"To Paris!" cried the duchess, to the coachman.

And the carriage returned toward the Faubourg St. Anto
after the conclusion of the treaty which gave up to death

ast friend of Fouquet, the last defender of Belle-Isle, the ancient friend of Marie Michon, the new enemy of the duchess.

Chapter 37 — THE TWO LIGHTERS

D'Artagnan had set off; Fouquet likewise was gone, and he with a rapidity which doubled the tender interest of his friends. The first moments of this journey, or, better to say, of this flight, were troubled by the incessant fear of all the horses and all the carriages which could be perceived behind the fugitive. It was not natural, in fact, if Louis XIV. was determined to seize his prey that he should allow it to escape; the young lion was already accustomed to the chase, and he had bloodhounds sufficiently ardent to allow him to depend upon them. But insensibly all the fears were dispersed; the surintendant, by hard traveling, placed such a distance between himself and his persecutors that no one of them could reasonably be expected to overtake him. As to his position, his friends had made it excellent for him. Was he not traveling to join the king at Nantes, and what did the rapidity prove but his zeal to obey? He arrived, fatigued, but reassured, at Orleans, where he found, thanks to the care of a courier who had preceded him, a handsome lighter of eight oars. These lighters, in the shape of gondolas, rather wide and rather heavy, containing a small, covered chamber, in shape of a deck, and a chamber in the poop, formed by a tent, then acted as passageboats from Orleans to Nantes, by the Loire, and this passage, a long one in our days, appeared then more easy and convenient than the highroad, with its post-hacks or its bad, scarcely hung carriages. Fouquet went on board this lighter, which set out immediately. The rowers, knowing they had the honor of conveying the surintendant of the finances, pulled with all their strength, and that magic word, the *finances*, promised them a liberal gratification, of which they wished to prove themselves worthy. The lighter bounded over the tiny waves of the Loire. Magnificent weather, one of those sun-risings that impurple landscapes, left the river all its limpid serenity. The current and the rowers carried Fouquet along as wings carry a bird, and he arrived before Beaugency, without any accident having signalized the voyage. Fouquet hoped to be the first to arrive at Nantes;

there he would see the notables and gain support among the principal members of the States; he would make himself necessary, a thing very easy for a man of his merit, and would delay the catastrophe, if he did not succeed in avoiding it entirely.

"Besides," said Gourville to him, "at Nantes you will make out, or we will make out the intentions of your enemies; we will have horses always ready to convey you to the inextricable Poiton, a bark in which to gain the sea, and when once in the open sea, Belle-Isle is the inviolable port. You see, besides that no one is watching you, no one is following you."

He had scarcely finished, when they discovered at a distance behind an elbow formed by the river, the masts of a large lighter, which was coming down. The rowers of Fouquet's boat uttered a cry of surprise on seeing this galley.

"What is the matter?" asked Fouquet.

"The matter is, monseigneur," replied the patron of the bark, "that it is a truly remarkable thing—that lighter comes along like a hurricane."

Gourville started, and mounted on the deck, in order to see the better.

Fouquet did not go up with him, but he said to Gourville with a restrained mistrust:

"See what it is, dear friend."

The lighter had just passed the elbow. It came on so fast that behind it might be seen to tremble the white train of its wake illumined with the fires of day.

"How they go!" repeated the patron, "how they go! They must be well paid! I did not think," he added, "that oars of wood could behave better than ours, but those yonder prove the contrary."

"Well they may," said one of the rowers, "they are twelve and we are but eight."

"Twelve rowers!" replied Gourville, "twelve—impossible!"

The number of eight rowers for a lighter had never been exceeded, even for the king. This honor had been paid to M. le Surintendant, much more for the sake of haste than of respect.

"What does that mean?" said Gourville, endeavoring to distinguish beneath the tent, which was already apparent, travelers which the most piercing eye could not yet have succeeded in discovering.

"They must be in a hurry, for it is not the king," said the patron.

Fouquet shuddered.

"By what do you know that it is not the king?" said Gourville.

"In the first place, because there is no white flag with fleurs-de-lis, which the royal lighter always carries."

"And then," said Fouquet, "because it is impossible it should be the king, Gourville, as the king was still in Paris yesterday."

Gourville replied to the surintendant by a look, which said: "You were there yourself yesterday."

"And by what do you make out they are in such haste?" added he, for the sake of gaining time.

"By this, monsieur," said the patron: "these people must have set out a long while after us, and they have already nearly overtaken us."

"Bah!" said Gourville, "who told you that they do not come from Beaugency or from Moit, even?"

"We have seen no lighter of that shape, except at Orleans. It comes from Orleans, monsieur, and makes great haste."

Fouquet and Gourville exchanged a glance. The patron remarked their uneasiness, and to mislead him, Gourville immediately said:

"Some friend, who was laid a wager he would catch us; let us win the wager, and not allow him to come up with us."

The patron opened his mouth to reply that that was impossible, when Fouquet said, with much hauteur:

"If it is any one who wishes to overtake us, let him come."

"We can try, monseigneur," said the patron timidly. "Come, you fellows, put out your strength; row, row!"

"No," said Fouquet, "stop short, on the contrary."

"Monseigneur! what folly!" interrupted Gourville, stooping toward his ear.

"Quite short!" repeated Fouquet.

The eight oars stopped, and, resisting the water, they created a retrograde motion in the lighter. It was stopped. The twelve rowers in the other did not, at first, perceive this maneuver, or they continued to urge on their boat so vigorously that it arrived quickly within musket-shot. Fouquet was short-sighted, Gourville was annoyed by the sun, which was full in his eyes; the patron alone, with that habit and clearness which are acquired by a constant struggle with the elements, perceived distinctly the travelers in the neighboring lighter.

"I can see them!" cried he; "there are two."

"I can see nothing," said Gourville.

"You will not be long before you distinguish them; in twenty strokes of their oars they will be within twenty paces of us."

But what the patron announced was not realized; the lighter imitated the movement commanded by Fouquet, and instead of coming to join its pretended friends, it stopped short in the middle of the river.

"I cannot comprehend this," said the patron.

"Nor I, neither," said Gourville.

"You, who can see so plainly the people in that lighter," resumed Fouquet, "try to describe them to us, patron, before we are too far off."

"I thought I saw two," replied the boatman. "I can only see one now, under the tent."

"What sort of man is he?"

"He is a dark man, large shouldered, short necked."

A little cloud at that moment passed across the azure of the heavens, and darkened the sun. Gourville, who was still looking, with one hand over his eyes, became able to see what he sought, and all at once, jumping from the deck into the chamber where Fouquet awaited him:

"Colbert!" said he, in a voice broken by emotion.

"Colbert!" repeated Fouquet. "Oh! how strange! But no, it is impossible."

"I tell you I recognized him, and he, at the same time, so plainly recognized me that he is just gone into the chamber on the poop. Perhaps the king has sent him to make us come back."

"In that case he would join us instead of lying by. What is he doing there?"

"He is watching us, without doubt."

"I do not like uncertainty," said Fouquet; "let us go straight up to him."

"Oh, monseigneur, do not do that, the lighter is full of armed men."

"He would arrest me, then, Gourville? Why does he not come on?"

"Monseigneur, it is not consistent with your dignity to go to meet even your ruin."

"But to allow them to watch me like a malefactor!"

"Nothing tells us that they are watching you, monseigneur; be patient."

"What is to be done, then?"

"Do not stop; you were only going so fast to appear to obey the king's order with zeal. Redouble the speed. He who lives will see!"

"That's just. Come!" cried Fouquet; "since they remain stock-still yonder, let us go on, on our part."

The patron gave the signal, and Fouquet's rowers resumed their task with all the success that could be looked for from men who had rested. Scarcely had the lighter made a hundred fathoms than the other, that with the twelve rowers, resumed its course equally. This position lasted all the day, without any increase or diminution of distance between the two vessels. Toward evening Fouquet wished to try the intentions of his persecutor. He ordered his rowers to pull toward the shore, as to effect a landing. Colbert's lighter imitated this maneuver, and steered toward the shore in a slanting direction. By the greatest chance, at the spot where Fouquet pretended to wish to land, a stableman from the Château of Langeais was following the flowery banks, leading three horses in halters. Without doubt, the people of the twelve-oared lighter fancied that Fouquet was directing his course toward horses prepared for his flight, for four or five men, armed with muskets, jumped from the lighter on to the shore, and marched along the banks, as if to gain ground on the horses and horseman. Fouquet, satisfied of having forced the enemy to a demonstration, considered it evident, and put his boat in motion again. Colbert's people returned likewise to theirs, and the course of the two vessels was resumed with fresh perseverance. Upon seeing this, Fouquet felt himself threatened closely, and in a prophetic voice:

"Well, Gourville," said he whisperingly, "what did I say at our last repast, at my house? Am I going, or not, to my ruin?"

"Oh, monseigneur!"

"These two boats, which follow each other with so much emulation, as if we were disputing, Monsieur Colbert and I, a prize for swiftness on the Loire, do they not aptly represent our two fortunes; and do you not believe, Gourville, that one of the two will be wrecked at Nantes?"

"At least," objected Gourville, "there is still uncertainty; you are about to appear at the States; you are about to show what sort of man you are; your eloquence and your genius for business are the buckler and sword that will serve to defend you, if not to conquer with. The Bretons do not know you; and when they shall know you your cause is won! Oh! let Monsieur Colbert look to it well, for his lighter is as much exposed as yours to being upset. Both go quickly, his faster than yours, it is true; we shall see which will be wrecked first."

Fouquet, taking Gourville's hand:

"My friend," said he, "everything considered, remember the proverb, 'First come, first served.' Well, Monsieur Colbert takes

care not to pass me. He is a prudent man, that Monsieur Col
bert!"

He was right; the two lighters held their course as far a
Nantes, watching each other. When the surintendant lande
Gourville hoped he should be able to seek refuge at once, an
have relays prepared. But, at the landing, the second lighte
joined the first, and Colbert, approaching Fouquet, saluted hir
on the quay with marks of the profoundest respect—marks s
significant, so public, that their result was the bringing of th
whole population upon La Fosse. Fouquet was completel
self-possessed; he felt that in his last moments of greatnes
he had obligations toward himself. He wished to fall from suc
a height that his fall should crush some one of his enemie
Colbert was there—so much the worse for Colbert. The surin
tendant, therefore, coming up to him, replied, with that a
rogant winking of the eyes peculiar to him:

"What! is that you, Monsieur Colbert?"

"To offer you my respects, monseigneur," said the latter.

"Were you in that lighter?" pointing to the one with twelv
rowers.

"Yes, monseigneur."

"Of twelve rowers!" said Fouquet. "What luxury, Monsie
Colbert! For a moment, I thought it was the queen mother c
the king."

"Monseigneur!" and Colbert blushed.

"This is a voyage that will cost those who have to pay for
dear, Monsieur l'Intendant," said Fouquet. "But you hav
happily, arrived. You see, however," added he, a moment afte
"that, I who had but eight rowers, arrived before you."

And he turned his back toward him, leaving him uncertai
whether all the tergiversations of the second lighter ha
escaped the notice of the first. At least, he did not give him th
satisfaction of showing that he had been frightened. Colber
so annoyingly attacked, did not give way.

"I have not been quick, monseigneur," he replied, "becaus
I followed your example whenever you stopped."

"And why did you do that, Monsieur Colbert?" cried Fo
quet, irritated by this base audacity; "as you had a superi
crew to mine, why did you not either join me or pass me?"

"Out of respect," said the intendant, bowing to the groun

Fouquet got into a carriage which the city sent to him, v
know not why or how, and he repaired to la Maison de Nante
escorted by a vast crowd of people, who for several days ha
been boiling with the expectation of a convocation of the State

Scarcely was he installed, when Gourville went out to go and order horses upon the route to Poitiers and Vannes, and a boat at Paimbœuf. He performed these various operations with so much mystery, activity, and generosity that never was Fouquet, then laboring under an access of fever, more near being saved, except for the cooperation of that immense disturber of human projects—chance. A report was spread during the night that the king was coming in great haste upon post-horses, and that he would arrive within ten or twelve hours at the latest. The people, while waiting for the king, were greatly rejoiced to see the musketeers, freshly arrived, with M. d'Artagnan, their captain, and quartered in the castle, of which they occupied all the posts, in quality of guard of honor. M. d'Artagnan, who was very polite, presented himself about ten o'clock at the lodgings of the surintendant, to pay his respectful compliments to him; and although the minister suffered from fever, although he was in such pain as to be bathed in sweat, he would receive M. d'Artagnan, who was delighted with that honor, as will be seen by the conversation they had together.

Chapter 38 — FRIENDLY ADVICE

Fouquet was gone to bed, like a man who clings to life, and who economizes as much as possible that slender tissue of existence, of which the shocks and angles of this world so quickly wear out the irreparable tenuity. D'Artagnan appeared at the door of his chamber, and was saluted by the surintendant with a very affable "good-day."

"*Bon jour*, monseigneur," replied the musketeer; "how did you get through the journey?"

"Tolerably well, thank you."

"And the fever?"

"But sadly. I drink, as you see. I am scarcely arrived, and I have already levied a contribution of *tisane* upon Nantes."

"You should sleep first, monseigneur."

"Eh! *corbleu!* my dear Monseigneur d'Artagnan, I should be very glad to sleep."

"Who hinders you?"

"Why, you, in the first place."

"I? Ah, monseigneur!"

"No doubt you do. Is it at Nantes as it was at Paris? do you not come in the king's name?"

"For Heaven's sake, monseigneur," replied the captain, "leave the king alone! The day on which I shall come on the part of the king, for the purpose you mean, take my word for it, I will not leave you long in doubt. You will see me place my hand on my sword, according to the ordonnance, and you will hear me say at once, in my ceremonial voice:

" 'Monseigneur, in the name of the king, I arrest you!' "

"You promise me that frankness?" said the surintendant.

"Upon my honor! But we are not to come to that, believe me."

"What makes you think that, Monsieur d'Artagnan? For my part, I think quite the contrary."

"I have heard speak of nothing of the kind," replied D'Artagnan.

"Eh, eh!" said Fouquet.

"Indeed, no. You are an agreeable man, in spite of your fever. The king ought not, can not help loving you, at the bottom of his heart."

Fouquet's face implied doubt.

"But Monsieur Colbert?" said he, "does Monsieur Colbert love me as much as you say?"

"I don't speak of Monsieur Colbert," replied D'Artagnan. "He is an exceptional man, is that Monsieur Colbert. He does not love you; that is very possible, but, *mordioux!* the squirrel can guard himself against the adder with very little trouble."

"Do you know that you are speaking to me quite as a friend," replied Fouquet; "and that, upon my life! I have never met with a man of your intelligence and your heart?"

"You are pleased to say so," replied D'Artagnan. "Why did you wait till to-day, to pay me such a compliment?"

"Blind as we are!" murmured Fouquet.

"Your voice is getting hoarse," said D'Artagnan; "drink, monseigneur, drink!"

And he offered him a cup of *tisane*, with the most friendly cordiality; Fouquet took it, and thanked him by a bland smile.

"Such things only happen to me," said the musketeer. "I have passed ten years under your very beard, while you were rolling about tons of gold. You were clearing an annual pension of four millions; you never observed me, and you find out there is such a person in the world just at the moment you——"

"I am about to fall," interrupted Fouquet. "That is true, my dear Monsieur d'Artagnan."

"I did not say so."

"But you thought so, and that is the same thing. Well, if I fall, take my word as truth, I shall not pass a single day without saying to myself, as I strike my brow, 'Fool! fool!— stupid mortal! You had a Monsieur d'Artagnan under your eye and hand, and you did not employ him, you did not enrich him!' "

"You quite overwhelm me," said the captain. "I esteem you greatly."

"There exists another man, then, who does not think as Monsieur Colbert does?" said the surintendant.

"How this Monsieur Colbert sticks in your stomach! He is worse than your fever."

"Oh, I have good cause," said Fouquet. "Judge for yourself."

And he related the details of the course of the lighters, and the hypocritical persecution of Colbert.

"Is not this a clear sign of my ruin?"

D'Artagnan became serious.

"That is true," he said. "Yes, that has a bad odor, as Monsieur de Tréville used to say."

And he fixed upon M. Fouquet his intelligent and significant look.

"Am I not clearly designated in that, captain? Is not the king bringing me to Nantes to get me away from Paris, where I have so many creatures, and to possess himself of Belle-Isle?"

"Where Monsieur d'Herblay is," added D'Artagnan.

Fouquet raised his head.

"As for me, monseigneur," continued D'Artagnan," I assure you the king has said nothing to me against you."

"Indeed?"

"The king commanded me to set out for Nantes, it is true, and to say nothing about it to Monsieur de Gesvres."

"My friend."

"To Monsieur de Gesvres, yes, monseigneur," continued the musketeer, whose eyes did not cease to speak a language different from the language of his lips. "The king, moreover, commanded me to take a brigade of musketeers, which is apparently superfluous, as the country is quite quiet."

"A brigade!" said Fouquet, raising himself upon his elbow.

"Ninety-six horsemen, yes, monseigneur. The same number as were employed in arresting Messieurs de Chalais, De Cinq-Mars, and Montmorency."

Fouquet pricked up his ears at these words, pronounced without apparent value.

"And besides?" said he.

"Well, nothing but insignificant orders; such as guarding the castle, guarding every lodging, allowing none of Monsieur de Gesvres' guards to occupy a single post. Monsieur de Gesvres, your friend."

"And for myself," cried Fouquet, "what orders had you?"

"For you, monseigneur?—not the smallest word."

"Monsieur d'Artagnan, the safety of my honor, and, perhaps, of my life, is at stake. You would not deceive me?"

"I?—and to what end? Are you threatened? Only there really is an order with respect to carriages and boats——"

" 'An order?' "

"Yes; but it cannot concern you—a simple measure of police."

"What is it, captain—what is it?"

"To forbid all horses or boats to leave Nantes, without a pass, signed by the king."

"Great God! but——"

D'Artagnan began to laugh.

"All that is not to be put into execution before the arrival of the king at Nantes. So that you see plainly, monseigneur, the order in nowise concerns you."

Fouquet became thoughtful, and D'Artagnan feigned not to observe his preoccupation.

"It is evident, by my thus confiding to you the orders which have been given to me, that I am friendly toward you, and that I endeavor to prove to you, that none of them are directed against you."

"Without doubt, without doubt!" said Fouquet, still absent.

"Let us recapitulate," said the captain, his glance beaming with earnestness. "A special and severe guard of the castle, in which your lodging is to be—is it not?"

"Do you know that castle?"

"Ah, monseigneur, a true prison. The total absence of Monsieur de Gesvres, who has the honor of being one of your friends. The closing of the gates of the city, and of the river, without a pass; but only when the king shall have arrived. Please to observe, Monsieur Fouquet, that if, instead of speaking to a man like you, who are one of the first in the kingdom, I were speaking to a troubled, uneasy conscience, I should compromise myself forever. What a fine opportunity for any one who wished to be free! No police, no guards, no orders; the water free, the roads free, Monsieur d'Artagnan obliged to lend his horses, if required. All this ought to reassur you, Monsieur Fouquet, for the king would not have left me thus independent, if he had had any evil designs. In truth, Monsieur Fouquet, ask me whatever you like, I am at your service; and, in return, if you will consent to it, render me a service, that of offering my compliments to Aramis and Porthos, in case you embark for Belle-Isle, as you have a right to do, without changing your dress, immediately, in your *robe de chambre*—just as you are."

Saying these words, and with a profound bow, the musketeer, whose looks had lost none of their intelligent kindness, left the apartment. He had not reached the steps of the vestibule, when Fouquet, quite beside himself, hung to the bell-rope, and shouted:

"My horses! my lighter!"

But nobody answered. The surintendant dressed himself with everything that came to hand.

"Gourville! Gourville!" cried he, while slipping his watch into his pocket. And the bell sounded again, while Fouquet repeated, "Gourville! Gourville!"

Gourville at length appeared, breathless and pale.

"Let us be gone! Let us be gone!" cried Fouquet, as soon as he saw him.

"It is too late!" said the surintendant's poor friend.

"Too late! Why?"

"Listen!"

And they heard the sounds of trumpets and drums in front of the castle.

"What does that mean, Gourville?"

"It is the king coming, monseigneur."

"The king?"

"The king, who has ridden double stages, who has killed horses, and who is eight hours in advance of your calculation."

"We are lost!" murmured Fouquet. "Brave D'Artagnan, all over, thou hast spoken to me too late!"

The king, in fact, was entering the city, which soon resounded with the cannon from the ramparts, and from a vessel which replied from the lower parts of the river. Fouquet's brow darkened; he called his *valets de chambre* and dressed ceremonial costume. From his window, behind the curtains, could see the eagerness of the people, and the movement a large troop, which had followed the prince, without its being to be guessed how. The king was conducted to the castle with great pomp, and Fouquet saw him dismount under the portcullis, and speak something in the ear of D'Artagnan, who

held his stirrup. D'Artagnan, when the king had passed under
the arch, directed his steps toward the house Fouquet was in;
but so slowly, and stopping so frequently to speak to his musketeers, drawn up as a hedge, that it might be said he was
counting the seconds, or the steps, before accomplishing his
message. Fouquet opened the window to speak to him in the
court.

"Ah!" cried D'Artagnan, on perceiving him, "are you still
there, monseigneur?"

And that word *still* completed the proof to Fouquet of how
much information, and how many useful counsels were contained in the first visit the musketeer had paid him. The surintendant sighed deeply.

"Good heavens! yes, monsieur," replied he. "The arrival of
the king has interrupted me in the projects I had formed."

"Oh, then, you know that the king has arrived?"

"Yes, monsieur; I have seen him, and this time you come
from him——"

"To inquire after you, monseigneur, and, if your health is
not too bad, to beg you to have the kindness to repair to the
castle."

"Directly, Monsieur d'Artagnan, directly?"

"Ah, *dame!*" said the captain, "now the king is come, there
is no more walking for anybody—no more free-will; the pass-
word governs all now, you as well as me, me as well as you."

Fouquet heaved a last sigh, got into his carriage, so great
was his weakness, and went to the castle, escorted by D'Artagnan, whose politeness was not less terrifying this time than
it had but just before been consoling and cheerful.

Chapter 39 — HOW KING LOUIS XIV. PLAYED HIS LITTLE PART

As Fouquet was alighting from his carriage, to enter the Castle
of Nantes, a man of mean appearance went up to him with
marks of the greatest respect, and gave him a letter. D'Artagnan endeavored to prevent this man from speaking to Fouquet
and pushed him away, but the message had been given to the
surintendant. Fouquet opened the letter and read it, and instantly a vague terror, which D'Artagnan did not fail to penetrate, was painted upon the countenance of the first minister

Fouquet put the paper into the portfolio which he had under his arm, and passed on toward the king's apartments. D'Artagnan, through the small windows made at every landing of the dungeon stairs, saw, as he went up behind Fouquet, the man who had delivered the note look around him on the place, and make signs to several persons, who disappeared in the adjacent streets, after having themselves repeated the signals made by the person we have named. Fouquet was made to wait for a moment upon the terrace of which we have spoken, a terrace which abutted on the little corridor, at the end of which the closet of the king was established. Here D'Artagnan passed on before the surintendant, whom, till that time, he had respectfully accompanied, and entered the royal cabinet.

"Well?" asked Louis XIV., who, on perceiving him, threw on to the table covered with papers a large green cloth.

"The order is executed, sire."

"And Fouquet?"

"Monsieur le Surintendant follows me," said D'Artagnan.

"In ten minutes let him be introduced," said the king, dismissing D'Artagnan again with a gesture.

The latter retired, but had scarcely reached the corridor at the extremity of which Fouquet was waiting for him, when he was recalled by the king's bell.

"Did he not appear astonished?" asked the king.

"Who, sire?"

"Fouquet," repeated the king, without saying monsieur, a particularity which confirmed the captain of the musketeers in his suspicions.

"No, sire," replied he.

"That's well!"

And a second time Louis dismissed D'Artagnan.

Fouquet had not quitted the terrace where he had been left by his guide. He reperused his note, which was thus conceived:

"Something is being contrived against you. Perhaps they will not dare to carry it out at the castle; it will be on your return home. The house is already surrounded by musketeers. Do not enter. A white horse is in waiting for you behind the esplanade."

Fouquet recognized the writing and the zeal of Gourville. Not being willing that, if any evil happened to himself, this paper should compromise a faithful friend, the surintendant was busy tearing it into a thousand morsels, spreed about by

the wind from the balustrade of the terrace. D'Artagnan found
him watching the flight of the last scraps into space.

"Monsieur," said he, "the king waits for you."

Fouquet walked with a deliberate step into the little corridor, where MM. de Brienne and Rose were at work, while
the Duc de St. Aignan, seated on a chair, likewise in the corridor,
appeared to be waiting for orders, with feverish impatience,
his sword between his legs. It appeared strange to Fouquet
that MM. de Brienne, Rose, and De St. Aignan, in general so
attentive and obsequious, should scarcely take the least notice
as he, the surintendant, passed. But how could he expect to
find it otherwise among courtiers, he whom the king no longer
called anything but "Fouquet?" He raised his head, determined to look every one and everything bravely in the face,
and entered the king's apartment, where a little bell, which we
already know, had announced him to his majesty.

The king, without rising, nodded to him, and with interest:

"Well, how are you, Monsieur Fouquet?" said he.

"I am in a high fever," replied the surintendant; "but I am
at the king's service."

"That is well; the States assemble to-morrow; have you a
speech ready?"

Fouquet looked at the king with astonishment.

"I have not, sire," replied he; "but I will improvise one.
am too well acquainted with affairs to feel any embarrassment
I have only one question to ask; will your majesty permit me?"

"Certainly, ask it."

"Why has your majesty done his first minister the honor to
give him notice of this in Paris?"

"You were ill; I was not willing to fatigue you."

"Never did a labor—never did an explanation fatigue me
sire; and, since the moment is come for me to demand an ex
planation of my king——"

"Oh, Monsieur Fouquet! an explanation upon what?"

"Upon your majesty's intentions with respect to myself."
The king blushed.

"I have been calumniated," continued Fouquet warmly, "and
I feel called upon to provoke the justice of the king to make
inquiries."

"You say all this to me very uselessly, Monsieur Fouquet;
know what I know."

"Your majesty can only know things as they have been told
to you; and I, on my part, have said nothing to you, while other
have spoken many and many times——"

"What do you wish to say?" said the king, impatient to put
an end to this embarrassing conversation.

"I will go straight to the fact, sire; and I accuse a man of
having injured me in your majesty's opinion."

"Nobody has injured you, Monsieur Fouquet."

"That reply proves to me, sire, that I am right."

"Monsieur Fouquet, I do not like people to be accused."

"Not when one is accused?"

"We have already spoken too much about this affair."

"Your majesty will not allow me to justify myself."

"I repeat that I do not accuse you."

Fouquet, with a half-bow, made a step backward.

"It is certain," thought he, "that he has made up his mind.
He alone who cannot go back can show such obstinacy. Not to
see the danger now would be to be blind indeed; not to shun it
would be stupid." He resumed, aloud: "Did your majesty send
for me for any business?"

"No, Monsieur Fouquet, but for some advice I have to give
you."

"I respectfully await it, sire."

"Rest yourself, Monsieur Fouquet; do not throw away your
strength; the session of the States will be short, and when my
secretaries shall have closed it I do not wish business to be
talked of in France for a fortnight."

"Has the king nothing to say to me on the subject of this
assembly of the States?"

"No, Monsieur Fouquet."

"Not to me, the surintendant of the finances?"

"Rest yourself, I beg you; that is all I have to say to you."

Fouquet bit his lips and hung down his head. He was evidently busy with some uneasy thought. This uneasiness struck
the king.

"Are you angry at having to rest yourself, Monsieur Fouquet?" said he.

"Yes, sire; I am not accustomed to take rest."

"But you are ill; you must take care of yourself."

"Your majesty spoke just now of a speech to be pronounced
to-morrow."

His majesty made no reply; this unexpected stroke embarrassed him. Fouquet felt the weight of this hesitation. He
thought he could read a danger in the eyes of the young prince,
which his fear would precipitate.

"If I appear frightened, I am lost," thought he.

The king, on his part, was only uneasy at the alarm of Fouquet.

"Has he a suspicion of anything?" murmured he.

"If his first word is severe," again thought Fouquet; "if he becomes angry, or feigns to be angry for the sake of a pretext how shall I extricate myself? Let us smooth the declivity a little Gourville was right."

"Sire," said he suddenly, "since the goodness of the king watches over my health to the point of dispensing with my labor, may I not be allowed to be absent from the council o. to-morrow? I could pass the day in bed, and will entreat the king to grant me his physician, that we may endeavor to find a remedy against this cursed fever."

"So be it, Monsieur Fouquet, as you desire; you shall have a holiday to-morrow, you shall have the physician, and shall be restored to health."

"Thanks!" said Fouquet, bowing. Then, opening his game "Shall I not have the happiness of conducting your majesty to my residence of Belle-Isle?"

And he looked Louis full in the face, to judge of the effec of such a proposal. The king blushed again.

"Do you know," replied he, endeavoring to smile, "tha you have just said, 'My residence of Belle-Isle?'"

"Yes, sire."

"Well, do you not remember," continued the king, in the same cheerful tone, "that you gave me Belle-Isle?"

"That is true again, sire. Only as you have not taken it, you will come with me and take possession of it."

"I mean to do so."

"That was, besides, your majesty's intention as well as mine and I cannot express to your majesty how happy and proud have been at seeing all the king's military household come from Paris for his taking possession."

The king stammered out that he did not bring the musketeer for that alone.

"Oh, I am convinced of that," said Fouquet warmly; "you majesty knows very well that you have nothing to do but t come alone with a cane in your hand, to bring to the ground a the fortifications of Belle-Isle."

"*Peste!*" cried the king, "I do not wish those fine fortifica tions, which cost so much to erect, should fall at all. No; le them stand against the Dutch and English. You would not gues what I want to see at Belle-Isle, Monsieur Fouquet; it is th pretty peasants and women of the lands on the seashore, wh

ance so well, and are so seducing with their scarlet petticoats.
I have heard great boast of your pretty tenants, Monsieur le
surintendant; well, let me have a sight of them."

"Whenever your majesty pleases."

"Have you any means of transport? It should be to-morrow,
if you like."

The surintendant felt this stroke, which was not adroit, and
replied:

"No, sire; I was ignorant of your majesty's wish; above
all, I was ignorant of your haste to see Belle-Isle, and I am
prepared with nothing."

"You have a boat of your own, nevertheless?"

"I have five; but they are all in the port, or at Paimbœuf;
and to join them, or bring them hither, we should require at
least twenty-four hours. Have I any occasion to send a courier?
Must I do so?"

"Wait a little; put an end to the fever—wait till to-morrow."

"That is true; who knows but that by to-morrow we may
not have a hundred other ideas?" replied Fouquet, now perfectly convinced, and very pale.

The king started, and stretched his hand out toward his little
bell, but Fouquet prevented his ringing.

"Sire," said he, "I have an ague—I am trembling with cold.
If I remain a moment longer I shall most likely faint. I request
your majesty's permission to go and conceal myself beneath
the bedclothes."

"Indeed, you are all in a shiver; it is painful to behold!
Come, Monsieur Fouquet, be gone! I will send to inquire after
you."

"Your majesty overwhelms me with kindness. In an hour I
shall be better."

"I will call some one to reconduct you," said the king.

"As you please, sire; I would gladly take the arm of any
one."

"Monsieur d'Artagnan!" cried the king, ringing his little
bell.

"Oh, sire," interrupted Fouquet, laughing in such a manner
as made the prince feel cold, "would you give me the captain
of your musketeers to take me to my lodgings? A very equivocal kind of honor, that, sire! A simple footman, I beg."

"And why, Monsieur Fouquet? Monsieur d'Artagnan conducts me often, and well."

"Yes, but when he conducts you, sire, it is to obey you;
while me——"

"Go on."

"If I am obliged to return home supported by the leader of the musketeers, it would be everywhere said you had had me arrested."

"Arrested!" replied the king, who became paler than Fouquet himself—"arrested! Oh!"

"And why would they not say so?" continued Fouquet, still laughing, "and I would lay a wager there would be people found wicked enough to laugh at it."

This sally disconcerted the monarch. Fouquet was skillful enough, or fortunate enough, to make Louis XIV. recoil before the appearance of the fact he meditated. M. d'Artagnan, when he appeared, received an order to desire a musketeer to accompany the surintendant.

"Quite unnecessary," said the latter; "sword for sword; I prefer Gourville, who is waiting for me below. But that will not prevent me enjoying the society of Monsieur d'Artagnan. I am glad he will see Bella-Isle, he who is so good a judge of fortifications."

D'Artagnan bowed, without at all comprehending what was going on. Fouquet bowed again, and left the apartment, affecting all the slowness of a man who walks with difficulty. When once out of the castle, "I am saved!" said he. "Oh, yes disloyal king; you shall see Belle-Isle, but it shall be when I am no longer there."

He disappeared, leaving D'Artagnan with the king.

"Captain," said the king, "you will follow Monsieur Fouquet at the distance of a hundred paces."

"Yes, sire."

"He is going to his lodgings again. You will go with him."

"Yes, sire."

"You will arrest him in my name, and will shut him up in a carriage."

"In a carriage? Well, sire?"

"In such a fashion that he may not, on the road, either converse with any one or throw notes to people he may meet."

"That will be rather difficult, sire."

"Not at all."

"Pardon me, sire, I cannot stifle Monsieur Fouquet, and if he asks for liberty to breathe, I cannot prevent him by shutting up glasses and blinds. He will throw out at the doors all the cries and notes possible."

"The case is provided for, Monsieur d'Artagnan; a carriage with a trellis will obviate both the difficulties you point out."

"A carriage with an iron trellis!" cried D'Artagnan; "but a carriage with an iron trellis is not made in half an hour, and your majesty commands me to go immediately to Monsieur Fouquet's lodgings."

"Therefore, the carriage in question is already made."

"Ah! that is quite a different thing," said the captain; "if the carriage is ready made, very well, then, we have only to set it going."

"It is ready, with the horses harnessed to it."

"Ah!"

"And the coachman, with the outriders, waiting in the lower court of the castle."

D'Artagnan bowed.

"There only remains for me to ask your majesty to what place I shall conduct Monsieur Fouquet."

"To the Castle of Angers, at first."

"Very well, sire."

"Afterward we will see."

"Yes, sire."

"Monsieur d'Artagnan, one last word; you have remarked that for making this capture of Monsieur Fouquet, I have not employed my guards, on which account Monsieur de Gesvres will be furious."

"Your majesty does not employ your guards," said the captain, a little humiliated, "because you mistrust Monsieur de Gesvres, that is all."

"That is to say, monsieur, that I have more confidence in you."

"I know that very well, sire; and it is of no use to make so much of it."

"It is only for the sake of arriving at this, monsieur, that if, from this moment, it should happen that by any chance, any chance whatever, Monsieur Fouquet should escape—such chances have been, monsieur——"

"Oh! very often, sire; but for others, not for me."

"And why not with you?"

"Because I, sire, have, for an instant, wished to save Monsieur Fouquet."

The king started.

"Because," continued the captain, "I had then a right to do so, having guessed your majesty's plan, without your having spoken to me of it, and that I took an interest in Monsieur Fouquet. Now, was I not at liberty to show my interest in this man?"

"In truth, monsieur, you do not reassure me with regard to your services."

"If I had saved him, then, I was perfectly innocent. I will say more, I should have done well, for Monsieur Fouquet is not a bad man. But he was not willing; his destiny prevailed; he let the hour of liberty slip by. So much the worse! Now I have orders, I will obey those orders, and Monsieur Fouquet you may consider as a man arrested. He is at the Castle of Angers, is Monsieur Fouquet."

"Oh! you have not got him yet, captain."

"That concerns me; every one to his trade, sire; only, once more, reflect. Do you seriously give me orders to arrest Monsieur Fouquet, sire?"

"Yes, a thousand times, yes!"

"Write it, then."

"Here is the letter."

D'Artagnan read it, bowed to the king, and left the room From the height of the terrace he perceived Gourville, who went by with a joyous air toward the lodgings of M. Fouquet

Chapter 40 — THE WHITE HORSE AND THE BLACK HORSE

"That is rather surprising," said D'Artagnan, "Gourville running about the streets so gayly, when he is almost certain that Monsieur Fouquet is in danger; when it is almost equally certain that it was Gourville who warned Monsieur Fouquet just now by the note which was torn into a thousand pieces upon the terrace, and given to the winds by Monsieur le Surintendant. Gourville is rubbing his hands; that is because he has done something clever. Whence comes Monsieur Gourville? Gourville is coming from the Rue aux Herbes. Whither does the Rue aux Herbes lead?"

And D'Artagnan followed along the tops of the houses of Nantes dominated by the castle the line traced by the streets as he would have done upon a topographical plan; only, instead of the dead, flat paper, the living chart rose in relief with the cries, the movements, and the shadows of men and things. Beyond the inclosure of the city, the great verdant plain stretched out, bordering the Loire, and appeared to run toward the impurpled horizon, which was cut by the azure of the waters and the dark green of the marshes. Immediately outside the gates of Nantes two white roads were seen diverging like the separated fingers of a gigantic hand. D'Artagnan, who had taken in all the panorama at a glance by crossing the terrace, was led by the line of the Rue aux Herbes to the mouth of one of those roads which took its rise under the gates of Nantes. One step more, and he was about to descend the stairs, take his trellised carriage, and go toward the lodgings of M. Fouquet. But chance decreed that at the moment of replunging into the staircase, he was attracted by a moving point which was gaining ground upon that road.

"What is that?" said the musketeer to himself; "a horse galloping—a runaway horse, no doubt. What a pace he is going at!"

The moving point became detached from the road, and entered into the fields.

"A white horse," continued the captain, who had just seen the color thrown out luminously against the dark ground, "and he is mounted; it must be some boy whose horse is thirsty and has run away with him to the drinking-place, diagonally."

These reflections, rapid as lightning, simultaneous with visual perception, D'Artagnan had already forgotten when he descended the first steps of the staircase. Some morsels of paper were spread over the stairs, and shone out white against the dirty stones.

"Eh! eh!" said the captain to himself, "here are some of the fragments of the note torn by Monsieur Fouquet. Poor man! he has given his secret to the wind; the wind will have no more to do with it, and brings it back to the king. Decidedly, Fouquet, you play with misfortune! the game is not a fair one—Fortune is against you. The star of Louis XIV. obscures yours; the adder is stronger and more cunning than the squirrel."

D'Artagnan picked up one of these morsels of paper as he descended.

"Gourville's pretty little hand!" cried he, while examining one of the fragments of the note. "I was not mistaken." And he read the word "horse." "Stop!" said he, and he examined another, upon which there was not a letter traced. Upon a third he read the word "white;" "white horse," repeated he, like a child that is spelling. "Ah, *mordioux!*" cried the suspicious spirit, "a white horse!" And, like to that grain of powder which, burning dilates into a centripled volume, D'Artagnan, enlarged by ideas and suspicions, rapidly reascended the stairs toward the terrace. The white horse was still galloping in the direction of the Loire, at the extremity of which, melted into the vapors of the water, a little sail appeared, balancing, like an atom.

"Oh! oh!" cried the musketeer, "there is but a man who flies who would go at that pace across plowed lands; there is but one Fouquet, a financier, to ride thus in open day upon a white horse; there is no one but the lord of Belle-Isle who would make his escape toward the sea while there are such thick forests on the land; and there is but one D'Artagnan in the world to catch Monsieur Fouquet, who has half an hour's start, and who will have gained his boat within an hour."

This being said, the musketeer gave orders that the carriage with the iron trellis should be taken immediately to a thicket situated just outside the city. He selected his best horse, jumped upon his back, galloped along the Rue aux Herbes, taking, not the road Fouquet had taken, but the bank itself of the Loire, certain that he should gain ten minutes upon the total of the distance, and, at the intersection of the two lines, come up with the fugitive, who could have no suspicion of being pursued in that direction. In the rapidity of the pursuit, and with the impatience of the persecutor animating himself in the case as in war, D'Artagnan, so mild, so kind toward Fouquet, was surprised to find himself become ferocious and almost sanguinary. For a long time he galloped without catching sight of the white horse. His fury assumed the tints of rage; he doubted of himself—he suspected that Fouquet had buried himself in some subterranean road, or that he had changed the white horse for one of those famous black ones, as swift as the wind, which D'Artagnan, at St. Mandé, had so frequently admired, and envied their vigorous lightness.

At these moments, when the wind cut his eyes so as to make the water spring from them, when the saddle had become burning hot, when the galled and spurred horse reared with pain, and threw behind him a shower of dust and stones, D'Artagnan, raising himself in his stirrups, and seeing nothing on the waters—nothing beneath the trees, looked up into the air like a madman. He was losing his senses. In the paroxysms of his eagerness he dreamed of aërial ways—the discovery of the following century; he called to his mind Dædalus and his vast wings, which had saved him from the prisons of Crete. A hoarse sigh broke from his lips, as he repeated, devoured by the fear of ridicule:

"I!—I, duped by a Gourville! I! They will say I am growing old—they will say I have received a million to allow Fouquet to escape!"

And he again dug his spurs into the sides of his horse; he had ridden astonishingly fast. Suddenly, at the extremity of some open pasture-ground, behind the hedges, he saw a white form which showed itself, disappeared, and at last remained distinctly visible upon a rising ground. D'Artagnan's heart leaped with joy. He wiped the streaming sweat from his brow, relaxed the tension of his knees—by which the horse breathed more freely—and, gathering up his reins, moderated the speed of the vigorous animal, his active accomplice in this manœunt. He had then time to study the direction of the road, and his position with regard to Fouquet. The surintendant had completely winded his horse by crossing the soft grounds. He felt the necessity of gaining a more firm footing, and turned toward the road by the shortest secant line. D'Artagnan, on his part, had nothing to do but to ride straight beneath the sloping shore, which concealed him from the eyes of his enemy; so that he would cut him off on the road when he came up with him. Then the real race would begin—then the struggle would be in earnest.

D'Artagnan gave his horse good breathing-time. He observed that the surintendant had relaxed into a trot, which was to say, he likewise was indulging his horse. But both of them were too much pressed for time to allow them to continue long at that pace. The white horse sprang off like an arrow the moment his feet touched firm ground. D'Artagnan dropped his hand, and his black horse broke into a gallop. Both followed the same route; the quadruple echoes of the course were confounded. Fouquet had not yet perceived D'Artagnan. But on issuing from the slope, a single echo struck the air, it was that of the steps of D'Artagnan's horse, which rolled along like thunder. Fouquet turned round, and saw behind him, within a hundred paces, his enemy bent over the neck of his horse. There could be no doubt—the shining baldrick, the red cassock—it was a musketeer. Fouquet slackened his hand likewise, and the white horse placed twenty feet more between his adversary and himself.

"Oh, but," thought D'Artagnan, becoming very anxious, "that is not a common horse Monsieur Fouquet is upon—let us see!"

And he attentively examined with his infallible eye the shape and capabilities of the courser. Round, full quarters, a thin, long tail, large hocks, thin legs, as dry as bars of steel, hoofs hard as marble. He spurred his own, but the distance between the two remained the same. D'Artagnan listened attentively;

not a breath of the horse reached him, and yet he seemed to cut the air. The black horse, on the contrary, began to blow like a blacksmith's bellows.

"I must overtake him, if I kill my horse," thought the musketeer; and he began to saw the mouth of the poor animal, while he buried the rowels of his merciless spurs in his sides. The maddened horse gained twenty *toises,* and came up within pistol-shot of Fouquet.

"Courage!" said the musketeer to himself, "courage! the white horse will perhaps grow weaker, and if the horse does not fall, the master must fall at last."

But horse and rider remained upright together, and gaining ground by degrees. D'Artagnan uttered a wild cry, which made Fouquet turn round, and added speed to the white horse.

"A famous horse! a mad rider!" growled the captain. "*Holá, mordioux!* Monsieur Fouquet, stop, in the king's name!"

Fouquet made no reply.

"Do you hear me?" shouted D'Artagnan, whose horse had just stumbled.

"*Pardieu!*" replied Fouquet laconically, and rode on faster.

D'Artagnan was nearly mad; the blood rushed boiling to his temples and his eyes.

"In the king's name," cried he, again, "stop, or I will bring you down with a pistol-shot!"

"Do!" replied Fouquet, without relaxing his speed.

D'Artagnan seized a pistol and cocked it, hoping that the noise of the spring would stop his enemy.

"You have pistols likewise," said he; "turn and defend yourself."

Fouquet did turn round at the noise, and, looking D'Artagnan full in the face, opened with his right hand the part of his dress which concealed his body, but he did not even touch his holsters. There were not more than twenty paces between the two.

"*Mordioux!*" said D'Artagnan, "I will not assassinate you; if you will not fire upon me, surrender. What is a prison?"

"I would rather die!" replied Fouquet; "I shall suffer less."

D'Artagnan, drunk with despair, hurled his pistol to the ground.

"I will take you alive!" said he; and by a prodigy of skill of which this incomparable horseman alone was capable, he threw his horse forward to within ten paces of the white horse; already his hand was stretched out to seize his prey.

"Kill me! kill me!" cried Fouquet; "it is more humane."

"No, alive—alive!" murmured the captain.

At this moment his horse made a false step for the second time, and Fouquet's again took the lead. It was an unheard-of spectacle, this race between two horses which were only kept alive by the will of their riders. It might be said that D'Artagnan rode, carrying his horse along between his knees. To the furious gallop had succeeded the fast trot, and that had sunk to what might be scarcely called a trot at all. And the chase appeared equally warm in the two fatigued *athletæ*. D'Artagnan, quite in despair, seized his second pistol, and cocked it.

"At your horse! not at you!" cried he to Fouquet.

And he fired. The animal was hit in the quarters; he made a furious bound, and plunged forward. At that moment D'Artagnan's horse fell dead.

"I am dishonored!" thought the musketeer; "I am a miserable wretch! For pity's sake, Monsieur Fouquet, throw me one of your pistols, that I may blow out my brains!"

But Fouquet rode on.

"For mercy's sake! for mercy's sake!" cried D'Artagnan, "that which you will not do at this moment, I myself will do within an hour; but here, upon this road, I should die bravely, I should die esteemed; do me that service, Monsieur Fouquet!"

M. Fouquet made no reply, but continued to trot on. D'Artagnan began to run after his enemy. Successively he threw off his hat, his coat, which embarrassed him, and then the sheath of his sword, which got between his legs as he was running. The sword in his hand even became too heavy, and he threw it after the sheath. The white horse began to rattle in his throat; D'Artagnan gained upon him. From a trot the exhausted animal sank to a staggering walk—the foam from his mouth was mixed with blood. D'Artagnan made a desperate effort, sprang toward Fouquet, and seized him by the leg, saying, in a broken, breathless voice:

"I arrest you in the king's name! Blow my brains out, if you like; we have both done our duty."

Fouquet hurled far from him, into the river, the two pistols which D'Artagnan might have seized and dismounting from his horse:

"I am your prisoner, monsieur," said he. "Will you take my arm, for I see you are ready to faint?"

"Thanks!" murmured D'Artagnan, who, in fact, felt the earth moving from under his feet, and the sky melting away over his head; and he rolled upon the sand, without breath or strength. Fouquet hastened to the brink of the river, dipped some water in his hat, with which he bathed the temples of the musketeer, and introduced a few drops between his lips. D'Artagnan raised himself up, looking round with a wandering eye. He saw Fouquet on his knees, with his wet hat in his hand, smiling upon him with ineffable sweetness.

"You are not gone, then?" cried he. "Oh, monsieur, the true king of royalty, in heart, in soul, is not Louis of the Louvre, or Philippe of Ste. Marguerite; it is you, the proscribed, the condemned!"

"I, who this day am ruined by a single error, Monsieur d'Artagnan."

"What, in the name of heaven, is that?"

"I should have had you for a friend. But how shall we return to Nantes? We are a great way from it."

"That is true," said D'Artagnan, gloomy and sad.

"The white horse will recover, perhaps; he is a good horse. Mount, Monsieur d'Artagnan; I will walk till you have rested a little."

"Poor beast! and wounded, too!" said the musketeer.

"He will go, I tell you; I know him; but we can do better still; let us both get up, and ride slowly."

"We can try," said the captain.

But they had scarcely charged the animal with this double load, than he began to stagger, then, with a great effort, walked a few minutes, then staggered again, and sank down dead by the side of the black horse, which he had just managed to come up to.

"We will go on foot—destiny wills it so—the walk will be pleasant," said Fouquet, passing his arm through that of D'Artagnan.

"*Mordioux!*" cried the latter, with a fixed eye, a contracted brow, and a swelling heart. "A disgraceful day!"

They walked slowly the four leagues which separated them from the little wood behind which waited the carriage with the escort. When Fouquet perceived that sinister machine he said to D'Artagnan, who cast down his eyes as ashamed of Louis XIV.

"There is an idea which is not that of a brave man, Captain d'Artagnan; it is not yours. What are these gratings for?" said he.

"To prevent your throwing letters out."

"Ingenious!"

"But you can speak, if you cannot write," said D'Artagnan. "Can I speak to you?"

"Why, certainly, if you wish to do so."

Fouquet reflected for a moment, then, looking the captain full in the face:

"One single word," said he; "will you remember it?"

"I will not forget it."

"Will you speak it to whom I wish?"

"I will."

"St. Mandé," articulated Fouquet, in a low voice.

"Well, and for whom?"

"For Madame de Belliere or Pellisson."

"It shall be done."

The carriage passed through Nantes, and took the route of Angers.

Chapter 41 — IN WHICH THE SQUIRREL FALLS—IN WHICH THE ADDER FLIES

It was two o'clock in the afternoon. The king, full of impatience, went to his cabinet on the terrace, and kept opening the door of the corridor, to see what his secretaries were doing. M. Colbert, seated in the same place M. le St. Aignan had so long occupied in the morning, was chatting, in a low voice, with M. de Brienne. The king opened the door suddenly, and addressing them:

"What do you say?" asked he.

"We were speaking of the first sitting of the States," said de Brienne, rising.

"Very well," replied the king, and returned to his room.

Five minutes after the summons of the bell recalled Rose, whose hour it was.

"Have you finished your copies?" asked the king.

"Not yet, sire."

"See, then, if Monsieur d'Artagnan is returned."

"Not yet, sire."

"It is very strange," murmured the king. "Call Monsieur Colbert."

Colbert entered; he had been expecting this moment all the morning.

"Monsieur Colbert," said the king, very sharply; "it must be ascertained what has become of Monsieur d'Artagnan."

Colbert, in his calm voice, replied:

"Where would your majesty desire him to be sought for?"

"Eh! monsieur, do you not know to what place I have sent him?" replied Louis acrimoniously.

"Your majesty has not told me."

"Monsieur, there are things that are to be guessed; and you, above all others, do guess them."

"I might have been able to imagine, sire; but I do not presume to be positive."

Colbert had not finished these words when a much rougher voice than that of the king interrupted the interesting conversation thus begun between the monarch and his clerk.

"D'Artagnan!" cried the king, with evident joy.

D'Artagnan, pale and in evidently bad humor, cried to the king, as he entered:

"Sire, is it your majesty who has given orders to my musketeers?"

"What orders?" said the king.

"About Monsieur Fouquet's house."

"None," replied Louis.

"Ah! Ah!" said D'Artagnan, biting his mustache, "I was not mistaken, then; it was monsieur here;" and he pointed to Colbert.

"What orders? Let me know," said the king.

"Orders to turn a house inside out, to beat Monsieur Fouquet's servants, to force the drawers, to give over a peaceful house to pillage! *Mordioux!* these are savage orders!"

"Monsieur!" said Colbert, becoming pale.

"Monsieur!" interrupted D'Artagnan, "the king alone, understand—the king alone has a right to command my musketeers; but, as to you, I forbid you to do it, and I tell you so before his majesty; gentlemen who wear swords are not fellows with pens behind their ears!"

"D'Artagnan! D'Artagnan!" murmured the king.

"It is humiliating!" continued the musketeer. "My soldiers are disgraced. I do not command *reîtres*, thank you, nor clerks of the intendance, *mordioux!*"

"Well, but what is all this about?" said the king, with authority.

"About this, sire: monsieur—monsieur, who could not guess your majesty's orders, and consequently could not know I was gone to arrest Monsieur Fouquet; monsieur, who has caused the iron cage to be constructed for his patron of yesterday—has sent Monsieur de Roncherat to the lodgings of Monsieur Fouquet, and, under pretense of taking away the surintendant's papers, they have taken away the furniture. My musketeers have been placed round the house all the morning; such were my orders. Why did any one presume to order them to enter? Why, by forcing them to assist in this pillage, have they been made accomplices in it? *Mordioux!* we serve the king, we do, but we do not serve Monsieur Colbert!"

"Monsieur d'Artagnan," said the king sternly, "take care; it is not in my presence that such explanations, and made in this tone, should take place."

"I have acted for the good of the king," said Colbert, in a faltering voice; "it is hard to be so treated by one of your majesty's officers, and that without vengeance, on account of the respect I owe the king."

"The respect you owe the king!" cried D'Artagnan, whose eyes flashed fire, "consists, in the first place, in making his authority respected, and making his person beloved. Every agent of a power without control represents that power, and when people curse the hand which strikes them, it is to the royal hand that God makes the reproach, do you hear? Must a soldier, hardened by forty years of wounds and blood, give you this lesson, monsieur? Must mercy be on my side, and ferocity on ours? You have caused the innocent to be arrested, bound, and imprisoned!"

"The accomplices, perhaps, of Monsieur Fouquet," said Colbert.

"Who told you that Monsieur Fouquet had accomplices, or even that he was guilty? The king alone knows that his justice is not blind! When he shall say, 'Arrest and imprison such and such people,' then he shall be obeyed. Do not talk to me, then, any more of the respect you owe the king, and be careful of your words, that they may not chance to convey any menace; for the king will not allow those to be threatened who do him service by others who do him disservice; and if in case I should have, which God forbid! a master so ungrateful, I would make myself respected."

Thus saying, D'Artagnan took his station haughtily in the king's cabinet, his eye flashing, his hand on his sword, his lips trembling, affecting much more anger than he really felt. Colbert, humiliated and devoured with rage, bowed to the king as if to ask his permission to leave the room. The king, crossed his pride and in his curiosity, knew not which part to take.

D'Artagnan saw him hesitate. To remain longer would have been an error; it was necessary to obtain a triumph over Colbert, and the only means was to touch the king so near and so strongly to the quick that his majesty would have no other means of extricating himself but choosing between the two antagonists. D'Artagnan then bowed as Colbert had done; but the king, who, in preference to everything else was anxious to have all the exact details of the arrest of the surintendant of the finances from him who had made him tremble for a moment—the king, perceiving that the ill-humor of D'Artagnan would put off for half an hour, at least, the details he was burning to be acquainted with—Louis, we say, forgot Colbert, who had nothing new to tell him, and recalled his captain of the musketeers.

"In the first place," said he, "let me see the result of your commission, monsieur; you may repose afterward."

D'Artagnan, who was just passing through the door, stopped at the voice of the king, retraced his steps, and Colbert was forced to leave the closet. His countenance assumed almost a purple line, his black and threatening eyes shone with a dark fire beneath their thick brows; he stepped out, bowed before the king, half-drew himself up in passing D'Artagnan, and went away with death in his heart. D'Artagnan, on being left alone with the king, softened immediately, and composing his countenance:

"Sire," said he, "you are a young king. It is by the dawn that people judge whether the day will be fine or dull. How, sire, will the people, whom the hand of God has placed under your law, argue of your reign, if, between them and you, you allow angry and violent ministers to act? But let us speak of me, sire, let us leave a discussion that may appear idle, and perhaps inconvenient to you. Let us speak of me. I have arrested Monsieur Fouquet."

"You took plenty of time about it," said the king sharply.

D'Artagnan looked at the king.

"I perceive that I have expressed myself badly. I announced to your majesty that I had arrested Monsieur Fouquet."

"You did; and what then?"

"Well, I ought to have told your majesty that Monsieur Fouquet had arrested me; that would have been more just. I re-establish the truth, then; I have been arrested by Monsieur Fouquet."

It was now the turn of Louis XIV. to be surprised. His majesty was astonished in his turn.

D'Artagnan, with his quick glance, appreciated what was ussing in the heart of his master. He did not allow him time put any question. He related, with that poetry, that pic- resqueness, which perhaps he alone possessed at that period, e evasion of Fouquet, the pursuit, the furious race, and, stly, the inimitable generosity of the surintendant, who might ve fled ten times over, who might have killed the adversary tached to the pursuit of him, and who had preferred impris- ment, and perhaps worse, to the humiliation of him who shed to ravish his liberty from him. In proportion as the le advanced, the king became agitated, devouring the narra- r's words, and knocking his finger-nails against one another.

"It results from this, then, sire, in my eyes, at least, that e man who conducts himself thus is a gallant man, and can- t be an enemy to the king. That is my opinion, and I repeat to your majesty. I know what the king will say to me, and I w to it: reasons of state—so be it. That, in my eyes, is very spectable. But I am a soldier; I have received my orders, y orders are executed—very unwillingly on my part, it is ue, but they are executed. I say no more."

"Where is Monsieur Fouquet at this moment?" asked Louis, ter a short silence.

"Monsieur Fouquet, sire," replied D'Artagnan, "is in the n cage that Monsieur Colbert had prepared for him, and is ing, as fast as four vigorous horses can drag him, toward gers."

"Why did you leave him on the road?"

"Because your majesty did not tell me to go to Angers. The of, the best proof of what I advance, is that the king de- ed me to be sought for but this minute. And then I have an- er reason."

"What is that?"

"While I was with him, poor Monsieur Fouquet would never empt to escape."

"Well!" cried the king, with stupefaction.

"Your majesty ought to understand, and does understand, tainly, that my warmest wish is to know that Monsieur uquet is at liberty. I have given him one of my brigadiers, most stupid I could find among my musketeers, in order t the prisoner might have a chance of escaping."

"Are you mad, Monsieur d'Artagnan?" cried the king, cross- his arms on his breast. "Do people speak such enormities, n when they have the misfortune to think them?"

"Ah! sire, you cannot expect that I should be the enemy of

Monsieur Fouquet, after what he has just done for you an
me. No, no; if you desire that he should remain under you
locks and bolts, never give him in charge to me; however closel
wired might be the cage, the bird would, in the end, fl
away."

"I am surprised," said the king, in a stern tone, "you hav
not followed the fortunes of him whom Monsieur Fouque
wished to place upon my throne. You had in him all you wan
—affection and gratitude. In my service, monsieur, you onl
find a master."

"If Monsieur Fouquet had not gone to seek you in th
Bastile, sire," replied D'Artagnan, with a deeply impressiv
manner, "one single man would have gone there, and that ma
would have been me—you know that right well, sire."

The king was brought to a pause. Before that speech of hi
captain of the musketeers, so frankly spoken and so true, th
king had nothing to offer. On hearing D'Artagnan, Louis re
membered the D'Artagnan of former times; him who, at th
Palais Royal, held himself concealed behind the curtains of hi
bed, when the people of Paris, led on by Cardinal de Reta
came to assure themselves of the presence of the king; th
D'Artagnan whom he saluted with his hand at the door of hi
carriage, when repairing to Notre Dame on his return to Paris
the soldier who had quitted his service at Blois; the lieutenan
whom he had recalled near his person when the death o
Mazarin restored him his power; the man he had always foun
loyal, courageous, and devoted. Louis advanced toward the doo
and called Colbert. Colbert had not left the corridor where th
secretaries were at work. Colbert appeared.

"Colbert, have you made a perquisition at the house of Mor
sieur Fouquet?"

"Yes, sire."

"What has it produced?"

"Monsieur de Roncherat, who was sent with your majesty'
musketeers, has remitted me some papers," replied Colbert.

"I will look at them. Give me your hand."

"My hand, sire!"

"Yes, that I may place it in that of Monsieur d'Artagna
In fact, Monsieur d'Artagnan," added he, with a smile, turı
ing toward the soldier, who, at the sight of the clerk, had r
sumed his haughty attitude, "you do not know this man; mal
his acquaintance." And he pointed to Colbert. "He has bee
but a moderate servant in subaltern positions, but he will be
great man if I raise him to the first rank."

"Sire!" stammered Colbert, confused with pleasure and fear.

"I have understood why," murmured D'Artagnan, in the king's ear; "he was jealous."

"Precisely, and his jealousy confined his wings."

"He will henceforth be a winged serpent," grumbled the musketeer, with the remains of hatred against his recent adversary.

But Colbert, approaching him, offered to his eyes a physiognomy so different from that which he had been accustomed to see him wear; he appeared so good, so mild, so easy; his eyes took the expression of an intelligence so noble that D'Artagnan, a connoisseur in physiognomies, was moved, and almost changed in his convictions. Colbert pressed his hand.

"That which the king has just told you, monsieur, proves how well his majesty is acquainted with men. The inveterate opposition I have displayed, up to this day, against abuses and not against men, proves that I had it in view to prepare for my king a great reign, for my country a great blessing. I have many ideas, Monsieur d'Artagnan; you will see them expand in the sun of public peace; and if I have not the certainty and good fortune to conquer the friendship of honest men, I am at least certain, monsieur, that I shall obtain their esteem. For their admiration, monsieur, I would give my life."

This change, this sudden elevation, this mute approbation of the king, gave the musketeer matter for much reflection. He bowed civilly to Colbert, who did not take his eyes off him. The king, when he saw they were reconciled, dismissed them. They left the room together. As soon as they were out of the cabinet the new minister, stopping the captain, said:

"Is it possible, Monsieur d'Artagnan, that with such an eye as yours you have not, at the first glance, at the first inspection, discovered what sort of man I am?"

"Monsieur Colbert," replied the musketeer, "the ray of the sun which we have in our eyes prevents us from seeing the most ardent flames. The man in power radiates, you know; and since you are there, why should you continue to persecute him who has just fallen into disgrace, and fallen from such a height?"

"I, monsieur?" said Colbert. "Oh, monsieur, I would never persecute him! I wished to administer the finances, and to administer then alone, because I am ambitious, and, above all, because I have the most entire confidence in my own merit; because I know that all the gold of this country will fall beneath my eyes, and I love to look at the king's gold; because, if I live thirty years, in thirty years not a *denier* of it will remain in my hands; because, with that gold I will build granaries, edifices, cities, and dig ports; because I will create a marine, will equip navies which shall bear the name of France to the most distant peoples; because I will create libraries and academies; because I will make of France the first country in the world, and the richest. These are the motives for my animosity against Monsieur Fouquet, who prevented my acting. And then, when I shall be great and strong, when France is great and strong, in my turn, then, will I cry 'Mercy!' "

"Mercy, did you say? Then ask his liberty of the king. The king only crushes him on your account."

Colbert again raised his head.

"Monsieur," said he, "you know that it is not so, and that the king has his personal enmities against Monsieur Fouquet; it is not for me to teach you that."

"But the king will be tired; he will forget."

"The king never forgets, Monsieur d'Artagnan. Hark! the king calls. He is going to issue an order. I have not influenced him, have I? Listen."

The king, in fact, was calling his secretaries.

"Monsieur d'Artagnan," said he.

"I am here, sire."

"Give twenty of your musketeers to Monsieur de St. Aignan, to form a guard for Monsieur Fouquet."

D'Artagnan and Colbert exchanged looks.

"And from Angers," continued the king, "they will conduct the prisoner to the Bastile, in Paris."

"You were right," said the captain to the minister.

"St. Aignan," continued the king, "you will have any one shot who shall attempt to speak privately with Monsieur Fouquet, during the journey."

"But myself, sire," said the duke.

"You, monsieur, you will only speak to him in the presence of the musketeers."

The duke bowed, and departed to execute his commission.

D'Artagnan was about to retire likewise; but the king stopped him.

"Monsieur," said he, "you will go immediately, and take possession of the isle and fief of Belle-Isle-en-Mer."

"Yes, sire. Alone?"

"You will take a sufficient number of troops to prevent delay, in case the place should be contumacious."

A murmur of adulatory incredulity arose from the group of ourtiers.

"That is to be done," said D'Artagnan.

"I saw the place in my infancy," resumed the king, "and I do not wish to see it again. You have heard me? Go, monsieur, and do not return without the keys of the place."

Colbert went up to D'Artagnan.

"A commission which, if you carry it out well," said he, "will be worth a maréchal's baton to you."

"Why do you employ the words, 'if you carry it out well?' "

"Because it is difficult."

"Ah! in what respect?"

"You have friends in Belle-Isle, Monsieur d'Artagnan; and it is not an easy thing for men like you to march over the bodies of their friends to obtain success."

D'Artagnan hung down his head, while Colbert returned to the king. A quarter of an hour after the captain received the written order from the king to blow up the fortress of Belle-Isle, in case of resistance, with the power of life and death over all the inhabitants or refugees, and an injunction not to allow one to escape.

"Colbert was right," thought D'Artagnan; "my baton of a maréchal of France will cost the lives of my two friends. Only they seem to forget that my friends are not more stupid than the birds, and that they will not wait for the hand of the fowler to extend their wings. I will show them that hand so plainly that they will have quite time enough to see it. Poor Porthos! Poor Aramis! No; my fortune shall not cost your wings a feather."

Having thus determined, D'Artagnan assembled the royal army, embarked it at Paimbœuf, and set sail, without losing a moment.

Chapter 42 — BELLE-ISLE-EN-MER

At the extremity of the mole, which the furious sea beats at evening-tide, two men, holding each other by the arm, were conversing in an animated and expansive tone, without the possibility of any other human being hearing their words, borne

away, as they were, one by one, by the gusts of wind, with the
white foam swept from the crests of the waves. The sun had
just gone down in the vast sheet of the reddened ocean, like a
gigantic crucible. From time to time one of these men, turning toward the east, cast an anxious, inquiring look over the
sea. The other, interrogating the features of his companion,
seemed to seek for information in his looks.

Then, both silent, both busied with dismal thoughts, they
resumed their walk. Every one has already perceived that
those two men were our proscribed heroes, Porthos and
Aramis, who had taken refuge in Belle-Isle, since the ruin of
their hopes, since the discomfiture of the vast plan of M.
d'Herblay.

"It is of no use your saying anything to the contrary, my
dear Aramis," repeated Porthos, inhaling vigorously the saline
air with which he filled his powerful chest. "It is of no use,
Aramis. The disappearance of all the fishing-boats that went
out two days ago is not an ordinary circumstance. There has
been no storm at sea; the weather has been constantly calm,
not even the lightest gale; and even if we had had a tempest,
all our boats would not have foundered. I repeat, it is strange.
This complete disappearance astonishes me, I tell you."

"True," murmured Aramis. "You are right, friend Porthos;
it is true, there is something strange in it."

"And, further," added Porthos, whose ideas the assent of
the bishop of Vannes seemed to enlarge; "and, further, have
you remarked that if the boats have perished, not a single
plank has been washed ashore?"

"I have remarked that, as well as you."

"Have you remarked, besides, that the two only boats we
had left in the whole island, and which I sent in search of the
others——"

Aramis here interrupted his companion by a cry, and by so
sudden a movement that Porthos stopped as if he were stupefied.

"What do you say, Porthos? What! you have sent the two
boats——"

"In search of the others, yes; to be sure I have," replied
Porthos, quite simply.

"Unhappy man! What have you done? Then we are indeed
lost!" cried the bishop.

"Lost! What did you say?" exclaimed the terrified Porthos.
"How lost, Aramis? How are we lost?"

Aramis bit his lips.

"Nothing! nothing! Your pardon, I meant to say——"

"What?"

"That if we were inclined—if we took a fancy to make an excursion by sea, we could not."

"Very good; and why should that vex you? A fine pleasure, *ma foi!* For my part, I don't regret it at all. What I regret is, certainly not the more or less amusement we can find at Belle-Isle—what I regret, Aramis, is Pierrefonds, is Bracieux, is Le Vallon, is my beautiful France! Here, we are not in France, my dear friend; we are—I know not where. Oh, I tell you, in the full sincerity of my soul, and our affection will excuse my frankness, but I declare to you I am not happy at Belle-Isle. No, in good truth, I am not happy!"

Aramis breathed a long but stifled sigh.

"Dear friend," replied he, "that is why it is so sad a thing you have sent the two boats we had left in search of the boats which disappeared two days ago. If you had not sent them away, we would have departed."

"Departed! And the orders, Aramis?"

"What orders?"

"*Parbleu!* Why, the orders you have been constantly, and on all occasions, repeating to me—that we were to hold Belle-Isle against the usurper. You know very well."

"That is true!" murmured Aramis again.

"You see, then, plainly, my friend, that we could not depart; and that the sending away of the boats in search of the others is not prejudicial to us in any way."

Aramis was silent; and his vague glance, luminous as that of a gull, hovered for a long time over the sea, interrogating space, and seeking to pierce the horizon.

"With all that, Aramis," continued Porthos, who adhered to his idea, and that the more closely from the bishop having found it correct—"with all that, you give me no explanation about what can have happened to these unfortunate boats. I am assailed by cries and complaints whichever way I go. The children cry at seeing the desolation of the women, as if I could restore the absent husbands and fathers. What do you suppose, my friend, and what ought I to answer them?"

"Suppose, then, my good Porthos, and say nothing."

This reply did not satisfy Porthos at all. He turned away, grumbling some words in a very ill-humor. Aramis stopped the valiant soldier.

"Do you remember," said he, in a melancholy tone, pressing the two hands of the giant between his own with an affectionate cordiality, "do you remember, my friend, that in the glorious days of your youth—do you remember, Porthos, when we were all strong and valiant—we, and the other two—if we had then had an inclination to return to France, do you think this sheet of salt water would have stopped us?"

"Oh!" said Porthos, "but six leagues!"

"If you had seen me get astride of a plank, would you have remained on land, Porthos?"

"No, *pardieu!* No, Aramis. But nowadays what sort of a plank should we want, my friend? I, in particular."

And the Seigneur de Bracieux cast a proud glance over his colossal rotundity, with a loud laugh.

"And do you mean seriously to say you are not tired of Belle-Isle also a little, and that you would not prefer the comforts of your dwelling—of your episcopal palace at Vannes? Come, confess."

"No," replied Aramis without daring to look at Porthos.

"Let us stay where we are, then," said his friend, with a sigh which, in spite of the efforts he made to restrain it, escaped with a loud report from his breast. "Let us remain! let us remain! And yet," added he, "and yet, if we seriously wished, but that decidedly—if we had a fixed idea, one firmly taken, to return to France, and there were no boats——"

"Have you remarked another thing, my friend—that is, since the disappearance of our barks, during the two days' absence of the fishermen, not a single small boat has landed on the shores of the isle?"

"Yes, certainly, you are right. I have remarked it also, and the observation was the more naturally made, for, before the last two fatal days, we saw barks and shallops arrive by dozens."

"I must inquire." said Aramis suddenly, and with great agitation. "And then, if I had a raft constructed——"

"But there are some canoes, my friend; shall I go on board one?"

"A canoe! a canoe! Can you think of such a thing, Porthos? A canoe to be upset in! No, no," said the bishop of Vannes; "it is not our trade to ride upon the waves. We will wait, we will wait."

And Aramis continued walking about with increased agitation. Porthos, who grew tired of following all the feverish movements of his friend—Porthos, who, in his calmness and belief, understood nothing of the sort of exasperation which as betrayed by his continual convulsive starts—Porthos stopped him.

"Let us sit down upon this rock," said he. "Place yourself here, close to me, Aramis, and I conjure you, for the last time, to explain to me in a manner I can comprehend—explain to me what we are doing here."

"Porthos!" said Aramis, much embarrassed.

"I know that the false king wished to dethrone the true king. That is a fact that I understand. Well——"

"Yes," said Aramis.

"I know that the false king formed the project of selling Belle-Isle to the English. I understand that, too."

"Yes."

"I know that we engineers and captains came and threw ourselves into Belle-Isle to take the direction of the works, and the command of ten companies levied and paid by Monsieur Fouquet, or rather, the ten companies of his son-in-law. All that is plain."

Aramis arose in a state of great impatience. He might be said to be a lion importuned by a gnat. Porthos held him by the arm.

"But what I cannot understand, what, in spite of all the efforts of my mind, and all my reflections, I cannot comprehend, and never shall comprehend, is, that instead of sending us troops, instead of sending us reinforcements of men, munitions, and provisions, they leave us without boats, they leave Belle-Isle without arrivals, without help; it is that, instead of establishing with us a correspondence, whether by signals, or written or verbal communications, all relations with us are interrupted. Tell me, Aramis, answer me, or rather, before answering me, will you allow me to tell you what I have thought? Will you hear what my idea is, what imagination I have conceived?"

The bishop raised his head.

"Well, Aramis," continued Porthos, "I have thought, I have had an idea, I have imagined that an event has taken place in France. I dreamed of Monsieur Fouquet all the night; I dreamed of dead fish, broken eggs, chambers badly furnished, meanly kept. Bad dreams, my dear D'Herblay; very unlucky, such dreams!"

"Porthos, what is that yonder?" interrupted Aramis, rising suddenly and pointing out to his friend a black spot upon the empurpled line of the water.

"A bark!" said Porthos; "yes, it is a bark! Ah! we shall have some news at last."

"There are two!" cried the bishop on discovering another mast; "two! three! four!"

"Five!" said Porthos, in his turn. "Six! seven! Ah, *mon Dieu! mon Dieu!* it is a whole fleet."

"Our boats returning, probably," said Aramis very uneasily, in spite of the assurance he affected.

"They are very large for fishing-boats," observed Porthos, "and do you not remark, my friend, they come from the Loire?"

"They come from the Loire, yes——"

"And look! everybody here sees them as well as ourselves; look! the women and children are beginning to get upon the jetty."

An old fisherman passed.

"Are those our barks yonder?" asked Aramis.

The old man looked steadily into the horizon.

"No, monseigneur," replied he, "they are lighter boats in the king's service."

"Boats in the royal service?" replied Aramis, starting. "How do you know that?" said he.

"By the flag."

"But," said Porthos, "the boat is scarcely visible; how the devil, my friend, can you distinguish the flag?"

"I see there is one," replied the old man; "our boats, or trade lighters, do not carry any. That sort of craft is generally used for the transport of troops."

"Ah!" said Aramis.

"*Vivat!*" cried Porthos, "they are sending us reinforcements; don't you think they are, Aramis?"

"Probably; unless it is the English coming."

"By the Loire? That would have an ill look, Aramis, for they must have come through Paris."

"You are right; they are reinforcements, decidedly, or provisions."

Aramis leaned his head upon his hands, and made no reply. Then, all at once:

"Porthos," said he, "have the alarm sounded."

"The alarm! do you think of such a thing?"

"Yes; and let the cannoneers mount to their batteries, let the artillerymen be at their pieces, and be particularly watchful of the coast batteries."

Porthos opened his eyes to their widest extent. He looked

attentively at his friend, to convince himself he was in his proper senses.

"I will do it, my dear Porthos," continued Aramis, in his most bland tone, "I will go and have these orders executed myself, if you do not go, my friend."

"Well, I will go instantly," said Porthos, who went to execute the orders, casting all the while looks behind him, to see if the bishop of Vannes were not deceived; and if, on returning to more rational ideas, he would not recall him.

The alarm was sounded, the trumpets brayed, and drums rolled; the great bell of the belfry was put in motion. The dikes and moles were quickly filled with the curious and soldiers; the matches sparkled in the hands of the artillerymen, placed behind the large cannon bedded in their stone carriages. When every man was at his post, when all the preparations for the defense were made:

"Permit me, Aramis, to try to comprehend," whispered Porthos timidly, in Aramis' ear.

"My dear friend, you will comprehend but too soon," murmured M. d'Herblay, in reply to this question of his lieutenant.

"The fleet which is coming yonder, with sails unfurled, straight toward the port of Belle-Isle, is a royal fleet, is it not?"

"But as there are two kings in France, Porthos, to which of these two kings does this fleet belong?"

"Oh! you open my eyes," replied the giant, stunned by this argument.

And Porthos, for whom the reply of his friend had just opened the eyes, or rather, thickened the bandage which covered his sight, went with his best speed to the batteries to overlook his people, and exhort every one to his duty. In the meantime, Aramis, with his eye fixed on the horizon, saw the ships continue to draw nearer. The people and the soldiers, mounted upon all the summits or irregularities of the rocks, could distinguish the masts, then the lower sails, and at last the hulls of the lighters, bearing at the masthead the royal flag of France. It was quite night when one of these vessels which had created such a sensation among the inhabitants of Belle-Isle was moored within cannonshot of the place. It was soon seen, notwithstanding the darkness, that a sort of agitation reigned on board this vessel, from the side of which a skiff was lowered, of which the three rowers, bending to their oars, took the direction of the port, and in a few instants struck land at the foot of the fort. The commander of this yawl jumped on shore. He had a letter in his hand, which he waved in the air, and seemed to wish to communicate with somebody. This man was soon recognized by several soldiers as one of the pilots of the island. He was the patron of one of the two barks kept back by Aramis, and which Porthos, in his anxiety with regard to the fate of the fishermen who had disappeared for two days, had sent in search of the missing boats. He asked to be conducted to M. d'Herblay. Two soldiers, at a signal from a sergeant, placed him between them, and escorted him. Aramis was upon the quay. The envoy presented himself before the bishop of Vannes. The darkness was almost complete, notwithstanding the flambeaus borne at a small distance by the soldiers who were following Aramis in his rounds.

"Well, Jonathan, from whom do you come?"

"Monseigneur, from those who captured me."

"Who captured you?"

"You know, monseigneur, we set out in search of our comrades?"

"Yes; and afterward?"

"Well, monseigneur, within a short league we were captured by a *chasse-marée* belonging to the king."

"Ah!" said Aramis.

"Of which king?" cried Porthos.

Jonathan started.

"Speak!" continued the bishop.

"We were captured, monseigneur, and joined to those who had been taken yesterday morning."

"What was the cause of the mania for capturing you all?" said Porthos.

"Monsieur, to prevent us from telling ·you," replied Jonathan.

Porthos was again at a loss to comprehend.

"And they have released you to-day?" asked he.

"That I might tell you they have captured us, monsieur."

"Trouble upon trouble," thought honest Porthos.

During this time Aramis was reflecting.

"Humph!" said he, "then I suppose it is a royal fleet blockading the coasts?"

"Yes, monseigneur."

"Who commands it?"

"The captain of the king's musketeers."

"D'Artagnan?"

"D'Artagnan!" exclaimed Porthos.

"I believe that is the name."

"And did he give you this letter?"

"Yes, monseigneur."

"Bring the flambeaus nearer."

"It is his writing," said Porthos.

Aramis eagerly read the following lines:

"Order of the king to take Belle-Isle, or to put the garrison to the sword, if they resist; order to make prisoners of all the men of the garrison; signed, D'ARTAGNAN, who, the day before yesterday, arrested Monsieur Fouquet, for the purpose of his being sent to the Bastile."

Aramis turned pale, and crushed the paper in his hands.

"What is it?" asked Porthos.

"Nothing, my friend, nothing."

"Tell me, Jonathan."

"Monseigneur?"

"Did you speak to Monsieur d'Artagnan?"

"Yes, monseigneur."

"What did he say to you?"

"That for more ample information he would speak with monseigneur."

"On board his own vessel."

"On board his vessel?" and Porthos repeated, "On board his vessel?"

"Monsieur le Mousquetaire," continued Jonathan, "told me to take you both on board my canoe, and bring you to him."

"Let us go at once!" exclaimed Porthos. "Dear D'Artagnan!"

But Aramis stopped him.

"Are you mad?" cried he. "Who knows that it is not a snare?"

"Of the other king?" said Porthos mysteriously.

"A snare, in fact. That's what it is, my friend."

"Very possibly. What is to be done, then? If D'Artagnan sends for us——"

"Who assures you that D'Artagnan sends for us?"

"Yes, but—but his writing——"

"Writing is easily counterfeited. This looks counterfeited—trembling——"

"You are always right; but, in the meantime, we know nothing."

Aramis was silent.

"It is true," said the good Porthos, "we do not want to know anything."

"What shall I do?" asked Jonathan.

"You will return on board this captain's vessel."

"Yes, monseigneur."

"And will tell him that we beg he will himself come into the island."

"Ah, I comprehend!" said Porthos.

"Yes, monseigneur," replied Jonathan; "but if the captain should refuse to come to Belle-Isle?"

"If he refuses, as we have cannon, we will make use of them."

"What! against D'Artagnan?"

"If it is D'Artagnan, Porthos, he will come. Go, Jonathan, go!"

"*Ma foi!* I no longer comprehend anything," murmured Porthos.

"I will make you comprehend all, my dear friend; the time for it has come. Sit down upon this gun-carriage, open your ears, and listen well to me."

"Oh! *pardieu!* I shall listen, no fear of that."

"May I depart, monseigneur?" cried Jonathan.

"Yes, be gone, and bring back an answer. Allow the canoe to pass, you men there!"

And the canoe pushed off to regain the fleet.

Aramis took Porthos by the hand, and commenced the explanations.

Chapter 43 — THE EXPLANATIONS OF ARAMIS

"What I have to say to you, friend Porthos, will probably surprise you, but it will instruct you."

"I like to be surprised," said Porthos, in a kindly tone. "Do not spare me, therefore, I beg. I am hardened against emotions; don't fear, speak out."

"It is difficult, Porthos, it is—difficult; for, in truth, I warn you a second time, I have very strange things, very extraordinary things, to tell you."

"Oh! you speak so well, my friend, that I could listen to you for days together. Speak, then, I beg—and—stop, I have a

ea; I will, to make your task more easy, I will, to assist you
telling me such things, question you."

"I shall be pleased at your doing so."

"What are we going to fight for, Aramis?"

"If you make me many such questions as that—if you would
nder my task the easier by interrupting my revelations thus,
rthos, you will not help me at all. So far, on the contrary,
at is precisely the Gordian knot. But, my friend, with a man
e you, good, generous, and devoted, the confession must be
de bravely. I have deceived you, my worthy friend."

"You have deceived me?"

"Good heavens! yes."

"Was it for my good, Aramis?"

"I thought so, Porthos; I thought so sincerely, my friend."

"Then," said the honest Seigneur of Bracieux, "you have
ndered me a service, and I thank you for it; for if you had
t deceived me, I might have deceived myself. In what, then,
ve you deceived me, say?"

"In that I was serving the usurper against whom Louis XIV.
this moment is directing his efforts."

"The usurper!" said Porthos, scratching his head. "That is
well, I do not too clearly comprehend that."

"He is one of the two kings who are contending for the
own of France."

"Very well. Then you were serving him who is not Louis
V.?"

"You have hit upon the matter in a word."

"It results that——"

"It results that we are rebels, my poor friend."

"The devil! the devil!" cried Porthos, much disappointed.

"Oh! but, dear Porthos, be calm; we shall still find means
getting out of the affair, trust me."

"It is not that which makes me uneasy," replied Porthos;
at which alone touches me is that ugly word *rebels*."

"Ah! but——"

"And so, according to this, the duchy that was promised
——"

"It was the usurper who was to give it to you."

"And that is not the same thing, Aramis," said Porthos ma-
tically.

"My friend, if it had only depended upon me, you should
ve become a prince."

Porthos began to bite his nails, after a melancholy fashion.

"That is where you have been wrong," continued he, "in

deceiving me; for that promised duchy I reckoned upon. Oh! I reckoned upon it seriously, knowing you to be a man of your word, Aramis."

"Poor Porthos! pardon me, I implore you!"

"So, then," continued Porthos, without replying to the bishop's prayer, "so, then, it seems, I have quite fallen out with Louis XIV.?"

"Oh, I will settle all that, my good friend, I will settle all that. I will take it upon myself alone."

"Aramis!"

"No, no, Porthos, I conjure you, let me act. No false generosity! No inopportune devotedness! You knew nothing of my projects. You have done nothing of yourself. With me it is different. I am alone the author of the plot. I stood in need of my inseparable companion; I called upon you, and you came to me, in remembrance of our ancient device. 'All for one, one for all.' My crime was being an egotist."

"Now, that is the word I like," said Porthos; "and, seeing that you have acted entirely for yourself, it is impossible for me to blame you. It is natural."

And upon this sublime reflection Porthos pressed the hand of his friend cordially.

In presence of this ingenuous greatness of soul, Aramis felt himself little. It was the second time he had been compelled to bend before real superiority of heart, much more powerful than splendor of mind. He replied by a mute and energetic pressure to the kind endearment of his friend.

"Now," said Porthos, "that we have come to an explanation, now that I am perfectly aware of our situation, with respect to Louis XIV., I think, my friend, it is time to make me comprehend the political intrigue of which we are the victims—for I plainly see there is a political intrigue at the bottom of all this."

"D'Artagnan, my good Porthos, D'Artagnan is coming, and will detail it to you in all its circumstances; but, excuse me, I am deeply grieved, I am bowed down by pain, and I have need of all my presence of mind, of all my reflection, to extricate you from the false step in which I have so imprudently involved you; but nothing can be more clear, nothing more plain than your position henceforth. The king, Louis XIV., has longer now but one enemy; that enemy is myself, myself alone. I have made you a prisoner; you have followed me, I day I liberate you; you fly back to your prince. You can perceive, Porthos, there is not a single difficulty in all this."

'Do you think so?" said Porthos.

'I am quite sure of it."

Then why," said the admirable good sense of Porthos, "then
, if we are in such an easy position, why, my friend, do we
pare cannon, muskets, and engines of all sorts? It seems to
it would be much more simple to say to Captain d'Artag-
: 'My dear friend, we have been mistaken; that error is to
repaired; open the door to us, let us pass through, and good-
!' "

'Ah! that," said Aramis, shaking his head.

Why do you say 'that?' Do you not approve of my plan, my
nd?"

'I see a difficulty in it."

'What is it?"

'The hypothesis that D'Artagnan may come with orders
ch will oblige us to defend ourselves."

What! defend ourselves against D'Artagnan? Folly! Against
good D'Artagnan?"

Aramis once more replied by shaking his head.

'Porthos," at length said he, "if I have had the matches
ted and the guns pointed, if I have had the signal of alarm
nded, if I have called every man to his post upon the ram-
ts, those good ramparts of Belle-Isle which you have so well
tified, it is for something. Wait to judge; or rather, no, do not
t——"

'What can I do?"

'If I knew, my friend, I would have told you."

But there is one thing much more simple than defending
selves—a boat, and away for France—where——"

My dear friend," said Aramis, smiling with a strong shade
sadness, "do not let us reason like children; let us be men in
ncil and execution. But, hark! I hear a hail for landing at
port. Attention, Porthos, serious attention!"

It is D'Artagnan, no doubt," said Porthos, in a voice of
nder, approaching the parapet.

Yes, it is I," replied the captain of the musketeers, run-
g lightly up the steps of the mole, and gaining rapidly the
e esplanade upon which his two friends waited for him. As
n as he came toward them Porthos and Aramis observed an
cer who followed D'Artagnan, treading apparently in his very
s. The captain stopped upon the stairs of the mole when
way up. His companion imitated him.

Make your men draw back," cried D'Artagnan to Porthos
Aramis: "let them retire out of hearing."

The order being given by Porthos, was executed immediately. Then D'Artagnan, turning toward him who followed him:

"Monsieur," said he, "we are no longer here on board the king's fleet, where, in virtue of your order, you spoke so arrogantly to me just now."

"Monsieur," replied the officer, "I did not speak arrogantly to you; I simply but rigorously obeyed what I had been commanded. I have been directed to follow you. I follow you. I am directed not to allow you to communicate with any one without taking cognizance of what you do; I mix myself, therefore, with your communications."

D'Artagnan trembled with rage, and Porthos and Aramis, who heard this dialogue, trembled likewise, but with uneasiness and fear. D'Artagnan, biting his mustache with that vivacity which denoted in him the state of an exasperation closely t[o] be followed by a terrible explosion, approached the officer.

"Monsieur," said he, in a low voice, so much the more impressive that, affecting a calm, it threatened a tempest—"monsieur, when I sent a canoe hither you wished to know what I wrote to the defenders of Belle-Isle. You produced a[n] order to that effect; and, in my turn, I instantly showed you th[e] note I had written. When the patron of the boat sent by m[e] returned, when I received the reply of these two gentlemen" (and he pointed to Aramis and Porthos), "you heard ever[y] word of what the messenger said. All that was plainly in yo[ur] orders, all that was well executed, very punctually, was it not[?]"

"Yes, monsieur," stammered the officer; "yes, without doub[t] but——"

"Monsieur," continued D'Artagnan, growing warm—"mo[n]sieur, when I manifested the intention of quitting my vessel [to] cross to Belle-Isle you required to accompany me; I did n[ot] hesitate; I brought you with me. You are now at Belle-Is[le] are you not?"

"Yes, monsieur; but——"

"But—the question no longer is of Monsieur Colbert, w[ho] has given you that order, or of whomsoever in the world y[ou] are following the instructions; the question now is of a man w[ho] is a clog upon Monsieur d'Artagnan, and who is alone with M[on]sieur D'Artagnan upon steps whose feet are bathed by th[e] feet of salt water; a bad position for that man, a bad positi[on] monsieur! I warn you."

"But, monsieur, if I am a restraint upon you," said the [of]ficer timidly, and almost faintly, "it is my duty which——"

"Monsieur, you have had the misfortune, you or those w[ho]

at you, to insult me. It is done. I cannot seek redress from ose who employ you—they are unknown to me, or are at too at a distance. But you are under my hand, and I swear that you make one step behind me when I raise my feet to go up those gentlemen, I swear to you by my name, I will cleave ur head in two with my sword, and pitch you into the water. ! it will happen, it will happen! I have only been six times gry in my life, monsieur, and, on the five times which have eceded this, I have killed my man."

The officer did not stir; he became pale under this terrible eat, but replied, with simplicity:

"Monsieur, you are wrong in acting against my orders."

Porthos and Aramis, mute and trembling at the top of the rapet, cried to the musketeer:

"Dear D'Artagnan, take care!"

D'Artagnan made them a sign to keep silence, raised his ot with a terrifying calmness to mount the stair, and ned round, sword in hand, to see if the officer followed him. e officer made a sign of the cross and stepped up. Porthos d Aramis, who knew their D'Artagnan, uttered a cry, and shed down to prevent the blow they thought they had already ard. But D'Artagnan passed his sword into his left hand.

"Monsieur," said he to the officer, in an agitated voice, "you a brave man. You ought better to comprehend what I am ng to say to you now than that which I have just said to u."

"Speak, Monsieur d'Artagnan, speak," replied the brave cer.

"These gentlemen we have just seen, and against whom you ve orders, are my friends."

"I know they are, monsieur."

"You can understand if I ought to act toward them as your tructions prescribe."

"I understand your reserve."

"Very well; permit me, then, to converse with them without itness."

"Monsieur d'Artagnan, if I yielded to your request, if I did t which you beg me to do, I should break my word; but if I not do it, I shall disoblige you. I prefer the one to the other. nverse with your friends, and do not despise me, monsieur, doing for the sake of you, whom I esteem and honor, do t despise me for committing for you, and you alone, an un- rthy act."

D'Artagnan, much agitated, passed his arms rapidly round

the neck of the young man, and went up to his friends. Th
officer, enveloped in his cloak, sat down on the damp, wee
covered steps.

"Well," said D'Artagnan to his friends, "such is my positio
judge for yourselves."

They all three embraced. All three pressed one another
their arms as in the glorious days of their youth.

"What is the meaning of all these rigors?" said Porthos.

"You ought to have some suspicions of what it is," sa
D'Artagnan.

"Not much, I assure you, my dear captain; for, in fact,
have done nothing, no more has Aramis," hastened the worth
baron to say.

D'Artagnan darted a reproachful look at the prelate, whic
penetrated that hardened heart.

"Dear Porthos!" cried the bishop of Vannes.

"You see what has been done against you," said D'Arta
nan; "interception of all that is coming to or going from Bell
Isle. Your boats all seized. If you had endeavored to fly, ye
would have fallen into the hands of the cruisers which plow th
sea in all directions, on the watch for you. The king wants ye
to be taken, and he will take you."

And D'Artagnan tore several hairs from his gray mustach
Aramis became somber, Porthos angry.

"My idea was this," continued D'Artagnan, "to make ye
both come on board, to keep you near me, and restore ye
your liberty. But now, who can say that when I return to m
ship I may not find a superior; that I may not find secret orde
which will take from me my command, and give it to anothe
who will dispose of me and you without hopes of help?"

"We must remain at Belle-Isle," said Aramis resolutely; "a
I assure you, for my part, I will not surrender easily."

Porthos said nothing. D'Artagnan remarked the silence
his friend.

"I have another trial to make of this officer, of this bra
fellow who accompanies me, and whose courageous resistan
makes me very happy; for it denotes an honest man, who, a
though an enemy, is a thousand times better than a complaisa
coward. Let us try to learn from him what he has the right
doing, and what his orders permit or forbid."

"Let us try," said Aramis.

D'Artagnan came to the parapet, leaned over toward t
steps of the mole, and called the officer, who immediately ca
up.

"Monsieur," said D'Artagnan, after having exchanged the ost cordial courtesies natural between gentlemen who know d appreciate each other worthily, "monsieur, if I wished to ke away these gentlemen from this place, what would you do?"

"I should not oppose it, monsieur; but having direct orders, rmal orders, to take them under my guard, I should detain em."

"Ah!" said D'Artagnan.

"That's all over," said Aramis gloomily.

Porthos did not stir.

"But still take Porthos," said the bishop of Vannes; "he n prove to the king—I will help him in doing so, and you can so prove, Monsieur d'Artagnan—that he has had nothing do in this affair."

"Hum!" said D'Artagnan. "Will you come? Will you follow e, Porthos? The king is merciful."

"I beg to reflect," said Porthos nobly.

"You will remain here, then?"

"Until fresh orders," said Aramis, with vivacity.

"Until we have an idea," resumed D'Artagnan; "and I now lieve that will not be long first, for I have one already."

"Let us say adieu, then," said Aramis; "but, in truth, my od Porthos, you ought to go."

"No," said the latter laconically.

"As you please," replied Aramis, a little wounded in his rvous susceptibility at the morose tone of his companion. nly I am reassured by the promise of an idea from D'Ar-gnan, an idea I fancy I have divined."

"Let us see," said the musketeer, placing his ear near Ara-s' mouth. The latter spoke several words rapidly, to which Artagnan replied:

"That is it, precisely."

"Infallible, then!" cried Aramis.

"During the first emotion that this resolution will cause, take re of yourself, Aramis."

"Oh, don't be afraid!"

"Now, monsieur," said D'Artagnan to the officer, "thanks, a ousand thanks! You have made yourself three friends for e."

"Yes," added Aramis.

Porthos alone said nothing, but merely bowed.

D'Artagnan, having tenderly embraced his two old friends, t Belle-Isle with the inseparable companion M. Colbert had ven him. Thus, with the exception of the explanation with

which the worthy Porthos had been willing to be satisfied
nothing had changed in appearance in the fate of the one or o
the other.

"Only," said Aramis, "there is D'Artagnan's idea."

D'Artagnan did not return on board without examining t
the bottom the idea he had discovered. Now, we know tha
when D'Artagnan did examine, according to custom, dayligh
pierced through. As to the officer, become mute again, he lef
him full measure to meditate. Therefore, on putting his foot o
board his vessel, moored within cannon-shot of the island, th
captain of the musketeers had already got together all his means
offensive and defensive.

He immediately assembled his council, which consisted o
the officers serving under his orders. These were eight in num
ber: a chief of the maritime forces, a major directing the artil
lery, an engineer, the officer we are acquainted with, and fou
lieutenants. Having assembled them in the chamber of th
poop, D'Artagnan arose, took off his hat, and addressed ther
thus:

"Gentlemen, I have been to reconnoiter Belle-Isle-en-Mer
and I have found in it a good and solid garrison; moreover
preparations are made for a defense that may prove trouble
some. I therefore intend to send for two of the principal officer
of the place, that we may converse with them. Having sep
arated them from their troops and their cannon, we shall b
better able to deal with them, particularly with good reasoning
Is this your opinion, gentlemen?"

The major of artillery rose.

"Monsieur," said he, with respect but with firmness, "I hav
heard you say that the place is preparing to make a trouble
some defense. The place is, then, as you know, determine
upon rebellion?"

D'Artagnan was visibly put out by this reply; but he was no
a man to allow himself to be subdued by so little, and resumed

"Monsieur," said he, "your reply is just. But you are i
norant that Belle-Isle is a fief of Monsieur Fouquet, and th
ancient kings gave the right to the seigneurs of Belle-Isle
arm their people."

The major made a movement.

"Oh, do not interrupt me," continued D'Artagnan. "You a
going to tell me that that right to arm themselves against th
English was not a right to arm themselves against their kin
But it is not Monsieur Fouquet, I suppose, who holds Bell
Isle at this moment, since I arrested Monsieur Fouquet th

day before yesterday. Now, the inhabitants and defenders of Belle-Isle know nothing of that arrest. You would announce it to them in vain. It is a thing so unheard-of and extraordinary, so unexpected, that they would not believe you. A Breton serves his master, and not his masters; he serves his master till he has seen him dead. Now, the Bretons, as far as I know, have not seen the body of Monsieur Fouquet. It is not, then, surprising that they hold out against that which is not Monsieur Fouquet or his signature."

The major bowed in sign of assent.

"That is why," continued D'Artagnan, "I propose to cause two of the principal officers of the garrison to come on board my vessel. They will see you, gentlemen; they will see the forces we have at our disposal; they will, consequently, know to what they have to trust and the fate that attends them, in case of rebellion. We will affirm to them, upon our honor, that Monsieur Fouquet is a prisoner, and that all resistance can only be prejudicial to them. We will tell them that the first cannon that is fired, there will be no mercy to be expected from the king. Then, I hope at least, they will no longer resist. They will yield without fighting, and we shall have a place given up to us in a friendly way, which it might cost us much trouble to subdue."

The officer who had followed D'Artagnan to Belle-Isle was preparing to speak, but D'Artagnan interrupted him.

"Yes, I know what you are going to tell me, monsieur; I know that there is an order of the king's to prevent all secret communications with the defenders of Belle-Isle, and that is exactly why I do not offer to communicate but in the presence of my staff."

And D'Artagnan made an inclination of the head to his officers, which had for object attaching a value to that condescension.

The officers looked at one another, as if to read their opinions in their eyes, with the intention of evidently acting, after they should have agreed, according to the desire of D'Artagnan. And already the latter saw with joy that the result of their consent would be sending a bark to Porthos and Aramis, when the king's officer drew from his pocket a folded paper, which he placed in the hands of D'Artagnan.

This paper bore upon its superscription the number 1.

"What, more still!" murmured the surprised captain.

"Read, monsieur," said the officer, with a courtesy that was not free from sadness.

D'Artagnan, full of mistrust, unfolded the paper, and read these words:

"Prohibition to Monsieur d'Artagnan to assemble any council whatever, or to deliberate in any way before Belle-Isle be surrendered and the prisoners shot.

"(Signed) LOUIS."

D'Artagnan repressed the movement of impatience that ran through his whole body, and, with a gracious smile:

"That is well, monsieur," said he; "the king's orders shall be complied with."

Chapter 44 — RESULT OF THE IDEAS OF THE KING AND THE IDEAS OF D'ARTAGNAN

The blow was direct. It was severe, mortal. D'Artagnan, furious at having been anticipated by an idea of the king's, did not, however, yet despair; and, reflecting upon the idea he had brought back from Belle-Isle, he augured from it a new means of safety for his friends.

"Gentlemen," said he suddenly, "since the king has charged some other than myself with his secret orders, it must be because I no longer possess his confidence, and I should be really unworthy of it if I had the courage to hold a command subject to so many injurious suspicions. I will go, then, immediately and carry my resignation to the king. I give it before you all, enjoining you all to fall back with me upon the coast of France, in such a way as not to compromise the safety of the forces his majesty has confided to me. For this purpose, return all to your posts; within an hour we shall have the ebb of the tide. To your posts, gentlemen; I suppose," added he, on seeing that all prepared to obey him, except the surveillant officer, "you have no orders to object this time?"

And D'Artagnan almost triumphed while speaking these words. This plan was the safety of his friends. The blockade once raised, they might embark immediately. and set sail for England or Spain, without fear of being molested. While they were making their escape D'Artagnan would return to the king, would justify his return by the indignation which the mistrusts of Colbert had raised in him; he would be sent back with full powers, and he would take Belle-Isle; that is to say, the cage, after the birds had flown. But to this plan the officer opposed a second order of the king's. It was thus conceived:

"From the moment Monsieur d'Artagnan shall have manifested the desire of giving in his resignation, he shall no longer be reckoned leader of the expedition, and every officer placed under his orders shall be held to no longer obey him. Moreover, the said Monsieur d'Artagnan, having lost that quality of leader of the army sent against Belle-Isle, shall set out immediately for France, in company of the officer who will have remitted the message to him, and who will consider him as a prisoner for whom he is answerable."

Brave and careless as he was, D'Artagnan turned pale. Everything had been calculated with a depth which, for the first time in thirty years, had recalled to him the solid foresight and the inflexible logic of the great cardinal. He leaned his head on his hand, thoughtful, scarcely breathing.

"If I were to put this order in my pocket," thought he, "who would know it, or who would prevent my doing it? Before the king had had time to be informed, I should have saved those poor fellows yonder. Let us exercise a little audacity. My head is not one of those which the executioner strikes off for disobedience. We will disobey!"

But at the moment he was about to adopt this plan, he saw the officers around him reading similar orders which the infernal agent of the thoughts of Colbert had just distributed to them. The case of disobedience had been foreseen, as the others had been.

"Monsieur," said the officer, coming up to him, "I await your good pleasure to depart."

"I am ready, monsieur," replied D'Artagnan, grinding his teeth.

The officer immediately commanded a canoe to receive M. d'Artagnan and himself. At sight of this he became almost mad with rage.

"How," stammered he, "will you carry on the direction of the different corps?"

"When you are gone, monsieur," replied the commander of the fleet, "it is to me the direction of the whole is committed."

"Then, monsieur," rejoined Colbert's man, addressing the new leader, "it is for you that this last order that has been remitted to me is intended. Let us see your powers."

"Here they are," said the sea-officer, exhibiting a royal signature.

"Here are your instructions," replied the officer, placing the folded paper in his hands; and, turning toward D'Artagnan, "Come, monsieur," said he, in an agitated voice (such despair did he behold in that man of iron), "do me the favor to depart at once."

"Immediately!" articulated D'Artagnan feebly, subdued, crushed by implacable impossibility.

And he let himself slide down into the little boat, which started, favored by wind and tide, for the coast of France. The king's guards embarked with him. The musketeer still preserved the hope of reaching Nantes quickly, and of pleading the cause of his friends eloquently enough to incline the king to mercy. The bark flew like a swallow. D'Artagnan distinctly saw the land of France profiled in black against the white clouds of night.

"Ah! monsieur," said he, in a low voice, to the officer to whom, for an hour, he had ceased speaking, "what would I give to know the instructions for the new commander! They are all pacific, are they not? and——"

He did not finish; the sound of a distant cannon rolled over the waters, then another, and two or three still louder. D'Artagnan shuddered.

"The fire is opened upon Belle-Isle," replied the officer.

The canoe had just touched the soil of France.

Chapter 45 — THE ANCESTORS OF PORTHOS

When D'Artagnan had quitted Aramis and Porthos the latter returned to the principal fort to converse with the greater liberty. Porthos, still thoughtful, was a constraint upon Aramis, whose mind had never felt itself more free.

"Dear Porthos," said he suddenly, "I will explain D'Artagnan's idea to you."

"What idea, Aramis?"

"An idea to which we shall owe our liberty within twelve hours."

"Ah, indeed!" said Porthos, much astonished. "Let us see it."

"Did you remark, in the scene our friend had with the officer, that certain orders restrained him with regard to us?"

"Yes, I did remark that."

"Well, D'Artagnan is going to give in his resignation to the king, and during the confusion which will result from his ab-sense, we will get away, or rather, you will get away, Porthos, if there is a possibility of flight only for one."

Here Porthos shook his head, and replied:

"We will escape together, Aramis, or we will remain here together."

"You are a generous heart," said Aramis, "only your melan-choly uneasiness afflicts me."

"I am not uneasy," said Porthos.

"Then you are angry with me."

"I am not angry with you."

"Then why, my friend, do you put on such a dismal counte-nance?"

"I will tell you: I am making my will."

And, while saying these words, the good Porthos looked sadly in the face of Aramis.

"Your will!" cried the bishop. "What, then, do you think yourself lost?"

"I feel fatigued. It is the first time, and there is a custom in our family."

"What is it, my friend?"

"My grandfather was a man twice as strong as I am."

"Indeed!" said Aramis; "then your grandfather must have been Samson himself."

"No; his name was Antoine. Well, he was about my age, when, setting out one day for the chase, he felt his legs weak, he who had never known this before."

"What was the meaning of that fatigue, my friend?"

"Nothing good, as you will see; for, having set out, com-plaining still of the weakness of his legs, he met a wild boar, which made head against him; he missed him with his arque-buse, and was ripped up by the beast, and died directly."

"There is no reason in that why you should alarm yourself, dear Porthos."

"Oh! you will see. My father was as strong again as I am. He was a rough soldier, under Henry III. and Henry IV.; his name was not Antoine, but Gaspard, the same as Monsieur de Coligny. Always on horseback, he had never known what lassitude was. One evening, as he rose from table, his legs failed him."

"He had supped heartily, perhaps," said Aramis, "and that was why he staggered."

"Bah! A friend of Monsieur de Bassompierre, nonsense! No, no; he was astonished at feeling this lassitude, and said to my mother, who laughed at him, 'Would not one believe I was going to meet with a wild boar, as the late Monsieur du Vallon, my father, did?' "

"Well?" said Aramis.

"Well, having this weakness, my father insisted upon going down into the garden, instead of going to bed; his foot slipped on the first stair; the staircase was steep; my father fell against a stone angle in which an iron hinge was fixed. The hinge opened his temple, and he lay dead upon the spot."

Aramis raised his eyes to his friend.

"These are two extraordinary circumstances," said he; "let us not infer that there may succeed a third. It is not becoming in a man of your strength to be superstitious, my brave Porthos. Besides, when were your legs seen to fail? Never have you been so firm, so superb. Why, you could carry a house on your shoulders."

"At this moment," said Porthos, "I feel myself pretty active; but at times I vacillate, I sink; and lately this phenomenon, as you say, has occurred four times. I will not say that this frightens me, but it annoys me. Life is an agreeable thing. I have money; I have fine estates; I have horses that I love; I have also friends that I love; D'Artagnan, Athos, Raoul, and you."

The admirable Porthos did not even take the trouble to dissimulate to Aramis the rank he gave him in his friendship. Aramis pressed his hand.

"We will still live many years," said he, "to preserve in the world specimens of rare men. Trust yourself to me, my friend; we have no reply from D'Artagnan; that is a good sign. He must have given orders to get the vessels together and clear the seas. On my part I have just issued directions that a bark should be rolled upon rollers to the mouth of the great cavern of Locmaria, which you know, where we have so often laid in wait for the foxes."

"Yes, and which terminates at the little creek by a trench which we discovered the day that splendid fox escaped that way."

"Precisely. In case of misfortunes, a bark is to be concealed for us in that cavern; indeed, it must be there by this time.

We will wait for a favorable moment, and, during the night, to sea!"

"That is a good idea; what shall we gain by it?"

"We shall gain by it—that nobody knows that grotto, or rather, its issue, except ourselves and two or three hunters of the island; we shall gain by it—that if the island is occupied, the scouts, seeing no bark upon the shore, will never imagine we can escape, and will cease to watch."

"I understand."

"Well, the legs?"

"Oh! excellent, just now."

"You see, then, plainly, that everything conspires to give us quietude and hope. D'Artagnan will clear the sea and make us free. No more royal fleet or descent to be dreaded. *Vive Dieu!* Porthos, we have still half a century of good adventures before us, and if I once touch Spanish ground, I swear to you," added the bishop, with a terrible energy, "that your brevet of duke is not such a chance as it is said to be."

"We will live in hope," said Porthos, a little enlivened by the renovated warmth of his companion.

All at once a cry resounded in their ears:

"To arms! to arms!"

This cry, repeated by a hundred voices, brought to the chamber where the two friends were conversing, surprise to the one, and uneasiness to the other. Aramis opened the window; he saw a crowd of people running with flambeaus. Women were seeking places of safety, the armed population were hastening to their posts.

"The fleet! the fleet!" cried a soldier, who recognized Aramis.

"The fleet?" repeated the latter.

"Within half cannon-shot!" continued the soldier.

"To arms!" cried Aramis.

"To arms!" repeated Porthos formidably.

And both rushed forth toward the mole, to place themselves within the shelter of the batteries. Boats, laden with soldiers, were seen approaching; they took three directions, for the purpose of landing at three points at once.

"What must be done?" said an officer of the guard.

"Stop them; and if they persist, fire!" said Aramis.

Five minutes after, the cannonade commenced. These were the shots that D'Artagnan had heard as he landed in France. But the boats were too near the mole to allow the cannon to aim correctly. They landed, and the combat commenced hand to hand.

"What's the matter, Porthos?" said Aramis to his friend.

"Nothing! nothing! only my legs; it is really incomprehensible! they will be better when we charge."

In fact, Porthos and Aramis did charge with such vigor, they so thoroughly animated their men, that the royalists re-embarked precipitately, without gaining anything but the wounds they carried away.

"Eh! but, Porthos," cried Aramis, "we must have a prisoner, quick! quick!"

Porthos bent over the stair of the mole and seized by the nape of the neck one of the officers of the royal army who was waiting to embark till all his people should be in the boat. The arm of the giant lifted up his prey, which served him as a buckler, and he recovered himself without a shot being fired at him.

"Here is a prisoner for you," said Porthos coolly, to Aramis.

"Well!" cried the latter, laughing, "have you not calumniated your legs?"

"It was not with my legs I took him," said Porthos, "it was with my arms."

Chapter 46 — THE SON OF BISCARRAT

The Bretons of the isle were very proud of this victory; Aramis did not encourage them in the feeling.

"What will happen," said he to Porthos, when everybody was gone home, "will be that the anger of the king will be roused by the account of the resistance; and that these brave people will be decimated or shot when they are taken, which cannot fail to take place."

"From which it results, then," said Porthos, "that what we have done is of no use."

"For the moment it may be of some," replied the bishop, "for we have a prisoner from whom we shall learn what our enemies are preparing to do."

"Yes, let us interrogate the prisoner," said Porthos, "and the means of making him speak are very simple. We are going to supper; we will invite him to join us; when he drinks he will talk."

This was done. The officer was at first rather uneasy, but became reassured on seeing what sort of men he had to deal with. He gave, without having any fear of compromising himself, all the details imaginable of the resignation and departure of D'Artagnan. He explained how, after that departure, the new leader of the expedition had ordered a surprise upon Belle-Isle. There his explanations stopped. Aramis and Porthos exchanged a glance which evinced their despair. No more dependence to be placed upon the brave imagination of D'Artagnan, consequently no more resources in the event of defeat. Aramis, continuing his interrogations, asked the prisoner what the leaders of the expedition contemplated doing with the leaders of Belle-Isle.

"The orders are," replied he, "to kill during the combat, and hang afterward."

Porthos and Aramis looked at each other again, and the color mounted to their faces.

"I am too light for the gallows," replied Aramis; "people like me are not hung."

"And I am too heavy," said Porthos; "people like me break the cord."

"I am sure," said the prisoner gallantly, "that we could have procured you what sort of death you preferred."

"A thousand thanks!" said Aramis seriously.

Porthos bowed.

"One more cup of wine to your health," said he, drinking himself. From one subject to another the chat with the officer was prolonged; he was an intelligent gentleman, and suffered himself to be led away by the charm of Aramis' wit and Porthos' cordial *bonhomie*.

"Pardon me," said he, "if I address a question to you; but men who are in their sixth bottle have a clear right to forget themselves a little."

"Address it!" said Porthos, "address it!"

"Speak!" said Aramis.

"Were you not, gentlemen, both in the musketeers of the late king?"

"Yes, monsieur, and of the best of them, if you please," said Porthos.

"That is true; I should say even the best of all soldiers, messieurs, if I did not fear to offend the memory of my father."

"Of your father?" cried Aramis.

"Do you know what my name is?"

"*Ma foi!* no, monsieur; but you can tell us, and——"

"I am called Georges de Biscarrat."

"Oh!" cried Porthos, in his turn, "Biscarrat! Do you remember that name, Aramis?"

"Biscarrat!" reflected the bishop. "It seems to me——"

"Try to recollect, monsieur," said the officer.

"*Pardieu!* that won't take me long," said Porthos. "Biscarrat—called Cardinal—one of the four who interrupted us the day on which we formed our friendship with D'Artagnan, sword in hand."

"Precisely, gentlemen."

"The only one," cried Aramis eagerly, "we did not wound."

"Consequently, a good blade," said the prisoner.

"That's true, very true!" exclaimed both the friends together. "*Ma foi!* Monsieur Biscarrat, we are delighted to make the acquaintance of such a brave man's son!"

Biscarrat pressed the hands held out to him by the two ancient musketeers. Aramis looked at Porthos as much as to say: "Here is a man who will help us, and without delay."

"Confess, monsieur," said he, "that it is good to have once been a good man."

"My father always said so, monsieur."

"Confess, likewise, that it is a sad circumstance in which you find yourself, of falling in with men destined to be shot or hung, and to learn that these men are old acquaintances—old hereditary acquaintances."

"Oh!" you are not reserved for such a frightful fate as that, messieurs and friends," said the young man warmly.

"Bah! you said so yourself."

"I said so just now, when I did not know you; but now that I know you, I say—you will avoid this dismal fate, if you like."

"How—if we like?" cried Aramis, whose eyes beamed with intelligence as he looked alternately at the prisoner and Porthos.

"Provided," continued Porthos, looking, in his turn, with noble intrepidity at M. Biscarrat and the bishop, "provided nothing disgraceful be required of us."

"Nothing at all will be required of you, gentlemen," replied the officer. "What should they ask of you? If they find you they will kill you; that is a settled thing. Try, then, gentlemen, to prevent their finding you."

"I don't think I am mistaken," said Porthos, with dignity "but it appears evident to me that if they want to find us, they must come and seek us here."

"In that you are perfectly right, my worthy friend," replied

mis, constantly consulting with his looks the countenance
Biscarrat, who was silent and constrained. "You wish,
nsieur de Biscarrat, to say something to us, to make us
ie overture, and you dare not—is not that true?"

Ah! gentlemen and friends, it is because in speaking I be-
v my duty. But, hark! I hear a voice which liberates mine
dominating over it."

Cannon!" said Porthos.

Cannon, and musketry, too!" cried the bishop.

)n hearing, at a distance, among the rocks, these sinister
orts of a combat which they thought had ceased:

What can that be?" asked Porthos.

Eh! *pardieu!*" cried Aramis, "this is just what I expected."

What is that?"

The attack made by you was nothing but a feint; is not
t true, monsieur? And while your companions allowed them-
es to be repulsed, you were certain of effecting a landing
he other side of the island."

Oh! several, monsieur."

We are lost, then," said the bishop of Vannes quietly.

Lost! that is possible," replied the Seigneur de Pierre-
ds, "but we are not taken or hung."

nd so saying, he rose from the table, went to the wall, and
lly took down his sword and pistols, which he examined with
care of an old soldier who is preparing for battle, and who
s that his life, in a great measure, depends upon the ex-
ence and the good condition of his arms.

.t the report of the cannon, at the news of the surprise
ch might deliver up the isle to the royal troops, the ter-
d crowd rushed precipitately to the fort to demand assis-
e and advice from their leaders. Aramis, pale and downcast,
ween two flambeaus, showed himself at the window which
ced into the principal court, full of soldiers waiting for or-
and bewildered inhabitants imploring succor.

My friends," said D'Herblay, in a grave and sonorous voice,
onsieur Fouquet, your protector, your friend, your father,
been arrested by an order of the king, and thrown into
Bastile."

long cry of fury and menace came floating up to the win-
at which the bishop stood, and enveloped him in a vibrat-
fluid.

Avenge Monsieur Fouquet!" cried the most excited of his
cers, "and death to the royalists!"

No, my friends," replied Aramis solemnly; "no, my friends;

no resistance. The king is master in his kingdom. The king is the mandatory of God. The king and God have struck Monsieur Fouquet. Humble yourselves before the hand of God. Love God and the king who have struck Monsieur Fouquet. But do not avenge your seigneur, do not think of avenging him. You would sacrifice yourselves in vain—you, your wives and children, your property, and your liberty. Lay down your arms, my friends—lay down your arms! since the king commands you so to do—and retire peaceably to your dwellings. It is I who ask you to do so; it is I who beg you to do so; it is I who now, in the hour of need, command you to do so, in the name of Monsieur Fouquet."

The crowd collected under the window uttered a prolonged growl of anger and terror.

"The soldiers of Louis XIV. have entered the island," continued Aramis. "From this time it would no longer be a combat between them and you—it would be a massacre. Be gone, then, be gone, and forget; this time I command you, in the name of the Lord!"

The mutineers retired slowly, submissive and silent.

"Ah! what have you just been saying there, friend?" said Porthos.

"Monsieur," said Biscarrat to the bishop, "you may save all these inhabitants, but you will neither save yourself nor your friend."

"Monsieur de Biscarrat," said the bishop of Vannes, with a singular accent of nobleness and courtesy, "Monsieur de Biscarrat, be kind enough to resume your liberty."

"I am very willing to do so, monsieur, but——"

"That would render us a service, for, when announcing to the king's lieutenant the submission of the islanders, you would perhaps obtain some grace for us on informing him of the manner in which that submission has been effected."

"Grace!" replied Porthos, with flashing eyes, "what is the meaning of that word?"

Aramis touched the elbow of his friend roughly, as he had been accustomed to do in the days of their youth, when he wanted to warn Porthos that he had committed, or was about to commit, a blunder. Porthos understood him, and was silent immediately.

"I will go, messieurs," replied Biscarrat, a little surprised likewise at the word "grace" pronounced by the haughty musketeer, of whom, some instants before, he had related boasted with so much enthusiasm the heroic exploits with which his father had delighted him.

"Go, then, Monsieur Biscarrat," said Aramis, bowing to him, "and at parting receive the expression of our entire gratitude."

"But you, messieurs, you whom I take honor to call my friends, since you have been willing to accept that title, what will become of you in the meantime?" replied the officer, very much agitated at taking leave of the two ancient adversaries of his father.

"We will wait here."

"But *mon Dieu!* the order is formal."

"I am bishop of Vannes, Monsieur de Biscarrat; and they no more shoot a bishop than they hang a gentleman."

"Ah, yes, monsieur—yes, monseigneur," replied Biscarrat; "it is true, you are right, there is still that chance for you. Then, I will depart; I will repair to the commander of the expedition, the king's lieutenant. Adieu! then, messieurs, or rather, to meet again, I hope."

The worthy officer, then jumping upon a horse given him by Aramis, departed in the direction of the sound of the cannon, and which, by bringing the crowd into the fort, had interrupted the conversation of the two friends with their prisoner. Aramis watched his departure, and when left alone with Porthos:

"Well, do you comprehend?" said he.

"*Ma foi!* no."

"Did not Biscarrat inconvenience you here?"

"No; he is a brave fellow."

"Yes; but the grotto of Locmaria—is it necessary all the world should know it?"

"Ah! that is true, that is true; I comprehend. We are going to escape by the cavern."

"If you please," replied Aramis joyously. "Forward, my friend Porthos; our boat awaits us, and the king has not caught us yet."

Chapter 47 — THE GROTTO OF LOCMARIA

The cavern of Locmaria was sufficiently distant from the mole to render it necessary for our friends to husband their strength to arrive there. Besides, night was advancing; midnight had struck at the fort. Porthos and Aramis were loaded with money and arms. They walked then across the heath, which is between the mole and the cavern, listening to every noise, and endeavoring to avoid ambushes. From time to time, on the road which they had carefully left on their left hand they passed fugitives coming from the interior at the news of the landing of the royal troops. Aramis and Porthos, concealed behind some projecting mass of rock, collected the words which escaped from the poor people who fled trembling, carrying with them their most valuable effects, and tried, while listening to their complaints, to draw something from them for their own interest. At length, after a rapid course, frequently interrupted by prudent stoppages, they reached the deep grottoes, into which the foreseeing bishop of Vannes had taken care to have rolled upon cylinders a good bark capable of keeping the sea at this fine season.

"My good friend," said Porthos, after having respired vigorously, "we are arrived, it seems. But I thought you spoke of three men, three servants, who were to accompany us. I don't see them—where are they?"

"Why should you see them, dear Porthos?" replied Aramis. "They are certainly waiting for us in the cavern, and no doubt are resting for a moment, after having accomplished their rough and difficult task." Aramis stopped Porthos, who was preparing to enter the cavern.

"Will you allow me, my friend," said he to the giant, "to pass in first? I know the signal I have given to these men, who, not hearing it, would be very likely to fire upon you or slash away with their knives in the dark."

"Go on, then, Aramis, go on—go first; you are all wisdom and prudence; go on. Ah! there is that fatigue again of which I spoke to you. It has just seized me again."

Aramis left Porthos sitting at the enterance of the grotto, and bowing his head, he penetrated into the interior of the cavern, imitating the cry of the owl. A little plaintive cooing, a scarcely distinct cry, replied from the depths of the cave. Aramis pursued his way cautiously, and soon was stopped by the same kind of cry as he had first uttered, and this cry sounded within ten paces of him.

"Are you there, Yves?" said the bishop.

"Yes, monseigneur; Goenne is here likewise. His son accompanies us."

"That is well. Are all things ready?"

"Yes, monseigneur."

"Go to the entrance of the grottoes, my good Yves, and you will there find the Seigneur de Pierrefonds, who is resting after the fatigue of our journey. And if he should happen not to be able to walk, lift him up, and bring him to me."

The three men obeyed. But the recommendation given to his servants was useless. Porthos, refreshed, had already himself commenced the descent, and his heavy step resounded among the cavities, formed and supported by columns of silex and granite. As soon as the Seigneur de Bracieux had rejoined the bishop, the Bretons lighted a lantern with which they were furnished, and Porthos assured his friend that he felt as strong as ever.

"Let us visit the canoe," said Aramis, "and satisfy ourselves at once what it will hold."

"Do not go too near with the light," said the patron, Yves; "for, as you desired me, monseigneur, I have placed under the bench of the poop, in the coffer you know of, the barrel of powder and the musket-charges that you sent me from the fort."

"Very well," said Aramis; and, taking the lantern himself, he examined minutely all parts of the canoe, with the precautions of a man who is neither timid nor ignorant in the face of danger. The canoe was long, light, drawing little water, thin of keel; in short, one of those which have always been so well constructed at Belle-Isle; a little high in its sides, solid upon the water, very manageable, furnished with planks which, in uncertain weather, form a sort of bridge over which the waves glide and which protect the rowers. In two well-closed coffers, placed beneath the benches of the prow and the poop, Aramis found bread, biscuit, dried fruits, a quarter of bacon, a good provision of water in leather bottles; the whole forming rations sufficient for people who did not mean to quit the coast, and could be able to revictual, if necessity commanded. The arms, eight muskets, and as many horse-pistols, were in good condition, and all loaded. There were additional oars, in case of accident, and that little sail called *trinquet*, which assists the speed of the canoe at the same time the boatmen row, which is so useful when the breeze is slack. When Aramis had seen all these things, and appeared satisfied with the result of his inspection, "Let us consult, Porthos," said he, "to know if we must endeavor to get the bark out by the unknown extremity of the grotto, following the descent and the shade of the cavern, or whether it be better, in the open air, to make it slide upon the rollers through the bushes, leveling the road of the little beach, which is but twenty feet high, and gives at its foot, in the tide, three or four fathoms of good water upon a sound bottom."

"It must be as you please, monseigneur," replied the patron Yves, respectfully; "but I don't believe that by the slope of the cavern, and in the dark, in which we shall be obliged to maneuver our boat, the road will be so convenient as in the open air. I know the beach well, and can certify that it is as smooth as a grass-plot in a garden; the interior of the grotto, on the contrary, is rough; without again reckoning, monseigneur, that at the extremity we shall come to the trench which leads into the sea, and perhaps the canoe will not pass down it."

"I have made my calculations," said the bishop, "and I am certain it would pass."

"So be it; I wish it may, monseigneur," continued the patron; "but your greatness knows very well that to make it reach the extremity of the trench, there is an enormous stone to be lifted—that under which the fox always passes, and which closes the trench up like a door."

"That can be raised," said Porthos, "that is nothing."

"Oh! I know that monseigneur has the strength of ten men," replied Yves; "but that is giving monseigneur a great deal of trouble."

"I think the patron may be right," said Aramis; "let us try the open-air passage."

"The more so monseigneur," continued the fisherman, "that we should not be able to embark before day, it would require so much labor, and that as soon as daylight appears a good *ve dette* placed outside the grotto would be necessary, indispensable even, to watch the maneuvers of the lighters or the cruiser that are upon the lookout for us."

"Yes, yes, Yves, your reasons are good; we will go by the beach."

And the three robust Bretons went to the boat, and were beginning to place their rollers underneath it to put it in motion, when the distant barking of dogs was heard, proceeding from the interior.

Aramis darted out of the grotto, followed by Porthos. Dawn just tinted with purple and white the waves and the plain; through the dim light the young melancholy firs waved their tender branches over the pebbles, and long flights of crows were skimming with their black wings over the thin fields of buckwheat. In a quarter of an hour it would be clear daylight; the awakened birds joyously announced it to all nature. The bark

gs which had been heard, which had stopped the three fisher-
en engaged in moving the boat, and had brought Aramis and
rthos out of the cavern, were prolonged in a deep gorge
thin about a league of the grotto.

"It is a pack of hounds," said Porthos; "the dogs are upon
scent."

"Who can be hunting at such a moment as this?" said Aramis.

"And this way, particularly," continued Porthos, "this way,
ere they may expect the army of the royalists."

"The noise comes nearer. Yes, you are right, Porthos, the
gs are on a scent. But, Yves," cried Aramis, "come here!
me here!"

Yves ran toward him, letting fall the cylinder which he was
out to place under the boat when the bishop's call interrupted
n.

"What is the meaning of this hunt, patron?" said Porthos.

"Eh! monseigneur, I cannot understand it," replied the
eton. "It is not at such a moment that the Seigneur de Loc-
aria would hunt. No, and yet the dogs——"

"Unless they have escaped from the kennel."

"No," said Goenne, "they are not the Seigneur de Locmaria's
unds."

"In common prudence," said Aramis, "let us go back into the
otto; the voices evidently draw nearer; we shall soon know
at we have to trust to."

They re-entered, but had scarcely proceeded a hundred steps
the darkness, when a noise like the hoarse sigh of a creature
distress resounded through the cavern, and breathless, rapid,
rrified, a fox passed like a flash of lightning before the
gitives, leaped over the boat, and disappeared, leaving behind
its sour scent, which was perceptible for several seconds un-
r the low vaults of the cave.

"The fox!" cried the Bretons, with the joyous surprise of
nters.

"Accursed chance!" cried the bishop, "our retreat is dis-
vered."

"How so?" said Porthos, "are we afraid of a fox?"

"Eh! my friend, what do you mean by that, and why do
u name the fox? It is not the fox alone, *pardieu!* But don't
u know, Porthos, that after the fox come hounds, and after
hounds men?"

Porthos hung his head. As if to confirm the words of Aramis,
y heard the yelping pack come with frightful swiftness upon

the trail of the animal. Six foxhounds burst out at once upon
little heath, with a cry resembling the noise of a triumph.

"There are the dogs, plain enough!" said Aramis, posted
the lookout behind a chink between two rocks; "now, who
the huntsmen?"

"If it is the Seigneur de Locmaria's," replied the patron, "
will leave the dogs to hunt the grotto, for he knows them, a
will not enter it himself, being quite sure that the fox will co
out at the other side; it is there he will go and wait for hir

"It is not the Seigneur de Locmaria who is hunting," repl
Aramis, turning pale in spite of his efforts to maintain a g
countenance.

"Who is it, then?" said Porthos.

"Look!"

Porthos applied his eye to the slit, and saw, at the summit
a hillock, a dozen horsemen, urging on their horses in the tr
of the dogs, shouting:

"Taïaut! taïaut!"

"The guards!" said he. "Yes, my friend, the king's guard

"The king's guards! do you say, monseigneur?" cried
Bretons, becoming pale in their turn.

"And Biscarrat at their head, mounted upon my gray hors
continued Aramis.

The hounds at the same moment rushed into the grotto I
an avalanche, and the depths of the cavern were filled with th
deafening cries.

"Ah! the devil!" said Aramis, resuming all his coolness
the sight of this certain, inevitable danger. "I am perfec
satisfied we are lost, but we have, at least, one chance left.
the guards who follow their hounds happen to discover there
an issue to the grotto, there is no more help for us, for on
tering they must see both us and our boat. The dogs must
go out of the cavern. The masters must not enter."

"That is clear," said Porthos.

"You understand," added Aramis, with the rapid precis
of command; "there are six dogs, which will be forced
stop at the great stone under which the fox has glided—but
the too narrow opening of which they shall be themsel
stopped and killed."

The Bretons sprung forward, knife in hand. In a few m
utes there was a lamentable concert of growls and mortal ho
ings—and then, nothing.

"That's well!" said Aramis coolly, "now for the masters!"

"What is to be done with them?" said Porthos.

"Wait their arrival, conceal ourselves, and kill them."

"Kill them?" replied Porthos.

"There are sixteen," said Aramis, "at least, at present."

"And well armed," added Porthos, with a smile of consolation.

"It will last about ten minutes," said Aramis. "To work!"

And with a resolute air, he took up a musket and placed his hunting-knife between his teeth.

"Yves, Goenne, and his son," continued Aramis, "will pass the muskets to us. You, Porthos, will fire when they are close. We shall have brought down eight before the others are aware of anything—that is certain; then all, there are five of us, we will dispatch the other eight, knife in hand."

"And poor Biscarrat?" said Porthos.

Aramis reflected a moment.

"Biscarrat the first," replied he coolly. "He knows us."

Chapter 48 — THE GROTTO

In spite of the sort of divination which was the remarkable side of the character of Aramis, the event, subject to the chances of things over which uncertainty presides, did not fall out exactly as the bishop of Vannes had foreseen. Biscarrat, better mounted than his companions, arrived the first at the opening of the grotto, and comprehended that the fox and the dogs were all ingulfed in it. Only struck by that superstitious error which every dark and subterraneous way naturally impresses upon the mind of man, he stopped at the outside of the grotto, and waited till his companions should have assembled round him.

"Well," asked the young men, coming up out of breath, and unable to understand the meaning of his inaction.

"Well, I cannot hear the dogs; they and the fox must be ingulfed in this cavern."

"They were too close up," said one of the guards, "to have lost scent all at once. Besides, we should hear them from one side or another. They must, as Biscarrat says, be in this grotto."

"But, then," said one of the young men, "why don't they give tongue?"

"It is strange!" said another.

"Well, but," said a fourth, "let us go into this grotto. Does it happen to be forbidden that we should enter it?"

"No," replied Biscarrat. "Only, as it looks as dark as a wolf's mouth, we might break our necks in it."

"Witness the dogs," said a guard, "who seem to have broken theirs."

"What the devil can have become of them?" asked the young men, in chorus.

And every master called his dog by his name, whistled to him in his favorite note, without a single one replying to either the call or the whistle.

"It is, perhaps, an enchanted grotto," said Biscarrat; "let us see."

And, jumping from his horse, he made a step into the grotto.

"Stop! stop! I will accompany you," said one of the guards, on seeing Biscarrat disappear in the shade of the cavern's mouth.

"No," replied Biscarrat, "there must be something extraordinary in the place—don't let us risk ourselves all at once. If in ten minutes you do not hear of me, you can come in, but not all at once."

"Be it so," said the young men, who, besides, did not see that Biscarrat ran much risk in the enterprise; "we will wait for you."

And, without dismounting from their horses, they formed a circle round the grotto.

Biscarrat entered then alone, and advanced through the darkness till he came in contact with the muzzle of Porthos' musket. The resistance which his chest met with astonished him; he naturally raised his hand and laid hold of the icy barrel. At the same instant Yves lifted a knife against the young man, which was about to fall upon him with all the force of a Breton's arm, when the iron wrist of Porthos stopped it halfway. Then, like low, muttering thunder his voice growled in the darkness:

"I will not have him killed!"

Biscarrat found himself between a protection and a threat, the one almost as terrible as the other. However brave the young man might be, he could not prevent a cry escaping him which Aramis immediately suppressed by placing a handkerchief over his mouth.

"Monsieur de Biscarrat," said he, in a low voice, "we mean you no harm, and you must know that, if you have recognized

; but at the first word, the first sigh, or the first breath, we all be forced to kill you as we have killed your dogs."

"Yes, I recognize you, gentlemen," said the officer, in a low ice. "But why are you here—what are you doing here? Unrtunate men, I thought you were in the fort!"

"And you, monsieur, you were to obtain conditions for us, I ink?"

"I did all I was able, messieurs, but——"

"But what?"

"But there are positive orders."

"To kill us?"

Biscarrat made no reply. It would have cost him too much to eak of the cord to gentlemen. Aramis understood the silence the prisoner.

"Monsieur de Biscarrat," said he, "you would be already ad if we had not had regard for your youth and our ancient sociation with your father; but you may yet escape from the ace by swearing that you will not tell your companions what u have seen."

"I will not only swear that I will not speak of it," said Biscarrat, "but I still further swear that I will do everything in e world to prevent my companions from setting foot in the otto."

"Biscarrat! Biscarrat!" cried several voices from the outside, ming like a whirlwind into the cave.

"Reply," said Aramis.

"Here I am!" cried Biscarrat.

"Now, be gone; we depend upon your loyalty."

And he left his hold of the young man, who hastily returned ward the light.

"Biscarrat! Biscarrat!" cried the voices, still nearer.

And the shadows of several human forms projected into the terior of the grotto.

Biscarrat rushed to meet his friends in order to stop them, d met them just as they were adventuring into the cave. amis and Porthos listened with the intense attention of men ose life depends upon a breath of air.

"Oh, oh!" exclaimed one of the guards, as he came to the ht, "how pale you are!"

"Pale!" cried another; "you ought to say livid."

"I?" said the young man, endeavoring to collect his faculs.

"In the name of Heaven! what has happened to you?" claimed all voices.

"You have not a drop of blood in your veins, my poo‍ friend," said one of them, laughing.

"Messieurs, it is serious," said another; "he is going t‍ faint; does any one of you happen to have any salts?"

And they all laughed.

All these interpellations, all these jokes crossed one anothe‍ round Biscarrat as the balls cross one another in the fire of *mêlee*. He recovered himself amid a deluge of interrogations.

"What do you suppose I have seen?" asked he. "I was to‍ hot when I entered the grotto, and I have been struck with th‍ cold; that is all."

"But the dogs, the dogs, have you seen them again—did yo‍ see anything of them—do you know anything about them?"

"I suppose they have gone out by another way."

"Messieurs," said one of the young men, "there is in tha‍ which is going on, in the paleness and silence of our friend, ‍ mystery which Biscarrat will not, or cannot reveal. Only, an‍ that is a certainty, Biscarrat has seen something in the grott‍ Well, for my part, I am very curious to see what it is, even ‍ it were the devil. To the grotto, messieurs, to the grotto!"

"To the grotto!" repeated all the voices. And the echo of th‍ cavern carried like a menace to Porthos and Aramis, "to th‍ grotto! to the grotto!"

Biscarrat threw himself before his companions.

"Messieurs, messieurs!" cried he, "in the name of Heaven‍ do not go in!"

"Why, what is there so terrific in the cavern?" asked sever‍ at once. "Come, speak, Biscarrat."

"Decidedly, it is the devil he has seen," repeated he who ha‍ before advanced that hypothesis.

"Well," said another, "if he has seen him, he need not b‍ selfish; he may as well let us have a look at him in our turns.‍

"Messieurs! messieurs! I beseech you," urged Biscarrat.

"Nonsense! let us pass!"

"Messieurs, I implore you not to enter!"

"Why, you went in yourself."

Then, one of the officers who—of a riper age than the othe‍ —had till this time remained behind, and had said nothing, a‍ vanced.

"Messieurs," said he, with a calmness which contrasted wit‍ the animation of the young men, "there is in this some perso‍ or something, that is not the devil; but which, whatever it ma‍ be, has had sufficient power to silence our dogs. We must kno‍ who this someone is, or what this something is."

Biscarrat made a last effort to stop his friends, but it was useless. In vain he threw himself before the most rash; in vain he clung to the rocks to bar the passage, the crowd of young men rushed into the cave, in the steps of the officer who had spoken last, but who had sprung in first, sword in hand, to face the unknown danger. Biscarrat, repulsed by his friends, not able to accompany them, without passing in the eyes of Porthos and Aramis for a traitor and a perjurer, with painfully attentive ear and still supplicating hands leaned against the rough side of a rock, which he thought must be exposed to the fire of the musketeers. As to the guards, they penetrated further and further, with cries that grew weaker as they advanced. All at once a discharge of musketry, growling like thunder, exploded beneath the vault. Two or three balls were flattened against the rock where Biscarrat was leaning. At the same instant cries, howlings, and imprecations burst forth, and the little troop of gentlemen reappeared—some pale, some bleeding—all enveloped in a cloud of smoke, which the outward air seemed to draw from the depths of the cavern.

"Biscarrat! Biscarrat!" cried the fugitives, "you knew there was an ambuscade in that cavern, and you have not warned us! Biscarrat, you are the cause that four of us have been killed! Woe be to you, Biscarrat!"

"You are the cause of my being wounded to death," said one of the young men, gathering his blood in his hand, and casting it into the face of Biscarrat. "My blood be upon your head!" And he rolled in agony at the feet of the young men.

"But, at least, tell us who is there?" cried several furious voices.

Biscarrat remained silent.

"Tell us, or die!" cried the wounded man, raising himself upon one knee, and lifting toward his companion an arm bearing a useless sword.

Biscarrat rushed toward him, opening his breast for the blow, but the wounded man fell back, not to rise again, uttering a groan which was his last. Biscarrat, with hair on end, haggard eyes, and bewildered head, advanced toward the interior of the cavern, saying:

"You are right. Death to me, who have allowed my companions to be assassinated. I am a base wretch!"

And, throwing away his sword, for he wished to die without defending himself, he rushed head foremost into the cavern. The others followed him. The eleven who remained out of sixteen imitated his example; but they did not go further than the first. A second discharge laid five upon the icy sand; and as it was impossible to see whence this murderous thunder issued, the others fell back with a terror that can be better imagined than expressed. But, far from flying, as the others had done, Biscarrat remained safe and sound, seated on a fragment of rock, and waited. There were only six gentlemen left.

"Seriously," said one of the survivors, "is it the devil?"

"*Ma foi!* it is much worse," said another.

"Ask Biscarrat, he knows."

"Where is Biscarrat?"

The young men looked round them, and saw that Biscarrat did not answer.

"He is dead!" said two or three voices.

"Oh, no!" replied another; "I saw him through the smoke, sitting quietly on a rock. He is in the cavern; he is waiting for us."

"He must know who are there."

"And how should he know them?"

"He was taken prisoner by the rebels."

"That is true. Well, let us call him, and learn from him whom we have to deal with."

And all voices shouted: "Biscarrat! Biscarrat!" But Biscarrat did not answer.

"Good!" said the officer who had shown so much coolness in the affair. "We have no longer any need of him; here are reinforcements coming."

In fact, a company of the guards, left in the rear by their officers, whom the ardor of the chase had carried away—from seventy-five to eighty men—arrived in good order, led by their captain and the first lieutenant. The five officers hastened to meet their soldiers; and, in a language the eloquence of which may be easily imagined, they related the adventure, and asked for aid. The captain interrupted them.

"Where are your companions?" demanded he.

"Dead!"

"But there were sixteen of you."

"Ten are dead. Biscarrat is in the cavern, and we are five."

"Biscarrat is, then, a prisoner?"

"Probably."

"No, for here he is—look!"

In fact, Biscarrat appeared at the opening of the grotto.

"He makes us a sign to come on," said the officer. "Come on!"

"Come on!" cried all the troop.

And they advanced to meet Biscarrat.

"Monsieur," said the captain, addressing Biscarrat, "I am assured that you know who the men are in that grotto, and who make such a desperate defense. In the king's name, I command you to declare what you know!"

"Captain," said Biscarrat, "you have no need to command me; my word has been restored to me this very instant, and I came in the name of these men."

"To tell me who they are?"

"To tell you they are determined to defend themselves to the death, unless you grant them good terms."

"How many are there of them, then?"

"There are two," said Biscarrat.

"There are two—and want to impose conditions upon us?"

"There are two, and they have already killed ten of our men."

"What sort of people are they—giants?"

"Better than that. Do you remember the history of the bastion St. Gervais, captain?"

"Yes; where four musketeers held out against an army."

"Well, these two men were of those musketeers."

"And their names?"

"At that period they were called Porthos and Aramis. Now, they are styled Monsieur d'Herblay and Monsieur du Vallon."

"And what interest have they in all this?"

"It is they who held Belle-Isle for Monsieur Fouquet."

A murmur ran through the ranks of the soldiers on hearing the two words, "Porthos and Aramis."

"The musketeers! the musketeers!" repeated they.

And among all these brave men, the idea that they were going to have a struggle against two of the oldest glories of the French army made a shiver, half enthusiasm, half terror, run through them. In fact, those four names—D'Artagnan, Athos, Porthos, and Aramis—were venerated among all who wore a sword; as, in antiquity, the names of Hercules, Theseus, Castor, and Pollux were venerated.

"Two men—and they have killed ten in two discharges! That impossible, Monsieur Biscarrat!"

"Eh! captain," replied the latter, "I do not tell you that they have not with them two or three men, as the musketeers of the bastion St. Gervais had two or three lackeys, but, believe me, captain, I have seen these men, I have been taken prisoner by them—I know they themselves alone could suffice to destroy a army."

"That we shall see," said the captain, "and that in a momen
too. Gentlemen, attention!"

At this reply no one stirred, and all prepared to obey. Bi
carrat alone risked a last attempt.

"Monsieur," said he, in a low voice, "believe me, let us pa
on our way. Those two men, those two lions you are going t
attack, will defend themselves to the death. They have alread
killed ten of our men; they will kill double the number, an
end by killing themselves, rather than surrender. What shall w
gain by fighting them?"

"We shall gain the consciousness, monsieur, of not havir
made either of the king's guards retire before two rebels. If
listened to your advice, monsieur, I should be a dishonore
man, and by dishonoring myself I should dishonor the arm
Forward, men!"

And he marched first as far as the opening of the grott
There he halted. The object of this halt was to give to Biscarr
and his companions time to describe to him the interior of th
grotto. Then, when he believed he had a sufficient acquaintan
with the places, he divided his company into three bodie
which were to enter successively, keeping up a sustained fi
in all directions. No doubt, in this attack they should lose fi
more men, perhaps ten; but, certainly, they must end l
taking the rebels, since there was no issue; and, at any rat
two men could not kill eighty.

"Captain," said Biscarrat, "I beg to be allowed to march
the head of the first platoon."

"So be it," replied the captain; "you have all the honor of
That is a present I make you."

"Thanks!" replied the young man, with all the firmness
his race.

"Take your sword, then."

"I shall go as I am, captain," said Biscarrat, "for I do n
go to kill, I go to be killed."

And, placing himself at the head of the first platoon, wi
his head uncovered and his arms crossed:

"March, gentlemen!" said he.

Chapter 49 — AN HOMERIC SONG

It is time to pass into the other camp, and to describe at once the combatants and the field of battle. Aramis and Porthos had gone to the grotto of Locmaria with the expectation of finding there their canoe ready armed, as well as the three Bretons, their assistants; and they at first hoped to make the bark pass through the little issue of the cavern, concealing, in that fashion, both their labors and their flight. The arrival of the fox and the dogs had obliged them to remain concealed. The grotto extended the space of about a hundred *toises*, to that little slope dominating a creek. Formerly a temple of the Celtic divinities, when Belle-Isle was still called Colonese, this grotto had seen more than one human sacrifice accomplished in its mysterious depths. The first entrance to the cavern was by a moderate descent, above which heaped-up rocks formed a low arcade; the interior, very unequal as to the ground, dangerous from the rocky inequalities of the vault, was subdivided into several compartments which commanded one another and joined one another by means of several rough, broken steps, fixed right and left, in enormous natural pillars. At the third compartment the vault was so low, the passage so narrow, that the bark would scarcely have passed without touching the two sides; nevertheless, in a moment of despair, wood softens and stone becomes compliant under the breath of human will. Such was the thought of Aramis, when, after having fought the fight he decided upon flight—a flight certainly dangerous, since all the assailants were not dead, and that, admitting the possibility of putting the bark to sea, they would have to fly in open day before the conquered, so interested, on recognizing their small number, in pursuing their conquerors. When the two discharges had killed ten men, Aramis, habituated to the windings of the cavern, went to reconnoiter them one by one—counted them, for the smoke prevented seeing outside; and he immediately commanded that the canoe should be rolled as far as the great cone, the closure of the liberating issue. Porthos collected all his strength, took the canoe up in his arms, and raised it up, while the Bretons made it run rapidly along the rollers. They had descended into the third compartment; they had arrived at the stone which walled up the outlet. Porthos seized this gigantic stone at its base, applied it to his robust shoulder, and gave a heave which made the wall crack. A cloud of dust fell from the vault with the ashes of ten thousand generations of sea-birds, whose nests stuck like cement to the rock. At the third shock the stone gave way; it oscillated for a minute. Porthos, placing his back against the neighboring rock, made an arch with his foot, which drove the block out of the calcareous masses which served for hinges and cramps. The stone fell, and daylight was visible, brilliant, radiant, which rushed into the cavern by the opening, and the blue sea appeared to the delighted Bretons. They then began to lift the bark over the barricade. Twenty more *toises*, and it might glide into the ocean. It was during this time that the company arrived, was drawn up by the captain, and disposed for either an escalade or an assault. Aramis watched over everything, to favor the labors of his friends. He saw the reinforcements, he counted the men, he convinced himself at a single glance of the insurmountable peril to which a fresh combat would expose them. To escape by sea, at the moment the cavern was about to be invaded, was impossible. In fact, the daylight which had just been admitted to the two last compartments had exposed to the soldiers the bark being rolled toward the sea, the two rebels within musket-shot, and one of their discharges would riddle the boat, if it did not kill the five navigators. Besides, supposing everything—if the bark escaped with the men on board of it, how could the alarm be suppressed—how could notice to the royal lighters be prevented? What could hinder the poor canoe, followed by sea and watched from the shore from succumbing before the end of the day? Aramis, digging his hands into his gray hair with rage, invoked the assistance of God and the assistance of the demon. Calling to Porthos, who was working alone more than all the rollers—whether of flesh or wood:

"My friend," said he, "our adversaries have just received a reinforcement."

"Ah, ah!" said Porthos quietly, "what is to be done, then?"

"To recommence the combat," said Aramis, "is hazardous."

"Yes," said Porthos, "for it is difficult to suppose that out of two one should not be killed, and certainly, if one of us were killed, the other would get himself killed also."

Porthos spoke these words with that heroic nature which, with him, grew greater with all the phases of matter.

Aramis felt it like a spur to his heart.

"We shall neither of us be killed, if you do what I tell you, iend Porthos."

"Tell me what."

"These people are coming down into the grotto?"

"Yes."

"We could kill about fifteen of them, but no more."

"How many are there in all?" asked Porthos.

"They have received a reinforcement of seventy-five men."

"Seventy-five and five, eighty. Ah, ah!" said Porthos.

"If they fire all at once they will riddle us with balls."

"Certainly they will."

"Without reckoning," added Aramis, "that the detonations ight occasion fallings-in of the cavern."

"Ay," said Porthos, "a piece of falling rock just now grazed y shoulder a little."

"You see, then!"

"Oh, it is nothing!"

"We must determine upon something quickly. Our Bretons ·e going to continue to roll the canoe toward the sea."

"Very well."

"We two will keep the powder, the balls, and the muskets ·re."

"But only two, my dear Aramis—we shall never fire three ·ots together," said Porthos innocently, "the defense by mus-·try is a bad one."

"Find a better, then."

"I have found one," said the giant eagerly; "I will place yself in ambuscade behind the pillar with this iron bar, and visible, unattackable, if they come in in floods, I can let my ·r fall upon their skulls, thirty times in a minute. *Hein!* what · you think of the project? You smile!"

"Excellent, dear friend, perfect! I approve it greatly; only ·u will frighten them, and half of them will remain outside to ·ke us by famine. What we want, my good friend, is the entire ·struction of the troop; a single man left standing ruins us."

"You are right, my friend; but how can we attract them, ·ay?"

"By not stirring, my good Porthos."

"Well, we won't stir, then; but when they shall be all to-·ether——"

"Then leave it to me, I have an idea."

"If it is thus, and your idea be a good one—and your idea ·most likely to be good—I am satisfied."

"To your ambuscade, Porthos, and count how many enter."

"But you, what will you do?"

"Don't trouble yourself about me; I have a task to perform.

"I think I can hear cries."

"It is they! To your post. Keep within reach of my voic and hand."

Porthos took refuge in the second compartment, which wa absolutely black with darkness. Aramis glided into the third the giant held in his hand an iron bar of about fifty poun weight. Porthos handled this lever, which had been used in rol ing the bark, with marvelous facility. During this time th Bretons had pushed the bark to the beach. In the enlightene compartment, Aramis, stooping and concealed, was busied i some mysterious maneuver. A command was given in a lou voice. It was the last order of the captain commandan Twenty-five men jumped from the upper rocks into the firs compartment of the grotto, and having taken their groun began to fire. The echoes growled, the hissing of the balls cu the air; an opaque smoke filled the vault.

"To the left! to the left!" cried Biscarrat, who, in his fir assault, had seen the passage to the second chamber, and wh animated by the smell of powder, wished to guide his soldier in that direction. The troop accordingly precipitated themselve to the left—the passage gradually growing narrower. Biscarra with his hands stretched forward, devoted to death, marched i advance of the muskets.

"Come on! come on!" exclaimed he; "I see daylight!"

"Strike, Porthos!" cried the sepulchral voice of Aramis.

Porthos breathed a heavy sigh—but he obeyed. The iron ba fell full and direct upon the head of Biscarrat, who was dea before he had ended his cry. Then the formidable lever ros ten times in ten seconds, and made ten corpses. The soldie could see nothing; they heard sighs and groans; they stum bled over dead bodies, but as they had no conception of th cause of all this, they came forward jostling one another. Th implacable bar, still falling, annihilated the first platoon, with out a single sound having warned the second, which was qu etly advancing, only this second, commanded by the captai had broken a thin fir, growing on the shore, and, with its resin ous branches twisted together, the captain had made a flam beau. On arriving at the compartment where Porthos, like th exterminating angel, had destroyed all he touched, the fir rank drew back in terror. No firing had replied to that of th guards, and yet their way was stopped by a heap of dead bo ies—they literally walked in blood. Porthos was still behind h pillar. The captain, on enlightening with the trembling flame of the fire this frightful carnage, of which he in vain sought the cause, drew back toward the pillar behind which Porthos was concealed. Then a gigantic hand issued from the shade, and fastened on the throat of the captain, who uttered a stifled rattle; his stretched-out arms beating the air, the torch fell and was extinguished in blood. A second after, the corpse of the captain fell close to the extinguished torch, and added another body to the heap of dead which blocked up the passage. All this was effected as mysteriously as if by magic. At hearing the rattling in the throat of the captain, the soldiers who accompanied him had turned round; they had caught a glimpse of his extended arms, his eyes starting from their sockets, and then the torch fell and they were left in darkness. From an unreflective, instinctive, mechanical feeling, the lieutenant cried:

"Fire!"

Immediately a volley of musketry flamed, thundered, roared in the cavern, bringing down enormous fragments from the vaults. The cavern was lighted for an instant by this discharge, and then immediately returned to a darkness rendered still thicker by the smoke. To this succeeded a profound silence, broken only by the steps of the third brigade, now entering the cavern.

Chapter 50 — THE DEATH OF A TITAN

At the moment when Porthos, more accustomed to the darkness than all these men coming from open daylight, was looking round him to see if in this night Aramis were not making him some signal, he felt his arm gently touched and a voice low as a breath murmured in his ear:

"Come!"

"Oh!" said Porthos.

"Hush!" said Aramis, if possible, still more softly.

And amid the noise of the third brigade, which continued to advance, amid the imprecations of the guards left alive, of the dying, rattling their last sigh, Aramis and Porthos glided imperceptibly along the granite walls of the cavern. Aramis led Porthos into the last but one compartment, and showed him, in a hollow of the rocky wall, a barrel of powder weighing from

seventy to eighty pounds, to which he had just attached a
match.

"My friend," said he to Porthos, "you will take this barrel,
the match of which I am going to set fire to, and throw it amid
our enemies; can you do so?"

"Parbleu!" replied Porthos, and he lifted the barrel with one
hand. "Light it!"

"Stop," said Aramis, "till they are all massed together, and
then, my Jupiter, hurl your thunderbolt among them!"

"Light it," repeated Porthos.

"On my part," continued Aramis, "I will join our Bretons
and help them to get the canoe to the sea. I will wait for you
on the shore; launch it strongly, and hasten to us."

"Light it," said Porthos a third time.

"But do you understand me?"

"Parbleu!" said Porthos again, with laughter that he did not
even attempt to restrain; "when a thing is explained to me, I
understand it; be gone, and give me the light."

Aramis gave the burning match to Porthos, who held out
his arm to him, his hands being engaged. Aramis pressed the
arm of Porthos with both his hands, and fell back to the outlet of the cavern where the three rowers awaited him.

Porthos, left alone, applied the spark bravely to the match.
The spark—a feeble spark, first principle of a conflagration—
shone in the darkness like a firefly, then was deadened against
the match which it inflamed, Porthos enlivening the flame with
his breath. The smoke was a little dispersed, and by the light
of the sparkling match objects might, for two seconds, be distinguished. It was a short but a splendid spectacle, that of this
giant, pale, bloody, his countenance lighted by the fire of the
match burning in surrounding darkness. The soldiers saw him—
they saw the barrel he held in his hand—they at once understood what was going to happen. Then, these men, already
filled with terror at the sight of what had been accomplished
—filled with terror at thinking of what was going to be accomplished—threw forth together one shriek of agony. Some endeavored to fly, but they encountered the third brigade which
barred their passage; others mechanically took aim and attempted to fire their discharged muskets; others fell upon
their knees. Two or three officers cried out to Porthos to promise him his liberty if he would spare their lives. The lieutenant
of the third brigade commanded his men to fire; but the guards
had before them their terrified companions, who served as a liv-

ng rampart for Porthos. We have said that the light produced
by the spark and the match did not last more than two seconds; but during these two seconds this is what it illumined—
in the first place, the giant, enlarged in the darkness; then, at
en paces from him, a heap of bleeding bodies, crushed, muti-
ated, in the midst of whom still lived some last struggle of
agony, which lifted the mass as a last respiration raises the
ides of a shapeless monster expiring in the night. Every breath
of Porthos, while enlivening the match, sent toward this heap
of bodies a sulphureous hue, mingled with streaks of purple.
In addition to this principal group, scattered about the grotto,
as the chance of death or the surprise of the blow had
stretched them, some isolated bodies seemed to threaten by
their gaping wounds. Above the ground, soaked by pools of
blood, rose, heavy and sparkling, the short, thick pillars of the
cavern, of which the strongly marked shades threw out the luminous particles. And all this was seen by the tremulous light
of a match attached to a barrel of powder, that is to say, a
torch which, while throwing a light upon the dead past, showed
he death to come.

As I have said, this spectacle did not last above two seconds. During this short space of time an officer of the third
brigade got together eight men armed with muskets, and,
through an opening, ordered them to fire upon Porthos. But
hey who received the order to fire trembled so that three
guards fell by the discharge, and the five other balls went hiss-
ng to splinter the vault, plow the ground, or indent the sides
of the cavern.

A burst of laughter replied to this volley; then the arm of
he giant swung round; then was seen to pass through the air,
like a falling star, the train of fire. The barrel, hurled a distance of thirty feet, cleared the barricade of the dead bodies,
and fell amid a group of shrieking soldiers, who threw themselves on their faces. The officer had followed the brilliant
rain in the air; he endeavored to precipitate himself upon the
barrel and tear out the match before it reached the powder it
contained. Useless devotedness! The air had made the flame
attached to the conductor more active; the match, which at
est might have burned five minutes, was consumed in thirty
seconds, and the infernal work exploded. Furious vortices, hiss-
ngs of sulphur and niter, devouring ravages of the fire
which caught to objects, the terrible thunder of the explosion,
his is what the second which followed the two seconds we

have described disclosed in that cavern, equal in horrors to a
cavern of demons. The rock split like planks of deal under the
ax. A jet of fire, smoke, and *débris* sprang up from the middle
of the grotto, enlarging as it mounted. The large walls of sile:
tottered and fell upon the sand, and the sand itself, an instru
ment of pain when launched from its hardened bed, riddled
the face with its myriads of cutting atoms. Cries, howling im
precations, and existences—all were extinguished in one im
mense crash.

The three first compartments became a gulf into which fel
back again, according to its weight, every vegetable, mineral
or human fragment. Then the lighter sand and ashes fell i
their turns, stretching like a gray winding-sheet and smokin
over those dismal funerals. And now, seek in this burning tomb
in this subterraneous volcano, seek for the king's guards wit
their blue coats laced with silver. Seek for the officers brillian
in gold; seek for the arms upon which they depended for thei
defense; seek for the stones that have killed them, the groun
that has borne them. One single man has made of all this
chaos more confused, more shapeless, more terrible than th
chaos which existed an hour before God had created the worl
There remained nothing of the three compartments—nothin
by which God could have known His own work. As to Portho
after having hurled the barrel of powder amid his enemies, h
had fled, as Aramis had directed him to do, and had gained th
last compartment, into which air, light, and sunshine pene
trated through the opening. Therefore, scarcely had he turne
the angle which separated the third compartment from th
fourth, than he perceived, at a hundred paces from him, th
bark dancing on the waves; there were his friends, there wa
liberty, there was life after victory. Six more of his formidabl
strides, and he would be out of the vault; out of the vaul
two or three vigorous springs, and he would reach the cano
Suddenly he felt his knees give way; his knees appeared pov
erless, his legs to yield under him.

"Oh, oh!" murmured he, "there is my fatigue seizing m
again! I can walk no further! What is this?"

Aramis perceived him through the opening, and unable t
conceive what could induce him to stop thus:

"Come on, Porthos! come on," he cried; "come quickly

"Oh!" replied the giant, making an effort which acted upo
every muscle of his body—"oh! but I cannot."

While saying these words, he fell upon his knees; but wit

his robust hands he clung to the rocks, and raised himself up again.

"Quick, quick!" repeated Aramis, bending forward toward the shore, as if to draw Porthos toward him with his arms.

"Here I am," stammered Porthos, collecting all his strength to make one step more.

"In the name of Heaven! Porthos, make haste! the barrel will blow up!"

"Make haste, monseigneur!" shouted the Bretons to Porthos, who was floundering as in a dream.

But there was no longer time; the explosion resounded, the earth gaped, the smoke which rushed through the large fissures obscured the sky; the sea flowed back, as if driven by the blast of fire which darted from the grotto as if from the jaws of a gigantic chimera; the reflux carried the bark out twenty *toises;* the rocks cracked to their base, and separated like blocks beneath the operation of wedges; a portion of the vault was carried up toward heaven, as if by rapid currents; the rose-colored and green fire of the sulphur, the black lava of the argellaceous liquefactions clashed and combated for an instant beneath a majestic dome of smoke; then, at first oscillated, then declined, then fell successively the long angles of rock which the violence of the explosion had not been able to uproot from their bed of ages; they bowed to one another like grave and slow old men, then, prostrating themselves, imbedded forever in their dusty tomb.

This frightful shock seemed to restore to Porthos the strength he had lost; he arose, himself a giant among these giants. But at the moment he was flying between the double edge of granite phantoms, these latter, which were no longer supported by the corresponding links, began to roll with a crash around this Titan, who looked as if precipitated from heaven amid rocks which he had just been launching at it. Porthos felt the earth beneath his feet shaken by this long rending. He extended his vast hands to the right and left to repulse the falling rocks. A gigantic block was held back by each of his extended hands; he bent his head and a third granite mass sunk between his two shoulders. For an instant the arms of Porthos had given way, but the Hercules united all his forces, and the two walls of the prison in which he was buried fell back slowly and gave him place. For an instant he appeared in this frame of granite like the ancient angel of chaos, but in pushing back the lateral rocks, he lost his point of support for the monolith

which weighed upon his strong shoulders, and the monolith, ly‐
ing upon him with all its weight, brought the giant down upon
his knees. The latteral rocks, for an instant pushed back, drew
together again, and added their weight to the primitive weight,
which would have been sufficient to crush ten men. The giant
fell without crying for help; he fell while answering Aramis
with words of encouragement and hope, for, thanks to the pow‐
erful arch of his hands, for an instant, he might believe that,
like Enceladus, he should shake off the triple load. But by de‐
grees Aramis saw the block sink; the hands strung for an
instant, the arms, stiffened for a last effort, gave way, the ex‐
tended shoulders sank, wounded and torn, and the rock con‐
tinued to lower gradually.

"Porthos! Porthos!" cried Aramis, tearing his hair. "Por‐
thos! where are you? Speak!"

"There, there!" murmured Porthos, with a voice growing
evidently weaker, "patience, patience!"

Scarcely had he pronounced these words, when the impulse
of the fall augmented the weight; the enormous rock sank
down, pressed by the two others which sank in from the sides,
and, as it were, swallowed up Porthos in a sepulcher of broken
stones. On hearing the dying voice of his friend, Aramis had
sprung to land. Two of the Bretons followed him, with each a
lever in his hand—one being sufficient to take care of the bark.
The last rattles of the valiant struggler guided them amid the
ruins. Aramis, animated, active, and young as at twenty, sprang
toward the triple mass, and with his hands, delicate as those of
a woman, raised by a miracle of vigor a corner of the immense
sepulcher of granite. Then he caught a glimpse, in the darkness
of that grave, of the still brilliant eye of his friend, to whom
the momentary lifting of the mass restored that moment of
respiration. The two men came rushing up, grasped their iron
levers, united their triple strength, not merely to raise it, but
to sustain it. All was useless. The three men slowly gave way
with cries of grief, and the rough voice of Porthos, seeing them
exhaust themselves in a useless struggle, murmured, in a jeer‐
ing tone, those supreme words which came to his lips with the
last respiration:

"Too heavy!"

After which the eye darkened and closed, the face became
pale, the hand whitened, and the Titan sank quite down,
breathing his last sigh. With him sank the rock, which, even
in his agony, he had still held up. The three men dropped the
levers, which rolled upon the tumulary stone. Then, breathless,

ale, his brow covered with sweat, Aramis listened, his breast
oppressed, his heart ready to break.

Nothing more! The giant slept the eternal sleep, in the
sepulcher which God had made to his measure.

Chapter 51 — THE EPITAPH
OF PORTHOS

Aramis, silent icy, trembling like a timid child, arose shiv-
ring from the stone. A Christian does not walk upon tombs.
But though capable of standing, he was not capable of walking.
t might be said that something of dead Porthos had just died
within him. His Bretons surrounded him; Aramis yielded to
heir kind exertions, and the three sailors, lifting him up,
arried him into the canoe. Then, having laid him down upon
the bench near the rudder, they took to their oars, preferring
o get off by rowing to hoisting a sail, which might betray
hem.

Of all that leveled surface of the ancient grotto of Locmaria,
f all that flattened shore, one single little hillock attracted
heir eyes. Aramis never removed his from it; and, at a dis-
ance out in the sea, in proportion as the shore receded, the
menacing and proud mass of rock seemed to draw itself up, as
ormerly Porthos used to draw himself up, and raise a smiling
nd invincible head toward heaven, like that of the honest and
valiant friend, the strongest of the four, and yet the first dead.
Strange destiny of these men of brass! The most simple of
eart allied to the most crafty; strength of body guided by
ubtlety of mind; and in the decisive moment, when vigor alone
ould save mind and body, a stone, a rock, a vile and material
veight, triumphed over vigor, and, falling upon the body, drove
ut the mind.

Worthy Porthos! born to help other men, always ready to
acrifice himself for the safety of the weak, as if God had only
iven him strength for that purpose; when dying he only
hought he was carrying out the conditions of his compact with
Aramis, a compact, however, which Aramis alone had drawn up,
nd which Porthos had only known to suffer by its terrible soli-
arity. Noble Porthos! of what good are the châteaus over-
owing with sumptuous furniture, the forests overflowing with
ame, the lakes overflowing with fish, the cellars overflowing

with wealth! Of what good are the lackeys in brilliant liveries
and in the midst of them Mousqueton, proud of the power dele
gated by thee! Oh, noble Porthos! careful heaper-up of treas
ures, was it worth while to labor to sweeten and gild life, to
come upon a desert shore, to the cries of sea-birds, and lay
thyself, with broken bones, beneath a cold stone? Was it worth
while, in short, noble Porthos, to heap so much gold, and not
have even the distich of a poor poet engraven upon thy monu
ment? Valiant Porthos! He still, without doubt, sleeps, lost
forgotten, beneath the rock which the shepherds of the heath
take for the gigantic abode of a *dolmen*. And so many twining
branches, so many mosses, caressed by the bitter wind of the
ocean, so many vivacious lichens have soldered the sepulchre
to the earth, that the passenger will never imagine that such a
block of granite can ever have been supported by the shoulders
of one man.

Aramis, still pale, still icy, his heart upon his lips, Aramis
looked, even till with the last ray of daylight the shore faded
on the horizon. Not a word escaped his lips, not a sigh rose
from his deep breast. The superstitious Bretons looked at him
trembling. The silence was not of a man, it was of a statue.
In the meantime, with the first gray lines that descended from
the heavens, the canoe had hoisted its little sail, which, swell
ing with the kisses of the breeze, and carrying them rapidly from
the coast, made brave way with its head toward Spain, across
the terrible Gulf of Gascony, so rife with tempests. But
scarcely half an hour after the sail had been hoisted the rowers
became inactive, reclining upon their benches, and making an
eye-shade with their hands, pointed out to each other a white
spot which appeared on the horizon as motionless as is in ap
pearance a gull rocked by the insensible respiration of the
waves. But that which might have appeared motionless to ordi
nary eyes was moving at a quick rate to the experienced eye of
the sailor; that which appeared stationary on the ocean was
cutting a rapid way through it. For some time, seeing the pro
found torpor in which their master was plunged, they did no
dare to rouse him, and satisfied themselves with exchanging
their conjectures in a low, disturbed voice. Aramis, in fact, so
vigilant, so active—Aramis, whose eye, like that of the lynx
watched without ceasing, and saw better by night than by day
—Aramis seemed to sleep in the despair of his soul. An hour
passed thus, during which daylight gradually disappeared but
during which also the sail in view gained so swiftly on the bark
that Goenne, one of the three sailors, ventured to say aloud

"Monseigneur, we are being chased!"

Aramis made no reply; the ship still gained upon them. Then, of their own accord, two of the sailors, by the direction of the patron, Yves, lowered the sail, in order that that single point which appeared above the surface of the waters should cease to be a guide to the eye of the enemy who was pursuing them. On the part of the ship in sight, on the contrary, two more small sails were run up at the extremities of the masts. Unfortunately, it was the time of the finest and longest days of the year, and the moon, in all her brilliancy, succeeded to this inauspicious daylight. The *balancelle*, which was pursuing the little bark before the wind, had then still half an hour of twilight, and a whole night almost as light as day.

"Monseigneur, monseigneur! we are lost!" said the patron. "Look! they see us although we have lowered our sail."

"That is not to be wondered at," murmured one of the sailors, "since they say that, by the aid of the devil, the people of the cities have fabricated instruments with which they see as well at a distance as near, by night as well as by day."

Aramis took a telescope from the bottom of the boat, arranged it silently, and passing it to the sailor:

"Here!" said he, "look."

The sailor hesitated.

"Don't be alarmed," said the bishop, "there is no sin in it; and if there is any sin, I will take it upon myself."

The sailor lifted the glass to his eye, and uttered a cry. He believed that the vessel, which appeared to be distant about a cannon-shot, had suddenly and at a single bound cleared the distance. But, on withdrawing the instrument from his eye, he saw that, except the way which the *balancelle* had been able to make during that short instant, it was still at the same distance.

"So," murmured the sailor, "they can see us as we see them."

"They see us," said Aramis, and sank again into his impassibility.

"How—they see us!" said Yves. "Impossible!"

"Well, patron, look yourself," said the sailor. And he passed to him the glass.

"Monseigneur assures me that the devil has nothing to do with this?" asked the patron.

Aramis shrugged his shoulders.

The patron lifted the glass to his eyes.

"Oh, monseigneur," said he, "it is a miracle; they are there;

it seems as if I were going to touch them. Twenty-five men, at least! Ah! I see the captain forward. He holds a glass like this, and is looking at us. Ah! he turns round, and gives an order; they are rolling a piece of cannon forward—they are charging it—they are painting it. *Miséricorde!* they are firing at us!"

And, by a mechanical movement, the patron took the glass off, and the objects, sent back to the horizon, appeared again in their true aspect. The vessel was still at the distance of nearly a league, but the maneuver announced by the patron was not less real. A light cloud of smoke appeared under the sails, more blue than they, and spreading like a flower opening; then, at about a mile from the little canoe, they saw the ball take the crown of two or three waves, dig a white furrow in the sea, and disappear at the end of that furrow, as inoffensive as the stone with which, at play, a boy makes ducks and drakes. That was at once a menace and a warning.

"What is to be done?" asked the patron.

"They will sink us!" said Goenne; "give us absolution, monseigneur!"

And the sailors fell on their knees before him.

"You forget that they can see you," said he.

"That is true," said the sailors, ashamed of their weakness. "Give us your orders, monseigneur; we are ready to die for you."

"Let us wait," said Aramis.

"How—let us wait?"

"Yes; do you not see, as you just now said, that if we endeavor to fly, they will sink us?"

"But, perhaps," the patron ventured to say, "perhaps, by the favor of the night, we could escape them."

"Oh!" said Aramis, "they have, little doubt, some Greek fire to lighten their own course and ours likewise."

At the same moment, as if the little vessel wished to reply to the appeal of Aramis, a second cloud of smoke mounted slowly to the heavens, and from the bosom of that cloud sparkled an arrow of flame, which described its parabola like a rainbow, and fell into the sea, where it continued to burn, illuminating a space of a quarter of a league in diameter.

The Bretons looked at one another in terror.

"You see plainly," said Aramis, "it will be better to wait for them."

The oars dropped from the hands of the sailors, and the bark, ceasing to make way, rocked motionless on the summits f the waves. Night came on, but the vessel still approached earer. It might be said it redoubled its speed with the darkess. From time to time, as a bloody-necked vulture rears its ead out of its nest, the formidable Greek fire darted from its ides, and cast its flame into the ocean like an incandescent now. At last it came within musketshot. All the men were on eck, arms in hand; the cannoneers were at their guns, the atches were burning. It might be thought they were about to oard a frigate and to combat a crew superior in number to heir own, and not to take a canoe manned by four people.

"Surrender!" cried the commander of the *balancelle*, with he aid of his speaking-trumpet.

The sailors looked at Aramis. Aramis made a sign with his ead. The patron, Yves, waved a white cloth at the end of a aff. This was like striking their flag. The vessel came on like race-horse. It launched a fresh Greek fire, which fell within wenty paces of the little canoe, and threw a stronger light upon hem than the most ardent ray of the sun could have done.

"At the first sign of resistance," cried the commander of the *alancelle*, "fire!"

And the soldiers brought their muskets to the present.

"Did not we say we surrender?" said the patron, Yves.

"Living! living! captain!" cried some highly excited soliers; "they must be taken living!"

"Well, yes—living," said the captain.

Then, turning toward the Bretons:

"Your lives are all safe, my friends!" cried he, "except the Chevalier d'Herblay."

Aramis started imperceptibly. For an instant his eye was xed upon the depths of the ocean, enlightened by the last ashes of the Greek fire—flashes which ran along the sides of he waves, played upon their crests like plumes, and rendered till more dark, more mysterious, and more terrible the abysses hey covered.

"Do you hear, monseigneur?" said the sailors.

"Yes."

"What are your orders?"

"Accept."

"But you, monseigneur?"

Aramis leaned still more forward, and played with the ends f his long, white fingers with the green water of the sea, to hich he turned, smiling as to a friend.

"Accept!" repeated he.

"We accept," repeated the sailors; "but what security have we?"

"The word of a gentleman," said the officer. "By my rank and by my name, I swear that all but Monsieur le Chevalier d'Herblay shall have their lives spared. I am lieutenant of the king's frigate, the Pomona, and my name is Louis Constant de Pressigny."

With a rapid gesture, Aramis—already bent over the side of the bark toward the sea—with a rapid gesture, Aramis raised his head, drew himself up, and with a flashing eye, and a smile upon his lips:

"Throw out the ladder, messieurs!" said he, as if the command had belonged to him.

He was obeyed. Then Aramis, seizing the rope-ladder, instead of the terror which was expected to be displayed upon his countenance, the surprise of the sailors of the *balancelle* was great when they saw him walk straight up to the commander, with a firm step, look at him earnestly, make a sign to him with his hand, a mysterious and unknown sign, at the sight of which the officer turned pale, trembled, and bowed his head. Without saying a word, Aramis then raised his hand close to the eyes of the commander, and showed him the collet of a ring which he wore on the ring-finger of his left hand. And while making this sign, Aramis, draped in cold, silent, and haughty majesty, had the air of an emperor giving his hand to be kissed. The commandant, who for a moment had raised his head, bowed a second time with marks of the most profound respect. Then, stretching his hand out, in his turn, toward the poop, that is to say, toward his own cabin, he drew back to allow Aramis to go first. The three Bretons, who had come on board after the bishop, looked at one another, stupefied. The crew were struck with silence. Five minutes after, the commander called the second lieutenant, who returned immediately, ordering the head to be put toward Corunna. While the given order was being executed Aramis reappeared upon the deck, and took a seat near the *bastingage*. The night had fallen, the moon had not yet risen, and yet Aramis looked incessantly toward Belle-Isle. Yves then approached the captain, who had returned to take his post in the stern, and said, in a low and humble voice:

"What course are we to follow, captain?"

"We take what course monseigneur pleases," replied the officer.

Aramis passed the night leaning upon the *bastingage*. Yves

n approaching him the next morning, remarked that "the night
must have been very humid, for the wood upon which the
bishop's head had rested was soaked with dew."

Who knows?—that dew was, perhaps, the first tears that had
ever fallen from the eyes of Aramis!

What epitaph would have been worth that? Good Porthos!

Chapter 52 — THE ROUND
OF M. DE GESVRES

D'Artagnan was not accustomed to resistance like that he had
just experienced. He returned, profoundly irritated, to Nantes.
Irritation with this vigorous man vented itself in an impetuous
attack, which few people hitherto, were they king, were they
giants, had been able to resist. D'Artagnan, trembling with
rage, went straight to the castle, and asked to speak to the
king. It might be about seven o'clock in the morning, and, since
his arrival at Nantes, the king had been an early riser. But on
arriving at the little corridor with which we are acquainted,
D'Artagnan found M. de Gesvres, who stopped him very politely, telling him not to speak too loud and disturb the king.

"Is the king asleep?" said D'Artagnan. "Well, I will let him
sleep. But about what o'clock do you suppose he will rise?"

"Oh, in about two hours; the king has been up all night."

D'Artagnan took his hat again, bowed to M. de Gesvres,
and returned to his own apartments. He came back at half past
nine, and was told that the king was at breakfast.

"That will just suit me," said D'Artagnan; "I will talk
to the king while he is eating."

M. de Brienne reminded D'Artagnan that the king would
not receive any one during his repasts.

"But," said D'Artagnan, looking askant at Brienne, "you do
know, perhaps, monsieur, that I have the privilege of *en-
rée* anywhere, and at any hour."

Brienne took the hand of the captain kindly, and said:

"Not at Nantes, dear Monsieur d'Artagnan. The king in this
journey has changed everything."

D'Artagnan, a little softened, asked about what o'clock the
king would have finished his breakfast.

"We don't know."

"How—don't know? What does that mean? You don't know

how much time the king devotes to eating? It is generally an
hour; and, if we admit that the air of the Loire gives an additional appetite, we will extend it to an hour and a half; that is
enough, I think. I will wait where I am."

"Oh, dear Monsieur d'Artagnan, the order is not to allow any
person to remain in this corridor; I am on guard for that purpose."

D'Artagnan felt his anger mounting a second time to his
brain. He went out quickly, for fear of complicating the affair by a display of ill-humor. As soon as he was out he began
to reflect.

"The king," said he, "will not receive me, that is evident.
The young man is angry; he is afraid of the words I may speak
to him. Yes; but in the meantime Belle-Isle is besieged, and
my two friends are taken or killed. Poor Porthos! As to Master Aramis, he is always full of resources, and I am quite easy
on his account. But, no, no; Porthos is not yet an invalid, and
Aramis is not yet in his dotage. The one with his arm, the other
with his imagination, will find work for his majesty's soldiers.
Who knows if these brave men may not get up for the edifica-
tion of his most Christian majesty a little bastion of St. Gervais! I don't despair of it. They have cannon and a garrison.
And yet," continued D'Artagnan, "I don't know whether it
would not be better to stop the combat. For myself alone, I
will not put up with either surly looks or treason on the part
of the king; but for my friends, rebuffs, insults, I have a right
to receive everything. Shall I go to Monsieur Colbert? Now
there is a man whom I must acquire the habit of terrifying. I
will go to Monsieur Colbert."

And D'Artagnan set forward bravely to find M. Colbert;
but he was told he was working with the king, at the Castle of
Nantes.

"Good!" cried he, "the times are returned in which I measured my steps from De Tréville to the cardinal, from the cardinal to the queen, from the queen to Louis XIII. Truly is it
said that men, in growing old, become children again. To the
castle then!"

He returned thither. M. de Lyonne was coming out. He
gave D'Artagnan both hands, but told him that the king had
been busy all the preceding evening and all night, and that orders had been given that no one should be admitted.

"Not even the captain who takes the order?" cried D'Artagnan. "I think that is rather too strong."

"Not even he," said M. de Lyonne.

"Since that is the case," replied D'Artagnan, wounded to the heart, "since the captain of the musketeers, who has always entered the king's chamber, is no longer allowed to enter it, his cabinet, or his *salle-à-manger*, either the king is dead, or his captain is in disgrace. In either case, he can no longer want him. Do me the favor, then, Monsieur de Lyonne, who are in favor, to return and tell the king plainly, I send him my resignation."

"D'Artagnan, beware of what you are doing!"

"For friendship's sake, go!" and he pushed him gently toward the cabinet.

"Well, I will go," said Lyonne.

D'Artagnan waited, walking about the corridor in no enviable mood. Lyonne returned.

"Well, what did the king say?" exclaimed D'Artagnan.

"He simply answered, 'That is well,'" replied Lyonne.

"That that was well!" said the captain, with an explosion. "That is to say, that he accepts it? Good! Now, then, I am free. I am only a plain citizen, Monsieur de Lyonne. I have the pleasure of bidding you good-by. Farewell, castle, corridor, antechamber! a bourgeois, about to breathe at liberty, takes his farewell of you."

And without waiting longer, the captain sprang from the terrace down the staircase where he had picked up the fragments of Gourville's letter. Five minutes after, he was at the hostelry, where, according to the custom of all great officers who have lodgings at the castle, he had taken what was called his city chamber. But when arrived there, instead of throwing off his sword and cloak, he took his pistols, put his money into a large leather purse, sent for his horses from the castle stables, and gave orders for reaching Vannes during the night. Everything went on according to his wishes. At eight o'clock in the evening he was putting his foot in the stirrup, when M. de Gesvres appeared at the head of twelve guards, in front of the hostelry. D'Artagnan saw all from the corner of his eye; he could not fail seeing thirteen men and thirteen horses. But he feigned not to observe anything, and was about to put his horse in motion. Gesvres rode up to him.

"Monsieur d'Artagnan!" said he, aloud.

"Ah, Monsieur de Gesvres! Good-evening!"

"One would say you were getting on horseback."

"More than that—I am mounted, as you see."

"It is fortunate I have met with you."

"Were you looking for me, then?"

"*Mon Dieu!* yes."

"On the part of the king, I will wager?"

"Yes."

"As I, three days ago, went in search of Monsieur Fouquet?"

"Oh!"

"Nonsense! It is of no use being delicate with me; that is all labor lost. Tell me at once you are come to arrest me."

"To arrest you? Good heavens, no!"

"Why do you come to accost me with twelve horsemen at your heels, then?"

"I am making my round."

"That isn't bad. And so you pick me up in your round, eh?"

"I don't pick you up; I meet with you, and I beg you to come with me."

"Where?"

"To the king."

"Good!" said D'Artagnan, with a bantering air; "the king has nothing to do at last!"

"For Heaven's sake, captain," said M. de Gesvres, in a low voice, to the musketeer, "do not compromise yourself! These men hear you."

D'Artagnan laughed aloud, and replied:

"March! People who are arrested are placed between the six first guards and the six last."

"But as I do not arrest you," said M. de Gesvres, "you will march behind, with me, if you please."

"Well," said D'Artagnan, "that is very polite, duc, and you are right in being so; for if ever I had had to make my rounds near your *chambre-de-ville*, I should have been courteous to you, I assure you, by the faith of a gentleman. Now, one favor more: what does the king want with me?"

"Oh, the king is furious!"

"Very well; the king, who has thought it worth while to be furious, may take the trouble of getting calm again; that is all. I shan't die of that. I will swear."

"No, but——"

"But—I shall be sent to keep company with poor Monsieur Fouquet. *Mordioux!* That is a gallant man, a worthy man! We shall live very sociably together, I will be bound."

"Here we are at our place of destination," said the duke. "Captain, for heaven's sake, be calm with the king!"

"Ah, ah! you are playing the brave man with me, duc," said D'Artagnan, throwing one of his defiant glances over De Gesvres. "I have been told that you are ambitious of uniting your guards with my musketeers. This strikes me as a capital opportunity."

"I will take devilish good care not to avail myself of it, captain."

"And why not?"

"Oh, for many reasons—in the first place, for this: if I were to succeed you in the musketeers, after having arrested you——"

"Ah! then you admit you have arrested me?"

"No, I don't."

"Say met me, then. So, you were saying, *if* you were to succeed me, after having arrested me?"

"Your musketeers, at the first exercise with ball cartridges, would all fire toward me, by mistake."

"Ah! as to that, I won't say, for the fellows do love me a little."

Gesvres made D'Artagnan pass in first, and took him straight to the cabinet, where the king was waiting for his captain of the musketeers, and placed himself behind his colleague in the antechamber. The king could be heard distinctly, speaking aloud to Colbert in the same cabinet where Colbert might have heard, a few days before, the king speaking aloud with M. d'Artagnan. The guards remained as a mounted picket before the principal gate; and the report was quickly spread through the city that M. le Capitaine of the Musketeers had just been arrested by order of the king. Then these men were seen to be in motion, as in the good old times of Louis XIII. and M. de Tréville; groups were formed, the staircases were filled; vague murmurs, issued from the court below, came rolling up to the upper stories, like the hoarse moaning of the tidewaves. M. de Gesvres became very uneasy. He looked at his guards, who, after being interrogated by the musketeers who had just got among their ranks, began to shun them with a manifestation of innocence. D'Artagnan was certainly less disturbed than M. de Gesvres, the captain of the guards, was. As soon as he entered he had seated himself on the ledge of a window, whence, with his eagle glance, he saw all that was going on, without the least emotion. None of the progress of the fermentation which had manifested itself at the report of his arrest had escaped him. He foresaw the moment when the explosion would take place; and we know that his previsions were pretty correct.

"It would be very whimsical," thought he, "if, this evening, my prætorians should make me King of France. How I should laugh!"

But, at the height, all was stopped. Guards, musketeers, officers, soldiers, murmurs, and uneasiness, all dispersed, vanished, died away; no more tempest, no more menace, no more sedition. One word had calmed all the waves. The king had desired Brienne to say:

"Hush, messieurs! you disturb the king."

D'Artagnan sighed.

"All is over!" said he; "the musketeers of the present day are not those of His Majesty Louis XIII. All is over!"

"Monsieur d'Artagnan, to the king's apartment!" cried an usher.

Chapter 53 — KING LOUIS XIV.

The king was seated in his cabinet, with his back turned toward the door of entrance. In front of him was a mirror, in which, while turning over his papers, he could see with a glance those who came in. He did not take any notice of the entrance of D'Artagnan, but laid over his letters and plans the large silk cloth which he made use of to conceal his secrets from the importunate. D'Artagnan understood his play, and kept in the background; so that, at the end of a minute, the king, who heard nothing, and saw nothing but with the corner of his eye, was obliged to cry:

"Is not Monsieur d'Artagnan there?"

"I am here, sire," replied the musketeer, advancing.

"Well, monsieur," said the king, fixing his clear eye upon D'Artagnan, "what have you to say to me?"

"I, sire!" replied the latter, who watched the first, blow of his adversary to make a good retort; "I have nothing to say to your majesty, unless it be that you have caused me to be arrested, and here I am."

The king was going to reply that he had not had D'Artagnan arrested, but the sentence appeared too much like an excuse, and he was silent. D'Artagnan likewise preserved an obstinate silence.

"Monsieur," at length resumed the king, "what did I charge you to go and do at Belle-Isle? Tell me, if you please."

The king, while speaking these words, looked fixedly at his

aptain. Here D'Artagnan was too fortunate; the king seemed o place the game in his hands.

"I believe," replied he, "that your majesty does me the onor to ask what I went to Belle-Isle to do?"

"Yes, monsieur."

"Well, sire, I know nothing about it; it is not of me that uestion should be asked, but of that infinite number of offi- ers of all kinds, to whom have been given an infinite number f orders of all kinds, while to me, head of the expedition, othing precise was ordered."

The king was wounded; he showed it by his reply.

"Monsieur," said he, "orders have only been given to such s were judged faithful."

"And, therefore, I have been astonished, sire," retorted the usketeer, "that a captain like myself, who ranks with a maré- hal of France, should have found himself under the orders f five or six lieutenants or majors, good to make spies of, pos- ibly, but not at all fit to conduct warlike expeditions. It was pon this subject I came to demand an explanation of your ajesty, when I found the door closed against me, which, the st insult offered to a brave man, has led me to quit your ajesty's service."

"Monsieur," replied the king, "you still believe you are liv- g in an age when kings were, as you complain of having been, nder the orders and at the discretion of their inferiors. You ppear too much to forget that a king owes an account of his ctions to none but God."

"I forget nothing at all, sire," said the musketeer, wounded y this lesson. "Besides, I do not see in what an honest man, hen he asks of his king how he has ill-served him, offends im."

"You have ill-served me, monsieur, by taking part with my nemies against me."

"Who are your enemies, sire?"

"The men I sent you to fight with."

"Two men the enemies of the whole of your majesty's rmy? That is incredible!"

"You have no power to judge of my will."

"But I have to judge of my own friendships, sire."

"He who serves his friends does not serve his master."

"I have so well understood that, sire, that I have respect- lly offered your majesty my resignation."

"And I have accepted it, monsieur," said the king. "Before

being separated from you, I was willing to prove to you that I know how to keep my word."

"Your majesty has kept more than your word, for your majesty has had me arrested," said D'Artagnan, with his cold, bantering air; "you did not promise me that, sire."

The king would not condescend to perceive the pleasantry, and continued seriously:

"You see, monsieur," said he, "to what your disobedience has forced me."

"My disobedience!" cried D'Artagnan, red with anger.

"That is the mildest name I can find," pursued the king. "My idea was to take and punish rebels; was I bound to inquire whether these rebels were your friends or not?"

"But I was," replied D'Artagnan. "It was a cruelty on your majesty's part to send me to take my friends and lead them to your gibbets."

"It was a trial I had to make, monsieur, of pretended servants, who eat my bread and ought to defend my person. The trial has succeeded ill, Monsieur d'Artagnan."

"For one bad servant your majesty loses," said the musketeer, with bitterness, "there are ten who have, on that same day, gone through their ordeal. Listen to me, sir; I am required to do ill. It was ill to send me in pursuit of two men whose lives Monsieur Fouquet, your majesty's preserver, had implored you to save. Still further, these men were my friends. They did not attack your majesty, they succumbed to a blind anger. Besides, why were they not allowed to escape? What crime had they committed? I admit that you may contest with me the right of judging of their conduct. But why suspect me before the action? Why surround me with spies? Why disgrace me before the army? Why me, in whom you have to this time showed the most entire confidence—me who for thirty years have been attached to your person, and have given you a thousand proofs of devotedness—for it must be said, now that I am accused—why reduce me to see three thousand of the king's soldiers march in battle against two men?"

"One would say you have forgotten what these men have done to me?" said the king, in a hollow voice, "and that it was no merit of theirs that I was not lost."

"Sire, one would say you forget I was there."

"Enough, Monsieur d'Artagnan, enough of these dominating interests which arise to keep the sun from my interests. I am founding a state in which there shall be but one master, as I promised you formerly; the moment is coming for keeping

promise. You wish to be, according to your tastes or your
endships, free to destroy my plans and save my enemies? I
ll thwart you, or will leave you—seek a more compliant mas-
. I know full well that another king would not conduct him-
f as I do, and would allow himself to be dominated over by
u, at the risk of sending you some day to keep company with
onsieur Fouquet and the others; but I have a good memory,
d for me, services are sacred titles to gratitude, to impunity.
u shall only have this lesson, Monsieur d'Artagnan, as the
nishment of your want of discipline, and I will not imitate
y predecessors in their anger, not having imitated them in
eir favor. And then other reasons make me act mildly to-
rd you; in the first place, because you are a man of sense,
man of great sense, a man of heart, and that you will be a
od servant for him who shall have mastered you; secondly,
cause you will cease to have any motives for insubordination.
ur friends are destroyed or ruined by me. These supports,
on which your capricious mind instinctively relied, I have
de to disappear. At this moment my soldiers have taken or
led the rebels of Belle-Isle."

D'Artagnan became pale.

"Taken or killed!" cried he. "Oh, sire, if you thought what
u tell me, if you were sure you were telling me the truth,
hould forget all that is just, all that is magnanimous in your
rds, to call you a barbarous king and an unnatural man. But
ardon you these words," said he, smiling with pride; "I par-
n them to a young prince who does not know, who cannot
mprehend what such men as Monsieur d'Herblay, Monsieur
Vallon, and myself are. Taken or killed! Ah! ah! sire, tell
, if the news is true, how much it has cost you in men and
ney. We will then reckon if the game has been worth the
kes."

As he spoke thus, the king went up to him in great anger,
d said:

'Monsieur d'Artagnan, your replies are those of a rebel.
ll me, if you please, who is King of France? Do you know
y other?"

"Sire," replied the captain of the musketeers coldly, "I very
ll remember that one morning at Vaux you addressed that
estion to many people who did not answer to it, while I, on
part, did answer to it. If I recognized my king on that day,
en the thing was not easy, I think it would be useless to ask
of me now, when your majesty is alone with me."

At these words Louis cast down his eyes. It appeared to him

that the shade of the unfortunate Phillippe passed betwee
D'Artagnan and himself, to evoke the remembrance of tha
terrible adventure. Almost at the same moment an officer er
tered and placed a dispatch in the hands of the king, who, i
his turn, changed color while reading it.

"Monsieur," said he, "what I learn here you would kno
later; it is better I should tell you, and that you should lear
it from the mouth of your king. A battle has taken place a
Belle-Isle."

"Oh! ah!" said D'Artagnan, with a calm air, though his hear
beat enough to break through his chest. "Well, sire?"

"Well, monsieur—and I have lost a hundred and ten men.
A beam of joy and pride shone in the eyes of D'Artagnan.

"And the rebels?" said he.

"The rebels have fled," said the king.

D'Artagnan could not restrain a cry of triumph.

"Only," added the king, "I have a fleet which closely block
ades Belle-Isle, and I am certain no bark can escape."

"So that," said the musketeer, brought back to his disma
idea, "if these two gentlemen are taken——"

"They will be hanged," said the king quietly.

"And do they know it?" replied D'Artagnan, repressing hi
trembling.

"They know it, because you must have told them yoursel
and all the country knows it."

"Then, sire, they will never be taken alive; I will answer f
that."

"Ah!" said the king negligently, and taking up his lette
again. "Very well, they will be dead then, Monsieur d'Artagna
and that will come to the same thing, since I should only tal
them to have them hanged."

D'Artagnan wiped the sweat which flowed from his brow.

"I have told you," pursued Louis XIV., "that I would on
day be an affectionate, generous, and constant master. You a
now the only man of former times worthy of my anger or m
friendship. I will not be sparing of either to you, according
your conduct. Could you serve a king, Monsieur d'Artagna
who should have a hundred kings his equals in the kingdon
Could I, tell me, do with such weak things, the great things
meditate? Have you ever seen an artist effect solid works wi
a rebellious instrument? Far from us, monsieur, those old lea
ens of feudal abuses! The Fronde, which threatened to ru
the monarchy, has emancipated it. I am master at home, Ca
tain d'Artagnan, and I shall have servants who, wanting pe

haps, your genius, will carry devotedness and obedience up to heroism. Of what consequence, I ask you, of what consequence is it that God has given no genius to arms and legs? It is to the head He has given it, and the head, you know, all the rest obey. I am the head."

D'Artagnan started. Louis XIV. continued as if he had seen nothing, although this emotion had not at all escaped him.

"Now let us conclude between us two that bargain which I promised to make with you one day when you found me very little at Blois. Do me justice, monsieur, when you think that I do not make any one pay for the tears of shame that I then shed. Look around you; lofty heads have bowed. Bow yours, or choose the exile that will best suit you. Perhaps, when reflecting upon it, you will find that this king is a generous heart, who reckons sufficiently upon your loyalty to allow you to leave him disssatisfied, when you possess a great state secret. You are a brave man; I know you to be so. Why have you judged me before term? Judge me from this day forward, D'Artagnan, and be as severe as you please."

D'Artagnan remained bewildered, mute, undecided for the first time in his life. He had just found an adversary worthy of him. This was no longer trick, it was calculation; it was no longer violence, it was strength; it was no longer passion, it was will; it was no longer boasting, it was council. This young man who had brought down Fouquet, and could do without D'Artagnan, deranged all the somewhat headstrong calculations of the musketeer.

"Come, let us see what stops you?" said the king kindly. "You have given in your resignation; shall I refuse to accept it? I admit that it may be hard for an old captain to recover his good-humor."

"Oh!" replied D'Artagnan, in a melancholy tone, "that is not my most serious care. I hesitate to take back my resignation because I am old in comparison with you, and that I have habits difficult to abandon. Henceforward, you must have courtiers who know how to amuse you—madmen who will get themselves killed to carry out what you call your great works. Great they will be, I feel—but if by chance I should not think them so? I have seen war, sire, I have seen peace; I have served Richelieu and Mazarin; I have been scorched with your father, at the fire of Rochelle, riddled with thrusts like a sieve, having made a new skin ten times, as serpents do. After affronts and injustices, I have a command which was formerly something, because it gave the bearer the right of speaking as

he liked to his king. But your captain of the musketeers will
henceforward be an officer guarding the lower doors. Truly,
sire, if that is to be the employment from this time, seize the
opportunity of our being on good terms, to take it from me.
Do not imagine that I bear malice; no, you have tamed me,
as you say; but it must be confessed that in taming me you
have lessened me; by bowing me, you have convicted me of
weakness. If you knew how well it suits me to carry my head
high, and what a pitiful mien I shall have while scenting the
dust of your carpets! Oh, sire, I regret sincerely, and you will
regret as I do, those times when the King of France saw in his
vestibules all those insolent gentlemen, lean, always swearing
—cross-grained mastiffs, who could bite mortally in days of
battle. Those men were the best of courtiers for the hand
which fed them—they would lick it; but for the hand that
struck them, oh! the bite that followed. A little gold on the
lace of their cloaks, a slender stomach in their *hauts-de-
chausses,* a little sprinkling of gray in their dry hair, and you
will behold the handsome dukes and peers, the haughty
maréchaux of France. But why should I tell you all this? The
king is my master; he wills that I should make verses, he wills
that I should polish the mosaics of his antechambers with satin
shoes. *Mordioux!* that is difficult, but I have got over greater
difficulties than that. I will do it. Why should I do it? Because
I love money? I have enough. Because I am ambitious? My
career is bounded. Because I love the court? No. I will remain
because I have been accustomed for thirty years to go and
take the orderly word of the king, and to have said to me,
'Good-evening, D'Artagnan,' with a smile I did not beg for.
That smile I will beg for. Are you content, sire?"

"Thanks, my old servant, my faithful friend," said he. "As,
reckoning from this day, I have no longer any enemies in
France, it remains with me to send you to a foreign field to
gather your maréchal's baton. Depend upon me for finding you
an opportunity. In the meanwhile, eat of my best bread, and
sleep tranquilly."

"That is all kind and well," said D'Artagnan, much agitated.
"But those poor men at Belle-Isle? One of them, in particular
—so good, so brave, so true!"

"Do you ask their pardon of me?"

"Upon my knees, sire!"

"Well, then, go and take it to them, if it be still time. But
do you answer for them?"

"With my life, sire."

"Go, then. To-morrow I set out for Paris. Return by that time, for I do not wish you to leave me in future."

"Be assured of that, sire," said D'Artagnan, kissing the royal hand.

And with a heart swelling with joy, he rushed out of the castle on his way to Belle-Isle.

Chapter 54 — THE FRIENDS OF M. FOUQUET

The king had returned to Paris, and with him D'Artagnan, who, in twenty-four hours, having made with the greatest care possible inquiries at Belle-Isle, had learned nothing of the secret so well kept by the heavy rock of Locmaria, which had fallen on the heroic Porthos. The captain of the musketeers only knew what those two valiant men—what those two friends, whose defense he had so nobly taken up, whose lives he had so earnestly endeavored to save—aided by three faithful Bretons—had accomplished against a whole army. He had been able to see, launched on to the neighboring heath, the human remains which had stained with blood the stones scattered among the flowering broom. He learned also that a bark had been seen far out at sea, and that, like a bird of prey, a royal vessel had pursued, overtaken, and devoured this poor little bird which was flying with rapid wings. But there D'Artagnan's certainties ended. The field of conjecture was thrown open at this boundary. Now, what could he conjecture? The vessel had not returned. It is true that a brisk wind had prevailed for three days; but the corvette was known to be a good sailer and solid in its timbers; it could not fear gales of wind, and it ought, according to the calculation of D'Artagnan, to have either returned to Brest or come back to the mouth of the Loire. Such was the news, ambiguous it is true, but in some degree reassuring to him personally, which D'Artagnan brought Louis XIV., when the king, followed by all the court, returned to Paris.

Louis, satisfied with his success, Louis—more mild and more affable since he felt himself more powerful—had not ceased for an instant to ride close to the carriage-door of Mlle. de la Vallière. Everybody had been anxious to amuse the two queens, so as to make them forget this abandonment of the son and

the husband. Everything breathed of the future; the past was
nothing to anybody. Only that past came like a painful and
bleeding wound to the hearts of some tender and devoted spirits. Scarcely was the king reinstalled in Paris when he received a touching proof of this. Louis XIV. had just risen and
taken his first repast, when his captain of the musketeers presented himself before him. D'Artagnan was pale and looked
unhappy.

"What is the matter, D'Artagnan?" asked Louis.

"Sire, a great misfortune has happened to me."

"Good heavens, what is that?"

"Sire, I have lost one of my friends, Monsieur du Vallon,
in the affair at Belle-Isle."

And, while speaking these words D'Artagnan fixed his falcon eye upon Louis XIV., to catch the first feeling that would
show itself.

"I knew it," replied the king quietly.

"You knew it and did not tell me!" cried the musketeer.

"To what good? Your grief, my friend, is so respectable! I
was my duty to treat it kindly. To have informed you of this
misfortune, which I knew would pain you so greatly, D'Artagnan, would have been, in your eyes, to have triumphed over
you. Yes, I knew that Monsieur du Vallon had buried himself
beneath the rocks of Locmaria; I knew that Monsieur
d'Herblay had taken one of my vessels with its crew, and had
compelled it to convey him to Bayonne. But I was willing you
should learn these matters in a direct manner, in order that
you might be convinced my friends are with me respected and
sacred; that always in me the man will immolate himself to
men, while the king is so often found to sacrifice men to his
majesty and power."

"But, sire, how could you know?"

"How do you yourself know, D'Artagnan?"

"By this letter, sire, which Monsieur d'Herblay, free and
out of danger, writes me from Bayonne."

"Look here," said the king, drawing from a casket placed
upon the table close to the seat upon which D'Artagnan was
leaning, "here is a letter copied exactly from that of Monsieur
d'Herblay. Here is the very letter, which Colbert placed in my
hands a week before you received yours. I am well served, you
may perceive."

"Yes, sire," murmured the musketeer, "you were the only
man whose fortune was capable of dominating the fortunes and

rength of my two friends. You have used, sire, but you will
t abuse it, will you?"

"D'Artagnan," said the king, with a smile beaming with kind-
ss, "I could have Monsieur d'Herblay carried off from the
rritories of the King of Spain, and brought here alive to
flict justice upon him. But, D'Artagnan, be assured I will not
eld to this first and natural impulse. He is free, let him con-
ue free."

"Oh, sire! you will not always remain so clement, so noble,
generous as you have shown yourself with respect to me
d Monsieur d'Herblay; you will have about you counselors
ho will cure you of that wickedness."

"No, D'Artagnan; you are mistaken when you accuse my
uncil of urging me to pursue rigorous measures. The advice
spare Monsieur d'Herblay comes from Colbert himself."

"Oh, sire!" said D'Artagnan, extremely surprised.

"As for you," continued the king, with a kindness very
common with him, "I have several pieces of good news to
nounce to you; but you shall know them, my dear captain,
e moment I have made my accounts all straight. I have said
at I wished to make, and would make, your fortune; that
omise will soon be a reality."

"A thousand times thanks, sire; I can wait. But I implore
u, while I go and practice patience, that your majesty will
ign to notice those poor people who have for so long a time
sieged your antechamber, and come humbly to lay a peti-
n at your feet."

"Who are they?"

"Enemies of your majesty."

The king raised his head.

"Friends of Monsieur Fouquet," added D'Artagnan.

"Their names?"

"Monsieur Gourville, Monsieur Pellisson, and a poet, Mon-
ur Jean de la Fontaine."

The king took a moment to reflect.

"What do they want?"

"I do not know."

"How do they appear?"

"In great affliction."

"What do they say?"

"Nothing."

"What do they do?"

"They weep."

"Let them come in," said the king, with a serious brow.

D'Artagnan turned rapidly on his heel, raised the tapestry which closed the entrance to the royal chamber, and, directing his voice to the adjoining room, cried:

"Introduce!"

The three men D'Artagnan had named soon appeared at the door of the cabinet in which were the king and his captain. A profound silence prevailed in their passage. The courtiers, at the approach of the friends of the unfortunate surintendant of the finances, the courtiers, we say, drew back, as if fearful of being affected by contagion, with disgrace and misfortune. D'Artagnan, with a quick step, came forward to take by the hand the unhappy men who stood trembling at the door of the cabinet; he led them to the front of the fauteuil of the king, who, having placed himself in the embrasure of a window, awaited the moment of presentation, and was preparing himself to give the supplicants a rigorously diplomatic reception.

The first of the friends of Fouquet that advanced was Pellisson. He did not weep, but his tears were only restrained that the king might the better hear his voice and his prayer. Gourville bit his lips to check his tears, out of respect for the king. La Fontaine buried his face in his handkerchief, and the only signs of life he gave were the convulsive motions of his shoulders, raised by his sobs.

The king had preserved all his dignity. His countenance was impassible. He had even maintained the frown which had appeared when D'Artagnan had announced his enemies to him. He made a gesture which signified, "Speak;" and he remained standing, with his eyes searchingly fixed upon these desponding men. Pellisson bowed down to the ground, and La Fontaine knelt as people do in churches. This obstinate silence, disturbed only by such dismal sighs and groans, began to excite in the king, not compassion, but impatience.

"Monsieur Pellisson," said he, in a sharp, dry tone. "Monsieur Gourville, and you, Monsieur—" and he did not name La Fontaine—"I cannot, without sensible displeasure, see you come to plead for one of the greatest criminals that it is the duty of my justice to punish. A king does not allow himself to be softened but by tears and remorse; the tears of the innocent, the remorse of the guilty. I have no faith either in the remorse of Monsieur Fouquet or the tears of his friends, because the one is tainted to the very heart, and the others ought to dread coming to offend me in my own palace. For these rea

ns, I beg you, Monsieur Pellisson, Monsieur Gourville, and
u, Monsieur——, to say nothing that will not plainly pro-
aim the respect you have for my will."

"Sire," replied Pellisson, trembling at these terrible words,
ve are come to say nothing to your majesty that is not the
ost profound expression of the most sincere respect and
ve which are due to a king from all his subjects. Your maj-
ty's justice is redoubtable; every one must yield to the sen-
aces it pronounces. We respectfully bow before it. Far from
be the idea of coming to defend him who has had the mis-
rtune to offend your majesty. He who has incurred your dis-
asure may be a friend of ours, but he is an enemy to the
te. We abandon him, but with tears, to the severity of the
ag."

"Besides," interrupted the king, calmed by that supplicat-
voice and those persuasive words, "my parliament will dele. I do not strike without having weighed a crime; my jus-
e does not wield the sword without having employed the
les."

"Therefore have we every confidence in that impartiality
the king, and hope to make our feeble voices heard, with the
nsent of your majesty, when the hour for defending an ac-
sed friend shall strike for us."

"In that case, messieurs, what do you ask of me?" said the
ag, with his most imposing air.

"Sire," continued Pellisson, "the accused leaves a wife and
family. The little property he had was scarcely sufficient to
y his debts, and Madame Fouquet, since the captivity of her
sband, is abandoned by everybody. The hand of your maj-
y strikes like the hand of God. When the Lord sends the
rse of leprosy or pestilence into a family, every one flies and
uns the abode of the leprous or plague-stricken. Some-
aes, but very rarely, a generous physician alone ventures to
oroach the accursed threshold, passes it with courage, and
oses his life to combat death. He is the last resource of the
ing, he is the instrument of heavenly mercy. Sire, we sup-
cate you, with clasped hands and bended knees, as a divinity
supplicated! Madame Fouquet has no longer any friends, no
ger any support; she weeps in her poor deserted house,
ndoned by all those who besieged its doors in the hour of
sperity; she has neither credit nor hope left. At least, the
aappy wretch upon whom your anger falls receives from
, however culpable he may be, the daily bread which is

moistened by his tears. As much afflicted, more destitute th
her husband, Madame Fouquet—she who had the honor
receive your majesty at her table—Madame Fouquet, the w
of the ancient surintendant of your majesty's finances, Mada
Fouquet has no longer bread."

Here the mortal silence which enchained the breath of P
lisson's two friends was broken by an outburst of sobs; a
D'Artagnan, whose chest heaved at hearing this humble pray
turned round toward the angle of the cabinet to bite his m
tache and conceal his sighs.

The king had preserved his eye dry and his countenar
severe; but the color had mounted to his cheeks, and the fir
ness of his look was visibly diminished.

"What do you wish?" said he, in an agitated voice.

"We come humbly to ask your majesty," replied Pelliss
upon whom emotion was fast gaining, "to permit us, with
incurring the displeasure of your majesty, to lend to Mada
Fouquet two thousand pistoles collected among the old frier
of her husband, in order that the widow may not stand in ne
of the necessaries of life."

At the word *widow,* pronounced by Pellisson while Fouq
was still alive, the king turned very pale; his pride fell; p
rose from his heart to his lips; he cast a softened look up
the men who knelt, sobbing, at his feet.

"God forbid!" said he, "that I should confound the innoc
with the guilty. They know me but ill who doubt my mer
toward the weak. I strike none but the arrogant. Do, messieu
do all that your hearts counsel you to assuage the grief
Madame Fouquet. Go, messieurs—go!"

The three men arose in silence with dried eyes. The te
had been dried up by contact with their burning cheeks a
eyelids. They had not the strength to address their thanks
the king, who himself cut short their solemn reverences by
trenching himself suddenly behind the fauteuil.

D'Artagnan remained alone with the king.

"Well," said he, approaching the young prince, who inter
gated him with his look. "Well, my master! If you had not
device which belongs to your sun, I would recommend you o
which Monsieur Convart should translate into Latin, 'M
with the lowly; rough with the strong.'"

The king smiled, and passed into the next apartment, af
having said to D'Artagnan: .

"I give you the leave of absence you must want to put t
affairs of your friend, the late Monsieur du Vallon, in orde

Chapter 55 — PORTHOS' WILL

At Pierrefonds everything was in mourning. The courts were deserted—the stable closed—the parterres neglected. In the basins, the fountains, formerly so spreading, noisy, and sparkling, had stopped of themselves. Along the roads around the château came a few grave personages mounted upon mules or farm nags. These were country neighbors, curés, and bailiffs of adjacent estates. All these people entered the château silently, gave their nags to a melancholy-looking groom, and directed their steps, conducted by a huntsman in black, to the great dining-room, where Mousqueton received them at the door. Mousqueton had become so thin in two days that his clothes moved upon him like sheathes which are too large, and in which the blades of swords dance about at each motion. His face, composed of red and white, like that of the Madonna of Vandyke, was furrowed by two silver rivulets which had dug their beds in his cheeks, as full formerly as they had become flabby since his grief began. At each fresh arrival Mousqueton found fresh tears, and it was pitiful to see him press his throat with his fat hand to keep from bursting into sobs and lamentations. All these visits were for the purpose of hearing the reading of Porthos' will, announced for that day, and at which all the covetousness and all the friendships connected with the defunct were anxious to be present, as he had left no relation behind him.

The visitors took their places as they arrived, and the great room had just been closed when the clock struck twelve, the hour fixed for the reading of the important document. Porthos' procureur—and that was naturally the successor of Master Coquenard—commenced by slowly unfolding the vast parchment upon which the powerful hand of Porthos had traced his sovereign will. The seal broken—the spectacles put on—the preliminary cough having sounded—everyone opened his ears. Mousqueton had squatted himself in a corner, the better to weep and the better to hear. All at once the folding-doors of the great room, which had been shut, were thrown open as if by a prodigy, and a manly figure appeared upon the threshold, splendent in the full light of the sun. This was D'Artagnan, who had come alone to the gate, and finding nobody to hold his stirrup, he had tied his horse to a knocker and announced himself. The splendor of the daylight invading the room, the murmur of all present, and, more than all that, the instinct of the faithful dog, drew Mousqueton from his reverie; he raised his head, recognized the old friend of his master, and, howling with grief, he embraced his knees, watering the floor with his tears. D'Artagnan raised up the poor intendant, embraced him as if he had been a brother, and, having nobly saluted the assembly, who all bowed as they whispered to one another his name, he went and took his seat at the extremity of the great carved oak hall, still holding by the hand poor Mousqueton, who was suffocating, and sunk down upon the steps. Then the procureur, who, like the rest, was considerably agitated, commenced the reading.

Porthos, after a profession of faith of the most Christian character, asked pardon of his enemies for all the injuries he might have done them. At this paragraph a ray of inexpressible pride beamed from the eyes of D'Artagnan. He recalled to his mind the old soldier; all those enemies of Porthos brought to the earth by his valiant hand, he reckoned up the numbers of them, and said to himself that Porthos had acted wisely not to detail his enemies or the injuries done to them, or the task would have been too much for the reader. Then came the following enumeration:

"I possess at this present time, by the grace of God:

"1. The domain of Pierrefonds, lands, woods, meadows, waters, and forests, surrounded by good walls.

"2. The domain of Bracieux, château, forests, plowed lands, forming three farms.

"3. The little estate Du Vallon, so named because it is in the valley." (Brave Porthos.)

"4. Fifty farms in Touraine, amounting to five hundred acres.

"5. Three mills upon the Cher, bringing in six hundred livres each.

"6. Three fish-pools in Berry, producing two hundred livres a year.

"As to my personal or movable property, so called because it can be moved, as is so well explained by my learned friend the bishop of Vannes"—(D'Artagnan shuddered at the dismal remembrance attached to that name)—the procureur continued imperturbably—"they consist:

"1. In goods which I cannot detail here for want of room,
and which furnish all my châteaus or houses, but of which the
list is drawn up by my intendant."

Every one turned his eyes toward Mousqueton, who was
absorbed in his grief.

"2. In twenty horses for saddle and draught, which I have
particularly at my château of Pierrefonds, and which are called
—Bayard, Roland, Charlemagne, Pépin, Dunois, La Hire, Ogier,
Samson, Milo, Nimrod, Urganda, Armida, Falstrade, Delilah,
Rebecca, Yolands, Finette, Grisette, Lisette, and Musette.

"3. In sixty dogs, forming six packs, divided as follows: the
first, for the stag; the second, for the wolf; the third, for the
wild boar; the fourth, for the hare; and the two others, for
setters and protection.

"4. In arms for war and the chase contained in my gallery
of arms.

"5. My wines of Anjou, selected for Athos, who liked them
formerly; my wines of Burgundy, Champagne, Bordeaux,
and Spain, stocking eight cellars and twelve vaults, in my various houses.

"6. My pictures and statues, which are said to be of great
value, and which are sufficiently numerous to fatigue the sight.

"7. My library, consisting of six thousand volumes, quite
new, and have never been opened.

"8. My silver plate, which is, perhaps, a little worn, but
which ought to weigh from a thousand to twelve hundred
pounds, for I had great trouble in lifting the coffer that contained it, and could not carry it more than six times round my
chamber.

"9. All these objects, in addition to the table and house-
linen, are divided in the residences I liked the best."

Here the reader stopped to take breath. Every one sighed,
coughed, and redoubled his attention. The procureur resumed:

"I have lived without having any children, and it is probable
I never shall have any, which to me is a cutting grief. And yet
I am mistaken, for I have a son, in common with my other
friends; that is Monsieur Raoul Auguste Jules de Bragelonne,
the true son of Monsieur le Comte de la Fere.

"This young nobleman has appeared to me worthy to suc-

ceed to the three valiant gentlemen, of whom I am the frien
and the very humble servant."

Here a sharp sound interrupted the reader. It was D'Ar
tagnan's sword, which, slipping from his baldric, had fallen or
the sonorous flooring. Every one turned his eyes that way
and saw that a large tear had rolled from the thick lid of D'Ar
tagnan on to his acquiline nose, the luminous edge of whic.
shone like a crescent enlightened by the sun.

"This is why," continued the procureur, "I have left all m
property, movable or immovable, comprised in the above enu
merations, to Monsieur le Vicomte Raoul Auguste Jule
de Bragelonne, son of Monsieur le Comte de la Fere, to conso
him for the grief he seems to suffer, and enable him to suppor
his name gloriously."

A long murmur ran through the auditory. The procureu
continued, seconded by the flashing eye of D'Artagnan, which
glancing over the assembly, quickly restored the interrupte
silence:

"On condition that Monsieur le Vicomte de Bragelonne d
give to Monsieur le Chevalier d'Artagnan, captain of the king
musketeers, whatever the said Chevalier d'Artagnan may de
mand of my property. On condition that Monsieur le Vicomt
de Bragelonne do pay a good pension to Monsieur le Chevalie
d'Herblay, my friend, if he should need it in exile. I leave t
my intendant, Mousqueton, all my clothes, of city, war, o
chase, to the number of forty-seven suits, with the assuranc
that he will wear them till they are worn out for the love o
and in remembrance of his master. Moreover, I bequeath t
Monsieur le Vicomte de Bragelonne my old servant and fait!
ful friend, Mousqueton, already named, providing that th
said vicomte shall so act that Mousqueton shall declare, whe
dying, he has never ceased to be happy."

On hearing these words, Mousqueton bowed, pale and trem
bling; his large shoulders shook convulsively; his countenanc
impressed by frightful grief, appeared from between his ic
hands, and the spectators saw him stagger and hesitate, as i
though wishing to leave the hall, he did not know the way.

"Mousqueton, my good friend," said D'Artagnan, "go an
make your preparations. I will take you with me to Atho
house, whither I shall go on leaving Pierrefonds."

Mousqueton made no reply. He scarcely breathed, as if everything in that hall would from that time be foreign. He opened the door, and disappeared slowly.

The procureur finished his reading, after which the greater part of those who had come to hear the last will of Porthos dispersed by degrees, many disappointed, but all penetrated with respect. As to D'Artagnan, left alone, after having received the formal compliments of the procureur, he was lost in admiration of the wisdom of the testator, who had so judiciously bestowed his wealth upon the most necessitous and the most worthy, with a delicacy that none among the most refined courtiers and the most noble hearts could have displayed more becomingly. When Porthos enjoined Raoul de Bragelonne to give to D'Artagnan all he would ask, he knew well, did that worthy Porthos, that D'Artagnan would ask or take nothing; and, in case he did demand anything, none but himself could say what. Porthos left a pension to Aramis, who, if he should be inclined to ask too much, was checked by the example of D'Artagnan; and that word *exile*, thrown out by the testator, without apparent intention, was it not the most mild, the most exquisite criticism upon that conduct of Aramis which had brought about the death of Porthos. But there was no mention of Athos in the testament of the dead. Could the latter, for a moment, suppose that the son would not offer the best part to the father? The rough mind of Porthos had judged all these causes, seized all these shades, better than the law, better than custom, better than taste.

"Porthos has a heart," said D'Artagnan to himself, with a sigh.

As he made this reflection he fancied he heard a groan in the room above him; and he thought immediately of poor Mousqueton, whom he felt it was a pleasing duty to divert from his grief. For this purpose he left the hall hastily to seek the worthy intendant, as he had not returned. He ascended the staircase leading to the first story, and perceived, in Porthos' own chamber, a heap of clothes of all colors and materials, upon which Mousqueton had laid himself down after heaping them together. It was the legacy of the faithful friend. Those clothes were truly his own; they had been given to him; the hand of Mousqueton was stretched over these relics, which he kissed with all his lips, with all his face, which he covered with his whole body. D'Artagnan approached to console the poor fellow.

"My God!" said he, "he does not stir—he has fainted!"

But D'Artagnan was mistaken—Mousqueton was dead. Dead, like the dog who, having lost his master, comes back to die upon his cloak.

Chapter 56 — THE OLD AGE OF ATHOS

While all these affairs were separating forever the four musketeers, formerly bound together in a manner that seemed indissoluble, Athos, left alone after the departure of Raoul, began to pay his tribute to that anticipated death which is called the absence of those we love. Returned to his house at Blois, no longer having even Grimaud to receive a poor smile when he passed through the parterre, Athos daily felt the decline of the vigor of a nature which for so long a time had appeared infallible. Age, which had been kept back by the presence of the beloved object, arrived with that cortège of pains and inconveniences which increases in proportion as it makes itself looked for. Athos had no longer his son to induce him to walk firmly, with his head erect, as a good example; he had no longer, in those brilliant eyes of the young man, an ever-ardent focus at which to regenerate the fire of his looks. And then, must it be said, that nature, exquisite in its tenderness and its reserve, no longer finding anything that comprehended its feelings, gave itself up to grief with all the warmth of vulgar natures when they give themselves up to joy. The Comte de la Fere, who had remained a young man up to his sixtysecond year; the warrior who had preserved his strength in spite of fatigues, his freshness of mind in spite of misfortunes, his mild serenity of soul and body in spite of Milady, in spite of Mazarin, in spite of La Valliere; Athos had become an old man in a week, from the moment at which he had lost the support of his latter youth. Still handsome, though bent; noble, but sad; gently, and tottering under his gray hairs, he sought, since his solitude, the glades where the rays of the sun penetrate through the foliage of the walks. He discontinued all the strong exercises he had enjoyed through life, when Raoul was no longer with him. The servants, accustomed to see him stirring with the dawn at all seasons, were astonished to hear seven o'clock strike before their master had quitted his bed. Athos

emained in bed with a book under his pillow, but he did not
sleep, neither did he read. Remaining in bed that he might no
longer have to carry his body, he allowed his soul and spirit to
wander from their envelope, and return to his son, or to God.

His people were sometimes terrified to see him, for hours
together, absorbed in a silent reverie, mute and insensible; he
no longer heard the timid step of the servant who came to the
door of his chamber to watch the sleeping or waking of his master. It often occurred that he forgot that the day had half
passed away, that the hours for the two first meals were
gone by. Then he was awakened. He rose, descended to his
shaded walk, then came out a little into the sun, as if to partake of its warmth for a minute with his absent child. And
then the dismal, monotonous walk recommenced, until, quite
exhausted, he regained the chamber and the bed, his domicile
by choice. For several days the comte did not speak a single
word. He refused to receive the visits that were paid him, and,
during the night, he was seen to relight his lamp and pass long
hours in writing or examining parchments.

Athos wrote one of these letters to Vannes, another to Fontainebleau; they remained without answers. We know why;
Aramis had quitted France, and D'Artagnan was traveling
from Nantes to Paris, from Paris to Pierrefonds. His *valet de
chambre* observed that he shortened his walk every day by
several turns. The great alley of limes soon became too long for
feet that used to traverse it formerly a hundred times in a day.
The comte walked feebly as far as the middle trees, seated
himself upon a mossy bank which sloped toward a lateral walk,
and there waited the return of his strength, or, rather, the return of night. Very shortly a hundred steps exhausted him. At
length Athos refused to rise at all; he declined all nourish-
ment, and his terrified people, although he did not complain,
although he had a smile on his lips, although he continued to
speak with his sweet voice—his people went to Blois in search
of the ancient physician of the late Monsieur, and brought him
to the Comte de la Fere in such a fashion that he could see the
comte without being himself seen. For this purpose they placed
him in a closet adjoining the chamber of the patient, and implored him not to show himself, in the fear of displeasing their
master, who had not asked for a physician. The doctor obeyed;
Athos was a sort of model for the gentlemen of the country;
the Blaisois boasted of possessing this sacred relic of the old
French glories. Athos was a great seigneur compared with such
nobles as the king improvised by touching with his yellow

fecundating scepter the dried trunks of the heraldic trees of
the province.

People respected, we say, if they did not love Athos. The
physician could not bear to see his people weep, and to see
flock round him the poor of the canton, to whom Athos gave life
and consolation by his kind words and his charities. He examined, therefore, from the depths of his hiding-place, the
nature of that mysterious malady which bent down and
devoured more mortally every day a man but lately so full of
life and a desire to live. He remarked upon the cheeks of Athos
the purple of fever, which fires itself and feeds itself; slow
fever, pitiless, born in a fold of the heart, sheltering itself behind that rampart, growing from the suffering it engenders, at
once cause and effect of a perilous situation. The comte spoke
to nobody, we say; he did not even talk to himself. His thought
feared noise; it approached to that degree of over-excitement
which borders upon ecstasy. Man thus absorbed, though he
does not yet belong to God, already belongs no longer to
earth. The doctor remained for several hours studying this
painful struggle of the will against superior power; he was
terrified at seeing those eyes always fixed, always directed toward an invisible object; he was terrified at seeing beat with
the same movement that heart from which never a sigh arose
to vary the melancholy state; sometimes the acuteness of
pain creates the hope of the physician. Half a day passed away
thus. The doctor formed his resolution like a brave man, like a
man of firm mind; he issued suddenly from his place of retreat
and went straight up to Athos, who saw him without evincing
more surprise than if he had understood nothing of the appari-
tion.

"Monsieur le Comte, I crave your pardon," said the doctor
coming up to the patient with open arms; "but I have a re
proach to make you—you shall hear me."

And he seated himself by the pillow of Athos, who had grea
trouble in rousing himself from his preoccupation.

"What is the matter, doctor?" asked the comte, after a
silence.

"Why, the matter is, you are ill, monsieur, and have had no
advice."

"I! ill!" said Athos, smiling.

"Fever, consumption, weakness, decay, Monsieur le Comte."

"Weakness!" replied Athos; "is that possible? I do no
get up."

"Come, come, Monsieur le Comte, no subterfuges; you are a good Christian?"

"I hope so," said Athos.

"Would you kill yourself?"

"Never, doctor."

"Well, monsieur, you are in a fair way of doing so; to remain thus is suicide; get well, Monsieur le Comte, get well."

"Of what? Find the disease first. For my part, I never knew myself better; never did the sky appear more blue to me; never did I take more care of my flowers."

"You have a concealed grief."

"Concealed!—not at all; I have the absence of my son, doctor; that is my malady, and I do not conceal it."

"Monsieur le Comte, your son lives, he is strong, he has all the future before him of men of his merit, and of his race; live for him——"

"But I do live, doctor; oh! be satisfied of that," added he, with a melancholy smile; "as long as Raoul lives, it will be plainly known, for as long as he lives, I shall live."

"What do you say?"

"A very simple thing. At this moment, doctor, I leave life suspended in me. A forgetful, dissipated, indifferent life would be above my strength, now I have no longer Raoul with me. You do not ask the lamp to burn when the spark has not enlightened the flame; do not ask me to live amid noise and light. I vegetate, I prepare myself, I wait. Look, doctor; remember those soldiers we have so often seen together at the ports, where they were waiting to embark; lying down, indifferent, half upon one element, half upon the other; they were neither at the place where the sea was going to carry them nor at the place the earth was going to lose them; baggages prepared, minds upon the stretch, looks fixed—they waited. I repeat it, that word is the one which paints my present life. Lying down, like the soldiers, my ear on the stretch for the reports that may reach me, I wish to be ready to set out at the first summons. Who will make me that summons? life or death? God or Raoul? My baggage is packed, my soul is prepared, I await the signal—I wait, doctor, I wait!"

The doctor knew the temper of that mind; he appreciated the strength of that body; he reflected for the moment, told himself that words were useless, remedies absurd, and he left the château, exhorting Athos' servants not to leave him for a moment.

The doctor being gone, Athos evinced neither anger nor vexation at having been disturbed. He did not even desire that all letters that came should be brought to him directly. He knew very well that every distraction which should arise would be a joy, a hope, which his servants would have paid with their blood to procure him. Sleep had become rare. By intense thinking, Athos forgot himself, for a few hours at most, in a reverie more profound, more obscure than other people would have called a dream. This momentary repose which this forgetfulness afforded the body fatigued the soul, for Athos lived a double life during these wanderings of his understanding. One night he dreamed that Raoul was dressing himself in a tent, to go upon an expedition commanded by M. de Beaufort in person. The young man was sad; he clasped his cuirass slowly, and slowly he girded on his sword.

"What is the matter?" asked his father tenderly.

"What afflicts me is the death of Porthos, ever so dear a friend," replied Raoul. "I suffer here of the grief you will feel at home."

And the vision disappeared with the slumber of Athos. At daybreak one of his servants entered his master's apartment, and gave him a letter which came from Spain.

"The writing of Aramis," thought the comte; and he read.

"Porthos is dead!" cried he, after the first lines. "Oh, Raoul, Raoul, thanks; thou keepest thy promise, thou warnest me!"

And Athos, seized with a mortal sweat, fainted in his bed, without any other cause than his weakness.

Chapter 57 — THE VISION OF ATHOS

When this fainting of Athos had ceased, the comte, almost ashamed of having given way before this supernatural event, dressed himself and ordered his horse, determined to ride to Blois, to open more certain correspondence with either Africa, D'Artagnan, or Aramis. In fact, this letter from Aramis informed the Comte de la Fere of the bad success of the expedition of Belle-Isle. It gave him sufficient details of the death of Porthos to move the tender and devoted heart of Athos to its last fibers. Athos wished to go and pay his friend Porthos a last visit. To render this honor to his companion in arms, he meant to send to D'Artagnan, to prevail upon him to recommence the painful voyage to Belle-Isle, to accomplish in his company that sad pilgrimage to the tomb of the giant he had so much loved, then to return to his dwelling to obey that secret influence which was conducting him to eternity by a mysterious road. But scarcely had his joyous servants dressed their master, whom they saw with pleasure preparing himself for a journey which might dissipate his melancholy; scarcely had the comte's gentlest horse been saddled and brought to the door, than the father of Raoul felt his head become confused, his legs give way, and he clearly perceived the impossibility of going one step further. He ordered himself to be carried into the sun; they laid him upon his bed of moss, where he passed a full hour before he could recover his spirits. Nothing could be more natural than this weakness after the inert repose of the latter days. Athos took a bouillon, to give him strength, and bathed his dried lips in a glassful of the wine he loved the best—that old Anjou wine mentioned by Porthos in his admirable will. Then, refreshed, free in mind, he had his horse brought again; but it required the aid of his servants to mount painfully into the saddle. He did not go a hundred paces; a shivering seized him again at the turning of the road.

"This is very strange!" said he to his *valet de chambre*, who accompanied him.

"Let us stop, monsieur—I conjure you!" replied the faithful servant. "How pale you are getting!"

"That will not prevent my pursuing my route, now I have once started," replied the comte.

And he gave his horse his head again. But suddenly the animal, instead of obeying the thought of his master, stopped. A movement, of which Athos was unconscious, had checked the bit.

"Something," said Athos, "wills that I should go no further. Support me," added he, stretching out his arms. "Quick! come closer. I feel all my muscles relax, and I shall fall from my horse."

The valet had seen the movement made by his master at the moment he received the order. He went up to him quickly, received the comte in his arms, and as they were not yet sufficiently distant from the house for the servants, who had remained at the door to watch their master's departure, not to perceive the disorder in the usually regular proceeding of the comte, the valet called his comrades by gestures and voice, and all hastened to his assistance. Athos had gone but a few steps on his return, when he felt himself better again. His strength seemed to revive, and with it the desire to go to Blois. He made his horse turn round; but, at the animal's first steps, he sank again into a state of torpor and anguish.

"Well, decidedly," said he, "it is *willed* that I should stay at home."

His people flocked around him; they lifted him from his horse, and carried him as quickly as possible into the house. Everything was soon prepared in his chamber, and they put him to bed.

"You will be sure to remember," said he, disposing himself to sleep, "that I expect letters from Africa this very day."

"Monsieur will, no doubt, hear with pleasure that Blasois' son is gone on horseback, to gain an hour over the courier of Blois," replied his *valet de chambre*.

"Thank you," replied Athos, with his bland smile.

The comte fell asleep, but his disturbed slumber resembled suffering more than repose. The servant who watched him saw several times the expression of interior torture thrown out upon his features. Perhaps Athos was dreaming. The day passed away. Blasois' son returned; the courier had brought no news. The comte reckoned the minutes with despair; he shuddered when those minutes had formed an hour. The idea that he was forgotten seized him once, and brought on a fearful pang of the heart. Everybody in the house had given up all hopes of the courier—his hour had long passed. Four times the express sent to Blois ‘had reiterated his journey, and there was nothing to the address of the comte. Athos knew that the courier only arrived once a week. Here, then, was a delay of eight mortal days to be endured. He commenced the night in this painful persuasion. All that a sick man, irritated by suffering, can add of melancholy suppositions to probabilities always sad, Athos heaped up during the early hours of this dismal night. The fever rose; it invaded the chest, where the fire soon caught, according to the expression of the physician, who had been brought back from Blois by Blasois at his last journey. It soon gained the head. The physician made two successive bleedings, which unlodged it, but left the patient very weak, and without power of action in anything but his brain. And yet this redoubtable fever had ceased. It besieged with its last palpitations the stiffened extremities; it ended by yielding as midnight struck.

The physician, seeing the incontestible improvement, returned to Blois, after having ordered some prescriptions, and declared that the comte was saved. Then commenced for Athos a strange, indefinable state. Free to think, his mind turned toward Raoul, that beloved son. His imagination painted the fields of Africa in the environs of Gigelli, where M. de Beaufort must have landed his army. They were gray rocks, rendered green in certain parts by the waters of the sea, when it lashed the shore in storms and tempest. Beyond, the shore, strewed over with these rocks like tombs, ascended in form of an amphitheater among mastick-trees and cactus, a sort of small town, full of smoke, confused noises, and terrified movements. All on a sudden, from the bosom of this smoke arose a flame, which succeeded, by creeping along the houses, in covering the whole surface of this town, and which increased by degrees, uniting in its red vortices tears, cries, arms extended toward heaven.

There was, for a moment, a frightful *pêle-mêle* of *madriers* falling to pieces, of swords broken, of stones calcined, of trees burned and disappearing. It was a strange thing that in this chaos, in which Athos distinguished raised arms, in which he heard cries, sobs, and groans, he did not see one human figure. The cannon thundered at a distance, musktetry cracked, the sea moaned, flocks made their escape, bounding over the verdant slope. But not a soldier to apply the match to the batteries of cannon, not a sailor to assist in maneuvering the fleet, not a shepherd for the flocks. After the ruin of the village, and the destruction of the forts which dominated it, a ruin and a destruction operated magically without the cooperation of a single human being, the flame was extinguished, the smoke began to descend, then diminished in intensity, paled, and disappeared entirely. Night then came over the scene; a night dark upon the earth, brilliant in the firmament. The large, blazing stars which sparkled in the African sky shone without lighting anything even round them.

A long silence ensued, which gave, for a moment, repose to the troubled imagination of Athos; and, as he felt that that which he saw was not terminated, he applied more attentively the looks of his understanding upon the strange spectacle which his imagination had presented. This spectacle was soon continued for him. A mild and pale moon arose behind the declivities of the coast, and streaking at first the undulating ripples of the sea, which appeared to have calmed after the roarings it had sent forth during the vision of Athos—the moon, say we, shed its diamonds and opals upon the briers and bushes of the hills. The gray rocks, like so many silent and attentive phantoms, appeared to raise their verdant heads to examine likewise the field of battle by the light of the moon, and Athos perceived that that field, entirely void during the combat, was now strewed over with fallen bodies.

An inexpressible shudder of fear and horror seized his soul when he recognized the white and blue uniform of the soldiers of Picardy, with their long pikes and blue handles, and their muskets marked with the fleur-de-lis on the butts. When he saw all the gaping, cold wounds, looking up to the azure heavens as if to demand back of them the souls to which they had opened a passage—when he saw the slaughtered horses, stiff, with their tongues hanging out at one side of their mouths, sleeping in the icy blood pooled around them, staining their furniture and their manes—when he saw the white horse of M. de Beaufort, with his head beaten to pieces, in the first ranks of the dead, Athos passed a cold hand over his brow, which he was astonished not to find burning. He was convinced by this touch that he was present, as a spectator without fever, at the day after a battle fought upon the shores of Gigelli by the army of the expedition, which he had seen leave the coast of France and disappear in the horizon, and of which he had saluted with thought and gesture the last cannon-shot fired by the duke as a signal of farewell to his country.

Who can paint the mortal agony with which his soul followed, like a vigilant eye, the trace of those dead bodies, and examined them, one after the other, to see if Raoul slept among them? Who can express the intoxication of joy with which Athos bowed before God, and thanked Him for not having seen him he sought with so much fear among the dead? In fact, fallen dead in their ranks, stiff, icy, all these dead, easy to be recognized, seemed to turn with complacency toward the Comte de le Fere, to be the better seen by him during his funeral inspection. But yet he was astonished, while viewing all these bodies, not to perceive the survivors. To such a point did the illusion extend that this vision was for him a real voyage made by the father into Africa, to obtain more exact information respecting his son.

Fatigued, therefore, with having traversed seas and continents, he sought repose under one of the tents sheltered behind a rock, on the top of which floated the white fleur-de-lised pennon. He looked for a soldier to conduct him to the tent of M. de Beaufort. Then, while his eye was wandering over the plain, turning on all sides, he saw a white form appear behind the resinous myrtles. This figure was clothed in the costume of an officer; it held in its hand a broken sword; it advanced slowly toward Athos, who, stopping short and fixing his eyes

upon it, neither spoke nor moved, but wished to open his arms,
because in this silent and pale officer he had just recognized
Raoul. The comte attempted to utter a cry, but it remained
stifled in his throat. Raoul, with a gesture, directed him to be
silent, placing his finger on his lips and drawing back by degrees, without Athos being able to see his legs move. The
comte, more pale than Raoul, more trembling, followed his
son, traversing painfully briars and bushes, stones and ditches,
Raoul not appearing to touch the earth, and no obstacle im-
peding the lightness of his march. The comte, whom the inequalities of the path fatigued, soon stopped, exhausted. Raoul
still continued to beckon him to follow him. The tender father,
to whom love restored strength, made a last effort, and climbed
the mountain after the young man, who attracted him by his
gesture and his smile.

At length he gained the crest of the hill, and saw, thrown
out in black upon the horizon whitened by the moon, the elongated aërial form of Raoul. Athos stretched out his hand to get
closer to his beloved son upon the plateau, and the latter also
stretched out his; but suddenly, as if the young man had been
drawn away in spite of himself, still retreating, he left the
earth, and Athos saw the clear blue sky shine between the feet
of his child and the ground of the hill. Raoul rose insensibly
into the void, smiling, still calling with a gesture; he departed
toward heaven. Athos uttered a cry of terrified tenderness. He
looked below again. He saw a camp destroyed, and all those
white bodies of the royal army, like so many motionless atoms.
And then, when raising his head, he saw still, still, his son beckoning him to ascend with him.

Chapter 58 — THE ANGEL OF DEATH

Athos was at this part of his marvelous vision when the charm
was suddenly broken by a great noise rising from the outward
gates of the house. A horse was heard galloping over the hard
gravel of the great alley and the sound of most noisy and
animated conversations ascended to the chamber in which the
comte was dreaming. Athos did not stir from the place he occupied; he scarcely turned his head toward the door to ascertain the sooner what these noises could be. A heavy step as-

cended the stairs; the horse which had recently galloped departed slowly toward the stables. Great hesitation appeared in the steps, which by degrees approached the chamber of Athos. A door then was opened, and Athos, turning a little toward the part of the room the noise came from, cried, in a weak voice:

"It is a courier from Africa, is it not?"

"No, Monsieur le Comte," replied a voice which made the father of Raoul start upright in his bed.

"Grimaud!" murmured he.

And the sweat began to pour down his cheeks. Grimaud appeared in the doorway. It was no longer the Grimaud we have seen, still young with courage and devotion, when he jumped the first into the boat destined to convey Raoul de Bragelonne to the vessels of the royal fleet. He was a stern and pale old man, his clothes covered with dust, with a few scattered hairs whitened by old age. He trembled while leaning against the door-frame, and was near falling on seeing, by the light of the lamps, the countenance of his master. These two men who had lived so long together in a community of intelligence, and whose eyes, accustomed to economize expressions, knew how to say so many things silently—these two old friends, one as noble as the other in heart, if they were unequal in fortune and birth, remained interdicted while looking at each other. By the exchange of a single glance they had just read to the bottom of each other's hearts. Grimaud bore upon his countenance the impression of a grief already old, of a dismal familiarity with it. He appeared to have no longer in use but one single version of his thoughts. As formerly he was accustomed not to speak much, he was now accustomed not to smile at all. Athos read at a glance all these shades upon the visage of his faithful servant, and in the same tone he would have employed to speak to Raoul in his dream:

"Grimaud," said he, "Raoul is dead, is he not?"

Behind Grimaud, the other servants listened breathlessly, with their eyes fixed upon the bed of their sick master. They heard the terrible question, and an awful silence ensued.

"Yes," replied the old man, heaving up the monosyllable from his chest with a hoarse, broken sigh.

Then arose voices of lamentation, which groaned without measure, and filled with regrets and prayers the chamber where the agonized father sought with his eyes for the portrait of his son. This was for Athos like the transition which led to his dream. Without uttering a cry, without shedding tear, patient, mild, resigned as a martyr, he raised his eyes toward heaven, in order to there see again, rising above the mountain of Gigelli, the beloved shade which was leaving him at the moment of Grimaud's arrival. Without doubt, while looking toward the heavens, when resuming his marvelous dream, he repassed by the same road by which the vision, at once so terrible and so sweet, had led him before, for, after having gently closed his eyes, he reopened them and began to smile; he had just seen Raoul, who had smiled upon him. With his hands joined upon his breast, his face turned toward the window, bathed by the fresh air of night, which brought to his pillow the aroma of the flowers and the woods, Athos entered, never again to come out of it, into the contemplation of that paradise which the living never see. God willed, no doubt, to open to this elect the treasures of eternal beatitude, at the hour when other men tremble with the idea of being severely received by the Lord, and cling to this life they know, in the dread of the other life of which they get a glimpse by the dismal, murky torches of death. Athos was guided by the pure and serene soul of his son, which aspired to be like the paternal soul. Everything for this just man was melody and perfume in the rough road which souls take to return to the celestial country. After an hour of this ecstasy Athos softly raised his hands as white as wax; the smile did not quit his lips, and he murmured low, so low as scarcely to be audible, these three words addressed to God or to Raoul:

"*Here I am!*"

And his hands fell down slowly, as if he himself had laid them on the bed.

Death had been kind and mild to this noble creature. It had spared him the tortures of the agony, the convulsions of the last departure; it had opened with an indulgent finger the gates of eternity to that noble soul worthy of every respect. God had no doubt ordered it thus that the pious remembrance of this death should remain in the hearts of those present, and in the memory of other men—a death which caused to be loved the passage from this life to the other by those whose existence upon this earth leads them not to dread the last judgment. Athos preserved, even in the eternal sleep, that placid and sincere smile—an ornament which was to accompany him to the tomb. The quietude of his features, the calm of his nothingness, made his servants for a long time doubt whether he had really quitted life. The comte's people wished to remove Grimaud, who, from a distance, devoured the face growing so pale, and did not approach, from the pious fear of bringing to him the breath of death. But Grimaud, fatigued as he was, refused to leave the room. He sat himself down upon the threshold, watching his master with the vigilance of a sentinel, and jealous to receive either his first waking look or his last dying sigh. The noises were all quieted in the house, and every one respected the slumber of their lord. But Grimaud, by anxiously listening, perceived that the comte no longer breathed. He raised himself with his hands leaning on the ground, and looked to see if there did not appear some motion in the body of his master. Nothing! Fear seized him; he rose completely up, and, at the very moment, heard some one coming up the stairs. A noise of spurs knocking against a sword—a warlike sound, familiar to his ears—stopped him as he was going toward the bed of Athos. A voice still more sonorous than brass or steel resounded within three paces of him.

"Athos! Athos, my friend!" cried this voice, agitated even to tears.

"Monsieur le Chevalier d'Artagnan!" faltered out Grimaud.

"Where is he? where is he?" continued the musketeer.

Grimaud seized his arm in his bony fingers, and pointed to the bed, upon the sheets of which the livid tints of the dead already showed.

A choked respiration, the opposite to a sharp cry, swelled the throat of D'Artagnan. He advanced on tiptoe, trembling, frightened at the noise his feet made upon the floor, and his heart rent by a nameless agony. He placed his ear to the breast of Athos, his face to the comte's mouth. Neither noise nor breath! D'Artagnan drew back. Grimaud, who had followed him with his eyes, and for whom each of his movements had been a revelation, came timidly, and seated himself at the foot of the bed, and glued his lips to the sheet which was raised by the stiffened feet of his master. Then large drops began to flow from his red eyes. This old man in despair, who wept, bent double without uttering a word, presented the most moving spectacle that D'Artagnan, in a life so filled with emotion, had ever met with.

The captain remained standing in contemplation before that smiling dead man, who seemed to have kept his last thought to make to his best friend, to the man he had loved next to Raoul, a gracious welcome even beyond life; and as if to reply to that exalted flattery of hospitality, D'Artagnan went and kissed Athos fervently on the brow, and with his trembling fingers closed his eyes. Then he seated himself by the pillow without

dread of that dead man, who had been so kind and affectionate
to him for thirty-five years; he fed himself greedily with the
remembrances which the noble visage of the comte brought to
his mind in crowds—some blooming and charming as that
smile—some dark, dismal, and icy as that face with its eyes
closed for eternity.

All at once, the bitter flood which mounted from minute to
minute invaded his heart, and swelled his breast almost to
bursting. Incapable of mastering his emotion, he arose, and
tearing himself violently from the chamber where he had just
found dead him to whom he came to report the news of the
death of Porthos, he uttered sobs so heartrending that the
servants, who seemed only to wait for an explosion of grief,
answered to it by their lugubrious clamors, and the dogs of the
late comte by their lamentable howlings. Grimaud was the only
one who did not lift up his voice. Even in the paroxysm of his
grief he would not have dared to profane the dead, or for the
first time disturb the slumber of his master. Athos had accustomed him never to speak.

At daybreak D'Artagnan, who had wandered about the lower
hall, biting his fingers to stifle his sighs—D'Artagnan went
up once more, and watching the moment when Grimaud turned
his head toward him, he made him a sign to come to him, which
the faithful servant obeyed without making more noise than
a shadow. D'Artagnan went down again, followed by Grimaud;
and when he had gained the vestibule, taking the old man's
hands:

"Grimaud," said he, "I have seen how the father died; now
let me know how the son died."

Grimaud drew from his breast a large letter, upon the envelope of which was traced the address of Athos. He recognized the writing of M. de Beaufort, broke the seal, and began to read, walking about in the first blue rays of day, in the
dark alley of old limes, marked by the still visible footsteps
of the comte who had just died.

Chapter 59 — THE BULLETIN

The Duc de Beaufort wrote to Athos. The letter destined for
the living only reached the dead. God had changed the address.

"My Dear Comte," wrote the prince, in his large, bad
schoolboy's hand—"a great misfortune has struck us amid
great triumph. The king loses one of the bravest of soldiers.
lose a friend. You lose Monsieur de Bragelonne. He has die
gloriously, and so gloriously that I have not the strength t
weep as I could wish. Receive my sad compliments, my dea
comte. Heaven distributes trials according to the greatness o
our hearts. This is an immense one, but not above your cou
age. Your good friend,

"Le Duc de Beaufort."

The letter contained a relation written by one of the prince'
secretaries. It was the most touching recital, and the most tru
of that dismal episode which unraveled two existences. D'Artag
nan, accustomed to battle emotions, and with a heart arme
against tenderness, could not help starting on reading the nam
of Raoul, the name of that beloved boy who had become, a
his father had, a shade.

"In the morning," said the prince's secretary, "monseigneu
commanded the attack. Normandy and Picardy had taken po
sition in the gray rocks dominated by the heights of the moun
tain, upon the declivity of which were raised the bastions o
Gigelli.

"The cannon beginning to fire, opened the action; the regi
ments marched full of resolution; the pikemen had their pike
elevated, the bearers of muskets had their weapons ready. Th
prince followed attentively the march and movements of th
troops, so as to be able to sustain them with a strong reserv
With monseigneur were the oldest captains and his aid-d
camp. Monsieur le Vicomte de Bragelonne had received orde
not to leave his highness. In the meantime, the enemy's can
non, which at first had thundered with little success agains
the masses, had regulated its fire, and the balls, better directe
had killed several men near the prince. The regiments forme
in column, and which were advancing against the rampart
were rather roughly handled. There was a sort of hesitation i
our troops, who found themselves ill-seconded by the arti
lery. In fact, the batteries which had been established the eve
ning before had but a weak and uncertain aim, on account o
their position. The direction from low to high lessened the jus
ness of the shots as well as their range.

"Monseigneur, comprehending the bad effect of this posi
tion of the siege artillery, commanded the frigates moored i
the little road to commence a regular fire against the plac

Monsieur de Bragelonne offered himself at once to carry this order. But monseigneur refused to acquiesce in the vicomte's request. Monseigneur was right, for he loved and wished to spare the young nobleman. He was quite right, and the event took upon itself to justify his foresight and refusal; for scarcely had the sergeant charged with the message solicited by Monsieur de Bragelonne gained the seashore, when two shots from long carbines issued from the enemy's ranks and laid him low. The sergeant fell, dyeing the sand with his blood, observing which, Monsieur de Bragelonne smiled at monseigneur, who said to him, 'You see, vicomte, I have saved your life. Report that, some day, to Monsieur le Comte de la Fere, in order that, learning it from you, he may thank you.' The young nobleman smiled sadly, and replied to the duke, 'It is true, monseigneur, that but for your kindness I should have been killed, where the poor sergeant has fallen, and should be at rest.' Monsieur de Bragelonne made this reply in such a tone that monseigneur answered him warmly, '*Vrai Dieu!* young man, one would say that your mouth waters for death; but, by the soul of Henri IV.! I have promised your father to bring you back alive, and, please the Lord, I will keep my word.' Monsieur de Bragelonne colored, and replied, in a lower voice, 'Monseigneur, pardon me. I beseech you; I have always had the desire to go to meet good opportunities; and it is so delightful to distinguish ourselves before our general, particularly when that general is Monsieur le Duc de Beaufort.'

"Monseigneur was a little softened by this; and, turning to the officers who surrounded him, gave his different orders. The grenadiers of the two regiments got near enough to the ditches and the intrenchments to launch their grenades, which had but little effect. In the meanwhile, Monsieur d'Estrées, who commanded the fleet, having seen the attempt of the sergeant to approach the vessels, understood that he must act without orders, and opened his fire. Then the Arabs finding themselves seriously injured by the balls from the fleet, and beholding the destruction and the ruins of their bad walls, uttered the most fearful cries. Their horsemen descended the mountain at the gallop, bent over their saddles, and rushed full tilt upon the columns of infantry, which, crossing their pikes, stopped this mad assault. Repulsed by the firm attitude of the battalion, the Arabs threw themselves with great fury toward the état-major, which was not on its guard at that moment.

"The danger was great; monseigneur drew his sword; his secretaries and people imitated him; the officers of the suite

engaged in combat with the furious Arabs. It was then Monsieur de Bragelonne was able to satisfy the inclination he had
manifested from the commencement of the action. He fought
near the prince with the valor of a Roman, and killed three
Arabs with his small sword. But it was evident that his bravery
did not arise from one of those sentiments of pride natural to
all who fight. It was impetuous, affected, forced even; he sought
to intoxicate himself with the noise and carnage. He heated
himself to such a degree that monseigneur called out to him to
stop. He must have heard the voice of monseigneur, because
we who were close to him heard it. He did not, however, stop,
but continued his course toward the intrenchments. As Monsieur de Bragelonne was a well-disciplined officer, this disobedience to the orders of monseigneur very much surprised everybody, and Monsieur de Beaufort redoubled his earnestness,
crying, 'Stop, Bragelonne! Where are you going? Stop!' repeated
monseigneur, 'I command you!'

"We all, imitating the gesture of Monsieur le Duc, we all
raised our hands. We expected that the cavalier would turn
bridle; but Monsieur de Bragelonne continued to ride toward
the palisades.

"'Stop, Bragelonne!' repeated the prince, in a very loud
voice; 'stop! in the name of your father!'

"At these words Monsieur de Bragelonne turned round, his
countenance expressed a lively grief, but he did not stop; we
then concluded that his horse must have run away with him.
When Monsieur le Duc had imagined the vicomte was not master of the horse, and had seen him precede the first grenadier,
his highness cried, 'Musketeers, kill his horse! A hundred pistoles for him who shall kill his horse!' But who could expect
to hit the beast without at least wounding his rider? No one
durst venture. At length one presented himself; he was a sharpshooter of the regiment of Picardy, named Luzerne, who took
aim at the animal, fired, and hit him in the quarters, for we
saw the blood redden the hair of the horse. Instead of falling,
the cursed jennet was irritated, and carried him on more furiously than ever. Every Picard who saw this unfortunate young
man rushing on to meet death, shouted in the loudest manner,
'Throw yourself off, Monsieur le Vicomte!—off!—off! throw
yourself off!' Monsieur de Bragelonne was an officer much
beloved in the army. Already had the vicomte arrived within
pistol-shot of the ramparts, a discharge was poured upon him
and enveloped him in its fire and smoke. We lost sight of him

e smoke dispersed; he was on foot, standing; his horse was
killed.

"The vicomte was summoned to surrender by the Arabs, but
he made them a negative sign with his head, and continued to
march toward the palisades. This was a mortal imprudence.
Nevertheless, the whole army was pleased that he would not
retreat, since ill-chance had led him so near. He marched a
few paces further, and the two regiments clapped their hands.
It was at this moment the second discharge shook the walls,
and the Vicomte de Bragelonne again disappeared in the smoke;
but this time the smoke was dispersed in vain; we no longer
saw him standing. He was down, with his head lower than his
legs, among the bushes, and the Arabs began to think of leaving
their intrenchments to come and cut off his head, or take his
body, as is the custom with the infidels. But Monseigneur le
Duc de Beaufort had followed all this with his eyes, and the
sad spectacle drew from him many and painful sighs. He then
cried aloud, seeing the Arabs running like white phantoms
among the mastick-trees, 'Grenadiers, piquers! will you let
them take that noble body?'

"Saying these words and waving his sword, he himself rode
toward the enemy. The regiments, rushing in his steps, ran in
their turns, uttering cries as terrible as those of the Arabs were
wild.

"The combat commenced over the body of Monsieur de
Bragelonne, and with such inveteracy was it fought that a hundred and sixty Arabs were left upon the field, by the side of at
least fifty of our troops. It was a lieutenant from Normandy
who took the body of the vicomte on his shoulders and carried
it back to the lines. The advantage was, however, pursued, the
regiments took the reserve with them, and the enemy's palisades were destroyed. At three o'clock the fire of the Arabs
ceased; the hand-to-hand fight lasted two hours; that was a
massacre. At five o'clock we were victorious on all the points;
the enemy had abandoned his positions, and Monsieur le Duc
had ordered the white flag to be planted upon the culminating
point of the little mountain. It was then we had time to think
of Monsieur de Bragelonne, who had eight large wounds
through his body, by which almost all his blood had escaped.
Still, however, he breathed, which afforded inexpressible joy
to monseigneur, who insisted upon being present at the first
dressing of the wounds and at the consultation of the surgeons.
There were two among them who declared Monsieur de Brage-

lonne would live. Monseigneur threw his arms round the
necks and promised them a thousand louis each if they coul
save him.

"The vicomte heard these transports of joy, and wheth
he was in despair, or whether he suffered much from his wound
he expressed, by his countenance, a contradiction, which ga
rise to reflection, particularly in one of the secretaries, whe
he had heard what follows. The third surgeon was the broth
of Sylvain de St. Cosme, the most learned of ours. He probe
the wounds in his turn, and said nothing. Monsieur de Brag
lonne fixed his eyes steadily upon the skillful surgeon, ar
seemed to interrogate his every movement. The latter, upc
being questioned by monseigneur, replied that he saw plain
three mortal wounds out of eight, but so strong was the co
stitution of the wounded, so rich was he in youth, and so merc
ful was the goodness of God, that perhaps Monsieur de Brag
lonne might recover, particularly if he did not move in tl
slightest manner. Frére Sylvain added, turning toward his a
sistants, 'Above everything, do not allow him to move even
finger, or you will kill him;' and we all left the tent in very lo
spirits. That secretary I have mentioned, on leaving the ten
thought he perceived a faint and sad smile glide over the lips
Monsieur de Bragelonne when the duke said to him, in a chee
ful, kind voice, 'We shall save you, vicomte, we shall save you

"In the evening, when it was believed the wounded youn
man had taken some repose, one of the assistants entered h
tent, but rushed immediately out again, uttering loud cries. W
all ran up in disorder, Monsieur le Duc with us, and the assi
tant pointed to the body of Monsieur de Bragelonne upe
the ground, at the foot of his bed, bathed in the remainder
his blood. It appeared that he had had some convulsion, son
febrile movement, and that he had fallen, that the fall had a
celerated his end, according to the prognostic of Frère Sylvai
We raised the vicomte; he was cold and dead. He held a lo
of hair in his right hand, and that hand was pressed tight
upon his heart."

Then followed the details of the expedition, and of the vi
tory obtained over the Arabs. D'Artagnan stopped at the a
count of the death of poor Raoul.

"Oh!" murmured he, "unhappy boy! a suicide!"

And turning his eyes toward the chamber at the châtea
in which Athos slept in eternal sleep:

"They kept their words with each other," said he, in a lc

voice; "now I believe them to be happy; they must be reunited."

And he returned through the parterre with slow and melancholy steps. All the village—all the neighborhood—were filled with grieving neighbors relating to each other the double catastrophe, and making preparations for the funeral.

Chapter 60 — THE LAST CANTO OF THE POEM

On the morrow, all the noblesse of the provinces, of the environs, and wherever messengers had carried the news, were seen to arrive. D'Artagnan had shut himself up, without being willing to speak to anybody. Two such heavy deaths falling upon the captain, so closely after the death of Porthos, for a long time oppressed that spirit which had hitherto been so inefatigable and invulnerable. Except Grimaud, who entered his chamber once, the musketeer saw neither servants nor guests. He supposed, from the noises in the house, and the continual coming and going, that preparations were being made for the funeral of the comte. He wrote to the king to ask for an extension of his leave of absence. Grimaud, as we have said, had entered D'Artagnan's apartment, and had seated himself upon a joint-stool near the door, like a man who meditates profoundly; then, rising, he made a sign to D'Artagnan to follow him. The latter obeyed in silence. Grimaud descended to the comte's bedchamber, showed the captain with his finger the place of the empty bed, and raised his eyes eloquently toward heaven.

"Yes," replied D'Artagnan, "yes, good Grimaud—now with the son he loved so much!"

Grimaud left the chamber, and led the way to the hall, where, according to the custom of the province, the body was laid out previously to its being buried forever. D'Artagnan was struck at seeing two open coffins in the hall. In reply to the mute invitation of Grimaud he approached, and saw in one of them Athos, still handsome in death, and in the other, Raoul, with his eyes closed, his cheeks pearly as those of the Pallas of Virgil, with a smile on his violet lips. He shuddered at seeing the father and son, those two departed souls, represented on earth by two silent, melancholy bodies, incapable of touching each other, however close they might be.

"Raoul here!" murmured he. "Oh, Grimaud, why did you not tell me this?"

Grimaud shook his head, and made no reply; but, taking D'Artagnan by the hand, he led him to the coffin, and showed him, under the thin winding-sheet, the black wounds by which life had escaped. The captain turned away his eyes, and judging it useless to question Grimaud, who would not answer he recollected that M. de Beaufort's secretary had written more than he, D'Artagnan, had had the courage to read. Taking up the recital of the affair which had cost Raoul his life, he found these words, which terminated the last paragraph of the letter:

"Monsieur le Duc has ordered that the body of Monsieur le Vicomte should be embalmed, after the manner practiced by the Arabs when they wish their bodies to be carried to their native land; and Monsieur le Duc has appointed relays, so that a confidential servant who brought up the young man might take back his remains to Monsieur le Comte de la Fere."

"And so," thought D'Artagnan, "I shall follow thy funeral my dear boy—I, already old—I, who am of no value on earth —and I shall scatter the dust upon that brow which I kissed but two months since. God has willed it to be so. Thou hast willed it to be so, thyself. I have no longer the right even to weep. Thou hast chosen death; it hath seemed to thee preferable to life."

At length arrived the moment when the cold remains of these two gentlemen were to be returned to the earth. There was such an affluence of military and other people that up to the place of sepulchre, which was a chapel in the plain, the road from the city was filled with horsemen and pedestrians in mourning habits. Athos had chosen for his resting-place the little enclosure of a chapel erected by himself near the boundary of his estates. He had had the stones, cut in 1550 brought from an old Gothic manor house in Berry, which had sheltered his early youth. The chapel, thus reedified, thus transported, was pleasant beneath its wood of poplars and sycamores. It was administered every Sunday by the curé of the neighboring bourg, to whom Athos paid an allowance of two hundred francs for this service; and all the vassals of his domain to the number of about forty, the laborers, and the farmers with their families, came thither to hear mass, without having any occasion to go to the city.

Behind the chapel extended, surrounded by two high hedges

f nut-trees, elders, white thorns, and a deep ditch, the little
closure—uncultivated, it is true, but gay in its sterility; be-
ause the mosses there were high, because the wild heliotropes
nd ravenelles there mixed their perfumes, because beneath
he tall chestnuts issued a large spring, a prisoner in a cistern of
arble, and that upon the thyme all around alighted thousands of
ees from the neighboring plants, while chaffinches and red-
hroats sang cheerfully among the flowers of the hedge. It was
this place the two coffins were brought, attended by a silent
nd respectful crowd. The office of the dead being celebrated,
he last adieus paid to the noble departed, the assembly dis-
ersed, talking, along the roads, of the virtues and mild death
f the father, of the hopes the son had given, and of his
elancholy end upon the coast of Africa. By little and little
ll noises were extinguished, like the lamps illumining the
umble nave. The minister bowed for a last time to the altar
nd the still fresh graves, then, followed by his assistant, who
ang a hoarse bell, he slowly took the road back to the pres-
ytery. D'Artagnan, left alone, perceived that night was coming
n. He had forgotten the hour while thinking of the dead. He
ose from the oaken bench on which he was seated in the
hapel, and wished, as the priest had done, to go and bid a last
dieu to the double grave which contained his two lost friends.

A woman was praying, kneeling on the moist earth. D'Ar-
agnan stopped at the door of the chapel, to avoid disturbing
his woman; and also to endeavor to see who was the pious
riend who performed this sacred duty with so much zeal and
erseverance. The unknown concealed her face in her hands,
hich were white as alabaster. From the noble simplicity of
er costume, she must be a woman of distinction. Outside the
closure were several horses mounted by servants, and a
raveling-carriage waiting for this lady. D'Artagnan in vain
ught to make out what caused her delay. She continued pray-
g, she frequently passed her handkerchief over her face, by
hich D'Artagnan perceived she was weeping. He saw her
trike her breast with the pitiless compunction of a Christian
oman. He heard her several times proffer, as if from a
ounded heart, "Pardon! pardon!" And as she appeared to
bandon herself entirely to her grief, as she threw herself down,
lmost fainting, amid complaints and prayers, D'Artagnan,
uched by this love for his so much regretted friends, made
few steps toward the grave, in order to interrupt the mel-
ncholy colloquy of the penitent with the dead. But as soon as

his step sounded on the gravel the unknown raised her head, revealing to D'Artagnan a face inundated with tears, but a well-known face. It was Mlle. de la Valliere!

"Monsieur d'Artagnan!" murmured she.

"You!" replied the captain, in a stern voice—"you here! Oh, madame, I should better have liked to see you decked with flowers in the mansion of the Comte de la Fere. You would have wept less—they, too—I, too!"

"Monsieur!" she said, sobbing.

"For it is you," added this pitiless friend of the dead—"it is you who have laid these two men in the grave."

"Oh, spare me!"

"God forbid, madame, that I should offend a woman, or that I should make her weep in vain; but I must say that the place of the murderer is not upon the grave of her victims."

She wished to reply.

"What I now tell you," added he coldly, "I told the king."

She clasped her hands.

"I know," said she, "I have caused the death of the Vicomte de Bragelonne."

"Ah! you know it?"

"The news arrived at court yesterday. I have traveled during the night forty leagues to come and ask pardon of the comte whom I supposed to be still living, and to supplicate God, upon the tomb of Raoul, that He would send me all the misfortunes I have merited, except a single one. Now, monsieur, I know that the death of the son has killed the father; I have two crimes to reproach myself with; I have two punishments to look for from God."

"I will repeat to you, mademoiselle," said D'Artagnan, "what Monsieur de Bragelonne said of you at Antibes, when he already meditated death: 'If pride and coquetry have misled her, I pardon her while despising her. If love has produced her error, I pardon her, swearing that no one could have loved her as I have done.'"

"You know," interrupted Louise, "that for my love I was about to sacrifice myself; you know whether I suffered when you met me lost, dying, abandoned. Well, never have I suffered so much as now; because then I hoped, I desired—now I have nothing to wish for; because this death drags away all my joy into the tomb; because I can no longer dare to love without remorse, and I feel that he whom I love—oh! that the law—will repay me with the tortures I have made other undergo."

D'Artagnan made no reply; he was too well convinced she was not mistaken.

"Well, then," added she, "dear Monsieur d'Artagnan, do not overwhelm me to-day, I again implore you. I am like the branch torn from the trunk, I no longer hold to anything in this world, and a current drags me on, I cannot say whither. I love madly, I love to the point of coming to tell it, impious as I am, over the ashes of the dead, and I do not blush for it—I have no remorse on account of it. This love is a religion. Only as hereafter you will see me alone, forgotten, disdained; as you will see me punished with that with which I am destined to be punished, spare me in my ephemeral happiness, leave it to me for a few days, for a few minutes. Now even, at the moment I am speaking to you, perhaps it no longer exists. My God! this double murder is perhaps already expiated!"

While she was speaking thus the sound voices and the steps of horses drew the attention of the captain. M. de St. Aignan came to seek La Valliere.

"The king," he said, "was a prey to jealousy and uneasyness."

St. Aignan did not see D'Artagnan, half-concealed by the trunk of a chestnut-tree which shaded the two graves. Louise thanked St. Aignan, and dismissed him with a gesture. He rejoined the party outside the inclosure.

"You see, madame," said the captain bitterly to the young woman, "you see that your happiness still lasts."

The young woman raised her head with a solemn air.

"A day will come," said she, "when you will repent of having so ill-judged me. On that day, it is I who will pray God to forgive you for having been unjust toward me. Besides, I shall suffer so much that you will be the first to pity my sufferings. Do not reproach me with that happiness, Monsieur d'Artagnan; it costs me dear, and I have not paid all my debt."

Saying these words, she again knelt down, softly and affectionately.

"Pardon me, the last time, my affianced Raoul!" said she. "I have broken our chain; we are both destined to die of grief. It is thou who departest the first; fear nothing, I shall follow thee. See, only, that I have not been base, and that I have come to bid thee this last adieu. The Lord is my witness, Raoul, that if with my life I could have redeemed thine, I would have given that life without hesitation. I could not give my love. Once more, pardon!"

She gathered a branch, and stuck it into the ground; then,

wiping the tears from her eyes, she bowed to D'Artagnan, and disappeared.

The captain watched the departure of the horses, horsemen, and carriage, then, crossing his arms upon his swelling chest:

"When will it be my turn to depart?" said he, in an agitated voice. "What is there left for man after youth, after love, after glory, after friendship, after strength, after riches? That rock, under which sleeps Porthos, who possessed all I have named; this moss, under which repose Athos and Raoul, who possessed still much more!"

He hesitated a moment, with a dull eye; then, drawing himself up:

"Forward! still forward!" said he. "When it shall be time God will tell me, as He has told others!"

He touched the earth, moistened with the evening dew, with the ends of his fingers, signed himself, as if he had been at the *bénitier* of a church, and retook, alone—ever alone—the road to Paris.

EPILOGUE

Four years after the scene we have just described two horsemen, well mounted, traversed Blois early in the morning, for the purpose of arranging a birding party which the king intended to make in that uneven plain which the Loire divides in two, and which borders on the one side on Meung, on the other on Amboise. These were the captain of the king's harriers and the governor of the falcons, personages greatly respected in the time of Louis XIII., but rather neglected by his successor. These two horsemen, having reconnoitered the ground, were returning, their observations made, when they perceived some little groups of soldiers, here and there, whom the sergeants were placing at distances at the openings of the inclosures. These were the king's musketeers. Behind them came, upon a good horse, the captain, known by his richly embroidered uniform. His hair was gray, his beard was becoming so. He appeared a little bent, although sitting and handling his horse gracefully. He was looking about him watchfully.

"Monsieur d'Artagnan does not get any older," said th

captain of the harriers to his colleague, the falconer; "with ten years more than either of us, he has the seat of a young man on horseback."

"That is true," replied the falconer. "I don't see any change in him for the last twenty years."

But this officer was mistaken. D'Artagnan in the last four years had lived twelve years. Age imprinted its pitiless claws at each angle of his eyes; his brow was bald; his hands, formerly brown and nervous, were getting white as if the blood began to chill there.

D'Artagnan accosted the officers with the shade of affability which distinguishes superior men, and received in return for his courtesy two most respectful bows.

"Ah! what a lucky chance to see you here, Monsieur d'Artagnan!" cried the falconer.

"It is rather I who should say that, messieurs," replied the captain, "for nowadays the king makes more frequent use of his musketeers than of his falcons."

"Ah! it is not as it was in the good old times," sighed the falconer. "Do you remember, Monsieur d'Artagnan, when the late king flew the pie in the vineyards beyond Beaugence? Ah! dame! you were not captain of the musketeers at that time, Monsieur d'Artagnan."

"And you were nothing but under-corporal of the tiercelets," replied D'Artagnan, laughing. "Never mind that, it was a good time, seeing that it is always a good time when we are young. Good-day, Monsieur the Captain of the Harriers."

"You do me honor, Monsieur le Comte," said the latter. D'Artagnan made no reply. The title of comte had not struck him; D'Artagnan had been a comte four years.

"Are you not very much fatigued with the long journey you have had, Monsieur le Capitaine?" continued the falconer. "It must be full two hundred leagues from hence to Pignerol."

"Two hundred and sixty to go, and as many to come back," said D'Artagnan quietly.

"And," said the falconer, "is *he* well?"

"Who?" asked D'Artagnan.

"Why, poor Monsieur Fouquet," continued the falconer, still in a low voice.

The captain of the harriers had prudently withdrawn.

"No," replied D'Artagnan, "the poor man frets terribly; he cannot comprehend how imprisonment can be a favor; he says that the parliament had absolved him by banishing him, and that banishment is liberty. He cannot imagine that they had sworn his death, and that to save his life from the claws of the parliament was to have too much obligation to God."

"Ah! yes; the poor man had a near chance of the scaffold," replied the falconer; "it is said that Monsieur Colbert had given orders to the governor of the Bastile, and that the execution was ordered."

"Enough!" said D'Artagnan pensively, and with a view of cutting short the conversation.

"Yes," said the captain of the harriers, drawing toward them, "Monsieur Fouquet is now at Pignerol; he has richly deserved it. He has had the good fortune to be conducted there by you; he had robbed the king enough."

D'Artagnan launched at the master of the dogs one of his evil looks, and said to him:

"Monsieur, if any one told me you had eaten your dogs' meat, not only would I refuse to believe it; but, still more, if you were condemned to the whip or the jail for it, I should pity you, and would not allow people to speak ill of you. And yet, monsieur, honest man as you may be, I assure you that you are not more so than poor Monsieur Fouquet was."

After having undergone this sharp rebuke, the captain of the harriers hung his head, and allowed the falconer to get two steps in advance of him nearer to D'Artagnan.

"He is content," said the falconer, in a low voice, to the musketeer; "we all know that harriers are in fashion nowadays if he were a falconer he would not talk in that way."

D'Artagnan smiled in a melancholy manner at seeing this great political question resolved by the discontent of such humble interests. He for a moment ran over in his mind the glorious existence of the surintendant, the crumbling away of his fortunes, and the melancholy death that awaited him; and to conclude:

"Did Monsieur Fouquet love falconry?" said he.

"Oh, passionately, monsieur!" replied the falconer, with an accent of bitter regret, and a sigh that was the funeral oration of Fouquet.

D'Artagnan allowed the ill-humor of the one and the regret of the other to pass, and continued to advance into the plain. They could already catch glimpses of the huntsmen at the issues of the wood, the feathers of the outriders, passing like shooting-stars across the clearings, and the white horses cutting with their luminous apparitions the dark thickets of the copse.

"But," resumed D'Artagnan, "will the sport be long? Pragive us a good swift bird, for I am very tired. Is it a heron or a swan?"

"Both, Monsieur d'Artagnan," said the falconer; "but you need not be alarmed, the king is not much of a sportsman; he does not sport on his own account, he only wishes to give amusement to the ladies."

The words "to the ladies" were so strongly accented that it set D'Artagnan listening.

"Ah!" said he, looking at the falconer with surprise.

The captain of the harriers smiled, no doubt with a view of making it up with the musketeer.

"Oh! you may safely laugh," said D'Artagnan; "I know nothing of current news; I only arrived yesterday, after a month's absence. I left the court mourning the death of the queen-mother. The king was not willing to take any amusement after receiving the last sigh of Anne of Austria; but everything has an end in this world. Well, then he is no longer sad? So much the better."

"And everything commences as well as ends," said the captain of the dogs, with a coarse laugh.

"Ah!" said D'Artagnan, a second time—he burned to know, but dignity would not allow him to interrogate people below him—"there is something beginning, then, it appears?"

The captain gave him a significant wink; but D'Artagnan was unwilling to learn anything from this man.

"Shall we see the king early?" asked he of the falconer.

"At seven o'clock, monsieur, I shall fly the birds."

"Who comes with the king? How is madame? How is the queen?"

"Better, monsieur."

"Has she been ill, then?"

"Monsieur, since the last chagrin he had, her majesty had been unwell."

"What chagrin? You need not fancy your news is old. I am but just returned."

"It appears that the queen, a little neglected since the death of her mother-in-law, complained to the king, who replied to her: 'Do I not sleep with you every night, madame? What more do you want?'"

"Ah!" said D'Artagnan, "poor woman! She must heartily hate Mademoiselle de la Valliere."

"Oh, no! not Mademoiselle de la Valliere," replied the falconer.

"Who then?"

The horn interrupted this conversation. It summoned the dogs and the hawks. The falconer and his companion set off immediately, leaving D'Artagnan alone in the midst of the suspended sentence. The king appeared at a distance, surrounded by ladies and horsemen. All the troop advanced in beautiful order, at a foot's pace, the horns of various sorts animating the dogs and the horses. It was a movement, a noise, a mirage of light, of which nothing now can give an idea, unless it be the fictitious splendor or false majesty of a theatrical spectacle. D'Artagnan, with an eye a little weakened, distinguished behind the group three carriages. The first was intended for the queen; it was empty. D'Artagnan, who did not see Mlle. de la Valliere by the king's side, on looking about for her saw her in the second carriage. She was alone with two of her women, who seemed as dull as their mistress. On the left hand of the king, upon a high-spirited horse, restrained by a bold and skillful hand, shone a lady of the most dazzling beauty. The king smiled upon her, and she smiled upon the king. Loud laughter followed every word she spoke.

"I must know that woman," thought the musketeer; "who can she be?"

And he stooped toward his friend, the falconer, to whom he addressed the question he had put to himself. The falconer was about to reply, when the king, perceiving D'Artagnan:

"Ah, comte!" said he, "you are returned, then! Why have I not seen you?"

"Sire," replied the captain, "because your majesty was asleep when I arrived, and not awake when I resumed my duties this morning."

"Still the same," said Louis, in a loud voice, denoting satisfaction. "Take some rest, comte; I command you to do so. You will dine with me to-day."

A murmur of admiration surrounded D'Artagnan like an immense caress. Every one was eager to salute him. Dining with the king was an honor his majesty was not so prodigal of a Henry IV. had been. The king passed a few steps in advance and D'Artagnan found himself in the midst of a fresh group among whom shone Colbert.

"Good-day, Monsieur d'Artagnan," said the minister, with affable politeness; "have you had a pleasant journey?"

"Yes, monsieur," said D'Artagnan, bowing to the neck of his horse.

"I heard the king invite you to his table for this evening," continued the minister; "you will meet an old friend there."

"An old friend of mine?" asked D'Artagnan, plunging painfully into the dark waves of the past, which had swallowed up for him so many friendships and so many hatreds.

"Monsieur de Duc d'Alméda, who is arrived this morning from Spain."

"The Duc d'Alméda?" said D'Artagnan, reflecting in vain.

"I!" said an old man, white as snow, sitting bent in his carriage, which he caused to be thrown open to make room for the musketeer.

"Aramis!" cried D'Artagnan, struck with perfect stupor.

And he left, inert as it was, the thin arm of the old nobleman hanging round his neck.

Colbert, after having observed them in silence for a minute, put his horse forward, and left the two old friends together.

"And so," said the musketeer, taking the arm of Aramis, "you, the exile, the rebel, are again in France?"

"Ah! and I shall dine with you at the king's table," said Aramis, smiling. "Yes, you will not ask yourself what is the use of fidelity in this world? Stop! let us allow poor Valliere's carriage to pass. Look, how uneasy she is! How her eye, dimmed with tears, follows the king, who is riding on horseback yonder!"

"With whom?"

"With Mademoiselle de Tonnay-Charente, now become Madame de Montespan," replied Aramis.

"She is jealous; is she, then, deserted?"

"Not quite yet, but it will not be long first."

They chatted together, while following the sport, and Aramis' coachman drove them so cleverly that they got up at the moment when the falcon, attacking the bird, beat him down, and fell upon him. The king alighted; Mme. de Montespan followed his example. They were in front of an isolated chapel, concealed by large trees, already despoiled of their leaves by the first winds of autumn. Behind this chapel was an inclosure closed by a latticed gate. The falcon had beat down his prey in the inclosure belonging to this little chapel, and the king was desirous of going in to take the first feather, according to custom. The cortège formed a circle round the building and the hedges, too small to receive so many. D'Artagnan held back Aramis by the arm, as he was about, like the rest, to alight from his carriage, and in a hoarse, broken voice:

"Do you know, Aramis," said he, "whither chance has conducted us?"

"No," replied the duke.

"Here repose people I have known," said D'Artagnan, much agitated.

Aramis, without divining anything, and with a trembling step, penetrated into the chapel by a little door which D'Artagnan opened for him.

"Where are they buried?" said he.

"There, in the inclosure. There is a cross, you see, under that little cypress. The little cypress is planted over their tomb; don't go to it; the king is going that way; the heron has fallen just there."

Aramis stopped and concealed himself in the shade. They then saw, without being seen, the pale face of La Valliere, who, neglected in her carriage, had at first looked on, with a melancholy heart, from the door, and then, carried away by jealousy, she had advanced into the chapel, whence, leaning against a pillar, she contemplated in the inclosure the king smiling and making signs to Mme. de Montespan to approach, as there was nothing to be afraid of. Mme. de Montespan complied; she took the hand the king held out to her, and he, plucking out the first feather from the heron, which the falconer had strangled, placed it in the hat of his beautiful companion. She, smiling in her turn, kissed the hand tenderly which made her this present. The king blushed with pleasure; he looked at Mme. de Montespan with all the fire of love.

"What will you give me in exchange?" said he.

She broke off a little branch of cypress and offered it to the king, who looked intoxicated with hope.

"Humph!" said Aramis to D'Artagnan, "the present is but a sad one, for that cypress shades a tomb."

"Yes, and the tomb is that of Raoul de Bragelonne," said D'Artagnan, aloud, "of Raoul, who sleeps under that cross with his father."

A groan resounded behind them. They saw a woman fall fainting to the ground. Mlle. de la Valliere had seen all, and heard all.

"Poor woman!" muttered D'Artagnan, as he helped the attendants to carry back to her carriage she who from that time was to suffer.

That evening D'Artagnan was seated at the king's table, near M. Colbert and M. le Duc d'Alméda. The king was very gay. H paid a thousand little attentions to the queen, a thousand kindnesses to madame, seated at his left hand, and very sad. I might have been supposed to be that calm time when the kin used to watch the eyes of his mother for the avowal or disavowal of what he had just done.

Of mistresses there was no question at this dinner. The king addressed Aramis two or three times, calling him M. l'Ambassadeur, which increased the surprise already felt by D'Artagnan at seeing his friend the rebel so marvelously well received at court.

The king, on rising from table, gave his hand to the queen, and made a sign to Colbert, whose eye watched that of his master. Colbert took D'Artagnan and Aramis on one side. The king began to chat with his sister, while Monsieur, very uneasy, entertained the queen with a preoccupied air, without ceasing to watch his wife and brother from the corner of his eye. The conversation between Aramis, D'Artagnan and Colbert turned upon indifferent subjects. They spoke of preceding ministers; Colbert related the feats of Mazarin, and required those of Richelieu to be related to him. D'Artagnan could not overcome his surprise at finding this man, with heavy eyebrows and a low forehead, contain so much sound knowledge and cheerful spirits. Aramis was astonished at that lightness of character which permitted a serious man to retard with advantage the moment for a more important conversation, to which nobody made any allusion, although all three interlocutors felt the imminence of it. It was very plain from the embarrassed appearance of Monsieur, how much the conversation of the king and madame annoyed him. The eyes of madame were almost red; was she going to complain? Was she going to commit a little scandal in open court? The king took her on one side, and in a tone so tender that it must have reminded the princess of the time when she was loved for herself:

"Sister," said he, "why do I see tears in those beautiful eyes?"

"Why—sire—" said she.

"Monsieur is jealous, is he not, sister?"

She looked toward Monsieur, an infallible sign that they were talking about him.

"Yes," said she.

"Listen to me," said the king; "if your friends compromise you, it is not Monsieur's fault."

He spoke these words with so much kindness that madame, encouraged, she who had had so many griefs for so long a time, was near bursting, so full was her heart.

"Come, come, dear little sister," said the king, "tell me your griefs; by the word of a brother, I pity them; by the word of a king, I will terminate them."

She raised her fine eyes, and, in a melancholy tone:

"It is not my friends who compromise me," said she; "they are either absent or concealed; they have been brought into disgrace with your majesty; they, so devoted, so good, so loyal!"

"You say this on account of De Guiche, whom I have exiled, at the desire of Monsieur?"

"And who, since that unjust exile, had endeavored to get himself killed once every day!"

"Unjust, do you say, sister?"

"So unjust, that if I had not had the respect mixed with friendship that I have always entertained for your majesty——"

"Well?"

"Well, I would have asked my brother Charles, upon whom I can always——"

The king started.

"What then?"

"I would have asked him to have had it represented to you that Monsieur and his favorite, Monsieur le Chevalier de Lorraine, ought not with impunity to constitute themselves the executioners of my honor and my happiness."

"The Chevalier de Lorraine," said the king; "that dismal face?"

"Is my mortal enemy. While that man lives in my household, where Monsieur retains him and delegates his powers to him, I shall be the most miserable woman in this kingdom."

"So," said the king slowly, "you call your brother of England a better friend than I am?"

"Actions speak for themselves, sire."

"And you would prefer going to ask assistance there——"

"To my own country!" said she, with pride; "yes, sire."

"You are the grandchild of Henry IV. as well as myself, my friend. Cousin and brother-in-law, does not that amount pretty well to the title of brother-germain?"

"Then," said Henriette, "act."

"Let us form an alliance."

"Begin."

"I have, you say, unjustly exiled De Guiche."

"Oh, yes!" said she, blushing.

"De Guiche shall return."

"So far, well."

"And now you say that I am wrong in having in your house-told the Chevalier de Lorraine, who gives Monsieur ill advice respecting you?"

"Remember well what I tell you, sire; the Chevalier de Lorraine some day— Observe, if ever I come to an ill end, I beforehand accuse the Chevalier de Lorraine; he has a soul capable of any crime."

"The Chevalier de Lorraine shall no longer annoy you—I promise you that."

"Then that will be a true preliminary of alliance, sire—I sign; but since you have done your part, tell me what shall be mine."

"Instead of imbroiling me with your brother Charles, you must make him my more intimate friend than ever."

"That is very easy."

"Oh! not quite so much so as you may think, for in ordinary friendship people embrace or exercise hospitality, and that only costs a kiss or a return, easy expenses; but in political friendship——"

"Ah! it's a political friendship, is it?"

"Yes, my sister; and then, instead of embraces and feasts, it is soldiers, it is soldiers all living and well equipped, that we must serve up to our friend; vessels we must offer, all armed with cannons and stored with provisions. It hence results that we have not always our coffers in a fit state to form such friendships."

"Ah! you are quite right," said madame; "the coffers of the King of England have been very sonorous for some time."

"But you, my sister, who have so much influence over your brother, you can obtain more than an ambassador could ever obtain."

"To effect that I must go to London, my dear brother."

"I have thought so," replied the king eagerly; "and I have said to myself that such a voyage would do your spirits good."

"Only," interrupted madame, "it is possible I should fail. The King of England has dangerous counselors."

"Counselors, do you say?"

"Precisely. If, by chance, your majesty had any intention —I am only supposing so—of asking Charles II. his alliance for a war——"

"For a war?"

"Yes, well, then the counselors of the king, who are to the number of seven—Mademoiselle Stewart, Mademoiselle Wells, Mademoiselle Gwyn, Miss Orchay, Mademoiselle Zunga, Miss Davies, and the proud Countess of Castlemaine—will represent to the king that war costs a great deal of money; that it is better to give balls and suppers at Hampton Court than to equip vessels of the line at Portsmouth and Greenwich."

"And then your negotiations will fail?"

"Oh! those ladies cause all negotiations to fail that they don't make themselves."

"Do you know the idea that has struck me, sister?"

"No; tell me what it is."

"It is that searching well around you, you might perhaps find a female counselor to take with you to your brother, whose eloquence might paralyze the ill-will of the seven others."

"That is really an idea, sire, and I will search."

"You will find what you want."

"I hope so."

"A pretty person is necessary; an agreeable face is better than an ugly one, is it not?"

"Most assuredly."

"An animated, lively, audacious character."

"Certainly."

"Nobility; that is, enough to enable her to approach the king without awkwardness—little enough, so as not to trouble herself about the dignity of her race."

"Quite just."

"And who knows a little English."

"*Mon Dieu!* why, some one," cried madame, "like Mademoiselle de Kéroualle, for instance!"

"Oh! why, yes!" said Louis XIV.; "you have found—it is you who have found, my sister."

"I will take her; she will have no cause to complain, I suppose."

"Oh, no; I will name her *séductrice plénipotentiaire* at once, and will add the dowry to the title."

"That is—well."

"I fancy you already on your road, my dear little sister, and consoled for all your griefs."

"I will go, on two conditions. The first is, that I shall know what I am negotiating about."

"This is it. The Dutch, you know, insult me daily in the gazettes, and by their republican attitude. I don't like republics."

"That may easily be conceived, sire."

"I see with pain that these kings of the sea—they call themselves so—keep trade from France in the Indies, and that their vessels will soon occupy all the ports of Europe. Such a power is too near me, sister."

"They are your allies, nevertheless."

"That is why they were wrong in having the medal you have heard of struck—a medal which represents Holland stopping the sun, as Joshua did, with this legend: 'The sun has stopped before me.' There is not much fraternity in that, is there?"

"I thought you had forgotten that miserable affair."

"I never forget anything, my sister. And if my true friends, such as your brother Charles, are willing to succeed me——"

The princess remained pensively silent.

"Listen to me; there is the empire of the seas to be shared," said Louis XIV. "For this partition, which England submits to, could I not represent the second party as well as the Dutch?"

"We have Mademoiselle de Kéroualle to treat that question," replied madame.

"Your second condition for going, if you please, sister?"

"The consent of Monsieur, my husband."

"You shall have it."

"Then consider me gone, my brother."

On hearing these words, Louis XIV. turned round toward the corner of the room in which D'Artagnan, Colbert, and Aramis stood, and made an affirmative sign to his minister. Colbert then broke the conversation at the point it happened to be at, and said to Aramis:

"Monsieur l'Ambassadeur, shall we talk about business?"

D'Artagnan immediately withdrew, from politeness. He directed his steps toward the chimney, within hearing of what the king was going to say to Monsieur, who, evidently uneasy, had gone to him. The face of the king was animated. Upon his brow was stamped a will, the redoubtable expression of which already met with no more contradiction in France, and was soon to meet with no more in Europe.

"Monsieur," said the king to his brother, "I am not pleased with Monsieur le Chevalier de Lorraine. You, who do him the honor to protect him, must advise him to travel for a few months."

These words fell with the crush of an avalanche upon Monsieur, who adored this favorite, and concentrated all his affections in him.

"In what has the chevalier been able to displease your majesty?" cried he, darting a furious look at madame.

"I will tell you that when he is gone," replied the impassible king. "And also when madame, here, shall have crossed over into England."

"Madame! into England!" murmured Monsieur, in a perfect state of stupor.

"In a week, my brother," continued the king, "while we two will go whither I will tell you."

And the king turned upon his heel, after having smiled in his brother's face, to sweeten a little the bitter draught he had given him.

During this time Colbert was talking with the Duc d'Alméda.

"Monsieur," said Colbert to Aramis, "this is the moment for us to come to an understanding. I have made your peace with the king, and I owed that clearly to a man of your merit; but as you have often expressed friendship for me, an opportunity presents itself for giving me a proof of it. You are, besides, more a Frenchman than a Spaniard. Shall we have, answer me frankly, the neutrality of Spain, if we undertake anything against the United Provinces?"

"Monsieur," replied Aramis, "the interest of Spain is very clear. To imbroil Europe with the United Provinces, against whom subsists the ancient malice of their conquered liberty, is our policy, but the King of France is allied with the United Provinces. You are not ignorant, besides, that it would be a maritime war, and that France is not in a state to make such a one with advantage."

Colbert, turning round at this moment, saw D'Artagnan, who was seeking an interlocutor during the "aside" of the king and Monsieur. He called him, at the same time saying, in a low voice, to Aramis:

"We may talk with D'Artagnan, I suppose?"

"Oh! certainly," replied the ambassador.

"We were saying, Monsieur d'Alméda and I," said Colbert, "that war with the United Provinces would be a maritime war."

"That's evident enough," replied the musketeer.

"And what do you think of it, Monsieur d'Artagnan?"

"I think that to carry that war on successfully you must have a very large land army."

"What did you say?" said Colbert, thinking he had ill understood him.

"Why such a land army?" said Aramis.

"Because the king will be beaten by sea if he has not the

English with him, and that when beaten by sea he will be soon invaded, either by the Dutch in his ports, or by the Spaniards by land."

"And Spain neutral?" asked Aramis.

"Neutral as long as the king shall be the stronger," rejoined D'Artagnan.

Colbert admired that sagacity which never touched a question without enlightening it thoroughly. Aramis smiled, as he had long known that in dipolmacy D'Artagnan acknowledged no master. Colbert, who, like all proud men, dwelt upon his fantasy with a certainty of success, resumed the subject:

"Who told you, Monsieur d'Artagnan, that the king had no navy?"

"Oh! I have taken no heed of these details," replied the captain. "I am but a middling sailor. Like all nervous people, I hate the sea; and yet I have an idea that with ships, France being a seaport with two hundred heads, we might have sailors."

Colbert drew from his pocket a little oblong book divided into two columns. On the first were the names of vessels, on the other the figures recapitulating the number of cannon and men requisite to equip these ships.

"I have had the same idea as you," said he to D'Artagnan, "and I have had an account drawn up of the vessels we have altogether—thirty-five ships."

"Thirty-five ships! that is impossible!" cried D'Artagnan.

"Something like two thousand pieces of cannon," said Colbert. "That is what the king possesses at this moment. With thirty-five vessels we can make three squadrons, but I must have five."

"Five!" cried Aramis.

"They will be afloat before the end of the year, gentlemen; the king will have fifty ships of the line. We may venture on a contest with them, may we not?"

"To build vessels," said D'Artagnan, "is difficult, but possible. As to arming them, how is that to be done? In France there are neither foundries nor military docks."

"Bah!" replied Colbert, with a gay tone. "I have instituted all that this year and a half past; did you not know it? Don't you know Monsieur d'Imfreville?"

"D'Imfreville?" replied D'Artagnan. "No."

"He is a man I have discovered; he has a specialty; he is a man of genius—he knows how to set men to work. It is he

who has founded cannon and cut the woods of Bourgogne. And
then, Monsieur l'Ambassadeur, you may not believe what I am
going to tell you, but I have a further idea."

"Oh, monsieur!" said Aramis civilly, "I always believe you."

"Figure to yourself, that calculating upon the character of
the Dutch, our allies, I said to myself, 'They are merchants,
they are friends with the king; they will be happy to sell to
the king what they fabricate for themselves; then the more
we buy—' Ah! I must add this: I have Forant—do you know
Forant, D'Artagnan?"

Colbert, in his warmth, forgot himself; he called the captain
simply D'Artagnan, as the king did. But the captain only smiled
at it.

"No," replied he; "I don't know him."

"That is another man I have discovered, with a genius for
buying. This Forant has purchased for me three hundred and
fifty thousand pounds of iron in balls, two hundred thousand
pounds of powder, twelve cargoes of northern timber, matches,
grenades, pitch, tar—I know not what, with a saving of seven
per cent. upon what all those articles would cost me fabricated
in France."

"That is a good idea," replied D'Artagnan, "to have Dutch
balls founded, which will return to the Dutch."

"Is it not with loss, too?"

And Colbert laughed aloud. He was delighted with his own
joke.

"Still further," added he, "these same Dutch are building
for the king, at this moment, six vessels after the model of
the best of their marine. Destouches— Ah! perhaps you don't
know Destouches?"

"No, monsieur."

"He is a man who has a glance singularly sure to discern,
when a ship is launched, what are the defects and qualities
of that ship—that is valuable, please to observe. Nature is
truly whimsical. Well, this Destouches appeared to me to be
a man likely to be useful in a port, and he is superintending
the construction of six vessels of seventy-eight, which the
provinces are building for his majesty. It results from all this,
my dear Monsieur d'Artagnan, that the king, if he wished to
quarrel with the provinces, would have a very pretty fleet.
Now, you know better than anybody else if the land army is
good."

D'Artagnan and Aramis looked at each other, wondering
at the mysterious labors this man had effected in a few years.

Colbert understood them, and was touched by this best of flatteries.

"If we, in France, were ignorant of what was going on," said D'Artagnan, "out of France still less must be known."

"That is why I told Monsieur l'Ambassadeur," said Colbert, "that Spain promising its neutrality, England helping us——"

"If England assists you," said Aramis, "I engage for the neutrality of Spain."

"I take you at your word," Colbert hastened to reply, with his blunt *bonhomie*. "And apropos of Spain, you have not the 'Golden Fleece,' Monsieur d'Alméda. I heard the king say the other day that he should like to see you wear the *grand cordon* of St. Michael."

Aramis bowed.

"Oh!" thought D'Artagnan, "and Porthos is no longer here! What ells of ribbon would there be for him in these largesses! Good Porthos!"

"Monsieur d'Artagnan," resumed Colbert, "between us two, you will have, I would wager, an inclination to lead your musketeers into Holland. Can you swim?"

And he laughed like a man in a very good humor.

"Like an eel," replied D'Artagnan.

"Ah! but there are some rough passages of canals and marshes yonder, Monsieur d'Artagnan, and the best swimmers are sometimes drowned there."

"It is my profession to die for his majesty," said the musketeer. "Only as it is seldom that in war much water is met with without a little fire, I declare to you beforehand that I will do my best to choose fire. I am getting old; water freezes me—fire warms, Monsieur Colbert."

And D'Artagnan looked so handsome in juvenile vigor and pride, as he pronounced these words, that Colbert, in his turn, could not help admiring him. D'Artagnan perceived the effect he had produced. He remembered that the best tradesman is he who fixes a high price upon his goods when they are valuable. He prepared, then, his price in advance.

"So, then," said Colbert, "we go into Holland?"

"Yes," replied D'Artagnan; "only——"

"Only?" said M. Colbert.

"Only," repeated D'Artagnan, "there is in everything the question of interest and the question of self-love. It is a very fine title, that of captain of the musketeers; but, observe this: we have now the king's guards and the military household of the king. A captain of musketeers ought, either to command

all that, and then he would absorb a hundred thousand livres a
year for expenses of representation and table——"

"Well, but do you suppose, by chance, that the king would
haggle with you?" said Colbert.

"Eh! monsieur, you have not understood me," replied
D'Artagnan, sure of having carried the question of interest;
"I was telling you that I, an old captain, formerly chief of the
king's guard, having precedence of the maréchaux of France
—I saw myself one day in the trenches with two other equals,
the captain of the guards and the colonel commanding the
Swiss. Now, at no price will I suffer that. I have old habits,
and I will stand to them."

Colbert felt this blow, but he was prepared for it.

"I have been thinking of what you said just now," replied
he.

"About what, monsieur?"

"We were speaking of canals and marshes in which people
are drowned."

"Well?"

"Well, if they are drowned, it is for want of a boat, a
plank, or a stick."

"Of a stick, however short it may be," said D'Artagnan.

"Exactly," said Colbert. "And, therefore, I never heard of
an instance of a maréchal of France being drowned."

D'Artagnan became pale with joy, and in a not very firm
voice:

"People would be very proud of me in my country," said
he, "if I were a maréchal of France; but a man must have
commanded an expedition in chief to obtain the baton."

"Monsieur," said Colbert, "here is in this pocketbook, which
you will study, a plan of a campaign you will have to lead a
body of troops to carry out in the next spring."

D'Artagnan took the book tremblingly, and his fingers meeting with those of Colbert, the minister pressed the hand of the
musketeer loyally.

"Monsieur," said he, "we had both a revenge to take, one
over the other. I have begun; it is now your turn."

"I will do you justice, monsieur," replied D'Artagnan, "and
implore you to tell the king that the first opportunity that shall
offer, he may depend upon a victory, or seeing me dead."

"Then I will have the fleur-de-lis for your maréchal's baton
prepared immediately," said Colbert.

On the morrow of this day, Aramis, who was setting out for

Madrid, to negotiate the neutrality of Spain, came to embrace D'Artagnan at his hotel.

"Let us love each other for four," said D'Artagnan, "we are now but two."

"And you will, perhaps, never see me again, dear D'Artagnan," said Aramis; "if you knew how I have loved you! I am old, I am extinguished, I am dead."

"My friend," said D'Artagnan, "you will live longer than I shall; diplomacy commands you to live; but, for my part, honor condemns me to die."

"Bah! such men as we are, Monsieur le Maréchal," said Aramis, "only die satiated with joy or glory."

"Ah!" replied D'Artagnan, with a melancholy smile, "I assure you, Monsieur le Duc, I feel very little appetite for either."

They once more embraced, and, two hours after, they were separated.

THE DEATH OF D'ARTAGNAN

Contrary to what always happens, whether in politics or morals, each kept his promise, and did honor to his engagements.

The king recalled M. de Guiche, and banished M. le chevalier de Lorraine; so that Monsieur became ill in consequence. Madame set out for London, where she applied herself so earnestly to make her brother, Charles II., have a taste for the political councils of Mlle. de Kéroualle, that the alliance between England and France was signed, and the English vessels, ballasted by a few millions of French gold, made a terrible campaign against the fleets of the United Provinces. Charles II. had promised Mlle. de Kéroualle a little gratitude for her good councils; he made her Duchess of Portsmouth. Colbert had promised the king vessels, munitions, and victories. He kept his word, as is well known. At length Aramis, upon whose promises there was least dependence to be placed, wrote Colbert the following letter, on the subject of the negotiations which he had undertaken at Madrid:

"MONSIEUR COLBERT: I have the honor to expedite to yo
the R. P. d'Oliva, general *ad interim* of the Society of Jesu
my provisional successor. The reverend father will explain t
you, Monsieur Colbert, that I preserve to myself the directio
of all the affairs of the order which concern France and Spain
but that I am not willing to retain the title of general, whic
would throw too much light upon the march of the negoti
tions with which his Catholic majesty wishes to intrust me.
shall resume that title by the command of his majesty, whe
the labors I have undertaken in concert with you, for the grea
glory of God and His Church, shall be brought to a good en
The R. P. d'Oliva will inform you likewise, monsieur, of th
consent which his Catholic majesty gives to the signature of
treaty which assures the neutrality of Spain, in the event of
war between France and the United Provinces. This conser
will be valid, even in England, instead of being activ
should satisfy herself with remaining neutral. As to Portuga
of which you and I have spoken, monsieur, I can assure you
will contribute with all its resources to assist the most Chri
tian king in his war. I beg you, Monsieur Colbert, to preser
to me your friendship, as also to believe in my profound a
tachment, and to lay my respect at the feet of his most Chri
tian majesty.

"(Signed)   LE DUC D'ALMÉDA."

Aramis had then performed more than he had promised;
remained to be known how the king, M. Colbert, and D'A
tagnan would be faithful to one another. In the spring, as Co
bert had predicted, the land army entered on its campaign.
preceded, in magnificent order, the court of Louis XIV., wh
setting out on horseback, surrounded by carriages filled wit
ladies, and courtiers, conducted the *élite* of his kingdom to th
sanguinary-*fête*. The officers of the army, it is true, had
other music but the artillery of the Dutch forts; but
was enough for a great number, who found in this war honor
advancement, fortune, or death.

M. d'Artagnan set out commanding a body of twelve tho
sand men, cavalry and infantry, with which he was ordered
take the different places which form the knots of that str
tegic network which is called La Frise. Never was an army co
ducted more gallantly to an expedition. The officers knew th
their leader, prudent and skillful as he was brave, would n
sacrifice a single man, nor yield an inch of ground without n
cessity. He had the old habits of war, to live upon the countr
keep his soldiers singing and the enemy weeping. The capta

of the king's musketeers placed his coquetry in showing that he knew his business. Never were opportunities better chosen, *coups de main* better supported, errors of the besieged taken better advantage of.

The army commanded by D'Artagnan took twelve small places within a month. He was engaged in besieging the thirteenth, which had held out five days. D'Artagnan caused the trenches to be opened without appearing to suppose that these people would ever allow themselves to be taken. The pioneers and laborers were, in the army of this man, a body full of emulation, ideas, and zeal, because he treated them like soldiers, knew how to render their work glorious, and never allowed them to be killed if he could prevent it. It should have been seen then with what eagerness the marshy glebes of Holland were turned over. Those turf-heaps, those mounds of potter's clay, melted at the word of the soldiers like butter in the vast frying-pans of the Friesland housewives.

M. d'Artagnan dispatched a courier to the king to give him an account of the last successes, which redoubled the good humor of his majesty and his inclination to amuse the ladies. These victories of M. d'Artagnan gave so much majesty to the prince that Mme. de Montespan no longer called him anything but Louis the Invincible. So that Mlle. de la Valliere, who only called the king Louis the Victorious, lost much of his majesty's favor. Besides, her eyes were frequently red, and for an Invincible nothing is more disagreeable than a mistress who weeps while everything is smiling around her. The star of Mlle. de la Valliere was being drowned in the horizon in clouds and tears. But the gayety of Mme. de Montespan redoubled with the successes of the king, and consoled him for every other unpleasant circumstance. It was to D'Artagnan the king owed this; and his majesty was anxious to acknowledge these services; he wrote to M. Colbert:

"MONSIEUR COLBERT: We have a promise to fulfill with Monsieur d'Artagnan, who so well keeps his. This is to inform you that the time is come for performing it. All provisions for this purpose you shall be furnished with in due time.
LOUIS."

In consequence of this, Colbert, who detained the envoy of D'Artagnan, placed in the hands of that messenger a letter from himself for D'Artagnan, and a small coffer of ebony inlaid with gold, which was not very voluminous in appearance, but which, without doubt, was very heavy, as a guard of five men was given to the messenger, to assist him in carrying it. These people arrived before the place which D'Artagnan was besieging, toward daybreak, and presented themselves at the lodgings of the general. They were told that D'Artagnan, annoyed by a sortie which the governor, an artful man, had made the evening before, and in which the works had been destroyed, seventy-seven men killed, and the reparation of the breaches commenced, had just gone with half a score companies of grenadiers to reconstruct the works.

M. Colbert's envoy had orders to go and seek M. d'Artagnan, wherever he might be, or at whatever hour of the day or night. He directed his course, therefore, toward the trenches, followed by his escort, all on horseback. They perceived M. d'Artagnan in the open plain, with his gold-laced hat, his long cane, and his large gilded cuffs. He was biting his white mustache, and wiping off, with his left hand, the dust which the passing balls threw up from the ground they plowed near him. They also saw, amid this terrible fire, which filled the air with its hissing whistle, officers handling the shovel, soldiers rolling barrows, and vast fascines, rising by being either carried or dragged by from ten to twenty men, covered the front of the trench reopened to the center by this extraordinary effort of the general animating his soldiers. In three hours all had been reinstated. D'Artagnan began to speak more mildly, and he became quite calm when the captain of the pioneers approached him, hat in hand, to tell him that the trench was again lodgeable. This man had scarcely finished speaking, when a ball took off one of his legs, and he fell into the arms of D'Artagnan. The latter lifted up his soldier, and quietly, with soothing words, carried him into the trench, amid the enthusiastic applause of the regiments. From that time, it was no longer ardor—it was delirium; two companies stole away up to the advance posts, which they destroyed instantly.

When their comrades, restrained with great difficulty by D'Artagnan, saw them lodged upon the bastions, they rushed forward likewise; and soon a furious assault was made upon the counterscarp, upon which depended the safety of the place. D'Artagnan perceived there was only one means left of stopping his army, and that was to lodge it in the place. He directed all his force to two breaches, which the besieged were busy in repairing. The shock was terrible; eighteen companies took part in it, and D'Artagnan went with the rest, within half cannon-shot of the place to support the attack by échelons.

The cries of the Dutch, who were being poniarded upon their guns by D'Artagnan's grenadiers, were distinctly audible. The struggle grew fiercer with the despair of the governor, who disputed his position foot by foot. D'Artagnan, to put an end to the affair, and silence the fire, which was increasing, sent a fresh column, which penetrated like a wimble through the posts that remained solid; and he soon perceived upon the ramparts, through the fire, the terrified flight of the besieged pursued by the besiegers.

It was at this moment the general, breathing freely and full of joy, heard a voice behind him, saying:

"Monsieur, if you please, from Monsieur Colbert."

He broke the seal of a letter which contained these words:

"MONSIEUR D'ARTAGNAN: The king commands me to inform you that he has nominated you Maréchal of France, as a reward of your good services, and the honor you do to his arms. The king is highly pleased, monsieur, with the captures you have made; he commands you, in particular, to finish the siege you have commenced, with good fortune to you, and success for him."

D'Artagnan was standing with a heated countenance and a sparkling eye. He looked up to watch the progress of his troops upon the walls, still enveloped in red and black volumes of smoke.

"I have finished," replied he to the messenger; "the city will have surrendered in a quarter of an hour."

He then resumed his reading:

"The *coffret*, Monsieur D'Artagnan, is my own present. You will not be sorry to see that while you warriors are drawing the sword to defend the king, I am animating the pacific arts to ornament the recompenses worthy of you. I commend myself to your friendship, Monsieur le Maréchal, and beg you to believe in all mine.   COLBERT."

D'Artagnan, intoxicated with joy, made a sign to the messenger, who approached, with his *coffret* in his hands. But at the moment the maréchal was going to look at it, a loud explosion resounded from the ramparts, and called his attention toward the city.

"It is strange," said D'Artagnan, "that I don't yet see the king's flag upon the walls, or hear the drums beat the *chamade*."

He launched three hundred fresh men, under a high-spirited officer, and ordered another breach to be beaten. Then, being more tranquil, he turned toward the *coffret,* which Colbert's envoy held out to him. It was his treasure—he had won it.

D'Artagnan was holding out his hand to open the *coffret,* when a ball from the city crushed the *coffret* in the arms of the officer, struck D'Artagnan full in the chest, and knocked him down upon a sloping heap of earth, while the fleur-de-lised baton, escaping from the broken sides of the box, came rolling under the powerless hand of the maréchal. D'Artagnan endeavored to raise himself up. It was thought he had been knocked down without being wounded. A terrible cry broke from the group of his terrified officers; the maréchal was covered with blood; the paleness of death ascended slowly to his noble countenance. Leaning upon the arms which were held out on all sides to receive him, he was able once more to turn his eyes toward the place, and to distinguish the white flag at the crest of the principal bastion; his ears, already deaf to the sounds of life, caught feebly the rolling of the drum which announced the victory. Then, clasping in his nerveless hand the baton, ornamented with its fleur-de-lis, he cast down upon i his eyes, which had no longer the power of looking upward toward heaven, and fell back, murmuring those strange words which appeared to the soldiers cabalistic words—words which had formerly represented so many things upon earth, and which none but the dying man longer comprehended:

"Athos—Porthos, farewell till we meet again! Aramis, adieu forever!"

Of the four valiant men whose history we have related, ther now no longer remained but one single body; God had resumed the souls.

Historical Fiction

(1600s)